DEMONIC SECT ELDER CULTIVATES RIGHTEOUS DISCIPLES

DEMONIC
SECT ELDER
CULTIVATES
RIGHTEOUS
DISCIPLES

Kalzara

Podium

Copyright © 2025 by Kalzara

Cover design by Dalia and Sam

ISBN: 978-1-0394-7149-8

Published in 2025 by Podium Publishing
www.podiumentertainment.com

Podium

DEMONIC SECT ELDER CULTIVATES RIGHTEOUS DISCIPLES

CHAPTER ONE

Urgh, what made me think that entering a pie-eating contest was a good idea?"

Zack found himself in an endless expanse of black, a void so complete and all-encompassing that it swallowed all senses. There was no ground beneath his feet, no air to feel against his skin, and no light to pierce the heavy shroud of darkness. It was as if he had been thrust into an abyss.

"Where am I?" Zack's voice echoed, sounding strange and distant in the vast emptiness. "Is this what the afterlife is? Just . . . nothingness?"

Suddenly, a bright blue box materialized before him.

System Activated

"W-what the . . . ?"

Welcome User
Searching for a vessel
. . .
. . .
. . .

"A vessel?" Zack muttered, his voice tinged with disbelief. "Is this some sort of isekai shit?"

2,732 possible matches found.
Determining compatibility.
. . .
. . .
Highest compatibility: 5%
Possibility of rejection is at 95%

"No way!" He scoffed. "Are you telling me that there aren't any more out-of-shape, lazy bums out there?"

Would you like to initiate Soul Migration?

His response was immediate, fueled by a mix of disbelief and panic. "No! Fuck no!"

Yet, no matter what he did, he could feel an inexorable pull, tugging at the very essence of his being.

"What the hell?! I said NO!"

For a moment, the force pulling at him hesitated, then halted.

> User has rejected Soul Migration.

So, the System does understand that no means no. Zack exhaled a shaky breath as he felt a sense of relief.

> Searching for an alternative vessel.
> . . .
> . . .
> . . .

"Yes, please do."

> 3,902 possible matches found.
> Determining compatibility.
> . . .
> . . .
> Highest compatibility: 97%
> Possibility of rejection: 3%

"How did it go from five percent to ninety-seven percent? Which unlucky fucker just died?"

> Would you like to initiate Soul Migration?

"Hell yeah! Give me that body!"

Before the System could send him into a new body, Zack thought about his past life. He remembered the dimly lit room of his parents' basement, the constant hum of the computer, and the countless web novels he devoured, each filled with tales of cultivators rising to unimaginable heights. Those stories were his refuge, a world where ordinary mortals transformed into immortals through hardships and trials. Yet, in his own life, he hadn't even managed to climb the proverbial steps out of his parents' basement.

He often heard their hushed whispers upstairs. "When will he get a job? What will become of him?" But Zack, ever buried in his fantasies of virtual worlds, ignored the real world's problems.

And then, there was the pie-eating contest. A fateful event he thought would finally show everyone that he had some worth. It was supposed to be his moment of glory.

In the village square, a large banner read, "Grand Pie-Eating Championship." Zack had smirked, thinking, *This is my chance!*

The contest started, and pies of various flavors lay before him. Blueberry, apple, cherry . . . each looked more delicious than the last. With a gleam in his eyes, he started devouring them at a pace that left spectators in awe.

"Go Zack!" cheered a kid, probably mistaking him for a local champion.

Halfway through, Zack felt full, but spurred on by the crowd's excitement and the thought of victory, he pushed on. With every bite, he felt closer to proving his worth.

However, soon his vision blurred. He felt a strange heaviness in his chest. The world began to spin. And as he took his last bite, with pie smeared all over his face and a foolish grin, Zack collapsed.

The crowd was in shock, and someone joked, "Guess he bit off more than he could chew!"

Zack had many regrets in life, too many to count, but his biggest was that he had been a disappointment, a leech upon his family.

"I won't waste this life," he vowed to himself, "I'll take this second chance that Go—"

Suddenly, a thought struck Zack. Where exactly was this System from? In all his memories from the web novels he'd read, Systems were usually gifts from divine beings, ancient treasures, or the author never got around to finishing the book . . .

"Hey, System, are any of those right?"

. . .

"Yeah . . . I knew you weren't going to reply, I'll probably find out a few thousand chapters later."

Soul Migration initiated. 1% . . . 10% . . . 45% . . .

"Erm, are you sure this is working? I can't feel anything . . ."
The numbers on the display continued to climb.

74% . . . 88% . . .

Just when he thought nothing was happening, he felt it—a sudden, violent pull at the core of his being. It was as if a cosmic hand grabbed hold of his soul and yanked it out of the abyss. Zack's formless essence twisted and spiraled through an interdimensional tunnel, a wormhole that distorted everything he thought he knew about existence.

The sensation was gut-wrenching, akin to the inexorable pull of a black hole. Zack's ethereal form felt compressed, as though he was being forced through an impossibly small opening. He experienced a whirlwind of thoughts and emotions as his soul contorted, trying to adapt to this foreign environment.

100% Soul Migration Complete

"That . . . that felt like plunging down the steepest drop of the world's most terrifying rollercoaster." *Rollercoasters* . . . he mused, a pang of nostalgia hitting him. *I haven't been allowed on one since I was a kid.*

A few minutes before.

"To think that my own disciple would turn against me."

In the midst of a barren wasteland, two figures confronted each other. The younger of the two, a dark-haired man with eyes that hinted at malevolence, sneered arrogantly at the elder before him. Blood oozed from the elder's wounds; he was gravely injured, clutching his bleeding arm and gasping for every breath. Yet, even in this state, the old master's presence exuded an aura of unyielding calmness and dignity.

"You have kept me on a leash for too long, old man," the young man responded, his voice dripping with resentment.

The master sighed. "The sect master does not take kindly to deserters, Tyrus. Come back with me."

Tyrus barked out a scornful laugh. "Always 'the sect master this, the sect master that.'" He tilted his head, eyes gleaming with newfound madness. "Let any come after me, and I'll send them to the netherworld! Starting with you, the sect master's lapdog!"

A shadow passed over the old man's face. He wasn't anyone's mere lapdog; his loyalty was pure, carved from centuries of dedication.

"Die, old man!" With a swift flick of his wrist, Tyrus unleashed a powerful burst of Sword Qi. It shot out like a streak of malevolent light, aimed straight at the old man's heart. The elder hastily began to form a protective qi barrier, however, the barrier barely took form before it was sliced through.

The strike found its mark, slamming into the old man's chest and propelling him backwards, his frail frame crashed violently into a large rock.

For a moment, the scene was still, except for the dust settling in the aftermath. The old man lay sprawled on the ground, convulsing as the wicked Sword Qi raged within his body. Like a sinister serpent, it sought to devour his very essence from the inside out.

"AAARRRRGHHHHHH."

But then, abruptly, his convulsions ceased. The elder's eyes, once alive with spirit and fire, glazed over.

The young man's face was an emotionless mask, and he watched with cold eyes as his master lay motionless. But within those black orbs, there was a glint of satisfaction.

Death by his own disciple. Such was the life of a demonic cultivator.

"This is the price of misplaced loyalty, old fool." With a scoff, Tyrus's form became blurry before he vanished.

Determining vessel status.
1% . . . 25% . . . 75% . . . 100%
Meridians crippled.
Vital organs malfunctioning.
Severe blood loss.
A brief pause was followed by more text:
Restoring body.
1% . . . 30% . . . 80% . . . 100%

As the System's progress bar reached completion, the lifeless body of the old man began to shudder. Twinges of sensation flooded through Zack. He attempted to pry his eyes open. After much struggle, they responded, revealing a world that was dim and out of focus.

Pain radiated from every part of him, and when he tried to move, he realized with a sinking feeling that he was completely immobilized. *Damn it! Did I really transmigrate only to be imprisoned immediately into a paralyzed body?*

The bright blue box emerged once more before him, presenting new information:

```
Name: Slifer
Race: Human
Alignment: Demonic
Cultivation: Body Tempering: 9th Stage
Lifespan Remaining: 24 Hours
Karmic Credits: 0
```

A cold dread filled him. *Only twenty-four hours? What the hell?* With the agony he was experiencing and his incapacitated state, what could he possibly achieve in a single day? Was he destined to simply lie here, waiting for the inevitable end? What kind of isekai story was that?

His mind raced, considering the information presented. He recognized the term "cultivation" from the xianxia tales he'd read. The ninth stage of Body Tempering suggested he'd only just begun his cultivation journey. He was probably in the body of a young MC who just got crippled by the villain. Any moment now he would find a way to not only recover but breakthrough multiple realms and kill that bastard who did this to him.

"Wait . . . demonic cultivator?" Zack's eyes narrowed as he contemplated the possibility that he had been transmigrated as the villain. Maybe he was the one who crippled the MC, who later came back and did the same to him?

"No, no, that can't be it. I have a . . . S-system. That's it! A System! There's no way a villain would have a System, right?" Zack attempted to console himself, but he knew in fact that villains could have a System.

Zack would rather be a side character than a villain, at least a side character could suck up to the MC and live. Villains? No matter what they did, they somehow offended the MC and ended up dead, along with nine generations of their family.

Determined to prove that he was in fact the protagonist, he did what all LitRPG protagonists do: obnoxiously shout at a blue box.

"Give me my power-up!"

```
. . .
```

"Erm . . . Hello? You there?"

```
. . .
```

"Any moment now would be nice."
No reply.
Did the System just throw him in a random body and leave?

Suddenly more text appeared in front of him.

> Beginning memory fusion.

"Ok. So, you haven't left. You're just choosing to ignore me."

> 1% . . .30% . . .58% . . .
> Critical Error: Essential memories absent.

"Oh, now that doesn't sound good . . ."

> Resuming fusion.

His eyes widened in disbelief. "Wait, you can't just leave out essential memories!"

> 76% . . . 99% . . . 100%
> Memory fusion complete.
> Alert: Host's essential memories are absent.

Suddenly, Zack let out a scream as his consciousness was flooded with a cascade of memories. The images played out like an aged reel, vivid, yet disjointed.

He saw a young, ambitious man, his eyes filled with determination, stepping into the intimidating gates of a demonic sect. Once inside, this shrewd and intelligent man recognized the importance of the sect elders and began to diligently curry favor with one of them. He was often seen bringing rare herbs to the elder, publicly supporting the elder's decisions, and committing heinous deeds that would make any sane person vomit, all while maintaining an air of subservience.

As years passed, the young man matured, climbing the ranks with the help of the elder, whom he'd supported unyieldingly. The elder, now the sect master, heavily relied on him, seeing in him a reflection of his younger self, or so the young man thought.

With the sect master's backing, the now-elderly man sought to achieve the next level of cultivation—a breakthrough to the Origin Realm!

Yet, despite all his preparations, and the sect master's support, his attempt was fraught with complications. The energy within him went haywire and he ended up failing. He was lucky to have survived the tribulation.

In the midst of his despair, his most promising disciple chose to leave. Feeling betrayed and worried about the sect master's reaction, the elder pursued his disciple.

The memories converged on a fateful confrontation. Zack saw a desolate landscape—the elder and the disciple, face to face, emotions running high. Words were exchanged, accusations thrown. And then, the tragic climax: the disciple unleashed a powerful Sword Qi, piercing straight through the old man's heart.

The intense pain that previously held Zack captive began to subside. Sensation flowed back into his limbs, each nerve awakening like a dormant beast. With tremendous effort, he pushed himself upright, wincing at the residual aches.

Thank the gods! I'm not crippled after all. As he took stock of his situation, realization dawned upon him. *This body . . . It was once at the Half-Step Origin Realm! How has it regressed so much to Body Tempering?*

Some would say that the title of cultivator was reserved for those who reached the Qi Refining Realm and could manipulate qi, whilst others would argue that only after building the foundations and entering the Foundation Establishment could one earn that title.

Regardless of which school of thought they followed, both groups agreed that a disciple at the Body Tempering stage did not have the right to call themselves a true cultivator.

Zack sighed in frustration, brushing off the rubble that clung to his aged robe. The System was able to bring this body back to life but didn't think to return its cultivation.

"I thought I got shafted into a young man's crippled body," he muttered to himself, "but an old man nearing the end of his time? That's a new one."

Stretching his arms wide, Zack grinned and spoke to the lingering spirit of Slifer, wherever it might be. "Don't worry, Grandpa. I'll take good care of this old thing."

Wait . . . it's best to think of myself as Slifer now. I'm in his body, after all. Can't afford any slipups. The very thought of what demonic cultivators would do to him if they discovered he was an impostor sent chills down his spine. He shuddered, imagining nefarious rituals or, worse, being turned into a demonic beast's snack.

Pausing for a moment, his thoughts wandered. Nascent Soul cultivators could live up to a millennium. But to surpass that, they must break through to the Origin Realm. A pang of regret hit him. Ah, that elusive Half-Step Origin . . . such a tease, offering power but no longevity.

"Wait . . . am I forgetting something?" Slifer's eyes widened as he recalled the System's earlier message about missing essential memories. A bitter laugh escaped his lips. "What could they possibly be? Knowing the typical xianxia tropes, it's probably a series of calamities."

His mind raced with potential scenarios:

Perhaps I offended the young master of a powerful sect by accidentally bumping into him during a festival?

Or what if . . . A mischievous glint appeared in his eyes. *I inadvertently peeped at a fairy bathing in a secluded pond?* Slifer burst into laughter at the thought of the old man creeping around.

Then his face turned comically grave. *Or even worse . . . I might have borrowed a rare herb from the garden of some reclusive old master. Turns out, it was his thousand-year-old tea leaf he'd been nurturing for his evening brew. I can already feel the wrath of a caffeine-deprived cultivator.*

Rubbing his chin, Slifer continued pondering. *And let's not forget the possibility of a forbidden romance. Did I elope with a celestial fairy from a righteous sect? No, wait, I'm a demonic grandpa. It's more likely that I flirted with the spirit of a cursed artifact and now it wants to tie the knot.*

Clearing his throat, he decided it was time to get back on track; twenty-four hours was not a long time, he could deal with those "essential memories" later . . . well, if he lived that long.

"System, I'm ready for my starter pack," he declared confidently. After all, wasn't it common knowledge that every System user was granted a starter pack?

3 Gift Packs Available:
Petite Pack

Median Marvel
Legendary Loot
User will receive one at random.

Slifer smirked, stretching his limbs as he prepared for his assured fortune. *As the main character, my luck has to be unrivaled. There's no way I won't get the Legendary Loot.*

He waited with bated breath, almost imagining the treasures he would soon hold. However, his thoughts were abruptly interrupted by the System's next message.

Congratulations!
You have received the Petite Pack.

Slifer's jaw dropped, his face a mix of shock and disbelief. "The . . . Petite Pack?" he stammered, feeling as though the universe had played a cruel joke on him.

"I'm the protagonist, darn it! Not some side character! And definitely NOT the villain!"

CHAPTER TWO

> Would you like to open the gift pack?

He tried to soothe himself. *Maybe, just maybe, this petite pack, despite its unimpressive name, has some Heaven-destroying bullshit items.*

> Congratulations!
> You have been gifted four items.

How many items could the other packs offer if even this petite one has four?
The System soon displayed the contents and their descriptions:

> Reversal Card x3
> This card devours the life energy in its vicinity to reverse the age of its user.
> Warning: Using demonic techniques will result in a Karmic Credit deduction.

Slifer's jaw dropped. "What kind of twisted logic is this?" he yelled, throwing his hands in the air. "You hand me this card and then penalize me for using it?! Next, you'll probably make me buy it from your Shop, then take away even more credits when I actually use it. Fantastic business model!"

> Peak Slifer Card x3
> Activate to harness Slifer's Peak cultivation for a duration of ten minutes.
> Warning: Using demonic techniques will result in a Karmic Credit deduction.

Slifer was nearly apoplectic now. "Are you kidding me?! From the memories I've seen, the old man practically breathed demonic techniques! It's as if this darned System is trying to kill me!"

He paused, taking a moment to steady his thoughts. *Alright, Slifer, remember the xianxia lore: the harder the trials an MC faces, the sweeter the rewards. Maybe there's a silver lining here somewhere.*

> Critical Block x3
> Passive Skill: Protects user from a critical strike.

"Hmm, not bad." Slifer could see this coming in handy.
With a mix of hope and trepidation, he looked at the final card.

> Random Skill Card
> When activated, 95% chance of granting user a random skill.
> Caution: When buying a Random Skill Card, beware of the risks associated with gambling.

"Oh, come on," Slifer muttered. "Really? Handing me a random skill card and then giving me a lecture on the dangers of gambling? As if *you* didn't just force me into this gamble!" He huffed, crossing his arms in exasperation. "This System . . . It's like offering candy and then lecturing about cavities."

Taking another deep breath, Slifer forced a grin. *Well, at least I don't have to worry about not seeing it after twenty-four hours.*

"Activate Reversal Card!"

Amidst the dense fog of the Yiru Mountains, three figures carefully observed Slifer from a discreet distance. Tenvil, a young man at the Early Core Formation Realm, fidgeted with nervous energy. Beside him stood Jornak and Quindel, both middle-aged cultivators at the Mid-Nascent Soul Realm. Overlooking them with a commanding presence was Elder Lornox, an old cultivator at the Late Nascent Soul stage.

"He's lost it!" Jornak whispered, trying to suppress a laugh. "Look at the elder of the Black Rose Sect, muttering to himself like a lunatic!"

Quindel smirked. "Seems like age and treachery have finally caught up with the old demon."

Tenvil, curiosity evident in his eyes, asked, "Can you hear what he's saying?"

Jornak shook his head. "No. We're staying far enough away so that old demon doesn't detect us. Trust me, Young Master, you don't want to be close when one of them has a meltdown."

Elder Lornox, deep in thought, commented, "I sense that his qi is extremely weak, barely detectable. Likely, he exhausted all of it to recover from his grave injuries." Turning his gaze to Tenvil, he continued, "Young Master Tenvil, this is our opportunity. We should strike now."

Quindel laughed. "Who would have thought? The elder of the Black Rose Sect nearly brought down by his very own disciple! Ah, the irony!"

Jornak chimed in, mimicking Slifer's voice for a comedic effect, "Ah, disciple, you dare betray me? After all those demonic bedtime stories I told you?"

Elder Lornox's eyes narrowed. "Enough jesting! We have the upper hand now. Young Master Tenvil, give the word, and we'll act."

Young Master Tenvil remembered the havoc wrought by the demonic cultivator. Villages pillaged, innocents sacrificed in grotesque rituals, and countless disciples of their revered Radiant Dawn Sect sent to early graves. The weight of responsibility pressed down on him. The elder of the Black Rose Sect posed a real and potent threat to the Radiant Dawn Sect's future.

Taking a deep breath, he began, "For the safety of our sect and the future of the innocent, we must end this menace now. On my order, we—"

But a sharp scream tore from his throat as he felt an intense drain, like the very essence of his being was being sucked out.

"No! What is this?!" Quindel exclaimed, his voice edged with panic. The pull of energy from him was slower than from Tenvil, but it was relentless.

Jornak grunted, trying to form a protective barrier, but it was futile. "Damn it! This . . . force . . . It's insidious!"

Elder Lornox's face twisted in pain. Drawing upon his Late Nascent Soul cultivation, he attempted to seal his meridians and keep his life energy from being siphoned away. His decades of cultivation granted him a momentary defense against the energy drain.

Struggling to speak, Lornox shouted, "It's him! That demon! He's using a forbidden technique, draining our life essences to rejuvenate himself!"

Sure enough, through his blurred vision, Lornox could see Slifer standing tall, laughing as he looked up at the heavens. The old demon was not muttering to himself, as they had thought; he had been conducting a demonic ritual!

Jornak, amidst his agony, cursed, "That cunning fox! He baited us, knew we would come, and now he's using us to heal himself!"

Tenvil, weakened and near his limit, choked out, "We . . . we need to retreat!"

Elder Lornox's voice was filled with regret as he said, "We underestimated him. Today, the Radiant Dawn Sect has truly seen the depths of the Black Rose Elder's cunning."

As the life energy drained from Tenvil, his eyes rolled back, and he began to collapse. Without hesitation, Elder Lornox lunged forward, catching the young master just in time. "Hold on, Young Master!" he urged.

Holding Tenvil tightly, Elder Lornox began retreating, swift as the wind. "He's not breathing!" Lornox's eyes widened in panic—the young master couldn't die, at least not under his watch! From his robe, he retrieved an assortment of jade pills and fed them to Tenvil. Each pill shimmered with a soft glow, releasing potent healing energy.

Meanwhile, unaware of the chaos unfolding not too far from him, Slifer roared with ecstasy. The influx of life energy coursed through him, rejuvenating every cell in his being. He laughed heartily, his voice echoing through the heavens. "So, this is what it feels like to be the MC! Such power!"

But as the elation started to wane, Slifer's grin turned upside down. He noticed his hand had become wrinkled and gray. "Wait a minute," he muttered, confused. "Shouldn't I be young and dashing by now?"

When he looked up, the stat screen blinked into existence.

Name: Slifer
Race: Human
Alignment: Demonic
Cultivation: Body Tempering—9th Stage
Lifespan Remaining: 50 Days
Karmic Credits: 0
Items: Reversal Cards x2, Peak Slifer Cards x3, Critical Block x3, Random Skill Card x1

Slifer's face turned crimson with fury. "Fifty days?" he hollered. "What good is that when I only have two Reversal Cards left? That's not even half a year! How am I supposed to reach the Origin Realm in such a short span of time?"

Before he could further lament his fate, another message flashed before him.

-25 Karmic Credits for using a demonic technique.

Slifer blinked. "Oh, come on! That's daylight robbery! Those Reversal Cards are a total rip-off!"

Another notification appeared.

-10 Karmic Credits for killing a Core Formation cultivator.

He looked around, confused and slightly paranoid. "Who? Where? I didn't kill anyone! There's literally no one here!"

Shaking his fist towards the heavens, Slifer shouted, "System! Are you playing tricks on me? Is this your idea of a sick joke?" But as expected, the System remained maddeningly silent.

Huffing in frustration, Slifer murmured, "If only this came with a terms and conditions page."

He then scratched his head, trying to formulate a plan. "Alright, think, think," he muttered. "First things first, getting back to the Black Rose Sect." It was an ironic twist of fate. For someone like him, the very heart of a demonic sect turned out to be the safest haven. Unlike other sects, Black Rose frowned upon its members killing each other. "Who'd have thought? A demonic sect with . . . rules!"

However, as Slifer surveyed his surroundings, a grim realization hit him. The sect was nestled deep within the formidable Mount Desolace. "With my current . . . limited abilities"—he grimaced—"it would take me nearly a hundred days on foot. And that's without counting the countless beasts, bandits, and other obstacles that might fancy an old man for dinner."

"Okay, what do MCs do in these situations?" he pondered aloud. An idea struck him. "Communication token! Yes! Every sect worth its salt has one!"

"Aha! My trusty ring should have it." Slifer beamed. He looked down at his hand, eyes locked onto the ornate storage ring gracing his finger. It shimmered with a subtle purple glow, adorned with intricate patterns of black roses. He recalled from the previous owner's memories that one had to channel their spiritual sense into the ring, unlocking its contents much like a key to a treasure chest.

"Simple enough," he thought, already anticipating the smooth journey ahead.

However, his jubilation was short-lived. As he tried to channel his spiritual sense, he paused, frowning. "Wait a minute . . . Body Tempering cultivators don't have a spiritual sense," he recalled, horror dawning on him. The spiritual sense was a trait gained during the Qi Refining stage.

"I'm fucked . . ."

Slifer glanced around, trying to come up with a plan. "Alright, let's see . . . walking will take an eternity," he muttered, rubbing his temples. "Maybe . . . just maybe, this skill card could help."

"Activate Skill Card!"

Come on, System. Do me a solid this time.

Randomizing Skill
Congratulations!
Skill Acquired—"Insight"

> Grants information about an object or person upon focus. Can be upgraded for more detailed insights.

"Ah, of course. Insight. Because that's precisely what I needed right now! Not teleportation, not a speed boost, but insight." Slifer sighed, his shoulders slumping in disappointment.

"But hey, could have been worse. I could've gotten 'Advanced Pebble Sorting' or something."

Although, he perked up at the thought of upgrades. *So, the System can upgrade skills. Noted.* It was a silver lining in an otherwise frustrating situation. Not every System out there had the luxury of this feature.

Still, the pressing matter of how to get back to the Black Rose Sect weighed on him. Slifer looked up to the heavens, half in jest, half in desperation. "Dear xianxia gods, if there ever was a time for a protagonist to catch a break, now would be it. So, if you could send a handy beast mount or a kind stranger with a super-fast chariot, I'd be eternally grateful. Also, a snack would be nice."

Not expecting a reply, he began his long journey. "One foot in front of the other. It's just a hundred days. A hundred long, tedious, danger-filled days. What could possibly go wrong?"

Fenlock soared through the sky, a glinting sword beneath his feet propelling him forward. The wind brushed past his short, jet-black hair, his sapphire eyes scanning the horizon for any sign of Elder Slifer.

He sighed heavily, a pitiable expression on his face. *Of all the times . . .* he thought. Fenlock had finally persuaded Junior Sister Lenvari to go sightseeing with him, but this blasted mission had to come up.

"Sightseeing," Fenlock muttered to himself. "Why in the Seven Heavens would anyone want to simply look at things they've seen a million times? Clouds, trees . . . other clouds."

But his seniors had sworn by the tactic.

"Women love it," Senior Brother Zonrak had said with a knowing wink. "Take them sightseeing, and they'll be eating out of your hand in no time."

Eating out of my hand? But why would she want to do that? Fenlock's naïvety was almost endearing.

Yet here he was, not gazing at clouds with Lenvari, but chasing after an old demonic cultivator. All thanks to his master's peculiar vendetta against Elder Slifer.

Why on earth does Master hate him so much?

He'd heard numerous wild theories from fellow disciples. Some whispered that Slifer had once borrowed a treasured teapot from the master and never returned it. Others claimed that both Elder Slifer and the master had once fallen for the same woman, a celestial beauty who chose neither and instead ascended to a higher realm, leaving them both in bitter rivalry.

Then there was that absolutely ridiculous rumor that Elder Slifer had once bested the master in a dumpling-eating contest. Fenlock chuckled at that. *If that's true, it explains a lot about Master's weight loss attempts.*

But of all the stories, Fenlock's favorite was the one about the legendary phoenix feather. Legend had it that back when they were disciples, Elder Slifer had gifted the master a phoenix feather, claiming it had the power of reincarnation. The master, in his enthusiasm, had showcased it everywhere only to later find out that it was a mere chicken feather painted in vibrant hues. The humiliation was said to be something he had never gotten over.

Fenlock shook his head, a grin on his face. *Who knew the world of cultivation would be filled with such . . . pettiness.*

Fenlock was brought out of his thoughts when Brolin, one of the younger disciples, spoke up, a hint of terror evident in his eyes. "Who's going to be the one to approach Elder Slifer?"

The group, all riding on their flying swords, exchanged uneasy glances. Yurna, a petite woman with fire-red hair, and Charn, a stocky man with a perpetual frown, simultaneously raised their hands and vigorously shook their heads.

"Oh no, not me," Yurna stated, shivering. "I've heard stories. Didn't Elder Slifer once vaporize a disciple because he sneezed too loudly?"

Charn gulped. "And I've heard he reduced another to ashes because the poor fellow complimented his robe. Turns out, it was the elder's least favorite outfit!"

Dentos, a tall and lanky disciple, chimed in, his voice squeaking more than usual. "Don't forget about that disciple who gifted him the 'Elixir of Everlasting Youth.' Turned out to be prune juice. That guy? Instantly turned into a statue and now serves as a garden ornament at the sect's entrance."

Everyone shuddered.

Fenlock shook his head. "Come on, these are just exaggerated tales! They're like the stories where Senior Brother Zontu reached the heavens by stacking chairs and climbing. Entertaining, yes, but hardly true."

Yet, deep down, he knew that the tales of Elder Slifer's temper and random bouts of punishments were what kept half the sect on their toes. Fenlock had the highest cultivation amongst the group, and their expectations weighed on his shoulders.

He finally nodded, trying to sound more confident than he felt. "Alright, alright. I'll do it. After all, how bad could it be?"

Dentos whispered to Yurna, "He's so brave. Or very, very foolish."

Yurna nodded. "Perhaps both."

Brolin looked visibly relieved. "Thank you, Fenlock. And if . . . well, if something does happen, I promise I'll personally dedicate a ballad in your name."

"Great," Fenlock replied, rolling his eyes, "just what I always wanted. But after this, all of you owe me big time. I'm missing my precious sightseeing date for this!"

Fenlock's eyes narrowed as he sensed a surge of powerful qi signatures rapidly approaching. "Formation!" he barked, startling the group.

Brolin, trying to maintain his balance on the sword, asked with a trembling voice, "What's wrong?"

"Nascent Soul cultivators are coming our way," Fenlock replied grimly, his hand instinctively going to the jade amulet he wore around his neck.

Dentos gulped. "Nascent Soul? Why couldn't it be a group of Core Formation juniors? We could've just intercepted them, maybe roughed them up a little for fun." He paused, a sheepish grin on his face. "You know, to . . . uh, relieve stress?"

Yurna nodded enthusiastically. "Right! That's what lower-stage cultivators are for. A good smack here, a pinch there. But Nascent Soul cultivators? They're just big bullies!"

Despite being Core Formation cultivators themselves, there were few at that stage who could threaten them. As long as an MC-like person didn't appear, they could treat other Core Formation cultivators like dirt.

Charn muttered, "The irony of our thoughts doesn't escape me, you know."

"We can't face them head-on!" Brolin exclaimed. "What do we do?"

Fenlock took a deep breath. "Get your life-saving treasures ready. If we're going down, we're taking at least one of them with us!"

Everyone nodded, determined expressions on their faces. Brolin clutched a tiny golden figurine, Yurna held a shimmering orb, Charn brandished a silver dagger, and Dentos was . . . well, he was rummaging in his pockets, cursing under his breath.

"I swear I had it here . . . maybe the other pocket . . ."

But inwardly, Fenlock's determination was far from genuine. *The moment things go south, I'm out. After all, Junior Sister is waiting. And nothing, not even Nascent Soul bullies, will keep me from that date*, he thought, sneaking a glance at the escape talisman in his palm.

The arrival of the three Nascent Soul cultivators from the Radiant Dawn Sect had the Black Rose Sect disciples tense.

Jornak spat disdainfully in the direction of the Black Rose disciples. "Scum!" he hissed.

Quindel snarled, "You lot will pay for the young master's death!"

But Elder Lornox, glancing around nervously, hissed back, "Quiet! *He* could be nearby!" Without waiting, he flew faster as he carried the corpse of the young master. He did not have the time to bother with mere Core Formation ants.

Watching them flee, the Black Rose Sect disciples exchanged puzzled looks. "Erm . . . what just happened?" Dentos whispered, rubbing the spot on his robe where the spit almost landed. "Who killed the Radiant Dawn Sect's young master?"

Charn gulped. "Do you think . . . it could be our elder?"

Yurna scoffed. "The elder? After the tribulation he faced during his last breakthrough? I doubt he's in any shape to fight a kid, let alone mid-stage Nascent Soul cultivators."

"No," Fenlock murmured, eyes widening in realization. "It must be Tyrus."

The group went silent, the mere mention of that name sending chills down their spines. Tyrus, the prodigious cultivator who had achieved the Nascent Soul stage at the young age of thirty and was now at its peak. Tales of his power and ruthlessness were legendary.

Dentos scratched his chin. "Tyrus? You mean, the 'I-can-practically-cultivate-in-my-sleep' Tyrus?"

"The very same," Brolin whispered, swallowing hard. "He's the only one they'd be this scared of."

"Regardless, we need to head there now," Fenlock replied as he urged them to follow him.

"Uh, found it!" Dentos pulled out a slightly squashed pastry from his pocket. He grinned, holding it up proudly.

Fenlock looked back, shaking his head in disbelief, and mumbled, "Seriously, we need to revise our emergency preparations." But there was no denying the relief in his voice. Another disaster averted, and the sightseeing date was still on!

Slifer moved effortlessly through the dense forest, admiring the vibrant canopy above. *At least I'm hidden now*, he thought, reflecting on the bare openness of the desolate region he had just traversed. *In a place like this, I would've been an all-you-can-eat buffet for any beast with even half-decent vision. And given this is xianxia, they probably have eagle eyes . . . or dragon eyes or whatever.*

The rustling of leaves and distant sounds of birds felt familiar, yet Slifer couldn't shake off the strangeness of this new body. Every step felt too light, every movement too fluid.

Man, I could probably jog for days in this body without even breaking a sweat, he thought.

His previous body was, well, more rounded. The sort of physique that got winded walking from the couch to the fridge. "The kind where just lifting a fork felt like weight training," he said aloud, chuckling.

He paused, struck by a sudden realization. *Isn't it weird? Here I am, an old man probably knocking on heaven's door any moment now, yet I'm more fit than I ever was as a middle-aged man on Earth. Go figure.*

He couldn't help but reminisce about his days on Earth. The nights spent binge-watching TV shows, the endless pizza boxes stacked up in the corner of his living room, the "marathon" sessions of moving from his bed to his gaming chair.

"Good times." He sighed.

Slifer's wandering mind was jolted back to the present as a voice proclaimed, "Found him." He nearly leapt out of his skin, looking up to find five young cultivators hovering on flying swords, sneering down at him. Their sharp eyes glinted with mischief, their robes flamboyantly adorned, and their hair various shades of vibrant colors, looking like the antagonists of a xianxia novel. Their oppressive auras pressed down on Slifer, making his knees buckle.

Activate Insight!

Name: N/A
Realm: Late Core Formation
Known Techniques: N/A
Known Affiliations: N/A
Disposition: N/A

Shit! Core Formation? I'm so dead. Slifer didn't see the point of using Insight on the others, one Core Formation was enough to snuff him out like a feeble candle in a tempest.

Oh, great. Just what I needed, Slifer thought bitterly, his eyes darting around for an escape route, even though he knew there was no escape, Slifer wasn't one to just give up. *This old geezer must've ticked off these punks. Now they're here to collect!*

The disciples exchanged glances, a myriad of thoughts racing through their heads.

Is . . . is this really the mighty Elder Slifer? Fenlock wondered, squinting at the seemingly frail figure before them. *I can't feel any qi emanating from him. Is he . . . is he hiding it? Or does he . . . not have any?*

Meanwhile, Dentos scratched his head in confusion. *Why is he . . . walking? Don't elders, you know, fly or teleport or whatever they do?*

The weight of their gazes bore into Slifer, making the hairs on the back of his neck stand on end. *Shit! Why are they looking at me like that?* His fingers twitched, thoughts racing to the only trump card he had left. *Am I going to have to use "it"?*

CHAPTER THREE

Slifer's mind raced as he considered the Peak Slifer Card. A surge of reluctance welled up in him; he only had three of those cards. *To waste one on mere Core Formation cultivators?* No, he wouldn't do it. Well, not unless he *absolutely* had to.

Pushing his shoulders back, he straightened his stance, injecting every ounce of arrogance he could summon into his expression. "You know," he began, lips curling into a confident smirk, even as an inner voice whispered, *Please buy it. Please buy it.* "My hands have been quite itching to give out a proper beating today."

The five disciples paled considerably. Panic written all over their faces, they descended hastily, nearly crashing in their hurry. Fenlock, Yurna, and the others began to kowtow in a rushed, almost comedic fashion. Dentos, in his haste, tripped over a stray root, face-planting into the ground. Without missing a beat, he shifted into a frantic kowtow as well.

I . . . I did not expect that. Slifer's arrogant façade was tested by the sheer absurdity of the situation. *Are they really this afraid of me?*

However, as they drew closer, Slifer could feel the oppressive weight of their Core Formation auras bearing down on him. His face turned a shade of deep crimson, and the world around him seemed to blur slightly. The pressure constricted his chest, making every breath a battle.

These fuckers, are they trying to kill me?

The disciples, noticing his reddening face, completely misunderstood his reaction. *Is he . . . is he getting even angrier?* Fenlock thought, feeling a cold shiver run down his spine.

Slifer managed to gasp out, "How dare you? Displaying your auras like that? Have you no respect?"

Damn it! We weren't even flaunting it! Yurna thought, bitterness evident in her eyes, even as she hastily retracted her aura. Beside her, Fenlock did the same, shooting a wary glance at Slifer. *The old demon's just looking for excuses to lash out*, he fumed.

Slifer felt the weight on his chest begin to lessen as their auras were retracted. He coughed, taking a few ragged breaths to compose himself. During this slight respite, Yurna, still trembling, hastily tried to placate the elder she believed was on the brink of fury. "Esteemed Elder Slifer, we truly meant no disrespect! Please, spare our insignificant lives!"

Catching a glimpse of the Black Rose emblem on their robes, a wave of relief washed over Slifer. *Ah, they are sect members. Ha ha, this could be my ticket out of here. Oh heavens, you really did hear my prayers!*

The question now was: how could he leverage this without giving away the fact that he had no idea what he was doing? After all, it would be odd for a an elder like him to ask for a ride.

"Enough!" Slifer bellowed, making the disciples stop their kowtowing and glance up timidly. "It appears that fate has brought us together for a reason."

Good, keep it vague and mysterious, Slifer thought.

Brolin, hesitatingly spoke up, "Elder Slifer, if there's anything we can assist you with . . ."

Slifer, seizing the opportunity, feigned contemplation. "I've been meaning to return to the sect. But . . . my recent meditation required me to abstain from flying for a while. You understand, don't you?"

The disciples nodded vigorously, none wanting to question such a bizarre stipulation. They had heard that Nascent Soul monsters would indulge in some odd habits. For instance, Elder Zantris meditated upside down for decades, believing that it would reverse his chi flow. Then there was the infamous Master Yanling who insisted on speaking backwards during the Waxing Moon phase, thinking it would align her energies. Compared to such eccentricities, Slifer's flying abstinence didn't seem too outlandish.

Fenlock hastily replied, "Of course, Elder! We can escort you back."

Slifer fought the urge to grin triumphantly. *Nailed it! And they say hitchhiking is hard.*

"Very well," he replied. "But *only* because the stars have decreed it."

Yurna, after a moment's hesitation, offered, "Elder, would you . . . like to share a sword with me?"

Slifer nodded as he put on an air of resigned tolerance, as though this arrangement was a minor but acceptable disruption to his grand spiritual pursuits.

But inside? Slifer was practically ecstatic. Sharing a sword with a real-life jade beauty? For a man who previously pursued the "Dao of Anime Courtship," this felt like he'd hit the cosmic jackpot. He quickly subdued his inner otaku, sternly reminding himself to maintain his composed façade.

"But remember," he cautioned, "if you fly too erratically, you'll disturb my meditative state." The truth, however, was far less dignified: he was more worried about hurling in midair or, heaven forbid, falling off the sword entirely. Either would be a mortifying way to go, especially for a supposed elder of his standing.

Soaring high in the skies, Slifer awkwardly stood behind Yurna on her flying sword, the wind tousling his hair. The vast expanse of blue beneath his feet gave him a feeling of both exhilaration and terror. Trying to keep balance was proving more challenging than he thought, and he swayed with each gust of wind, fighting the urge to clutch onto Yurna for support.

Why didn't anyone mention sword-flying was this tricky?

Slifer was doing his best to keep up the façade of an elder of the sect—an expert who had ridden countless swords before. However, the genuine look of panic in his eyes betrayed his true feelings.

When Yurna made a swift turn, Slifer, unprepared, nearly lost his balance. With a gasp, he instinctively grabbed onto her waist to steady himself.

Yurna stiffened immediately. Her thoughts raced; *I've heard stories of old cultivation experts with . . . ulterior motives. Could Elder Slifer be . . . ?*

"E-Elder, are you okay?" she stammered, her voice betraying the calm façade she tried to project, a fragile smile painted on her face.

Trying to ease the palpable tension and regain his pride, Slifer nodded, attempting to appear unperturbed. "I am indeed, thank you. I must say," he began, thinking he'd divert the topic to something more casual, "you have an impressive physique. Yes, very . . . curvy, which surely must aid in flying."

Time seemed to stop. Yurna's forced smile faltered and then disappeared entirely. Her worst fears were confirmed. *Elder Slifer is after my body!* Her posture stiffened, panic evident in her eyes.

Seeing her reaction, Slifer mentally kicked himself. *Idiot! This is what happens when your only experience with females comes from virtual dating sims!* He groaned inwardly. *Smooth move, Casanova.*

Feeling the need to clarify, Slifer coughed awkwardly. "Erm, I meant that in a purely cultivation-related sense, of course! Your physique suggests you've done an excellent job in maintaining your meridians, vital for qi flow . . . or . . . something . . ."

Yurna looked unconvinced, but before she could voice any concerns, Slifer, sensing he was digging himself into a deeper hole, quickly interjected, "Let's just focus on getting to the sect, shall we?"

Fenlock watched Elder Slifer's precarious balancing act on Yurna's sword, raising an eyebrow in the process. *Seriously, what's this elder's deal? Does he have motion-sickness or is this some high-level cultivation technique?* He pondered for a moment, then thought, *Well, as long as he's not after Junior Sister Lenvari, it's fine by me.* He gave a shrug, deciding that whatever weirdness the elder had in mind for Yurna was not his concern.

His thoughts soon turned to the enigma that was Tyrus. *How to broach the topic without setting off the possibly unhinged elder? Did Elder Slifer give Tyrus a one-way ticket to the netherworld?*

However, glancing at the uninjured Elder Slifer, Fenlock dismissed the idea. *No, no way Tyrus would be taken down that easily. They must have missed each other or I'm pretty sure this old fool would be dead.*

Suddenly, a thunderous roar split the air. "You dare!"

Whipping his head up, Fenlock's eyes met the spectacle of a bald, topless old man descending from the skies. Despite his age, the elder's physique was impressive, rippling with muscles that seemed to be chiseled from granite. The sunlight gleamed on his shiny head, making it almost blinding.

It was Elder Tarnyx, the renowned body cultivator from the Radiant Dawn Sect!

Fenlock's pupils dilated in shock. *Elder Tarnyx?! Wasn't he supposed to be in secluded cultivation, preparing for his breakthrough to the Origin Realm? What's he doing here?* he thought, scrambling to put pieces of the puzzle together.

The palpable might emanating from Tarnyx was suffocating. Slifer, already struggling to maintain his expert façade, could feel cold beads of sweat forming on his forehead. The immense pressure was almost too much to bear. *What on earth does this hulking bald guy want with me?* he wondered.

Insight!

Name: N/A
Realm: Half-Step Origin Realm
Known Techniques: N/A
Known Affiliations: N/A
Disposition: N/A

H-Half-Step Origin Realm?! What the hell did the original do?! Slifer felt like fate was playing a cruel trick on him, he could not catch a break.

As Tarnyx floated, the air around him trembled. "Slifer!" he boomed, his face an alarming shade of crimson. "How dare you lay hands on the flesh and blood of Tarnyx!"

Tarnyx? Slifer blinked, taken aback not just by the accusation but also by Tarnyx's peculiar way of speaking. *D-did he just talk about himself in the third person?*

Swallowing his amusement and gulping down his nervousness, he replied, "Your flesh and blood? I have no idea what you're—"

"You think you can just kill the heir of Tarnyx and go about your day?" The elder seethed, recalling how he had been in deep meditation when the sudden extinguishing of his son's Soul Lamp jolted him awake. Abandoning everything, he had traveled from the sect to exact revenge.

Slifer was inwardly fuming at the situation he found himself in. *By the heavens,* he thought, *how many enemies did this old coot make? Am I going to have to dodge vengeful relatives every time I step outside?*

Fenlock stepped forward, clearing his throat. "Elder Slifer," he began cautiously, "I believe Elder Tarnyx is referring to the Radiant Dawn Sect's young master."

Slifer blinked. "Young master? What young master? I haven't killed anyone this ti—" His voice trailed off as a memory surged into his mind. Right, the System *had* mentioned something about a Core Formation cultivator falling victim to the Reversal Card's power.

Slifer reluctantly turned to Tarnyx, an apologetic grimace on his face. "Elder Tarnyx, by any chance was your son in the Core Formation Realm?"

Tarnyx's face contorted in rage, his aura crackling around him like a gathering storm. "Yes! And you dared to harm him!" The atmosphere around them grew heavy as Tarnyx's aura intensified, turning the surrounding space into a swirling vortex of oppressive energy.

Slifer's heart raced. He hadn't intended for this. He didn't even know anyone had been around when he used the Reversal Card! "Elder Tarnyx, I assure you it was an accident. I had no intention of harming a mere Juni—"

His words were cut off by the roar of Elder Tarnyx, who in a flash, appeared behind Slifer. With an enraged bellow, Tarnyx delivered a powerful blow, the space around it warping and distorting under the sheer force.

Fucked. I'm so fucked, Slifer thought but then a sudden notification rang out.

Ding!
Critical Block Activated

To his astonishment, Tarnyx's attack rebounded off an invisible shield, sending the bald elder staggering back from the recoil.

The force of the rebound also blew away Dentos, who had for some strange reason been trying to get a closer look. He landed face-first into a mud puddle. "Not again!" he mumbled, spitting out some mud.

Slifer exhaled, his legs feeling like jelly. *Whew, good thing that's a passive skill,* he thought, still reeling from the shock of Tarnyx's blinding speed. *He was right in front of me, and the next thing I know, he's behind me! That bald lightning bolt.*

Yurna, maintaining her balance on the sword beside Slifer, inwardly cursed. *Why did I offer this old man a ride?* She had thought she would be able to curry favor with the elder, unlike the other Core Disciples here, she and Dentos didn't have a strong backing. But, it turns out, not only was the elder a pervert but he also had a death wish!

> *Ding!*
> Kill Your Attacker
> Reward: 75 Karmic Credits
> Failure: Death

Slifer's eyes widened. *75 credits? Is that a lot?* He assumed so, killing a cultivator a half a step into the Origin Realm was no small feat but then again, he did have a System and with these Systems, you could never be certain.

He glanced warily at Tarnyx, whose face was twisted with anger. But a new conundrum plagued Slifer's mind: the last time he had killed, he lost credits. So, either killing was allowed as self-defense or the System was messing with him. *Could it be that I can only kill when the System gives the green light?*

He sighed heavily. If he were to stand any chance against the raging bald behemoth before him, he'd have to pull out the Peak Slifer Card. But the very thought of it made his heart race for all the wrong reasons. The probable credit deductions for invoking those dreaded demonic techniques could cost him dearly.

Why is this so complicated? Can't the System make up its mind? he thought exasperatedly.

Tarnyx's aura began to swell again as he prepared for another attack. Slifer took a deep breath, knowing he couldn't wait any longer.

"Slifer," Tarnyx roared, his bald head gleaming menacingly, "prepare to face your end!"

Slifer rolled his eyes. "Really? You couldn't come up with a better line?"

Tarnyx's face turned an even deeper shade of red, if that was possible. "Silence! This is your last moment, and—"

Before the bald elder could complete his clichéd sentence, Slifer, seeing no other option, activated the Peak Slifer Card. *System, activate the overpowered, and credit-eating, Peak Slifer Card. And if I see a ridiculous amount of credits disappear, we're going to have a long chat!*

Almost instantly, an overpowering aura began to emanate from Slifer's very core. It first shattered the Qi Refining Realm, sending ripples through the surroundings. Not stopping there, it surged upwards, breaking through the Foundation Establishment. Trees rustled and birds took flight in alarm. As it further breached the Core Formation Realm, the clouds in the sky began to swirl and change, reacting to the sudden outburst of energy. And then, with an overwhelming surge, it touched the Nascent Soul Realm, causing a sonic boom that echoed across the area.

But the climax was when it stopped at Half-Step Origin. The aura released a shockwave so potent that it caught Yurna off guard, she was sent flying off her sword. Her scream echoed briefly before being lost in the wind.

The disciples' eyes widened in sheer disbelief. Fenlock, eyes bulging, stammered, "I . . . I thought Elder was injured!"

Slifer felt the raw, unbridled power in every fiber of his being. It was exhilarating. He could sense everything—the rustling of each leaf, the heartbeat of a bird flapping its wings, even the soft hum of energy in the distant mountains. *So this is spiritual sense,* he marveled, *It's like seeing the world with the eyes of a god.*

In his newfound clarity, he also sensed Yurna's trajectory. An awkward pang of guilt hit him. *Oops. Hope she's okay.*

Pulling his focus back to Tarnyx, Slifer was met with an unimpressed glare. The old man scoffed, "All these theatrics and for what? It won't change your fate today."

What is this cannon fodder yapping about? Slifer thought as he relished in the feeling of the power surging within him.

> *Ding!*
> 10 Minutes Remaining

Slifer glanced at the dwindling time limit of the Peak Slifer Card. He felt a surge of urgency. The clock was ticking, and he had to defeat Tarnyx before the card's effects ran out.

His mind raced, sifting through the memories of the original Slifer to recall the most potent techniques. Just as he solidified a plan, Tarnyx lunged forward, using the move he was best known for, the "Titan's Crushing Palm."

Slifer, reacting quickly, summoned one of original's most powerful defensive techniques: Darkflame Ward.

Flames as black as the night sky rose around him, creating a barrier meant to consume any attack. However, unfamiliar with the technique's intricacies, Slifer's control wavered. Instead of a solid wall of fire, the flames flickered like erratic candlelight. *Shit, that was not what I was expecting.*

The Titan's Crushing Palm broke through the flimsy barrier and connected squarely with Slifer, sending him flying back, crashing into trees and leaving a path of destruction in its wake.

Slifer hit the ground with a thud, feeling as though every bone in his body had shattered. He tried to suppress a scream, gritting his teeth and taking short, sharp breaths. As a couch potato, he was not used to pain . . . or exercise for that matter.

But as the pain reached its peak, it suddenly . . . vanished. Surprised, Slifer inspected himself to find not a single scratch on him. Even more shockingly, his qi, which he expected to be greatly diminished, was pulsating at full capacity.

Amidst his astonishment, he began laughing uproariously. The sound of his laughter echoed through the forest, causing the Black Rose disciples to exchange uneasy glances.

Fenlock whispered to the disciple beside him, "Is . . . is Elder Slifer losing his mind?"

Dentos replied in a hushed voice, "It must be the trauma from the attack. I've heard of cultivators laughing like madmen after surviving near-death experiences."

Yurna just stared wide-eyed, her earlier fear replaced with pure confusion.

Reveling in his newfound realization, Slifer thought to himself, *So, the Peak Card keeps me in Slifer's optimal state! It's as if I'm immortal!* He grinned, wiping away a tear from laughing so hard. "Oh, Tarnyx," he said with a mocking tone, "you truly are outmatched today. Immortality is quite the feeling!"

I'm just going to spam powerful attacks one after another, let's see how you deal with that! With a flick of his wrist, Slifer summoned the Shadow Serpent Inferno.

A colossal, shadowy serpent manifested from the dark mist around him, slithering through the air with menacing grace. As it moved, dark flames trailed behind, painting the sky with a dance of darkness.

However, when Slifer attempted to direct the serpent towards Tarnyx, the creature, instead of following a straight path, made a detour and circled around, narrowly avoiding Dentos, who yelped in surprise. *Oops, gotta practice my control,* Slifer thought, inwardly cringing at the serpent's wayward movements. *Don't want another accidental death on my hands.*

Tarnyx, seeing the incoming attack, quickly used his prized defensive technique, Aegis Titan Shell. A rock-solid protective barrier enveloped his body. But the shadow serpents, persistent and relentless, wrapped around the shell, constricting and tightening around him. Tarnyx's once-confident face twisted in alarm.

From a distance, Brolin whispered to Yurna, "Did . . . did Elder Slifer just mess up a legendary technique and still manage to make it work?"

Yurna, who was picking out the leaves and twigs in her hair, could only nod. "It's like watching someone trip and accidentally perform a perfect somersault," she mumbled.

Without giving his opponent a moment's respite, Slifer unleashed another technique: Stellar Cascade Fury. The skies above darkened momentarily before a shower of glittering stars rained down, each star a concentrated ball of spiritual energy, destined to explode upon impact.

"How in the Seven Heavens . . ." Tarnyx started, incredulous, "can you continue using such advanced techniques without pause?"

Before he could finish his rant, the onslaught of stars struck him, drowning out his voice and leaving only the resounding booms of the explosions in the air.

Oh, Tarnyx, Slifer smirked internally, *I hope this teaches you not to mess with someone who has an overpowered cheat System at his disposal.*

As the brilliant shower of stars began its descent, Slifer's smirk faded, replaced by a look of utter disbelief. He had just realized that he'd accidentally included himself in the attack's trajectory.

Well, this is awkward, he thought, watching the dazzling stars zooming towards him. *If one of those stars obliterates me in a single strike, that Peak Card healing perk might be useless.*

With little time to think, Slifer summoned the Darkflame Ward again. Dark, ethereal flames enveloped him, forming a protective barrier. As the stars made contact, bright explosions erupted upon the ward's surface, sending shockwaves in all directions. Although the barrier did an excellent job of deflecting most of the impacts, a few managed to break through, scorching Slifer's robes and leaving light burn marks on his arms and chest. Before he could even wince, the burns began to fade, rapidly healed by the card's power.

Meanwhile, the disciples exchanged bewildered glances, trying to make sense of what they'd just witnessed.

"Did . . . did he just attack himself?" Brolin whispered, his eyes wide in confusion.

Yurna responded with a hushed chuckle, "Seems like the elder's taken a liking to pain. A bit of a masochistic streak, perhaps?"

Dentos added, "If reaching Nascent Soul means turning this . . . unpredictable, I think I might be content in Core Formation."

From the crater created by Slifer's attack, a severely injured Tarnyx began to rise. His once robust and muscular frame now bore deep gashes and charred skin, his robes tattered and singed. Blood dripped from his wounds, and his bald head, which previously gleamed menacingly, was now smeared with dirt and ash.

"You . . ." He coughed, pointing a shaky finger at Slifer. "This isn't over, Slifer. I will be back, and you will rue the day you crossed paths with Tarnyx of the Radiant Dawn Sect."

He really does sound like a typical xianxia villain, complete with the exit lines.

Slifer hesitated, his hand hovering in midair. Back on Earth, the closest thing to murder he'd committed was annihilating a double bacon cheeseburger. Now here he was, contemplating actual killing.

His gaze sharpened as he shook off the hesitation. *But in xianxia logic, if I don't finish him off, he'll just come back with an even bigger grudge and a Power-Up Orb or something. And that's a headache I don't need right now.* He took a deep breath. "I can't let you leave here alive," he finally stated, extending his hand with newfound resolve. *I've read enough to know you don't let a vengeful cultivator skulk away. It's like rule number one. Plus, I really do need those credits.*

Instantly, an overwhelming force of darkness emanated from him, swiftly expanding outwards and surrounding Tarnyx.

Tarnyx's eyes widened in horror. He never expected this. "A D-domain? At Nascent Soul Realm? Impossible!" He tried to dash out, but as the shadows thickened, he quickly found himself enclosed in an inky void, hitting an unseen barrier.

A cultivator of Tarnyx's experience immediately recognized the terrifying power of a domain. Yet, such a capability was commonly reserved for the Venerable cultivators of the Origin Realm. Only the rarest of prodigies in the Nascent Soul Realm could command such power. And from what Tarnyx knew of Slifer, he was no prodigy.

The darkness consumed Tarnyx, severing his senses one by one. He was rendered blind, deaf, robbed of smell and even his spiritual sense. Desperation gripped him, and panic set in as only his sense of touch remained. He tried to use short-distance teleportation, an ability characteristic of the Nascent Soul Realm, to break free, but his attempts repeatedly failed.

If only I had known . . . Tarnyx thought, his heart pounding. *If only I knew this monster could command a domain. I would never have dared to challenge him.* The realization that domains provided a nearly insurmountable advantage weighed on him. With such power, Slifer could easily decimate numerous cultivators of a similar rank.

Heir? Bah! What use is an heir in the face of death? I, Tarnyx of the Radiant Dawn Sect, can sire countless heirs under the heavens!

"Oh, what did I do to deserve such an unfilial son?" Tarnyx cursed under his breath, wishing this son of his had never crossed paths with this calamity of a cultivator.

From the outside, the disciples could only see a vast expanse of darkness, like a blotch of ink splattered against the landscape. Their faces registered shock and awe.

"I . . . I didn't know Elder Slifer had a domain," Yurna murmured, her voice quivering.

"If Elder has this kind of power, then Tyrus . . . he must truly be gone," Dentos added.

Fenlock, his eyes never leaving the dome of darkness, muttered, "This changes everything. Master must be informed."

With a thought, Slifer attempted a short-distance teleportation, aiming to appear right before Tarnyx. Instead, he materialized upside down, momentarily flailing before righting himself.

That . . . was not how it's supposed to go, he thought, clearing his throat and straightening his robes, grateful no one had seen his unintended acrobatics. He could not think of any excuse that could explain it.

"Erm, anyways, time to earn me some credits!"

CHAPTER FOUR

Slifer looked towards Tarnyx, who was currently deaf and oblivious to the outside world. "Sorry, old man," Slifer mumbled.

Sifting through the sea of memories within himself, Slifer came across several soul-annihilating techniques the original had mastered. They were, to put it mildly, intense. If the System wasn't going to reward him with extra credits for this kill, was using these techniques justifiable? Particularly when some felt like, well, absolute overkill.

One technique, dubbed the Eternal Abyss Seal, would tear a soul apart and imprison it within an endless chasm of anguish. Another, named Soul Shatter Rite, fragmented the soul into countless shards, casting them into myriad realms, rendering reincarnation almost impossible.

He exhaled a heavy sigh, his moral compass pointing away from these heinous methods. After all, he was the one who'd inadvertently ended the life of Tarnyx's son. "Well," Slifer mused, a sardonic grin forming, "I suppose I'll be seeing you in about a hundred chapters or so."

After continuing to look through his internal catalogue of techniques for a little longer, he finally found one that seemed slightly less horrifying.

"Hmm, this doesn't seem too bad, and apparently it gives me a power boost!" He had decided to use a technique named Bloodshadow Chains.

Crimson chains, born from his own blood, burst forth from his body. Each link that formed sent a sharp pain through his body, causing him to grimace.

"Are all demonic cultivators masochists?"

The chains lunged towards the blinded Tarnyx, wrapping around him and seeping into his skin. Tarnyx's screams echoed through the domain as the chains began their relentless draining. With every passing moment, his muscular form shrunk, his vitality sapped away, until he crumbled into dust.

Slifer sighed, a bitter smile forming on his lips. "You know, with all the killing that happens in this world, it's a wonder they haven't discovered the concept of therapy. Maybe if people talked through their issues, there'd be less need for all this bloodshed."

Just as the words left his lips, a Nascent Soul materialized from the ashen remnants of Tarnyx's body. It was a silvery, luminescent figure that had a vague resemblance to Tarnyx, and its voice was tinged with rage. "You slay my son and attempt to end my existence, and you speak of conversation?"

Slifer's eyes widened in disbelief. *Can he . . . see and hear me? Damn, I must've botched this technique too! I knew getting it right on my first try seemed too good to be true!*

Coughing lightly in embarrassment, Slifer tried to clarify. "Look, like I said before, the thing with your son was an unfortunate accident, alright? As for you, it was self-defense. Believe me, I have better things to do than go around offing old men."

The Nascent Soul glared at him and for a moment, their gazes locked in a silent standoff between the two. Then, with a final roar of fury, the soul declared, "I'll be back! I'll kill you and your descendants for nine generations!" Its ethereal form began to shoot upwards as it searched for a weakness in the domain.

Chasing behind it, Slifer grumbled, "Why do they always have to make these threats?"

Despite his initial surprise, Slifer's Half-Step Origin cultivation was no joke. In a flash, he was upon the Nascent Soul. With an outstretched hand, he delivered a fierce slap. The impact resonated with a thunderous boom.

Hovering in the sky, Slifer stared at the dissipating remnants of the Nascent Soul. A momentary pang of guilt passed through him. Had he gone too far?

He descended gently to the ground and sighed deeply. "It's done," he whispered to himself. "But at least, old man, you can still find another life." He looked to the sky, his thoughts drifting towards the endless cycle of birth, death, and rebirth. "Without using a soul-exterminating technique, Tarnyx can still enter the wheel of reincarnation. He'll probably come back as a turtle or something."

Slifer turned to see the crimson chains of blood reenter his body, he felt a rush, a powerful surge of qi swirling within him. His eyes gleamed with anticipation, relishing the newfound strength. *Ah, now this is the good stuff!* But just as he began to absorb this new energy, a System notification popped up.

Ding!
Warning: Peak Slifer form cannot be enhanced further.

His smirk faded. "You've got to be joking," he muttered. "Now what am I supposed to do with all this excess qi?"

Slifer attempted to force out the qi, but it clung to his insides like an unwanted guest at a party. It tried merging with him, but his current Half-Step Origin state resisted. Glancing at the timer for the Peak Slifer Card, a sinking feeling set in. Only five minutes left. Panic bubbled up. *If I don't sort this out, this foreign qi's going to tear me apart when the card runs out.*

He chastised himself: "Of all the times to get greedy, Slifer!"

Amidst the mounting desperation, a sliver of hope emerged from the depths of his memories—the Qi Condensation Seal. This method allowed a cultivator to condense excess qi and temporarily store it within the fortified channels of their body. But the word "temporarily" halted his relief. While this would buy him time, he was merely delaying the inevitable explosion.

Left with no better options, Slifer initiated the Qi Condensation Seal. He started channeling the surging energy, compressing it bit by bit. His muscles tightened and veins bulged as he systematically trapped the excess qi in specific spots within his body, sealing it away.

It was grueling, and more than once, Slifer felt the qi might break free. But as time passed, his control over the technique improved, and after what felt like an eternity, he had successfully condensed and stored the chaotic energy.

Taking a deep, shaky breath, Slifer examined himself for any abnormalities. To his relief, everything seemed stable, at least for now. However, he was acutely aware this was a temporary fix. The sealed qi pockets would eventually demand release, and he would have to face this challenge again.

Warning: 5 Seconds Remaining

"I'm going to miss this feeling." Slifer sighed. This was the first time he had felt true power; he could now understand why those cultivation maniacs would spend centuries behind closed doors—the boost was addicting.

Just as he was about to dispel the domain, a horrid thought crossed his mind: *What if the Qi Condensation Seal vanishes along with the Peak Slifer form?*

He tried rationalizing. "Techniques that have already been cast and that don't require more qi should stay in effect, right?" But the seeds of doubt had taken root. He looked at the timer. Only one second remained. As he closed his eyes, expecting an imminent explosion, there was only one thought going through his mind.

Fuck you, System!

The oppressive Domain of Darkness around them started to fade, showing the clear sky behind the blackness. Slifer could feel the power he had commanded moments ago slipping away. From Half-Step Origin, his cultivation plummeted downwards to Nascent Soul, then Core Formation, Foundation Establishment, Qi Refining, and finally halted at Ninth Stage Body Tempering.

Slifer slowly opened his eyes, surprised by the lack of, well, an explosion. He found himself the center of attention, with curious eyes staring at him. He cleared his throat. "Ah, I was . . . meditating for inner peace after such a fierce battle."

Dentos nodded sagely, a glint of admiration in his eyes. "Indeed, Elder. It's said that only through the act of killing can one truly achieve inner peace."

Slifer blinked, startled. That was definitely not the response he'd expected. *This kid's got a strange idea of inner peace.* Smiling awkwardly, he replied, "Ah, yes. Exactly as you say, young man. Inner peace through . . . killing." Slifer winced internally but kept up his profound-expert façade.

Whispers of agreement echoed amongst the demonic disciples, making Slifer question whether he really wanted to return to the sect.

"Elder, where is the corpse?" Yurna suddenly asked, looking around for any signs of the fallen cultivator.

Dentos's eyes lit up with excitement, "A corpse of a Half-Step Origin body cultivator would fetch a small fortune on the black market!"

Before Slifer could respond, Fenlock stepped forward. "Dentos! Show some respect. The spoils of battle belong to the elder. It's his choice whether to keep or dispose of them."

Slifer's mind raced. *Corpse? Sell?* A pang of regret hit him. He hadn't considered the value of the remains. With an inward groan, he realized the potential treasure he'd overlooked. Without access to the original's storage ring, he was basically broke, he would take anything he could get.

Well, isn't this a familiar feeling? Broke in one life, broke in another.

However, he had to maintain his image. Composing himself, Slifer replied with an air of indifference, "I saw no need for spoils. The body has been destroyed."

There was an audible gasp from the disciples. Destroying the corpse of a Half-Step Origin body cultivator was a feat that required immense power, usually only achievable by those in a higher realm.

Dentos, momentarily forgetting his greed, exclaimed, "Elder, your might is unparalleled! To think you could effortlessly destroy such a powerful body! Truly, our sect is blessed to have you."

Fenlock and Yurna exchanged glances, both clearly unimpressed by Dentos's blatant attempt at flattery.

Fenlock muttered under his breath, "Does he think we're blind? It's like he's wearing a sign that says, 'I'm brownnosing.'"

Yurna wrinkled her nose. "Some people just have no subtlety."

Mission Completed
75 Karmic Credits Added

Slifer felt a brief moment of elation, but then the message continued.

Use of multiple demonic techniques detected.
Deducting 25 Karmic Credits

He sighed, causing a few disciples to shoot him curious glances. A net gain of fifty credits wasn't all bad. He mentally patted himself on the back, thinking, *Not bad, Slifer. Not bad at all.*

However, his optimism wavered a bit when he looked at his stat screen. He only had fifty days left and he was already down one Peak Slifer Card.

Name: Slifer
Race: Human
Alignment: Demonic
Cultivation: Body Tempering: 9th Stage
Lifespan Remaining: 50 Days
Karmic Credits: 15
Skills: Insight (Basic)
Items: Reversal Cards x2, Peak Slifer Card x2, Critical Block x2

At least I'm no longer in the negatives!

He hadn't explored the System's Shop yet; only after checking its prices would he have a better idea if seventy-five credits *was* a good deal for killing a Half-Step Origin cultivator, but he had a sneaking suspicion it wasn't.

Clearing his throat, he addressed the still awestruck disciples. "Let's return to the sect." He did not want to stay outside any longer, especially given the unpredictable nature of this world.

Knowing my luck, a mystical beast in the midst of a thousand-year-long nap would be disturbed by the ruckus of our fight and come seeking vengeance.

Or worse, a heavenly maiden, while picking herbs, would accidentally drop her precious Heaven-Dew Elixir which he would inadvertently step on. And then she, backed by her overprotective sect, would hunt him down for compensation.

Nope, not today!

As they moved, Slifer couldn't help but look around cautiously, half-expecting some kind of disaster to unfold at any second. Yurna, who had been observing Elder Slifer intently, was bewildered.

This elder . . . he's not at all like the rumors, Yurna thought, scratching her head. *They say he's a ruthless, unapproachable figure, but he seems . . . well, honestly, he seems a bit neurotic right now.*

Nestled amidst the towering peaks was the Black Rose Sect. The main hall, made of obsidian stone, shimmered under the sun, a contrast to the white snowy mountain peaks that surrounded it. Its elegant architecture echoed the intricate patterns of black roses, the symbol of the sect.

Disciples in black robes were everywhere, some meditating under the ancient trees, while others practiced their sword techniques in open courtyards.

Contrary to popular belief regarding demonic sects, the Black Rose Sect was a peaceful sect. Well, as peaceful as a demonic sect could be.

Two junior disciples, Jorik and Lenis, were in the midst of a sparring session. Jorik dodged a move and laughed. "You're still too slow, Lenis!"

Lenis huffed. "You just wait. One day, I'll surpass you!"

Another disciple, Elara, was nearby, humming a soft tune as she watered the sect's famous Black Rose bushes. "Stop fooling around, you two! The elder won't be pleased if you trample on the roses again," she chided.

Suddenly, a shadow was cast overhead. All three looked up as one disciple, Dael, pointed skyward. "Look!"

High above them was Elder Slifer, surprisingly seated behind Yurna on her flying sword, followed by the other four disciples soaring close by. The spectacle was unusual to say the least.

Jorik sent a spiritual transmission to Lenis. "Isn't Elder Slifer a peak expert? Why is he on Yurna's sword? Do you think she's . . . you know . . . his woman now?"

Lenis chuckled inwardly, replying, "Well, with Elder's rumored short lifespan, I'd do the same. Enjoy every moment, right? Gather as many *roses* as you can, if you catch my drift."

Slifer's feet touched the ground, the cold stone of the Black Rose Sect beneath him. As soon as he landed, whispers spread like wildfire. The surrounding disciples seemed taken aback, their eyes widening as they realized they couldn't sense any qi emanating from him. It was a far cry from the usual overbearing aura Elder Slifer liked to parade around.

"Do you feel that?" Lorn, a mid-level disciple whispered to his friend, Orin.

Orin furrowed his brow. "Feel what? That's just it, I don't feel anything from Elder Slifer. Maybe he's turned over a new leaf?"

Perra, standing a little distance away, overheard them and scoffed. "You naïve fool. He's probably scheming. You'll see; by tomorrow, he'll be slapping some junior disciple for not bowing deeply enough."

A nearby disciple, Raela, shot them both a warning glance. "Quiet down! If the elder hears you, you're done for." Her words sent shivers down the spines of the nearby listeners.

Slifer felt a pang of annoyance. Even without sensing their exact words, he could guess the content. The whispers, the concealed laughter, the sideways glances; it all screamed mockery.

What fools! If I was the real Elder Slifer, they'd be in the afterlife right now. This demon killed someone for forgetting to address him as Elder!

As Slifer grumbled inwardly, a haughty laugh echoed through the grounds, cutting through the subtle whispers. A domineering aura descended, pressing down on the surroundings. It was the kind of pressure that made lesser cultivators feel as if a mountain rested on their shoulders, and it was now targeted at Slifer.

"E-Elder Fron . . ." one of the disciples choked out, the overwhelming pressure making it difficult to breathe.

Slifer's head snapped up to identify the source. The suffocating aura emanated from a familiar face, a fellow elder of the Black Rose Sect known for his arrogance and disdain for others.

"Elder Slifer." The man sneered, his lips curled into a smirk. "How the mighty have fallen. No longer flaunting your qi, I see? Or could it be . . . you've become a cripple?"

Struggling to maintain his air of profoundness, Slifer's heart raced as the old man's Peak Nascent Soul aura washed over him. In a bid to understand the old man before him better, he activated his Insight skill.

Name: Fron
Realm: Peak Nascent Soul
Known Techniques: N/A
Known Affiliations: Black Rose Sect
Disposition: N/A

Well, this is just fantastic, Slifer thought, feeling the weight of an impending xianxia trope about to play out. *This must be like that time the protagonist was forced by a jealous rival to kneel in the public square, only for some hidden power to kick in later. But unfortunately, I don't have that luxury right now.*

He raised his eyes, meeting the old man's gaze. "Elder Fron," Slifer began, "only a coward finds joy in oppressing the weak while trembling in the face of the strong. Must you really burden these young disciples with your aura?"

The old man's face turned a shade redder, clearly taken aback by Slifer's words. "Oh, please! You're one to talk." Elder Fron scoffed. "Just last week, I heard you made some poor disciple vomit by strangling him with your aura. Hypocrite much?"

The surrounding disciples murmured amongst themselves, while Slifer's eyes widened momentarily. *Oh right, the old demon did do that,* he thought, feeling a touch guilty.

Clearing his throat, Slifer replied with as much profundity as he could muster, "Ah, well, that was the action of a younger man."

Elder Fron laughed, his eyes gleaming with amusement. "Younger man? You're practically knocking on death's door! That *younger man* would have been, what, a few days younger?"

Slifer winced, reminding himself to remain calm. "Age," he replied slowly, "is but a perspective, Elder Fron. One must always strive to better oneself with each passing day."

The old man's gaze shifted, and a smirk formed on his lips. "Where's that disciple of yours, Tyrus?" he asked, a mocking tone evident.

Slifer's face remained impassive as he stayed silent.

Seeing the lack of response, Elder Fron's smirk grew even wider. "He betrayed the sect, didn't he? Oh, Slifer, you've truly lost your touch," he taunted. "To think that the *mighty* Elder Slifer couldn't even keep a simple disciple in check."

A wicked gleam appeared in Elder Fron's eyes. "You know, my own disciple tried to abandon our sacred Black Rose Sect about a decade ago," he boasted. "I broke every bone in his body and threw him into our dungeon. To this day, he's still down there, pleading for my forgiveness and mercy."

Is he . . . really bragging about that? Slifer pondered, feeling a mix of pity and disbelief.

He responded with an air of scholarly wisdom. "Every disciple needs to experience the world in their own way. Tyrus's path has diverged, but only by exploring it can he truly grow. When the time is right, I'll guide him back to our sect."

That's such utter nonsense; how do I even come up with this stuff? Slifer thought. *But then again, if that punk Tyrus hadn't offed the original me, I wouldn't have this body . . . Perhaps I owe him a twisted thank-you?*

Elder Fron's mocking laughter rang out once again. "What in the heavens has come over you? Has old age muddled your mind? The Slifer I knew a hundred years ago would've flattened that brat with a mere slap."

With a slow shake of his head, Slifer replied, "Ah, but that was the folly of a rash young man."

Elder Fron's face turned an even deeper shade of red, veins popping on his forehead. "Young man?! What is this young man nonsense?" He spluttered. "You haven't been a 'young man' for nine hundred and seventy years!"

Just as Slifer was about to retort, several System messages flashed before his eyes, causing his gaze to momentarily drift, looking distracted.

Ding!
New Task
Kill the Demonic Elder
Reward: 50 Karmic Credits
Failure: Possibly Death

N-no, I can't kill this guy, I'm not using another Peak Slifer Card! Slifer hoped that death would be due to the old man killing him and not the System instantly ending his life if he refused to follow along. At least with the old man, he could try talking his way out of it but if the System wanted to kill him, well then he was screwed.

Ding!
Alternative Task
Reeducate the Demonic Elder
Reward: 500 Karmic Credits
Failure: N/A

---

500 credits?! So, the System wants me to convert these bad guys into good guys? And if that doesn't work then I should just kill them? Sounds fair . . .

Slifer noticed that there was no consequence for failing that mission, then maybe he did have a chance to talk himself out of this.

Elder Fron, meanwhile, misinterpreted Slifer's distracted look. His own face reddened further, interpreting Slifer's momentary lack of focus as blatant disrespect. "You dare to ignore me?!"

Fenlock, sensing the escalating danger, quickly darted behind his master, sending a hurried spiritual transmission. "Master, you must be careful! Elder Slifer annihilated Elder Tarnyx! Not even a shred of his body remains."

Elder Fron's color drained from his face upon hearing this, and his eyes widened in shock. Tarnyx, a Half-Step Origin expert, was a sub-realm above him, and if Slifer had disposed of him so easily, he would be no match. He had been confident mocking Slifer earlier, assuming his power had waned significantly and that this was the best time to humiliate him, but now he realized the perilous miscalculation he made.

Whipping around in panic, Elder Fron raised his hand and slapped Fenlock hard. The slap sent him crashing into a sect building, but the building's protective ward sent him bouncing back, tumbling ungracefully to the ground.

"You fool!" Elder Fron roared. "You call yourself a disciple of mine?! Why didn't you inform me sooner?"

Rubbing his sore face, Fenlock mumbled, "I . . . I just arrived, Master."

"You dare speak back to me!" Elder Fron's eyes blazed with fury. "You are no longer worthy to be my disciple!" he thundered, disowning Fenlock in one sweeping declaration.

Fenlock's head drooped low, his body quivering like a leaf in a storm. Without the backing of an elder, not only would all benefits exclusive to favored disciples be stripped away, but he would also become an easy target. In a world where the law of the jungle reigned supreme, lacking an elder's protection was akin to walking on a threadbare rope over a bottomless abyss. No one would bat an eye if he were to vanish into thin air.

Seeing the desolate expression on Fenlock's face, the surrounding disciples whispered among themselves, many shooting him pitiful glances while others wore malicious smirks, clearly happy about his misfortune.

Slifer shook his head in disbelief. *Geez, talk about an overreaction. Why is this old man so dramatic? That poor disciple . . . His future looks grim.* He shrugged, turning his gaze away. *Well, not my problem. I already have enough on my plate.*

Swallowing hard and trying to salvage his pride, Elder Fron turned back to Slifer, clearing his throat. "Ah, Elder Slifer, I just recalled an extremely crucial matter that needs my urgent attention."

Slifer raised an eyebrow, surprised by the quick turn of events. "Oh? And what might that be?"

"Ah, Elder Slifer, it was our conversation. It has brought . . . um, a sudden enlightenment! Yes! I must immediately retreat to my meditation chamber to grasp this new understanding. Your words . . . they might have just nudged me towards my next breakthrough. How . . . um, fortuitous!" With a stiff nod, and without wasting another second, Elder Fron zipped away, practically vanishing into thin air.

Watching him go, Slifer shook his head, almost facepalming at the sudden retreat.

Beside him, Dentos exclaimed, "I have also received enlightenment from the wise elder's speech!"

Ah, these disciples weren't useless after all. Not only did I get a free ride, but they can spread tales of my awesomeness.

Just as Slifer was about to leave, a System message appeared before his eyes.

> Congratulations!
> New Feature Unlocked
> Disciple Management

Before he could even consider what that entailed, another message popped up.

> *Ding!*
> New Task
> Take the young Fenlock as your disciple.
> Reward: 25 Karmic Credits
> Failure: N/A

Oh, great. Now I have to babysit? Slifer sighed, muttering under his breath, "Turns out it is my problem after all."

He quickly skimmed the details and saw the reward: a generous number of credits. *Hmm, not bad. Can't really say no to credits,* he mused, imagining ways to delegate any disciple-related chores. *Maybe there are some sect errands I can send him on. Or perhaps some annoying elder I can have him fetch tea for.*

Approaching the dejected Fenlock, Slifer channeled his inner sage and wrapped himself in a profound aura. "Young one," he began with a deep, resonant voice, "it appears that the heavens have decided our paths shall intertwine."

Fenlock blinked and looked up, confusion clouding his eyes. *What on earth is this elder babbling about? Isn't he the reason I'm in this mess?*

Perceiving the silence as the young lad being too shocked to answer, Slifer continued, "Would you, by chance, be interested in becoming my disciple?"

Fenlock's face drained of color. In his mind, the only predicament worse than being under Elder Fron would be to serve under the unpredictable Elder Slifer. But meeting the piercing gaze of the elder, a sense of inevitable surrender washed over him. Stammering, he bowed low, "D-disciple greets . . . Master."

It's over, he mourned. *From one disaster straight into another.*

> *Ding!*
> Mission Completed
> Congratulations on gaining a new disciple!
> 25 Karmic Credits Added

A triumphant grin spread across Slifer's face. *That went smoother than anticipated. Isn't my reputation as a "difficult" elder supposed to precede me?* He shrugged, silently commending himself. *Maybe I'm just that charismatic.*

A few feet away, Yurna watched the scene unfold with barely concealed envy. *If it were me, I wouldn't think twice. Being under any elder, even if it is Elder Slifer, is far better than having no elder at all.* She sighed internally, yearning for the prestige and protection that came with being an elder's disciple.

Dentos, having observed Fenlock's sudden change in fortune, promptly dropped to his knees. "Elder Slifer!" he exclaimed. "Please, allow me to become your disciple too!"

Slifer glanced upwards, half-expecting another System prompt to guide his next actions. However, no notifications came. *Well, I'm not taking in freeloaders without a reward,* he mused with a slight frown.

Misinterpreting the frown, Dentos hastily blurted out, "I know I'm not much now, Elder, but I promise to change for you! I'll become the disciple you deserve!"

Why does that sound like a line from a bad breakup? Slifer pondered, mildly amused. *Sorry, buddy, I'm not looking for that kind of commitment.*

Clearing his throat, Slifer began, "Young Dentos, I believe our fates are not . . ."

Before he could finish, Dentos interrupted, almost desperate, "But Elder! We, as demonic cultivators, defy the heavens! We're not meant to talk about fate!"

Slifer froze. *Damn, he's got a point. Why am I blabbering about fate? I need to be more . . . demonic. Righteous cultivators and their fate talk . . .* He huffed internally, rebuking himself for the lapse in character.

Recomposing himself, he pondered how to display his demonic nature convincingly. The images of various methods of torture flashed across his mind. But they all seemed a bit . . . over the top.

Opting for a simpler approach, he scoffed dismissively, his tone dripping with disdain. "You're right. You're not worthy."

Dentos's face turned purple, as though he'd swallowed a bitter pill. He collapsed onto the ground, pounding his fists against the earth. "Ah, even Elder Slifer has rejected me! Am I truly doomed to be a mediocre disciple, forever without an elder's guidance? How shall I face my ancestors? How shall I even face myself?"

He then started crawling on all fours, picking up a handful of dirt and letting it slip through his fingers as if contemplating the sands of his rapidly diminishing future. "Even the earth rejects me," he wailed, tossing the dirt away.

Slifer watched the display, fighting back a smirk. *Honestly, with all this angst and passion, this kid would probably fit in better at one of those holier-than-thou righteous sects,* he mused. *There, they'd probably call this "profound introspection" or something.*

Seated atop a plush cultivation cushion in his quarters, Slifer couldn't help but marvel at its comfort. *No wonder cultivators can stay immobile for years. This feels like a cloud!* He pressed the soft fabric, allowing himself a momentary indulgence.

Rubbing his hands together gleefully, he murmured, "Finally, a safe haven." The warmth of the sect's protective array provided a peace he hadn't felt since he entered this world. "I don't think I'll be stepping outside anytime soon." He chuckled to himself, looking forward to a quiet period of reclusiveness. After all, there was no way he would risk his hide before regaining his cultivation.

His mood on the upswing, Slifer prepared to dive back into cultivation. "Regaining my power should be simple enough," he murmured, optimism coating every word. *This body has been cultivating for centuries, it surely remembers the methods.*

The real issue that concerned him was the lack of time; he would need to milk his disciples if he wanted to survive.

"Eh, I can think about that later. Right now, I need to at least enter the Qi Refining Realm. Without any spiritual qi, I'm basically useless."

Delving into the recesses of the original Slifer's memories, he attempted to find the primary cultivation technique. Frustratingly, the memories seemed hazy, almost as if covered by a fine mist.

"Why can't I recall the primary cultivation method? Wouldn't the old geezer have been using it every day? It's like forgetting how to brush your teeth!" he grumbled, his brows furrowing.

Ah, wait a minute... A sudden realization struck him. *This must be one of those "essential memories" the System mentioned I'd be missing. Well, that's just perfect.*

After a few futile minutes, a secondary cultivation method surfaced in the sea of memories: the Sinful Karma Absorption. As he read the technique's introduction, he felt his heart sink. The method was gruesome, to say the least. *To actually harness wicked deeds as energy... That's messed up.*

Demonic cultivators using this method would purposely commit unthinkable crimes, accumulating an abundance of dark karma. This malevolent energy would then be harnessed and converted into cultivation power, elevating them through different cultivation stages.

Slifer felt a shiver run down his spine. Merely thinking of the vile acts listed as requirements for each breakthrough turned his stomach. *Even for a demonic cultivator, the original Slifer was one twisted soul,* he thought. *If the sect discovered even a fraction of these deeds, they'd probably banish him on the spot.*

"I'm NOT using this damned method," Slifer spat vehemently, his voice echoing through his chamber. With a deep breath, he composed himself. There had to be another way.

Still unsettled from reading the Sinful Karma Absorption technique, Slifer continued sifting through the memories, looking for a less detestable option. Finally, his eyes landed on another technique: the Abyssal Heart Resonance.

As he delved into the technique's intricacies, he found it relatively benign for a demonic method. This technique channeled one's inner darkness, syncing it with the surrounding shadows and night energy. The harmonic resonance would then be absorbed and refined to boost one's cultivation.

With a resigned sigh, he decided. "Guess I don't have much choice here." *At least this doesn't involve breaking any moral codes.* Preparing to immerse himself in the Abyssal Heart Resonance's depths, he was interrupted by an all-too-familiar chime.

Ding!
Deduction Alert
Use of demonic cultivation methods will result in a loss of Karmic Credits.

"Are you kidding me?!" Slifer exclaimed, glaring at the message. "This method's hardly even demonic! Heck, some might even call it a force for good!"

Despite his protests, the System remained ominously silent. Frustration bubbled within him. It felt as though the universe was against his every move.

With a heavy sigh, he mumbled, "Alright then, System. It's clear that there's only one way left, show me your Shop."

After all, if he couldn't cultivate the traditional way, he might as well see if the System had some shortcuts. Granted, he only had forty credits, but it was time to see what this Shop was like. Who knows, maybe it even had some affordable techniques that would bypass its pesky rules.

At the thought of "affordable," Slifer almost burst into laughter. *Ah, what a concept. I'll probably find a Level One Basic Qi Pill for a thousand credits or some nonsense like that.*

He thought back to all the stories he'd heard of LitRPG Systems. There was always that cliché where the System conveniently had a sale right after you spent all your credits. Or the special "limited edition" items which, oddly enough, seemed to be available all the time.

Slifer shook his head, his laughter slowly subsiding. *Well, I've delayed enough. Time to see if the System is a scam artist or if it actually has some valuable treasures.*

CHAPTER FIVE

The Shop interface appeared before Slifer.

Shop
Cards
Cultivation Methods
Treasures
Pills and Elixirs
Mystic Techniques
Martial Techniques
Bloodlines and Ancestries
Constitutions
Spirit Roots
Beasts and Familiars
Create

There were cultivation methods, cultivation resources, treasures, pills, martial techniques, and more. Everything a cultivator could dream of was listed. There was even a "Create" option!

Slifer's eyes darted straight to the cultivation methods. Curious, he tapped on the cultivation methods category. *Even though the System can comprehend my intentions, there's an oddly pleasing sensation in the act of selecting it myself.*

Cultivation Methods
Heaven
Earth
Mortal

He was greeted by an array of options, all seemingly righteous in nature. *No surprise there*, he mused, recalling the System's earlier reprimand about demonic techniques. As he skimmed through the vast collection, he quickly found the cheapest technique for each tier.

Heavenly Celestial Breath Method
Description: Channels the power of celestial stars into pure cultivation energy.
Price: 500 Karmic Credits
Earthly Vital Core Condensation
Description: Condenses the vital energy in the dantian, aiding rapid cultivation breakthroughs.

Price: 200 Karmic Credits
Mystic Heart Purity Method
Description: Purifies the heart and soul of the practitioner, ensuring a sturdy foundation
for future cultivation.
Price: 100 Karmic Credits

Slifer's eyebrows furrowed. *Is this System trying to rob me blind?* "One hundred credits for a basic mortal technique? You'd think I was shopping in a luxury sect boutique!" he huffed.

With only forty credits to his name, the situation was dire. "To afford even the most basic technique, I'd need to take down a Core Formation cultivator," he muttered in frustration. "If I wanted anything more than that, then I'll have to go on a killing spree, and that's certainly not happening!"

Feeling defeated, he thought about exploring other sections of the Shop but was hesitant. "If the techniques are priced higher than a celestial mountain, I might end up doing that stereotypical xianxia blood-vomiting move out of sheer exasperation."

He chuckled bitterly, realizing that he'd always found those scenes in xianxia novels to be overly dramatic. But now? *Seems I'll be joining the club of blood vomiters soon.*

With a flick of his finger, he closed the System Shop's interface. "I've had enough of this for today. I'll have to think of another way."

A smirk formed on his lips as an idea sprouted in his mind. "Time to utilize my underlings," he murmured. After all, he had an array of eager lackeys ready to do his bidding, not even counting his actual disciples.

He tried to recall the names of his disciples but then just decided to open up the Disciple Management Panel.

Disciple Overview
Number of Disciples: 5
Disciple Capacity: 5

Promote/Demote
Outer Disciples: 4
Inner Disciples: 0
Core Disciples: 1
Legacy: 0

Current Disciples
Amelia: Active
Caelum: Active
Fenlock: Inactive
Hughie: Active
Tyrus: Inactive

Slifer examined the overview with a discerning eye, noting the unfamiliar names. *Only five disciples? And I've only met the newly minted Fenlock?* He was slightly taken aback. *What was the original even doing?* he mused, especially intrigued by the "Outer Disciples" category. Elders usually took in young talents as Core Disciples, and if they had the aptitude of a genius, they'd be ranked as Legacy Disciples. However, knowing the original's paranoia, Slifer doubted he would give away his own personal cultivation methods.

He rubbed his temples. *Maybe the original just didn't care enough.* Though, from the fragmented memories he'd accessed, it seemed they all reaped the same benefits as Core Disciples.

He decided to click on Amelia's profile and a new panel appeared.

Disciple Panel			
Character Profile		**Cultivation Profile**	
Name:	Amelia	Current Cultivation:	Mid-Core Formation
Age:	20	Primary Cultivation Method:	N/A
Sex:	Female	Subsidiary Skills:	N/A
Background:	Unknown	Constitution:	N/A
Affiliation:	Black Rose Sect	Bloodlines:	N/A
Alignment:	Demonic	Spiritual Roots:	N/A
Comprehension:	5	Management Options:	
Luck:	6	Current Quest:	
Talent:	7	Training Plan:	
Will:	4	Loyalty:	69%

Eyeing the profile, he realized that not all the information was accessible. *Unknown background? Spiritual Roots not available? Great, that's helpful.*

He squinted at the character profile. "Why are some sections missing?"

> Disciple Management must be upgraded to access additional information and features.

Slifer sighed dramatically, rolling his eyes. "Of course, there's an upgrade. There's always an upgrade. So, I buy this with credits, right?"

> Disciple Management is upgraded by gaining experience in managing disciples.

Slifer raised an eyebrow, slightly amused. "So, I get 'XP' for this, huh?"

The System remained silent.

Typical. They always leave you hanging when you start asking the right questions.

Then, his attention shifted to the character statistics.

"System," he started, scratching his chin, "these numbers . . . I mean, they're out of ten, right? So what's the benchmark here?"

> Numbers range from 1–10
> 1–3 is Mortal Rank
> 4–6 is Earth Rank
> 7–9 is Heaven Rank

Slifer arched an eyebrow, his curiosity piqued. *And what about ten?* he wondered. The System remained silent on the matter, offering no further clarification.

Probably some mythical, universe-bending, deity-level stuff. They always love throwing in those crazy tiers.

Looking at Amelia's stats, Slifer nodded in approval. "Not too shabby. Probably a pseudo-protagonist."

He assumed that protagonists would have mainly Heaven Rank stats, if only he could look at his own stats then he could find out what he really was.

He then clicked on Hughie.

Disciple Panel			
Character Profile		**Cultivation Profile**	
Name:	Hughie	Current Cultivation:	Late Core Formation
Age:	25	Primary Cultivation Method:	N/A
Sex:	Male	Subsidiary Skills:	N/A
Background:	Unknown	Constitution:	N/A
Affiliation:	Black Rose Sect	Bloodlines:	N/A
Alignment:	Demonic	Spiritual Roots:	N/A
Comprehension:	2	Management Options:	
Luck:	8	Current Quest:	
Talent:	8	Training Plan:	
Will:	3	Loyalty:	55%

Slifer's brows raised as he decided to look at Hughie's stats. *Wow, both comprehension and will are trash. How is this guy even . . .* His thoughts trailed off as he caught sight of Hughie's luck, which stood tall at a staggering eight.

"Eight?! This guy's luck is almost at the peak of Heaven Rank?!" he exclaimed, his voice raising a few octaves. He held his head in his hands, looking genuinely distressed. "Ah, a protagonist! A real one!"

Protagonists! Why does it always have to be protagonists? Slifer mused. *Sure, pseudo-protagonists are a handful, but they're manageable. But true protagonists? They're calamity magnets, walking, talking disaster zones.*

He recalled tales from classic xianxia stories. *Let's see, the beloved master meets a tragic end, the sect gets obliterated, the loved ones either perish or get kidnapped . . .* The list went on. The thought of one of those tropes landing on his doorstep made his skin crawl.

Oh no, what do I do with this guy? Do I have to die tragically for his character development?

The only reason he wanted to be a protagonist in the first place was because the number one rule of any xianxia was that the protagonist always wins. Yeah, granted, he might have to suffer for thousands of chapters but he'd be the one who finally got the jade beauties and basically became a god, right?

Seeking a change from the mind-boggling stats, he clicked on Caelum's profile.

Disciple Panel			
Character Profile		**Cultivation Profile**	
Name:	Caelum	Current Cultivation:	Late Core Formation

Age:	25	Primary Cultivation Method:	N/A
Sex:	Male	Subsidiary Skills:	N/A
Background:	Unknown	Constitution:	N/A
Affiliation:	Black Rose Sect	Bloodlines:	N/A
Alignment:	Demonic	Spiritual Roots:	N/A
Comprehension:	7	Management Options:	
Luck:	6	Current Quest:	
Talent:	6	Training Plan:	
Will:	6	Loyalty:	50%

The numbers were more balanced, much to his relief. "Ah, Caelum, at least you don't seem like you'll be the death of me," he muttered.

Slifer's eyes narrowed. "Wait a minute. How did the original even manage to recruit all these talented disciples? It's like he was collecting young prodigies like trading cards." The thought unsettled him. *And why did Tyrus kill him? I mean, sure, the old me wasn't winning any "Master of the Year" awards, but still . . . The original definitely was doing some sketchy stuff . . .* His thoughts trailed off, unable to pinpoint exactly what he was concerned about.

Shaking his head, Slifer mumbled, "All I know is each and every one of these disciples is way too important. Like, plot-twist-important." He sighed. "Especially Tyrus. Why else would the old man chase him right after failing a breakthrough? Urgh, I'm thinking about this too much." Slifer shook his head and then decided to check Fenlock's stats, the System wouldn't make him accept a nobody as a disciple, right?

> Error
> Unauthorized Access
> Complete Master-Disciple Ceremony

Slifer squinted at the screen, momentarily taken aback by the denied access. "System, aren't you being a tad too formal? It's not like I'm trying to hack his bank account," he muttered.

He then scratched his chin as he thought of the details of the Master-Disciple Ceremony. *The ceremony usually involves pouring spiritual tea into jade cups. Both parties sip the tea and form a spiritual bond, eternally connecting their fates—or at least until one of them inevitably dies in some gruesome manner, because that seems to be the only way people die in this world.*

"Eh, I can do that later." He remembered how Fenlock had scurried off, muttering about some "junior sister."

Clearly, they both had more important things to do.

Looking back at the names, Slifer was struck by an odd realization. "Hughie? Caelum? Amelia?" he muttered, incredulous. Even though their features were unmistakably Asian, their names were decidedly . . . Western.

Now that I think about it, I have yet to meet anyone with a traditionally Asian name. Why would they . . . ? Oh, wait. An absurd realization hit him. *Xianxia with Western names? Are you kidding me?* In his mind's eye, he pictured his disciples: Asian faces with names that wouldn't be out of place in an English pub. *What's next, a cultivator named Bob?*

A frown crossed his face. *It's those Western authors! Trying to make everything convenient for themselves. Taking sacred Eastern traditions and . . . ahem . . . perverting them.* He conveniently skipped over that one time he, a Western guy, tried writing a xianxia tale, only to find himself drowning in a sea of Chinese names. Choosing to name his characters "John" and "Lily" to save his sanity was a memory he'd rather forget.

"Now, how should I call them?" Slifer muttered, staring at the empty room. Normally, he would use a spiritual transmission or activate a communication token, but both required spiritual qi. Being in the Body Tempering stage, his reserves were as empty as a beggar's bowl at a feast.

With a heavy sigh, he got up and made his way outside. His quarters were protected by all sorts of mystical runes, designed to keep external noises and unwanted spiritual senses at bay.

It's like living in a self-made prison of silence.

His quarters opened into a large courtyard, filled with exotic plants and blooming spirit flowers. Even the pathways were crafted from spirit stones, glistening softly in the ambient qi. Ponds were filled with spiritual fish that emitted faint glows. Everything was just perfect for a cultivation sect's main headquarters.

Clearing his throat, he decided to do it the old-fashioned way. "Hughie! Amelia! Caelum! Get over here!" he shouted, his voice echoing through the courtyard.

After a short pause, he could hear hurried footsteps approaching. A young Chinese man, appearing around twenty-five, rushed forward. "Master, is something wrong?"

"Ah, Hughie, I need you to do something urgent for me."

Hughie, who was in fact Caelum, decided against clarifying the mix-up. Past memories flooded in—memories of the elder flying into a rage over minor details, of innocent bystanders who fell victim to Slifer's unpredictable temper. *Better to be Hughie for today than not be at all,* he reasoned.

Breaking his reverie, Slifer cast a scrutinizing gaze at Hughie (still, actually Caelum). "Where's Morvran?" he demanded, recalling the elderly Core Formation cultivator who was Slifer's right-hand man and, in many ways, a butler. The old man was nearing the end of his three-hundred-year lifespan; he was raised by Slifer as a death warrior and if Slifer wanted something done, then he was the man for the job.

Gulping, Caelum was startled by the question. *Doesn't Master already know this?* "Master, Boss Morvran . . . umm . . . he's on an errand you assigned him," he replied hesitantly. *Is this some sort of test?*

Slifer nodded, keeping his facial expression carefully controlled but inwardly, he was a jumble of confusion. *What on earth did I—I mean, the original—send Morvran to do? Rob a spirit herb garden? Steal a divine beast? Start a sect war for fun?* A sense of dread filled him. *Knowing that old demon, it's probably something that'll give me a headache for a decade . . . if I live that long.*

"Very well," Slifer said aloud, feigning satisfaction. "Once Morvran returns, let me know immediately."

"Of course, Master," Caelum replied, barely masking his relief. He really thought that the master was looking for an excuse to beat him.

Slifer handed Caelum a jade token. "Take this to the elder's section in the sect archives. I want you and the others to find some righteous cultivation methods and bring them to me."

Caelum stared, genuinely shocked. *Righteous methods? For Master?* The very idea was so out of character for Slifer, it was like asking a lion to go vegan. Risking a quick glance upwards, he found Slifer's eyes fixed on him. Panic surged through Caelum, and he instantly dropped his gaze to the ground, his entire body rigid as a statue.

Slifer stared at his disciple, perplexed. *What's wrong with him? Did I pick a defective one?*

Several heartbeats passed, and when nothing occurred, Caelum slowly opened his eyes. Seeing his master merely waiting, his breathing eased, though there was a sheen of sweat on his forehead.

"What are you waiting for?" Slifer waved his hand dismissively. "Go, get on with it." But as Caelum began to retreat, Slifer added, "Oh, and do remember to grab some dumplings on your way back, the ones with the spicy filling."

Caelum blinked, not sure whether to be more surprised by the request for righteous methods or dumplings. He nodded so fervently that Slifer worried he might dislocate something. "Understood, Master. Righteous methods and . . . dumplings, it shall be."

Then, using a movement technique, he vanished in a blur, grateful for his master's unusual benevolence. *Thank the Immortal Lords he's in a good mood today, even if he might be acting a little strange,* he thought as he rushed off.

Slifer sighed. *He moved so fast, I couldn't even see him. Guess that's what happens when you're stuck at the bottom of the cultivation ladder.* Shaking his head, he began to make his way back to his quarters. *I would've just used a righteous method from the original Slifer's memory if it weren't so foggy! The only clear thing was how quickly the old demon sold off those righteous methods.*

Slifer reclined on his cultivation pillow, indulging in delicate spirit fruits he had discovered in his quarters. The juicy, radiant blue fruit burst in his mouth, releasing an aromatic essence that calmed his senses. However, his indulgence left him with sticky hands and a trail of juice dripping down his chin.

Just as he was about to take another bite, a voice resonated in his mind, clear and direct. "Master, we have completed the task."

Was that . . . in my head? Slifer mused, momentarily taken aback. The sensation of a spiritual transmission, something he hadn't felt before, was oddly invasive. Knowing he couldn't respond through the same medium, he hastily set aside the half-eaten fruit, brushing off the juicy crumbs and wiping his mouth.

Exiting his quarters and stepping into the courtyard, Slifer was met with the sight of two familiar figures kneeling. One was Hughie, the twenty-five-year-old he had met earlier. Beside him was a girl who appeared around sixteen, with big luminous eyes, flowing silver hair, and an ethereal glow around her, much like an anime character straight out of his previous world's TV shows. She even had those absurdly long eyelashes. Just the sight of her made Slifer feel uneasy. He wasn't used to being around beautiful women . . . or any type of women for that matter.

Hughie extended his hand, offering a storage ring. "Master, we found one hundred and thirty-two righteous cultivation methods in the sect archives, as instructed."

Taking the ring, Slifer's eyes shimmered with anticipation. *Surely, out of all these, there must be one suitable for me.* He nodded. "Good job."

Amelia's eyes widened in disbelief as she heard Slifer say, "Good job."

Did Master just . . . compliment us? she thought, stunned. She shot a quick glance at Hughie, whose eyes were equally wide.

Why are they making me wait? Don't they understand that a man can die from starvation!

Clearing his throat, Slifer fixed Hughie with a slightly annoyed look. "Hughie, I specifically mentioned dumplings. Where are they?"

Hughie froze, a deer caught in headlights. "Master," he stammered, "it was Caelum you spoke to regarding the dumplings. He's fetching them right now. We thought it best to deliver the scrolls first."

Slifer blinked, taking a second to process. *Wasn't this the same fellow I spoke to earlier? Do they have an army of look-alikes or is he deceiving me?* He wondered if the disciples had detected he wasn't the original and were testing him. But, he brushed that off. *They wouldn't dare. If they suspected me, they'd have thrown me into the deepest dungeon, not handed over prized scrolls.*

Seeing her master's indecision, Amelia quickly chimed in, hoping to defuse the situation. "Indeed, Master. Caelum is getting them."

Slifer squinted at her, then at Hughie. *They're either very loyal or very good actors.*

Insight!

```
Name: Hughie
Realm: Late Core Formation
Known Techniques: N/A
Known Affiliations: Black Rose Sect
Disposition: N/A
```

He finally nodded, sighing. "Ah, yes. Very well."

Slifer glanced at the storage ring in his hand, in his hands it was basically useless. He then looked at Amelia. "Open this," he ordered, feigning a tone of indifference as if such menial tasks were beneath him.

Amelia's heart soared with relief. Not only had they escaped punishment, but they had also been entrusted with a new task. Eager to please, she quickly channeled her qi and, with a flick of her wrist, the scrolls from the storage ring materialized in front of Slifer.

Taking a deep breath, Slifer activated his Insight skill. Instantly, a System notification popped up in his vision.

```
Cultivation Method
Moonlit Pathway
Rank: Low Mortal
```

Low Mortal Rank? Seriously? Slifer thought, frustration evident in his features. He rapidly toggled through the notifications for the next scroll and the next.

```
Cultivation Method
Windswept Harmony
Rank: Mid-Mortal
```

Cultivation Method
Sunset Echo
Rank: High Mortal

Yet, the one that caught his eye, though still not up to his expectations, was:

Cultivation Method
Celestial Dawn's Awakening
Rank: Peak Mortal

Such grandiose names for mere Mortal Rank techniques, Slifer scoffed inwardly.

The disciples exchanged puzzled looks, watching Slifer's bizarre behavior with growing curiosity. To them, it seemed as if their master possessed such prodigious spiritual senses that merely staring at a scroll allowed its content to be discerned. Each time Slifer dismissed a scroll with increasing displeasure, their anxiety spiked.

How is this possible? Not a single Earth Rank, let alone Heaven? His face tightened with each scroll, his eyes narrowing in irritation.

"Useless," Slifer finally muttered, tossing the last scroll to the ground as if it were garbage. The tension among the disciples shot up; they braced themselves, certain they'd be blamed for the so-called "useless" finds.

Amelia, desperate to deflect potential punishment, stammered, "Master, I overheard Zarius bragging that he found a Heaven Rank Cultivation Method. He said he got it from a fallen Core Disciple of a righteous sect."

Slifer's gaze snapped to her. "Zarius? That braggart? Perhaps he might have something of use after all." The master's mood seemed to lift slightly at the prospect of a stronger method.

Hughie chanced a comment. "Master, should we retrieve it from him?"

Slifer pondered for a moment, weighing the information. *If what Amelia says is true, then that scroll could be the solution to all my problems.*

The mere mention of "Heaven Rank" seemed to lift a cloud from Slifer's brow. His eyes twinkled like stars on a moonless night. "You two, go negotiate with Zarius. Give him whatever he demands. I must have that scroll."

Ding!
Congratulations!
Your disciples have been assigned their first task—retrieve the scroll!
Reward: 5 Karmic Credits
5 Bonus Karmic Credits

Slifer's eyebrows shot up in surprise. *Bonus credits? Really? This frugal System is now handing out bonuses? Well, color me impressed. And an official task at that. Up until now, the System barely blinked when I sent them out for those useless scrolls, or when I asked Caelum for some dumplings,* he reflected, a touch of irony seeping into his thoughts.

Just think about it—what if every trivial command turned into an official task? A smirk tugged at his lips as his imagination began to run wild. *I'd be racking up credits by sending them on errands. Heck, I could even get credits for demanding a foot massage!*

Unaware of their master's whimsical thoughts, Hughie and Amelia exchanged solemn nods before vanishing in the blink of an eye, leaving their elder in solitude.

As the minutes ticked by, an audible rumble echoed from Slifer's belly, causing him to cast an annoyed glance at the courtyard's entrance. "Where is that lazy lackey with my dumplings?" he mumbled under his breath.

Almost as if summoned by complaint, a gust of wind swept across his face. Kneeling before him was Caelum, hands outstretched and trembling as they offered a plate of steaming dumplings. *He really does look just like the other one,* he mused. *Wait. Am I . . . am I being racist for not being able to tell them apart?* Slifer shook his head, inwardly reassuring himself. *No, no. Even their mothers would struggle to tell the difference.*

Insight!

Name: Caelum
Realm: Late Core Formation
Known Techniques: N/A
Known Affiliations: Black Rose Sect
Disposition: N/A

Oh, they really were two different people . . .

Catching the slight upward twitch of Slifer's lips, Caelum hesitated, unsure of his master's mood.

Slifer, realizing he should remain stoic and in command, quickly composed himself, shooting Caelum a stern glare. "You've taken quite a bit of time, haven't you?" he remarked.

Caelum trembled as if a cold wind had just blown through him. "F-forgive me, Master," he stammered, a silent prayer racing through his mind that he'd escape further reprimand.

Slifer ignored him and swiped the plate of dumplings from his outstretched hands. "Go catch up with the others. Make sure they don't mess this up," he ordered, unable to hide the undertone of eagerness in his voice.

The quicker this brat leaves, the quicker I can eat!

"As you wish, Master," Caelum replied, vanishing as quickly as he'd appeared. The less time he needed to spend with his master, the better!

The moment he stepped back into his quarters, Slifer's stern façade crumbled like a poorly baked cookie. A grin as wide as the crescent moon stretched across his face. *Ah, servants, dumplings, and a Heaven Rank Cultivation Method. Life is good.*

Clutching the plate to his chest like a treasure, he shut the door behind him.

Zarius strutted through the winding paths of the sect, reveling in the way lower-rank disciples scattered out of his way. Outer disciples, inner disciples, even some Core Disciples—all dipped their heads and made room for him to pass.

Catching sight of his own reflection in a nearby pond, he couldn't help but stop and admire himself. *Ah, being a Legacy Disciple certainly has its advantages,* he mused, his eyes lingering on his perfectly symmetrical face and striking features. *But let's not forget the main perk: me. It's like the heavens themselves carved this face to grace the sect with unparalleled beauty.*

With that self-congratulatory note, he continued his strut as his thoughts shifted to the upcoming auction. He was eager to auction off the Heaven Rank Cultivation Method he had "found" during his last expedition.

Oh, how they'll scramble to bid for it. He smirked, but sighed soon after, though. As much as he wanted to, he couldn't use the Heaven Rank method himself. His cultivation method was only at the Earth Rank, and the methods weren't compatible. *I'll need to find a compatible Heaven Rank Demonic Method someday.*

His musings were interrupted when three Core Formation cultivators descended from the sky on their flying swords. Behind them were five more in various stages of Core Formation. He narrowed his eyes, recognizing the uniforms they wore.

Disciples of Elder Slifer. Great. He frowned, contemplating whether to vanish into thin air. *They say cultivators nearing the end of their lifespan become erratic and crazy. I don't need that sort of problem.*

The male, who Zarius now recognized as Hughie, stepped forward with a grin. "Zarius! Fancy meeting you here," he said, feigning cheerfulness.

Zarius attempted nonchalance. "Hughie. And . . . Amelia, was it? What brings Elder Slifer's . . . esteemed disciples to this part of the sect?"

Amelia responded with an almost sly smile. "We heard you acquired a little . . . trinket? A Heaven Rank Cultivation Method, perhaps?"

Zarius gulped, attempting to maintain composure. "I have many treasures. You'll have to be more specific."

Hughie chuckled, "Come now, Zarius. Don't play coy. The whole sect has heard about it by now."

Amelia's eyes twinkled as she took a step closer. "Would you mind if Big Sister took a quick look at this Heaven Rank method?"

Zarius blinked, taken aback by Amelia's sudden switch to familial terms. *Big sister? She's got to be kidding.* The word made him cringe. If she was "big sister," then what did that make him? *Little Brother Zarius?* The very thought made his skin crawl.

Forcing a strained smile, Zarius replied, "Ah, well, you see, it's going to be up for auction soon. I wouldn't want any . . . accidental damage."

The cheerfulness in Amelia's eyes dimmed and her smile turned almost robotic. "You think I'd damage it?"

Zarius laughed nervously, "No, no, that's not what I meant. My master said I can't show it to anyone." *Lie! Big lie!* Zarius inwardly panicked. He had been flaunting the method around for days, but invoking the name of his master, a grand elder, might make them back down.

Amelia let out a melodic laugh. "How funny! My master, Elder Slifer, said he'd really like a sneak peek at it. And you know, when he wants something . . ."

Zarius felt a cold sweat forming on his brow—when had he, a Heaven's Chosen been pressed like this? But the name "Elder Slifer" held a weight that was hard to ignore. "Look, I'd happily hand it over for Elder Slifer to peruse, but my master . . . he's very particular. Maybe you could discuss it with him?" he suggested, hoping to divert the responsibility.

Amelia's smile vanished. "I tried to be nice, Zarius, really I did."

Zarius could swear he heard thunder crackling somewhere, even though the sky was clear.

"I tried to be the kind of big sister who asks politely," Amelia continued, her eyes narrowing, "but it seems you don't respond well to niceness."

This is bad. This is really bad, Zarius thought, cursing his earlier hesitation.

Beside the group, Fenlock shifted uncomfortably, playing with his fingers. *This isn't how I envisioned my day going*, he mused, recalling the soft laughter of Junior Sister Lenvari as they strolled together, talking about their future. It had been a rare, tranquil moment amidst the sect's constant strife, and he had cherished it. But the sudden arrival of his new senior brother and sister had thrown that all into chaos.

"*Hey, Junior Brother Fenlock*," Hughie had said, "*Wanna join us for a little bit of fun?*" Before Fenlock could even protest, he found himself being dragged away from Lenvari, leaving behind a trail of confusion.

Now, he cleared his throat, trying to defuse the tense situation. "Senior Sister, Senior Brother . . . maybe we should, you know, not resort to . . . um, strong measures?"

Zarius eyed Fenlock with a hint of surprise. He'd heard about Elder Slifer's newly acquired disciple but hadn't expected him to be so . . . meek?

"Seems your junior has some sense, no?" Zarius tried to divert the conversation, hoping to exploit any discord.

Hughie chuckled, patting Fenlock's shoulder. "Junior Brother, you're too soft! This is the demonic path! We take what we want when we want. Isn't that right?"

Fenlock's face flushed. "It's not about having a soft heart. It's about not creating unnecessary trouble. We could maybe . . . trade? Or borrow it for a while?"

Amelia and Hughie exchanged glances, then burst into laughter. "You really are a funny one, Fenlock," Hughie managed between chuckles. "But in all honesty, you think this snob would agree to a trade?"

Fenlock's ears turned an even deeper shade of red. "I . . . I just thought . . ."

Amelia waved him off. "It's cute that you tried. Now, Zarius, last chance. Hand over the method, or things might get . . . uncomfortable."

Before Zarius could reply, Caelum appeared with a whoosh of air. "Amelia, what's taking so long? Master doesn't have all day!" He released his Late Core Formation aura with a flourish, and the energy in the area intensified further.

Amelia nodded, unleashing her own aura. "Right. Time to wrap this up."

Hughie and the others also released their auras, each one radiating with Core Formation energy. Then they started yelling.

"Teach him a lesson!"

"How dare he defy our master!"

"Let's settle this!"

Zarius took a step back as his Mid-Stage Core Formation aura unfurled. *I could take any of them one-on-one, but all at once? This is bad.* He glanced around, hoping for some support, but was met with derisive smiles from other disciples. *Great, even the spectators are against me.*

Fearing the worst, Zarius activated a movement technique to flee. Just as he thought he'd escaped, Amelia appeared before him like a wisp of smoke.

"Going somewhere?" she said, her grin more dangerous than ever.

With a flash of her hand, she attacked. Zarius hastily defended, feeling the force of her strike reverberate through his arms. *This is a bad, bad day.*

"Was it something I said?" Amelia taunted, pulling back for another strike.

"Listen, can't we just talk about this?" Zarius stammered. *They're all mad! One little scroll and they've turned into rabid beasts.*

"Talking time was over when you refused to give us the scroll," Caelum chimed in, landing beside Amelia.

Hughie and the others circled Zarius, their auras swelling like storm clouds. "Last chance," Hughie warned. "Hand it over and we might just let you walk away."

Before Zarius could utter a word, a barrage of attacks rained upon him. Fists, kicks, palm strikes—all coming from different directions, each hit landing with a thud.

This is it, Zarius thought, *this is how I become a laughingstock.*

Suddenly, a ground-shaking roar echoed, "STOP!"

The beating ceased instantly.

A bald, fat Asian man appeared as if from thin air. His aura was intense; he had eyes like burning coals, and cheeks so flushed he looked perpetually angry, or perhaps sunburned. "What's going on here?" he thundered.

Amelia brightened. "Boss Morvran! How wonderful to see you. Master said the Heaven Rank Cultivation Method this disciple has is urgently needed. But this little guy is refusing to give it up."

Morvran's face darkened. "You lot! Have I taught you nothing about subtlety and tact?"

With a movement faster than anyone could track, Morvran was in front of the beaten Zarius. Without hesitation, his foot descended onto Zarius's ribs with a sickening crunch. Zarius let out a bloodcurdling scream.

Morvran then turned to Amelia and the others, shaking his head like a disappointed teacher. "Always go for the bones. Break them one by one and ensure prolonged agony. Have I not taught you this?"

Amelia's previously confident smile wavered. *Both him and Master . . . so similar in their viciousness*, she thought. *I still have much to learn!*

Hughie chimed in. "We'll, uh, remember that for next time."

Morvran looked at Zarius, who was writhing in pain on the ground, and then back to his subordinates. "Well, since you all seem to need a lesson in finesse, let's use this as a teaching moment."

Hughie stepped forward first, slightly nervous but eager to please. He raised his foot and hesitated. "Like this, boss?"

"Aim for the collarbone," Morvran instructed, "and twist your foot on impact for maximum pain."

Hughie nodded enthusiastically and brought his foot down on Zarius's collarbone. A crunching sound echoed, and Zarius screamed louder than before. Hughie turned for approval.

"Acceptable," Morvran noted. "But your form could be cleaner. Work on that."

Caelum stepped up next, his foot hovering over Zarius's arm. "How's this, boss?"

"Extend your leg a bit more for leverage," Morvran said, scrutinizing Caelum's stance as if judging a piece of art.

Caelum adjusted his stance and stomped, breaking the bone with another sickening crunch.

"Better," Morvran approved. "But never forget: a clean break leads to quicker healing, which is not what we want. Make it messy."

Make it messy? Caelum thought. *Where did he learn all this?*

Amelia, sporting a playful pout, said, "Boss, any tips for me?"

"Imagine you're stepping on a piece of delicate glassware," Morvran said, the corners of his mouth turning down even further in disdain. "You don't want to crush it immediately. You want to feel it crack and give way under your foot. Savor it."

Amelia nodded, took a deep breath, and followed Morvran's instructions to the letter. The sound of Zarius's bone-breaking was followed by a guttural howl of agony.

"Splendid," Morvran commented. "You catch on fast."

Amelia beamed. "Thank you, Boss!"

Morvran's gaze finally landed on Fenlock, who had been standing at the back of the group, trying to blend into the scenery. "You there, you're up next. Complete the lesson."

Fenlock blinked in disbelief. *Me? Really? I just wanted a simple, peaceful date with Junior Sister Lenvari. Now I have to break bones? These people are crazy!* "Uh, I think I'll pass," he said hesitantly, eyeing Zarius's mangled form on the ground with distaste.

Morvran raised an eyebrow. "Pass? Are you saying you don't want to learn from the best?"

Hughie chuckled. "Don't be shy, Fenlock. Learning from the boss is a privilege."

Amelia winked at him. "Consider it your initiation, Junior Brother. Most would kill for such a hands-on lesson."

Initiation? More like hazing, Fenlock thought, feeling his stomach churn.

Reluctantly, Fenlock stepped forward. Zarius looked up at him, his eyes filled with terror and pain, pleading silently for mercy.

Morvran gestured towards Zarius's unbroken leg. "Go on, give it a try. Remember, aim for the joints. They break easier and hurt more."

This is insane. What am I doing here? Fenlock thought, his foot hovering uncertainly above Zarius's leg.

Seeing his hesitation, Morvran sighed deeply, like a chef disappointed in a student who couldn't even chop an onion properly. "Lift your leg higher. You'll need the gravity to assist the break."

Feeling peer-pressured and not seeing any way out, Fenlock finally stomped down, his eyes squeezing shut as he heard the predictable crunch and Zarius's ensuing scream.

"Ah, there you go!" Morvran exclaimed, clapping his hands together. "Not bad for a first-timer, but your form could use some work. Still, you'll get plenty of practice, don't worry, I'll make sure of it."

Fenlock stepped back, feeling his face flush with a mixture of shame and nausea. *Is this what it means to be one of Elder Slifer's disciples? What have I gotten myself into?*

Morvran looked at the disciples, their faces beaming with pride. "Now, we have what we came for. And you have all learned a valuable lesson in the art of . . . dissuasion."

They collected the much-sought-after scroll from Zarius, leaving him as a heap of misery on the ground.

"As for you"—Morvran looked down at the defeated Zarius—"maybe this will teach you not to reject Master."

Slifer sat on his cultivation pillow, his face smeared with dumpling sauce. With every bite, he moaned in satisfaction, lost in the flavors that danced on his tongue. Pushing aside the sinking feeling in his gut, he thought, *Eh, it's probably just the dumplings.*

Slifer was about to grab another dumpling when a notification popped up in his vision.

Ding!

> Congratulations!
> Due to Hughie's actions, you have received 1 Karmic Credit.

Slifer paused, his hand frozen midair, chopsticks dangling from his fingers. *What the heck is Hughie up to that gets me extra credits?* Intrigued but not overly concerned, he shrugged and continued savoring his meal.

> *Ding!*
> Congratulations!
> Due to Caelum's actions, you have received 1 Karmic Credit.

Slifer grinned, the food momentarily forgotten. *And I thought the System was stingy!*

> *Ding!*
> Congratulations!
> Due to Amelia's actions, you have received 1 Karmic Credit.

By now, his grin had evolved into a full-on smile. *This is getting ridiculous. But ridiculously good.*

> *Ding!*
> Congratulations!
> Due to Fenlock's actions, you have received 1 Karmic Credit.
> Error
> Recalibrating
> . . .
> . . .
> Cannot receive credits until Master-Disciple Ceremony is complete.

Slifer burst into laughter, not bothered by the latest notification. "I'll have to ask them what happened. Getting extra credits while just sitting here and eating? That's the life!"

Rubbing his hands together in anticipatory glee, he mumbled, "Ah, the farming season has officially commenced."

However, for some reason, the nagging feeling in his gut only grew stronger . . .

CHAPTER SIX

Finishing the last dumpling, Slifer leaned back, contentedly patting his belly. The burp that followed echoed in the room, resonating with his deep satisfaction. "Ah!" He sighed. "Eating is truly one of life's simplest pleasures." Then, smirking, he thought, *Just because this body doesn't demand food, doesn't mean I'll starve it of its ten meals a day.*

Suddenly, the familiar voice buzzed in his head once more. "Master, I have returned."

Startled, Slifer quickly wiped his face with his sleeve, hoping to look a bit more presentable, though the sauce stains still lingered. Rushing into the courtyard, he saw Amelia, Fenlock, the "identical twins"—Caelum and Hughie—and a bald, fat old man who looked like an older, plumper version of the twins.

Are all my lackeys from the same family? Do they have a family discount on loyalty or something?

His chain of thoughts was broken when Morvran stepped forward, presenting a scroll. Slifer's eyes lit up immediately. "Is this . . . ?" he began.

"The Heaven Rank scroll, Master," Morvran confirmed.

> *Ding!*
> Congratulations!
> Your disciples have completed their first task!
> You have gained 5 Karmic Credits.
> You have gained an additional 5 Karmic Credits.

Trying to maintain a calm exterior, though his excitement bubbled just below the surface, Slifer asked, "And how many spirit stones did it cost us?"

A brief pause filled the air.

Amelia, wearing a smug grin, remarked, "Actually, Master . . . we got it for free!"

Slifer's eyebrows shot up. *Free? In this world, nothing's truly free. There's always a catch. Did they threaten someone? Or maybe they promised a favor? Oh, not the ominous "favor to be redeemed later." That's always a recipe for disaster!*

Eyes narrowing, Slifer mused aloud, "So . . . no cost, you say? That's . . . unusual."

Amelia, taken aback by her master's reaction, blinked a couple of times. *He usually loves it when we acquire things without spending a dime. Why the suspicion now?* She tried to regain her composure. "Yes, Master. It was a very . . . generous donation."

Caelum cleared his throat nervously. "Well, Master, the disciple initially wasn't keen on parting with the scroll. But, we managed to . . . persuade him."

Slifer's gaze remained fixed on Caelum, waiting for him to elaborate.

But before Caelum could continue, Morvran cut in, his voice dripping with a stern pride. "Master, we did what we do best. We demonstrated precisely why he should not refuse you."

A bead of sweat trickled down Slifer's forehead. *Oh no, what did they do this time?* Composing himself, he inquired, "You beat him up, didn't you?"

Morvran nodded proudly. "Yes, Master. That young man won't be leaving his bed for at least a week."

Slifer's thoughts raced. *In a world where minor injuries can be healed with a mere drop of elixir, what in the heavens did they do to him?*

Amelia chimed in, her voice tinged with righteousness, "Frankly, he was lucky. For showing such disrespect towards Master, he deserved much worse."

Hold up. If they did that, why did the System reward me with credits? I thought it had an aversion to anything even slightly demonic. Then it hit him. *Oh, the System doesn't dock me for violence against demonic cultivators. It's like a cosmic vigilante, putting its crusade against darkness above all else.*

Just then, a System notification popped up:

> Congratulations!
> You have uncovered your main quest: eradicate or reform all demonic cultivators!
> Reward: Hidden
> Failure: Hidden

Slifer's jaw dropped in disbelief. *Eradicate or reform ALL demonic cultivators? That's absurd!* The Black Rose Sect's cultivators were practically Boy Scouts compared to some of the more sinister factions out there. How could one possibly be expected to change or eliminate every single one of them?

His thoughts spiraled. *This is insane. What's with the hidden reward and failure? Is the System trying to trap me?* His skepticism grew, feeling that the System was acting in bad faith. *If the penalty for failure is death, then this is pretty much a guaranteed death sentence. How can anyone even hope to accomplish such a quest?*

And then another concern surfaced. *Wait a minute, there's no time limit mentioned . . .* He thought fast, his mind racing. *Nope, System, you've got the wrong guy. Why couldn't I have gotten a System that gives me credits for, say, mastering culinary arts or tasting exotic foods? Now, that's a main quest I could get behind! Well . . . as long as it doesn't involve a pie-eating contest.*

A shudder ran down his spine as he recalled his past life's untimely demise. As he shook off the memories and processed his outrageous mission, a tentative voice interrupted his tumultuous train of thought.

Fenlock, who'd been looking ashamed and guilt-ridden, finally mustered the courage to speak. "Master, I . . . I didn't want any part in this. *They* made me!"

Morvran shot him a sharp glare, while Amelia huffed.

"Really, Junior Brother? Snitching on us now?"

Slifer quickly raised a hand, trying to regain his composure. "From now on," he began with a deliberately calm tone, "there will be no more . . . aggressive negotiations. Or killings! Unless I give explicit orders, understood?"

The disciples looked at one another, their faces a canvas of confusion. Wasn't violence always their go-to solution? The universal fixer of problems?

Slifer sighed, running a hand through his hair. *While the few credits from the System might seem like a boon now, they're negligible in the grand scheme of things. Especially when weighed against the potential repercussions.* The image of an angered Great Elder came to his mind.

And what if they keep this up? He imagined a future where, by beating up every disciple who crossed their path, they eventually ran into a protagonist-type. Antagonizing such a character meant nothing but certain doom. The mere thought made his heart flutter.

Amelia tilted her head. "Master, aren't those . . . techniques . . . what you taught us? To always make sure your wishes are fulfilled?"

Hughie nodded in agreement. "Yeah, the 'persuade till they agree' method."

Slifer almost rolled his eyes. *I have a lot of retraining to do.*

Morvran, ever the serious one, added, "It is always effective, Master. A touch of pain can be quite enlightening."

Slifer waved his hands frantically. "That's not what I meant! Well, not to that extent. I want you to be diplomatic."

Hughie scratched his head. "Diplo-what now?"

Caelum nodded sagely. "Ah, I've heard of that. It's where you talk things out before using your fists, right?"

Morvran's eyebrows drew together—diplomacy was a whole new realm for him. "I . . . see."

Do cultivators get brain fog or something from cultivating too much? Slifer thought. *Or maybe, given their long lifespans, they just take a few centuries longer to catch on to basic concepts. These disciples of mine . . . Not the brightest lot. Perhaps if I can distract them with a task . . . ?* He quickly opened the Disciple Management Panel and selected the option to assign a task. A list of missions, ranging in difficulty, appeared before him.

A holographic list shimmered before him:

Current Quests Available
Quest Name: Difficulty
Gather rare Moonlit Herbs: Qi Condensation
Protect the Sacred Altar from wild beasts during full moon: Foundation Establishment
Save Lushan Village from bandits: Core Formation
Retrieve the Mystic Phoenix Feather from the Azure Mountain   Nascent Soul.

"I've got a special assignment for the three of you," Slifer declared to Amelia, Caelum, and Hughie, adopting the tone of a quest master who handed out world-saving missions— except in this case, the heroes might be more villainous than valiant. "The village of Lushan needs your 'expertise.' Bandits have been wreaking havoc there, and you're the ones who'll put an end to it."

Amelia, Caelum, and Hughie exchanged glances before nodding in unison. "Understood, Master."

Slifer quickly turned his attention to Fenlock, who looked like he'd rather be anywhere but here. "Fenlock," Slifer began, "get everything prepared for the Master-Disciple Ceremony. We need to make this official."

Ding!
Task Assigned: Prepare for the Master-Disciple Ceremony
Karmic Credits: 10

The sooner I get this ceremony done, the sooner I can put this one to work— But Slifer's thoughts were abruptly interrupted as a sudden chill permeated his very being, making his blood run cold.

An icy voice echoed in his mind. *Come to my quarters, now.*

Slifer quickly turned, his face paling, ensuring his disciples couldn't see his obvious fear. *That voice. It's unmistakably the sect master.* He cursed inwardly, berating the disciples in his mind for causing such a ruckus that it reached the sect master's ears. *Of all the times, why now? I just got here, damn it!*

A deeper, more terrifying thought struck him. *What if he's discovered that I'm not the real Slifer? That I'm an impostor?* He felt the weight of panic set in, his heart thudding wildly against his chest.

Alright, Slifer, you've been in tighter spots before . . . okay, that's a blatant lie, but how bad could this be?

He winced at his own thoughts. *I really need to stop asking questions I don't want answers to.*

Gathering his composure, he turned back to face his disciples. "I have urgent matters to attend to with the sect master. Focus on your missions, don't cause trouble."

Morvran nodded sternly. "Understood, Master."

Amelia chimed in, trying to cheer him up, "Don't worry, Master. The sect master probably just wants to congratulate you on acquiring the Heaven Rank scroll!"

Yeah, I'm sure he just wants to congratulate me on putting that kid in hospital . . . or whatever it is they have here.

Slifer trudged along the path leading to the sect master's quarters. Along the way, his eyes landed upon a pristine lake. Its waters, clear as crystal, shone under the sun. The stillness of the surface momentarily distracted him from his troubles.

Wait a minute, he thought, chuckling lightly to himself. *Isn't it a ritual in these isekai situations to gaze into a water reflection or a mirror and finally see what you've become?* He knew, thanks to the memories he had inherited, exactly what he looked like. But what was the harm in indulging in a little cliché?

Taking a moment, he approached the water's edge. Bending down, he allowed his reflection to slowly come into view. An aged Asian face stared back, with long white hair that flowed gracefully to his shoulders, matching the thick white beard and mustache that adorned his face. His eyes, however, still held the spark of youth.

Slifer nodded in approval. "Just as I expected."

Yet, as his gaze drifted down to the rest of his reflection, his brow furrowed in discontent. His robe hung loosely on his slender frame, and Slifer could make out the sharp edges of bones, giving away his emaciated state.

"Did this old man even remember to eat?" he murmured, raising an eyebrow. *Ah right, Nascent Soul cultivators live off qi. Who needs food when you can inhale energy?*

"No! That's no excuse!" he exclaimed, shaking his head. "A healthy man ought to have a healthy belly!" And by "healthy," Slifer distinctly meant a generously rotund belly. One that would jiggle with every step and be a testament to many indulgent meals.

He gently patted his stomach, as if consoling it. "Don't you worry, little one," he murmured, "we'll get you nice and plump soon."

Suddenly aware of how ridiculous he must seem, he shot a glance around, half-expecting someone to have witnessed his soliloquy. Fortunately, the coast seemed clear.

As he resumed his journey, fragments of memories began to surface. They pieced together an image of the original Slifer's dynamics with the sect master.

His brows knitted in disapproval. *Oh heavens, what was that weasel-like behavior?* He cringed at the thought. The former Slifer was a man of many faces, in front of almost everyone, he was proud and imposing—but in the presence of the sect master, he turned into a groveling, fawning mess.

Ugh! I refuse to bow down like that! Slifer thought, his face scrunching in disgust. *Well . . . I guess if my life depends on it, then maybe a little bow won't hurt.*

Finally, he arrived at the cave's entrance. It was an ominous hole in the mountain, shrouded in dark mists and guarded by eerie formations of rocks that looked like demonic faces.

Very edgy, Slifer noted, amused. The sect master was the only one in the sect who lived in a cave. *Maybe it's a status thing?* he mused. *You know, being a demonic sect's leader and living in a creepy cave to add to the aesthetic?* But Slifer quickly dismissed that. *Honestly, why would anyone trade a comfortable bed for cold, hard stone? If I were the sect master, I'd at least have a proper mattress in there.*

Slifer had to hand it to him: before the sect master's reign, the sect was a chaotic mess. Disciples stabbing each other in the back—literally—elders mysteriously vanishing, and chaos reigning supreme.

However, the events seven hundred and fifty years ago necessitated change. The demonic invasion was a cataclysmic event that not only reshaped the landscape but also altered the balance between the demonic and righteous sects. Slifer remembered it clearly, having just broken into the Nascent Soul Realm. The invasion was repelled, but at a heavy cost. The aftermath saw the sect master taking the reins, but it also garnered intense scrutiny from the righteous factions who became extremely wary of any demonic activity.

The sect master transformed the sect in a way that nobody had thought possible, making it more similar to that of a righteous sect. He had instigated strict rules, regulated inter-disciple fights to official dueling grounds, and even established a merit-based System that reduced the number of mysterious "accidents" dramatically. More importantly, he had re-strategized their operations to be covert, focusing on resource accumulation and secret alliances rather than wanton violence and flashy displays of demonic prowess.

It's a rather relaxed sect now, Slifer mused, *well, if you can call doing demonic rituals and annihilating innocents relaxed.*

Slifer heaved a sigh of relief, grateful for the cosmic luck of transmigrating into an elder's body instead of some unfortunate outer disciple. *Being a main character in these stories usually means years of abuse. There's always that one time where they find a heaven-defying cultivation manual or some old master's soul, and then—boom!—they're overpowered. But until then, it's all about being stomped on.*

Suddenly, a voice jolted him from his daydream. "Elder Slifer." A disciple approached and bowed deeply. "The sect master awaits."

Taking a deep breath, Slifer entered the cave. Inside, it was exactly what he would have imagined for a demonic sect master in a xianxia novel. *Skulls? Check. Dark, creepy lighting? Check. A distinct, otherworldly air of menace? Double-check.*

When Slifer's eyes landed on the sect master, he did a double take. Seated on an obsidian throne, etched with intricate patterns, was a man who looked . . . well, ordinary. The sect master could easily pass for the friendly guy who used to work at the local Chinese restaurant—average build, hair neatly combed back, and a face that said "Would you like spring rolls with that?" rather than, "I am the master of dark arts."

Is that Mr. Chen? No, wait, focus. This guy is a demonic sect master, not your go-to for Kung Pao chicken.

But then the sect master lifted his gaze, and those eyes—far from the warm, inviting eyes of a man who'd offer you an extra egg roll—were piercing and full of ancient cunning. His skin, though it looked typical, was a front; Slifer knew the man sitting before him had been alive for over a thousand years.

The sect master was currently smiling warmly at a disciple who looked incredibly uneasy. "You seem to have taken your time arriving after I summoned you," the sect master commented, his voice soft, yet edged with a hint of mockery. The perpetual smile on his face was chilling to those who truly knew him.

Slifer knew the deceptive nature of the sect master's seemingly jovial disposition; he was as calculating as they came. The smile never reached his eyes, which remained cold and scrutinizing.

"Forgive me, Sect Master, I . . ." The disciple's voice quivered, his face a mask of confusion and fear. This was his first time being summoned by the sect master. He had no idea what the master meant by being late; he had appeared as soon as he was summoned.

"No need for long explanations. You won't be late again, I assure you," the sect master said, his smile widening. With a casual flick of his wrist, the disciple was engulfed in flames. His scream was agonizingly brief as he was reduced to ashes.

A cold sweat formed on Slifer's brow. *Was that a message for me?* he pondered, his heart racing. He sent a silent apology to the disciple, sensing that he was likely the true target of the sect master's ire.

The sect master's eyes, still beaming pleasantly, fixed on Slifer. "Now, Elder Slifer, why did you keep me waiting?" His tone was mild, but the underlying threat was evident.

Oh, fuck! That poor kid wasn't even late, was he? Slifer gulped mentally. "Sect Master, I . . . I departed immediately upon receiving your message," Slifer said, voice shaking slightly.

The sect master's eyes twinkled with mischief. "Yet, it took you four hours."

Not my fault your cave is a four-hour walk away! Some of us can't just fly around, okay? Slifer raged internally but restrained himself. "I . . . walked here," Slifer replied, a touch of awkwardness evident in his voice. *Walking is great and all, but four hours on a mountain is a bit much. If not for this Peak Body Tempering, my feet would be riddled with blisters by now.*

The sect master blinked, looking genuinely surprised for a split second. "This once, you're forgiven," he said, his smile never faltering.

Slifer bowed his head, muttering a respectful, "It won't happen again, Sect Master." *Yeah, no promises there until I can fly.*

Unable to hold back his curiosity, he activated his Insight skill.

Name: Malachar (True Name Unknown)
Realm: Peak Ascendant Realm
Known Techniques: N/A

Known Affiliations: Black Rose Sect
Disposition: N/A

Slifer's eyes widened slightly, his heart rate quickening. *The Peak Ascendant Realm . . .* Slifer recalled what he knew of the cultivation realms. The Ascendant Realm was two realms above the Nascent Soul Realm and was whispered to be the pinnacle of the Human Realms. Once a cultivator broke past that formidable realm, they transcended to the Immortal Realm. Legends spoke of those immortals living for hundreds of thousands of years, if not more.

And he's in the "Peak" stage of that realm. Just how close is he to becoming an immortal?

It was likely that the next time Slifer met the sect master, he would have already joined the ranks of the immortals.

A notification from the System popped into his mind.

Warning: Demon Identified
Eliminate
Reward: 50,000 Karmic Credits

Slifer felt his knees go weak. *A d-demon? He's an actual demon?* His mind raced to connect the dots. *The changes in the sect, the need to stay under the radar . . . He's scheming something massive. Shit, what the hell have I gotten myself into?!*

The sect master, unaware that his true identity had been discovered, continued, "You've been keeping yourself busy lately, I heard you had your underlings rough up a Legacy Disciple. Is that true?"

Ah, there it is. Cold sweat trickled down Slifer's spine.

Dropping his head even lower, Slifer stammered, "This—this foolish elder admits his mistake, Sect Master."

The sect master shook his head but not in disappointment. "It's good to remind those below you of who's in charge."

Is that what you're doing to me right now, you old fiend? Slifer thought bitterly.

However, the sect master's next words gave him slight relief. "The grand elder is not pleased with your actions, but he's chosen to stay out of this matter. He believes the Legacy Disciple could stand to face some of life's . . . challenges."

Challenges? Slifer snorted inwardly. *With rumors of me finishing off Elder Tarnyx circulating, he'd rather steer clear. Plus, who in their right mind would want to confront a cultivator on the brink of death? Hell, I wouldn't go anywhere near one, they'd drag you down with them if given a chance.*

Despite his inner turmoil, Slifer bowed once again. "Thank you, Sect Master, for your wisdom and understanding."

But inside, Slifer's thoughts were anything but thankful. He wanted to get as far away from this demon as possible!

The sect master continued to stare at Slifer. "Something about you has changed," he finally stated, eyes narrowing suspiciously. "Your trip seemed to have given you quite a gift—a technique that completely conceals your aura. I can't sense even a trace of qi from you."

Slifer gulped. "Indeed, Sect Master. My travels have been . . . enlightening."

Enlightening is quite the understatement. From the original's untimely demise to this whole isekai business, it's been one wild ride.

The warmth of the sect master's smile contrasted sharply with the frosty undertone of his words. "If I hadn't learned about Elder Tarnyx's *unfortunate* end, I would've assumed that you had lost your cultivation base entirely. For your contribution, I've given you five hundred merits." Leaning slightly forward in his obsidian throne, the sect master's façade barely concealed his raw curiosity. "But this newfound ability," he added, an unmistakable note of longing evident in his voice. "Do elaborate."

Slifer could hear the subtle hunger in the sect master's tone, and immediately realized the dangerous situation he was in. *Oh heavens,* Slifer thought, anxiety churning in his stomach. *This isn't a technique, I've really just lost my cultivation.*

Attempting to play it cool, Slifer hesitated, and after a few moments, managed to reply, "It's . . . well, it's not that significant, Sect Master. Just a minor trick I picked up. It's not even perfected yet." He tried to wave it off.

The sect master chuckled lightly. "Perhaps, after I emerge from my closed-door cultivation, I could offer my insights on this 'minor trick.' It would indeed be regrettable if you never had the opportunity to perfect it."

Swallowing hard, Slifer paused once more before asking, "And . . . how long would that be, Sect Master?"

The sect master waved his hand dismissively. "A decade at most. You'd best stay out of trouble till then."

Slifer bowed obediently, but internally, his mind was racing. *System, you'd better have a technique like that in the Shop, or a way to eliminate a demon two major realms above my peak form. Or else I'm as good as dead. No—much worse—he would probably torture my soul for eternity looking for a technique that doesn't even exist!*

Slifer sat on his cultivation cushion in the dim confines of his chamber, still mulling over his unsettling encounter with the sect master. *That request for the "technique" could be a big problem,* he thought, shaking his head. *But that's a concern for future me. First, I need to make it through the next two months.*

His mood brightened as his gaze landed on the exquisite scroll resting beside him. A smirk spread across his face. "Thought you could play me, System? Well, I've finally gotten one over on you!" Triumphantly, he unfurled the Heaven Rank scroll, eager to see the secrets contained within.

Activating his Insight skill, a System notification emerged:

Heavenly Radiance Cultivation Art
Rank: Mid-Earth Rank
Gathers the Essence of the Sun and Moon, Providing a Balance in One's Qi

---

His elated expression crumbled, replaced with shock and rage. "Mid-Earth Rank?!" Slifer's face reddened, and in his anger, he hurled a nearby teacup against the wall, shattering it.

That damned Legacy Disciple tricked me! But another thought stopped him in his tracks. *Or did my lackeys betray me?* He quickly discarded the thought. *No, they wouldn't dare. The consequences would be too severe. It must be that kid!* "That wretch! He deserved more than a mere beating for this deception!" Slifer glared at the scroll.

A sudden thought halted his brewing anger. *Could it be the System's grading that's different? It wouldn't be too far-fetched. Perhaps the locals deemed it Heaven Rank due to a scarcity of superior techniques.*

Rubbing his temples, Slifer attempted to calm himself. *Alright, an Earth Rank technique will have to do for now.* He took a deep breath, reassuring himself. "I saved a hundred credits, and this should be enough to help me break through to the Qi Refining Realm. It's not the worst outcome."

Seating himself in the traditional cultivation position, Slifer began to methodically absorb the words of the technique. He let them seep deep into his consciousness. Closing his eyes, he stretched out his senses, trying to attune himself to the omnipresent qi of the heavens and earth.

There it is . . . The familiar, yet always elusive, sensation of the natural world's energy grazed his senses. Slifer guessed that his body, having nearly touched the Origin Realm, was more receptive to this qi, making it easier for him to detect.

Tapping into the original's memories, Slifer recollected that the Qi Refining Realm marked the first stage of cultivation. It all revolved around harnessing the universal qi present in everything—from the smallest pebble to grand celestial bodies like the sun and the moon. Specific cultivation techniques, such as the Heavenly Radiance Cultivation Art, aimed to target a particular source of qi, converting it into a form his human body could assimilate, commonly known as "Anima Qi."

To advance to the first stage of Qi Refining Realm, one had to undergo nine cycles of absorbing and converting qi. As you climbed each level within this realm, the cycles required for the next breakthrough would multiply by nine.

"Ah, the significance of the number nine," Slifer mused. "Always cropping up in Chinese culture."

He then began to direct the qi, focusing on gathering the essence of the sun and moon. The sun's energy was easy to collect, feeling warm and vibrant as it flowed into him. However, the moon's essence proved elusive. Despite the daylight, the moon hung faintly in the sky, its energy weaker and much harder to grasp.

Ah, so that's the catch. Slifer sighed internally. *During the day, the sun's essence is abundant, but at night, the moon's essence is stronger. This balance makes it a challenge. No wonder it's only Earth Rank.*

Nevertheless, Slifer continued his cultivation. He gathered, refined, and cycled the qi through his meridians, performing one complete cycle, then another. By the time he completed the ninth cycle, something profound shifted within him.

His body vibrated as if resonating with the universe. A barrier in his spirit seemed to crumble, making room for a greater influx of qi. The sensations culminated in a breakthrough: he had reached the Qi Refining Realm.

Instantly, a wave of new sensations washed over him. He could sense the environment around him within a small radius.

When using the Peak Slifer Card, he had been too focused on the battle to take much notice of his spiritual sense, but the influx of information was overwhelming; he had to momentarily sever the connection to regain his clarity. *This is disorienting but amazing.*

Opening his eyes, Slifer felt a gentle flow of qi circulating through his meridians. It was slow, almost negligible, but it was there.

"Finally, I'm a cultivator," he whispered to himself, a satisfied grin spreading across his face. "I guess it wasn't that hard. Then again, I am in this old demon's body."

Congratulations on achieving a major breakthrough!
You Have Gained 10 Karmic Credits

His triumph was short-lived as he looked up at his stat screen:

Name: Slifer
Race: Human
Alignment: Demonic
Cultivation: Qi Refining—1st Stage
Lifespan Remaining: 49 Days
Karmic Credits: 63
Skills: Insight (Basic)
Items: Reversal Cards x2, Peak Slifer Card x2, Critical Block x2

"Forty-nine days left." His expression darkened. *Time's running out.*

"I need to speed this up," he mumbled, resuming his cultivation stance. With newfound urgency, he started channeling qi through his meridians again, sticking strictly to the Earth Rank method from the scroll.

No need to worry about Qi Deviation at this stage, he assured himself. Firstly, the Earth Rank technique was less prone to such risks. Secondly, his body, well-acclimated to qi manipulation, could handle it more efficiently.

Amelia, Hughie, and Caelum soared through the skies on their swords, the wind brushed against their faces, creating ripples in their robes as they made their way towards Lushan Village.

Hughie let out a hearty laugh. "It's been a while since Master sent us to wipe out a village, eh?"

Amelia nodded, her lips curving into a playful smirk. "I was beginning to think the master was getting soft in his old age," she said, alluding to the recent scolding they had received for breaking Zarius's bones.

Caelum looked at both of them, his brow raised in surprise. "Wait, you two think Master sent us to wipe out the village?" he asked incredulously. "He told us to *save* the villagers, not kill them."

Hughie shook his head, a confident gleam in his eyes. "No, no, Senior Brother. Master said to use our 'expertise.' And Hughie's expertise is killing."

Amelia chimed in, "Exactly, Master said to 'put an end to it.' He didn't specify what 'it' is. So why not the whole village? Don't overthink it, Senior Brother."

Caelum rubbed his temples, a deep sigh escaping his lips. *Why are my juniors so dense?* He felt a pang of responsibility. After all, he was the Senior Brother. "Listen," he began, "Master wants us to put an end to the havoc, not the villagers."

"But if we kill the villagers, then the havoc ends. Isn't that like killing two birds with one stone?" Hughie replied, genuinely believing his logic was sound.

Caelum took a deep breath, trying to contain his exasperation. *They've never been asked to save anyone before. This is new territory for them.* He understood where their confusion was coming from; their master's orders often involved destruction and chaos. "No," he asserted firmly, "no killing villagers. The bandits are fair game, though."

Amelia pouted, floating closer to Caelum. "Senior Brother is no fun."

Just then, a light bulb seemed to go off in Hughie's head. "Ah, I get it! The villagers are like Master's cattle, and the bandits are wolves trying to prey on them. Master wants us to shoo away the wolves so he can fatten the cattle for some . . . demonic ritual later!"

Caelum, despite himself, nodded hesitantly. "That . . . actually does sound like something Master would do."

CHAPTER SEVEN

Deep into his cultivation trance, the growl of Slifer's stomach echoed louder than the ancient chants of his ancestors. He cracked open one eye, then the other, and sighed. Hunger, it seemed, was the true ancient enemy of cultivators.

Ding!
Congratulations!
You Have Advanced to the Next Stage
You Have Gained 1 Karmic Credit

"Show stats."

Name: Slifer
Race: Human
Alignment: Demonic
Cultivation: Qi Refining—7th Stage
Lifespan Remaining: 48 Days
Credits: 69
Skills: Insight (Basic)
Items: Reversal Cards x2, Peak Slifer Card x2, Critical Block x2

Checking his stat screen, a proud grin spread across his face. "Seventh Stage of Qi Refining!" He cheered internally. "Just think, if my belly wasn't so rebellious, I might've reached Foundation Establishment!"

Exiting his quarters, the sight of Morvran waiting in the courtyard caught his attention. Slifer quirked an eyebrow. *Has this guy been standing here all these hours? Does he not get bored?*

Morvran, seeing his master's inquisitive glance, hurriedly knelt. "Master! The mission you assigned . . . it was successful."

Slifer blinked. *Ah, the mission that Hughie—or Caelum—mentioned.* Slifer still had no idea what it was. But deciding to play along, he adopted a sagely air, stroking his beard. "Ah, yes, excellent. Now, do enlighten me about the . . . intricate details. It's always prudent to ensure no loose ends, after all."

Relieved that his master seemed in a good mood, Morvran nodded. "Of course, Master. As per your command, we have successfully kidnapped the daughter of Grand Elder Olakin from the Black Heart Sect."

Slifer's eyes nearly popped out of their sockets, but he managed, with considerable effort, to maintain a placid exterior. *Holy sacred turtles! Kidnapping the daughter of an Origin Realm expert? This isn't an everyday errand! It's a ticket to the afterlife!*

Back when Morvran joined his disciples in beating up that annoying Legacy Disciple, Slifer realized that it was only his own actions or that of his disciples that influenced Karmic Credits, so he was unable to rely on the System to warn him if Morvran committed any evil actions—like kidnapping a girl.

He took a deep breath, trying to calm the whirlwind of emotions and scenarios running in his mind. *Let me guess,* he thought sarcastically, *next, the beautiful, misunderstood daughter and I will share a deep, soulful connection. We'll bond over . . . I don't know, shared affinity for dumplings or something? And then, just when we're about to sip tea together under the moonlight, Elder Olakin will burst onto the scene, hell-bent on turning me into a human pancake.*

Wait a moment . . . I'm an old man! There's no way the girl would even glance my way, unless it's to identify my corpse after her father kills me. So, maybe, just maybe, that particular xianxia trope won't apply here.

In a voice that trembled just the slightest bit, he asked, "And where, pray tell, is this esteemed guest?"

Morvran, oblivious to Slifer's internal turmoil, replied, "In the dungeon, Master."

Slifer gulped. *Of course, she's in the dungeon. Why not make her stay more miserable? I need to somehow turn this trope around before it's too late.*

Slifer activated his Insight skill to assess Morvran, just to be sure.

Name: Morvran
Realm: Peak Core Formation
Known Techniques: N/A
Known Affiliations: Slifer's Chief Subordinate
Disposition: N/A

His brow furrowed in confusion. *He really is at the Core Formation Realm. How could he possibly . . .*

He voiced his doubts. "Morvran, she must have been guarded by Nascent Soul cultivators. How did you manage to kidnap her under their watch?"

"Master, I made use of the treasures you generously bestowed upon me. They proved more than effective in dispatching her protectors."

Slifer's face darkened at the mention of the dead Nascent Soul cultivators. Those were not mere foot soldiers; their deaths would send ripples through any sect.

"And did you, by any chance, leave evidence pointing back to me?"

Morvran nodded solemnly. "Of course, Master. I made sure to leave enough clues so that they know it was you who orchestrated this."

Is this man out of his mind? No, wait, maybe he's trying to get me killed. Or . . .

Slifer's complexion went from dark to a sickening pale in seconds. He asked in a slow, dangerously calm voice, "And why would you do that?"

Morvran bowed even lower. "You instructed me so, Master. It is not my place to question."

So, it isn't Morvran who has it out for me, but it was the original Slifer. That old coot clearly had some bizarre death wish! And now I'm caught up in his whirlwind of madness!

"Why didn't you inform me of this sooner?"

Morvran scratched the back of his bald head, looking slightly embarrassed. "Well,

Master, I got distracted. There was that Legacy Disciple who needed some . . . discipline. By the time I remembered to inform you, you were already deep in closed-door cultivation."

If I knew earlier, I could have tried to free the girl, explained the situation . . . Slifer's thoughts trailed. He sighed deeply, realizing the gravity of the situation. *But with the deaths of the Nascent Soul cultivators, would the Black Heart Sect even listen? They might just see this as a deliberate act of aggression from us, and I can't even blame them because they would absolutely be right.*

"Alright, Morvran, take me to the girl," Slifer said decisively, standing up. But as he did, his stomach growled loudly.

Morvran's unwavering expression seemed to falter for a split second, a hint of surprise showing in his eyes. Nascent Soul cultivators didn't typically need sustenance. "Master, are you . . . hungry?"

Slifer gave an awkward laugh. "Erm, yes. The breakthrough took more out of me than I thought. Any chance you could get me some . . . dumplings?"

Morvran bowed. *Master's cultivation may appear stagnant to outsiders, but it seems that he is still making progress and experiencing breakthroughs.* "Of course, Master. Would you prefer the celestial cloud dumplings or the golden phoenix ones?"

Slifer blinked, a bit taken aback. "We have celestial cloud dumplings? What in the heavens are those?"

"They are a delicacy made from the finest ingredients, steamed atop a cloud during a rare celestial event, giving them a unique taste," Morvran explained.

Slifer stared at him, momentarily speechless. *Then why have I been eating regular meat-filled dumplings this whole time?*

"Bring me the celestial cloud ones and, oh, a pot of immortal brew tea."

Morvran nodded. "Very well, Master. I'll have them brought to you promptly."

The dungeon was a dark and gloomy place, the walls made of cold gray stone, dimly illuminated by flickering torches. The suffocating scent of dampness and despair permeated the air. On either side of the narrow path, prisoners were chained up, their gaunt faces bearing the signs of intense torment. Some of them were whimpering, others groaning, and a few appeared to have given up altogether, their eyes vacant.

Amidst the sea of anguish, one particular prisoner stood out.

A young, beautiful lady named Leah. Her robes were in tatters, her pale skin marred with blood and bruises, yet the fire in her eyes hadn't been entirely extinguished. With raven-black hair that cascaded down her back, eyes that shimmered like the purest of amethysts, and a grace only matched by celestial beings, she was the epitome of sect royalty. Men wanted her, women envied her, and cultivators from other sects respected her solely because of her father's fearsome reputation.

Born into unimaginable privilege, she never had to struggle. Everything was given to her, from the rarest cultivation resources to the ancient scripts holding the sect's secrets. Under the protective gaze of her powerful father, and benefitting from the sect's resources, she achieved the Core Formation Realm in a mere eighteen years.

However, here she was, humiliated, injured, and imprisoned. She felt a fury and shame she had never experienced before. Her current state was so far removed from her past life that it seemed like a cruel joke played by the heavens. Never in her worst nightmares had she envisioned a fate like this.

Slifer strolled into this scene, a plate of dumplings in one hand. He tried to maintain the elegance and poise befitting an elder as he nibbled on them, but he was having a hard time managing the chopsticks. *How do people even eat with these infuriating things?* he wondered as he fumbled, almost dropping a dumpling.

But his culinary frustrations took a backseat as his eyes fell on the injured lady. He paused mid-chew, his demeanor changing instantly. *This is horrendous! She's been here for what, a day? Morvran, what the hell did you do?*

She looked up at him, a fierce hatred burning in her eyes. "So, the demon finally makes an appearance."

Slifer ignored her, his mind raced as he tried to recall classic xianxia reasons for such a capture. *Is it leverage? A hostage to extract some treasure or technique from the Black Heart Sect? Or maybe it's revenge, making Elder Olakin suffer by harming his beloved daughter.* His thoughts took a darker turn. *It couldn't be the blood sacrifice trope, could it? Using her pure blood for some forbidden ritual?*

His train of thought was rudely interrupted when she, after gathering strength, spat out a mouthful of blood in his direction. He dodged just in time, narrowly evading the flying projectile.

Whew! That would've been embarrassing.

Morvran's expression darkened. "How dare you!" he bellowed, stepping forward and entering her cage with speed. With a swift motion, he slapped her across the face. Slifer's eyes widened in horror, unaccustomed to seeing a woman get beaten.

"Enough!" Slifer shouted, raising his hand.

Morvran's hand froze midair. He immediately stepped back and bowed deeply to Slifer. "As you command, Master."

This is getting out of hand, Slifer thought. *Not only do I have to figure out why she's here, but I also have to rein in Morvran before he turns this whole thing into an even bigger disaster.*

"Step out, Morvran. I need to speak with the young lady alone," Slifer said, his tone severe.

Morvran nodded, exiting the dungeon and standing guard outside, his face still flushed but obedient.

Slifer turned his attention back to the woman. "So," he began, setting aside the now forgotten dumplings, "let's sort this out."

There was an awkward silence between Slifer and the young woman. *What do I even do with her?* he wondered. Releasing her without getting anything in return would raise suspicions among the sect, after all, when had Elder Slifer ever just let a prisoner go? But holding her was a bigger issue; it would risk the wrath of her father and the Black Heart Sect, and that was definitely something he was not equipped to deal with.

There must be a middle ground. Finally, he sighed. *Blackmail it is, then. But first, let's see what we're working with.*

Insight!

Name: Leah
Realm: Early Core Formation
Known Techniques: N/A
Known Affiliations: Black Heart Sect
Disposition: N/A

Suddenly, another notification chimed in.

Ding!
Rare Cultivation Body Discovered

A rare cultivation body? That makes things more complicated. It seems that the previous Slifer had an eye for rare treasures, he thought as his gaze traveled up and down her form, suspecting the original Slifer's intentions for kidnapping Leah. The plot thickened. But try as he might, he couldn't recall any relevant memories that could shed light on this plan. It was like groping in the dark.

Ding!
You Have Gained 5 Credits

He raised an eyebrow at the sudden credit gain. *This System . . . is giving me credits for discoveries now?* He smirked, a hint of suspicion twinkling in his eyes. *Is it trying to tempt me to leave the safety of the sect in search of more rare phenomena?* But he was cautious. He knew the System all too well. Only something truly special or out of the ordinary would lead to a reward. He would not foolishly leave the sect, hoping that he could get credits for discovering something basic, like a new location.

Lost in thought, he failed to notice the young lady shivering under his intent gaze.

Why is he staring at me like that? she fretted.

Clearing his throat, Slifer began his first ever attempt at blackmail. "I apologize for the way you've been treated." He paused as her resentful eyes pierced into him, then took a deep breath and pushed on. "But if your father provides me with a Heaven Rank Righteous Cultivation Method, I will ensure your release."

Her face contorted into a mixture of disbelief and anger. "Really? All of this . . . for a Heaven Rank method? That's the only reason?" Her pride was wounded. She was a woman in the prime of her youth, and to think that her only worth in this situation was to be bartered for a cultivation method was deeply insulting.

Slifer raised an eyebrow, he sensed her rising indignation but misunderstood its root. *What did she expect, a poetic declaration?* "You don't really have anything else of value to me."

She scoffed, her inner thoughts practically screaming, *I am a beautiful young woman! Surely there's more to me than just some ransom material!*

Realization struck Slifer like a slap in the face. *Wait a minute! Is she expecting me to . . . coerce her?* Panic edged his thoughts—he was not *that* kind of guy. *I'm just trying not to get killed here, woman! It's my life versus your beauty, and honestly, right now, life is winning by a landslide!*

"Listen," he continued, "if your father gives me the method, you're free to go. No harm, no foul. And you can get back to . . . whatever it is you do when you're not being kidnapped."

Seeing that Slifer wasn't swayed by her beauty, she retorted, "Nothing will save you from my father's wrath when he finds out how I've been treated."

Slifer inwardly cursed. *Girl, why are you making things difficult for me? I don't even want you here.* Hoping to regain some semblance of control, he decided to put on the demonic sect elder act and fixed her with an ominous glare. "If your father's revenge is inevitable, then perhaps I should end this now and be done with you."

She visibly paled, any remnants of her previous bravado melting away. Eyes wide, she fell silent, perhaps realizing that she was not in the position she thought she was.

Nodding his approval, Slifer softened slightly. "Be a good girl, and maybe we can all walk away from this relatively unscathed."

Turning on his heel, he made his way out of the cell. But just as he was about to step out into the corridor, a pitiable sight from the corner caught his attention. Amongst the prisoners, one stood out as particularly wretched. It was Elder Fron's disciple.

The man was a shadow of his former self. His skin clung to his bones, giving him a skeletal appearance. His clothes were tattered, and every inch of his visible skin seemed to be covered in welts, bruises, and cuts. Most disturbingly, his eyes—once bright and alert—now stared blankly ahead, as if the very essence of his soul had been drained.

Slifer winced internally. *So, the old man wasn't exaggerating. He really did this to his own disciple. How heinous!*

As he stepped out of the dungeon, Slifer couldn't help but feel that life had dealt him a complicated hand. Turning to Morvran, who had been waiting patiently, he said, "Put her in one of the guest quarters but keep an eye on her. Oh, and get into contact with her father, tell him if he wants to see his daughter again, to bring me a Heaven Rank Cultivation Method."

"Yes, Master."

Back in the tranquility of his quarters, Slifer settled down, lost in his contemplations. His thoughts naturally wandered to his disciples and their mission. It was the first time he had anyone under his care; it was a strange feeling and not something he had gotten used to yet.

Ding!
Your Disciple Hughie Has Killed a Demonic Foundation Establishment Cultivator
You Have Gained 5 Karmic Credits

Seeing the notification, a smile appeared on Slifer's face. He'd been seeing similar notifications pop up throughout the day, and his credits were rising rapidly. However, he couldn't help but feel like he was missing something.

He idly tapped his fingers on the armrest of his chair, but as the moments passed, an unsettling realization dawned upon him.

Wait a minute . . .

In the world of cultivation, even if there was no apparent danger, a protagonist would somehow attract it. Like moths to a flame.

And then it hit him—a typical xianxia trope.

When the protagonists get into trouble, someone usually swoops in to save them. His face paled. *That "someone" is usually their master . . . which would be me.* "System!" he exclaimed, a clear sense of urgency in his voice.

Responding to his call, a holographic screen floated before him, showcasing various items available for purchase. His eyes scanned the list, looking for something—anything— that could potentially save him if the situation arose.

He quickly scanned through the options. Cultivation techniques, weapons, talismans . . . they all had their own prerequisites, be it a certain cultivation level or a set duration for mastery. None of which he had the luxury of time for.

Then his eyes landed on the "Cards" section. These cards were mostly single-use items that didn't rely on cultivation levels to activate, making them perfect for the situation. He found a few that he could see come in handy and others that he found interesting.

Card	Description	Cost
Random	25% chance of gaining a card.	10
Reversal	Devours the life energy in its vicinity to reverse the age of its user.	50
Critical Heal	Heals 30% of wounds.	100
Random Skill	When activated, 95% chance of granting user a random skill.	200
Critical Block	Protects user from a critical strike.	900
Impeccable Defense	Provides 10 seconds of damage immunity.	1,200
Reflection Barrier	Creates energy barrier that reflects incoming ranged attacks back at the attacker for 20 seconds.	1,500
Peak Slifer	Harness Slifer's Peak Cultivation for a duration of 10 minutes.	10,000
Heavenly Tribulation Strike	Lightning bolt at the level of: Nascent Soul Realm (69%), Origin Realm (25%), Astral Awakening Realm (5%), Ascendant Realm (1%), and Immortal Realm (0.0001%).	85,000
Deadly Strike	Deliver a fatal blow to the target.	100,000
Second Life	Activates automatically when user dies.	1,000,000

The price range, however, had him heaving a sigh. *Of course, nothing good comes cheap.*

He had limited options, given that he only had 239 Karmic Credits. His eyes then fell upon the Random Card, which cost only 10 credits but had a catch: a twenty-five percent chance of giving him a useful card and a seventy-five percent chance of leaving him empty-handed.

His smile was tinged with irony. *Ah, gambling. We meet again.*

If he was being honest with himself, the System's previous warning against gambling wasn't unwarranted. His past experiences with gambling weren't *entirely* positive. A couple of big wins were overshadowed by greater losses, thanks to his tendency to double down. He wasn't a gambling addict or anything, well that's at least what he assured himself.

Okay, so if I spend on three Random Cards, I'll still have enough for four Reversal Cards just in case things go south with my lifespan. He paused for a moment, making sure he had not missed anything. *Well, if there's a time to gamble, it's now.*

Muttering a quick prayer to whatever deities watched over gamblers and desperate cultivators alike, he selected "Random Card" and spent the 10 Karmic Credits. *Let's hope luck's on my side this time.*

Ding!

Random Card Acquired
Activate now?
(Yes/No)

Holding his breath, Slifer mentally chose "yes."

The anticipation as he activated it was palpable. A faint glow enveloped the card, but as the light faded, Slifer was greeted with a hollow echo.

Ding!
Unsuccessful
Better Luck Next Time

His face fell, and a curse escaped his lips. "Of course, my luck wouldn't be that great on the first try."

Taking a deep breath to calm himself, he tried to muster some optimism. *Come on. Second time's the charm.* With that hopeful thought, he bought another Random Card.

Ding!
Random Card Acquired
Activate now?
(Yes/No)

Again, he selected "yes."

Ding!
Successful!
You Have Acquired: Heavenly Tribulation Strike Card
Description: Lightning Bolt at the Level of: Nascent Soul Realm (69%), Origin Realm (25%), Astral Awakening Realm (5%), Ascendant Realm (1%), Immortal Realm (0.0001%)

Slifer's eyes widened in astonishment. His heart rate picked up, adrenaline pumping through his veins. "By the heavens!" he exclaimed.

This card was a game changer. It was guaranteed to be effective against Nascent Soul cultivators, and if his luck was good, then perhaps it could even one-shot more powerful cultivators! This was the ray of hope he needed, something to even the odds should a threat arise.

His eyes darted back to the Shop. The temptation to gamble for a third card was intense. The familiar itch to take a risk coursed through him. *Maybe, just maybe, I can strike gold twice in a row*, he thought, his hand hovering over the buy option. *Should I press it?*

"No," he said, clenching his fingers into a fist as he pulled his hand back. "Enough is enough." *I know how this works. The house always wins in the end. The third one will most likely be a dud, and then I'll regret it.*

He leaned back in his chair, satisfied yet still buzzing from the adrenaline of the gamble. "I have something that can protect them, and that's what matters. No need to push my luck further."

And so, reining in his desire to gamble, Slifer turned his focus back to the matters at hand. With Heavenly Tribulation Strike now in his inventory, he felt a smidgen more secure, both for himself and for his wayward disciples. *May this card never need to be used*, he thought. But he knew that in the dangerous world of cultivation, it was always better to be safe than sorry.

CHAPTER EIGHT

As Slifer rested in his quarters, contemplating his next move, a sudden spiritual transmission interrupted his thoughts.

"Apologies for the interruption, Master," Morvran's voice echoed, "but Valeriana has made a breakthrough to the Nascent Soul Realm. She eagerly awaits your arrival."

Valeriana? Slifer delved deep into the recesses of the original's memories, trying to recall any hint of this individual. *Nothing. Not a single hint. Just who is this Valeriana?* "That's splendid news, Morvran," he responded with feigned enthusiasm. "Lead the way."

Inwardly, Slifer couldn't help but grumble like an old man. *What does this woman's breakthrough have to do with me? Is this some flex of her cultivation?*

As Slifer was lost in thought, Morvran effortlessly leaped onto his sword and started to ascend. However, he soon noticed that Slifer was just standing there, staring up at him with an awkward smile on his face.

"Master, is everything alright?" Morvran asked, slightly confused.

With a light chuckle, Slifer adjusted his robes and adopted a sagely demeanor. "Ah, Morvran. I've sworn off flying for the time being. A personal decision."

Morvran looked taken aback, then offered, "Would you like a ride then, Master?"

Slifer nodded in gratitude. "That would be most kind." And with that, he hopped onto the sword, securing himself behind Morvran.

As they flew higher, a sense of unease settled in Slifer's chest. *Something doesn't feel right. It's as though we're being watched by some hidden predator.* The sky darkened slightly, which only added to his discomfort.

Their destination was evident when a massive cave loomed in the distance. But the nauseating smell of rotting flesh wafting from it made Slifer's stomach churn. *Who in the world would choose to live in such a place? Is this Valeriana a madwoman?*

A sudden gust of warm air, redolent with that awful odor, billowed out of the cave, almost knocking Slifer off his feet.

Morvran, apparently unfazed, remarked, "Valeriana must be in a particularly good mood today."

Slifer grimaced, fighting the urge to retch. *By "good mood," does he mean she's . . . cooking something? Human meat perhaps?*

Slifer's feet had barely touched the ground when a vibrant little dragon, smaller than a housecat, came flying out of the cave. The creature was orange, its scales reflecting light like tiny suns. It had large, innocent eyes and tiny wings flapping energetically as it circled around Slifer.

Well, regardless of how weird this Valeriana is, she sure has an adorable pet, Slifer mused.

Reaching out, he gently patted the tiny dragon's head. "Hello there, little fella!"

However, to his astonishment, the cute baby dragon scrunched up its face into an adorably angry expression and said, "Master, you know me, girl, not boy!"

Slifer staggered back, his eyes widening. *It talks?*

"Master is just teasing, Valeriana," Morvran reassured the young dragon.

Slifer's eyebrows shot up. *This . . . This is Valeriana? The one who reached the Nascent Soul Realm?* Staring intently at the dragon, he tried reconciling the idea of a mighty Nascent Soul beast with this pocket-sized bundle of cuteness. *I was expecting something menacing . . . But this? Maybe she can't intimidate opponents, but she could certainly distract them with adorability.*

Rapidly sifting through the original's memories, Slifer recalled that most beasts, prior to reaching the Core Formation level, were essentially mindless, functioning on basic instincts alone. Once they entered the Core Formation Realm, they were able to talk, but their vocabulary was limited to just their names. *Kind of like a . . . Pokémon.*

Upon reaching the Nascent Soul Realm, they would attain the intellectual capacity of a child. Only after stepping into the Ascendant Realm would they gain full maturity. So, the little dragon in front of him was still a baby.

Valeriana, still a tad peeved but wanting to clarify her identity, proudly declared, "Me . . . Val . . . Valer . . . Ugh! Name too long. Me just Val now."

Slifer felt sorry for the poor thing, even in the Nascent Soul Realm, she was still struggling to pronounce her name. "It's okay, Val. Names can be hard, especially long ones."

Valeriana swelled with pride, puffing out her tiny chest. "Master, me break through! Val big dragon now!"

Slifer couldn't help but chuckle at her endearing bragging. He leaned down, playfully pinching her chubby cheek. "Oh, absolutely! You're the biggest dragon I've ever seen!" he teased, a smirk playing on his lips. Technically, he was not lying, she was the *only* dragon he has seen.

Valeriana tilted her head, looking at Slifer with those large, innocent eyes. "M-Master, why you look make funny face? Val no scary?"

"Oh, you're plenty 'scary,' alright," Slifer teased, struggling to keep a straight face.

The only time I see this gentle side of Master is with little Val. Morvran's usually stoic expression softened. *To outsiders, Master Slifer is a ruthless, unyielding force. But those few close to him see the duality—the gentleness he displays to those he cares for.*

However, it seemed that Valeriana was able to tell that Slifer wasn't taking her seriously, as her tiny body suddenly began to shimmer and ripple.

In a swift transformation, her once tiny form expanded rapidly, wings stretching out and growing vast, while her body elongated and thickened. Her once cute, beady eyes were replaced by two large, piercing orbs that glinted dangerously. The adorable orange baby dragon had transformed into a colossal and majestic creature with scales that gleamed like molten gold in the sunlight.

Caught off guard by the sudden change, Slifer's eyes widened in horror. He took an involuntary step back, his heart racing, as the mighty dragon reared her head and let out a deafening roar. The roar's force alone was enough to push him several steps back, making his robes flutter wildly.

What in the Nine Heavens . . . ?!

The huge dragon then halted abruptly, her menacing gaze shifting to one of sheer excitement. "Master scared?" Valeriana questioned in her usual babyish tone, although her voice now had a rumbling undertone because of her colossal size.

Morvran, stepping forward, replied, "Yes, you've scared Master." He nodded approvingly.

Ah, Master's playing along. Little Val lacks confidence. It's like a lion pretending to be scared when its cub pounces. Nicely done, Master.

Valeriana, regaining her smaller form, hopped around Slifer gleefully, puffing out her chest in pride. "Me did it! Me scared Master big-big!" Her tail wagged with delight, and she chirped joyfully. She believed that her master was the scariest person in the world, and if she could scare her master then she could scare anyone.

Though still slightly rattled, Slifer couldn't help but chuckle at the enthusiastic little dragon. He crouched back down to her level, his voice gentle, "Yes, you did. You really are the mightiest dragon I've ever met."

Valeriana chirped, "Master, follow me! Me have something to show!" With a flap of her tiny wings, she led Slifer deeper into the cave.

As he entered, the overwhelming stench of decaying corpses only grew stronger. Laid out before him were the remains of many humans, too many to count.

She's small and cute, but she's still a dragon. Complaining about her eating habits would be like those vegans back on Earth who called me a murderer for eating a hamburger. Slifer couldn't help but chuckle inwardly. *Trust me, vegans, nothing could ever keep me away from a good burger.*

Wandering deeper into the cave, Slifer's eyes widened at the sight of mountains of gold coins, shimmering jewels, and other treasures strewn about. *So, the old tales were right. Dragons do have a thing for hoarding treasures.*

"Look, Master, look!" Valeriana flew over to a small alcove and nudged a ruby pendant towards him. "Pretty, yes?"

Slifer smiled, indulging her excitement. "Yes, it's very pretty, Valeriana."

She has diamonds and all sorts of other precious gems here, yet she's excited about a ruby? Slifer thought. But then, a little voice in the back of his mind nudged him. *Might as well use Insight on it. What's the harm?*

He focused his spiritual sense on the pendant, activating the skill.

> Error
> Insight Skill Level Too Low
> Upgrade to Identify Object

His eyes widened. *What the . . . ? There must be something special about this ruby.*

"Master like it?" Valeriana looked up at him, clearly seeking approval.

Slifer, still taken aback by the unexpected failure of his Insight skill, replied, "I like it very much, Valeriana."

"You keep!" Valeriana nudged the ruby pendant towards him. "Gift for Master!"

His eyes widened. *She's giving it to me? Well, if she insists.* "Thank you, Valeriana. It's a beautiful gift."

Valeriana buzzed around happily. "Master happy, me happy!"

Slifer couldn't help but smile at her simplicity. Despite her quirks and the rather morbid environment she called home, she was a fascinating creature—equal parts terrifying and adorable.

"Val, where did you find this ruby?" Slifer asked, his curiosity piqued.

"Val munching cultivator. Bite dis by accident," she said, making a biting motion with her tiny jaws. Valeriana's face suddenly turned sad. She opened her mouth to reveal a chipped tooth. "Tooth break."

Slifer's eyes narrowed. *An object that can't be identified by Insight and strong enough to chip a dragon's tooth. What on Earth is this thing?*

Valeriana's face lit up again. "But it pretty. Master like, so me forgive it!"

Slifer couldn't help but smile at her innocent joy. "You did the right thing, Val. It is a very special ruby."

He turned to Morvran. "Morvran, do you think you can find any information on what this ruby might be?"

Morvran nodded, his expression turning serious. "I can try to consult the sect's archives or speak with some artifact appraisers. It is indeed curious that it could chip Valeriana's tooth."

Slifer then turned back to Val and focused, activating his Insight skill.

Congratulations!
You Have Discovered a Higher Being
You Have Gained 5 Credits
Would You Like to Take the Being as a Disciple?

A smirk spread across Slifer's wrinkled face. *A Nascent Soul being as a disciple?* The credits he could farm from her would solve many of his problems. Eagerly, he mentally replied, *Yes.*

Error
Soul Bond Required
Upgrade to Identify Object
A Soul Bond Can Be Purchased at the Shop for 900 Karmic Credits

---

Of course. Slifer sighed inwardly. *The System always knows how to tease me. Just when I think I'm about to get something good, there's a catch.*

Valeriana, oblivious to Slifer's internal dialogue, tilted her head, her eyes brimming with childlike curiosity. "Master, why you look sad?"

Slifer, momentarily pulled from his thoughts, gave Val a pat on the head, chuckling, "Ah, little one, just the world playing its tricks on an old man."

"Hughie, watch out!" Caelum called out.

Engaged in a fierce duel with a Mid-Core Formation expert, Hughie barely maneuvered out of harm's way. The blade slashed, narrowly missing the spot where Hughie's head had been a mere moment earlier.

Laughing, he taunted the two assailants, the other being an Early Core Formation expert. "Is that the best you two can manage? Double-teaming and you still miss!"

The Early Core Formation expert retorted, "You talk too much!"

The other sneered. "We'll shut that mouth for good."

They both channeled their qi and activated their combined skill, Twin Celestial Strike.

The Mid-Core expert produced a luminous white blade from thin air, and the Early Core expert's hands transformed into fiery phoenix claws. The two charged simultaneously from opposite directions, attempting to trap Hughie in a pincer attack.

With a gleam in his eye, Hughie shouted, "Come on then! Give me everything you've got!"

Instead of evading, he stood his ground. He fortified his vital organs with a barrier of qi but allowed the rest of the attacks to hit. The blade sliced his side, and the phoenix claws scorched his skin. The combined force sent him hurtling backwards, crashing into a boulder, leaving him bloodied and bruised, but remarkably, with no fatal wounds.

The bandits laughed. "Look at him," the Mid-Core expert jeered. "All he's good for is bullying those Foundation Establishment weaklings. All bark and no bite."

However, as Hughie slowly began to rise, his laughter, tinged with madness, echoed across the village.

The two bandits exchanged bewildered glances. *Has he lost his mind?* thought the Early Core Formation bandit.

A shocking transformation began. Hughie's injuries started healing at an inhuman speed. Crimson veins appeared and pulsated across his form, and his muscles bulged and expanded. He clenched his fists, and they emitted a pulsing, menacing aura.

Towering over them, Hughie smirked. "Thank you for the warm-up. Now, it's my turn."

Startled by Hughie's sudden transformation, the two bandits instinctively stepped back. But in a blink of an eye, Hughie appeared before the Mid-Core Formation expert. With an exaggerated wind-up and a grin, he threw a punch at the first one. The bandit was unable to dodge and Hughie's punch landed squarely on his chest. The impact was so overwhelming that the bandit's body instantly flattened, disintegrating into a violent explosion of blood and gore.

The scene looked like an artist's palette of red . . . if the artist was particularly morbid.

The Early Core Formation bandit was frozen in sheer terror for a moment, but instinct quickly kicked in. He turned to flee, his voice quivering as he shouted, "Y-you're a demon!"

Laughing maniacally, Hughie's form flickered and he appeared right in front of the fleeing bandit, catching him by the neck with one massive hand. Effortlessly lifting him off the ground, Hughie whispered into the terrified bandit's ear, "Going somewhere?"

As the bandit gasped and choked, Hughie said with mock solemnity, "Boss Morvran would be so proud of this. You ready?"

Without waiting for an answer, Hughie began to repeatedly slam the bandit onto the ground. After each slam, he would lift him up, inspect the damage, and comment as if he was testing the durability of a new toy. "Hmm, still intact . . . Let's try that again."

By the time Hughie was done, the once fearsome bandit was reduced to a jumble of battered bits and pieces. Hughie, catching his breath, looked at his handiwork and nodded appreciatively. "Now that's what I call a stress-relief exercise!"

Caelum watched the aftermath of Hughie's explosive display and sighed deeply. *Why can't Junior Brother ever approach things with a bit more caution?* he thought. In the world of cultivation, underestimating an opponent, no matter how weak they seemed, was a ticket to an early grave. Caelum had never considered cultivating like Hughie. Hughie's method, although potent, was simply too volatile, too fraught with the danger of a misstep that could end one's life.

His thoughts were interrupted as the bandit leader before him spoke. The man was a Late Core Formation cultivator. Like any typical bandit, he was broad-shouldered and had a twisted scar on his face. "Why is the Black Rose Sect aiding this insignificant village?" The leader sneered.

Caelum's eyes narrowed, his expression growing cold. "That is none of your concern." Drawing his sword from its sheath, the blade shimmered under the sunlight. Its hilt was intricately designed, embedded with black roses. It was a gift from his master, given to him when he began his journey as a sword cultivator.

Closing his eyes, Caelum channeled his qi into the sword, whispering softly, "Awaken, Bloodthorn."

The silvery blade began to morph, turning a deep shade of crimson, almost as if it was thirsting for blood. Dark, sinister patterns emerged along the blade, giving it a demonic appearance.

"This skirmish has dragged on for far too long," Caelum remarked.

Even though they both stood at the Late Stage of Core Formation, as a sword cultivator, Caelum possessed a naturally superior offensive capability. Moreover, unlike these bandits, whose cultivation techniques were hardly worth mentioning, Caelum was a disciple of the Black Rose Sect. His methods, refined and potent, were all ranked within the esteemed Earth Rank.

It's time to end this, Caelum thought, his grip tightening around Bloodthorn.

The bandit leader sensed the imminent danger, his instincts screaming that Caelum intended to finish the battle with a single, decisive strike. In a desperate move, he activated his own technique, Inferno Vortex, gathering fire elemental energy in his palms and shaping it into a swirling column of raging flames.

However, just as he lunged forward, Caelum's eyes snapped open, now red and demonic. In a flash of scarlet light, Caelum appeared behind the bandit leader, as swift as a ghost. The fiery attack, devoid of its intended target, veered off course and slammed into a nearby tree. The tree instantly caught fire, its wood hissing and cracking as it was consumed by the blaze.

The bandit leader's eyes widened in disbelief. Before he could even process what had happened, his body tensed, and in the next moment, his head cleanly separated from his torso, falling to the ground with a dull thud.

Caelum sighed, casting a glance at Bloodthorn, now stained with the bandit leader's blood. The sword seemed to pulse with life as it absorbed the fresh blood, glowing a vibrant crimson for a brief moment before reverting back to its original, elegant form.

As efficient as ever, Bloodthorn, Caelum thought, sheathing the sword once more

"It took you long enough," a voice drawled, tinted with amusement.

Both Caelum and Hughie turned to see Amelia perched atop a grotesque mountain of dead Core Formation and Foundation Establishment cultivators.

Hughie let out a hearty laugh, his previously enraged form now settled back to its normal state. "Ah, Senior Sister, these poor souls really drew the short straw having to face you."

Caelum raised an eyebrow at the comment, thinking to himself, *Getting pulverized to death by Junior Brother doesn't sound like a picnic either.* But his gaze upon Amelia sharpened. *Still, Hughie's got a point. Soul techniques are the worst. Not only do they inflict excruciating pain, but they rob a cultivator of their chance at reincarnation. Just the perfect arsenal for our sadistic junior sister.*

Suddenly, a half-dead cultivator who'd been playing possum began to scramble away.

Amelia laughed gleefully. "Ah, I was waiting for one of you to try something!"

In one fluid motion, she launched a dagger. It cut through the air with deadly precision, piercing the escaping cultivator's head and continuing its flight, shattering a window in one of the nearby village houses. A bloodcurdling scream followed.

Amelia's eyes widened. "Oh, spirits, I didn't mean to—"

Caelum shook his head. "Master will not be pleased with this collateral damage, Amelia."

She scowled and shot both of them a threatening glare. "Master isn't going to hear about this. Understand?"

Hughie rubbed the back of his neck awkwardly. "I, uh, didn't see anything. Did you, Brother Caelum?"

This is going to be a long day, Caelum thought, suppressing a sigh.

The village leader, a frail old man with a crooked back and white, wispy hair, approached them cautiously, his legs visibly trembling. With a deep bow, he said, "Esteemed cultivators, our humble village owes you a great debt for driving away those ruffians. We are eternally grateful."

Conveniently, he made no mention of the unfortunate villager who met an untimely death.

Hughie grinned awkwardly. "Ah, no need to thank me, old man. I had a blast."

The village leader managed a strained smile but inwardly quivered. *Why did these cultivators from the demonic sect save us? What could they possibly want?* Fearing that they might take offense if not offered something, he cleared his throat. "Um, we have some gold that—"

Amelia waved a dismissive hand. "Old man, keep your gold. We're not interested."

The village leader's face paled. *If not gold, then what . . . ?*

Swallowing hard, he blurted out, his voice tinged with shame, "We can also offer some young women to—" His eyes darted nervously between Caelum and Hughie, gauging their reactions.

Amelia raised an eyebrow. "Women? Why not men? Why not *old* men?" She shot the village leader a playful glance, making the elder's blood run cold.

Before the situation could get more awkward, Caelum interrupted, his voice calm yet assertive. "Our master sent us on this mission. We have no desire for any offerings from the villagers. Our job is done."

Hearing this, the village leader let out a sigh of profound relief, his knees almost buckling from the weight lifted off his shoulders.

Thank the gods they're leaving. I don't think our village could handle any more "help" from demonic cultivators, he thought, still shaking from the whole ordeal.

"Ah, I've finally found you."

All eyes darted upwards, locking onto the figure of an old man hovering in the air. His long gray hair cascaded down to his waist, swaying gently in the wind. Dressed in weathered martial arts robes, he looked like a relic from a bygone era.

Yet the most startling thing about him was the presence he radiated; it was as if the world itself bent to his will. Trees, that had stood tall for centuries, now seemed to lean towards him, almost like disciples bowing before a master. The very air felt heavier, filled with a pressure that made even breathing feel like a challenge.

Caelum's eyes widened in realization, his voice trembling as he whispered, "Origin Realm . . ."

CHAPTER NINE

Elder Olakin's voice boomed, echoing through the air like thunder. "The Black Rose Sect has truly crossed the line this time!" His face contorted with anger. "To think that your master, a mere Nascent Soul cultivator, dared to kidnap *my* precious daughter!"

With each word he spoke, the trio of disciples felt their chests tighten. An invisible pressure weighed them down, making it hard to breathe. But when the word "daughter" escaped Elder Olakin's lips, it was like a boulder had been dropped onto them. They collapsed to their knees, gasping for breath, while the village leader, standing nearby, simply exploded, leaving nothing except a mist of red.

Of course, Master would be the one to kidnap the daughter of an Origin Realm expert, Caelum thought, a bitter smile twisting his lips.

Hughie's mind raced frantically. *Just my luck! Getting bullied by an old man!*

Amelia, on the other hand, seemed genuinely surprised. *Master kidnapped someone? That's new. He usually just . . . kills them.*

Elder Olakin continued, "You will remain here while your master returns with my daughter." With a wave of his hand, three Nascent Soul cultivators appeared beside him in the sky, bowing deeply. "Send word to their sect."

One of the Nascent Soul cultivators hesitated, voice trembling, "My lord, what if the Black Rose Sect sends reinforcements?"

Elder Olakin chuckled. "Do you truly think the Black Rose Sect would risk war for an elder on his last breath? No, he shall be their sacrificial lamb."

The Nascent Soul cultivators nodded in agreement, vanishing as quickly as they appeared.

Elder Olakin then turned his gaze back to the fallen disciples. "As for you three, you can only blame your own master for the fate that awaits you."

The elder then raised his hand, and the very earth seemed to respond to his will. Vines erupted from the ground, shooting towards the disciples like green serpents.

"Awaken, Bloodthorn," Caelum whispered urgently.

His blade, bathed in a familiar demonic glow, lashed out at the encroaching vines, trying to sever them. But it was all in vain. Even a casual move by an Origin expert was too strong, too overwhelming. Before the other two could even react, the vines coiled around them, holding them in place.

Satisfied, Elder Olakin closed his eyes, sinking into a meditative state as he waited. But only a few moments later, he suddenly tensed. A disturbance in the heavens above caught his attention. Opening his eyes, Elder Olakin saw the silhouettes of two figures locked in battle. "Astral Awakening Realm . . ." he whispered, a hint of envy in his voice.

What are they doing here? he pondered. *Such beings usually prefer secluded, closed-door cultivation. Something significant must've occurred to draw them out.*

His thoughts were interrupted as the two figures above clashed, sending a stray streak of white fire plummeting towards him. Elder Olakin's eyes widened; he shifted to the side just in time, narrowly avoiding the inferno. The fire streaked past him, missing him by inches. Beads of sweat materialized on his brow as he realized how dangerously close he had come to death.

By the time the white flames reached ground level, they had diminished to a flickering spark.

Hughie, constricted by the vines and entirely helpless, watched the spark approach him with a sense of impending doom. Closing his eyes, he braced for the end. But the end never came. When he dared to open his eyes again, he found the vines that had bound him reduced to mere ashes. Miraculously, he himself was unscathed. He was free!

Wasting no time, Hughie shouted, "Senior Brother, Senior Sister, I'm going to get help!" Without a backwards glance, he made a mad dash away from the scene.

Elder Olakin's eyes locked onto Hughie's retreating form. "You think you can escape, boy?" With a burst of energy, he surged forward, determined to capture the escaping disciple. But as if the heavens themselves intervened, another radiant streak descended from the celestial brawl above, a blazing white fire even fiercer than the previous.

"Not again!" Elder Olakin spat, desperately trying to evade the oncoming onslaught. But this time, he was a fraction of a second too slow. The fire struck him squarely on the back, sending him tumbling out of the sky and crashing into the ground, where he formed a small crater upon impact.

Lying there, Elder Olakin desperately called upon one of his strongest defensive measures. "Aqua Barrier Cascade!" he coughed out. The air around him moistened as a swirling barrier of water formed, enveloping him in its embrace.

However, the celestial white fire seemed to scoff at his defenses. It lapped hungrily at the watery shield, threatening to evaporate it entirely as it continued its relentless approach towards the elder.

How can this be? Elder Olakin thought in disbelief.

But as abruptly as the attack began, it subsided. The ethereal flames dissipated, leaving a charred and shaken Elder Olakin amidst the ruins.

Slowly, very slowly, he rose to his feet. He chose not to pursue Hughie, at least not for now.

Twice in such a short span? Is this mere chance or . . . His eyes darted to Hughie's receding figure, suspicion brewing. *That boy . . . Could he . . . ?*

He cast a wary glance skyward, worried that he, an Origin Realm expert, would be killed as collateral damage.

"Such power . . ."

Slifer was engrossed in conversation with Morvran and Val when a sudden message interrupted his thoughts.

Ding!
Warning: Your Disciple Amelia Is in Mortal Danger

Slifer's eyes widened in shock. He had only sent Amelia and the other disciples on a task of Core Formation difficulty. What could've gone so wrong?

Another two notifications popped up in quick succession causing his heart to drop.

> *Ding!*
> Warning: Your Disciple Hughie Is in Mortal Danger
> *Ding!*
> Warning: Your Disciple Caelum Is in Mortal Danger

Slifer's eyes narrowed as he tried to piece together the puzzle. Given the life-saving treasures they possessed, bestowed by the original, only cultivators of the Origin Realm or above had the power to endanger them. *Could it be . . . did the bandits have a backing even the sect wasn't aware of?*

Without hesitation, he asked the System, *Where are the disciples now?*

> Error
> Increase Disciple Loyalty to 95% or Upgrade Disciple Management Panel to Obtain More Information

With no time or credits to worry about upgrades, Slifer sighed. *I need to go to Lushan Village.*

> *Ding!*
> New Task: Save Your Disciples From Imminent Danger
> Reward: 1000 Karmic Credits

The sight of so many credits up for grabs made Slifer's face turn pale. The System wouldn't offer such a prize unless the danger was sky-high. *Am I walking into my own grave?*

He shook his head, banishing the dread that crept into his thoughts. *Credits or no credits, I'd go save them. They're not just disciples; they're my lifeline. No disciples means no credits, and no credits means a short life for me.*

A smile crossed his face as he thought of Hughie. *That boy has protagonist-level luck. If the Heavenly Tribulation Strike reaches Astral Awakening or even the Ascendant level, we just might stand a chance.*

> *Ding!*
> Your Disciple Hughie Is No Longer in Mortal Danger

Seeing the notification, Slifer's smile faltered, he decided to wait for a few more seconds to see if the situation had resolved itself, maybe he wouldn't need to interfere after all.

However, seeing no further notifications, a frown appeared on his face. *Should I be relieved or worried? If Hughie isn't in danger, can I still count on his protagonist-level luck to aid me?*

He sighed, the weight of uncertainty pressing on him. *Why won't the System let me see my own stats? Knowing my own luck could ease my mind or . . . make it worse.*

"Master?" Morvran's voice pulled him from his thoughts. "You seemed disturbed. Is everything okay?"

"The disciples are in danger," Slifer revealed with a heavy sigh, "I must go save them."

Morvran's eyes widened slightly. "Could it be that one of their life-saving treasures was activated?"

Slifer blinked, momentarily caught off guard by the plausible excuse Morvran provided. *That's . . . a better explanation than anything I could have come up with.*

"Yes," he replied with a firm nod. "That's exactly what happened."

Morvran's face took on a determined look. "Master, is there anything I can do to help?"

Slifer forced a smile, though his worry was clear in his eyes. "Prepare a grand feast for my return." *If I return,* he added internally. Just then his belly gave an inopportune rumble, and a hint of embarrassment crossed his face. *With everything going on, I think a feast is the least I deserve.*

Val, having overheard, approached him with large, worried eyes. "Master go? Val help?"

He smiled at the tiny dragon. "Yes, Val. I need you to change into your bigger form. Will you give me a ride?"

Val nodded energetically. "Yes, Master! Val be big and fly!" With that, she darted out of the cave. In moments, her smaller form was replaced by the magnificent sight of her large, majestic size.

Slifer couldn't help but feel a rush of excitement. *Riding a dragon . . . It's the stuff of childhood dreams.*

As he prepared to climb onto Val, he noticed Fenlock descend from the clouds. "Master! I've set up the Master-Disciple Ceremony!"

Ding!
Task Complete
You Have Gained 10 Karmic Credits

Slifer quickly waved him off. "Your senior brothers and sister are in danger, the ceremony can wait." Without waiting for a response, Slifer leaped onto Val, who readied her wings for flight.

Fenlock stood still for a moment, processing the situation. But then, his face broke into a grin. "This means . . . more time with Junior Sister Lenvari!" With newfound energy, he dashed off, shouting joyfully, "Junior Sister! Wait for me!"

Flying high in the sky, Slifer's sharp eyes scanned the landscape below. In the distance, he spotted a small figure hurrying away from Lushan Village. *Wait a minute . . . isn't that . . . Hughie?*

He decided to activate the Insight skill to confirm.

Name: Hughie
Realm: Late Core Formation
Known Techniques: N/A
Known Affiliations: Black Rose Sect
Disposition: N/A

"Val, let's intercept Hughie," Slifer ordered.

Val tilted her head. "Huwie there? We say hi-hi!"

With a burst of enthusiasm, she swooped down, her vast shadow casting a dark veil over Hughie, who was so wrapped up in his own world that he nearly leapt out of his boots when Val landed in front of him.

"Holy dragon scales, Val! You nearly gave me a heart attack," Hughie exclaimed, clutching his chest dramatically.

Val giggled. "Oopsie! Val scared Huwie!"

Then, lifting his gaze, Hughie spotted Slifer. "Master!" he exclaimed in relief. "I was heading to the Black Rose Sect to find you. Some creepy old man attacked us, and he's taken Senior Brother and Senior Sister hostage. I was taken too, but . . . well . . . I managed to escape," he finished with a sheepish laugh.

Slifer's eyes narrowed. *As I suspected, Hughie's high luck stat saved him.* "Get on, and show us the way," he instructed.

Scratching the back of his head, Hughie pointed towards Lushan Village. "They're that way. It's really not that far, Master. I'm sure you could find it yourself."

Slifer scrutinized him. *With a luck stat of eight, there's no way I'm letting you go.* His face hardened. "What kind of junior brother are you, refusing to aid your seniors?"

Hughie's head dropped as he realized that his plans of escaping were exposed. "I . . . I thought I'd be in the way," he mumbled.

Slifer dismissed his excuse with a shake of his head. "Just get on. And make sure to stay close to me the whole time, no matter what happens."

Hughie hesitated, then nodded. *Urgh, why is Master punishing me?* he thought, misunderstanding Slifer's instructions.

Slifer smirked inwardly. *I don't know if luck is contagious, but having Hughie near me certainly can't hurt.*

"Me fly fast! Hold strong!" Val chirped, her wings spreading wide as she sped towards the village.

Elder Olakin, hovering in the air, felt the weight of the world lift slightly with the departure of the Astral Awakening seniors. His gaze drifted to the two struggling disciples, their will unwavering despite their dire circumstances. A glint of admiration sparkled in his eyes. *In another time and place, perhaps they would have been worthy of being my disciples.*

His gaze then darted in the direction of the Black Rose Sect. Any moment now, his servants would reach their destination. He didn't expect the sect's elder to face him directly; after all, challenging an Origin Realm cultivator like him was akin to courting death. But he did expect that the foolish elder would hand over his daughter without resistance. The captured disciples below were just the price to be paid for their master's audacity.

A frown creased his brows. *But if he dares to harm even a single strand of her hair . . . The heavens themselves won't be able to save him.*

His thoughts were abruptly interrupted by the unmistakable silhouette of a dragon, cutting through the skies. Squinting, Olakin's enhanced vision focused on the figure of Elder Slifer and that annoying disciple riding the mighty beast. *Where is she? What has that demon done?*

Hughie, seeing the elder staring at him, gave an uncomfortable wave, his expression screaming, "I'd rather be anywhere else right now."

As for Slifer, he calmly met the elder's gaze. *So, another old man with a grudge. But which of the original's enemies could this be?*

Insight!

Name: N/A

Realm: Late Origin Realm
Known Techniques: N/A
Known Affiliations: Black Heart Sect
Disposition: N/A

Late Origin Realm? Slifer pondered his options, he would rather save his cards if possible. *Talking my way out would be the best course here, but demonic cultivators are rarely the diplomatic type. I shouldn't get my hopes up.*

He then looked down to see two of his disciples bound by vines.

Caelum shook his head in disbelief. "Why did Master come? He can't possibly best an Origin Realm expert."

Amelia, never one to hold her tongue, smirked at her captor. "Well, now that our master is here, you'll soon be begging him to spare your pathetic life, old man."

Do all disciples nowadays take Courting Death 101? Slifer's heart nearly jumped out of his chest at her bold proclamation. *And she's trying to take me down with her!*

"Slifer," Olakin spat out, "where is my daughter?"

Daughter? Origin Realm expert . . . Slifer's thoughts raced, connecting the dots. *Elder Olakin! If I had known it was him, I'd have brought the girl.* But as he recalled the wounds Morvran had inflicted on her, a chill ran down his spine. *Then again, given her current state, that might've ended badly for me anyway.*

Clearing his throat, Slifer spoke with feigned calm. "She is currently a guest at our sect."

A mocking laughter escaped Olakin's lips. "Guest? You expect me to believe you'd kill Nascent Soul experts just to accommodate a Core Formation cultivator?"

Slifer didn't respond. The biting truth in Olakin's words made him inwardly curse the original Slifer for getting him into such a predicament. Gathering his courage, he proposed, "Return my disciples, and I'll ensure your daughter's safe return."

Olakin shook his head dismissively. "You misunderstand, Slifer. I'll personally retrieve my daughter. As for you and your disciples, you won't live to see another day."

As Slifer opened his mouth, searching for the right words to defuse the volatile situation, Elder Olakin suddenly attacked.

"Emerald Vine Strike!"

The technique burst forth, a verdant vine shot directly at Slifer with breathtaking speed, too fast for his eyes to track. *Only the Critical Block Card can save me now,* he thought frantically.

Val let out a panicked, "No hurt Master!" She swiftly tried to dodge, but the vine's relentless speed caught her off guard and the sharp tip grazed her flank. "Owie!" she cried out as she began to lose control and spiral towards the earth.

As she descended rapidly, both Slifer and Hughie clung to her desperately. The wind whipped past them, roaring in their ears. But just as the ground seemed ominously close, Val's large form began to shrink.

In this moment of crisis, Hughie's reflexes kicked in. He reached into his storage ring, drawing forth his sword. With a nimble move, he landed on the flat of the blade, suspending himself in midair. Looking quite pleased with himself, he exclaimed, "Well, that was close!"

Below, Slifer's heart raced. As Val continued to decrease in size, he managed to grab hold of the now tiny dragon, wrapping her in his arms. He braced for impact, tucking and rolling to distribute the force of their landing.

Breathing heavily, he examined the tiny dragon, and noticed that her orange scales were tarnished by a dark, oozing wound on her flank. "Val, are you okay?"

Val sniffled, her large, teary eyes looking up at Slifer. "Val hurt, but Val strong," she whispered.

I don't have any pills that could heal a dragon, Slifer thought bitterly, a sinking feeling gripping his chest. The sect was the only place with the resources to heal her.

"Rest now, Val," he whispered tenderly, cupping the baby dragon's face. "I'll be back soon."

Her eyes, misty with pain, gazed into his. She nodded weakly, her trust in her master unwavering.

Seeing little Val like this caused something to snap inside of Slifer. Gazing at the sky, his face twisted with hatred. *Damn you, old man. You just signed your death warrant.*

He had been sympathetic towards Elder Olakin, understanding that the original Slifer was the one that kidnapped his daughter and caused all this. But the moment the elder injured Val, all bets were off. Despite their short time together, he had developed a fondness for the little dragon that he simply couldn't ignore.

Activate Heavenly Tribulation Strike Card!

Ding!
Heavenly Tribulation Strike Card Activated
Randomizing Power Level

. . .

. . .

Power Level: Origin Realm

Slifer clenched his fists. *Please let this be enough*, he thought.

The atmosphere shifted dramatically. The sky turned an ominous shade of gray as storm clouds rapidly converged. A deafening rumble of thunder echoed, chilling the very bones of those who heard it. Elder Olakin's initially smug expression morphed into one of grave concern. Sensing the potent aura gathering above, he prepared himself.

"Golden Shield Array! Spirit Wind Cloak! Earth Essence Guard!" Olakin chanted, summoning layer upon layer of defense around himself. Each protective aura was distinct: one was a golden barrier, another like an ethereal cloak of wind, and the last a sturdy shell formed of condensed earth essence.

Witnessing the impending catastrophe, Hughie's eyes widened with fear. Without a second thought, he descended rapidly, seeking safety from the storm.

With a blinding flash, the thunderbolt descended. It tore through the sky with unmatched fury, smashing through Elder Olakin's defenses one by one. The sheer force sent him hurtling backwards, crashing into the ground with a colossal impact, and a thick cloud of dust rose from the newly formed crater.

Slifer's eyes widened, his heart pounding. *Was it enough? Did I . . . ?*

But his heart sank when he saw a bloodied hand emerge from the dust, followed by the battered figure of the old man as he pulled himself out from the crater. His aura, although weakened, still resonated with the overwhelming power of the Origin Realm.

Managing a weak chuckle, Olakin spat out a mouthful of blood. "Impressive, Slifer. You've managed to keep your breakthrough a secret." Pausing for a moment, his eyes narrowed and darkened. "But that was your only chance. I'm done playing around."

The elder's words sent a chill down Slifer's spine. *W-what do I do now?*

CHAPTER TEN

Slifer grit his teeth, weighing his options. *If this were an anime, perhaps the "talk no jutsu" would've been my way out. It always seems to work wonders in these types of situations.* But, unfortunately for him, this was a xianxia world, where it was strength that did all the talking.

Slifer's gaze settled on his cards. Among them, the Reversal Card caught his attention. The memory of when he first entered this world flashed in his mind. *The Reversal Card managed to kill a Core Formation cultivator the last time I used it, but could it be powerful enough to deal with an Origin Realm expert?*

As he was about to activate the card, a thought hit him. *The range of this card is too big. What if it hurts my disciples . . . or Val?* His eyes glanced at Val's tiny form on the ground, her chest moving up and down with shallow breaths. *No, it's not worth the risk.*

Seeing Slifer deep in thought, Elder Olakin scoffed, "You dare get distracted in front of me!" In a swift motion, he summoned another attack.

"Verdant Lash of Desolation!" Green tendrils, imbued with the very essence of the earth, surged forward. Their speed was incomprehensible, and before Slifer could react, they were nearly upon him.

But just as the lethal tendrils were about to pierce his heart, a System notification sounded.

Ding!
Critical Block Activated

The attack rebounded as if hitting an invisible barrier, dissipating into harmless wisps of energy.

Elder Olakin's eyes widened in disbelief. "What . . .?" he muttered, a hint of unease evident in his voice. "Even if you've reached the Origin Realm . . . this should not be possible."

Slifer, trying to buy more time, replied coolly, "There's much you don't know, Elder. Perhaps it's time we talk this through."

Elder Olakin's face darkened further; he had heard tales that this Elder Slifer was as bloodthirsty as they come, but here he was, wanting to chat.

Slifer's eyes darted to his stat screen, noticing the 269 credits. *I need a good card from the Shop, and fast!*

Ding!
Random Card Acquired
Activate now?
(Yes/No)

Without hesitation, he activated the Random Card function.

Ding!
Successful!
You Have Acquired: Critical Block Card
Description: Protects user from a critical strike.

Not bad but it would only prolong the inevitable.
Slifer's hands were clammy as he saw Elder Olakin move for another strike.

"Thorny Coffin of Eternal Slumber!" the elder announced, summoning thick vines, bristling with deadly thorns, that moved like serpents in the air. This was his most powerful plant-based attack, one that trapped and strangled the life out of his enemies.

Slifer's eyes widened as the thorny vines shot towards him. *I have to rely on another Critical Block Card.* With a desperate click, he purchased one more Random Card as he braced for impact.

Ding!
Unsuccessful
Better Luck Next Time
Ding!
Critical Block Activated

Just as the thorny vines were about to envelope him, much like the previous attack, they ricocheted off the invisible shield.

Elder Olakin's face turned crimson with rage and disbelief. "Impossible!" he spat, but doubt gnawed at him. *If I can't even touch him, and he can conjure that thunderbolt again . . . I'm finished.*

This isn't working, my luck stat must be too low! Slifer's attention turned to Hughie, who had taken refuge behind a tree. *Does he really think that hiding under a tree will save him from lightning?* "Hughie!" Slifer yelled. "Get over here, now!"

Peeking out from his hiding spot, Hughie spotted Slifer's grave expression. He gulped audibly and flew over. "Master, I . . . umm—"

"No time to talk, hold my hand!" Slifer cut him off.

As Hughie grabbed Slifer's hand, his eyes were full of questions, but he knew better than to ask them at this moment.

Come on, give me something good. Slifer sent a desperate plea to the fickle gods of luck.

Just as he triggered another Random Card purchase, Elder Olakin let out an earth-shaking roar and summoned his domain: "Entwined Forest of Desolation!"

Suddenly, the entire area transformed. Giant trees erupted from the ground, their branches intertwining to create a vast, impenetrable canopy above, while below, thick vines twisted and turned, crawling towards everyone like ravenous serpents.

Slifer felt the crushing pressure of Elder Olakin's domain as the world around him turned into an endless forest. *So, this is a true Origin Realm domain,* he thought, momentarily comparing it to his own fledgling Nascent Soul Realm domain, which paled in comparison.

If he could visualize his own stats, he was certain there'd be a glaring debuff staring back at him. But then again, as a Qi Refining cultivator, his base power was already insignificant against Elder Olakin.

Beside him, Hughie quivered like a leaf in a storm. *Is this how it ends?* he wondered, glancing over at Slifer with wide-eyed panic. *Why on earth does Master want our final moments to be hand in hand?*

A fleeting thought of how he'd imagined his own end crossed Hughie's mind: comfortably old, surrounded by a doting harem, each competing to feed him grapes, not . . . clutching his master's hand in some backwards village.

As these thoughts swirled in Hughie's mind, Slifer was already taking action. He repositioned himself protectively in front of Hughie and focused intently on the System screen.

Ding!
Critical Block Activated

As anticipated, the vines harmlessly deflected off Slifer.

"Why?!" Elder Olakin's roar of frustration echoed through the vicinity. Assuming Slifer possessed some magical item that defended against distant assaults, the elder decided on a more direct approach. "Let's see if you can fend off a close-quarters attack!" Elder Olakin shouted, charging at Slifer with a fist aimed straight for his face.

Why do they always announce their moves? Slifer wondered. *It would be so much more effective if he just attacked without warning.* But then, recalling his own battles, he realized he too enjoyed shouting out his moves. *Guess I can't really fault him for it.*

Slifer knew that the Critical Block Card worked against any form of attack, so he wasn't concerned. However, when he took a look at his remaining cards, he noticed that he was out of Critical Block Cards. His eyes widened in panic as the old man appeared before him.

Suddenly, another System notification appeared.

Ding!
Successful!
You Have Acquired: Deadly Strike Card
Description: Deliver a fatal blow to the target.
Warning: Effect Only Applies to Beings below the Immortal Realm

---

Without a moment's hesitation, Slifer activated the card.

Randomizing Attack
. . .
Sword Strike: Peak Ascendant Realm

Before he could even skim through the second notification, a surge of intangible Sword Qi erupted from his hand, piercing straight through Elder Olakin. The elder, now just a foot away from Slifer, froze.

Time seemed to stand still, then, with a loud thud, Elder Olakin's head toppled over, followed by his lifeless body collapsing onto the ground.

The Plant Domain around them shattered like a fragile glass globe, its fragments disappearing into wisps of plant essence.

Ding!
Task Complete
You Have Gained 1000 Karmic Credits
Ding!
You Have Killed an Origin Realm Cultivator
You Have Gained 200 Karmic Credits

Hughie, mouth agape, stared at the fallen elder, then at his master. "Master . . . you . . . how did you . . .?"

Slifer looked at Hughie, then at Elder Olakin's fallen body, and finally at his own hands, still feeling the residual tingling from the Deadly Strike Card. *That was too close. Way too close.*

"Sometimes, it's all about luck," Slifer muttered, seemingly lost in thought.

Hughie looked down at their still-clasped hands, then back up to Slifer. "Uh, Master, can you let go of my hand now?"

Slifer blinked, realizing he was still gripping Hughie's hand tightly. He cleared his throat awkwardly and released his disciple's hand. "My apologies." He chuckled, giving Hughie a playful pat on the back. "You're quite the lucky charm."

Hughie forced a smile, his thoughts running wild. *If it weren't for Master, I'd be miles away from this mess. But . . .* "Of course, Master," he said out loud, though a little hesitantly.

"Quickly, store that corpse in your storage ring," Slifer instructed, pointing to the decapitated Elder Olakin.

With a swift motion, Hughie complied. Slifer then rushed to where little Val lay. He gently picked up the tiny dragon, her snores filling the air.

"Master has taken care of the bad man," he murmured, brushing his fingers over her smooth scales. Val just snored louder, her adorable face deep in slumber, utterly oblivious to the events that had just transpired.

As the suffocating vines disappeared, Amelia strode over, a triumphant smile playing on her lips. "I always knew Master would come through," she bragged, tossing her hair.

Beside her, Caelum dropped into a deep bow. "Forgive me, Master," he said, voice shaking. "This disciple doubted you."

Since when was Master a swordsman? Caelum wondered. *That Sword Qi . . . it had Will. Isn't that an Astral Awakening Senior's ability?*

Slifer studied them both, hiding a small smile. Just as Caelum raised his head, a System notification popped up.

Ding!
Congratulations!
Your Actions Have Affected Your Disciples
Your Disciple Amelia's Loyalty Has Increased By 11%
Your Disciple Caelum's Loyalty Has Increased By 20%
Your Disciple Hughie's Loyalty Has Increased By 5%

Increasing their loyalty . . . I need to delve deeper into this. Apart from the obvious reasons for desiring loyalty, he remembered there were additional benefits, like pinpointing their exact location via the System. *What other advantages might there be?*

Slifer turned his attention to Amelia, there was something he needed to make clear. "You need to stop belittling cultivators more powerful than yourself. There may come a time when even I can't save you." *If she keeps this up, she might draw trouble that not even Hughie's bizarre luck can get us out of.*

Amelia lowered her head, a shadow of regret passing over her face. But then, a mischievous glint appeared in her eyes. "Alright, Master! I promise to only pick on those weaker than me."

Slifer raised an eyebrow. A hint of exasperation crept into his voice as he replied, "No, Amelia, that's not the point. No bullying anyone."

She huffed, looking away in disappointment. "Master, you're no fun."

Before he could reply, a prior System notification replayed in his mind. He recalled being deducted 10 credits because Amelia had taken an innocent life. "Amelia," he began, "why did you kill a villager? Didn't I explicitly state to *not* take an innocent life?"

She froze, her eyes widening in shock. "M-Master . . . it was an accident," she stammered, clearly caught off guard, she had not expected him to find out, especially so soon.

Slifer exhaled deeply, pinching the bridge of his nose. The idea of sending Amelia outside the sect to save lives flashed through his mind, but after what happened this time, he shook it off. He didn't know which enemy of the original would come after him next and he did not want to find out.

"Your punishment will be to assist in the Medicine Hall, saving ten lives to atone for the one you took," he declared.

"But Master, I don't know anything about—"

Slifer cut her off with a stern look, stopping her in her tracks. "You will learn," he said firmly.

Her shoulder's slumped down as she nodded, accepting her punishment. "Yes, Master," she mumbled.

This might be a good way to earn credits while guiding her on a righteous path, Slifer thought optimistically. *I might actually be getting the hang of being an elder.*

Ding!
Task Assigned: Save 10 Lives
Disciple: Amelia
Status: 0/10
Reward: 10 Karmic Credits

Slifer's eyebrows furrowed at the notification. *Only one credit for a life?* He sighed. *Sometimes, this System truly doesn't make sense.*

Whilst her master was once again lost in thought, Amelia cast a suspicious glance at Caelum and then at Hughie. *It must have been Hughie who ratted me out. Senior Brother was with me the whole time.*

Catching her glare, Hughie paled, raising his hands defensively. "Hey, it wasn't me!"

Amelia didn't seem convinced, her eyes narrowing further.

Ignoring the little exchange, Slifer looked down at Caelum. The truth was, Caelum had been correct in his initial assessment. Against an Origin Realm expert, Slifer would have been severely outmatched. But Slifer wasn't one to waste an opportunity to acquire more credits, even if it meant employing creative disciplinary measures.

"Caelum," Slifer began, "your lack of faith in your master is disappointing. As your punishment, you will complete ten tasks within the sect." Pausing, Slifer added, "I won't list them out for you. Unlike the other two, I trust you can pick them yourself."

Caelum's eyes widened briefly before he nodded solemnly, accepting the task. "Yes, Master."

Ding!
Task Assigned: 10 Righteous Deeds
Disciple: Caelum
Status: 0/10
Reward: ???

Slifer ignored the notification as he looked over at Hughie. There was no need to punish him; after all, Hughie was his lucky charm. *Would punishing a protagonist affect my luck? Perhaps it's best not to test those waters.*

His eyes softened as he looked down at Val's small form cradled in his arms. "We must return to the sect," he declared. The severity of Val's injury concerned him—a strike from an Origin Realm expert was not to be taken lightly.

However, Amelia interjected, pointing in a particular direction. "Master, the Nascent Soul servants went that way. They'll likely be back soon. Shouldn't we . . . take care of them?"

We? More like me. I've had enough action for tonight . . . heck, enough for the next century, Slifer thought. Without another word, he started heading in a different direction, aiming to circle back to the sect and avoid them monsters.

Confused, Amelia hastened to keep up with him. "Master, why are we leaving them alive? Aren't they a threat?"

Assuming a wise and profound expression, Slifer shook his head slowly. "There's been enough death today," he intoned gravely. However, Slifer knew that he would lose more credits than he would gain if he were to kill them. *Peak Slifer cards don't come cheap.*

Amelia looked at her master, genuine confusion evident in her eyes. *Why would the man who brought entire sects to their knees think a single death is too many?*

The three Nascent Soul cultivators from the Black Heart Sect swiftly made their way back to Lushan Village. Their journey was interrupted by a sudden vibration from their communication tokens. As the glowing light shone, they saw the message that froze their steps.

"The grand elder . . . he's dead?" the first one stammered, voice shaking.

Another simply shook his head, his eyes filled with disbelief. The reality of Elder Olakin's death was impossible to digest. "Could the elder from the Black Rose Sect have done this? Could he have killed the grand elder?"

The third just whispered, almost inaudibly, "No, it can't be. Elder Slifer failed to breakthrough to the Origin Realm, everyone knows that."

But the next moment shattered their doubts. The communication token lit up, showing the last moments of Elder Olakin's life playing out before their eyes. They watched as Elder Slifer, previously thought to be a dying cultivator, raised his hand and released an explosive Sword Qi that effortlessly decapitated the grand elder.

"How is this possible?! Elder Olakin, taken down with just one strike?" The three of them gasped in unison, as the reality of the situation sank in.

"Ascendant Realm," one muttered, his voice quivering.

The leader, snapping out of his daze, clenched his fists. "We must return to the sect immediately," he declared. "The emergence of a new Ascendant cultivator could upheave the balance among the sects. We need to prepare for the worst."

The second nodded, adding, "Especially when that cultivator is that demon Slifer."

Slifer returned to his private quarters, his heart heavy with a mixture of relief and apprehension. He had just placed little Val in a specialized healing chamber, and now there was nothing left to do but wait.

He settled down on a plush cushion, his thoughts drifting back to the confrontation. *It's true what they say in those xianxia novels*, he mused, a wry smile forming on his lips. *Personal power is everything in this world.* If he had been an Astral Awakening Senior, perhaps Elder Olakin wouldn't have been so audacious.

"He wouldn't have even thought of taking my disciples hostage," Slifer murmured to himself, shaking his head in frustration.

Suddenly, the memory of Amelia's taunting words surfaced in his mind. He chuckled bitterly. "Bullying the weak is the norm here, huh? It's as if the powerful take pleasure in the misery of others."

His expression hardened, determination lighting up his eyes. *I need to increase my cultivation. Having those rare cards might give me an edge, but in the end, my own strength is the most reliable.*

Eagerly, he activated the Shop interface.

Shop
Cards
Cultivation Methods
Treasures
Pills and Elixirs
Mystic Techniques
Martial Techniques
Bloodlines and Ancestries
Constitutions
Spirit Roots
Beasts and Familiars
Create

I need a Heaven Rank Cultivation Method if I'm going to make any significant leaps in my cultivation.

His fingers danced across the interface, pulling up the methods available for purchase. The cheapest methods, like the Heavenly Celestial Breath Method, were priced at 500 credits. Now that he had a few more credits to spend, perhaps he could aim higher.

He scrolled through the options, noting the price tags. But when he looked at the Mid-Heaven Rank Methods—like Nine Heavens Soul Refinement and Celestial Ascent Scripture—they all required 1000 credits. The High Heaven Rank Methods, such as Eternal Dao Enlightenment and Primordial Essence Codex, were an even steeper 2500 credits. As for the Peak Methods, like Universe Mastery Technique, they were an astronomical 5000 credits.

Slifer exhaled sharply, a hint of annoyance evident in his features. "No matter how much I earn," he muttered, "it never seems to be enough." *Choices, choices.* He gazed at the glowing interface. *What path should I take?*

Slifer sighed and redirected his attention to the "Create" option on the Shop interface.

He delved deeper into the option and found that it allowed a cultivator to fuse methods they had mastered to form a new, potentially stronger technique. The cost? A mere 10 Karmic Credits.

"That sounds incredibly overpowered," Slifer mumbled to himself. *But then again, mastering even one method takes an eternity. How would I ever master multiple?*

He spotted another option that grabbed his attention. It permitted him to fuse cultivation methods he was familiar with, but had not yet mastered. There was, however, a catch: the cost in Karmic Credits would increase significantly.

"System," Slifer inquired, "how much would it cost to merge the Heavenly Radiance Cultivation Art with the Heavenly Celestial Breath Method?"

Heavenly Radiance Cultivation Art Mastery: 5%
Heavenly Celestial Breath Method Mastery: 0%
Calculating Cost

. . .

350 Karmic Credits

Slifer nodded slowly, processing the information. "And the rank of the resulting method?"

Mid-Heaven Rank

A satisfied smile crept onto Slifer's face, his earlier frustration melting away. "Now, that's a deal I'm willing to take."

Without hesitation, Slifer acquired the Heavenly Celestial Breath Method for 500 credits. With the method in his possession, he navigated to the "Create" option and initiated the merging process.

Are You Sure You Wish To Proceed?

"Yes, proceed," Slifer affirmed.

The System took a moment, its interface swirling with myriad colors before it finally announced:

Merging Process Complete
Please Provide a New Name for Your Cultivation Method

Slifer paused, pondering. He needed a name that resonated with the essence of both methods yet sounded profound and mysterious, befitting the xianxia world.

"Let's call it the 'Celestial Radiance Breathing Art,'" he declared with a satisfied nod. It might not sound as impressive as some of the other Heaven Rank Methods but Slifer felt like it did the job.

With a Heaven Ranked Method, I should be able to reach Foundation Establishment in one step.

Taking a deep breath, he murmured, "Time to break through." But as he began to cycle the energy, a nagging sensation tugged at the edges of his consciousness. *Am I forgetting something?* he wondered, trying to pinpoint the source of his unease.

Unable to identify the elusive thought, he shook his head, choosing to immerse himself in his cultivation. "Distractions won't aid my breakthrough," he muttered.

Meanwhile, in the guest quarters, Leah paced the room, growing more impatient with each step. Suddenly, she paused, and a cruel smirk appeared on her face. "Father will come soon," she muttered, "and he'll teach that old pervert a lesson."

Then her thoughts turned to Morvran, causing her face to darken. "And that buffoon," she spat out, "how dare he lay a hand on me?" A vivid image of Morvran's bald head on a spike flashed in her mind, bringing the smirk back to her face.

CHAPTER ELEVEN

In a dimly lit chamber, Zarius lay on a wooden bed, covered in white bandages that wrapped tightly around his body. His breaths were shallow and the slightest movement caused pain to course through his body.

"Elder Slifer and his pathetic disciples," he cursed, his voice raspy and weak. Memories flashed, the bald, plump servant demonstrating to the disciples how to inflict the most pain upon him. "And to think that fat oaf had the audacity to join them." He grimaced. It was one thing to get ambushed by fellow disciples but to be struck by a mere servant? Unacceptable.

Gritting his teeth, Zarius recalled his precious Heaven Rank Cultivation Method. The very treasure he had risked everything to steal, now gone, taken by Elder Slifer's underlings.

His jaws tightened as he recalled the severity of his injuries. *If not for Master's Earth Rank healing pellet and those other pills, I'd probably be floating in the river of the afterlife.*

He exhaled deeply, glancing at the bandages that crisscrossed his body. The potent medicines were working, and he could sense his strength slowly returning. *Just a few more days, and I'll be back to my peak.*

That old man might be out of my reach, but those disciples? They'll pay dearly. Zarius's face darkened.

The faint creak of the door interrupted his vengeful thoughts. Looking up, Zarius caught sight of a young, lanky disciple with a perpetually confused expression entering the chamber.

Another one? Zarius thought, irked. "What do you want?" he snapped, recalling the horde of disciples trying to win his favor during his vulnerable state.

The newcomer, unperturbed by Zarius's cold reception, began placing talismans at each corner of the room, all the while maintaining that idiotic smile.

What is he up to? Zarius's suspicion continued to grow. "Hey! What are you doing here?"

The disciple turned to face him, an oddly satisfied smirk on his face. "Now that the noise suppression talismans are up," he began, muttering more to himself than anyone else, "no one will interrupt us."

Zarius's eyes widened in alarm. As the disciple moved closer, a sense of dread settled in. "Do you even know who I am?" Zarius blurted out, attempting to use his status to deter the strange disciple. "Stay away! My master, a grand elder, won't stand for this!"

The disciple—Dentos—let out a sigh. "Ah, 'Master,'" he murmured, a faraway look in his eyes. "How I wish I had a master. If I did, I wouldn't be doing . . . well, this."

Zarius, now confused and increasingly concerned, tried to pull away but his injuries held him back. Dentos firmly grabbed onto Zarius's arm. "The heavens have been so unfair to me," Dentos lamented, as he oddly began to massage Zarius's fingers.

Suddenly, with a swift and eerie precision, he bent one of Zarius's fingers backwards.

The sharp pain made Zarius gasp, his face contorting in agony. But Dentos was relentless. As he moved to the next finger, breaking it with the same deliberate cruelty, Zarius let out a shrill cry, his eyes moistening with tears of pain and disbelief. *Oh heavens, why is this happening to me?!*

"Missed my golden opportunity with Boss Morvran," Dentos mused, seemingly unfazed by the torment he was inflicting. With each word, another finger met its unfortunate fate, and Zarius's breath came in ragged pants, his body quivering. "But perhaps, if Boss Morvran learns of my . . . dedication, he'll put in a good word with Elder Slifer. And then, I'll have a master!"

"So . . . you're doing all this . . . just because you don't have a master?" Zarius, between screams, managed to ask.

Dentos nodded earnestly. "You see, it's just unbearable in this sect without one."

"What happened to the other elders?" Zarius tried to distract him, hoping that someone would come check up on him.

Dentos started reminiscing about his various "good deeds" to help the elders. A half-smile played on his face, as if he genuinely believed they were acts of kindness.

"You know," he began, "I once heard Elder Karna mention he had a sore back. Thinking this was my chance, I went to his chambers at midnight. I wanted to give him a massage. He, uh, didn't appreciate my initiative. The new pond in the garden? That was me being blasted into the earth."

" . . . "

"Ah, then there was Elder Mira!" Dentos continued. "She always struck me as distant, perhaps a tad chilly. I reckoned a hug would do wonders. At a sect meeting, I went for it, hugging her from behind. She didn't take it too well. It took three elders to pry her off. Trust me, it wasn't the warm embrace I'd imagined."

How . . . How is this guy still alive after all this? Zarius blinked in disbelief.

Dentos looked down at Zarius's pained face. "See? It's really hard for me. No one appreciates my good intentions. That's why I have to impress Elder Slifer this way. Maybe then, finally, I'll have a master."

This guy is a calamity on two legs, Zarius thought to himself. *As for Elder Slifer and his disciples—they're all lunatics. Forget revenge, I never want to cross paths with them again!*

With a last apologetic glance, Dentos murmured, "Sorry, this is just a necessary evil. You understand, right?"

Before Zarius could answer, Dentos continued with his bone-breaking, all in his misguided quest for a master.

CHAPTER TWELVE

Ding!
Congratulations!
You Have Advanced to the Next Stage
You Have Gained 1 Karmic Credit

Slifer stepped out of his private chambers, his feet landing silently on the cool, stone-paved courtyard. The crescent moon overhead seemed to mirror his frustration, casting a dim, silvery glow upon the ground. With a deep scowl etched onto his face, he thought about his recent failed attempts at cultivation.

For the past few hours, he had tried every method he could think of to advance to the Foundation Establishment Realm but they had all been in vain.

He was stuck at the Peak Ninth Stage of Qi Refining.

It was maddening.

A cultivator at the Qi Refining stage would need to condense their dispersed qi into a solid pillar, a foundation upon which their future cultivation would rest. Only by forming this foundation could one step into the realm of Foundation Establishment, and be recognized as a true cultivator.

As for those lucky enough to possess a Foundation Establishment pill, they could potentially expedite this breakthrough. These pills contained condensed qi essence that could aid in forming the qi pillar, offering a smoother transition from Qi Refining to Foundation Establishment.

Well, that was the theory behind it but for Slifer, they seemed to do nothing.

All those stories I read about young masters fighting tooth and nail, even competing in grand tournaments just to lay their hands on a single Foundation Establishment Pill, he recalled, shaking his head in exasperation. *And here I am, swallowing them like candy to no avail.*

Slifer absentmindedly rolled the now-empty vials of the Foundation Establishment Pills in his hand as his mind drifted back to the Heaven Rank Cultivation Method. He had experienced the leap in efficiency.

A Low Heaven Rank method is supposedly nine times more effective than a Peak Earth Rank one, he pondered. As for his own Mid-Heaven Rank method, the Celestial Radiance Breathing Art, he couldn't precisely gauge its efficiency, but he knew it was nothing to scoff at.

The Heavenly Radiance Cultivation Art had its merits but was tricky, with its reliance on the balance of sun and moon qi. In contrast, the Celestial Radiance Breathing Art tapped into the energy of various celestial bodies. No need to worry about balance; he could just keep absorbing and converting qi.

"But what good is a faster cultivation speed if I can't break through?" With a snort, he muttered, "Heaven Rank Methods, huh? More like heavenly overrated!"

After his futile attempts to break through, Slifer decided to rummage through his storage ring, hoping to find anything that might aid him. However, most of the items within had been destroyed, whether by the Origin Realm Tribulation or by Tyrus, Slifer could only guess.

His mood lightened a tad as his fingers brushed against the small cache of spirit stones that had survived the tribulation's wrath. A soft sigh escaped him. Just like in the countless cultivation novels he had read, spirit stones were the currency of this world, their values tiered by their quality.

One high-quality spirit stone for one thousand medium ones . . . and one medium for one thousand low quality. Simple mathematics, he mused, a fleeting smirk gracing his lips as he reached out for what he presumed to be the finest among them. Holding it to the light, he couldn't help but marvel at its lustrous sheen.

"This," he whispered to himself, "has to be a high-quality spirit stone."

Spirit Stone Rank: Medium

The smirk that adorned Slifer's face vanished as swiftly as it had appeared. He had only five of these and around a hundred that he assumed were low-quality stones. In contrast, an elder of his standing should've had a stash of a few hundred high-quality spirit stones. His shoulders slumped as a sigh of resignation left him.

"From rags in my past life to . . . well, rags in this one too," he lamented aloud. The cruel irony wasn't lost on him; to be deprived of wealth in two successive lives seemed a tad excessive.

Status Name: Slifer Race: Human Alignment: Demonic Cultivation: Qi Refining—9th Stage Lifespan Remaining: 47 Days Credits: 650 Skills: Insight (Basic) Items: Reversal Cards x2, Peak Slifer Card x2

Slifer sighed heavily as he glanced at the dwindling lifespan counter. He still had two Reversal Cards that could prolong it, yet the more pressing issue was the Origin Realm Qi swirling within his body. The prison he'd constructed for it was tenuous at best.

Card	Description	Cost
Primal Expulsion Card	Channels the rogue Origin Realm Qi out of your body, expelling it into the void to prevent internal damage.	5000

| Realm's Fury Blaster | Harnesses the volatile qi to fuel a single, devastating attack against foes, showcasing the fury of the realms. | 5300 |
| Eternal Calm Lotus (Redux) | Absorbs the rogue qi, converting its turbulent force into a calming aura that enhances your meditation and cultivation experience. | 6800 |

His breaths grew heavier with each passing second. "Is a higher cultivation really the answer to all this?" The realization that he was among the fifty percent who couldn't break through the first realm tightened the knot of anxiety in his chest.

A chilling thought passed through his mind: *Is it my age? Could it be that being in the body of an old man somehow affects the chance of breakthrough?*

Slifer wasn't sure of all the factors that could affect cultivation, he knew that in some webnovels, the older you were, the lower your potential. *But surely, even if that were the case, being in the body of a former Nascent Soul monster would counter that?*

Distracted by his spiraling thoughts, a sudden System notification jolted him.

Ding!
Breakthrough Requirements Updated
Convert 1 Demonic Foundation Establishment Cultivator to the Righteous Path
Alternative Requirement
Exterminate 3 Demonic Foundation Establishment Cultivators

Slifer's eyes widened. *That's it? That's surprisingly straightforward. Maybe I could ask Caelum to—*

Before he could finish the thought, another message from the System interrupted him.

Ding!
User Must Personally Complete Task
Assistance from Others Is Not Permissible

Is the System being serious? Why? "Fine, I'll head to the dungeon and seek out someone deserving of execution. Wait . . . what am I saying, they're demonic cultivators, it'd be more surprising to find one that *doesn't* deserve death."

Ding!
The challenge must be issued to an appropriate demonic cultivator, demonstrating the supremacy of the righteous path.

Slifer, seeing the conditions piling on, threw his hands up in exasperation. "Oh, so now it's a righteous battle, is it? And what next? Should I ask them to sign a waiver too?"

He felt that the System was being unreasonable, how was he meant to defeat multiple cultivators above his cultivation realm with no help? Especially considering that he had no techniques, no legit battle experience, and a time limit.

"It wants me to keep using up my cards!" Slifer grumbled under his breath.

Shop
Cards
Cultivation Methods
Treasures
Pills and Elixirs
Mystic Techniques
Martial Techniques
Bloodlines and Ancestries
Constitutions
Spirit Roots
Beasts and Familiars
Create

Slifer sat down near the lotus pond and opened the System panel once again, his eyes meticulously scanning through the list of cards available for purchase. His hopes of finding a reasonably priced solution were dashed as each card seemed to boast a price tag steeper than the climb to the heavens.

Why did I expect anything different? he thought bitterly.

His attention then drifted to the Reversal Card, a tiny shred of hope fluttered within him. However, the unease of using such a potent card against mere Foundation Establishment cultivators soured the idea quickly. It was like employing a phoenix to catch a rabbit: excessive and unreliable.

"This isn't the path," Slifer murmured, he knew that he couldn't keep relying solely on the cards. *I need a foundation, something that doesn't vanish after one use.* His eyes darted back to the System panel, dismissing the options of spirit roots, bloodlines, and constitutions. Those were investments for a distant future, and he needed power now.

His gaze shifted towards the list of techniques, martial and mystic. His eyes narrowed as he sifted through the offerings, but he quickly brushed the idea away. *Learning a new technique would take weeks if not months, and that's assuming I could even grasp it quickly, like these young geniuses. Time isn't a luxury I possess.*

With a sigh, Slifer tapped on the treasures tab, eyes immediately seeking the offensive treasures that were suitable for Foundation Establishment cultivators. As a Peak Qi Refining cultivator, it would be a waste to buy anything weaker.

Treasure	Description	Cost
Thunderclap Hammer	A mighty hammer imbued with the essence of a thunderstorm. Each strike echoes with the roar of thunder, capable of disrupting qi and causing severe internal injuries.	9000
Heaven's Fall Axe	An axe said to have the weight of the heavens, able to smash through any obstacle with unstoppable force.	8500

Sky Piercing Bow	An ancient bow known for its ability to shoot arrows that pierce the skies, capable of penetrating strong protective barriers with ease.	7500

These prices . . . they're astronomical! Slifer grumbled, his face darkening. A sharp cough escaped his lips, and for a moment, he feared he'd see blood, such was his rage.

Biting back his frustration, he whispered, "Perhaps the old way is best." The sect's archives held ancient techniques, and as an elder, he had almost unrestricted access. It might not be the quick fix he'd hoped for, but it was a start.

If I run out of time, I'll have to use the Reversal Cards. He felt a pang of guilt at the thought, muttering a silent apology to anyone who might become unintended collateral.

A soft ping echoed in Slifer's mind—a spiritual transmission from Morvran.

"Master, the feast is prepared."

A smile broke across Slifer's face, a genuine moment of relief. *I promised myself a feast if I lived through this*, he thought, patting his stomach. *And I am very much alive. Maybe for a few hours, I can forget about this cultivation madness.*

As Slifer stepped into the kitchen, the rich aroma of cooked delicacies hit him. The place was bustling with activity, with servants moving hurriedly, their faces tense, ensuring every detail was perfect. Boss Morvran stood overseeing the operations with a satisfied expression on his face. The feast table was a sight to behold, loaded with assorted dishes from the mystic cloud rice pilaf to the Heavenly Beast meat stew, and celestial fruit platters among others.

Stammering slightly, the chef, a chubby middle-aged man previously enjoying a laid-back life in the sect thanks to the original Slifer's preferences, approached. "Master Slifer, if any dish isn't to your liking, please let me know, and I'll prepare something else right away."

Looking around at the flurry of activity, Slifer coughed to get everyone's attention. "I'd prefer some privacy." Though his exterior was stern, his inner thoughts screamed, *What's about to unfold isn't very elder-like!*

At his words, everyone scurried out, leaving him alone with the feast. Morvran mentioned he'd be right outside should Slifer need anything, to which he nodded.

Once alone, the solemn expression on Slifer's face melted away. He rubbed his hands together, beaming at the feast before him.

"Finally, you're all mine." He chuckled, diving into the spread like a starved beast. He tore into the meat stew, its rich flavors exploding in his mouth. "Oh, this is divine," he murmured, almost inhaling the dish. He then moved to the mystic cloud rice pilaf, its subtle aroma and delicate flavors made him let out moans of appreciation.

After an hour, Slifer leaned back, patting his now bloated belly with contentment. *This alone is worth getting isekai'd for*, he thought. However, as he glanced down, he could almost see his metabolism working at an absurd rate, the bulge in his stomach flattening swiftly.

With a sigh, he picked up a dumpling, resigned to the fact that no matter how much he ate, his physique remained stick-thin. *Eternal skinniness*, he thought ruefully.

As he was about to take a bite out of the dumpling, thoughts of Fenlock and the Master-Disciple Ceremony crossed his mind. "I've spent a fortune on that useless Heaven cultivation method," he muttered, "I need to put that lad to work."

Without further delay, he sent a spiritual transmission to Morvran. "Bring Fenlock to me."

He continued to munch on his dumplings, eagerly awaiting the disciple's arrival. However, the scene that followed was not what he expected. As he popped another dumpling into his mouth, the doors were thrust open. Fenlock stumbled in, crashing to the floor, closely followed by a clearly irritated Morvran.

Slifer almost choked on his dumpling, eyes wide at the sudden commotion.

Morvran snorted. "I found this little one"—he pointed at Fenlock—"attempting to summon a minor demon."

Fenlock, gingerly rubbing his sore spots from the fall, looked up with eyes awash in bewilderment. "But Senior Brother Zonrak said it would win her heart . . ." he mumbled.

The innocence, or sheer ignorance, reflected in Fenlock's voice was like a punch to Slifer's guts. *Is there a dense cultivator factory somewhere churning these characters out?* He mentally facepalmed. His sigh wasn't an external one this time, but it resonated within him, through the core of his very being.

He eased the last bit of the dumpling down his throat, preparing himself for what felt like an unavoidable mentoring moment. "Fenlock," he began, striving to infuse his words with a mix of wisdom and assurance, "you've been misled. Girls, in general, fancy heroes. Ones who can stand between them and lurking dangers, not those who invite malevolent beings into this realm."

The words flowed easily but carried a dissonance that echoed within Slifer. *What a load of hogwash. The allure of the bad boys has been a tale as old as time. "Good guys finish last" didn't emerge out of thin air,* his mind retorted. Yet here he was, feeding his disciple the sort of fantastical narrative that had kept virgins like himself in perpetual ignorance for generations.

Fenlock's eyes widened at the revelation. However, he seemed reluctant to fully accept it. He bowed his head nonetheless, fearing that contradicting his master might result in punishment.

Slifer saw the reluctance but decided to not press further. Who was he to offer relationship advice?

"I recall you have the Master-Disciple Ceremony prepared?" he inquired, changing the subject.

Fenlock quickly nodded, his hands nervously removing the ceremonial items from his storage ring. There were three cups, one larger than the other two, a pot of fragrant tea, and a set of incense sticks. These were typical items used in a Master-Disciple Ceremony.

The Master-Disciple Ceremony was a sacred tradition in the cultivation world, it was held even by demonic cultivators. It set the foundation for a lifelong bond between a master and disciple. It was marked by a series of rituals that included the exchange of tea, a symbolic gesture of respect and acceptance.

The disciple, on his part, offered tea to the master, showcasing humility and eagerness to learn, while the master accepting the tea signified his acceptance of the disciple and the responsibilities entailed.

He watched as Fenlock carefully poured tea into the largest cup, offering it with both hands, his head bowed in reverence.

Slifer accepted the tea, sipped it, and then nodded. "From today onwards, you are my disciple."

Ding!

Congratulations!
Young Fenlock Is Officially Your Disciple
Reward: Hidden
To Unlock Your Reward, Summon Your Loyal Disciples

Summoning the disciples, that's a new one. Slifer raised an eyebrow. He had come across hidden rewards before, but the requirement to unlock this one seemed a bit unorthodox. *Either this is a significant reward, or the System is having a good laugh at my expense once again.*

His gaze lowered to Fenlock, who was now awaiting any further instruction. It was time to get a better understanding of why the System picked him.

Insight!

Disciple Panel			
Character Profile		**Cultivation Profile**	
Name:	Fenlock	Current Cultivation:	Late Core Formation
Age:	28	Primary Cultivation Method:	
Sex:	Male	Subsidiary Skills:	
Background:	Unknown	Constitution:	N/A
Affiliation:	Black Rose Sect	Bloodlines:	N/A
Alignment:	Demonic	Spiritual Roots:	N/A
Comprehension:	4	Management Options:	
Luck:	6	Current Quest:	
Talent:	8	Training Plan:	
Will:	3	Loyalty:	55%

Not too shabby, Slifer mused. *His talent and will are quite decent, I can see why the System chose him.*

Ding!
Warning: Disciple's Loyalty Is Low
Increasing Loyalty Is Advised
Failure to maintain loyalty at 10% or above will render the disciple inactive, resulting in a penalty.

The System seems to have endless reasons to punish me. Slifer sighed inwardly.

Fenlock, still kowtowing, was growing anxious with each passing silent moment, his forehead pressed against the cold floor. *Why is Master not saying anything? Did I do something wrong already?*

The silence was broken when Morvran cleared his throat. "Master, urgent news. The prisoner attempted an escape."

"Prisoner?" Slifer echoed.

"Elder Olakin's daughter, Leah," Morvran clarified.

Oh, shit . . . that's the mess I forgot. Slifer frowned. The task of explaining to the innocent girl that he had orphaned her was daunting. *Maybe being the villain is easier,* he thought, almost defeatedly.

"Take me to her," Slifer commanded.

Just as he was about to leave, another System notification rang.

Ding!
Your Disciple Fenlock Is Close to a Breakthrough
Provide Guidance to Ensure a Successful Breakthrough
Reward: Hidden

Is this supposed to be funny? he thought bitterly. *I, who can't even advance to Foundation Establishment, am to guide his breakthrough?*

Slifer shook his head and turned to Fenlock, who had finally raised his head. "Stay away from your junior sisters, and do not leave your quarters until you break through."

As the silhouette of his master faded away, Fenlock muttered with a tinge of sadness, "But Junior Sister Lenvari . . ."

Upon reaching the location, Slifer and Morvran found Amelia in a heated argument with Leah.

"You are nothing but a cockroach, scuttling in the shadows of your father," Amelia sneered with disdain.

"At least I had a father who cared, not a monster who had to be put down!" Leah retorted.

Amelia's smile turned cold as ice. "You know, watching your father's head fall to the ground was rather satisfying. The way it bounced . . . like a child's plaything."

Leah's face contorted with a mixture of rage and pain. Her voice shook as she spat out, "You . . . you heartless witch!"

"Oh, save your tears. It's a dog-eat-dog world, sweetie," Amelia retorted.

The spiteful words hung heavily in the air. Slifer sighed inwardly. *This . . . this is a mess.*

As Amelia spotted him, her demeanor shifted instantly. She whirled around and sprinted towards Slifer, her face blossoming into an innocent smile. "Master, I've completed the mission," she declared with a hint of pride twinkling in her eyes.

He nodded in response, but he couldn't help but be baffled by the stark contrast between the angelic demeanor Amelia now displayed and the spiteful harpy who was spewing venom just moments ago.

He shivered involuntarily. *Was she a . . . yandere?* The notion unnerved him, sending a chill racing down his spine.

Leah's eyes shifted to Slifer, blazing with fury. "You . . . you killed my father!" Her voice trembled with a mix of rage and grief. Overcome by emotions, she charged at Slifer.

Slifer wasn't alarmed; with her cultivation suppressed by the qi-restraining cuffs, she posed no real threat. *Finally, an opportunity to look cool for a change,* he smirked inwardly. He envisioned catching her fist midair just before it could land on him, just like the scenes from the action movies he enjoyed.

However, before his fantasy could turn into reality, a swift blur shot past him. Amelia had darted forward, her hand connecting sharply with Leah's face. The force was so immense that Leah's body made an imprint on the ground as she fell.

Should've seen that coming, Slifer thought, sweat trickling down his brow as he watched

Leah struggle to lift herself from the ground, her cheek red from the force of the slap. It was apparent Amelia had been itching for an opportunity to put Leah in her place.

Amelia sneered down at Leah. "How dare you attempt to attack *my* master."

Leah groaned, clutching her cheek, pain and humiliation evident in her eyes. "You . . . you . . ."

Seeing how the situation had derailed, Slifer rubbed his temple, feeling a headache coming on. *This isn't going to be easy.*

CHAPTER THIRTEEN

Slifer walked over to where Leah lay. He released a sigh. "I never wished to kill your father, but he didn't leave much room for conversation."

Moaning with the effort, Leah pushed herself to her feet, steadying her shaky legs. "If you hadn't taken me away," she spat, eyes alight with anger, "he would never have come after you in the first place."

He winced internally. She wasn't wrong. But it wasn't actually him who had made the choice; it was his predecessor. *How can I explain to her that it was not "me" but another "me"?* he mused. Unfortunately, he couldn't very well tell her the truth of the situation.

He cleared his throat, attempting to find the right words. "Actually, Leah, I . . . I wanted you as a disciple."

She looked at him as if he had grown a second head. "Then why," she began, voice trembling, "did you slaughter those who were sworn to protect me?"

He took a deep breath, searching for the right words. "You possess an incredibly rare cultivation body. With my teachings, you could reach heights you've never imagined. Your father, and even you, I presumed, wouldn't willingly let you be my disciple. So, I . . . I had to use alternative methods."

Inside, Slifer cringed at his own words. *The truth is, the original Slifer probably wanted her for darker purposes. To use her as a cultivation furnace, perhaps.* The thought left a bad taste in his mouth.

Leah's eyes held a mixture of disbelief and shock. "So, you're saying . . . you killed them . . . all for me?"

Slifer hesitated, then nodded slowly. "Yes, in a way."

He paused for a moment. "Would you consider being my disciple?"

Internally, he almost chuckled. *She'll say no, for now at least. But I can play the long game.* Slifer knew the nature of demonic cultivators too well; they were notorious for exploiting any situation to their advantage, even if it meant sacrificing their own kin.

Leah's eyes widened a tad, and he could see the gears turning within her mind. The fall of her father left her vulnerable in the Black Heart Sect, a place where her privileged status had earned her a host of enemies. The Black Heart Sect's lethal competitiveness was a stark contrast to the relatively tame Black Rose Sect. A return to her sect, he understood, meant a death sentence awaited her, and it would be those who seemed the most loyal to her to be the first ones to stab her in the back.

Amelia, who'd been quietly observing the exchange, finally broke her silence. "Master, you already have so many disciples . . . Isn't Amelia enough for you?"

Slifer's skin crawled a bit under Amelia's gaze, which was perhaps a tad too possessive. Before he could respond, a System message popped up.

> *Ding!*
> Maximum Disciple Capacity Reached
> No More Disciples Can Be Accepted

He dismissed the alert with a thought, its message irritating but irrelevant. *I don't need the System's approval to guide her. If Leah accepts my offer, we can work around the formalities.*

His objective was clear: persuade Leah to accept him, mend the fractured relationship, and hopefully, prevent further conflict. He did not like the idea of a young genius dedicating their life to get revenge on him, he couldn't hide behind Hughie's luck forever.

But ending her life . . . could I really do it?

The more he observed Leah's young face, the more he realized he couldn't stomach the idea of bringing her any more pain. *She's practically a child in the grand scheme of things. The last thing I want is to add her blood to my already stained hands.*

Leah seemed to ponder the offer, her face going through a range of emotions. It was apparent that she was at a crossroad, faced with a choice between vengeance and survival. The world of cultivation was cruel, and sometimes, one's mortal enemies turned into unlikely allies under the harsh laws of survival.

> Exceeding Disciple Limit Will Result in Continuous Credit Deduction

Slifer's face darkened, the System's limitations ever testing his patience.

Yet, another notification followed almost immediately:

> Task: Kill or Reform the Demonic Cultivator
> Description: Having orphaned a young demonic cultivator, resentment now brews in her heart. It falls upon you to cleanse her spirit, either through the release of death or the path of reform.
> Reward for Kill: 20 Credits
> Reward for Reform: Extra Disciple Slot

His eyes widened at the potential reward for reforming Leah. *So, the System isn't totally against me taking Leah as a disciple. But first, she needs to be "reformed." Challenge accepted.*

He shifted his focus back to Leah, whose seemed to have made a decision.

"I'll never accept you as my master! Not after you took my father from me!" She spat at him with all the venom she could muster.

With a casual tilt of his head, Slifer effortlessly dodged the unsavory projectile. *What's with this girl and spitting?* he thought, almost amused. *Would she like a taste of her own medicine?*

Before he could react, Amelia's hand struck Leah's face again, snapping, "You don't deserve to have him as your master!"

Frowning at the escalating situation, Slifer put on a stern mask, addressing Morvran. "Keep her under house arrest. If she doesn't come around in a while, she can rot in the dungeon."

Morvran acknowledged with a sharp nod, then reached out and grasped Leah's hair, lifting her to her feet. She let out a piercing scream and kicked at Morvran's legs, shouting, "Let go of me, you bald-headed oaf!"

Slifer watched as Morvran dragged the thrashing Leah away, his bald head gleaming in the light as it bore the brunt of Leah's verbal onslaught.

He shook his head, a plan forming in his mind to turn Leah's loyalties towards him. *Kidnappers manage to do it all the time. It's just a matter of breaking and reshaping. Stockholm syndrome, that's what they call it.*

As he began to walk away, with Amelia closely tailing him, a System notification blinked into existence:

Ding!
Congratulations!
Your Disciple Fenlock Has Broken Through
Reward: 25 Credits

He raised an eyebrow. *It hasn't even been an hour. How on earth did the lad manage a breakthrough so quickly?*

Fenlock emerged from his quarters, the aura of Peak Core Formation radiating off him in vigorous waves. He clenched his fists tightly and his face hardened with resolve as he muttered fiercely, "Junior Sister, no one will keep me away from you, not even Master."

Slifer sat cross-legged on the ground in his courtyard, a circle of disciples surrounding him. Amelia had stubbornly claimed the seat to his right, an almost protective aura about her. On his left, Caelum was seated, his gaze flitting between Bloodthorn and his master, with an unspoken query swirling in his eyes.

Opposite to Slifer sat Fenlock and Hughie; the former emanated a newfound aura of confidence after his breakthrough, while the latter seemed to wish for nothing but the earth to swallow him whole, distancing him from the scrutinizing gaze he imagined from his master.

The silence was palpable as they all waited for Slifer to speak, yet he seemed to be lost in another world. His face cycled through an array of expressions—surprise, annoyance, and then a trace of glee.

Within the stillness, Caelum's thoughts roamed wild. *Is Master experiencing some sort of enlightenment? I've heard rare geniuses undergo such states. It's not something one can seek, it just . . . happens. Could Master be one of those rare geniuses?*

Hughie, on the other hand, sat in growing discomfort. *Is Master staring at me?* The thought nagged at him, causing his gaze to drop to his hands. He remembered the touch, shuddering at the recollection. *If only Master were a beautiful woman,* the thought fleeted, but he banished it immediately. *But I had to be chosen by an old man, an ugly one at that. Heavens no.*

In reality, Slifer's focus was entirely occupied by the System notifications that floated before his eyes.

Ding!
Congratulations!
You Have Completed the Requirements to Unlock Your Reward

What could it be? His heart skipped a beat as another notification emerged.

You Have Gained the Ability to Learn Your Disciples' Skills
Ability: Mirror Mastery
Description: "I taught you everything you know, not everything I know."
Techniques Will Be Converted to a Righteous Version, Showcase to Your Disciples the Power of the Righteous Path

---

Slifer's eyes widened in realization. *This sounds so OP! So, the System doesn't hate me after all.* Relief washed over him. *With this, maybe there's a chance to break through . . .*

Current Skill Level: 1
User can only take 1 skill per disciple, only the skill they most commonly use.
The conversion of this skill incurs a cost.

His smile briefly faltered. *Ah, all these conditions. Now, this is the System I am accustomed to,* he thought with a tinge of sarcasm.

Focus your attention on a disciple and activate your ability.

Slifer redirected his attention to his disciples. Clearing his throat, he crafted a believable excuse for this gathering. "It's been a while since I've checked on your progress," he said calmly, his eyes shifting to Hughie. *Hughie is the only disciple that definitely has protagonist-level potential, surely he has multiple OP techniques.* "Hughie, how has your cultivation method progressed?"

Hughie froze for a split second. *I knew he'd pick me,* he thought bitterly, rubbing the back of his head. "Master, I . . . I have yet to break through to the second layer," he awkwardly confessed, his voice tinged with embarrassment.

Slifer observed as the technique manifested before him through the System.

Technique: Bloodforge Ascension
As injuries accumulate, the user's body becomes a conduit for malevolent energy, morphing them into a nightmarish titan of destruction.
Current Level: 1—Enhances stats by 1 substage, defense and regeneration enhanced by 2 substages.
Warning: High likelihood of death due to injuries being a requirement for activation.
Warning: Low will stat can lead to loss of control.

Interesting technique, I wonder what the righteous version is like.

Technique: Thunderstrike Ascension
The user, when struck by Heavenly Lightning, becomes a conduit for celestial energy, morphing into a mighty titan of righteous fury.
Current Level: 1—Enhances stats by 1 substage, defense and regeneration enhanced by 2 substages.

> Warning: Requires a high luck stat to survive the strike of Heavenly Lightning.
> Warning: Low will stat can lead to loss of control.

Slifer's face darkened as he mulled over the revised technique's description. *Such a technique would have been perfect, but the high luck stat . . . I'd be dead before activating it.*

Hughie, witnessing the shift in his master's demeanor, felt a chill run down his spine. As his master seemed lost in thought, Hughie hastily mentioned, "Master, I . . . I just need a little more time, a little more experience. I can feel the breakthrough nearing."

Slifer's attention drifted as he pondered the possibility of acquiring more skills from Hughie, yet a System notification cut through his thoughts.

> Upgrade Insight to Learn More

Slifer shook his head, knowing full well that he could not afford to spend credits on upgrades now. *There isn't the luxury of credits for Insight . . .*

Misinterpreting the gesture, Hughie deflated, thinking the head shake was directed at him. *He's going to use this as an excuse to punish me.*

However, to Hughie's surprise, Slifer directed his gaze towards Fenlock. "Fenlock, share your cultivation method."

Fenlock cleared his throat, his hands awkwardly producing a flute from his robe. "My . . . my previous master found me suited for Sound cultivation. I . . . I have some talent in music," he shared hesitantly, his face a shade of red. The memories of mockery from other demonic cultivators, who called him "soft," plagued his confidence.

With a mental command, Slifer activated the ability the System had granted him.

> Technique: Demonic Path of Emotions
> Through the medium of music, the cultivator channels destructive attacks.

Fenlock watched his master's face for any sign of approval or disapproval, while Slifer marveled at the uniqueness of the cultivation method. *Music as a conduit for destruction . . .* It was something truly profound in its own right.

Slifer, with a raised brow, inquired, "Can you only use offensive attacks with this technique?"

Fenlock hesitated briefly, then shook his head. "No, Master. The effects of the attacks depend on my emotions and my will at the time."

Ah, that makes sense why his will stat is high, Slifer thought.

As he opened his mouth to speak, Fenlock hastily interrupted him. "Master, I don't need any guidance."

Fenlock was worried that his master would use cultivation as an excuse to keep him locked in his quarters, he couldn't allow that to happen, not again.

Slifer blinked, momentarily taken aback. Inwardly, he exhaled in relief. *Good, I wasn't going to offer any guidance anyway. I'm hardly familiar with ordinary cultivation, let alone the nuances of sound cultivation.* However, not wanting to seem negligent, he responded, "It's the duty of a master to ensure the progress of his disciple. Demonstrate your technique."

With a hesitant nod, Fenlock directed his gaze to a nearby tree, he took a deep breath, summoning his feelings—particularly the annoyance of his master's perceived attempts to keep him away from his junior sister. With this emotion fueling his technique, he played a haunting melody on his flute.

As the notes flowed from the flute, they seemed to take on a sinister life of their own. The air around Fenlock vibrated with the intensity of his emotions, and the melody grew louder, more menacing. The soundwaves condensed into visible, pulsating ripples, like ethereal snakes, and they streaked towards the unsuspecting tree with terrifying speed.

The notes condensed into visible soundwaves that streaked towards the tree, smashing into it with a resonating shockwave. The bark shattered, leaves disintegrated, and the solid wood splintered into fragments, erasing the tree from existence.

Slifer watched the display, his expression unreadable. *Impressive. But this technique . . . it isn't for me.* He knew his limitations. Music had never been his forte, and the System, in its typical fashion, would likely require him to painstakingly level the skill himself.

"That was impressive, Fenlock," Slifer began, attempting to offer constructive feedback. "Perhaps, for greater control, you could intertwine the essence of your soul with your flute. Let the medium become an extension of your spirit." He was winging it, but from his vast reading experience, geniuses in these types of novels gained inspiration from the most ridiculous sayings. *Let's see if this holds true here.*

Fenlock bowed deeply, thanking Slifer. "Thank you, Master. Your insight is invaluable."

Slifer turned his gaze towards the spot where the mighty tree once stood. *Perhaps,* he thought, *I should be more careful around trees in this sect. I certainly don't want to get on the bad side of a demonic tree.*

CHAPTER FOURTEEN

Slifer shifted his focus onto Amelia, and felt a tad uncomfortable when she inched closer to him.

"So, Amelia, how goes your cultivation?"

Amelia's brows creased in mild frustration. "Master, I need more victims. To break through to the Late Core Formation, I need to devour the souls of three Late Core Formation cultivators."

Ding!
Your Disciple Is Struggling to Break Through
Bring Your Disciple 3 Late Core Formation Souls
Reminder: Righteous Souls Will Result in Credit Deduction
Reward: 50 Karmic Credits

Slifer's eyes narrowed as he read the System notification. His mind churned with thoughts. *Using a Peak Slifer Card just to get her these souls? Not happening.* His thoughts drifted momentarily to Val. *Once she's healed . . . if Amelia hasn't progressed by then, perhaps Val could assist her.*

He collected himself and refocused on Amelia. The hidden cost of her cultivation method had the potential to chip away at his painstakingly earned credits. That was a risk he couldn't take. "Amelia, you must ensure the souls you devour are not of innocent beings."

A look of genuine confusion spread across Amelia's face. "But Master, how can I know who is innocent and who isn't?"

Slifer paused, taken aback by her question. *She does have a point.* He knew that it was the System that decided what was good and what was evil. Wanting to play it safe, he replied, "Target mostly demonic cultivators. When it comes to righteous cultivators, only act against them if they threaten you, or if you're sure they've harmed mortals."

He nodded to himself, his thoughts running along the lines of universal laws. *In most realms like this, the heavens frown upon the killing of mortals by cultivators. I hope the System aligns with this logic.*

Amelia responded with an angelic smile. "Understood, Master." Yet, the glint in her eyes made Slifer uneasy. He hoped she wouldn't provoke others to assault her just to have a reason to claim their souls . . .

Mind Mirror!
Technique: Soul Render
Description: Unleash a blade of soul energy to slice through the enemy's spiritual essence, causing profound damage at the soul level.

This is intriguing, Slifer mused, *a soul-based technique.*

"Show me your progress with the Soul Render technique."

Amelia gleefully agreed, her eyes scanning the courtyard for a target. Realizing there was none, she muttered, "One moment," and vanished.

Wait a minute, is she . . . The thought barely took form before Amelia reappeared, dragging a trembling Qi Refining disciple along. His eyes were wide with terror.

Slifer's eyes widened as realization struck. He opened his mouth to halt her, but he was a moment too late. Amelia had already activated the technique. A ghostly blade formed from her fingertips, slashing through the air to strike the disciple. His tormented scream echoed through the courtyard as his soul was viciously shredded by the ethereal blade. The poor disciple collapsed onto the ground, unconscious, his face twisted in lingering anguish.

Amelia turned to face her master, a triumphant smile brightening her features. Yet the smile faded quickly as she met Slifer's darkened gaze. His heart pounded heavily. Witnessing such a brutal technique against a Qi Refining cultivator like himself was frightening.

Only a Qi Refining cultivator . . . *The level of pain she could inflict was beyond belief.* His heart shivered at the thought, his disciples' previous acts of violence paling in comparison. Ignoring the one credit gain notification, his eyes narrowed.

"Master . . ." Amelia stuttered, sensing that she had angered Slifer.

"Didn't I make it abundantly clear to stop bullying lower-ranked cultivators?" Slifer's voice cut through the silence like a sword.

Amelia's eyes widened in fear. "I-I wasn't bullying him, Master. He agreed to let me practice the technique on him for you to see."

Agreed? More like he was coerced, he thought bitterly. The boundary between consent and coercion was thin and murky in the cruel world of cultivation.

Slifer shook his head, feeling a prick of concern about Amelia's practice methods. "When you practice this technique, what do you normally do?" *Surely there must be a different method.*

"Oh, quite a few of the junior brothers volunteer," she replied nonchalantly, brushing a lock of hair behind her ear.

Slifer paused. *Are these guys so desperate that they'd endure soul torture just to spend time with a girl?* He shook his head in disbelief at their pathetic desperation, a term from his previous world echoing in his thoughts—*simp behavior.*

He sighed heavily. "Amelia, my intention was for you to demonstrate on an animal, not on another disciple. You left before I could give proper instructions."

Amelia lowered her gaze. "I'm sorry, Master. I should have waited for your guidance."

Slifer waved his hand dismissively.

Ding!

Righteous Alternative: Soul Harmony Strike

Description: By tuning one's soul to the righteous energies of the heavens, the cultivator can channel a harmonious strike that seeks to purify the malicious intent within the target. The strike resonates with the opponent's soul, diminishing their malicious energies and weakening their offensive capabilities for a short duration. The effectiveness of this technique increases with higher cultivation levels.

Slifer read the description, taking a moment to let the information sink in. *Soul Harmony*

Strike . . . it sounds less sinister compared to Amelia's soul devouring technique. However, it still deals with the soul, a realm that I am not yet ready to tread upon.

He was apprehensive. The soul was a delicate and profound essence of a being, meddling with it without sufficient understanding was akin to treading on thin ice. While the righteous version seemed to have a noble intent, the underlying manipulation of soul energies was something that he didn't take lightly.

He concluded that he would not be copying this technique, at least not until he was better versed in the intricacies of soul cultivation.

Slifer turned his gaze to Caelum, hoping against hope that his disciple had a technique that could prove useful. "Caelum, how goes your cultivation?"

A shadow of disappointment cast across Caelum's face, his shoulders drooping. "Master," he began, his voice filled with self-reproach, "I have failed as a swordsman. I did not even recognize my own master was a cultivator of the sword."

Slifer blinked in confusion, momentarily taken aback. Then it dawned on him. *Ah, the Deadly Strike Card that manifested Sword Qi. I hope he doesn't ask me for guidance, along with the others. I might be able to mumbo jumbo my way out of it, but Caelum isn't as gullible.*

Caelum, in his desperation, began to kowtow before Slifer. "Please, Master, guide me! My own sword cultivation feels shallow and incomplete. Witnessing your strike has shown me the true path of the sword."

His head lowered, Caelum awaited Slifer's response with bated breath. He wished for his master's guidance but was realistic about his expectations. *Master has always given us freedom, only intervening when he felt we were neglecting our cultivation. What are the chances he'd guide me now?*

But Slifer, at the moment, was engrossed in a System message, not truly catching any of Caelum's impassioned plea.

Technique: Shadowstep Slash
Description: This technique uses the blood essence of the user to teleport instantly to their target's shadow, delivering a deadly, unexpected strike.

A grin slowly spread across Slifer's face. *This . . . This is it. Such a technique would be ideal to confront cultivators of higher realms. And being a sword cultivator? It does have a certain ring to it. Aren't sword cultivators known for being able to fight above their realms?*

Meanwhile, Caelum, who had raised his head in the meantime, misinterpreted Slifer's smile as an approval to his earlier request. His face brightened and he began thanking Slifer profusely. "Oh, thank you, Master! I knew you would guide me. Your benevolence is as boundless as the endless heavens . . ."

Slifer blinked, pulled out from his trance by Caelum's ecstatic gratitude. *Wait a minute, what's happening now?* He realized he had been so engrossed in the technique acquisition that he hadn't paid attention to a word Caelum had been saying. *Oh no, what did I just agree to?* Slifer thought, a sudden pang of unease striking him. He looked down at Caelum who was still in the midst of expressing his heartfelt gratitude, utterly oblivious to the internal panic seizing his master.

"I shall put in twice the effort, thrice the discipline to live up to your expectations, Master," Caelum was saying, his eyes shimmering with unshed tears of joy.

The reality of the situation began sinking in for Slifer. *Oh heavens, what sort of sword guidance is he expecting now? I can't even tell a hilt from a blade.* He had never seen such emotion from his usually composed disciple.

Not wanting to shatter Caelum's newfound enthusiasm, Slifer nodded vaguely, hoping the System would provide further assistance when the time came. Eager to familiarize himself with the new technique's nuances, he gestured to Caelum. "Demonstrate the technique for me."

Caelum, visibly elated, nodded eagerly. "Certainly, Master." He stood up and focused his gaze on a nearby tree, preparing to launch his technique.

However, Slifer's eyes widened in alarm. He hastily interrupted, "Wait! We never practice on trees, especially not within the sect grounds."

Caelum, a tad perplexed, complied. His eyes swept over his fellow disciples, wondering who would volunteer. Hughie slowly stood up, a fearless grin etched across his face. He seemed to welcome the chance to taste a bit of pain.

Slifer, recognizing an opportunity to also witness Hughie's technique, fought to suppress a smile. He gestured for them to proceed.

Standing opposite Caelum, Hughie chuckled. "Don't hold back, Senior Brother."

Caelum shook his head at the daring enthusiasm of his junior brother. He lowered his gaze to his sword, murmuring softly, "Awaken, Bloodthorn." The sword responded, its form contorting into a demonic appearance. With a swift intake of breath, Caelum's eyes flashed red, and in a whisk, he vanished, reappearing behind Hughie in a streak of red.

Hughie burst into laughter. "Didn't even feel that!" However, the laughter caught in his throat as he abruptly coughed up blood, clutching his chest where a ghastly hole had been punctured.

Anger coursed through him, triggering his technique. "Bloodforge Ascension!" Hughie roared. His frame swelled, and he morphed into a terrifying figure as malevolent energy surged through his veins. His skin reddened and veins bulged menacingly as he turned towards Caelum, an avatar of rage.

With a bellow, Hughie swung a gargantuan fist towards Caelum. A nimble dodge saved Caelum from a crushing blow. The ground where the fist landed cracked and cratered, sending shards of rock flying.

"Master, I didn't mean for this to happen!" Caelum shouted, keeping a wary eye on the transformed Hughie.

Slifer frowned, deep in thought. *Perhaps I should intervene before things escalate further but is it worth using up a card . . . ?*

The Bloodforge Ascension technique had its dangers, and losing control was a common one among transformation techniques that dabbled with demonic energy. Slifer remembered that Hughie had a measly will of 3; losing control was probably normal for him.

Yeah . . . I'd rather not get involved, at least not yet.

Amelia, who had been silently observing the mayhem unfold, smirked. "I could easily put him down, you know."

As for Fenlock, he shook his head. *I hope this isn't an everyday affair here.* Even with his superior cultivation, Hughie's aura sent a shiver down his spine.

"Caelum," Slifer called out, "you must subdue him. As his senior brother, this responsibility is *yours*."

Caelum nodded, his face tightening with resolve. As Hughie launched himself towards Caelum with a ground-shaking roar, Caelum nimbly hopped onto his other sword which lifted him into the air, narrowly evading the lethal swipe from Hughie.

Hughie, in his demonic frenzy, seemed to have forgotten his own ability to fly, opting to leap off the ground in an attempt to snatch Caelum out of the sky.

With a swift maneuver, Caelum activated a technique, and suddenly, the air was filled with nine images of him, each wielding its own Bloodthorn.

Is this a mirage technique? Slifer wondered, but as each image descended upon Hughie with a vengeance, the reality of the situation hit him—they were all real, or at least capable of inflicting real damage.

Despite Hughie's inexplicable luck, which helped him evade most of the strikes, the sheer number and ferocity of the attacks had a few land on target. Each strike that landed echoed with a sharp cry of agony from Hughie as he spiraled downwards, crashing into the earth with a deafening thud.

The coordination . . . impressive, Slifer thought.

The images of Caelum merged back into one as he descended cautiously to inspect the fallen disciple.

As Hughie staggered back to his feet, his body was a scene of carnage, riddled with gashes oozing dark blood. But as the Bloodforge Ascension technique continued to work its malicious magic, the wounds started healing, albeit painfully, while Hughie's form expanded even further, his musculature bulging grotesquely. His eyes, now pools of boiling rage, shot up to the sky as he bellowed, "Die!"

A surge of demonic qi erupted from him, the blast force strong enough to send Caelum staggering back.

Caelum steadied himself, his eyes hardening. "I apologize, Junior Brother, but it seems I must stop holding back."

CHAPTER FIFTEEN

C aelum readied himself, inhaling deeply. With determination burning in his eyes, he activated his most potent technique. "Bloodthorn Feast," he whispered, his voice barely audible. At his command, an eerie, elongated tongue sprouted from the blade of Bloodthorn.

Without any hesitation, Caelum plunged the sword deep into Hughie's belly, who, caught in the midst of his transformation, couldn't dodge in time. The grotesque tongue wiggled its way in, hungrily devouring the rampant demonic energy coursing through him.

Hughie's screams echoed throughout the training grounds. His eyes, filled with agony, watched his monstrous form revert. As the transformation receded, his body grew smaller, and the color of his skin started to normalize. With fleeting clarity returning to his gaze, Hughie mustered enough strength to look at Caelum. "Senior Brother . . . beat me again," he murmured weakly, before collapsing into unconsciousness.

Caelum caught Hughie before he could hit the ground. "It's not befitting for a senior brother to lose to his junior," he softly remarked, gently cradling the defeated disciple in his arms. To expedite Hughie's recovery, Caelum placed a few rejuvenating pills in his mouth.

Slifer, standing at a distance, let out a concealed sigh of relief. *I'm just glad I didn't have to waste any cards. And I was lucky Hughie targeted only Caelum, not me.*

Caelum turned to his master, a hint of anticipation in his eyes, hoping for some insights or pointers on his sword technique.

Slifer caught his disciple's expectant gaze, quickly racking his brain for a profound yet sufficiently vague piece of advice. "Your technique, Bloodthorn Feast, carries the essence of both purification and devastation," Slifer remarked, weaving together words that seemed intricate, yet were vague. "Remember, the blade is an extension of the self. Its potential is bound only by your own comprehension of the truth within the sword's essence."

Caelum's eyes widened in revelation. "Thank you, Master, for your invaluable guidance!" he said, clasping his hands together in gratitude.

Slifer gave a small nod, pleased that he was able to get away with his nonsense. His mind then focused on the new technique he had acquired. *I need to get them out of here so I can practice*, he thought. But then the missions he assigned to his disciples came to mind. "Caelum, have you completed your mission?" He navigated to the System panel, clicking on Caelum's name.

> Disciple: Caelum
> Mission Status: In Progress
> 8/10 Completed

Caelum sighed, looking downcast. "This disciple has yet to complete the mission. There were two left, but then I was summoned here."

Slifer nodded in understanding. "Complete them and then return here. I will require your assistance for a little trip outside the sect."

Caelum's eyes widened momentarily, hope flickering within. *Perhaps Master will provide more personal guidance*, he thought. But Slifer's next words dashed that hope as he addressed Fenlock.

"Fenlock, stabilize your cultivation and await my call. You will also be joining me," Slifer instructed.

Slifer's gaze then landed on Amelia. "And young lady, didn't you claim your mission was complete?"

Amelia bobbed her head enthusiastically. "Yes, Master! You can ask around at the Medicine Hall. They'll vouch for me!"

Slifer's lips tightened as a System message blinked before him.

Disciple: Amelia
Mission Status: Incomplete
0/10 Completed

Slifer sighed deeply, his patience thinning with Amelia's deceit. The girl had claimed no prior experience, yet here she was, claiming to have completed the mission within a day. The previous Slifer's leniency had unfortunately bred a sense of entitlement. It was obvious she was lying.

"Foolish girl, do you think you can lie to me? I know you haven't saved a single life at the Medicine Hall," Slifer said sternly, his face hardened by disappointment.

Amelia's eyes widened, and panic swirled in them as she stammered to find an excuse. *Who betrayed me at the Medicine Hall?* she thought bitterly, plotting revenge on the yet unknown perpetrator. Outwardly though, she pouted, "I . . . I apologize, Master . . ."

Displeased with her response, Slifer's voice grew colder. "I should send you to Thunderclap Peak for your insolence."

The name of the dreaded mountain sent shivers down Amelia's spine. It was where the original sent the disciples for punishment. The dangers that lurked there were well known, especially to Core Formation cultivators. While no disciple had died, they surely returned battered and bruised.

Although the original found the Thunderclap Peak useful for Hughie's special technique, Slifer found it barbaric. He only intended to bluff, and the terror in Amelia's eyes told him it worked.

Amelia's face paled considerably, recalling the state Hughie returned in from that cursed place. Her voice quivered, "No, Master, I . . . I'll complete the mission. I promise."

Just then, a System notification appeared before Slifer:

Discipline Administered Correctly
5 Karmic Credits Awarded

Slifer felt a spark of pride. *Doing my job right*, he thought, not surprised by the Karmic Credit gain. It was the System's way to nurture righteousness within disciples. He would have been more taken aback had he not received any credits.

He looked at his disciples one last time before dismissing them.

With his disciples gone, Slifer's full attention was focused on the System screen that floated before him.

Righteous Version: Sunrise Slash
Description: This technique harnesses the pure essence of Light Qi, allowing the user to teleport instantly to their target's shadow to deliver a strike.

Slifer's eyes widened. The righteous version was indeed different from the original, no longer tainted by the use of blood essence.

Cost: 100 Karmic Credits
20% Discount Due to Caelum's Loyalty Rating Exceeding 80%

A twenty percent discount, not bad at all, Slifer thought, his lips curving into a satisfied smile. *It seems having disciples with high loyalty does come with its own advantages.*

Deciding to buy the technique, Slifer mentally tapped the "Purchase" option on the System screen.

As he confirmed his choice, the System promptly responded.

Sunrise Slash (Level 1) Added
80 Karmic Credits Deducted

As the technique was added, Slifer felt a peculiar sensation, a gentle pulse of energy that seemed to ripple through his mind. His vision blurred momentarily as knowledge and details about the Sunrise Slash technique flowed into his consciousness. When his sight cleared and the transfer of information ceased, he had a basic understanding of the technique.

It's time to put this technique to the test, Slifer smirked. However, to truly practice, he needed a blade in his hand. The System's outrageous prices for treasures made it impractical to purchase one. So, he'd previously asked Morvran to fetch a sword from the Armory.

Not long after, Morvran arrived, holding a carefully wrapped item. As the wrapping came off, a sword was revealed. Slifer carefully took hold of the sword, his eyes drawn to its unique orange hilt. *I've not seen that before.* As he unsheathed the blade, its polished surface revealed its quality—a Peak Foundation Establishment treasure.

The sword required the qi of a Foundation Establishment cultivator to unleash its full potential, but with his Qi Refining stage qi, Slifer would have to channel more energy to compensate for the lack of quality. This excessive channeling could drain his qi swiftly, and might have potentially impaired his physique. However, he wasn't worried. With the Sunrise Slash technique and a Foundation Establishment sword, he would be able to end the battle in one strike.

Slowly he swung the sword around, trying to get the feel of it. The imbalance and awkwardness in his form were glaringly obvious, even to his untrained eyes.

Morvran, who stood there watching, found his master's interest in such a mundane weapon surprising, yet he knew better than to comment. The sight of Slifer swinging the sword with such atrocious form was almost painful to watch, but Morvran consoled himself thinking that his master must be creating a new technique. *After all, someone capable of killing an Origin Realm expert with a single blow of Sword Qi couldn't possibly be inept with a sword.*

Catching Morvran's lingering presence, Slifer cleared his throat, a hint of embarrassment in his tone. "Morvran, I'd appreciate some privacy for now."

"Understood, Master." Morvran nodded, adding, "I'll stand guard outside to ensure no disturbances."

Once Morvran departed, Slifer's focus shifted to a new System notification that appeared before him.

Sword Mastery: 0%

The swing of the sword felt more alien with each movement. He was sure the System would have a function to boost his mastery or levels using credits, yet such a feature seemed locked at the moment. *And even if it was accessible*, he mused, *the cost would likely be astronomical.*

Slifer spent a good amount of time familiarizing himself with the sword, feeling its weight, and growing accustomed to its length. He would have been lying if he said that the sword already seemed to have become an extension of himself. But after about an hour, he felt it was time to practice the technique.

His eyes glanced over the dummies Morvran had arranged around the courtyard. He positioned himself a reasonable distance from one, thinking back to how Caelum activated his Shadowstep technique.

He took a deep breath, channeled qi into his sword, and closed his eyes. With a soft murmur, he whispered, "Sunrise Slash."

Upon opening his eyes, a bright light glowed within them. And in a fraction of a second, he vanished from his spot, reappearing far from his intended target, stumbling a bit before tumbling to the ground.

Brushing off the dirt and twigs from his robes, Slifer chuckled lightly. "Not bad," he commented. "It'd probably get me killed in battle, but not a bad first attempt."

He eyed the dummy again. *Alright, once I get this right, I'll treat myself to a bowl of Celestial Lotus Soup*, he thought.

The technique demanded a precise control of qi, which he unfortunately did not have, causing each failed attempt to drain him bit by bit. However, with every new attempt, Slifer noted the minute improvements. His teleportation distance became more accurate, the flash of light during his transitions less blinding, and his landing sturdier.

However, it wasn't long before exhaustion finally caught up with him. Slifer collapsed onto a stone bench, his body slick with sweat and his breathing heavy.

He felt a warm satisfaction in his chest as he looked up to see a System message:

Sword Mastery: 1%
Sunrise Slash Leveled Up

A weary smile stretched across his face. "Looks like level two means I've got the basics down. But there's still a long road ahead if I want to use it in battle."

At the far end of a cave sat a throne, enveloped in shadows. Upon it, a hooded figure sat, its presence a cold void that repelled the meager light attempting to infiltrate the dark lair.

The soft patter of hurried footsteps broke the silence, growing louder as they approached the chamber.

A figure, visibly anxious, made its entrance and quickly knelt before the hooded entity. "Master," he gasped, his voice tinged with a mix of fear and urgency. "My lord, I have news."

The hooded entity shifted ever so slightly, and for a brief moment, a pair of eyes beneath the hood glowed a deep, menacing red. "Speak," it commanded, its voice chillingly calm.

Swallowing hard, the kneeling man began, "Grand Elder Olakin from the Black Heart Sect . . . he's been killed."

A shadow of a frown creased the hooded figure's concealed face. "And how does this concern me?"

The young man hesitated momentarily, gathering his courage. "It is said . . . Elder Slifer is the one responsible." Taking a shaky breath, he added, "The grand elder was killed in a single strike."

A tense silence settled in the chamber. Suddenly, the hooded figure's eyes flashed red again, this time more intensely. Its fingers tightened around the throne's armrests, the stone beneath its grip groaning in protest. "Impossible," it hissed. "I killed him myself. I made certain his Nascent Soul was annihilated."

As the words left its mouth, an overwhelming aura surged from the hooded figure, pressing down on the already trembling man kneeling before it.

Gasping for breath, the man's eyes widened in realization. "Origin Realm . . ." he whispered, awe and fear evident in his voice, before succumbing to the pressure and collapsing on the cavern floor.

The sudden thud snapped the hooded figure out of its revelry. Quickly, it reined in its aura. *I must contact the others*, it thought. *We can't delay any longer.*

Without a moment's hesitation, the figure vanished in a burst of demonic energy, leaving the unconscious messenger lying on the cold, hard floor, the cave once again swallowed by silence.

CHAPTER SIXTEEN

Morvran awoke with the early rays of dawn, pulling himself from the bed that barely held the imprint of his body. As a Core Formation expert, sleep was more a luxury than a necessity; a few hours per week sufficed.

He plodded over to the basin, fetching a jug of water to freshen his face and rinse his mouth.

Stepping in front of the mirror, a bald and chubby-yet-serious face greeted him back. His features, distinctly Chinese, wore an expression of profound contemplation.

He opened a drawer, retrieving a small jar of cream. The price he paid for it had been rather steep, costing him a few medium spirit stones. But the renowned alchemist who created it had promised it would give his bald head a sheen like no other.

As he rubbed the cream into his scalp, he murmured, "As Master Slifer's right hand, one must always appear impeccable."

Slipping into his grand robes, he opened the door to his quarters, and was immediately greeted by a sight of three young men, clad in dark robes with their faces shrouded, kneeling in wait.

These were Master Slifer's death warriors—elite guardians raised from childhood to lay down their lives for their revered master when the hour called for it.

Morvran let out a heavy sigh. *If it weren't for Master Slifer, these souls would've met a cruel fate in some forgotten alley, their existence devoured by the wilderness of the world.*

His master had been a savior to many, a beacon of change in the merciless world they navigated. He too, like these death warriors, was an orphan taken under Master Slifer's wings. A ripple of gratitude surged through his veins, as Morvran knew he owed every shred of his being to his master.

Morvran cleared his throat, bringing himself back from his thoughts. "Speak," he commanded the death warriors.

One of the young men responded, his voice steady but filled with concern. "Boss, last night an intruder attempted to break into Master's quarters."

Morvran raised an eyebrow. In the past, such audacity was unheard of, but after news spread of Master Slifer's failed breakthrough, and his subsequent weakened state, there had been a trickle of bold attempts against him. As Slifer's right-hand man, Morvran was the shield between his master and any threats; a role he undertook with grave seriousness.

"Where is this intruder now?" Morvran inquired, his voice a slow drawl conveying an icy calmness.

The young man hesitated for a brief moment before answering, "It wasn't an assassin, boss. It was . . . a disciple."

Morvran's eyes narrowed into slits. *Sending a disciple . . . this smells of a clever ploy by one of the elders*, he thought.

"Bring me to him," Morvran commanded, his voice leaving no room for question.

Without a word, the quartet moved, their figures blurring as they darted through the sect with a speed that made them near-invisible to the naked eye.

The dungeon was dimly lit, the few torches on the walls providing an eerie illumination that flickered as a cold draft swept through the underground chambers.

A young voice echoed through the halls, pleading with a fervent passion. "Let me out! Don't you understand? He is *my* master!"

Upon entering, Morvran's eyes landed on a tall, lanky disciple. This young man's frame was riddled with bruises, yet there was a defiant gleam in his eyes, and an almost-cocky smile stretched across his face. The moment the lad's gaze settled on Morvran, recognition lit up his features. "Boss Morvran!" he exclaimed, joy evident in his voice.

So, the would-be assassin recognizes me, he thought grimly. Without a word, Morvran approached and, without warning, delivered a powerful slap across the boy's face. Blood splattered, and the boy's head jerked to the side, but the grin remained.

"Who sent you?" Morvran demanded coldly, suspicion clear in his eyes.

Still smiling, the lad, who was Dentos, laughed. "I wasn't here to harm anyone. I simply wanted to deliver a meal I had made for my master."

"And who, exactly, is this 'master' of yours?" Morvran's tone was skeptical.

Dentos looked straight into Morvran's eyes and declared confidently, "Master Slifer, of course."

Morvran's patience was wearing thin. With a swift motion, he struck Dentos again, this time with more force. The boy's head collided with the cage's bars, the metal clanging upon impact. "Stop with the lies, boy," Morvran warned, his gaze piercing through Dentos, taking in the boy's battered physique and mentally marking which bones he'd target next.

Through the haze of pain, Dentos chuckled, albeit with bitterness tingeing his voice. "Elder Slifer *is* my master," he claimed, pausing briefly before adding, "he just doesn't know it yet . . ."

Morvran stayed his hand momentarily. The idea of someone yearning to be his master's disciple was new to him. He had always known Master Slifer to be a great man, but the world had its way of slandering the worthy. His doubts lingered, but he knew for his master's sake, he *had* to make sure.

With a swift motion, Morvran seized Dentos by the neck, his fingers pressing into the soft flesh. "This 'meal,' is it poisoned? Is this your plan to assassinate my master?" he hissed.

Gasping for breath, Dentos managed to choke out, "No . . . I heard Master has taken a liking to food recently . . . I just . . . wanted to gift this to him."

Behind Morvran, one of the death warriors approached, handing him a meticulously wrapped package. "We found this in the boy's storage ring," the warrior said, his voice devoid of emotion.

Morvran unwrapped the package to reveal a meal: delicate dumplings with a hint of celestial herbs, a soup that emitted a gentle aroma hinting at rare earthbound mushrooms, and a portion of heavenly glazed fish. It was a feast fit for a revered master.

Turning to Dentos, Morvran spoke sternly, "We shall see if you speak the truth, boy." He signaled to the death warrior who nodded and began cautiously tasting the food.

At the same time, another death warrior darted off towards the Medicine Hall to summon a healer, in case the food indeed was poisoned.

As the death warrior took the first bite, Dentos's eyes widened in terror. "Stop!" he shouted, straining against the chains that bound him, his face twisted in a desperate plea. "It isn't meant for you!"

But his plea fell on deaf ears. Morvran watched the warrior continue to taste the meal, and then nodded in silent affirmation to Dentos, convinced now of the poisonous intent.

The boy's desperate reaction . . . it only confirms the deceit, Morvran thought, the grim realization settling within his chest as he looked at Dentos with eyes hardened like the cold, merciless steel of a blade.

Morvran turned to the death warrior who had sampled the meal. "How was it?" he inquired.

The death warrior, though his face was concealed by the mask, seemed to carry a rare smile in his eyes as he responded, "Delicious. It tastes how I imagine a mother's cooking would be."

Morvran scowled. "But have you noticed any adverse effects?"

The warrior shook his head. "No, there has been no change in my health or my qi."

Morvran muttered under his breath, "Must be a slow-acting poison." His gaze shifted as the healer hurriedly approached them, applying a technique to ascertain the presence of any toxins. After a brief moment of scanning, the healer looked up, shaking his head.

"No poison detected," the healer confirmed.

"So, no poison?" Morvran mumbled to himself, his eyes not leaving Dentos. *Perhaps this boy does have what it takes to be Master's disciple.* The thought darted through his mind, surprising him. His thoughts quickly jumped to Fenlock, and he scoffed inwardly. *At least he'll be better than that lovesick brat.*

He sighed and commanded his men, "Release him."

The clank of chains falling to the cold floor resonated in the silent room as Dentos was freed from his bonds. He slowly rose to his feet, rubbing his wrists to ease the soreness.

Morvran looked at Dentos with a newfound curiosity. "It seems there was a misunderstanding. You may go," he said. His voice was stern yet carried a trace of unspoken apology.

Dentos, however, didn't move. His eyes were fixed on Morvran as he defiantly said, "I want to see Master Slifer."

CHAPTER SEVENTEEN

Slifer sat cross-legged in his quarters, eagerly devouring the bowl of Celestial Lotus Soup that he had promised himself. Each mouthful was a delightful explosion of rich flavors, making the tedious practice worthwhile. As he relished the heavenly taste, his concentration was broken by a sudden spiritual transmission.

"Master, the grand elder has extended an invitation for tea," Morvran's voice echoed in Slifer's mind.

Slifer paused, the spoon halfway to his mouth. *grand elder . . . Isn't that young brat Zarius's master?* he thought, a hint of displeasure clouding his thoughts. *The sect master mentioned that the grand elder had let the previous incident slide. Now what could he possibly want?*

With a resigned sigh, he lifted the bowl to his lips and in one hearty gulp, drained the remaining broth. His face turned a shade of red from the effort, but it was followed by a satisfied burp. A small victory before whatever it was that awaited him.

He rose from his seat, setting down the empty bowl. It was time to look presentable for the meeting ahead. He straightened his robes and made sure that there was no incriminating soup evidence. *Clean. Nice.*

"This old man better not have any thoughts of bullying me," he muttered, adjusting the collar of his robe. "And the tea . . . It better be top-notch."

The entrance to Grand Elder Tenzin's courtyard was nothing short of breathtaking. A serene pond filled with blooming lotuses dominated the scene. Silver koi swam gracefully beneath the surface, casting ripples that reflected the soft glimmer of hanging lanterns. Surrounding it were vibrant gardens filled with rare spiritual herbs that emitted a gentle fragrance. Slifer exhaled deeply, *If only I had reincarnated as a grand elder. This place . . . it's just like a slice of heaven.*

As he approached the main hall, a servant in elegant robes stepped forward, about to speak. Before a word could leave the servant's mouth, a middle-aged figure with refined features, clad in a majestic robe depicting dragons intertwined with phoenixes, appeared out of thin air.

Insight!

Name: Tenzin
Realm: Early Origin Realm
Known Techniques: N/A
Known Affiliations: Black Rose Sect
Disposition: N/A

"Leave us," Grand Elder Tenzin commanded, dismissing the servant with a wave. He then turned to Slifer, his voice surprisingly humble. "A figure of Elder Slifer's stature deserves to be welcomed by someone more significant than a mere servant. Even if that someone is as insignificant as little me."

Slifer blinked, taken aback by the warm welcome. *This isn't the Tenzin I remember*, he thought. From the snippets of memories he retained from the original, Grand Elder Tenzin was known to be arrogant, much like his young disciple, Zarius.

Greeting the grand elder, Slifer bowed his head slightly. "It's an honor, Grand Elder Tenzin."

Tenzin's face reddened a bit, and he awkwardly cleared his throat. "Ah, Senior has shown this junior too much respect."

Senior? Slifer thought, utterly confused. *Despite how I might look, this grand elder is surely millennia older than me.*

As the two walked deeper into the courtyard, Tenzin's brow was slick with perspiration, his mind racing. *Damn that Zarius! If he hadn't so rashly provoked this demon over the Heaven Rank method, I wouldn't be in this humiliating position.* He swallowed hard, recalling the gruesome image that had spread like wildfire throughout the sect—Slifer effortlessly decapitating an Origin Realm expert with an Ascendant level strike. The mere thought sent shivers down Tenzin's spine.

Upon reaching the center of the courtyard, two thrones stood facing each other. With a polite gesture, Grand Elder Tenzin gestured for Slifer to sit on the larger one, while he himself took the smaller seat. As they settled, servants bustled forward, pouring a clear, aromatic liquid into their cups—Immortal Tea.

Eagerly, Tenzin watched as Slifer took a sip. The subtle changes in Slifer's expression didn't go unnoticed; his eyes widened slightly, and his lips curled into a small smile of appreciation. *Ah, this . . . this is far superior to what Morvran usually serves me*, Slifer mused, taking another sip. *Being a grand elder truly is worlds apart from a mere elder.*

"I trust the tea meets Senior's tastes?" Tenzin inquired with a soft smile.

Slifer nodded slowly. "Indeed, it's exceptional." Yet inwardly, he questioned, *What's with calling me Senior? Is this old fool mocking me?*

The grand elder cleared his throat before continuing. "Elder Slifer, I wanted to discuss the recent . . . incident between my disciple and yourself." He glanced at Slifer, noting the brief flash of annoyance in his eyes.

Slifer's eyes narrowed, his previous appreciation for the tea momentarily forgotten. *I knew it, he seeks retribution for that brat.*

Seeing the change in Slifer's demeanor, a bead of sweat trickled down Tenzin's temple. *As feared, this demon holds grudges.*

Desperate to alleviate the tension, Tenzin forced a smile. "The disputes between juniors should indeed remain among them, don't you agree?"

Slifer responded with a hesitant nod. "I believe so."

Tenzin carried on, "However, I was hoping a modest gift might ensure no ill feelings remain between us."

The expression on Slifer's face darkened. *Blackmailing me? As if I have much to offer.*

Tenzin's heart pounded as he witnessed Slifer's displeasure. *Even a gift isn't appeasing this demon!* He cursed inwardly as he let out a nervous chuckle.

With a snap of his fingers, a servant emerged, cradling a sublime sword. The black blade carried a haunting elegance, the hilt adorned with a red rose.

Slifer's eyes widened as he activated Insight on the sword.

Treasure
Grade: Origin Realm
Type: Sword
Conditions: Perfect

He shook his head in disappointment. *Useless. With my cultivation, it'll be a while before I can use it.*

Grand Elder Tenzin observed Slifer's dismissive reaction and concealed a frown, he was not surprised that an Origin Realm treasure wasn't worth an Ascendant cultivator's attention. But it had been centuries since he had been humbled like this, he felt like a servant attempting to please a king with a handful of gold.

Nevertheless, he forced a smile and began elaborating on the sword's rich past.

"This is the Midnight Rose," he said, "an heirloom of the Lotus Peak Sect that I . . . acquired. It was forged from Black Meteoric Iron by Grandmaster Shen, adorned with a Vermilion Blood Rose from the Heavenly Garden. It's a humble offering, but the best this junior could muster."

Slifer dipped his head slightly. "Thank you, Grand Elder."

Yet, he noticed Tenzin's lingering gaze upon him. *Stare all you want, old man, but I have nothing to give you*, he thought, his face unmoved. He doubted the grand elder would attack him outright, if there was a high likelihood of that happening then he wouldn't be as composed as he was right now.

Noticing the displeasure creeping upon Slifer's face, Tenzin hurriedly changed the topic.

"Congratulations, Elder Slifer, on your recent breakthrough to the Ascendant Realm. Truly, you now stand as a supreme elder," he managed, trying to inject warmth into his tone.

Slifer's eyes momentarily widened, a flicker of genuine surprise. *Ascendant Realm . . . me?*

Tenzin caught that split second of vulnerability. *Ah, the wolf wished to hide among the sheep a while longer*, he thought bitterly.

Now it all makes sense, Slifer thought, nearly cursing out loud. *The death of Elder Olakin, an Origin Realm expert, certainly alerted the sect. They must have viewed his Soul Lamp and seen me delivering the fatal blow. That news must've led Grand Elder Tenzin to approach me with such caution.*

He managed a nonchalant smile. "Thank you, Grand Elder. But really, it's no great feat."

Yet inside, Slifer raged at the unwanted attention. *How am I supposed to behave like an Ascendant cultivator? That level of prowess is usually reserved for sect leaders!*

However, a smirk curled on the edge of his thoughts. *But, "supreme elder" does have a nice ring to it.*

Tenzin broke through Slifer's musings, "While the sect master remains in seclusion, your title of supreme elder won't be formally acknowledged within the sect."

Slifer's heart lightened, secretly pleased. *Perfect. I'm not prepared for the burdens that come with higher recognition. Being an elder is already too much of a stretch.*

However, Tenzin, ever the diplomat, added, "But, in my eyes, you'll always be a supreme elder."

The grand elder then dropped a tidbit that piqued Slifer's interest. "Given the sect master's absence, during the Disciple Selection Ceremony in a week, *you* will have the privilege of the first pick."

Before Slifer could digest this news, a System notification appeared in front of him.

> *Ding!*
> Save a Poor Disciple from the Clutches of These Demons
> You Have Been Given an Extra Disciple Slot
> Rewards: ???

If the System handed this task to me, there must be a protagonist-caliber disciple among the participants.

Curiosity piqued, he asked the System, *Can I identify protagonists among the participants?*

> Upgrade the Insight skill to gather more intricate details about targets.

Slifer mulled over this information. *If I could see their stats, I could snatch the protagonist from right under the noses of the other elders.* He recalled how Hughie's protagonist status had unintentionally saved him. *Maybe, having another protagonist disciple isn't that bad of an idea.*

He suppressed a chuckle at a wicked thought. *I wonder if combining the luck of two protagonists and using the Random Card could yield a jackpot? Maybe something worth one hundred thousand credits?*

"Is something amusing, Senior?" Tenzin asked, feeling that the newly ascended elder was mocking him.

"Oh, nothing." Slifer waved off the question, the trace of a smirk playing on his lips. "I was just pondering the prospects of the upcoming Disciple Selection Ceremony. It seems there are interesting times ahead."

The grand elder nodded slowly before his face grew serious. "Senior, now that you've broken through, the nearby sects will undoubtedly be on guard," he remarked, the worry etched across his features.

Slifer frowned, not liking where the conversation was headed.

Tenzin continued, "The Black Heart Sect and the Black Death Sect, being demonic in nature, are less inclined to make a move against us. Especially after you eliminated their Elder Olakin. However." Tenzin sighed, his gaze distant. "The three major righteous sects—Heaven's Light Sect, Pure Soul Sect, and White Tiger Sect—won't take kindly to this development."

Slifer groaned internally. *Great, as if I don't already have enough on my plate, now I've got to deal with these righteous hypocrites.*

Sensing Slifer's annoyance, Tenzin pressed on. "With the Inter-Sect Tournament nearing, we'll gain an extra slot for the Sealed Realm, thanks to your breakthrough."

Slifer nodded. The original's memories laid out the rules clearly. Each Ascendant cultivator earned their sect a slot. Typically, only twenty slots were allotted. After dividing them among the six sects, the righteous ones usually hoarded the most, leaving scraps for the demonic sects. The strongest among the righteous sects, boasting three Ascendant cultivators, snagged three slots.

The remaining ten were fought for in the inter-sect competitions—five for Core Formation cultivators and five for Foundation Establishment cultivators. Now, one would be directly allocated to the Black Rose Sect, reducing the competed slots to nine.

"Only those beneath the Nascent Soul stage may enter the realm," Tenzin elaborated. "I advise caution in selecting your new disciple, Senior. With your new status, many eyes will scrutinize both you and your disciples. It would be a significant boon to our sect if you could nurture a Foundation Establishment cultivator to secure one of those spots."

Slifer met the Grand Elder's warm gaze. *This old man isn't so bad,* he thought. *Ah, who am I kidding? He's only being this courteous because he believes I'm an Ascendant Realm cultivator.* "I appreciate the insight, Junior," he responded, still finding it odd to address someone so much older with that title.

As he stood to leave, his thoughts turned to the new task that he had received. Given that the System wanted him to acquire another disciple, he was set on doing so, but he'd be damned if he settled for anything less than the best.

After all, I didn't grow up in capitalist America just to miss out on maximizing profits. He smirked. *Every capable disciple is a walking, talking credit machine.*

Whilst heading back to his quarters, the looming worries of the Inter-Sect Tournament and the slots kept gnawing at Slifer's mind. *Would I need to negotiate with other Ascendant cultivators?* he wondered. The thought of deceiving beings that were a breath away from the Immortal Realm seemed next to impossible. *It's a matter for the future,* he thought. *Who knows what cards I'd have by then, maybe I can handle the situation.*

He shook his head, shifting his focus, and decided it was time to meet the criteria for breaking through to the Foundation Establishment Realm. A bitter laugh escaped him as he imagined the whispers about the newly ascended Ascendant cultivator, Slifer, going around challenging Foundation Establishment juniors.

Summoning Morvran through a spiritual transmission, he awaited his arrival. Soon, the fat man stood before him.

"Has Val awakened?" Slifer asked, hopeful.

With a somber shake of his head, Morvran responded, "She remains in deep hibernation, her body is still recovering."

Slifer sighed deeply. *With little Val by my side, there would be fewer worries.*

He composed himself and instructed Morvran, "Inform Caelum and Fenlock to meet me at the sect entrance in an hour."

Morvran nodded and vanished in a blur of speed, leaving Slifer in his silent contemplation.

As he began his preparation, Slifer muttered to himself, "Like hell am I going anywhere without some bodyguards."

CHAPTER EIGHTEEN

Nestled amidst lush green hills, a day's journey away from the sect, was Willowbrook Village. A charming haven for the weary traveler, yet an easy target for bandits, the latter being the reason Slifer had chosen the location for this little trip of his.

As they entered the village, Fenlock turned to Slifer, a look of curiosity etched on his face. "Master, why have we traveled to this place?"

With a semblance of profundity, Slifer replied, "The journey to Enlightenment is diverse, young Fenlock. The Dao beckons us to gain experience from every corner of life." He paused, letting his eyes scan the villagers working away. "Many cultivators overlook the impoverished and the weak, yet, it is they who possess the mightiest of wills."

Yet, his real intentions were far from noble. *When the bandits attack, eliminating a few Foundation Establishment Realm bandits will not only earn me credits for my breakthrough but also for saving a village. Two birds, one stone.* He smiled.

Slifer had ensured through Morvran that these bandits were not backed by some aged powerful cultivator. *The last thing I need is an irate grandpa appearing out of thin air.* Slifer shuddered at the classic xianxia trope.

Walking deeper into the village, the trio felt numerous eyes fall on them. The villagers, with their sun-beaten faces and wary eyes, observed them with a mix of curiosity and dread. The emblem on their robes—the Black Heart Rose—was well known in the region and *not* for the best reasons.

An elderly man with a limp, who Slifer assumed to be the village elder, approached them. His frail frame trembled slightly as he coughed into his wrinkled hands before introducing himself. "I am Baelin, the leader of this humble abode. How . . . how may this poor old man assist the esteemed guests?"

Caelum and Fenlock exchanged glances. Each was as clueless as the other. Their eyes turned to Slifer, awaiting an explanation.

With a gentle smile, Slifer addressed the village leader. "We have simply come for my disciples to gain some experience from this village. There is no cause for concern."

Suddenly, a young man, tall and robust with sharp features and green piercing eyes, stepped forward, his stride carrying an air of righteousness. His jet-black hair flowed with the wind, and his eyes held a fierce determination.

Insight!

```
Name: N/A
Realm: Early Foundation Establishment
Known Techniques: N/A
Known Affiliations: Willowbrook Village—Righteous
Disposition: N/A
```

Ah, the brave, outspoken, and possibly not-too-bright hero archetype. Slifer sighed.

The young man chuckled disdainfully. "A demonic cultivator instructing his disciples in a secluded village like this? Doesn't exactly instill confidence within us."

Caelum's gaze grew icy. He could hardly believe that a mere Foundation Establishment cultivator would have the audacity to insult his master. Advancing a step, he released his overwhelming Core Formation aura. "If you're suggesting that my master has ill intentions towards this village, know that had he desired, everyone here would have been long dead."

The pressure of the Core Formation aura bore down on the young man, making his legs tremble, but he stood his ground. With great effort, he released his Foundation Establishment aura, looking unflinchingly into Caelum's eyes.

Sensing the rising tension, the village leader immediately intervened. "Ziven!" he scolded the young man. "Show respect to our esteemed guests!"

Slowly, Ziven lowered his head, offering an apology, yet the fire in his eyes remained unquenched.

Slifer, observing this, couldn't help but crack a small smile. Yet, he wondered if retreat was the better choice to avoid entangling with a potential protagonist character—he had personally experienced their absurd luck work for him and he certainly did *not* want to be on the receiving end.

No . . . we're here for the bandits, not a confrontation with a budding hero. As long as the disciples don't do anything dumb, it shouldn't be an issue.

Waving his hand slightly, Slifer signaled Caelum to stand down. Immediately, Caelum suppressed his aura, stepped back, and offered a deferential bow to Slifer.

Turning to the gathered villagers, Slifer spoke up. "I've heard the Shadow Veil Bandits have been tormenting this village lately. I thought it would be a valuable lesson for my disciples to assist in this situation."

Hearing Slifer's reply, the village elder's face twisted into a hesitant expression. The notion of demonic cultivators offering aid was a challenging concept to accept, however, he didn't have much of a choice, Willowbrook Village had no power to refuse the Black Rose Sect.

Huffing, the young man, Ziven, walked away with heavy steps. "I'd rather face death than take assistance from the likes of demonic cultivators!" he declared, his voice filled with anger and disdain.

Immediately, the village leader fell into a begging posture, deeply apologetic. "Forgive young Ziven's outburst." He trembled as he spoke. "His family was slaughtered by demonic cultivators, their souls devoured before his very eyes."

Slifer's nod was almost imperceptible. *A tragic backstory, check. Heroic demeanor, check. Foolish enough to challenge forces beyond comprehension, check.* He mentally ticked off the checklist that screamed of a protagonist's traits.

The thought of taking the young lad as a disciple crossed Slifer's mind. Although his character seemed a bit abrasive, Slifer believed he could mold him into something more . . . tolerable. But as if reading his mind, a System notification appeared before him:

Ding!
Maximum Disciple Capacity Reached
No More Disciples Can Be Accepted

Slifer sighed softly, he was aware of the limit, but he had held a slender hope that the System might carve out an exception for a potential protagonist. His eyes roamed over the retreating figure of Ziven and then back to the elder still holding a humble bow.

"I understand the grudges held by the young man; it is the tragic reality of the cultivation world. Nevertheless, our intention here is genuine, village elder."

Baelin, now slowly regaining his composure, nodded, though the uncertainty in his eyes was hard to miss.

Regardless, the village elder led them towards his humble abode.

When they arrived, Baelin turned to Slifer and mentioned, "The bandits haven't struck for several moons now."

Slifer nodded as he pondered his words. *If they haven't attacked for months, it's very likely they'll strike soon. The sooner I can end this, the quicker I can return to the sect's security.*

The elder's home was modest, bearing the true essence of rural life. Earthen walls, wooden beams, and a low-hanging roof made from thick straw. The center of the main room had a rustic wooden table surrounded by stools.

The elder quickly ushered Slifer to the seat of honor, a slightly elevated wooden chair.

As Slifer seated himself, a "lavish" feast was presented before him. The village, in their undeniable generosity—or perhaps, sheer terror of angering a demonic cultivator—had sacrificed their precious livestock.

As he picked at the humble meat dish, he couldn't help but feel a twinge of guilt. These folks were hanging on by a thread, yet here they were, offering what little they had to please him.

It's only fair to compensate them for their loss before we leave, he thought, nibbling at a piece of the rough-cut meat that tasted of genuine struggle and survival. A brief pause later, a memory of his own lack of wealth dawned on him, bringing a grimace to his face. *Oh, right . . . my storage ring resembles a barren wasteland.*

His eyes darted towards Fenlock, who was surveying the room with a detached look. *I'm sure Fenlock could spare a few spirit stones.* A smirk appeared on his face once again. *That would save him from squandering them on that junior sister he's been swooning over lately.*

As Slifer ate, he relished every bite, thinking, *For all the lavish feasts back at the sect, there's something comforting about this simple homemade fare.*

Lost in his thoughts, he failed to notice the incredulous stares he was receiving from Fenlock, Caelum, and the village elder, as he devoured the meal like a starved beast.

Is this really an elder from the Black Rose Sect? Baelin thought.

After a short while, Fenlock stiffened, his attention snapping towards the door. *Bandits!* But as his gaze shifted to his still-feasting master, he decided to keep silent. *If I sensed them just now, Master must have detected them long ago.*

Suddenly, a loud crash interrupted Slifer's gluttonous feast. The wooden door burst open as a battered figure slammed into Slifer's table, sending food and dishes flying. Gravy dripped from shattered bowls, and Slifer's plate of meat lay ruined amidst the debris.

No, not my food, Slifer thought mournfully. He had always held a deep-seated belief, bordering on a sacred rule, that no morsel of food should ever meet an unjust end, especially not before meeting the end of his chopsticks.

Slifer's eyes narrowed as they landed on the intruder: it was Ziven, battered, his clothes torn, and bruises covering his body. He looked up at Slifer, pain evident in his eyes. His lips parted, trying to relay a message, but before any words could emerge, he succumbed to unconsciousness.

What kind of protagonist loses to a mere bandit? he thought. He paused. *Right, their early years usually consist of regular public humiliations. How typical.*

"The villagers!" cried the village elder, fear replacing the initial shock as he darted outside.

Wiping the food stains from his robes, Slifer sighed. "It wasn't personal before, but now"—he glared at the splintered door—"now it's very personal."

The bandits had just committed a cardinal sin—ruining his meal.

Slifer and his disciples emerged from the house, their eyes scanning the chaotic scene before them, and they found the cries of the frightened mixed with the defiant shouts of men who were ready to die to protect their homes. These brave men brandished whatever weaponry they could muster—be it a rusty sword, a worn-out axe, or even farming tools.

Slifer observed the ragtag assembly of fighters. Most were mere Qi Refining cultivators with just a handful at the Foundation Establishment level.

But what caught Slifer's eye was the village elder. The previously humble and weak aura that had surrounded him had vanished. With a steely resolve evident in his eyes, he released an aura that was at the peak of Foundation Establishment. Without a second's hesitation, he charged towards a sinister-looking figure, presumably the bandit leader.

It's always the old men to be wary of, Slifer mused, a common notion in a world where survival was the supreme law.

Caelum's hand tightened on the hilt of his sword as he watched the bandits wreak havoc on the village. He turned to Slifer; the question evident in his eyes. "Master, should we engage?"

Fenlock too seemed eager to join the fray, but Slifer hesitated. He saw the various techniques being thrown around on the battlefield, some of which were potent enough to one-shot a Qi Refining cultivator like himself. *I can't afford to let them leave my side,* he decided, *even for a split second.*

Donning a sage-like demeanor, Slifer replied with an excuse he had prepared, "We can easily eliminate these bandits within a few breaths, but our goal here transcends mere fighting. It's about gaining enlightenment through restraint."

Fenlock tilted his head, confusion evident. "How do we achieve that, Master?"

Slifer flashed a knowing smile. "By challenging ourselves against our foes, restricting our cultivation as we do so. Remain close and observe."

Fenlock's eyes widened at the prospect of his master joining the battle, unlike the other disciples, he had never seen his master fight before.

Forsaking the ego to hone the blade. Brilliant. Caelum's eyes sparkled with understanding.

Slifer ignored his disciples as he assessed the battleground. His gaze landed on a particular bandit, who was smirking arrogantly to himself. It was clear to Slifer that this was the ruffian responsible for Ziven's sorry state—and more importantly the destruction of his meal.

Insight!

Name: N/A
Realm: Early Foundation Establishment

Known Techniques: N/A
Known Affiliations: Affiliation: Shadow Veil Bandits—Demonic
Disposition: N/A

Early Foundation Establishment? Perfect!

Ding!
Breakthrough Requirements
Appropriate Target Detected
Would you like to issue a challenge?

Slifer's lips curved in a predatory grin. "Challenge," he murmured.

Challenge Accepted
Begin

Upon seeing the prompt from the System, a smirk graced Slifer's face. He was not foolish enough to announce his presence. As long as the System viewed it as a challenge, that was enough. He knew that to kill a Foundation Establishment cultivator, there could be no playing around, he needed to end the battle with a single strike.

With a fluid motion, Slifer unsheathed his sword, its blade gleaming ominously under the flickering flames that had caught onto some nearby huts. He then closed his eyes briefly and activated a skill—the Sunrise Slash.

When his eyes snapped open, they gleamed with a brilliant golden hue.

"Consider this payback for a meal so rudely interrupted," Slifer whispered as he vanished into thin air, leaving only a fleeting trace of golden light behind.

"This . . . this is my technique . . ." Caelum's eyes widened in disbelief.

Shadowstep Slash.

Despite some slight differences, to the creator of the technique, the sequence was unmistakable.

"How can Master use it?" Caelum was certain that his master had only seen him perform the technique once.

I-is this the comprehension of an Ascendant Realm expert?

CHAPTER NINETEEN

Slifer soundlessly materialized behind the bandit.

The bandit, previously leering at a woman with a disgusting grin, froze in place. His eyes widened in terror, but before he could even register the danger, his head separated from his body, landing on the ground with a soft thud.

> *Ding!*
> Successfully Killed a Demonic Foundation Establishment Cultivator
> Reward: 5 Karmic Credits
> Breakthrough Requirements: 1/3

Slifer smoothly sheathed his sword, turning to face his disciples. A smirk played on his lips. "Flawless victory," he whispered more to himself than to anyone in particular.

However, his satisfaction was short-lived. From the corner of his eye, he noticed a pair of bandits turning his way, fury evident in their eyes for having killed their comrade.

One of them, with tattoos snaking up his arms and a face twisted in anger, barked, "Old man, you'll pay for that!"

Insight!

> Name: N/A
> Realm: Late Foundation Establishment
> Known Techniques: N/A
> Known Affiliations: Shadow Veil Bandits
> Disposition: N/A

Late Foundation Establishment? I might have bitten off more than I can chew. Without missing a beat, he coughed lightly, directing his disciples' attention to the hostile bandits. "Well, what are you waiting for? It's your turn now."

Caelum and Fenlock exchanged glances before nodding in unison. Conscious of Slifer's earlier lesson, they suppressed their cultivation to match their opponents.

With a fierce battle cry, Caelum lunged at his opponent, blade singing as it cut through the air. The bandit parried the blow, but the sheer force behind the strike pushed him several steps back, the ground beneath his feet cracking. Regaining his balance, the bandit looked Caelum up and down, a lewd grin spreading across his face. "I'll have fun with a pretty boy like you."

Caelum simply shook his head, retorting sharply, "You should worry less about my looks and more about keeping your head attached."

Meanwhile, the bandit charged at Fenlock with a maniacal glint in his eyes. But instead of drawing a weapon, Fenlock raised his flute to his lips. The resulting melody was grating and harsh, far from harmonious tone you would expect.

The bandit suddenly stumbled, clutching his head in agony. "What . . . what is that sound?! Stop it!" he shrieked.

Yet, it wasn't just noise that was tormenting the bandit. The Sound Qi from Fenlock's flute was insidiously seeping into the bandit's body, tearing apart his insides.

Having ensured his disciples were occupied, Slifer subtly withdrew to a quieter corner, eager to try his luck at the gacha-like System.

> *Ding!*
> Successful
> You Have Aquired: Critical Block Card
> Description: Protects user from a critical strike.

Yes!" Slifer whispered, his face lighting up. "A Critical Block Card." Having lost his previous ones, Slifer had felt naked without them.

> *Ding!*
> Successful
> You Have Aquired: Critical Block Card
> Description: Protects user from a critical strike.

With a delighted grin, Slifer exclaimed, "Another one? My luck's been on fire lately!" He felt like he could never have too many of them. However, his joy was short-lived. The next card turned out to be a dud.

> *Ding!*
> Successful
> You Have Aquired: Whimsical Wind Card
> Description: When activated, makes the user's hair blow dramatically even in the absence of wind.

Slifer cocked an eyebrow, staring at the card in disbelief. *What in the heavens . . . ?* He couldn't help but shake his head in exasperation. "When would this ever be of use?" he muttered.

Determined to get something more valuable, he continued his card buying spree. After a few repeated failures, he finally won something interesting.

> *Ding!*
> Successful
> You Have Aquired: Mirror Wave Card
> Description: Allows the user to redirect any incoming attack back to its origin.

Slifer's eyes widened in excitement, but as he read the fine print, his enthusiasm dwindled.

Only effective against attacks below the Nascent Soul Realm? Heaving a sigh, he commented, "Well, it's still better than that ridiculous Whimsical Wind Card."

Despite the mixed results, the thrill of gambling spurred him on. But after several more fruitless attempts, Slifer decided it was time to rejoin the battle, after all, he still had two Foundation Establishment cultivators left to kill.

His gaze settled on Caelum's fight, and a frown formed on his face. Instead of the swift, decisive moves he expected from his disciple, Caelum seemed to be drawing out the fight, toying with his opponent like a cat with a mouse. He danced around, evading blows effortlessly and countering with teasing strikes, never landing a finishing blow.

"That's not the Caelum I remember," Slifer commented. "He's usually so . . . serious."

As he looked at Caelum's opponent, the System chimed in, startling him slightly.

Ding!
Appropriate Target Detected
Would you like to initiate a challenge?

Slifer blinked in surprise. "How? He's already in battle." But a thought occurred to him. Caelum hadn't actually inflicted any damage. *Is that the reason? Or is the System just being unusually generous today?*

Regardless of the reasons, Slifer wasn't one to decline an advantage. He chuckled. "I'll take whatever I can get."

"Challenge!"

Challenge Accepted
Begin

Slifer closed his eyes briefly, activating the Sunrise Slash. In the blink of an eye, he materialized behind Caelum's opponent. The man's eyes widened in shock and just as he tried to utter the word "coward," he began coughing violently. He grasped at his throat, only for his head to drop off moments later.

Ding!
Successfully Killed a Demonic Foundation Establishment Cultivator
Reward: 5 Karmic Credits
Breakthrough Requirements: 2/3

Slifer turned his gaze to Caelum, who looked taken aback by the sudden intervention. "A sword cultivator must aim for efficiency," he commented crisply. *Has Hughie's influence made Caelum toy with opponents?*

Bowing his head slightly, Caelum responded, "Thank you, Master."

Fenlock soon joined the duo, an air of satisfaction around him. His opponent's scoffing remarks about him being "soft" as a sound cultivator had cost him his life.

A sudden System notification interrupted their brief respite.

Ding!

Alert: The Village Is Under Attack
Task: Save The Villagers
Reward: Based on Number of Villagers Saved

I was wondering when this would show up, Slifer thought. Turning to his disciples, he stated with a firm voice, "We've had our fun. Now, it's time to get serious and protect these people. Leave any Early Foundation Establishment cultivators alive."

Caelum and Fenlock exchanged puzzled glances but nodded. They weren't sure why they should spare those cultivators, but they trusted their master's judgment. With a shimmer, they unleashed their Core Formation aura and jumped back into the fray.

Good, they understand, Slifer thought, nodding in approval. *Now, I just need to locate one more Foundation Establishment bandit, then I can make my exit.*

As if on cue, a voice rang out, "Old man!"

Slifer turned to find a young bandit confronting him. The youth was striking with sharp features, clear skin, and a cocky glint in his eyes.

Laughing mockingly, the bandit sneered and said, "What's a useless Qi Refining cultivator like you doing here?"

Slifer raised an eyebrow. *This fool could have taken me by surprise. Granted, not in one hit, thanks to my Critical Block Cards. But still . . .*

Shaking his head, Slifer responded with a smirk, "You might want to reconsider your strategy if you plan on surviving long in this world, young man."

The young bandit's laughter echoed, rich with disdain. "You're already one foot in the grave. Let me help you take that last step."

Slifer cocked an eyebrow. "Didn't your parents teach you to respect your elders?"

The bandit's face darkened. "My parents are dead, killed by Black Rose Sect scum."

Slifer sighed inwardly. *When will I finally face someone without a vendetta against me or my sect?*

With a smirk, the young bandit taunted, "Prepare to join them, *elder.*"

Matching his humor, Slifer retorted, "I should be saying that to you, *boy.*"

Without further ado, he activated his Sunrise Slash once more, reappearing behind his opponent. Swinging his sword downwards, he fully expected to take the bandit's head. Yet, his eyes went wide with shock as the bandit managed to turn in time, their swords clashing with a resounding ring.

With a sneer, the young fighter jeered, "Did you really think I would fall for that?"

Oh, shit. As Slifer hastily leapt backwards, he was painfully aware of his limitations. Lacking proper sword techniques and martial arts knowledge, he felt like a fish out of water.

His thoughts darted to the new card in his possession. *Guess I have to rely on you now.* With only one such card available, he needed to ensure he used it optimally. He had to provoke the bandit enough for him to unleash a devastating attack; then, with the card's power, Slifer would redirect it and finish the fight.

Slifer racked his brain. *Now how do I rile up a hot-headed teenager?* Several ideas sprung to mind but as he pondered, a chuckle escaped his lips. *Wait a minute. If teenagers here are anything like they were back home, practically anything will set them off.*

Slifer decided to go with a time-tested tactic: the insult aimed at one's family. With a playful smirk, he remarked, "Such fiery anger. Is it inherited from your parents, or did they leave you too early to pass it on?"

The young bandit's face went from pale to deep crimson. Veins popped out on his neck as he screamed, "Blazing Fire Dragon Strike!"

That's it, Slifer thought, preparing to use the card at the right moment. *Come at me with all you've got.*

From the bandit's sword, a gigantic, roaring, fire dragon emerged, its infernal heat causing the very air around it to shimmer. It lunged straight for Slifer, the intensity of its flames threatening to incinerate anything in its path.

What an idiot. With a mental command, Slifer activated the card.

Mirror Wave Card Activated

Immediately, an invisible barrier sprung up before him.

The fire dragon collided with the barrier, attempting to pierce it with its fiery fangs and claws. However, instead of breaking through, the dragon began to be pulled in, swirling and spiraling as if it were being sucked into a vortex. Within moments, it vanished completely, leaving behind an eerie silence.

The bandit paused, confusion painting his features. But before he could comprehend what had happened, a thunderous roar echoed. From behind the barrier, the very same fire dragon reappeared, this time facing its original master. Its eyes glowed brighter, and its flames seemed even more intense as it surged forward.

The bandit's eyes shot open in pure terror, realizing the danger he was in. He raised his arms in a feeble attempt to shield himself, but the sheer surprise of seeing his own technique turned against him made him too slow to react effectively. The fire dragon slammed into him with a fury, wrapping its burning body around him and drowning him in an ocean of flames.

When the inferno subsided, only the charred remains of the once-arrogant bandit were left, smoke still rising from the scorched earth.

Slifer sighed. *And that's why you never underestimate an old man.*

Ding!
Successfully Killed a Demonic Foundation Establishment Cultivator
Reward: 5 Karmic Credits
Breakthrough Requirements: 3/3
Enter Closed-Door Cultivation to Initiate Breakthrough

Ziven groggily regained consciousness, his head throbbing from the impact. As awareness returned, the distant sounds of battle echoed in his ears. Pushing himself to his feet, he stumbled out of the house, his vision blurry. When it cleared, the sight that met him was both terrifying and infuriating. A massive fire dragon was consuming a young bandit, and standing a short distance away was the old demonic cultivator, Slifer.

"No . . . it can't be . . ." Ziven's eyes widened in shock. Grief and anger clouded his vision as he recognized the young bandit. "*Xander!*"

With a bellow of fury, he launched himself at Slifer, executing the Windblade Vortex, a swirling tornado of sharp wind blades aimed directly at the old man.

Catching the movement in his peripheral vision, Slifer's eyes widened just a fraction. *What the hell is he attacking me for?* Before the attack could land, Critical Block activated, repelling the young man's assault.

Ziven, momentarily disoriented, pushed himself up and, fueled by rage, roared, launching himself at the elder once more.

I don't have the time for this. Slifer gritted his teeth. *If only the System allowed for mid-battle advancements. Is this brat really going to make me use one of my precious Peak Slifer cards?*

Yet, as Ziven drew near, a familiar figure appeared between them, parrying Ziven's onslaught with practiced ease.

The village leader's voice boomed, "Ziven! Stop this madness!"

But Ziven's eyes, clouded with grief, glared past him. "Move! He *killed* Xander! I promised I'd bring him back!"

Slifer, observing from the side, couldn't help but think, *Did that hit on the head earlier make him even more of an idiot?*

The village leader tried to soothe the anguished young man. "Ziven, Xander had turned. He was with the bandits. It's heartbreaking, but we *have* to face the truth."

Tears streamed down Ziven's face, raw emotion choking his voice, "H-he was my best friend. I *swore* I'd save him."

Slifer just stared, an incredulous expression forming. *Is this some Naruto-Sasuke situation playing out in front of me?*

Ding!
Warning: You Are Now the Target of a Son of Heaven's Wrath
Your Luck Stat Has Been Appropriately Adjusted

W-what?!

CHAPTER TWENTY

Ding!
Warning: You Are Now the Target of a Son of Heaven's Wrath
Your Luck Stat Has Been Appropriately Adjusted
Recommendation: Purchase the "Heaven's Shield Card" to Protect Yourself Against Heaven's Displeasure

---

This kid really was a protagonist, but to be able to affect my stats . . . Slifer's left eye twitched in irritation.

Ding!
Luck Is Not a Fixed Stat
It Is Swayed by the Will of Heaven

Heaven's Will . . . Slifer racked his brain. His experience from other xianxia worlds was that the Heaven's Will was an abstract concept, a guiding force that governed the fate of everything in its domain. *But what if the Heaven's Will in this world isn't the same? Perhaps only immortals have some understanding of Heaven's Will.* Slifer shook his head as he focused on his immediate concern.

Slifer quickly opened his System panel to check the cost of the recommended Heaven's Shield Card.

Card: Heaven's Shield
Description: Once activated, it forms an invisible barrier around the user, protecting them from the direct wrath of Heaven's Displeasure. The shield lasts for one month or until Heaven's Wrath is appeased.
Note: The card does not provide full protection against breakthrough tribulations, but it can lessen their intensity.
Note: It does not guarantee safety from agents or beings carrying out Heaven's Will. Repeated offenses against Heaven may weaken the card's efficacy.
Cost: 1000 Karmic Credits

The System . . . *really has a knack for stirring up trouble and then conveniently providing solutions—at an extortionate price, of course. How typical.* Slifer let out an exasperated sigh.

System, are any of my other stats compromised? He needed to ensure he wouldn't suddenly become less perceptive, rendering him as clueless as his more . . . challenged disciples.

Ding!

Negative
Only the Luck Stat Can Be Affected By Heaven's Will

Slifer exhaled deeply, the tension leaving his body. *Thank the heavens I won't end up a dimwit.* Glancing over at the enraged Ziven, Slifer pondered, *Now, how am I going to deal with this kid?*

A sudden memory flashed through his mind. It was a betrayal from his past, not in this world but in an online game.

It was the raid on Naxxramas. Slifer's guild had spent weeks planning and preparing to vanquish Kel'Thuzad. They were on the brink of victory, with the boss's health dwindling to *just* five percent.

But at that crucial moment, DrizztMagic, their primary healer, inexplicably chose to roll need on The Phylactery of Kel'Thuzad and then . . . promptly logged out.

That backstabbing— Slifer shook his head, pulling himself from the memory. *It was a game, yes. But trust is trust.*

Looking back at Ziven, Slifer's expression softened. "Betrayal is a bitter pill, young one. But be wary. Dwelling too deeply on such emotions can form a Dao demon."

Ziven glared back, tears streaking his face, "Y-you don't understand, old man. You can't!"

That's true . . . I've never experienced such a deep loss before. Slifer sighed, realizing that perhaps comparing his gaming experience to Ziven's pain might not have been the right approach.

Ding!
A Son of Heaven Poses a Threat to Your Noble Task
Action: Eliminate
Reward: 500 Karmic Credits
Warning: Killing a Son of Heaven Will Affect Your Luck

Slifer blinked at the abrupt notification, momentarily caught off guard. *Kill a Son of Heaven?* His eyes narrowed, deep in thought. *Aren't the System and the Sons of Heaven aligned on the righteous path? Why would the System want him dead? And offering such a high reward . . . what's the catch?* His attention refocused on the scene in front of him.

Ziven pushed the village leader away, his expression one of raw pain. "Remember this, old demon," he said, his voice low and threatening, "I will avenge Xander, even if it's the last thing I do."

The village leader's face turned ashen. He mumbled to himself, "Does this child wish to court death?"

Before Slifer could form a reply, a sharp pain lanced through his chest. His hand instinctively reached to clutch at the pain point as the imprisoned Origin Realm energy within him rebelled. The turbulent energy then quieted, but the fleeting pain had been sharp and unexpected.

Caelum rushed to his side, a worried expression on his face. "Master, are you alright?"

Masking his distress, Slifer waved dismissively. "I am pained that such a young soul can carry so much hatred."

Internally, Slifer frowned. *The Origin Realm energy shouldn't have acted up. Could the reduced luck stat have caused this instability?*

Seeing Slifer's darkening expression, the village leader grew even more anxious. "Esteemed Elder, please understand, Ziven is young and has faced much pain. Please, I beg you, show mercy."

Slifer barely heard him. Instead, he asked, "When did the boy begin cultivating?"

The old man, taken aback by the sudden question, stammered, "About . . . two years ago, after the death of his parents."

Foundation Establishment in just two years? Slifer's eyebrows shot up in surprise. *That's no small feat. This kid, if he's been cultivating for such a short time and reached this level, is definitely a genius.*

As Slifer contemplated the young prodigy's potential, a growing unease settled in the pit of his stomach.

I can't give him the chance to grow, Slifer thought. The guilt began to weigh on him, the idea of killing Ziven conflicted with his every moral fiber. Yet, he told himself, for survival's sake, it was necessary. *This kid could be the death of me.*

The vivid memory of novels he read, where lone protagonists obliterated entire sects to avenge a single person, sent shivers down his spine. The future was uncertain, and Slifer did not want to risk everything just because he felt bad for the kid.

Slifer turned to his disciples. "Caelum, Fenlock. Kill him."

The disciples hesitated, exchanging unsure glances.

Fenlock asked, "Both of us, Master?"

"Yes," Slifer's voice was cold and decisive.

"But Master," Caelum said, his voice wavering, "he's only at the Foundation Establishment Realm. Just one of us should suffice."

Slifer's expression darkened further, his tone leaving no room for discussion. "Attack together. Kill him in one blow."

I'm not taking any chances with a protagonist, he thought wryly. *If I'm going to kill him, I'm going all out.*

With a melancholic smile, Caelum thought, *Master remains as ruthless as ever,* before he and Fenlock lunged forward in sync.

The village elder's face went pale. "Please, have mercy! He's just—" he began, stepping forward to plead. But Slifer's raised hand silenced him. The elder hesitated, torn between helping the young cultivator and self-preservation. Finally, with a heavy sigh, he stepped back.

Ziven . . . This path was of your choosing.

Caelum lunged forward, aiming straight for Ziven's heart. However, just as steel was about to meet flash, a brilliant light burst from Ziven's body.

It was a treasure—a jade pendant emitting a radiant, protective shield. Caelum's sword collided with the barrier, causing a deafening clang and a violent rebound.

Slifer, watching intently, chuckled ruefully. *A treasure of that caliber? In the hands of a mere village boy? Only protagonists . . .*

From the other side, Fenlock's flute emitted a piercing sound wave. The barrier began vibrating violently under the sonic assault. Ziven's body shook, sweat beading on his forehead as he tried to withstand the combined might of the two assailants.

After a few seconds, the barrier shattered, propelling Ziven backwards. Fueled by desperation and rage, he roared at the heavens, and the skies responded with a thunderous echo. The familiar yellow aura surrounding him began to thicken, becoming denser, more radiant. There was a moment of absolute silence, then a burst of energy came off him.

Ziven had broken through to the Mid-Foundation Establishment Realm.

Slifer's eyes narrowed in envy. *Of course. Mid-battle breakthroughs. Always so dramatic and timely. It's a shame the System never lets me have such moments.*

Caelum, witnessing this transformation, shook his head and commented dryly, "A Mid-Foundation Establishment cultivator is still just a Foundation Establishment cultivator."

With the newfound strength from his breakthrough, Ziven knew that even then, he stood no chance against the combined might of Fenlock and Caelum.

Desperation forced him to act, and he activated another treasure—a smooth, jet-black marble. It pulsated with energy, ready to teleport him out of harm's way.

"You'll pay for this," Ziven spat, even as the darkness of the marble began to envelop him. "I swear, I'll come back and end you all!"

However, before the escape treasure could fully work its magic, Fenlock put his lips to his flute. The haunting notes pierced the air, causing Ziven to sway and stumble as he clutched his head in pain.

Seizing the opportunity, Caelum dashed in front of the staggered Ziven. Their eyes met—one filled with determination, the other with disbelief.

"No!" Ziven shouted, but his plea was cut short as Caelum's blade descended, severing his head from his body in one fluid motion.

Caelum, with practiced ease, returned his blade to its sheath and bowed deeply to Slifer. "It is done, Master."

Slifer blinked in surprise. *I had expected him to make a narrow escape. Protagonists and their pesky knack for slipping away . . .* He concealed his thoughts behind an impassive face, nodding at Caelum.

As Slifer prepared to depart, an ethereal white apparition—not quite a soul, but a shadow of Ziven's essence—emerged from the fallen body. Before Slifer could react, it merged with a peculiar token that manifested from Ziven's spirit ring.

No . . . Not this, Slifer thought, recognizing the importance of the token. *I cannot let him flee, not in any form.*

He reached for his Peak Slifer Card, ready to obliterate any trace of Ziven's essence. But before he could act, a rift in the very fabric of space manifested, swallowing the mysterious token whole.

Slifer sighed heavily. *That token . . . Could it be one of those clichéd xianxia treasures? Maybe an old master sealed within, awaiting to mentor the chosen one? Or perhaps it's a gateway to a hidden cultivation realm? Or could it be an infinite reservoir of qi?* His mind raced with possibilities. *If only I could've claimed that token for my own,* Slifer mused. But after a moment of contemplation, he grinned sardonically. *Although, the last thing I need is some elderly mentor inside a token. That'd be quite the sight—me, an old man, guided by another old man.*

Ding!
You Have Destroyed the Body of a Son of Heaven
Your Luck Stat Has Been Appropriately Adjusted
Reward: 250 Karmic Credits

Slifer's eyebrows shot up in surprise. *So, the System's feeling generous today?* he thought with a hint of suspicion. But before he could further dwell on it, another message popped up.

Ding!
The Son of Heaven Has Escaped
Warning: With Each Escape, Your Chances of Killing a Son of Heaven Decreases

---

These protagonists . . . they're like cockroaches. Slifer sighed deeply. *Resilient and ever returning.* He shook his head with a hint of exasperation. *Next time, I'll have little Val devour him whole. That should do the trick.*

Caelum stepped forward, head lowered. "Master, I apologize for my negligence. I let Ziven escape."

Fenlock, following Caelum's lead, quickly bowed as well. "It was *our* failure, Master."

Slifer motioned for them to rise. "It's unexpected," he continued, "that the young man would possess a treasure protecting his soul."

Suddenly, another message from the System popped up in Slifer's vision:

Task Complete
Calculating Reward

. . .

554 Villagers Saved
Reward: 554 Karmic Credits

Slifer's eyes widened at the notification. *Why is the System granting me a credit for each life? When I saved Lushan Village, the reward was but a fraction . . . Just what game is the System playing?*

His thoughts were interrupted as the village leader approached, kneeling before him in deep gratitude. "Elder, we owe you our lives."

Slifer gestured for him to rise. "Stand, village leader."

Then, turning to Fenlock, he commanded, "Give him five medium spirit stones."

Fenlock hesitated, a flash of panic in his eyes. *Why me?* He reluctantly took out the spirit stones from his storage ring, lamenting inwardly, *How will I be able to afford my date with Junior Sister?*

Handing over the stones, Slifer saw the village leader's face brighten with gratitude. He would have been more generous, but the encounter with Ziven had annoyed him.

The village leader, seemingly having forgotten Slifer's earlier intentions towards Ziven, beamed, holding the spirit stones. "Thank you, benefactor!" he exclaimed, bowing repeatedly.

Slifer waved him off dismissively. "Enough. It's time we left." He then addressed his disciples, "Prepare to depart." His gaze shifted in the direction of the sect, and a determined thought filled his mind: *It's finally time to break through!*

CHAPTER TWENTY-ONE

Amelia hesitantly stepped into the Medicine Hall, her eyes scanning the unfamiliar surroundings. It was her first time inside these walls. She had never needed the services of this place; any injury she received was healed using the pills her master had given her. Ironically, *she* was the reason many disciples ended up here.

To think I would be here to heal them, she thought, shaking her head in disbelief.

Inside, disciples bustled about, tending to the injured. The clatter of medicinal pots, the soft whispers, and the gentle laughter painted a peaceful picture, contrasting sharply with what one would expect from a typical demonic sect.

However, the moment Amelia entered, the atmosphere shifted. The noise quieted down as the disciples paused their tasks and turned their gaze towards her. Their expressions ranged from curiosity to caution, and for some, fear.

One particular disciple, a young girl with fair skin and braided hair, caught Amelia's gaze. Recognition flashed across both their faces. This girl had tasted Amelia's fist just a week ago, for daring to slander her beloved master. The sheer terror in the girl's eyes was apparent. She had believed *this* hall, of all places, would be her safe haven from her tormentor.

Seeing Amelia glare at her, the girl's face paled and her eyes rolled back as her body went limp.

What a weakling. She won't last long in the sect. Amelia snorted softly, her lips curling in disdain.

The head disciple, a young man with an earnest face and wearing a pristine white robe, approached her hesitantly. His eyes betrayed a mixture of respect and fear. He clasped his hands and bowed. "The grand elder is not present at the moment. To what do we owe the honor of hosting Elder Slifer's disciple in our humble Medicine Hall?"

Her master's voice echoed in her mind: *Strike first, be it words or fists*. This was the first lesson he imparted after he found her as a scared little girl. Taking a deep breath, Amelia puffed up her chest and looked down her nose at him.

"Listen closely," she began, her voice cold and haughty. "My master has assigned me a mission to save ten lives. I'm here to fulfill that task." She glanced dismissively around the hall. "Let's make this quick. There are other matters I must attend to."

A single droplet of sweat trailed down the head disciple's forehead. *Healing isn't something that can be mastered in mere hours*, he thought anxiously.

However, he wisely chose to keep his thoughts to himself. *I'd rather not be the one to deal with her,* he reflected, deciding to redirect Amelia's newfound enthusiasm to someone else.

He led Amelia to his junior sister, a delicate young woman with deep blue eyes.

"Amelia, meet Clara," he introduced.

Offering a smile that seemed somewhat forced, Clara greeted, "Welcome, Amelia."

Amelia returned the greeting with a curt nod, her posture radiating confidence, yet her eyes hinting at uncertainty. "I'm here to learn . . . healing."

Clara took a moment, choosing her words with care. "Have you practiced any healing techniques before?"

Amelia hesitated. Admitting ignorance wasn't something she was fond of, and the weight of Clara's gaze was becoming increasingly uncomfortable. But truth had its way, and she reluctantly shook her head.

Clara's smile wavered momentarily. "Very well," she said, trying to keep her voice steady. "Perhaps it would be best if you observed me today. Tomorrow, you can begin practicing on your own."

Amelia merely nodded in agreement, eager to get the day over with.

Clara then led her to their first patient: a young man. His arm was swollen, angry red marks suggesting a bad fracture. His pale face showed clear signs of pain, his eyes barely focusing on the newcomers.

Clara motioned for Amelia to come closer. "For starters, I'll use the Essence Mend technique. It's the most basic of healing techniques. By channeling my qi into the patient, it stimulates their own qi to expedite the healing process."

Amelia watched with rapt attention as Clara took a deep breath, her hands glowing faintly as she gently placed them over the patient's injured arm. Slowly but surely, the swelling started to subside, the redness fading away. The fractured bone was aligning itself, and the young man's painful grimace gradually transformed into a look of relief.

This . . . is incredible. Not as potent as Master's pills, but impressive nonetheless. Amelia's eyes widened in amazement.

Clara glanced up, catching Amelia's astounded expression. She smiled softly. "It takes time and practice. But soon, you'll be able to do it too."

Over the next couple of hours, Amelia shadowed Clara, closely watching as she healed a variety of patients. Each ailment was unique: from deep gashes to burns, from fractures to internal injuries. But after the fifth or sixth patient, Amelia's interest began to wane. The monotonous cycle of observation without participation was proving to be a tiresome affair.

Eventually, stifling a yawn, Amelia turned to Clara. "I think I've seen enough for today. I'll be heading out."

Clara, who by now seemed more at ease around Amelia, offered her a warm smile. "You did well."

Amelia paused mid-stride, eyebrows furrowed in confusion. "What do you mean? I just stood there."

"No," Clara replied, shaking her head with a soft chuckle, "you were part of the team. By being present and showing interest, you lent your support."

Amelia tilted her head slightly, processing the words. "So, you're saying I helped *heal* those patients?"

Clara hesitated for a moment, choosing her words carefully. "I guess, in a way, you did."

A bright smile blossomed on Amelia's face, one that Clara hadn't seen before. "Then you can vouch for me," she stated more than asked.

Clara nodded, laughing softly. "Of course."

I've fulfilled my task, and with time to spare! A mischievous glint appeared in Amelia's eyes. *Perhaps now I can find a lucky soul to devour.*

With a lively bounce in her step and a carefree wave to Clara, Amelia turned to leave.

The next day, Amelia stormed back into the Medicine Hall, her footsteps echoing loudly against the polished marble floor.

Whispers circulated as disciples tending to patients paused and exchanged worried glances. All remembered her from the day prior, but today she seemed more . . . volatile.

Clara looked up and met Amelia's eyes. A hint of surprise flashed across her face. "I didn't think you'd be back."

How could she act so innocent? Such two-faced behavior!

Amelia's eyes were cold and piercing as she shot back, "It must've been you who tattled to Master!" Without warning, her clenched fist launched at Clara.

The unexpected move caught the healer off guard, and with no time to react, Clara felt the full force of the blow. She was sent flying, crashing hard into the formation-reinforced wall. The impact rebounded her forward, leaving her motionless on the ground.

The room grew deathly silent, shock evident on every face.

"I never thought you'd betray me." The unfamiliar sting of betrayal gnawed at her insides. Amelia had thought, maybe, just maybe, that she had found her first friend in the sect.

Before the situation could escalate further, a rift in space tore open, revealing a stern-looking woman. With flowing raven-black hair, sharp eyes that missed no detail, and an air of authority that demanded respect, she was none other than Grand Elder Lydia, the head of the Medicine Hall.

Amelia felt a pang of unease from the immense pressure emanating from the elder. However, she remembered her master's teachings and forced herself to maintain eye contact, refusing to appear weak.

Lydia's gaze darted between the unconscious Clara and Amelia. Her lips pressed together in a thin line. "Even if you're the disciple of an Ascendant cultivator," Lydia began sternly, "I will not tolerate such behavior in my hall."

Amelia, trying to reign in her boiling emotions, retorted, "She *betrayed* my trust. She got what she deserved."

Grand Elder Lydia shook her head slowly. "Clara was here all night. When would she have found the time to run to your master?"

Amelia froze. Conflicting emotions warred within her. *If not Clara . . . then how did Master find out?*

Elder Lydia sighed, her expression softening slightly. "If you have come to learn the ways of healing, you will shadow *me* today." She paused, casting a glance back at Clara. "Let us begin with her."

She lowered herself beside Clara's unconscious form, examining the bruises and contusions that marred her pale skin. "I heard Clara introduced you to the Essence Mend technique yesterday," she stated without looking up.

Amelia hesitated briefly before nodding. "Yes, she did."

With a slight nod, Lydia commanded, "Use it. Show me."

Amelia blinked, taken aback. While she had observed the technique, executing it was an entirely different matter. But her innate talent for quickly mastering techniques bolstered her confidence. She recalled the many instances when her rapid comprehension had impressed her master.

Drawing a deep breath, she began to channel her qi, focusing on the basic principles Clara had explained. Her hands began to glow a faint blue, moving rhythmically over Clara's injuries.

However, Clara's body reacted adversely. She started twitching, her face contorting in pain, and her soft groans echoed throughout in the silent hall.

In Slifer's quarters, his meditation was interrupted by a notification:

> *Ding!*
> Due to Amelia's actions, you have received 1 Karmic Credit.

Slifer heaved a resigned sigh, rubbing his temples. *Always trouble, that one.*

Back at the Medicine Hall, Lydia immediately intervened. "Your flow is too forceful. Gentle! Like a breeze, not a storm. Focus on guiding, not forcing."

Amelia gritted her teeth, adjusting her approach. Drawing upon the Essence Mend technique's foundational principles, she began to realign her qi, pouring it with a gentler, more nurturing touch.

As the minutes passed, Clara's whimpers faded and were gradually replaced by steady breathing. Her eyelids fluttered open, revealing confusion and lingering pain. When her gaze met Amelia's, there was also a hint of fear.

Feeling a tightness in her chest, something she hadn't often experienced, Amelia offered a hesitant smile. "I'm . . . sorry, Clara."

Clara nodded slowly, her eyes still wary but also holding a trace of gratitude. "Thank you . . . for healing me."

Another one scared off. Amelia let out a sigh, feeling a sting of regret.

CHAPTER TWENTY-TWO

Seated on a plush cushion in his quarters, Slifer took a moment to reflect. The journey back had not been a comfortable one for him. He had found himself constantly looking around and upwards, half-expecting a disaster at every turn.

With my luck stat decreasing twice, it's a wonder the heavens didn't send a bolt down to finish me, he thought with a shudder. To his relief, the only real threats they encountered on their return were a few Core Formation beasts. But those were dispatched with ease by his disciples.

But with them around, at least I don't need to worry about the minor nuisances.

Taking a deep breath, Slifer leaned back and considered the events of the past day. Ever since his return, his mind had been preoccupied with preparing for the breakthrough.

Cultivation . . . A path of defiance against the very heavens, he pondered. Every cultivator, in their bid to ascend to greater power, had to face a tribulation imposed by the heavens. This was their way of testing and challenging the audacity of mortals who dared to tread too close to godhood.

Breakthroughs below the Immortal Realm, he contemplated, *are not created equal.* His mind separated the tribulations into five distinct grades. *The first grade*, he thought. *The Azure Pinnacle Tribulation.* A mental image of azure clouds gathered in his mind. These sky-blue formations indicated the arrival of a Grade 1 tribulation. The tribulation consisted of three lightning strikes, one following the other. The intensity of these strikes was determined by the level the cultivator was advancing to. In Slifer's case, it would be at the Foundation Establishment level.

His thoughts shifted to the next. Grade 2, a tribulation he was all too familiar with, was the Crimson Wave Tribulation. Contrary to its name, it wasn't a wave of water. Instead of successive strikes, five lightning bolts would come crashing down simultaneously, like a sudden tidal wave.

Surviving the Crimson means a touch of the heavens' own qi. Slifer remembered. Cultivators who endured this grade were rewarded. Merging with just a hint of that divine qi, their Foundation Establishment pillars became more fortified.

A twenty to thirty percent increase in qi quality and quantity . . .

The difference between the Azure and the Crimson could mean the difference between mediocrity and superiority.

Slifer sighed, the original had faced this very tribulation. Even among top sects where the Crimson was somewhat common, it was no mere spectacle. The intensity of the Grade 2 Origin Realm tribulation had nearly claimed the original's life.

The Grade 3 Tribulation, known as the Golden Crown Tribulation, was reserved for the true geniuses of the top sects. As the name suggested, a brilliant, mesmerizing gold would cover the skies, akin to a monarch's crown.

For this tribulation, nine lightning strikes would descend. It was as if the heavens gave a guided tour through the Foundation Establishment Realm. The first three strikes, representing the Early stage, were challenging but not insurmountable. The middle trio, symbolizing the Mid-Stage, were potent and ferocious. But it was the final trinity, signifying the Late Stage, that truly tested a cultivator's mettle.

"Beyond the increase in qi quality and quantity, there's the chance for Enlightenment," he murmured aloud. This brief but profound moment allowed cultivators to either birth a brand-new technique or master an existing one. It was a coveted opportunity as entering the state of Enlightenment naturally was almost impossible.

Caelum's Shadowstep Slash . . . Slifer wondered, deep in thought. The memory was hazy, but he felt certain that his disciple had created his signature move during that brief moment.

His thoughts then shifted to Amelia. She, too, had undergone the tribulation, and he couldn't help but wonder about the insights she might have gleaned. Unfortunately for him, the memories of the original Slifer were hazy, incomplete.

"Either the original didn't bother to ask, or the memories were lost," Slifer sighed. "Actually, given Amelia's nature," he murmured, "it's best if I remain in the dark. With her tendencies, it's likely some strange soul technique, and some things are better left undiscovered."

"The Obsidian Monarch . . ." he whispered as his thoughts turned to the fourth grade. The skies during such a tribulation would turn a deep, inky black, as if the heavens themselves were consumed by darkness.

Thirteen strikes, he thought, a knot of dread forming in his stomach. The initial nine mirrored the Golden Crown Tribulation, but it was the subsequent blows that were terrifying. "A blow from a Peak Foundation Establishment cultivator," he whispered, trying to fathom its intensity. Yet, the ultimate test was the thirteenth strike, a blow powerful enough to have come from a Core Formation expert.

"How can the heavens expect a Foundation Establishment cultivator to bear such an onslaught?" he muttered, frustration evident in his voice. "Is it a trial or a death sentence?"

His fingers tapped the armrest in contemplation. "But the reward . . ." he said, his voice trailing off.

"It includes the enlightenment of Grade 3 and something more," he whispered in awe. "A bloodline."

Bits and pieces of memories floated to the surface of Slifer's consciousness. *Hughie,* he thought. The young genius likely faced this tribulation, Slifer would need to subtly ask him later what bloodline he received. But there was *another* face intertwined with those memories, a face that left a bitter taste in his mouth—Tyrus.

Did Tyrus rely on insane luck, like Hughie? Or did he possess some other technique, some hidden strength that saw him through? If Tyrus had indeed faced and surpassed the Obsidian Monarch Tribulation, it meant he now had a bloodline. A bloodline that made him even more dangerous.

The significance wasn't lost on Slifer. A cultivator's bloodline was the essence of their identity, an intrinsic power inherited from birth.

"To acquire one," he murmured, "only the Obsidian Monarch Tribulation can grant such a reward . . . and now the System."

Obviously, those that underwent a Grade 4 tribulation at the Foundation Establishment

Realm received a weaker bloodline than those encountering it at higher realms. Still, in the eyes of the sects, even the faintest of bloodlines was a treasure. They'd leverage such disciples, essentially transforming them into the founders of new, powerful clans.

"I mean, who wouldn't want to sire an entire clan?" Slifer thought out loud, an amused smirk on his face. "Being surrounded by ethereal beauties, that'd be a dream for any vir—" He paused, chuckling. " . . . Well, for someone like me."

But that dreamlike scenario had a dark flip side. The odds of survival for these tribulations, even for prodigious talents, were abysmally low. The mere notion of facing such dire odds, especially with his recent stroke of misfortune, made Slifer's skin glisten with nervous sweat.

The perks of higher-grade tribulations—bloodlines, constitutions, enhanced spiritual roots—they all paled in comparison to the threat of obliteration. "With the System by my side, I could buy those blessings, can't I?" he whispered, trying to reassure himself. "And if I consider their actual value . . . it's a bargain."

Drawing a deep breath, Slifer tried to center himself. *Hughie's extraordinary luck should balance out my misfortune.* He tried to convince himself of the likelihood of facing a more manageable tribulation, perhaps Grade 2 or even Grade 3.

A thought suddenly struck him. "If only I could get my disciples to bear the brunt of the tribulation for me," he said, a hint of mischief in his voice. "Imagine Val and the others fending off a Grade 4 tribulation. I'd simply reap the rewards." But he quickly sobered up. The memories of the original Slifer warned against such folly. Interference in another's tribulation wasn't just discouraged; it was catastrophic.

Interfering with another's tribulation invites one's own, he shuddered at the thought.

"I don't even want to imagine what a protagonist's tribulation would be like."

Slifer's mind drifted to the Celestial Prism Tribulation, the highest grade. He almost scoffed, it wasn't worth even considering. It was a legend, an enigma; its trials and tribulations remained shrouded in mystery.

"I don't even know why it's considered part of the grades," Slifer mumbled, "the original has never met anyone who has witnessed it. I doubt even the elders of ancient sects have any reliable records of it."

Regardless, anything related to the heavens can go so wrong, he thought, rubbing his temples. *It's always best to be as prepared as possible.* And for Slifer, preparation translated to ensuring that he had enough credits on hand. He needed to be in a position to instantly buy a card if the situation called for it.

However, the System's generosity in providing Karmic Credits lately was suspicious.

It's too quiet . . . Too . . . generous. Something is amiss.

He felt the weight of impending doom, though, thankfully, it wasn't a heart attack. Slifer chuckled to himself. *Can cultivators even die from heart issues?* He pondered for a moment before grinning wryly. *Although, given what I've read, dying by furiously coughing up blood seems to be all the rage.*

His thoughts then drifted to Amelia. When she had mentioned her new healing technique, an idea had taken root in his mind and he had immediately sent her back. *If she refines that technique, perhaps I can harness its potential through my Mirror skill*, he thought. *A righteous healing technique without any need for conversion? That's savings right there.*

He nodded to himself, a plan forming. The side benefit?

Perhaps some time in the Medicine Hall will tone down Amelia's . . . aggressiveness. Slifer chuckled at the notion. The girl had a fire in her, but sometimes, even fires needed to be controlled.

If all goes well, I'll have a new technique and a less volatile disciple.

Ding!
Your Disciple Hughie Has Completed a Task
Reward: 50 Karmic Credits

Good timing, Slifer nodded. *He should be back soon.*

While waiting for Hughie's arrival, a thought popped up. "System, when can I view my own stats?"

The System Is Currently at Version 1
Upgrade to Version 2 to Access Additional Features

Raising an eyebrow, Slifer contemplated. *Interesting, an upgradable System. Just how OP can this thing become?*

Keen on pursuing this line of thought, he asked, "How do I upgrade you?"

Requirements For Upgrade:
  1. Kill a demonic cultivator. Status: Complete.
  2. Convert at least one demonic cultivator to the righteous path. Status: Incomplete.
  3. Upgrade Disciple Management Function. This will occur when all disciples achieve a breakthrough to the next major realm. Status: 0/4 Complete.

"Sounds reasonable enough."

All my disciples are exceptional in their own rights. Their breakthroughs shouldn't take too long. Slifer rubbed his chin thoughtfully. *But breaking through to the Nascent Soul Realm from Peak Core Formation . . . even for prodigies like them, it can take decades.*

He sighed. "Time isn't on my side. I need to speed things up. The faster they achieve their breakthroughs, the sooner I can upgrade."

Looking at the second requirement, he smirked. *Converting a demonic cultivator to the righteous path . . . Well, I've got that covered. It's only a matter of time.*

Status!

Name: Slifer
Race: Human
Alignment: Demonic
Cultivation: Qi Refining—9th Stage
Lifespan Remaining: 45 Days
Karmic Credits: 1300
Skills: Insight (Basic)
Items: Reversal Cards x2, Peak Slifer Card x2, Critical Block Card, Whimsical Wind Card

Abilities: Mirror Mastery: Level 1
Techniques: Sunrise Slash: Level 2
Weapon Mastery: Sword: 1%

Slifer's eyes darted over his stats, noting the healthy number of credits he had accumulated. *Having all four disciples working in tandem is a real game changer.*

He had previously compiled a list of beneficial cards to potentially utilize during the tribulation.

Critical Heal Card
Cost: 100 Karmic Credits
Description: Heals 30% of wounds instantly.

This could be crucial, especially if I face a Grade 3 Tribulation, Slifer thought.

Thunder's Ward Card
Cost: 500 Karmic Credits
Description: Grants 30% Resistance to lightning for 1 minute.

Considering the essence of the tribulations, this card seemed invaluable.

Critical Block Card
Cost: 900 Karmic Credits
Description: Protects user from a critical strike.

I won't have the luxury to gamble in the heat of tribulation. I already have one but it couldn't hurt to have another.

Impeccable Card
Cost: 1200 Karmic Credits
Description: Provides 10 seconds of absolute damage immunity.

Ten seconds of damage immunity. That could make or break the tribulation. Still, there's no urgency to buy now, he thought, trying to curb his enthusiasm. *Maybe, with Hughie around, I won't even have to spend these credits.*

The reason he hadn't picked up the Heaven's Shield Card to balance out his luck stat wasn't out of negligence. *Even with normal luck, if I face an insurmountable tribulation . . . Better to save and strategize,* he mused, relying on Hughie's luck to shield him.

His thoughts were suddenly interrupted by a familiar voice. "Master, you called for me?" Hughie hesitated at the entrance of Slifer's chamber.

It's time.

Slifer exited his quarters to find Hughie standing nervously. Slifer could sense the confusion emanating from the young man.

Clearing his throat, Slifer tried to find a logical explanation. "Hughie, I've been delving into a few . . . unique techniques. I might have drawn the attention of the heavens."

Hughie's eyes widened. *Why am I involved in this?* his posture seemed to question.

Reading Hughie's unease, Slifer reassured with a smile, "Remember the battle against Elder Olakin? I need you by my side, just like then." With a beckoning gesture, Slifer motioned for Hughie to come closer.

Hughie gulped. *He wants to . . . hold my hand? Why did the heavens bless me with such looks?* He thought frantically for a way out. "Master, perhaps Senior Brother Caelum would be better suited for this? He's quite handsome too, although maybe not at my level . . ."

Slifer's face scrunched in bewilderment. *What in the world do looks have to do with this?* He shook his head, dismissing the thought. "No, Caelum won't suffice. It has to be *you*."

Hughie's shoulders drooped, and he murmured, mostly to himself, "Senior Brother attracts all the ladies, while I . . . I keep drawing old men."

Choosing to dismiss Hughie's peculiar muttering, Slifer decided to focus on the task at hand. Grasping Hughie's hand firmly, he closed his eyes, allowing his spiritual sense to delve into his being. As he began the process of condensing his qi, a subtle shift in the atmosphere enveloped them.

Ding!
Warning: Heavenly Tribulation Triggered

Opening his eyes, Slifer noticed the sky transforming. The formation of ominous red clouds heralded the incoming tribulation.

CHAPTER TWENTY-THREE

O nly a Grade 2 tribulation," Slifer murmured with relief, watching the electric dance of the clouds with a hint of amusement. *This shouldn't take too long.*

Turning to Hughie, he clapped a heavy hand onto the boy's back, causing him to wince. "You really are my lucky charm," Slifer declared, a broad grin on his face.

Confusion marred Hughie's features. He couldn't fathom why his master needed him for what appeared to be a Foundation Establishment Realm tribulation. It all seemed so . . . ordinary.

Slifer's gaze wandered to the Critical Block Card. The Crimson Wave Tribulation was ideal for his current predicament. The fact that his disciples hadn't primarily trained in defensive techniques meant he couldn't use the Mirror technique to replicate any form of protective measure.

Just one card . . . he thought, hoping it would be enough.

Finally, the charged clouds released their pent-up fury. Five brilliant, red lightning strikes, like the fingers of an angered deity, snaked their way down from the heavens, aimed directly at Slifer.

Hughie's eyes widened in disbelief as he observed his master, who made no move to prepare any defensive technique. *Can an Ascendant cultivator's body withstand such strikes without any protection?* he wondered, doubt clouding his mind.

In the next heart-stopping moment, the five lightning bolts descended as one, aiming straight for Slifer. Just as they were about to make contact, the Critical Block Card activated. An invisible barrier shimmered into existence around him, just in time to intercept the heavenly onslaught. The lightning was easily repelled by the barrier and sent shooting outwards, striking the courtyard with deafening cracks.

The dust settled slowly, and there stood Slifer, unscathed, with a triumphant grin plastered across his face.

Hughie had seen such a phenomenon before, where attacks seemed to refuse to land on his master. *Is it even possible for a lower realm attack to touch an Ascendant Realm master?* he wondered, utterly baffled.

As Slifer absorbed traces of the heavenly qi, he felt a profound sense of satisfaction. The energy merged with his nascent pillar, a feeling that left him momentarily lost in its pleasure. Gazing at the dissipating remnants of the tribulation, Slifer scoffed. "I didn't even need to prepare for this."

Hughie could only manage a nervous sweat. *Why is Master so proud of overcoming a tribulation meant for the Foundation Establishment Realm?* he thought, not daring to voice it out loud.

But then, Slifer's expression abruptly changed. His self-satisfied smile faltered, replaced by a frown of confusion. *Wait a minute, why hasn't my first pillar been completed?* he thought anxiously.

It was common knowledge that the Foundation Establishment Realm consisted of nine qi pillars. Surviving the tribulation should have solidified the first one. Yet, nothing happened.

Determined, Slifer attempted to manually complete the pillar by manipulating his qi. Despite his efforts, frustration mounted as the pillar stubbornly remained ninety percent complete. After several failed attempts, he couldn't help cursing under his breath, suspecting the System's involvement. *Is the System preventing my progress?*

His thoughts, however, were abruptly interrupted by Hughie's soft muttering. "Obsidian Monarch Tribulation," the disciple whispered, seemingly to himself, but the words caught Slifer's attention immediately.

Slifer snapped his head towards Hughie. "What did you just say?" he asked sharply, the previous issue with the pillar momentarily forgotten.

Hughie's hand trembled as he pointed upwards, drawing Slifer's gaze to the heavens. The elder cultivator's eyes widened in disbelief, taking in the sight of an unnaturally darkened sky. Midday, yet the heavens were consumed by an inky black. An unmistakable sign of . . . the Obsidian Monarch Tribulation.

Ding!
Warning: Heavenly Tribulation Triggered

Shit . . . this . . . this isn't even fair, Slifer cursed inwardly. He had scoured the original's memories and found no mention of facing multiple tribulations in succession.

With an accusing glance towards Hughie, Slifer muttered, "I expected more from you."

Bewildered, Hughie responded, "Master, what did you want from me?" His thoughts raced. *If Master feels lonely, surely the sect has many maidens eager for his company. Why drag me into this?*

Slifer's thoughts raced even as the tribulation gathered momentum. *I need that Impeccable Card now.* But when he tried to purchase it, an unwelcome message from the System interrupted him.

Error: Shop Unavailable During Tribulation

He stood there, stunned, face turning a shade of red from frustration. *The System . . . It knew! It knew my plan all along!* His thoughts were abruptly halted by the sight of the first black lightning strike descending upon him.

Without wasting another moment, Slifer activated the Peak Slifer Card. Immediately, nine sturdy qi pillars took shape within him but just as swiftly as they formed, they shattered, coalescing into a golden core. The core quickly dissolved, giving way to a Nascent Soul, which expanded continuously, threatening to burst from the immense power it contained.

"I missed this," Slifer whispered, a surge of near-Origin realm power coursing through him, invigorating every fiber of his being.

The first lightning bolt hurtled towards him with alarming speed. Reacting instantly, Slifer channeled qi into his palms and forcefully slapped the strike away, redirecting it into a nearby tree. Watching the tree burst into a fiery blaze, Slifer's eyes widened in alarm. *Not a tree . . . anything but a tree!* he chastised himself.

Almost instantly, two more lightning bolts rushed at him. With swift reflexes, Slifer diverted them upwards, redirecting their trajectory back towards the heavens. *Take that!* he thought defiantly, fully aware that such an act couldn't possibly injure the heavens, but the symbolic gesture still brought him satisfaction.

The onslaught ceased momentarily after the third bolt, and Slifer lifted his gaze to the skies. He recognized the pattern—every three strikes grew in ferocity. Taking a deep breath, he shouted, "Come on! Give me your best shot!" Every second counted with the Peak Slifer Card's time constraint.

The heavens responded with a thunderous roar, sending three more bolts. With graceful motions, Slifer repelled them one by one. But the presence of the thirteenth strike was undeniable, even Hughie shifted uncomfortably from the aura it released.

With a resounding crack, Slifer met the strike head-on, deflecting it with a powerful swipe of his hand. After the last assault, he inspected his hand, noting the scorch marks with a pained grimace.

As the last remnants of the tribulation clouds disappeared with a roar, Slifer sighed in relief. *It's finally over.*

However, his relief was short-lived. Peering within himself, he discovered the Foundation Establishment pillar was stuck at ninety-nine percent.

He shot a wary glance at the sky, squinting against the dissipating clouds. *Don't you dare send another one*, he mentally warned the heavens.

The heavens didn't seem to have taken Slifer's warnings seriously as a multi-colored cloud began to take shape in the sky.

"No," Slifer whispered, dread apparent in his eyes. Beside him, Hughie, already pale, stammered, "Ce . . . Celestial Prism."

Yet, to their astonishment, the swirling cloud didn't coalesce. Instead, it crumbled apart, the sky gradually returning to the calm blue of midday.

Slifer's body sagged with relief. *That was too close. A strike from the Nascent Soul Realm . . .* he mused, shuddering at the mere thought.

However, before he could process the turn of events further, an overwhelming dizziness gripped him. Clutching his head in bewilderment, he tried to steady himself. When his vision cleared, he found himself surrounded by an endless expanse of white, the familiar surroundings nowhere in sight.

Outside, Hughie's demeanor shifted to an unusual seriousness. He recognized the signs—his master had entered a state of Enlightenment. Grasping Slifer's hand more firmly, he stood guard. Any disturbance during such a pivotal moment could have grave consequences.

Where am I? Slifer wondered, but then a sliver of memory from his predecessor surfaced. During Enlightenment, a cultivator's consciousness transcended, supposedly establishing a faint link with the heavens.

With this realization, Slifer closed his eyes, surrendering to the meditative state that he'd become familiar with through countless cultivation sessions. But nothing could have prepared him for what followed. An influx of information, vast and dense, cascaded into his mind with crushing weight. He felt as though his mind would be pulverized under the relentless torrent of knowledge.

I must focus, he reminded himself amidst the chaos, recognizing the monumental opportunity before him. This was more than just survival; it was his chance to create a technique of his own.

Slifer decided on creating a defensive sword technique. He already possessed the Sunrise Slash, an attack method, and he reasoned that a corresponding defense technique would make a complete set.

The light essence from the Sunrise Slash was already a part of his repertoire. *It only makes sense to continue down this path. Light is both illuminating and forceful,* he thought. There weren't clear guides or structured lessons in the information, but rather raw and powerful insights about the sword's essence.

The accelerated speed of his thoughts astounded him, making complex tasks seem simple. He swiftly sifted through the overwhelming influx of information, zeroing in on details related to sword techniques and the light element.

Condense light through sword strikes . . . create a shield . . . explode outwards upon impact . . . Slifer pondered, his mind working feverishly. He envisioned a technique that channeled light through the sword, solidifying into a radiant shield. This shield would then burst outwards when struck, repelling incoming attacks.

The number of strikes determines the shield's potency, he surmised. *The first strike could probably hold off an Early Foundation Establishment attack, and with the third strike, it could resist even a Late Foundation Establishment assault.*

He fine-tuned his method, occasionally discarding certain steps. "The angle of the second slash needs to be sharper," he murmured, "and the timing between the strikes . . . it's crucial. Too fast, and the light won't condense properly. Too slow, and the defense will be riddled with gaps."

After what felt like a lifetime, Slifer felt his consciousness begin the journey back to his physical form as the separation between the Enlightenment state and the tangible world blurred, then solidified. The sounds and scents of the outside world flooded back to him.

Opening his eyes, a contented sigh left him, and he whispered the name of his newly crafted technique, Stellar Nova Strike. Though the name hinted at aggression, the "strikes" were, in fact, the foundation of his defense.

Upon hearing his master's whisper, Hughie's eyes sparkled with a trace of respect. *A new technique crafted by an Ascendant being,* he thought, filled with wonder. *Perhaps Peak Earth Rank, or maybe even Heaven Rank.*

Hughie was curious about what sort of heaven-defying technique his master had created during his state of Enlightenment, but he held his tongue, aware of his master's . . . slight paranoia.

Slifer sighed, a hint of longing in his breath. He missed the exhilarating clarity of Enlightenment; now, his thoughts trudged along at a pace that felt painfully slow. He looked down, surprised to find his hand still clasped in Hughie's. He quickly released it. *Best not give my disciples the wrong idea.*

Congratulations on creating a new technique!
Reward: 200 Karmic Credits
Technique Name: Stellar Nova Strike
Rank: Mid-Earth
Description: A light-element defensive sword technique that harnesses consecutive strikes to form an explosive shield of condensed light.

Mid-Earth Rank. Not too shabby. Slifer nodded with satisfaction.

Congratulations on successfully breaking through to the Foundation Establishment Realm!
Reward: 100 Karmic Credits

One step closer to the original's cultivation, Slifer thought. *Foundation Establishment might be insignificant, but for an out-of-shape man from another world, it's a huge accomplishment. Though this blasted System's a double-edged sword . . .*

With a simple wave of his hand, Slifer dismissed Hughie, who didn't waste any time scampering off.

Once alone, Slifer entered his quarters and with a faint smile, summoned his status screen.

Name: Slifer
Race: Human
Alignment: Demonic
Cultivation: Early Foundation Realm (1/9)
Lifespan Remaining: 45 Days
Karmic Credits: 1600
Skills: Insight (Basic)
Items: Reversal Cards x2, Peak Slifer Card, Whimsical Wind Card
Abilities: Mirror Mastery: Level 1
Techniques: Sunrise Slash: Level 2, Stellar Nova Strike: Level 1
Weapon Mastery: Sword: 5%

However, his grin quickly turned into a frown as he saw there was no change in his lifespan, not even by a single day.

Typically, reaching the Foundation Establishment Realm should've added a century to my life. But since this body already achieved that once . . . He mused, the realization sinking in. *Makes sense, I suppose. Otherwise, we'd all just yo-yo between realms for eternal life.*

With a resigned sigh, he muttered, "I'll have to rely on those Reversal Cards then."

Slifer then shifted his focus to the anticipated new bloodline—a reward for conquering the Obsidian Monarch Tribulation.

A Peak Slifer Card for a bloodline? Definitely worth the trade. He consoled himself, still somewhat skeptical. Yet, his anticipation turned to annoyance when he found no trace of any new bloodline. *Did the heavens scam me?*

Congratulations on acquiring a new bloodline!
Bloodline Name: ???
Requirements to Unlock: ???

CHAPTER TWENTY-FOUR

Congratulations on acquiring a new bloodline!
Bloodline Name: ???
Requirements to Unlock: ???

Slifer frowned, letting out an exasperated grunt. "Great! A mysterious bloodline that I can't even access. How very . . . helpful."

Just watch, I'll be on the brink of death, cornered by some lord from the netherworld, and THEN this overpowered bloodline will kick in to save the day. He rolled his eyes.

Pushing the bloodline to the back of his mind, Slifer turned his focus to his new technique. He summoned his sword from his storage ring. Though it was the same sword with the familiar orange hilt, something felt . . . different.

As he gripped the hilt, a sensation coursed through him, like the sword was whispering to him. *Kill, kill, kill . . .* It wasn't the most pleasant of feelings, but what could he expect from a blade that originated from a demonic sect?

Ding!
Congratulations on comprehending Sword Intent!
Reward: 100 Karmic Credits

His eyes widened slightly. *So, this is Sword Intent?* he pondered, understanding that the bond between blade and bearer was crucial to a sword cultivator's true power. Sword Intent marked the first step in sword cultivation, potentially boosting a cultivator's attack by an entire sub-realm.

"Not bad," he muttered appreciatively.

As Slifer swung his sword around, he could feel a significant difference due to the four percent increase in his sword mastery. The air itself seemed to part more smoothly before the blade, every motion more fluid and precise.

Closing his eyes, he channeled his qi and intent into the sword, channeling the Sunrise Slash technique. In an instant, he was before a dummy, and with a swift, clean movement, its head tumbled to the ground.

Grinning at the effortless cut, he couldn't help but boast a little. "At this rate, I might just stand a chance against a Peak Foundation Establishment cultivator. Well . . . that is, if I catch them off guard."

Energized, he readied himself to test out the Stellar Nova Strike technique. Positioning himself, he performed three deliberate sword strikes. Each motion gathered the ambient light element, focusing and refining it until a radiant shield of condensed light blossomed around him. Observing the shield critically, he nodded in satisfaction but recognized its current limitations.

He paused for a moment. "Needs to be stronger," he reflected, aware that the technique was still in its initial phase, merely at level 1. "And I'll do that the best way I know how." He took a breath, adding, "By facing real threats." A brief hesitation followed before he corrected himself. "Well, maybe not a *real* battle. After all, I can't risk getting killed. It's not like I have an endless stash of cards to rescue me . . . But one of my disciples will do just fine."

A spiritual transmission abruptly pulled Slifer out of his musings. Morvran's voice echoed in his mind, "Master, Val has woken up."

A grin spread across Slifer's face. "Guess I've got a training buddy now," he commented out loud.

He arrived at the beast chamber, a place designated for housing beasts below the Core Formation Realm. The beasts of Core Formation Realm and above usually dwelled in their own habitats, like Val with her . . . cave. He felt a slight shudder run down his spine at the memory.

Slifer scanned his surroundings, seeing magnificent beasts, that he had believed to be only in fairy tales, caged like this made Slifer shake his head in disapproval. *Such primitive ways of taming beasts,* he thought sadly.

He had always had an affinity for animals, and while these beasts weren't exactly . . . pets, Slifer believed there had to be a better way to tame them. "Maybe once I get my stuff sorted, I'll see if I can change some stuff around," he mumbled to himself.

A disciple approached and offered a respectful bow. "Senior Slifer, your beast awaits you in one of the healing chambers."

Slifer barely held back a sigh. To him, it made more sense to treat these beasts as partners rather than mere tools. *A deeper connection would surely yield better results in combat.* "It's all about synergy, like Kiba and Akamaru," he muttered.

The disciple looked up in confusion. "Elder?"

Slifer waved him off. "Never mind, just take me to Val."

As they entered the healing chamber, his eyes were immediately drawn to the center. There lay little Val surrounded by a series of intricate formations, too complex for Slifer to even attempt to decipher.

Feeling her master's presence, Val lifted her head and her eyes lit up with delight. With a joyful squeak, she swiftly rose and flew straight into Slifer's waiting arms.

Turning to the disciple, who stood awkwardly observing the reunion, Slifer gave him a blank stare. The young man cleared his throat awkwardly. "I shall take my leave, Elder." With a swift bow, he quickly exited the chamber.

Immediately, Slifer's stern exterior melted away, replaced by a look of tender concern. "How are you feeling?" he asked, his fingers gently brushing over the spot where Val had been injured.

Val tilted her head, attempting to muster a serious expression. "Me all bettew now."

Noticing the absence of even a faint scar, Slifer nodded in relief. "Master is glad. Val had us all worried."

Val blinked her large eyes. "How Mastew? Val wowwied Mastew huwt."

A warm smile spread across Slifer's face. "Master is good, little one. I got rid of the big bad guy who hurt you."

Val's round eyes widened even more. "Bad man hit Val for no weason."

"That's right," Slifer affirmed, hugging the baby dragon a bit tighter. "Val didn't deserve that."

The little dragon shook her head earnestly, her eyes still shining with innocence. "Val good."

Slifer's eyes sparkled with mischief. "But guess what? Master has a present for you!"

"Pwesent? What pwesent?"

"It's a surprise," Slifer teased.

Val's face scrunched up in a pout. "No supwise!" she declared adamantly.

After a playful pause, Slifer continued, "How would you . . . like to be my *disciple*?"

Val blinked, clearly confused. "Me monsta. How can monsta be disciple?"

Slifer sighed inwardly. *From the original's memories, I never heard of beasts becoming disciples. And about beasts taking human forms? Either that doesn't exist here, or it's reserved for those in the Immortal Realm.*

He gently patted Val's head, trying to reassure her. "Master doesn't see you as a monster." After a moment's pause, he softly added, "So, what do you think?"

Tears brimmed in Val's eyes as she whispered, "Val be Mastew disciple."

Slifer smiled as he swiftly opened up the Shop and scrolled through until he found the card he was looking for.

Name: Soul Bond Card
Description: Establishes a telepathic link between the user and the creature. The card grants the user the ability to utilize a random ability from the creature once a day.
Warning: If the creature is killed, the user's soul will be severely damaged.
Cost: 900 Karmic Credits

Slifer looked down at Val, her big eyes filled with hope and trust.

She's worth it. Without hesitation, Slifer made the purchase, applying the Soul Bond Card to Val.

Almost immediately, a burning sensation seared his chest, causing him to look beneath his robes. He was met with the mark of a dragon. This mark, however, wasn't just skin deep—it was as if it had imprinted itself onto his very spirit.

Ding!
Soul Bond Successful
Randomizing Ability
. . .
Ding!
You Have Gained the Ability "Firebreath"

I can breathe fire? That's pretty cool!

Congratulations on gaining a special disciple!
Your Disciple Capacity Has Been Adjusted
You have gained 100 Karmic Credits.

Good, she didn't take up a traditional disciple slot, Slifer thought with a hint of relief. *I still need an open spot for the upcoming Disciple Selection Ceremony. There's no telling who or what potential I might encounter there.*

Closing his eyes, Slifer decided to focus on the newly formed bond. He could sense Val's feelings, her immense joy and overwhelming emotion, and he knew he could pinpoint her location regardless of the distance.

As he opened his eyes, he saw a similar mark on Val. But it wasn't the image of Slifer—it was a blurry outline of a young man. *That's . . . Zack. My original body. So even in this form, my soul retains its original identity*, he thought, taken aback by the revelation.

Val's voice interrupted his thoughts. "Val feel . . . funny."

Slifer, recovering quickly, pinched her plump cheek affectionately. "We now have a Soul Bond."

Val's already wide eyes seemed to grow even larger with wonder. She knew that Soul Bonds were rare, transforming the typical master-servant dynamic to something far more profound, almost akin to equals. Tears formed in her eyes as she stammered, "Val so . . . so happy."

Hugging her closer, Slifer whispered, "Master is happy too." After enjoying the peaceful moment, Slifer coughed slightly to regain composure. "Master needs help practicing a defensive technique."

Val's head popped up, her eyes filled with eagerness. "Val help!"

Yet, seeing her overwhelming enthusiasm, Slifer hesitated, second-guessing his request. *Is it really a smart idea to ask a Nascent Soul level beast to attack me?*

Val seemed to pick up on his hesitation. "Val pwomise be gentle," she mumbled, her tiny snout drooping slightly.

A small chuckle escaped Slifer's lips, though doubts still danced in his mind. *Does she even know her own strength?* Yet, looking into those innocent eyes, Slifer couldn't resist nodding in agreement. *Eh, maybe I'll get to use her own firebreath attack against her.* He smirked, imagining the look of surprise on Val's face. *Now, that'll be an interesting sight.*

CHAPTER TWENTY-FIVE

Back at Slifer's courtyard, he turned to Val, his expression serious. "Val, I need you to restrict your cultivation to the Early Foundation Establishment stage."

Val's large, round eyes blinked in confusion. "Why, Mastew?"

Slifer pondered how best to explain it, then chose a slightly convoluted explanation. "It's because by tempering the technique against a milder flame, we can detect more subtle flaws."

Val's expression only grew more puzzled, but she stubbornly nodded. "Okay. Val stay small."

Slifer pressed his lips together to keep from smiling. *The ego of a dragon*, he thought, *always too proud to admit when they don't understand.*

He observed closely as Val's Nascent Soul aura began to recede. It shrank to the Core Formation level and continued dropping until it stabilized at the Foundation Establishment stage. Cultivators could suppress their power, but without a formation or seal, it was merely a temporary measure. Any loss of concentration could lead to an accidental release of their true strength and *that* could be deadly,

Slifer exhaled in relief upon noticing he still possessed a Critical Block Card. *You never know, this might come in handy.*

Eager to begin, Val's wings flapped vigorously. "Mastew, weady?"

Gripping his sword firmly, Slifer nodded. "Yes. Attack me with your firebreath."

With a graceful leap, little Val soared into the air. She paused, hovering, then opened her small mouth. A moment later, she exhaled a concentrated fireball, its heat distorting the air as it barreled towards Slifer.

He took a slow, deep breath, centering himself. Channeling his qi into his sword, Slifer danced through the three movements of the Stellar Nova technique with swift precision. Just as the firebreath was about to make contact, a barrier of light formed around him. The next moment, Val's fireball crashed against the barrier. Instead of swallowing him, the impact caused the barrier to burst outwards in a radiant explosion, and a thick layer of smoke and dust flew into the air, masking his vision.

As the dust faded, he glanced down and couldn't help but smirk at the lack of any injuries on himself. But then, an annoyed squeak echoed.

Looking up, Slifer saw Val, her cute face covered in soot. "Dat not nice, Mastew," she muttered, her voice carrying a hint of a whine.

Slifer's laughed, "Try again, Val. This time, Late Foundation Establishment level."

Her little face contorted in annoyance. Taking a deep breath, she spat out fire just as Slifer completed his third sword movement. The fire seemed stronger, and when it met Slifer's defense, a larger explosion followed, sending more dust into the air.

A triumphant giggle echoed. "Got Mastew, now Mastew diwty."

As the dust began to clear, Slifer located the source of the voice: Val, sitting proudly on a tree branch.

Yet when she saw Slifer, untouched by smoke or dirt, her joy turned to a pout. "Dis boring," she declared with a hint of frustration. "Take dis!"

To Slifer's surprise, Val began morphing into her more menacing form. She unleashed a roar, and then, an inferno from her mouth.

"Stop!" Slifer shouted, but Val was too engrossed.

No choice. I won't waste a card on this. Focusing on the Soul Bond skill, Slifer felt a powerful heat build up within him. The sensation was overwhelming, as if the very core of Val's essence was melding with his own. He opened his mouth, and to his amazement, a brilliant stream of fire erupted at the Nascent Soul level.

The two fire streams met in the air, clashing and swirling in a tempestuous dance. However, Slifer's firebreath slowly began to overpower Val's. The fiery onslaught struck her directly, and her roar of defiance turned into a pained whimper. She shrank back to her original size, the powerful beast reduced once again to a small, delicate creature.

Slifer hurriedly closed his mouth, dashing towards Val as she gently floated down onto the ground. He hesitated for a moment, seeing her crunched up posture, her face turned away. "Val?" he asked softly, extending a cautious hand to turn her face towards him.

Suddenly, Val turned, letting out a small roar. Her eyes twinkled mischievously. "I twick Mastew!" she giggled.

Slifer exhaled deeply, a mixture of relief and exasperation. "You always trying to trick Master, Val. But one day, Master might get hurt."

She blinked. "But Mastew most powewful," she mumbled.

Shaking his head, Slifer replied, "Master is old, Val. You need to take care of Master."

As he watched her, Slifer could see the wheels turning in her head. "Mastew old, Mastew die?" she asked with a touch of fear.

Slifer couldn't help but laugh at her sincere concern. "If you sneak attack me like that, then maybe one day I die."

Val's eyes widened, and she quickly nodded, her expression serious. "Val, pwomise no sneak attack. Val pwotect old Mastew."

Smiling, Slifer gently rubbed her head. "Yes, protect Master." But as he gazed into the distance, a sobering thought crossed his mind. *No, seriously. If she keeps up with these "tricks," she might actually kill me.*

His gaze drifted around the courtyard. Morvran had just recently cleaned up the aftermath of the tribulation. Now, due to their playful skirmish, it looked like a mess. Slifer felt a pang of guilt. *Poor Morvran. He'll have to clean this all up. Again.*

Taking Val to the sect's training grounds would have been a safer option, but the last thing Slifer wanted was prying eyes observing their every move. In front of Val, he could maintain an air of mastery, but in front of others . . . *Others are more astute. I can't risk looking foolish.*

Grrrrowl.

Both Slifer and Val snapped their heads towards the origin of the sound. Their eyes met, a hint of embarrassment evident in Slifer's gaze. Clearing his throat, Slifer quickly said, "Val trained hard today. Val deserves a snack."

Val's eyes sparkled with excitement. "Val want . . . umm, fingies? Or tasty eaw? Or, or . . . tendew toesies?" she babbled, her words not quite hitting the mark.

Slifer's face turned a shade paler, realizing she was referring to what a dragon would naturally prefer—human meat. He hastily interrupted her, "Uh, I was thinking maybe some . . . dumplings?"

Val pondered for a moment, then nodded enthusiastically. "Val wike dumpwings."

Oh, thank the heavens, Slifer thought with a deep sigh of relief. *Because I definitely don't have any pieces of "hoomans" laying around.*

In the easternmost pavilion of the sect, surrounded by majestic silver pine trees, sat a middle-aged man, his stern face framed by a meticulously trimmed goatee. He had sharp cheekbones, a hawk-like nose, and piercing black eyes.

A light knock echoed, and a frail-looking messenger timidly entered the room, bowing deeply. "Honorable Grand Elder Darius," he began hesitantly, "a tribulation has occurred at Supreme Elder Slifer's pavilion."

Darius's eyes narrowed dangerously, and with a flicker of his intent, the messenger began to choke, clutching at his neck desperately. The pressure from the elder's aura felt like a noose tightening. "That brat is no supreme elder," Darius growled.

The messenger, face turning blue, managed a croak. "Apologies, Grand Elder!"

Ah, Slifer, Darius mused, memories flooding back. *Always the sect master's pet, his faithful lapdog.*

Releasing his aura's stranglehold, Grand Elder Darius sighed, a hint of annoyance still evident. "To think that a brat from the sect master's camp broke through to the Ascendant Realm," he thought aloud, shaking his head.

Failed tribulation, damaged cultivation base, that brief flicker of the Soul Lamp, and now an attack at the Ascendant Realm? What game is the sect master playing? Could it be . . . He hesitated for a moment, the mere thought sending chills down his spine. *Has a demon lord from the Nether Realm taken over that fool's body?*

Coming back to the present, Grand Elder Darius fixed his gaze on the messenger. "Contact Grand Elder Wyatt for a meeting," he ordered.

The messenger hesitated for a moment, seemingly gathering courage, then asked, "W-what about Grand Elder Lydia or Grand Elder Tenzin?"

Darius let out a derisive snort, his face twisted in contempt. "The Medicine Hall doesn't meddle in politics," he retorted bitterly. "As for that weasel, he has already caved in to the brat's whims. No spine, as expected."

The messenger nodded quickly, ready to depart, when he heard Darius mutter under his breath, "There's not enough room in this sect for another supreme elder . . . especially one that isn't me."

There were four distinct camps that had emerged within the sect over the years: the sect master's camp, and the factions of the three grand elders. Each wielded power, overseeing various resources that made the sect function. The unexpected emergence of a supreme elder threatened this balance, potentially diluting their influence.

If this new "supreme elder" takes root, Darius pondered, *the share of resources for my camp will shrink.*

Scowling, he rose from his seat, pacing the empty room. "We must suppress this so-called supreme elder. And fast." His fingers grazed a worn amulet lying on the nearby table. As he picked it up and put it on, he whispered to himself, "At least for now—until I break through."

* * *

Slifer strolled towards Leah's quarters, munching on dumplings with little Val perched on his shoulder. Val, though she loved the treat, had a knack for accidentally scorching half her share just by breathing a tad too hard. It was both amusing and frustrating. By the time they reached Leah's door, only a few dumplings remained in their containers.

Slifer gave her a sideways glance and mumbled, "Maybe try less fire, more eat."

Val turned her big, innocent eyes towards him, a visible pout forming on her messy mouth, "Val sowwy."

Slifer chuckled, patting her tiny head. "It's okay. Just remember for next time."

Arriving outside Leah's quarters, Slifer decided to go old-school and knocked. It felt weird. *Why knock when you could send a mental memo via spiritual transmission?*

After what seemed like forever (but was probably just ten seconds), the door creaked open a smidge, revealing a cautious eye.

"Ah, Leah," Slifer greeted with a smile, "I hope you have reconsidered my offer."

Leah's face twisted into a scowl, her body tensing for what Slifer guessed was another attempt to spit at him. But suddenly, her eyes widened, and a high-pitched squeal escaped her lips. She flung the door wide open and lunged towards Slifer.

Is this some ploy to attack me? Slifer wondered, tensing up. But he relaxed slightly, remembering the qi-restraining cuffs she wore. Though they looked much like mundane cuffs from Earth, these were especially designed for cultivators. The inscriptions on them made even mountain-shattering cultivators as harmless as toddlers.

"SO CUTE!" Leah shrieked.

Slifer backpedaled, pulling Val protectively closer. But Val, unused to being the center of such frenzied attention, toppled from his shoulder.

Leah, quick as a flash, caught the tiny dragon in her arms, hugging her close and cooing, "You're staying with me."

Slifer shook his head slowly. "Val doesn't belong to anyone," he began, and silently added, *Except me.*

Leah, seemingly oblivious to his disapproval, pinched Val's chubby cheeks, cooing, "But she's just a baby, she needs someone to take care of her."

Slifer watched the scene, a knot of confusion forming in his stomach. This was the same haughty, self-centered girl who had been hurling death threats at him just days ago, and now here she was, fawning over his . . . disciple? *It must be true*, he nodded, *cuteness is indeed a girl's biggest weakness.*

Val, however, didn't seem to appreciate Leah's affections. With a scowl, she wriggled out of Leah's hold and flew to hover beside Slifer. Puffing out her tiny chest, she proclaimed with babyish dignity, "Val big dwagon."

Leah looked down at Val, a chuckle threatening to spill from her lips. Clearly, she found the pint-sized dragon's bravado endearing.

Val's eyes flared, and she looked ready to transform into her massive form, but a gentle pat from Slifer calmed her down.

His gaze then shifted to Leah, her playful demeanor melting away as their eyes met. The air grew cold, charged with tension. *Ah, there's the Leah I remember*, he thought.

Slifer had been careful over the past few days to ensure Leah's comfort. Though she was under house arrest and far from the pampered life she'd known at the Black Heart Sect, he'd instructed the servants to cater to her every need. *A bit of carrot before the whip*, he'd mused.

His face hardened as he addressed her. "I warned you, girl. If you don't accept my offer, the dungeon awaits you," he said, pausing for effect before adding, "and Morvran . . . He's expressed a rather keen interest in 'visiting' you there."

Leah's face paled as she remembered the death warrior who was all too eager to see her suffer. Still, defiance sparked in her eyes as she tried to bargain. "Maybe, if you give me the dragon," she motioned towards Val, "I'll consider your offer."

Val's orange-scaled face turned a deeper shade of red, indignation clear in her eyes. The audacity of the human before her was incomprehensible.

Slifer's laugh echoed gently, cutting through the tension. "Like I've said, no one owns her." Internally, he sized up Leah. *She's sharp and has had time to understand her predicament. The only thing holding her back is her ego, but with just a slight nudge, her stubborn pride will give in.*

He turned his attention to Val, offering a suggestion with a gleam in his eyes. "Why not spend some time with Leah?"

Val tilted her head defiantly. "Val no wike cwazy lady."

Slifer couldn't help but smile at her straightforwardness. Leaning closer to Val, he whispered, "Master needs Val's help to keep an eye on her. Will you do that for Master?"

The tiny dragon, feeling a surge of responsibility, puffed out her chest proudly. "Val make suwe cwazy lady no escape." With renewed purpose, she darted over to hover near Leah, casting wary glances at her.

Once Val warms her up, all I need is the perfect setup, Slifer schemed internally. The idea was already taking shape: *I'll engineer a scenario where I rescue Leah from her old sect, making her feel indebted to me.* His plan was forming, and the pieces were slowly coming into place.

Ding!
Task Assigned: Dragon Babysitting a Crazy Lady
Disciple: Val
Task Description: Ensure Val stays beside Leah for . . . 7 days!
Reward: 70 Karmic Credits

Slifer blinked in surprise. *Seventy credits for such a simple task?*

He quickly sent a spiritual transmission directly to Val. "Master needs you to stay with her for seven days."

Just as Val opened her mouth, probably to bombard him with protests, Slifer turned on his heel and disappeared around the corner.

After all, he had more pressing concerns to think about. *The Disciple Selection Ceremony is drawing closer*, he remembered. *I guess it's about time for another master-disciple circle.*

CHAPTER TWENTY-SIX

Amelia's eyes darted around the circle, settling for a moment on each disciple. The last time Master Slifer had summoned them all was only a few days ago, as for before that it was . . . she couldn't remember, it had been too long. "What could be so urgent?" she whispered, leaning towards Caelum.

Caelum merely shrugged, his focus fixed on Bloodthorn, the sword on his lap. The faint red glow of the blade mirrored in his eyes as he tried to deepen the connection between them.

Hughie shifted uneasily in his seat, deliberately positioning himself in such a way that Slifer would have to turn to face him directly. "I really have to find a way to divert Master's attention from me." The recent attention from Slifer was . . . unsettling.

Across the circle, Amelia shot Fenlock a venomous glare. "You should address me as *Senior* Sister," she hissed under her breath, her pride wounded. *It doesn't matter if he's older or has a higher cultivation realm. I've been Master's disciple longer.*

Fenlock stiffened, feeling the intensity of Amelia's gaze. *I hope Junior Sister Lenvari doesn't hear about this*, he thought worriedly. *She might get the wrong impression.* Trying to appear nonchalant, he averted his eyes from Amelia, gazing at the ground instead.

The creaking sound of a door interrupted their individual musings. Every head turned as Slifer emerged from his quarters, he had a blank expression and the disciple noticed a few crumbs clinging to his robes.

Hughie whispered to Amelia, nodding subtly at the crumbs. "Master has been . . . eating?"

Amelia stifled a giggle, responding, "Seems like that's all he does these days."

Caelum raised an eyebrow but said nothing, silently hoping the crumbs had nothing to do with their urgent summons, he really couldn't afford to waste time bringing his master another meal.

Slifer's eyes scanned the group, stopping momentarily on Hughie, who swallowed hard and looked away. "I have a pressing announcement," he began.

Each disciple had their own thoughts rush in. Caelum gripped the hilt of Bloodthorn, his eyes reflecting a steely glint. *Is the sect on the brink of war?*

Amelia felt a pang in her heart. *Could Master be telling us he's nearing his end?* she feared.

Hughie's palms grew clammy. His eyes darted around nervously. *Will Master reveal to everyone his . . . feelings for me?*

Slifer, drawing out the suspense a tad longer, finally said, "I will be entering a period of closed-door cultivation."

There was a collective moment of silence, then Amelia broke it, her voice dripping with disbelief. "All this suspense just for that?"

Caelum frowned. "Master, you've secluded yourself countless times before. Why the need for this meeting?"

Hughie sighed in relief, his worst fears not coming to pass. *Thank goodness, it's just that.*

Fenlock barely reacted, his mind already wandering back to Lenvari, though he noted the peculiar nature of this announcement.

Noting their baffled expressions, Slifer cleared his throat. "That's not all," he started, trying to regain some authority. "While I'm away, I've assigned tasks for each of you. If they remain incomplete upon my return, well . . ." He left the threat hanging in the air.

Amelia exchanged a glance with Caelum, the same thought crossing their minds. *Master has never been this involved in our training. What's changed?*

Hughie, still in a daze from earlier, asked, "Master, what tasks have you prepared for us?"

Slifer's gaze landed on Amelia. "You need to complete your breakthrough requirements," he began, his tone slightly uneasy. *Three souls of Late Core Formation cultivators . . .* He internally sighed. "When I return, I want to see you in the Late Stage of Core Formation. But ensure your . . . *acquisitions* are demonic cultivators. Preferably, ones without any substantial backing."

Amelia frowned, her usually feisty nature shining through. "Master, you've always told me not to fret over backings."

Slifer pinched the bridge of his nose, regretting that Amelia always took the original's teachings so literally. *Why does she always challenge every single instruction?*

"Indeed, I did say that," he admitted, "but the dynamics have shifted. With me as an Ascendant cultivator, your actions now reflect upon the entire sect. Killing someone with powerful allies might be interpreted as an act of aggression. Do *you* wish to drag our sect into a war?"

To his astonishment, Amelia's eyes sparkled with excitement. "Yes! Wars mean more battles. More battles mean more souls for me to consume!"

Slifer rubbed his temples, mentally chiding himself for posing such a question to Amelia. *Of course, a battle maniac like her would relish the idea of inciting a war.* Deciding to change tactics, he pressed, "Do you want to achieve your breakthrough or not?"

"Yes, Master, I do," she replied, her tone slightly subdued.

"Then follow my instructions and don't dwell on the reasons," Slifer countered. "And don't forget, the Medicine Hall still requires your . . . expertise."

Amelia made a sound of protest, but her eyes betrayed her. *She probably enjoys her time there more than she'd ever admit,* Slifer thought amusedly.

His attention then shifted to Hughie. The younger disciple shrank under the intensity of his master's gaze. *Why does Hughie always act so nervous? He's got protagonist qualities; he should exude confidence.*

"Assist Amelia in her tasks," Slifer instructed. "Protect her."

Ding!
Task Assigned: Protect Your Senior Sister
Reward: 50 Karmic Credits
Bonus Requirements: Hidden
Bonus Reward: Hidden

The hidden bonus details caught his attention, causing the edges of his lips to twitch downwards. *Hidden requirements, huh? That's never a simple matter,* he mused. The System was notorious for its unpredictable demands, and hidden tasks typically spelled complications, often unfolding in the most inconvenient of ways.

Amelia, oblivious to the internal commotion her master was experiencing, stuck her chin out defiantly. "I don't need my junior brother's protection," she huffed.

But Hughie was already nodding eagerly, relief evident on his face. The chance to be away from the sect—and Slifer—was like a breath of fresh air. "Understood, Master. I'll make sure Senior Sister is safe."

Watching their exchange, Slifer held his tongue. *It's not about gender or strength. It's all about luck. Amelia's fiery nature will undoubtedly land them in trouble, but Hughie's inexplicable good fortune might just pull them through.*

Yet, the possible implications of the hidden requirements lingered. *Unless Amelia is destined to die a brutal death so that Hughie can unlock some latent power . . . Tch, these xianxia tales, they can be so unpredictable at times.* Shaking away the ominous thought, he comforted himself. *Amelia's own luck should be enough to shield her.*

Deciding to rely once again on Hughie's luck, Slifer put the thought to the back of his mind as his gaze shifted to Caelum, who was eyeing him expectantly, obviously hungry for some profound sword wisdom that he most definitely would not be able to offer.

"Caelum," Slifer began, "you need to hone your sword skills. Go out, kill as many demonic cultivators as you can, but restrain your cultivation. Rely only on your sword techniques."

Ding!
Task Assigned: The Way of the Sword—Achieve a Breakthrough
Reward: 100 Karmic Credits

Caelum nodded. His intention had always been to follow his master's teachings, but the constant tasks had tethered him to the sect.

"Why does Caelum get the fun task?" Amelia piped up, her voice tinged with envy.

Isn't slaughtering three cultivators thrilling enough? Slifer wondered, perplexed by her insatiability.

Caelum, in his stoic fashion, responded solemnly, "I do not take pleasure in killing, but if it aids my journey to becoming a great swordsman, then it is a path I must walk."

Slifer paused, a thought striking him. *I need to copy more of his sword techniques.* "One more thing, Caelum," he added quickly. "You are forbidden to use the Shadowstep Slash technique."

"Why not, Master?" Caelum questioned, perplexed.

Clearing his throat, Slifer improvised. "Relying too heavily on one technique will only hinder your comprehensive understanding of the sword."

Caelum's eyes widened in realization. *Master is right! This must be the bottleneck in my training,* he thought, committing himself to his master's words with a firm nod.

Slifer couldn't help but smile. *If only all my disciples were as compliant as Caelum.* His attention shifted to Fenlock just as a System message materialized before him:

Ding!
Your Disciple is Getting Bullied by Demonic Cultivators

Option 1: Eliminate the tormentors.
Reward: 100 Karmic Credits
Option 2: Cultivate your disciple's resilience, enabling him to confront his adversaries.
Reward: 100 Karmic Credits

Slifer exhaled, slightly exasperated. *I'm his mentor, not a guardian angel,* he complained. *How on earth is Fenlock, a Peak Core Formation cultivator, getting bullied?*

It was difficult to fathom. Slifer was certain no Nascent Soul or higher-ranked cultivator would dare harass one of his disciples. A grimace formed on his face as a possibility came to mind. *It must be those self-proclaimed "senior brothers" that he mentioned.*

"Fenlock," Slifer addressed him with a stern look, "it has come to my attention that you've been facing some . . . challenges with your peers." His voice was laced with slight irritation, more at the situation than at his disciple. "It's time you learned to stand up for yourself. I won't always be around to fend off your bullies."

"I-I'm not being bullied," Fenlock stammered in a low voice, but Slifer dismissed his protest.

"Your 'senior brothers' aren't your friends," he countered sharply. "Imagine what your junior sister would feel, seeing you in such a state."

Shame washed over Fenlock as he lowered his head. *Could Master be right?*

"I want you outside the sect for the foreseeable future, focusing solely on hunting demonic cultivators," Slifer continued.

This will kill two birds with one stone, Slifer thought inwardly. *Not only will it get me some much-needed Karmic Credits, but it'll also, hopefully, help Fenlock gain some confidence.*

Fenlock's heart grew heavy as he wondered if this was another one of his master's schemes to separate him from his junior sister. *What has Master got against our love?*

Feeling satisfied with how the meeting went, Slifer dismissed them with a wave. "I will emerge once I have made my breakthrough."

The disciples exchanged glances of astonishment. *Another breakthrough for Master?*

But before they could disperse, Slifer added, "And remember, don't cause *any* trouble during my seclusion."

"Of course, Master," the disciples replied, leaving to get on with their tasks.

As Slifer retreated to his quarters, multiple notifications popped up:

Ding!
Your Disciple Amelia's Loyalty Has Increased By 2%
Your Disciple Caelum's Loyalty Has Increased By 3%
Your Disciple Fenlock's Loyalty Has Increased By 2%
Your Disciple Hughie's Loyalty Has Increased By 1%

What prompted that? Slifer paused, pondering over the message. His thoughts then turned to the tasks he had assigned his disciples, and he let out a resigned sigh. While he hoped for a peaceful period during his closed-door cultivation, Slifer couldn't shake the nagging suspicion that things wouldn't be so simple.

I really hope they don't stir up any unnecessary problems during my closed-door cultivation. But knowing how these xianxia tales unfold, I will probably come out to a catastrophe of their making.

CHAPTER TWENTY-SEVEN

Veloria City was a stronghold for the White Tiger Sect, with their grand elder serving as the City Lord. Despite this, it was also home to two other major powers: the Valdorian Clan and the Eldric Clan. These three titans coexisted in a precarious equilibrium and always seemed as though they were at the brink of war.

Caelum entered through the grand South Gate, taking in the bustling scenes of the marketplace and the shouts of vendors selling exotic treasures. His mind, however, was a whirlwind of thoughts. *Eight . . . I've eliminated eight demonic cultivators at the Core Formation Realm while restricting my cultivation to the Foundation Establishment.*

But Caelum knew that he needed a final battle, a life-and-death confrontation with a Peak Core Formation expert. He could feel it, a breakthrough to the Sword Soul Realm was imminent.

The majority of Caelum's generation were still struggling in the Sword Qi Realm, while a select few had just tasted the early stages of the Sword Aura realm. But Caelum was different. He stood at the cusp of entering the Sword Soul Realm.

Achieving the Sword Soul Realm within just ten years of cultivation would not only be a personal triumph but would also mark him as one of the most prodigious swordsmen of his generation, a feat he hoped would make his master proud.

I need to find him. Caelum's eyes narrowed with determination.

His previous victim was . . . kind enough to give the whereabouts of a suitable target that met his master's requirements. However, whether he would find his target was a different matter, finding one individual in a sprawling city of over a hundred thousand souls was no trivial task.

If only I had his qi signature, Caelum sighed.

Every cultivator had a unique qi signature, a distinctive energetic imprint shaped by their cultivation techniques and the elements they harnessed. It was as unique to each person as fingerprints were to mortals.

With a qi signature and an appropriate treasure to amplify its traces, locating his target would be effortless. But without such aids, Caelum was facing a scenario akin to searching for a needle in a haystack.

As Caelum looked around, the familiar structures and sounds brought a wave of nostalgia. His village was only a few miles from here, and memories of visiting this city with his parents all those years ago flooded back.

It all seemed so simple then, he mused.

His trip down memory lane was suddenly interrupted by a frantic shout. "Move! Outta the way!"

Whirling around, Caelum's gaze landed on a boy, not older than twelve, dashing towards him. The boy's clothes were tattered, his straw hat perched precariously atop a mop of unruly hair. Clutched in his hands were various food items. Caelum sidestepped smoothly, allowing the child to hurtle past and hide behind a large merchant cart.

Their eyes met for a brief second. The boy, eyes wide with desperation, pressed a finger to his lips.

A street rat, Caelum thought.

As shouts grew louder, Caelum turned to face the oncoming commotion. A group of burly men emerged, muscles rippling beneath their grubby shirts. Halting in front of Caelum, the leader, with a scar running down his cheek, demanded, "Did ya see a brat runnin' this way with some food?"

Caelum raised an eyebrow but before he could answer, the aggressive man lunged forward, and another man yanked his comrade back by the wrist.

"Look at him, you fool!" the second man hissed, nodding towards Caelum.

Caelum wore a green robe but what caught their attention the most was the insignia on his chest—a beautifully embroidered black rose.

Recognition flashed in the aggressive man's eyes, and a cold sweat formed on his forehead. "I-immortal!" he stammered, dropping into a deep bow. "Forgive me! I didn't know—"

Caelum, slightly amused, raised a hand, motioning him to stop. "The child you're looking for went that way." With a nonchalant gesture, he pointed them in the opposite direction.

Gratitude filled the men's faces. They bowed profusely. "Thank you, Immortal!" they repeated, before hastily retreating in the direction Caelum had indicated.

"You can come out now," Caelum called out a few moments later, his voice steady yet gentle.

After a moment's hesitation, the boy emerged from his hiding spot, eyes wary but curious. Caelum sighed softly. He understood all too well the life this kid was leading; it wasn't so long ago he'd been in a similar situation, before his master had found him.

"Thank you, mister," the boy said, bowing quickly before turning to scamper off.

However, just as the boy thought he was free, a blur moved in front of him. Stopping dead in his tracks, he stared wide-eyed at Caelum, who had reappeared with an almost imperceptible swiftness. Falling onto his backside, fear evident in his eyes, the boy stammered, "M-mister?"

Caelum's gaze softened. *They often know more than they let on*, he thought. He knew the value of information that these city children could provide, often being overlooked by the cultivators who saw them as nothing but ants.

"I've helped you," Caelum began, "now it's your turn to help me."

The boy's eyes darted around warily, his face shadowing with apprehension. He had heard stories from other street kids about men with *strange* requests.

Reading the fear in the boy's eyes, Caelum quickly added, "I need your help finding someone."

The boy relaxed ever so slightly. "Who?" he asked, drawing himself up a bit.

"A group of demonic cultivators," Caelum replied.

The boy shrugged dismissively. "Demonic cultivators come and go in Veloria all the time."

Caelum nodded. "These are different. They each bear a specific mark on their face." He traced the shape of the tattoo with his fingers.

Recognition flickered in the kid's eyes. "I've seen 'em," he said, his voice a whisper.

Caelum's lips curled up into a faint smile. "Help me find them, and I'll reward you." As he spoke, he twirled a golden coin between his fingers. It was unusual for cultivators to carry coins, as their currency was spirit stones, but Caelum's past made him an exception, so he always kept some coins in his storage ring.

The boy's eyes fixed on the coin, and a goofy grin spread across his face. He nodded eagerly. "Deal."

In a cramped corner of a small tavern, a group of four men drank as their crude laughter and banter filled the air. They were a rough-looking bunch, with leathery skin and cold eyes, the kind who a law-abiding citizen would try to stay clear of.

"If he doesn't want to give up his daughter, he can forfeit his life," one jeered, a wicked gleam in his eyes.

The apparent boss, a burly man with a tattoo tracing down his cheek, laughed heartily and slapped his subordinate on the back. "Either way, she'll be our *plaything* by nightfall," he declared.

The tavern owner couldn't help but shoot nervous glances at the group, regretting ever letting them inside.

The door creaked open, revealing Caelum and the young boy. Scanning the room, Caelum's gaze landed on the boss. The distinctive mark on his face was unmistakable. Without a word, he flipped a few golden coins towards the boy, who caught them with ease.

"Thanks, mister!" The boy grinned, dashing out, knowing better than to stay for what was to come.

Suspicion flitted across the eyes of the four men, especially upon noting Caelum's Black Rose Sect insignia. The rat-faced man sneered. "What you looking at?"

But Caelum didn't respond, his gaze locked onto the boss.

The boss, sensing Caelum's profound spiritual energy, felt a hint of unease. Though he was at the Peak Core Formation realm, he was acutely aware that sect cultivators were often not to be trifled with. *Could this kid be one of those prodigies?* he wondered.

"Get out of here, kid, while you still can," the boss growled, trying to mask his uncertainty with bravado.

The tall man laughed boisterously. "You heard the boss!" Rising from his chair, he swaggered towards Caelum, a cruel glint in his eyes. But in a heartbeat, the man's head separated from his body, dropping with a grim thud, his eyes reflecting sheer disbelief.

One of the other men stammered, voice trembling, "I . . . I didn't even see him move."

Caelum's expression remained impassive, his sword sheathed as quickly as it had been drawn. He turned his attention back to the boss. "Face me in a duel," he stated calmly.

The boss cursed his luck under his breath. Had he been alone, he would have fled without a second thought. But with his men watching, he had to maintain a façade of confidence. He gulped down his drink, the jug hitting the table with a thud as he stood up. Wiping his mouth, he sneered, "Next year today will be your death anniversary, kid."

The tavern owner, a bead of sweat trickling down his forehead, nervously interjected, "Could you please take this outside?"

A deadly glare from the boss made him regret his words, but Caelum smoothly intervened. "He's right. Let's not dirty the tavern floors," he said, already heading for the door.

Scoffing, the boss followed, his remaining two men trailed behind, leaving behind their comrade's corpse.

Once outside, under the moon's ghostly glow, Caelum and the boss faced each other. The boss unleashed his aura, the oppressive might of a Peak Core Formation cultivator. "I am Dravon," he introduced himself with a wicked grin.

Restraining his power to the Peak Foundation Establishment level, Caelum clapped his hands together in a formal greeting. "I am Caelum," he responded. But as he bowed slightly, Dravon lunged forward, his right hand enveloped in roaring flames.

Sword Aura, Caelum thought, activating the technique. The third realm of sword cultivation, Sword Aura, allowed practitioners to envelop themselves in an invisible aura, enhancing their speed, agility, and reflexes.

With heightened senses, Caelum dodged the fiery strike with ease and counterattacked. Their attacks clashed, but the force from Dravon's blow drove Caelum back several steps.

This will be a difficult battle, he acknowledged silently, eyes narrowing.

Dravon laughed maniacally, growing in confidence. "Restricting your cultivation as a training exercise? You're just guaranteeing your death, kid!" He then sent a wave of fire towards Caelum.

Caelum's sword, infused with both his Sword Qi and aura, swung forward, shattering the oncoming inferno and scattering flames into the night. He realized, with his cultivation restricted, Dravon's attacks were faster and stronger. Even with Sword Aura, he had to be alert at all times and maintain a tight defense to even survive this duel.

One of the followers yelled, "That's right, boss! Show that brat his place!"

The boss charged forward, his fists engulfed in flames, launching a mixture of martial arts and fiery attacks. Caelum found himself retreating, each clash leaving him with bruises and burns. His back brushed against the cool night air as he narrowly evaded a particularly vicious strike.

Realizing the need for a different approach, Caelum initiated the Nine Shadows Mirage technique. In an instant, eight other images of him flickered into existence, each grasping their own version of the Bloodthorn sword.

"A mere mirage technique won't save you, boy!" the boss scoffed, undeterred.

Yet, to his surprise, all nine Caelums lunged into action, each capable of launching its own attack. The boss found himself fighting off multiple adversaries, grunting as he dispelled one image after another with powerful strikes. However, the effort cost him; he sustained several cuts, his own blood now dripping onto the ground.

When he finally struck the real Caelum, the impact was massive. Caelum went flying, crashing painfully into a tree before slumping to the ground.

"You seem to enjoy taking a beating, boy," the boss remarked, walking towards the fallen Caelum but remaining cautious. He knew better than to underestimate a sect cultivator's resilience.

Caelum, with blood trickling from the corner of his mouth, wondered whether he should release his cultivation's restrictions to gain an upper hand. *No*, he quickly chided himself, *I have to push my limits. I have to trust in Bloodthorn*. Gripping the hilt of his sword tightly, Caelum poured his emotions, his grievances, and his resolve into the weapon.

In response, a peculiar sensation enveloped him, as though a monumental shift had just occurred within his very being. As he gazed at the advancing bandit, a phrase emerged from the depths of his heart, echoing in his soul: "Awaken the Sanguine Nightmare, Bloodthorn."

Whispering the phrase like a sacred vow, he clutched his sword as it began to glow with a sinister red hue. A low growl, almost inaudible, resonated from the blade.

Without warning, Bloodthorn stretched out, bridging the distance between Caelum and Dravon in an instant. The blade pierced through Dravon's chest, its tip emerging from his back.

Dravon's eyes widened in disbelief, blood bubbling from his mouth. He could accept not being able to handle Caelum's true cultivation, but he never imagined he'd be killed even with the kid's self-imposed limitations.

"Impossible," he choked out, his body swaying before toppling over, lifeless.

Upon witnessing the death of their leader, the two remaining followers exchanged a terrified glance. Without hesitation, they activated their respective escape techniques, vanishing into opposite directions, hoping that Caelum would pursue the other.

Lost in thought, Caelum barely registered their escape. He felt a profound connection with Bloodthorn that he'd never experienced before.

I've finally reached the Sword Soul Realm . . .

In this realm, his consciousness and Bloodthorn had fused, enabling him to communicate with the weapon on a deeper level and harness some of its abilities.

The technique that had dispatched Dravon so effortlessly was the Thorned Lash, it allowed Bloodthorn to elongate and contort its blade, striking from a distance with deadly precision.

Gently wiping the blade, he thought, *Bloodthorn is now an extension of my soul. We're linked in a manner deeper than ever before. But this bond is a double-edged sword.* He knew that the destruction of Bloodthorn would reverberate within his very soul, causing potentially irreparable damage.

We will be together till the end . . . I promise.

Far from the city, in his secluded cultivation quarters, Slifer received a System notification.

Ding!
Congratulations!
Your disciple Caelum has broken through to the Sword Soul Realm.
Reward: 500 Karmic Credits

Engrossed in his meditation, the message went unnoticed.

Back in the city, as Caelum walked away from the scene of the battle, an intense pressure weighed down on him. His body instinctively tensed, and he raised his eyes to see a young woman descending gracefully from the heavens. Her robes bore the symbol of the White Tiger Sect, and her pretty face was twisted into an ugly scowl.

"You think you can *walk* away after causing such a ruckus?" she demanded, her voice as sharp as the blade at Caelum's waist.

Caelum arched an eyebrow, meeting her gaze. "Who might you be?"

"Typical of demonic scum to wreak havoc and then play ignorant." She shook her head, disgust evident on her face. "You have two choices: accompany me to the dungeons for your crimes, or face your death here and now."

Can we handle a Nascent Soul cultivator, Bloodthorn? Caelum pondered, his gaze dropping to the sword in his hand.

In response, Bloodthorn let out a low growl in agreement.

CHAPTER TWENTY-EIGHT

Caelum's aura surged to Late Core Formation as he prepared for what seemed to be the greatest challenge in his life thus far.

In the Peak Foundation Establishment Realm, he had managed to kill a cultivator at the Peak Core Formation, but Caelum wasn't deluded. He knew that the chasm between a Core Formation expert and a Nascent Soul cultivator was vast, immeasurably so.

Perhaps, with Bloodthorn's assistance, he might be able to battle to a standstill against this Early Nascent Soul Realm girl, but Caelum knew that with one misstep, his life would forfeit.

The girl, sensing his desire to battle, laughed coldly. "You truly don't grasp the difference between the heavens and the earth. I'll flatten you in a single move." With a wave of her hand, a gargantuan hand, made of densely compacted earth and stones, rose from the ground. Towering over Caelum, it raced towards him with crushing intent.

Caelum's eyes narrowed, understanding that the girl was dead serious—she intended to kill him. In a low voice, he invoked, "Awaken the Sanguine Nightmare, Bloodthorn."

The blade was engulfed in a swirling crimson energy and began to expand exponentially in size, rushing to meet the gargantuan hand. This was another ability of Bloodthorn, known as the Crimson Vortex technique, that he had gained access to after reaching the Sword Soul Realm.

As the blade clashed with the earthen palm, Caelum and the young woman stood locked in a fierce stalemate, a deafening roar echoed and a whirlwind of dust and debris spiraled around them, stinging their faces. However, as the two techniques continued to strain against each other, a soft yet firm voice echoed through the vicinity.

"Enough!"

Instantly, their respective techniques crumbled, and their bodies locked in place, frozen by an overwhelming force.

From the heavens, a stunning woman, who looked to be in her thirties, descended. She wore azure robes, decorated with the emblem of the white tiger, that flowed around her like water. Her beauty was breathtaking, and her navy-blue eyes seemed to have the power to soften even the hardest of hearts.

Under the immense pressure, the Nascent Soul cultivator's confident demeanor crumbled, her voice quivering as she cried out, "C-City Lord Alina!"

"Liora." The woman smiled gently at the young girl, withdrawing her aura. She then shifted her gaze to Caelum. "The disciple of Supreme Elder Slifer is always welcome here in our city," she spoke gently.

"This junior greets the City Lord." Caelum clasped his hands respectfully.

Meeting an Origin Realm cultivator again . . . if she harbored any ill intent, there'd be no escape for me. Noticing the friendly demeanor of the City Lord, Caelum let out a sigh of relief.

However, the girl, whom Alina addressed as Liora, was not as forgiving. Her eyes flashed with indignation. "He blatantly disregarded our city's laws," she protested, her voice dripping with disdain. "He not only dared to attack, but he also took a *life*!"

Alina motioned for Liora to calm down. "I had intended to send a few to deal with the ruckus those lone cultivators were causing. This young man merely addressed the issue before we could." Turning to Caelum, she said, "Thank you for assisting with our city's troubles."

Hearing this, Liora's expression darkened further. She shot a glare at Caelum. "If not for the treaty between the sects, demonic cultivators like you would be hunted down like stray dogs."

Alina's face turned grave, and her aura sharply focused on Liora. "You might be a prodigy and an elder of our sect, but remember, Liora, this is *my* domain. *I* am the City Lord."

The pointed reminder made Liora shiver. A hint of fear reflected in her eyes. She bowed deeply, her tone respectful yet strained. "I . . . will abide by the City Lord's command."

However, as she prepared to leave, she shot Caelum a final warning glance. "Just pray to the heavens that we don't cross paths outside this city's walls."

Watching Liora retreat, Caelum sighed inwardly. *Why does she have such a vendetta against me?*

Alina, observing the retreating figure of the young girl, turned her attention back to Caelum. "Pay her no mind. Youth often blinds one with hatred, especially between the righteous and demonic paths. Eventually, she will see there is not much difference."

Caelum clasped his hands and bowed slightly, expressing his gratitude. "Thank you for your understanding, City Lord."

She waved a dismissive hand, a small smile playing on her lips. "There is no need for formalities, I am acquainted with your master. We are . . . old friends."

Caelum's eyes widened in genuine surprise. *Master knows the City Lord?* The revelation was startling, he didn't know his master had any . . . friends.

But before he could voice his thoughts, she interrupted. "I'm sure, young one, you have more pressing matters than speaking with an old woman like me."

"Thank you for your assistance." Caelum gave another respectful bow.

Just as he was about to leave, he paused for a moment. "The young boy in the city . . . he has potential. Do look out for him." He had no doubt Alina knew whom he referred to. He suspected she had been watching since he had set foot in the city.

Without waiting for a reply, Caelum vanished from the spot.

Alina's gaze drifted to the aftermath of the battle. The markings on the ground showed subtle signs of the sword technique slowly overpowering the gigantic earthen hand.

"No disciple of an Ascendant cultivator," she murmured to herself, "is simple."

Caelum stared at the entrance of Hearthbrook village. It felt like an eternity since he'd last set foot here, he was but a child when his master took him under his wing. *It feels like just yesterday,* he mused, a sigh escaping his lips. Time, for cultivators, seemed to warp and twist, years passing like fleeting moments.

Would they even recognize me now? He had always yearned to return, but the potential dangers held him back. Cultivators, particularly demonic cultivators, would exploit the weak to get to the strong, and so his master had strictly warned him against visiting. But now, an inexplicable pull tugged at his soul. "Perhaps it's Heaven's Will," he whispered, drawing strength from the thought.

Walking inconspicuously, like any other mortal, he traversed the village's cobblestone paths, relying on distant memories to guide him home. He easily masked his presence, remaining undetected by the unaware villagers. While urban folk held some knowledge about the world of cultivation, these villagers remained blissfully ignorant, unable to differentiate between immortal and demonic cultivators.

Ahead, he noticed an old, worn-down house, its wooden planks showing signs of weathering and its roof made of straw, still holding up despite the evident years it had seen. An elderly man entered the dwelling, and as Caelum extended his spiritual sense, he found an aged woman lying on a bed, her life's flame dimming, while the man cared for her tenderly.

"Mother," he whispered, emotion constricting his voice. Witnessing the fragility of the parents he once saw as pillars was gut-wrenching.

He hadn't anticipated this. They should have been healthier, stronger. The life-extending pills that his master had provided should have granted them a century of good health.

Whispering softly, he murmured, "I'm sorry." Hesitantly, he extended his spiritual sense to scan his mother's fragile form. Such an action was deeply intimate, considered an invasion of one's privacy. He felt a pang of guilt, even if she remained oblivious to his actions.

I need to find out what is wrong, Caelum thought with resolve.

After a few moments of silent observation, his eyes widened in shock. "H-how is this possible?" Caelum muttered under his breath.

His mother's body harbored a poison—but this was no ordinary affliction. It was a vicious poison known to cultivators as Cultivator's Bane, infamous for its cruelty. This sinister toxin lurked undetected within a victim, sapping their life force gradually until nothing but a husk remained.

For cultivators with extended lifespans and enhanced physiques, the venom's effects could unfold unnoticed over decades or even centuries. But in his mother's mortal body, the poison's devastation had been swift and merciless. It had manifested fully within mere months.

Caelum's face twisted into a grimace. *Who could have done this to her?* he thought, feeling an unfamiliar surge of rage.

Driven by a sudden impulse, he began to approach the house. He wanted to be there, to comfort and protect, but he halted mid-step, his heart heavy. *Revealing myself now would change nothing*, he thought despairingly.

The bitter truth was, he carried no cure. Worse, the Cultivator's Bane had a cruel trait: it thrived and intensified its potency when exposed to healing elixirs. Caelum's face contorted in anguish. The only way to counteract its effects was with the rare antidote known as Essence of Dawn.

The perpetrator could be near, observing their handiwork, he considered. His spiritual sense expanded outwards like a ripple, scanning the surroundings for any sign of malicious watchers. After detecting no immediate threats, Caelum felt a pang of relief.

If they used this poison instead of an outright attack, then my family is likely safe . . . for now. With one last, lingering look at the place he once called home, Caelum walked away.

He needed the antidote, and he needed it fast.

CHAPTER TWENTY-NINE

H ey, can you hurry things up?" a voice called out lazily.

Amelia easily sidestepped a ferocious punch aimed at her, resulting in a sizable dent forming on the ground where she once stood. Grinning mischievously, she retorted, "Where's the fun in that?" Her eyes landed on Hughie, who was nonchalantly lounging on a tree branch, an apple in hand.

Her opponent, a burly middle-aged man at the Late Core Formation stage, sneered, launching a palm strike her way. "You'll be the one begging for mercy, little girl, when I have my way with you tonight," he leered.

I'd rather face death than let this filthy swine lay a hand on me. Amelia wrinkled her nose in disgust.

Without warning, she executed her Soul Render technique. A razor-sharp blade of soul energy materialized, slashing through the man's spiritual essence. He paused, confusion written across his face as he inspected himself for physical harm. Then his eyes widened in horror, blood spurted from his mouth, and he stumbled backwards. "S-soul attack . . ." he gasped.

Amelia hadn't given the slightest hint of being a soul cultivator throughout the battle.

Feel that? That's your essence being shredded. Her lips curled into a cruel smirk as she approached the agonized man, who was doubled over in pain. The torment he experienced was not of the flesh but the soul. It felt as if molten lava flowed through his veins, and icy daggers pierced his essence repeatedly.

With a fluid motion, Amelia leapt high into the air before descending rapidly, her fingers dug into the man's hair as she mercilessly slammed his head against the ground, rendering him unconscious.

"I didn't kill you because there's so much fun to look forward to," she whispered, almost tenderly.

Hughie sighed, observing as Amelia knelt beside the unconscious man, her palm covered in a soothing blue qi. This wasn't new; her last two opponents had endured the same fate. She'd pummel them into unconsciousness, then meticulously use her Essence Mend technique to heal their physical traumas, only to repeat the process once they awoke.

Amelia's fingers danced with precision, the blue energy weaving into the man's wounds, stitching flesh, and mending bone. The process was delicate and paradoxically caring, contrasting starkly with the violence that had preceded it and the violence that was to follow . . .

"Boss Morvran would be proud," Hughie murmured, taking another bite of his apple.

In a place not too far away, an old man received a distressing alert. His grandson's Soul Lamp flickered perilously close to extinguishment. Rushing to the soul chamber, he watched, heart in throat, as the light bravely battled back to life. He exhaled in relief, a prayer of thanks on his lips, only for his smile to falter as the glow diminished once again to a mere spark.

Just as he was about to leave to seek revenge, the light flared up once again, only to dim down once more. This cycle repeated several times, and with each iteration, the old man's face grew hotter.

"Enough!" he exclaimed. Unable to stand it any longer, he shot into the sky like a comet, hurtling towards his grandson's location.

"I'll make the nine generations of my son's tormentor pay," he growled.

Meanwhile, back at the battle site, Hughie yawned, clearly unimpressed. "Can you finish up already? There's an auction nearby, and I'm itching to get my hands on a sword like Caelum's."

Amelia paused, her hands still glowing with healing energy. "Alright," she said with a sigh. With a swift motion, she initiated her cultivation technique—the Voidswallow Incantation.

Hughie involuntarily took a step back, feeling a chill run down his spine. No matter how many times he witnessed it, he found that Amelia's transformation was nothing short of horrifying. Her once radiant skin grew pale and sallow, her eyes hollowed out, leaving only an eerie blue glow in their wake. Veins turned black, tracing macabre patterns across her skin. The most disturbing change, however, was her mouth. It expanded in a grotesque caricature, revealing a gaping maw lined with sharp, jagged teeth.

It's like staring into an abyss, Hughie thought, a shudder coursing down his spine.

The horrifying mouth acted like a black hole, and the soul of the unconscious man began to swirl towards it like water down a drain. He awoke with a start, his screams piercing the air as his soul was violently wrenched from his body. Amelia's maw snapped shut, the deed done, and as quickly as she had changed, she returned to her normal appearance.

She then turned to Hughie, a twisted grin plastered on her face. "Delicious," she purred, licking her lips.

Hughie barely had time to process her words when a thunderous roar shook the air. "How dare you?!" bellowed the voice, fraught with fury and grief.

Their heads snapped in the direction of the sound, only to see an enraged elder flying towards them, his face a mask of wrath.

Uh-oh, Hughie thought, glancing at Amelia's nonchalant demeanor. "Boss Morvran would indeed be proud."

A sudden surge of energy erupted from Amelia, its intensity revealing her cultivation level of the Late Core Formation Realm. "What did you say, old man?" she quipped, a hint of playful arrogance in her tone. "I was busy eating." She then paused, releasing an exaggerated burp.

The elderly figure's face darkened, his anger barely contained. With a roar that seemed to shake the very heavens, he violently tore off his robe, unveiling a surprisingly sculpted physique. A potent pressure descended upon them—the intimidating aura of a Mid-Nascent Soul cultivator.

Hughie leaned in, whispering to Amelia, "Even with your recent breakthrough, this might be too much."

With a huff, Amelia responded, "Run if you're scared. I'll handle this."

"What would I even tell Master?" Hughie countered, his gaze never leaving their formidable adversary. But before more could be said, the elder appeared in front of Hughie in a blur, delivering a resounding slap. Hughie was propelled backwards, crashing into a boulder before falling to the ground. His body was a mess of bruises and blood, bones fractured in places he didn't even know could break. Pain radiated through him, making even the slightest movement feel like torture.

"You'll regret that, old man!" Amelia unleashed her Soul Render technique, sending a blade of Soul Qi hurtling towards the elder. But he dodged with ease, his movements a blur.

Amelia's heart raced. *Body cultivators . . . dangerous up close*, she mentally noted, stealing a glance at Hughie's state. *Can't let him land a hit.*

Despite the excruciating pain, Hughie managed to push himself upright. "You got me good, old man," he croaked, grimacing. The force of the slap had met the requirements to activate the Bloodforge Ascension technique. His form shifted, growing taller, muscles expanding as his skin reddened and veins bulged prominently. Looking down at his newly transformed body, a smirk played on his lips as he noticed the injuries rapidly healing.

However, glancing at his surroundings, a shiver ran down his spine. *Being on this mountain edge . . . one misstep, one heavy blow, and it's a long fall down.*

Meanwhile, the old man had found it increasingly challenging to close the distance between him and Amelia. Her consistent assault of soul blades forced him to remain on the defensive, each strike narrowing his options. Seizing a momentary pause in her onslaught, he mustered his qi, dodging her next blade while simultaneously darting forward. Striking with a palm, the sheer force expelled the air from her lungs, sending her spiraling into a tree, shattering its trunk upon impact.

Amelia lay amidst the splinters, her clothing torn, revealing dark bruises beneath. Blood trickled from a cut on her forehead, and her breathing came in ragged gasps. As she tried to push herself upright, a shadow loomed above her. The old man, his face twisted with vindictive satisfaction, sneered. "Now you'll know how my grandson felt."

Before Amelia could react, he gripped her throat, lifting her effortlessly off the ground. The world around her started to blur, air failing to reach her lungs. However, just as darkness threatened to consume her vision, the old man was sent flying off his feet by a powerful blow. Gasping, Amelia crumpled to the ground, her eyes finding Hughie's enlarged form.

"No one hurts Senior Sister on my watch," Hughie growled, his voice filled with protective rage.

The old man, hardly perturbed, swiftly regained his footing. Brushing the dirt off his exposed torso, a small bruise evident on his temple, he met Hughie's gaze without a hint of fear.

Realizing the old man's resilience, Hughie turned urgently to Amelia. "Escape," he barked. "I'll hold him back." Without waiting for her reply, he charged.

Lying amidst the debris, Amelia's hand instinctively moved to her injuries. *I'm no coward.* The thought was steadfast in her mind. *How can I let my junior brother protect me? It's my duty as a senior.*

As she watched the ensuing brawl, it became evident that despite Hughie's size advantage, the old man's superior martial skill and cultivation began to tilt the fight in his favor. Hughie's strikes, though mighty, often found only air, while the old man's blows landed with precise and brutal efficiency. The sound of flesh meeting flesh echoed, with each blow Hughie took leaving a fresh mark, deepening his wounds.

Amelia, watching with a mixture of admiration and concern, murmured, "Hughie . . ."

She held back a sigh; she wished their master had given them a life-saving treasure, but unfortunately Slifer was well known for being stingy.

As the old man's foot connected with Hughie's torso, sending him spiraling through the air, Amelia saw an opening. With a shout, she seized her chance, unleashing her Soul Rendering technique. The blade of Pure Soul energy sped through the air and lodged into the old man's back.

He faltered momentarily, taking a staggering step forward, clutching his heart. A trickle of blood seeped from the corner of his lips, yet he seemed mostly unscathed. Turning his gaze to Amelia, a smirk crept onto his face. "Had you been at the Nascent Soul Realm, that attack might have damaged my Nascent Soul," he remarked coldly.

My soul attacks . . . they're useless against him. Amelia remembered that Nascent Soul cultivators held a more profound connection to their souls, granting them resilience against basic soul attacks.

The old man's foot shifted in the dirt, hinting at his next move towards Amelia. But a thunderous roar interrupted his advance. He, along with Amelia, shifted their gaze towards the source: Hughie. He had undergone a monstrous transformation, growing even larger. His veins threatened to break through his skin, now a sickly shade of purple-red. His eyes, once sharp with intelligence, now glazed over with pure, unadulterated bloodlust.

"Die!"

An aura equivalent to an Early Nascent Soul cultivator surged from Hughie.

The old man's eyes tightened. "This young one has surprises," he murmured. The rational part of him whispered caution, to consider the background of these formidable Core Formation cultivators. But the seething anger, fueled by the pain of his grandson's violent death, overpowered his judgment.

As the two giants collided, the very ground beneath them trembled.

Hughie, in his berserk state, launched a series of ferocious punches. The first one aimed straight for the old man's chest. But with a swift sidestep, the elder dodged, delivering a palm strike to Hughie's side. Hughie retaliated with a sweeping leg kick, hoping to knock the old man off his feet. But the old man leapt upwards, avoiding the sweep, and descended with a powerful elbow strike. Hughie managed to block it just in time, but the force sent him skidding backwards.

The old man, with his superior speed, danced around Hughie, landing jabs and kicks. Yet, for each strike that connected, Hughie, with his newfound strength, would retaliate with a blow of his own.

"Your strength is impressive," the old man commented, ducking a particularly fierce swing and countering with a swift elbow to Hughie's side. "But raw power won't best experience!"

Hughie, unyielding, caught the old man's next punch, his hand closing around the elder's wrist with crushing force. But the old man was nimble, using his trapped arm as leverage to deliver a kick that sent Hughie crashing sideways.

Just as the old man took a step forward to attack Hughie whilst he was down, another Soul Render sliced through the air, striking the old man on the back. He growled in pain, glaring at Amelia from a distance. Drawing a sleek spear from his storage ring, he poised himself and hurled the weapon with all his might.

Amelia's eyes widened as the spear cut through the air with a whistle, closing the distance between them rapidly. *It's too fast,* she thought, frozen, realizing escape was impossible given her injuries.

But in that split second, a massive figure interposed itself between Amelia and the incoming spear. Hughie, with clarity restored to his eyes, took the brunt of the attack, his chest pierced by the spear. His eyes, no longer filled with the wildness of his former state, now had a clarity to them, but his voice . . . it carried a guttural, demonic tone.

"Master told me to protect you," he rasped, blood dribbling from the corner of his lips. "How can I face him if I fail?"

Before Amelia could reply, Hughie swiftly slapped a tag, inscribed with runes, onto her chest. Memories flooded Amelia's mind; she recalled Hughie discovering the tag and choosing not to share its existence with their master. She remembered him playfully recounting tales of previous treasures he had "loaned" to their master and never seen again.

Hoping to lighten the gravity of the situation, Hughie smirked, his demonic voice making the attempt at humor eerie. "Was hoping for more . . . action, but guess this'll have to do," he quipped, hinting at the intimate placement of the tag.

"You . . . idiot!" Amelia choked out, tears streaming down her face. "I *won't* leave you behind!"

But before she could rip the tag from her chest, it began glowing. A brilliant flash of lightning enveloped her, and in the next instant, she vanished. Hughie, left behind, smiled bitterly at the empty space she once occupied.

The grandpa, his eyes blazing with fury at Amelia's escape, spewed curses at Hughie. "You meddlesome fool!" he roared, appearing before the massive figure in a blink. With a vicious yank, he retrieved the spear from Hughie's chest, the act exacerbating the wound immensely.

Hughie couldn't help but let out a deep, guttural growl, the pain searing through every fiber of his being.

The old man, bereft of any semblance of mercy, hurled Hughie to the ground with immense force. "You let her go!" he snarled, each word punctuated by a brutal stomp or punch. "You will pay for her actions, for my grandson's suffering!"

Hughie's body was nothing more than a canvas for the old man's rage, each hit painting a bruise or gash. After what felt like an eternity, the assault ceased. The old man glared down at Hughie, his body now barely more than a battered, bloody heap. Slowly, the hulking form that was Hughie shrank back to its original size, his breaths shallow and labored.

So, this is how it ends? Hughie thought, the edges of his vision darkening. *I'm sorry, Master, Amelia . . .*

Disgust contorted the old man's features as he spat on the broken figure before him. "Not even worthy to die by my hand." Gripping Hughie's neck with a single hand, he dragged him to the edge of the mountain.

Is this the end? Hughie wondered, feeling the cold air rush past his face as the mountain's edge approached.

Looking down at the abyss, the old man hoisted up Hughie's limp body. "A dog's death for a dog's intervention," the old man said, sneering. Without a shred of compassion, he hurled Hughie's limp body off the edge. The mountain's precipice swallowed him, and he plummeted downwards.

With a huff, the old man turned away, his figure slowly swallowed by the mist.

Ding!
Alert: Critical Condition Detected

Disciple Designation: Hughie
Status: Fatally Wounded
Task: Administer Advanced Healing to Hughie
Time Limit: 1 Hour
Warning: If Disciple Hughie remains untreated within the specified time frame, it will result in the disciple's unfortunate demise.
Caution: Death of a disciple incurs severe consequences.
For specifics:
- Hidden
- Hidden
- Hidden

However, the System's plea for immediate action went unseen, as Slifer, deeply immersed in his meditation, remained oblivious to the events of the outside world.

CHAPTER THIRTY

The room was simple, with plain wooden walls, a bed, and a small wooden table beside it. There wasn't much in the way of decoration, only the essentials. A young woman was leaning over the bed, her hands delicately tending to a young man swathed in white bandages.

"Father told me that if you don't show signs of waking soon, he'll throw you right back into that river," she whispered with a soft chuckle. Brushing a stray lock of hair from his forehead, she continued, "He also mentioned he's not too happy about how much time I've been spending with you. Says you're nothing but trouble. It's just . . . there was something about you, I feel like I can't leave your side."

She paused for a moment, as if gathering her thoughts, before confessing further, "I know I shouldn't be saying all this to an unconscious stranger, but . . . you're a good listener."

A small smile played on her lips. "It's weird to think that just a week ago, father fished you out from that lake. Had he not acted so quickly, you would've either succumbed to your grave injuries or . . ." She shuddered at the thought. "Become a meal for one of those monstrous creatures in the lake."

Engrossed in her monologue, she failed to notice the young man's eyelids flutter open. As his eyes adjusted to the dim light of the room, he found himself staring into the beautiful face of his caretaker. *A beauty like this . . . in the Mortal Realm?* he thought, awestruck.

"It's time to change the bandages on this leg," she mumbled, moving to undo the bandages wrapped around Hughie's thigh. Suppressing his excitement, Hughie closed his eyes, feigning unconsciousness.

The room's stillness was broken when the door burst open with a bang. An older man stormed in, his eyes narrowing at the scene before him. Without a word, he marched up to the bed and delivered a resounding slap to Hughie's face.

Hughie, caught off guard, winced from the sharp sting and exclaimed, "What the hell was that for, old man?"

The young woman, her face flushed with surprise and anger, stood up to confront her father. "Father! Why would you do that?"

The old man, unmoved by his daughter's outburst, glanced disdainfully at Hughie. "I knew he was pretending. Trouble indeed. But now that the scoundrel's awake, *he* can change his own bandages."

Hughie's eyes darted around, realizing he had given himself away. He hastily closed his eyes again, trying to feign unconsciousness. However, sensing the imminent arrival of the old man's fist towards his face, he hastily blurted, "Alright, alright, I'm awake."

"Father, he's still too injured," the young woman, concern evident in her voice, interjected. Hughie nodded fervently in agreement.

The father's face darkened as he addressed his daughter. "Oliviare, it isn't proper for a young woman like you to be doing this." His gaze then shifted mischievously to Hughie, a somewhat lecherous grin forming on his lips. "I'll handle this," he declared, grabbing a set of fresh bandages.

Hughie's eyes widened in alarm. *Why do the old geezers always take a liking to me?* he thought desperately. Pain flared across his body as he raised his hand in a stopping gesture. "Uncle is right, I can do it myself."

The old man laughed heartily and tossed the bandages at Hughie, who caught them despite the jolt of pain from the sudden movement. Oliviare smiled softly, providing him a blanket for modesty as he changed his bandages.

"I'm Oliviare, and this stubborn old man is my father, Brom," she introduced them, explaining that they had found him a week ago, washed up by the lake.

A week? Hughie was taken aback, not just by the time he'd been out, but also by the fact that mere mortals had managed to save him. *I was sure I'd be dead unless some heaven-defying treasure intervened.*

Noticing his confusion, Oliviare added, "When we found you, there was a healing herb, Starbloom Euphorbia, attached to your body. I guess it must have been carried by the current."

A sigh of relief escaped Hughie. *Of course. Another one of those serendipitous occurrences in my life*, he thought, trying to recall the moments leading up to the river. He had grown accustomed to these bizarre strokes of luck. *In fact*, he mused, *I'd probably be more startled if these strange events stopped happening.*

Two days had slipped by in what seemed like moments. Hughie sensed that activating his Bloodforge Ascension technique might now fully heal him. Yet, an unfamiliar feeling settled in his heart, he realized he wasn't quite ready to return to the sect. There was something that urged him to linger in this village, and as he listened to Oliviare animatedly discuss the upcoming Moon Blossom Festival, the reason became clearer.

"I can't wait for the Moon Blossom Festival!" she said, her eyes shining with excitement. "The entire village gathers, there's music, dance, and the best food you can imagine!"

I don't want to leave her yet, he thought wistfully. Hughie's mind wandered to his past—a time before the sect and the comfort it brought. Having been an orphan, he was familiar with loneliness until his master had found him, giving his life purpose. The thought of the sect made him wonder if anyone would truly miss him. When images of his master and senior siblings flitted through his mind, he dismissed them. *They would probably be better off without me.*

His train of thought was abruptly halted when Oliviare, her cheeks tinted a delicate shade of pink, asked, "Would you . . . perhaps, like to accompany me to the festival?"

Caught off guard, Hughie scratched the back of his head, a bit flustered. "I'd love to, Oliviare."

The door burst open, and in marched Brom, grumbling, "Don't think I won't have my eye on you, lad."

Hughie groaned internally. *This old man is really something.*

As nightfall wrapped the village in its embrace, Hughie found himself alone in his room. Laid out for him were the clothes Oliviare had provided—simple yet elegant village attire. He swapped his cultivator robes for them, noting that the bandages across his chest remained concealed beneath.

Gazing at his reflection, he wondered, *Is this what people consider . . . a date?*

He retrieved a small locket from his storage ring. It was an odd treasure he'd stumbled upon years ago, one that suppressed a cultivator's qi. *Why would anyone want to seal off their cultivation?* he had often thought, leaving the locket untouched within his ring. Now, he saw its purpose.

Slowly, he placed the locket around his neck. For a brief instant, it emitted a soft purple glow, and Hughie felt his connection to his cultivation cut off, as if severed by an unseen hand. "Hughie, the cultivator, is dead," he muttered to himself. "Tonight, I am Hughie, the mortal."

A gentle knock on the door drew him from his musings.

"Enter," he called.

Oliviare stepped in, and Hughie felt his breath catch in his throat. She was dressed in a beautiful gown that accentuated her milky white skin and large brown eyes. She looked radiant and ethereal.

"What do you think?" she asked shyly, her eyes twinkling like the first stars of the evening.

Hughie stammered, momentarily lost for words. "You . . . you look stunning," he managed finally.

Just as he spoke, Brom appeared at the doorway. His frown deepened as he caught Hughie's words. "You'd better take good care of her," the father warned sternly.

Oliviare's face scrunched into a pout. "Father! Don't be so hard on Hughie."

Brom shook his head, chuckling despite his feigned annoyance. "If I'm not careful, I'll have to answer to your mother in the next life," he said, a hint of longing in his voice.

At the mention of her mother, Oliviare's head dipped, a shadow briefly crossing her face.

Hughie, seeing her sudden sadness, found himself at a loss for words. *What should I say?* But then, as quickly as it had come, her gloom lifted. She raised her head, a determined spark in her eyes.

"Are you ready?" she asked, her voice regaining its earlier excitement.

Hughie nodded, offering her a reassuring smile. "Yes, let's go."

The festival was a grand affair. Lanterns of every hue illuminated the village square. Musicians played their traditional instruments, filling the air with melodies both haunting and upbeat. Stalls lined the perimeter, offering an array of treats from steamed buns to skewered meats. Children ran around with joyous laughter, while the older villagers danced to the beat of the drums.

Amidst this jubilation walked Hughie and Oliviare, side by side, their arms almost touching but not quite. They moved through the crowd, occasionally stealing glances at each other but quickly looking away whenever their eyes met.

"It's lovely, isn't it? The Moon Blossom Festival only comes once a year, but it always feels magical." Oliviare tried to initiate conversation, her voice a mix of cheerfulness and nervous energy.

"Yes, it's quite different from what I'm used to," Hughie responded, his attention partially on the festivities and partially on her.

Gathering her courage, Oliviare asked the question that had been burning in her mind. "What is it like . . . being an immortal?"

He sighed, a sound tinged with unexpected sorrow. "Lonely," was all he said.

"And if you had a companion? Would you still feel lonely then?" she asked, her voice barely above a whisper.

Hughie gave her a sad smile. "I've not found an immortal who has captured my heart." *I always thought I'd build a harem of celestial beauties*, he mused internally, then chuckled silently at his own foolishness. *But then, plans have a funny way of changing, don't they?*

"Hughie, do you think a mortal could . . . steal your heart?" she asked hesitantly.

Time seemed to slow as he gazed deeply into her eyes, causing a rush of color to her cheeks. "I believe she already has," he confessed softly.

Just as Hughie leaned forward, their lips nearly touching, a loud commotion shattered the moment. They turned to see four cultivators descending from the sky, riding swords of gleaming energy.

Hughie's expression hardened as he gripped Oliviare's hand. "Stay behind me," he whispered, a surge of protectiveness overwhelming him.

The cultivators landed with arrogant grace. The leader, brimming with the powerful aura of the Core Formation stage, exuded the haughtiness typical of a young master. His entourage, though only at the Foundation Establishment stage, shared his overbearing demeanor.

"Have any of you villagers seen an injured immortal around here?" one of the lackeys demanded loudly.

A brave villager shook his head. "No, sir, no immortals here."

In a swift, threatening motion, the lackey grabbed the villager by the neck. "You'd best not be lying, old man," he snarled.

Fear took hold, and the poor villager soiled himself, shaking his head frantically in terror. *Things are about to get complicated*, Hughie thought, preparing for what might come next.

CHAPTER THIRTY-ONE

The leader, his eyes previously closed in concentration, opened them slowly, a hint of frustration evident. "I can't sense him," he murmured. "Either he's dead or he never came here."

Another lackey, more composed than his peers, spoke up. "We received word of a body thrown into the lake. We're wondering if it washed up here." He paused, eyeing the villagers. "There's a reward of one hundred gold coins for any information."

Eyes widened among the villagers, a flicker of greed flashing across several faces. They knew of the stranger Oliviare and her father had taken in. One villager, eager for the reward, pointed directly at Hughie. "It's him!"

The leader's gaze snapped towards Hughie, trying to probe for any signs of cultivation but finding none. He frowned, puzzled, and gestured to one of his men.

The lackey strode forward, stopping so close to Hughie that his breath brushed against his face. Hughie released Oliviare's hand, whispering, "Don't interfere, no matter what."

The lackey scrutinized Hughie, then turned back to his leader, shaking his head. "This one doesn't seem like a cultivator," he said, indicating Hughie's plain clothes and the absence of any detectable qi.

"That's the outsider. Found him half-dead in the lake," a villager piped up, eager to share information for the reward.

Hughie, feigning innocence, shrugged. "I'm just a hunter who had an accident. Don't know anything about these immortals you speak of."

The leader, however, seemed unconvinced. He gestured, and the lackey grabbed Hughie roughly, dragging him forward. "We'll take him back to grandpa. Even if he isn't the one, I'm in need of a new servant."

"No, don't take him!" Oliviare's voice cut through the tension.

The leader's attention diverted to Oliviare as she stood defiantly, her beauty striking him visibly. His eyes gleamed with a different kind of greed now. "Bring the girl," he ordered his men, his voice oily. "But be gentle. She will be . . . mine."

The second the lackey began his approach towards Oliviare, Hughie acted without hesitation. Tearing off the locket, it vanished seamlessly into his storage ring. With a breath, the Bloodforge Ascension technique surged to life within him, transforming his physique. His skin adopted a fiery hue as his injuries healed at a breathtaking speed. The potent aura of a Late Core Formation cultivator swept the area, causing the approaching lackey to stagger back in surprise.

"Stay away from her!" Hughie's voice was a growl, barely coherent, saturated with a rage he hadn't known he possessed. He lunged, driven by a burgeoning bloodlust. In a flash, he was upon the hapless Foundation Establishment cultivator.

The man, caught off guard, didn't stand a chance.

Hughie's hand, large and unyielding, clamped onto the man's face, and with a ferocious slam, he drove the lackey's head into the ground. The impact was catastrophic, the earth splintering while the man's skull caved in, brain matter seeping into the cracked soil.

A shrill scream pierced the air. "Demon!" A villager's voice echoed with terror, setting off a chain reaction of fear. Villagers scattered, seeking shelter.

Oliviare staggered back, her eyes wide with horror.

The sight stabbed him. *She's afraid . . . of me,* Hughie realized, heart sinking. He hadn't wanted her to witness this side of him, the side that veered closer to demonhood than the immortal cultivator she imagined. A battle began inside him: the beast craving bloodshed against the part of him that yearned to protect Oliviare.

His self-reflection was shattered by the leader's enraged bellow. "Get him!" he ordered, his command rallying the remaining two Foundation Establishment cultivators to encircle Hughie.

Each step they took, each battle stance they adopted, only fed the beast inside Hughie. But a sliver of his consciousness, fading fast, reminded him to finish it quickly. He struggled to think. *Oliviare . . . keep her safe.*

The leader unsheathed his sword, taunting, "You've done me a favor by killing my cousin, making me the heir, but—" His words ended abruptly when, in a flurry of motion, Hughie was upon him. His fingers, more claw than human, gripped the leader's throat. The man's frantic struggles only served to stoke Hughie's desire for violence.

Gasping, the leader tried wielding his sword. But with a feral snarl, Hughie batted it away. As his bloodlust threatened to consume him entirely, the leader's desperate pleas filtered through. "Please . . . you don't have to . . ."

But Hughie's grip only tightened, the rage blinding him to reason. With a sickening crack, the leader's neck snapped. Hughie tossed the lifeless body aside like it was nothing more than a ragdoll.

The two remaining lackeys, faces pale with horror, turned to flee, but Hughie was faster. In one fluid motion, he seized the leader's fallen sword, hurling it with deadly precision. It sailed through the air, impaling one lackey through the chest, pinning him to a tree. The man's eyes went wide as the life slowly left him.

The second lackey didn't even get a moment to process the scene. As he unleashed a blazing fire arrow attack, Hughie was already upon him. With a swift motion, Hughie brushed the fiery projectile aside, landing a powerful blow on the cultivator. The punch sent the man sprawling to the ground. But Hughie's wrath didn't stop there. With a powerful leap, he descended, foot first, onto the cultivator's skull. There was a wet, sickening sound as the head was pulverized, fragments of bone and gore scattering in all directions.

Chest heaving, he scanned the area. His bloodred eyes landed on Oliviare, standing alone beneath a market stall. A sinister urge prodded him forward. In a heartbeat, he was before her, teeth bared.

Hurt her, hurt her, hurt her, the whispers in his mind chanted.

Yet as he stared deep into her eyes, a hint of clarity pierced the fog of his rage. The weight of what he had nearly done bore down on him. "Am I . . . am I a monster?" he murmured.

Closing his eyes, he struggled to keep the tears at bay. *I am a man. Cultivators don't shed tears. Not here, not now. Especially not in front of her.* But the jovial mask he wore in the sect, the cheerful demeanor that masked his true feelings, was crumbling.

Suddenly, soft, warm arms wrapped around him. He felt Oliviare's comforting embrace.

"You're not a monster," she whispered into his ear, voice shaking but firm. "You protected the village, you . . . protected me."

Sh-she doesn't realize how close I was to . . . Hughie shook his head, not able to complete the thought.

He tentatively hugged her back as his demonic form slowly receded. "How can you *not* be afraid of me?" he whispered back.

Her voice, tender, carried a weighty confession. "Father was right, you are trouble . . . but you're my trouble now."

Hughie shook his head, a wave of sadness washing over him. "I have to leave this village. Staying will only endanger you, and I . . . I can't bear that thought."

Oliviare clung tighter to him, her voice brimming with emotion. "But I don't want you to go."

"And I don't want to leave," he admitted, his voice breaking.

"Why can't we stay like this forever?" she murmured, her breath warm against his bare chest.

Hughie remained silent, lost in thought. Just a few days ago, he'd tried a simple qi sensitivity technique on her. *All she had to do was sense the qi flow*, he recalled. But like many others, she didn't show any signs of the gift. He wished things were different.

If she could cultivate . . . he mused, *I could bring her to the sect, and perhaps we could have a future. But being with me, as a mortal? Too risky. I can't be selfish.*

"I . . . I wanted to tell you that . . . I mean, I think . . . I . . . uh . . ." Words began to tumble from him, a jumbled mess of emotions he tried to shape into a confession. But his tongue seemed to have a mind of its own, tripping over the syllables like a novice on the training field.

She gently placed a finger on his lips, silencing him. "I understand," she said softly. From the folds of her clothes, she took out a pitch-black ring. Plain, without any ornate designs, it looked . . . well, rather unimpressive.

"This has been in my family for generations," she explained, pressing the ring into his hand. "It's always been with me, close to my heart. And now, it's yours."

He stared at the ring, his thoughts whirling. *Seriously? Who in the world would craft a ring this . . . bleak?* "I can't take this," he blurted, the words escaping before he could catch them. And not just because of propriety. The ring was . . . *ugly. So very, very ugly.*

"Just take it." She smiled, shyly.

His hand closed around the ring, the metal cool against his skin. *Ugly or not, I'll treasure it. Because it's from her.* He couldn't help but smile back.

She leaned forward, her lips briefly touching his cheek. "Something to remember me by, Mr. Immortal," Oliviare teased. As she slowly moved away, she murmured, "I will always be waiting for you. Always."

Just before she vanished from his line of sight, she hesitated and turned back. Her face was slightly flushed, and her fingers nervously played with the edge of her dress. "And when you come back," she added, mustering the courage, "I expect you to propose with that ring."

Hughie stood there, the warmth of her kiss lingering on his skin, watching her retreating figure until it disappeared. He sighed deeply, sliding the unattractive ring onto his finger. *This is going to be an interesting story to tell the guys back at the sect*, he mused, a bitter smile tugging at his lips.

And then, out of the blue, a disgruntled voice echoed inside his mind. "Insolent young-ster! Daring to charm and woo my precious descendent! And you! Oliviare! How could you hand our ancestral ring to this . . . this stranger?!"

Hughie blinked, trying to comprehend the sudden intrusion. *Am I . . . am I hearing voices now?* he thought.

The voice continued to rant. "Back in my days, we valued traditions, not like these unfilial descendants. Gifting away family treasures to the first charming face they see! Bah! To think that our noble immortal lineage would produce such . . . such mortals."

The voice was old and cranky, and Hughie imagined a grumpy old man shaking his fist at the sky.

Has the ring got some sort of curse that includes a nagging ancestor?

"Hello?" Hughie ventured, hoping he wasn't going mad.

"What? You can hear me?!" The voice responded with genuine surprise.

Hughie nodded, then realizing that the voice probably couldn't see him, he verbalized his response. "Yes, I can hear you."

A throaty chuckle emerged from the ring. "Well, then, lad. It seems it's your lucky day. I am a true immortal. Not one of those half-baked 'I've lived for two centuries and now I'm enlightened' ones. Nope! A genuine, bona fide immortal!" The voice paused, a sort of smug-ness emanating through the connection. "You know, if you manage to impress me—which is no small feat, mind you—I might just consider taking you on as a disciple."

Ding!

Your Disciple Hughie Has Found a Heaven Rank Treasure

Alert: Your Disciple's Loyalty Is Being Tested

Special Condition Activated: For every action, there's a reaction. Should your disciple Hughie prove loyal, you will be rewarded. However, if his loyalty falters, you will face consequences.

Reward for Disciple's Loyalty:

- 1000 Karmic Credits
- Comprehension Card (Level 1)

Consequences of Losing a Disciple:

- Hidden
- Hidden
- Hidden

CHAPTER THIRTY-TWO

Hughie couldn't help but let out a small, incredulous chuckle. "I appreciate the generous offer," he replied with a hint of sarcasm, "but I already have a master, thank you very much."

The old man's laughter boomed in Hughie's mind, so loud Hughie wondered if others could hear it. "Fine, fine! No need to be so formal. How about this: I'll take your master as a disciple too! With my unparalleled wisdom, I'm sure they'll leap at the chance to learn from a true immortal. Who wouldn't?"

Hughie's mouth twitched. *This ring isn't just ugly, it's eccentric too!* "I'm not quite sure he'd go for that," Hughie retorted. "He's a bit old-fashioned. Doesn't believe in switching masters willy-nilly, especially for ones living in . . . uh, jewelry."

The old man harrumphed, the sound vibrating through Hughie's skull. "Living in jewelry! I'll have you know, this is a highly sophisticated form of existence! Free from the mundane needs of the flesh! And besides, what's not to love? I'm like a wise mentor you can carry in your pocket!"

Hughie's eyebrows knitted as he glanced at the ring on his finger. "How did you end up in a ring in the first place?"

The old man cleared his throat, an awkwardness seeping into his usually boisterous tone. "Ah, well, you see, there was a minor incident where my body got, er, destroyed."

Hughie raised an eyebrow. "And you couldn't find anything better than a ring to inhabit?"

The old man's voice bristled with indignation. "Now, young man, I'm sure many respectable elders get trapped in rings! It's probably quite common in the higher realms, you know!" In his mind's eye, Hughie could easily imagine the old man shaking his fist at him, trying to appear intimidating while stuck in an accessory.

Sighing, Hughie asked, "Alright, what's your name? I don't want to keep calling you 'old man.'" *I have enough old men in my life*, he thought bitterly.

Puffing up with pride, the old man announced, "I am Li Fenghao, the illustrious sect leader of the Heavenly Cloud Sect!" He paused for dramatic effect, letting his words hang in the air. "A Ninth Stage Greater Immortal, I'll have you know!"

Hughie looked at him, or rather the ring, a little confused. "Never heard of it," he replied dismissively.

Li Fenghao laughed heartily. "It would surprise me more if anyone from such a . . . backwards place like this had heard of it."

Hughie smirked. "You talk big for someone stuck in a ring, *former* Sect Master." He emphasized the word "former," drawing out each syllable.

The old man quieted for a second, then muttered, "If it wasn't for that damned chicken, I—" He halted, then cleared his throat. "Never mind that. Just know I'll be out of here soon."

Not entirely convinced, Hughie simply nodded. "Sure."

Li Fenghao, sensing the skepticism, pounced on the opportunity to reassert his prestige. "Aren't you the least bit impressed? Me, a greater immortal, Ninth Stage at that! Almost at the—"

Hughie waved his hand dismissively, cutting him off. "Listen here, old man. How do I know you're not just trying to trick me? Anyone can talk a big game. Why don't you prove your grand claims?"

Li Fenghao spluttered. "Prove it? I'm in a ring! How do you suggest I do that?"

Hughie had to bite his lip to keep from smirking. *Time to swindle an old monster.* Memories of his younger days flitted across his mind—those times he'd scam unsuspecting victims out of their money. Initially, it was to fend off starvation, but eventually, it became a game. A game he was *really* good at.

With a contemplative expression, Hughie mused aloud, "Hmm, let me think . . ." He feigned deep thought for a moment before leveling his gaze at the ring. "You say you're a greater immortal at . . . what was it again?"

Li Fenghao's voice interrupted with a mixture of pride and impatience, "Ninth Stage!"

"Yeah, yeah." Hughie waved dismissively. "So, as a greater immortal, you must know some Heaven Rank techniques. I mean, any immortal worth their salt would surely possess one."

Li Fenghao burst out laughing, the sound echoing strangely in Hughie's mind. "Boy, I practically breathe Heaven Rank techniques! Heavens, I even know a few Obsidian Rank techniques."

Hughie's eyes narrowed ever so slightly. *Obsidian Rank?* He'd never heard of such a thing. Yet he kept his expression neutral. "All I've heard so far is a lot of bragging, old man. Where's the proof? Show me these techniques!"

The old man huffed, sounding somewhat defensive. "Fine! Since you're so insistent, I'll teach you the Dimensional Slide. It's an Obsidian R—" he began, then stopped abruptly. "Wait just a moment! You're trying to pull one over on this old man, aren't you?"

Shaking his head with exaggerated innocence, Hughie retorted, "If anyone's attempting any tricks, it's you. Why on earth would a 'greater immortal' be desperate to take on someone like me as a disciple? Unless . . . you're hoping I might help free you from your . . . ring-shaped prison?"

Li Fenghao fell silent. *How did this seemingly simple-minded brat figure it out?* the old man wondered, genuinely taken aback.

Hughie leaned in, a sly smirk on his face. "I think you need to prove your worth to me. In fact," he said with feigned magnanimity, "maybe, just maybe, if you impress me enough, *I'll* consider taking you on as a master."

Trapped for millennia, the old man had grown frustrated, even as a greater immortal. No matter how powerful he was, life had its limits, and his was inching closer to its end. Not a single one of his descendants, neither cultivator nor mortal, had ever sensed his presence in the ring.

"You know, in my prime," the old man began, sounding irritable, "disciples would climb mountains, cross vast oceans, just for a chance to learn from me. And here you are, demanding a technique like you're asking for pocket change! You really have some nerve, brat." With a sigh that sounded suspiciously like a defeated groan, he continued, "But so be it. You want to learn the technique? I'll teach you."

Hughie couldn't help the grin spreading across his face. *Another one swindled*, he thought gleefully. In truth, he wasn't entirely sure he could assist the old man, but it seemed his bluff had spectacularly paid off.

Li Fenghao started detailing the technique. "It's called the Dimensional Slide. It allows the user to momentarily traverse into a pocket dimension, enabling them to instantaneously appear at another location." He paused, seriousness creeping into his voice. "But this dimension is not a sanctuary. It's a viper's nest with its own perils. Linger too long, and it might just be the death of you."

Hughie's eyes widened in awe. *This is leagues beyond anything I imagined he'd cough up.*

Noticing Hughie's impressed expression, the old man couldn't help but chuckle, a sound that seemed to warm him slightly. "With this technique, lad, you'll be untouchable. No one could catch up to you."

Yet Hughie couldn't resist poking fun. "And yet, it didn't save you from a chicken."

Li Fenghao's voice caught in his throat, a mixture of irritation and embarrassment. "That was no ordinary farmyard fowl! That chicken was . . ."

Hughie interrupted, a playful smirk on his face, "A chicken is still a chicken, old man."

The old man let out an exasperated sigh. "Regardless of your . . . poultry opinions, know this: With the Dimensional Slide, you'll be unmatched in speed. Absolutely no one in *this* realm will be able to catch you."

"Hmm, let's test that out," Hughie declared, searching for a suitable spot for training. After wandering for a bit, he found a secluded area distant from the village. Standing at the village's edge, he cast a lingering glance backwards, nostalgia briefly touching his eyes. *Will I ever return here?*

Li Fenghao, seemingly oblivious to Hughie's introspection, piped up with, "Your talent shines brightly, lad. Quite impressive . . . at least for this realm," he mumbled under his breath. Clearing his throat, he continued, "I believe you'll grasp the Dimensional Slide without much difficulty."

Awkwardly rubbing the back of his head, Hughie couldn't help but feel a bit guilty. Yes, breakthroughs in cultivation came somewhat easily to him, but learning new techniques? That was a different story. He'd always envied how his senior brother Caelum seemed to master numerous sword techniques effortlessly while he struggled. Hughie decided it was best to keep this bit of information from the old man.

"Now, listen closely," the old man started, his tone serious. "First, you need to focus your qi, but don't rush it. Let it build steadily, feel it flow through your body, ready to burst forth, but under your complete control . . ."

As the old man continued, detailing the intricacies of the Dimensional Slide, Hughie found his teachings surprisingly clear and intuitive. But despite that, his mind stubbornly refused to grasp the concept. *It's like trying to catch fish with your bare hands,* he thought in frustration.

Sensing Hughie's readiness—or at least what he mistook for readiness—the old man asked, "Are you prepared to give it a go?"

Swallowing his apprehension, Hughie nodded. Taking a deep breath, he tried to summon the image the old man had described, focusing on his feet and visualizing . . . something. But instead of a rift, all he managed was a small puff of dust as his foot stomped the ground.

The old man's chuckle filled the air. "Well, at least you've managed to master the 'Dusty Foot Stomp.' Very impressive!"

Hughie grimaced, feeling a pang of embarrassment. "Well, practice makes perfect, right?"

The old man continued to chuckle, clearly enjoying himself. "Indeed, brat. But perhaps let's start with something simpler . . . like standing still."

After a few grueling hours of practice, Hughie had nothing to show for his efforts. Not even a hint of a rift had materialized.

Fed up, he flung his hands up, "Are you certain this move isn't exclusive to Nascent Soul cultivators?" He groaned. Nascent Soul practitioners held the ability to create minor rifts in space, albeit only stretching across short distances. The Dimensional Slide, on the other hand, offered access to the vast expanse of the void, a wholly different dimension.

Li Fenghao snorted. "Why, I utilized this technique all the time when I was at the Core Formation stage." He paused, his brows knitting in thought. "Although, now that you mention it, I don't recall anyone else managing it until they'd reached Nascent Soul . . ."

Hughie's eye twitched in exasperation. *This ring-wearing, rambling old geezer . . .* "So," he mumbled, "the technique's practically useless then?"

The old man's voice took on an intrigued tone. "Hmm, hold that thought, I might have a little idea to speed up your progress."

Suspicion flared in Hughie's eyes. "What sort of idea?"

Li Fenghao responded, "I'll impart my comprehension of the technique directly to you. An information dump of sorts."

Hughie's face scrunched in confusion. "If you could do that all along, why waste hours watching me fail repeatedly?"

The old man's lamenting sigh sounded almost like a deflating balloon. "You youngsters have no patience. Who even is your master? Didn't he teach you anything about the Dao?" He paused to gather his thoughts. "Imparting comprehension directly can be a double-edged sword. Yes, it can speed up initial learning, but it might hinder your personal understanding of the Dao later on. The Dao isn't a one-size-fits-all; it needs to be understood and interpreted by each cultivator individually."

Hughie grimaced, clearly unimpressed. "Everyone always goes on and on about the Dao. I just want to get stronger, plain and simple." He paused, tilting his head slightly. "What's so great about this Dao everyone keeps yammering about anyway?"

Li Fenghao's voice turned contemplative. "Ah, lad, the Dao is . . . well, it's many things. But that's a lesson for another day. Everyone's got a different answer, and it's up to each to find their own."

Then, in a more biting tone, he added, "Now, cease your relentless questions and let me concentrate!"

After a few moments, a surge of green qi spiraled out of the ring, it slowly made its way to Hughie's temple, embedding itself there. It was like a river of knowledge, every twist and turn, every ripple, explaining the intricacies of the Dimensional Slide. For Hughie, it felt like thousands of pages of instruction compacted into mere moments of understanding.

After processing the flood of information, Hughie blinked a couple of times, looking bewildered. "Old man, why didn't you explain it like this from the start? It's so straightforward!"

Li Fenghao merely huffed, rolling his eyes. "Arguing with a fool is truly a waste of breath." He then nudged Hughie forward. "Give it another try. If my comprehension doesn't help you open a rift now, then I'm afraid nothing will."

Ignoring the jab, Hughie took a deep breath and began channeling the technique. The air around him seemed to shimmer, and then, with a tearing sound, a rift appeared. It was like a doorway to another world, the edges glowing with a bluish tint, and the center was pure, endless darkness.

"Do I just . . . walk in?" Hughie questioned, pointing towards the rift.

Li Fenghao's voice dripped with sarcasm. "No, you dance your way in. Of course, you walk!"

Hughie scowled. "Hey, I'm just being cautious. What if it leads to the Abyss of Ten Thousand Demons or something?"

"If you had been paying attention," Li Fenghao responded with a huff, "you'd remember it leads to the void plane. From there, you can decide where to emerge next."

Hughie mumbled, "Sounds like an unnecessary extra step . . ."

Taking a tentative step, Hughie entered the rift. The world around him shifted. Everything was in stark black and white, like an old photograph. It was eerily silent. Just as he was about to question the aesthetics of the void plane, a cold shiver ran down his spine.

A massive, ethereal beast hovered in the distance. It was translucent, its body like that of smoke, but its form was clear. The beast possessed twisted, antler-like protrusions atop its head, long, jagged claws, and piercing eyes that seemed to glow.

Though it was a distance away, Hughie felt ensnared by its gaze, like a rabbit facing a predator.

Li Fenghao's voice screamed in Hughie's mind. "Move, you imbecile! MOVE!"

But Hughie felt paralyzed, ensnared by the otherworldly gaze of the phantom beast. All he could think was, *Why didn't the old man mention this?*

Ding!
Your Disciple Hughie Has Encountered an Otherworldly Being
Warning: Your Disciple Is in Mortal Danger
Task: Save Hughie
Reward:
  • Disciple Loyalty Increases
  • 10,000 Karmic Credits
Failure:
  Outcome 1: Death of Disciple
  Outcome 2: Your Disciple Has Been Saved By Another, Disciple Loyalty Will Be Adjusted

CHAPTER THIRTY-THREE

Move, boy, MOVE!" The old man's urgent voice reverberated in Hughie's head. Seeing the young man remain rooted to the spot, Li Fenghao released an exasperated sigh. "This is going to set me back *decades*!"

Suddenly, the ring on Hughie's finger glowed a soft green. He felt a rush of unfamiliar energy coursing through him, startling him back into action. Without a second thought, he leaped backwards into the rift, reemerging in the training ground.

Catching his breath, Hughie heard the weakened voice of Li Fenghao grumbling, "You truly have dogshit luck!"

Hughie's ears reddened. No one had ever accused him of being unlucky before. Everywhere he went, people often envied his fortune. "What . . . what was that creature?" His voice trembled.

The sheer pressure from the being was unlike anything Hughie had ever experienced before. Not even the Origin Realm expert he had encountered made him feel so . . . insignificant.

Li Fenghao let out a deep sigh. "They are called Voidwalkers, beings that inhabit the void plane. It's exceedingly rare to come across one, especially for a first-timer like you."

Hughie shuddered at the thought. If the old man had mentioned that these creatures were common in the void, he might've sworn off the technique altogether.

The old man continued, "Even greater immortals tread lightly around them." Trying to sound comforting, though in a peculiar way, he added, "Given your current cultivation, you're no more than an ant in its eyes. Had it truly noticed you as a threat, not even I could've saved you."

Hughie looked even more pale. "So . . . every time I use the technique, there's a chance I'll run into them?"

The old man chuckled. "Well, technically, yes. But think of it as crossing a busy street. You might get hit by a carriage, but with experience, you'll know when to walk."

That's his version of reassurance? Hughie grimaced.

Seeing Hughie's reaction, Li Fenghao huffed. "You youngsters need thicker skin. In my time, we faced Voidwalkers with just a twig and some good intentions!"

Hughie raised an eyebrow. "Really?"

The old man sighed. "No, not really. But it sounded good, didn't it?"

Hughie shook his head at the old man's antics. "Anyways, thanks for saving me back there."

The old man smirked, puffing up his chest. "As your *master*, it's my solemn duty to protect my disciples."

"Like I said, I've already got a master. And with that little adventure over, I think it's time for me to head back." Hughie hesitated, his thoughts drifting to Amelia. *She probably thinks I'm dead by now.*

Trying to reel Hughie back, the old man persisted. "You sure about going back to your so-called master? What stage of the Immortal Realm is he at, anyway?"

Hughie scratched the back of his neck. "Uh, he's in the Ascendant Realm."

Li Fenghao paused, his eyes widening in mock shock. And then, out of nowhere, a roaring laughter erupted from him. "Ascendant Realm? Ha ha! Your master would kneel and beg for me to take him in as a disciple! Why, back in my prime, Ascendants used to shine my boots!"

Hughie couldn't help but roll his eyes. Trying to change the subject, he asked, "What kind of name is Li Fenghao, anyway?"

The old man's laughter died down instantly, his face reddening as if he'd been slapped. "In the Immortal Realm, we have names fit for men! As for here . . . well, you lot have the peculiar names." With a look of distaste, he tried to mimic Hughie's name with a mocking tone. "Hooo-ghie? Sounds like someone choking on a fish bone!"

Hughie chuckled. "Well, 'Li Fenghao' sounds like someone sneezing during a poetry reading."

Li Fenghao huffed. "You have no appreciation for the elegance and depth of an immortal's name!"

Hughie laughed heartily. "You really are something, old man."

"I'm just speaking the truth. And remember, brat, it's 'Master Li' to you."

Hughie smirked. "In your dreams, Grandpa."

The old man grumbled, muttering something about "disrespectful youngsters."

Ding!
Congratulations!
You Have Reached Late Foundation Establishment Realm
Reward: 200 Karmic Credits

Slifer emerged from his closed-door cultivation session, rubbing his stomach. The rumbling in his belly was hard to ignore. *Ah, the worldly needs of the flesh.* Stretching his limbs, he thought with satisfaction, *It won't be long until I enter the Core Formation Realm.* His confident smile, however, quickly faded when a System notification caught his eye.

Ding!
Alert: Critical Condition Detected
Disciple Designation: Hughie
Status: Fatally Wounded
Task: Administer Advanced Healing to Hughie
Time Limit: 1 Hour
Warning: If Disciple Hughie remains untreated within the specified time frame, it will result in the disciple's unfortunate demise.
Caution: Death of a disciple incurs severe consequences.
For specifics:
  • Hidden
  • Hidden
  • Hidden

Slifer's heart nearly stopped, but the real shock was that the alert had appeared *five* days ago!

In a frenzy, he quickly checked the status of all his disciples on the System. When he saw that they were all safe and sound, he let out a sigh of relief.

"I *told* that boy to stay out of trouble!" he exclaimed, exasperated. He shook his head, *Of course, this is the kind of drama I should expect when mentoring a protagonist disciple. I wonder how he managed to wiggle out of this one though*, he pondered. Several tropes came to his mind: *A sudden power surge? An unexpected ally arriving in the nick of time? Or maybe a hidden legacy awakening within him?*

Shaking his head, he decided to scroll through more notifications, it wasn't long before another one caught his eye.

Ding!

Your Disciple Hughie Has Found A Heaven Rank Treasure

Alert: Your Disciple's Loyalty Is Being Tested

Special Condition Activated: For every action, there's a reaction. Should your disciple Hughie prove loyal, you will be rewarded. However, if his loyalty falters, you will face consequences.

Reward for Disciple's Loyalty:
  • 1000 Karmic Credits
  • Comprehension Card (Level 1)

Consequences of Losing a Disciple:
  • Hidden
  • Hidden
  • Hidden

Slifer frowned, wondering. *What kind of Heavenly Treasure could possibly test his loyalty?* He tried to piece together the events. *Could the Heavenly Treasure be the reason he survived?* But when Slifer compared the timestamps, the events were days apart. *Nah, probably not related. But what could that treasure be?*

He took one last glance at the notifications, shook his head, and decided to grab a bite. *After all*, he reasoned, *an empty stomach won't help in deciphering Hughie's antics.*

As Slifer left his courtyard, a sudden tear in space appeared before him. Reflexively, he retreated several steps, ready to defend himself. A woman with raven-black hair and piercing eyes stepped out of the spatial rift. The singular word that flashed in Slifer's mind to describe the woman was "matron." The emblematic Black Rose Sect symbol on her robes made him swallow hard and straighten, feigning nonchalance as though her abrupt appearance hadn't fazed him in the slightest.

Sheesh, you can't just pop out of nowhere like that, he thought.

"Ah," the woman remarked in a poised tone, "just who I was looking for."

Slifer raised an eyebrow, a hint of sarcasm in his thoughts. *Why make it sound like a surprise when you literally appeared outside my courtyard?* He was about to address her when he realized he couldn't recall her name. The original's memories were fragmented at best. Yet, from the aura she radiated, he figured she was a grand elder.

"Grand Elder," Slifer began, clasping his hands together and giving a slight nod, "what brings you here?"

The stern expression on the woman's face transformed into an awkward smile. "Supreme Elder Slifer is too polite," she said, waving off his formality.

Regaining his composure and recalling his newfound status, Slifer coughed lightly. "While my cultivation may have advanced, in terms of age and wisdom, I remain your junior."

The grand elder's eyebrows raised in surprise. The Slifer she remembered was notoriously arrogant. But his cunning nature also came to mind. *This must be one of his games,* she deduced.

She then gestured to the rift, and another figure emerged. "Regrettably," she declared, "Amelia will no longer be welcome at the Medicine Hall."

Slifer's eyes widened as he gazed upon Amelia. The young disciple appeared distant, her normally radiant face now pale, her eyes tinged with redness.

What on earth happened to her? he wondered, his gaze shifting between the grand elder and the disheveled Amelia.

Grand Elder Lydia continued, her tone heavy with disappointment. "Amelia has perverted the Essence Mend technique. She's broken the sacred oath taken by all healers—to never bring harm to patients. Instead, she's used it malevolently to torture disciples who were in desperate need of healing."

Slifer's eyes darted to the oath's specific wording. *It specifies not to harm patients but says nothing about others.* Every demonic sect boasted a division of healers. These disciples, unlike their brethren, weren't inherently malevolent. If they were, who would dare seek their medical expertise? Yet, these same healers didn't strictly tread the path of righteousness either. They existed in a gray zone; neutral when you were under their care, but possibly dangerous if you crossed them outside the healing chambers.

While Slifer mulled this over, memories of his recent notifications flooded back. Among them were several notifications of "Karmic Credit Earned." The only act he recalled that granted a single Karmic Credit was . . . torture.

He let out a weary sigh, not surprised in the least. "I see."

Slifer gestured for Amelia to approach him. She shuffled her feet, her eyes blank, and took her place beside her master. The ensuing silence was palpable as Slifer and Grand Elder Lydia locked eyes, each waiting for the other to break the tension.

Does she expect an apology? Slifer thought. Clearing his throat, he turned to Amelia. "Apologize to the grand elder."

Amelia's voice was hollow, devoid of emotion. "I apologize, Grand Elder Lydia."

The grand elder nodded slightly but kept her gaze fixed on Slifer. The air grew thick with expectation.

She wants me to apologize too, Slifer surmised, his annoyance flaring. *She can wait forever. It wasn't me who twisted Amelia this way. That blame rests squarely on the original Slifer.*

As seconds ticked by, Grand Elder Lydia's patience waned. Without another word, she stepped back into the spatial rift. Just before she vanished, she muttered, "Seems you truly haven't changed, Supreme Elder."

Eh, she'll get over it, Slifer thought dismissively, but his gaze softened as he turned to Amelia. He'd never imagined seeing his spirited disciple in such a despondent state. A sudden realization struck him. *Could she be blaming herself for Hughie's "death"?*

"What is troubling you, Amelia?" Slifer inquired gently.

Hidden beneath her cascade of silver hair, Amelia's voice came out as a whisper, "I'm a terrible senior sister."

Slifer, trying to exude patience and understanding, gently prodded, "Why do you believe that?" *I feel like some school therapist. Next thing I know, I'll be asking her about her childhood.*

"Because of me . . . Hughie . . ." Amelia's voice cracked as she struggled to get the words out. " . . . died."

Ah, there it was. Slifer had suspected as much. With a gentle smile, he reassured her, "Hughie is not dead."

She shook her head vigorously, a hint of anger in her eyes. "You don't know, Master! During our mission, a Nascent Soul cultivator attacked us. Hughie . . . he sacrificed himself for me."

Suppressing a chuckle, Slifer mused, *A single Nascent Soul cultivator? Please, it would take an army of them to threaten a protagonist like Hughie. If she had said a horde of them were after him, maybe I would've been more convinced.*

"Did you check his Soul Lamp?" he asked, eyebrow raised.

"Why would I? He couldn't possibly have survived that!" she retorted.

"You underestimate our Hughie." Slifer grinned. "He is like a cockroach. Indestructible."

A slow smile spread across Amelia's face. With a delighted squeal, she leapt into Slifer's arms. "Hughie's alive?!"

Slifer's body stiffened. *Oh no, why did I stand so close?*

While Amelia's embrace tightened around Slifer, a sharp chime resonated in his mind. A System notification floated before his eyes:

Ding!
Your Disciple Hughie Has Encountered An Otherworldly Being
Warning: Your Disciple Is in Mortal Danger
Task: Save Hughie
Reward:
  • Disciple Loyalty Increases
  • 10,000 Karmic Credits
Failure:
  Outcome 1: Death of Disciple
  Outcome 2: Your Disciple Has Been Saved By Another, Disciple Loyalty Will Be Adjusted

---

His focus shifted from the clinging Amelia—who, for some reason, was burrowing her face into his neck with a peculiar grin—to the message. He sighed. *Guess I won't be getting food anytime soon.*

For a brief moment, he contemplated the idea of anchoring Hughie to the sect with some mystical chains. *At least then, I wouldn't be on constant rescue missions.* However, another thought wormed its way into his consciousness. *With rewards like these, perhaps letting him loose and playing the hero isn't such a bad idea.*

The weight of the reward troubled him. *10,000 Karmic Credits? I might need a miracle to save him this time. Like . . . a Deadly Strike Card.*

Slowly, Slifer tried to disentangle himself from Amelia, who gave a reluctant pout. "I need to fetch Hughie," he explained, rubbing the back of his neck. *Before some savior swoops in and steals his loyalty.*

Amelia's face fell a little. "Can I come with you?"

Slifer was quick to shake his head. "No. And when I return, we will discuss your ban from the Medicine Hall. You will face consequences."

As he began to move away, his thoughts raced. He would need to get to Hughie as fast as possible.

I guess it's time to see Val!

CHAPTER THIRTY-FOUR

As Slifer arrived outside the guest quarters, where Leah was currently staying, the scene before him left him momentarily stunned. Val, in her smaller dragon form, was energetically chasing Leah around the courtyard, breathing out mini fireballs that Leah barely evaded.

Of all the things to walk into, Slifer thought, rolling his eyes. However, as Val transformed into her enormous form, Slifer's amusement turned to alarm. The fireball forming in her mouth was nothing to scoff at. *S-she's going to kill her!* Slifer thought in alarm, knowing that Leah did not have access to her cultivation.

"Val, stop!" Slifer commanded as he took a hasty step back; he did *not* want to get caught in the blast.

Val froze in midair, reverting back to her smaller form. With a wobbling lip and teary eyes, she squeaked, "Mastew shout at Val."

Slifer sighed, rubbing the bridge of his nose. "I told you to watch over Leah, not turn her into a roasted duck."

Val, shaking her small head, protested, "Val only playin thow."

Slifer's attention shifted to Leah, who appeared rather peeved at him.

Upon receiving a quizzical look from Slifer, she grumbled, "Yeah we were having fun. Until *someone* ruined it."

Val can't control herself. If I hadn't intervened, you would've been ashes by now, Slifer thought as he remembered the time that Val had gone overboard in their training session. Clearing his throat, he offered diplomatically, "Master didn't want our guest harmed. Perhaps there was a misunderstanding."

Val's eyes grew round. "Mastew sowwy?"

Slifer had to stop himself from sighing aloud. *Why does everyone expect an apology from me?* "Yes," he reluctantly muttered, "Master is sorry." But internally, he added, *Well, not really.*

Val's gloomy expression shifted to one of delight. "Val fowgive Mastew."

Smiling gently at the dragon, Slifer tempted, "Since Val forgives Master, would Val like to go on a mission?"

Val's enthusiastic nodding made it clear she was thrilled at the idea.

Slifer glanced towards Leah, whose posture tightened at his attention. "I trust you enjoyed your stay here?" he said.

She offered a timid nod, her gaze drifting to Val, her reluctance to let the dragon leave apparent.

Slifer shook his head inwardly. *Yet another heart bewitched by Val.*

Ding!
Task Name: Dragon Babysitting a Crazy Lady

Task Description: Ensure Val stays beside Leah for . . . 7 days!
Status: Complete
You have received 70 Karmic Credits.

Suppressing a grin, Slifer felt a slight satisfaction. Not only had he earned Karmic Credits, but Val had indeed softened Leah's edges. *At least she didn't try to spit on me this time.*

Val's voice cut through Slifer's thoughts. "What our mission, Mastew? Val gettin tweats?"

The mention of "tweats" drained the color from Slifer's face. A chilling memory surfaced: the original Slifer would take Val hunting for . . . humans. Hastily, he replied, "No, we're searching for your junior brother."

"Huwie missin?" Val's vibrant energy dimmed a little.

Slifer nodded solemnly. "Yes, and only Val can rescue him."

Val's dragon pride surged, her chest puffing out in a show of determination. With a majestic transformation, she expanded to her gigantic form.

Without hesitation, Slifer leaped onto her back, signaling her to take off.

"Val save Huwie!" she roared, launching herself into the skies.

A sense of exhilaration washed over him as they soared. *No matter how many times I experience this, the thrill never fades.* As Val carried him away from the sect, he still felt Leah's lingering gaze upon them.

Hours of flying turned into a rhythmic blur, but Slifer's patience was running thin. *There's still so much ground to cover,* he thought with a sigh.

To assist in the search, he had been using a special treasure—a Soul Compass. The item connected with the fragment of soul inside the Soul Lamp, revealing the whereabouts of a cultivator. Yet, its limitations were glaringly evident. Instead of pinpointing an exact location, it marked a broad region. Not to mention, there was a delay of about fifteen minutes, making tracking a moving Core Formation expert like finding a needle in a haystack.

Ding!
Task: Save Hughie
Status: Failed
Your Disciple Has Been Saved By Another
Hughie's Loyalty Has Decreased By 30%

The sudden task notification caused Slifer to sigh. *I was too late.* He took a moment to gather his thoughts, then shrugged. *At least the boy survived.* Glancing at Val, he said, "Find a secluded spot, away from any humans."

Val tilted her head. "Huwie here?"

Shaking his head, Slifer responded, "Your junior brother is safe for now. I have something else on my mind." He couldn't help but glance at the dwindling timer indicating his remaining lifespan.

Lifespan Remaining: 23 Days

The urgency to use one of his Reversal Cards bore down on him. He'd been saving them, hoping to use several together when the right time came. But now, time itself seemed to be running thin.

When will I next leave the sect? he pondered. *It's not like I can use it within the sect unless I'm fine with wiping out half the disciples as collateral.*

Once Val touched down in a forest clearing, Slifer leapt off her back. "Val," he began, "stay away until I call for you."

With the Soul Bond, he wasn't worried about losing her.

Val's eyes lit up with mischief. "Val look for food?"

Slifer hesitated for a moment. He knew her predatory nature all too well. "No humans," he emphasized, "but anything else is fair game."

The idea of Val hunting humans made him uneasy. *She's a dragon, and it's natural for her*, he rationalized. However, the concern that she might go too far and attract unwanted attention was real. *Yet the last thing I need is a vengeful protagonist on my doorstep due to Val's dietary preferences.*

Val pouted. "Master mean!" Without waiting for a reply, she flapped her wings and soared away.

After making sure Val had truly left, Slifer chose a spot and sat down. He wondered briefly, *Is the lifespan given by the Reversal Card always the same fixed amount or does it vary with the amount of life essence it collects? Well, I guess there is only one way to find out.* Taking a deep breath, he activated the Reversal Card.

Instantly, a brilliant white aura emanated from him, pulsating outwards like ripples in a pond. As the light touched the plants, they wilted almost instantly. Tall trees, once teeming with life, became gaunt as their leaves crisped away and their bark turned gray and lifeless.

The creatures of the forest weren't spared either. As the aura reached them, they frantically attempted to escape, but their efforts were in vain. Birds dropped mid-flight from the sky, their life essence sapped. Insects on leaves paused, then stilled forever. Even the small mammals that had been hidden in burrows and underbrush met the same fate, their life force drawn into the white aura.

The further the aura reached, the more desolate the clearing became. What was once a lively and verdant place was now rapidly turning into a barren wasteland, devoid of life.

Slifer felt the surge of life essence flow into him. The sensation was intoxicating, a heady mix of vitality and power. Drawing in a deep breath, he couldn't help but exclaim, "This . . . this is true sustenance!" *This . . . this is far better than any delicacy I've ever tasted*, he thought, a grin forming on his face. And for someone like him, who was known for his insatiable appetite, that meant something.

Hughie focused intently on the Dimensional Slide technique, silently praying that he wouldn't stumble into another Voidwalker. As the portal to the Void Realm appeared and he cautiously entered, a sigh of relief escaped him upon realizing that the space was free of those phantom-like beings. *If there was one waiting for me, I would seriously question my luck.*

Closing his eyes, he envisioned the sect's entrance and opened another breach. However, when he stepped through the new rift, he found himself amidst towering mountains and thick forests, certainly not at the sect's entrance.

Before he could fully comprehend his surroundings, Hughie felt a terrifying force attempting to pull the very life essence out of him. "W-what's happening?" he whispered, clutching his chest.

Li Fenghao's eyes widened in shock as his ethereal vision locked onto an elderly figure seated cross-legged in a clearing, casually absorbing the life essence around him.

How is this even possible?

The heavens hadn't merely forbidden the absorption of life essence through strict mandates, but had ensured it was fundamentally unattainable. Heavenly Tribulation was the sole genuine method to lengthen one's lifespan without drawbacks. Over the eons, many cultivators had sought alternate ways to prolong their lives, yet they all had severe, sometimes debilitating repercussions.

Li Fenghao's vision went blurry as he felt a tug on his own life force. "Escape! Use the technique and escape NOW!" he shouted mentally at Hughie as a sliver of his life essence made its way to the mysterious figure.

Without wasting another moment, Hughie created another fissure in space. This time, he reappeared right outside his sect. Panting, he tried to regain his composure.

The old man couldn't contain his frustration. "Boy! In all my years, I've never seen someone with luck as horrid as yours! How can it be that every time you use the technique, you narrowly escape death? Do you have a death wish?"

Hughie's ears turned a shade of crimson. He felt the sting of the old man's words, but there was no counter to it. The old man was right, his recent encounters had been nothing short of catastrophic.

Is my luck truly that terrible? he wondered. He then recalled his master's attempts at holding his hand during past lessons. *Did those touches somehow curse me?* he shivered.

Li Fenghao continued to grumble, "I've taught numerous disciples and traveled countless realms. But never . . . NEVER have I seen a lad attract disaster like a moth to flame! Is this some special talent of yours?"

"I . . . I don't know," Hughie mumbled.

Ding!
Warning: You Are Attacking Your Disciple Hughie

Hughie? Slifer's eyes snapped open in surprise. *Of course, it's Hughie. Where did that boy suddenly pop up from?* Despite extending his spiritual sense, he couldn't find any traces of the young cultivator.

While the delicious stream of life essence continued to flow into him, he kept an eye out for Hughie. *I mean, if he could dodge some strange being from another dimension, a tiny life essence tug should be like a gentle pat on the back . . . right?*

Ding!
Cease Your Attack
The Death of a Disciple By Your Own Hand Will Have Severe Repercussions

---

The message from the System felt like a slap in the face. As per the System's design, the Reversal Card, or any other card, once activated, could not be stopped midway.

Oh, come on, System! You're the one who gave me these cards! Why couldn't you add a "pause" button for those things? Slifer began to feel a hint of anxiety; he genuinely wasn't sure if even a protagonist, however lucky, could escape the System's grip entirely.

He better be okay . . . For both our sakes.

Ding!
Congratulations!
You Have Absorbed 0.000001% Life Essence of a Greater Immortal

---

CHAPTER THIRTY-FIVE

A rush of pure life essence unlike any other Slifer had ever felt surged through him, leaving him gasping, "G-greater immortal?" The intensity of the energy sent him into a state of euphoria so potent that focusing on anything else became a herculean task.

But survival instincts kicked in, forcing his eyes wide open as he scanned his surroundings fearfully. *A greater immortal... here?* The thought was as terrifying as it was perplexing. *Aren't they supposed to be in the higher realms, not meddling in the affairs of ants like me?*

He half-expected the offended immortal to materialize from the ether, delivering a slap potent enough to end his existence for the audacity of stealing even a sliver of their precious life essence. Slifer knew all too well that none of his cards could save him from a greater immortal's wrath.

Deadly Strike Card against a greater immortal? Might as well throw pebbles at a mountain. Fight or flight? Both seem equally futile before such a being, he thought grimly.

But as moments ticked by and no divine retribution descended upon him, Slifer's tense muscles began to relax. *That's odd . . .* His thoughts began drifting back to Hughie. *Could there be a connection?* Shaking his head, he decided to find out how much lifespan he gained. *Status!*

Name: Slifer
Race: Human
Alignment: Demonic
Cultivation: Late Foundation Establishment
Lifespan Remaining: 10 Years
Karmic Credits: 5700
Skills: Insight (Basic)
Items: Reversal Card, Peak Slifer Card, Whimsical Wind Card
Abilities: Mirror Mastery: Level 1
Techniques: Sunrise Slash: Level 2, Stellar Nova Strike: Level 1
Weapon Mastery: Sword: 5%

That 0.000001 percent gave me a whole decade? Good heavens, what kind of monstrous longevity do these greater immortals have? Slifer mused, his eyes widening in disbelief. *Man, if only that greater immortal had been feeling a tad more generous. A tiny bit more and I could've seen the next ice age!*

His train of thought was cut short by a sharp pain that pierced through his chest. He quickly extended his spiritual sense inwards, examining his body. There, he saw the chaotic swirl of Pseudo Origin Realm energy battering against the Qi Condensation Seal, which now showed alarming signs of fracturing.

Dammit, is this backlash from clashing with Hughie's luck? he wondered, his thoughts punctuated by pain.

A barrage of System notifications popped up, but Slifer dismissed them with a flick of his mind. Doubled over in agony, he hurriedly opened the System Shop, seeking something—anything—that could stabilize the situation.

The following cards appeared before his eyes:

Qi Purge Seal: When activated, this seal creates a temporary pathway for the excess qi to flow out of the body. Cost: 500 Karmic Credits

Qi Storm Dispersion Array: When activated, this array disperses the excess qi in the form of controlled energy storms. Cost: 700 Karmic Credits

Qi Conversion Meditation: Convert the unstable qi into pure spiritual energy, accelerating cultivation progress. Cost: 1,000 Karmic Credits

Qi Armor Manifestation: Gain the ability to manifest a protective Qi Armor around the body to enhance defense, strength and agility. Cost: 1,500 Karmic Credits

---

"Purging the Pseudo-Origin Realm qi would be a waste," Slifer muttered under his breath. *With risk comes reward, after all.* The options to absorb the qi were tempting, promising an immediate breakthrough, but he knew it was an unnecessary shortcut with his Heaven Rank Cultivation Method and pills. *If only it promised a breakthrough to the Nascent Soul Realm . . .*

Without any hesitation, he purchased the Qi Armor Manifestation. Without any Critical Block Cards left, a reliable defense was paramount.

Stellar Nova Strike probably isn't enough.

Activating the card, he felt the rampaging qi within him quell, transforming into a smoke-like Qi Armor. It enveloped him, creating a defensive shell at the Peak Nascent Soul level. The minute traces of Origin Realm energy, overwhelmed by the conversion, was lost in the process.

With his body only at the Body Tempering Realm, the armor's effect was clearly evident, he could already feel it enhancing his physical abilities. "With this, Core Formation cultivators shouldn't pose much of a threat," he muttered, a smirk forming on his lips. But as he moved, the armor fractured, fissures spreading across its smoky form until it dissipated into nothingness.

Slifer sighed, a touch of frustration in his voice. "Seems my body can't handle this armor for more than ten seconds." He shook his head, it seemed he would need to focus on body cultivation.

Slifer thought about the difference between body cultivators and their spiritual counterparts. Body cultivators tempered their flesh, bones, and blood through arduous and, more often than not, torturous training, transforming their very bodies into weapons.

As for spiritual cultivators, they sought internal harmony, meditating to refine their spiritual energy and qi.

One path is like forging iron under relentless hammer blows, while the other is like nurturing a delicate flower. He shuddered at the thought of undertaking the brutal regimen body cultivators endured. *But if I want to extend the Qi Armor's duration, I have no choice but to strengthen my physique,* he concluded. With a shake of his head, dismissing the unpleasant thoughts, he decided it was time to return to the sect. He reached out with his Soul Bond, calling for Val.

Within moments, he noticed the silhouette of the little dragon in the distance, flying quickly towards him. But something was amiss. Val's posture was slouched, her head lowered, wings drooping slightly—she had the look of a child who knew she'd done something wrong.

"What's wrong, Val?" Slifer asked, though part of him wasn't sure he wanted to know.

Val covered her face shyly with her wings, her body language screaming of guilt.

Time to check the notifications, Slifer thought with a growing sense of dread. As he feared, he was met with multiple identical messages.

Ding!
Your Disciple Has Attacked a Righteous Cultivator
120 Karmic Credits Have Been Deducted

Had it been one message, perhaps Slifer wouldn't need to worry, but attacking three righteous cultivators would definitely spell trouble.

"Val." Slifer sighed, rubbing his temples. "What did you do?"

Val peeked through her wings, her eyes big and round. "Pwomise Mastew won't be mad?"

Heaving another sigh, Slifer said, "Alright, I promise. What happened?"

Val looked up, her eyes shimmering with unshed tears. "Val made wickle miswake. Now bad men chase Val."

Slifer's heart sank. *Just what I needed. More trouble.* However, seeing Val's earnest eyes, he couldn't find it in himself to scold her. "Alright, Master will deal with it," he said, forcing a smile. *I really hope it's something minor. It would be quite the scene if an Ascendant cultivator had to flee from "lesser" cultivators—*

His thoughts were interrupted by a distant shout. Looking up, Slifer saw a group of five Nascent Soul cultivators flying towards him, led by an old man whose aura suggested he was at the Origin Realm.

Oh, Val, you're going to be the death of me, Slifer groaned internally.

One of the Nascent Soul cultivators laughed derisively. "You finally gave up running," he taunted.

Another nodded in agreement, sneering. "Your master will pay for your sins, beast."

"You dare devour my grandson," a third accused, his voice thick with grief.

Realizing that not even the last Peak Slifer Card could save him from the situation, Slifer felt a tremor of fear threaten to shake his legs, but he held his ground, and knew that he had to give off the aura of an expert if he wanted to bluff his way out of the situation.

Behind him, Val cowered, peeking out from her hiding spot. "Mastew, mean men," she whispered, pointing a small talon at them.

The Nascent Soul cultivators paused as their leader raised his hand. He squinted at Slifer, sensing something familiar. As recognition dawned, his complexion turned ashen, and he plummeted to the ground, bowing his head in a submissive posture. "Forgive me! Forgive me!" he cried out in horror.

What just happened? Slifer's brow arched in surprise at the sudden turn of events.

Two hundred years ago, the old man remembered with a pang of fear. He had been ambushed by none other than Slifer. The attack was swift, merciless, and almost took his life. By a twist of fate and sheer luck, he managed to escape with his life, but his treasured Luminance Blade was left behind. That cherished heirloom, passed down through generations, was taken by Slifer, who then corrupted its pure nature and left it to gather dust for years before bestowing it upon one of his disciples as a casual gift.

Foolish! The old cultivator chastised himself. He had always intended to retrieve his family's blade and seek revenge on Slifer. But news that Slifer had advanced to the Ascendant Realm changed everything. *It's certain death to provoke an Ascendant, especially one as ruthless as Slifer,* he agonized.

Seeing the old man's reaction, the Nascent Soul cultivators exchanged confused glances. Their leader, on his knees and begging for mercy? This was a sight none of them had expected.

"W-what are you doing, Sect Master?"

The old man, his forehead still pressed against the ground, motioned with his hand, urging his followers to mimic his actions. Taking a deep, shaky breath, he addressed Slifer, "Had I known the dragon was under the protection of Ascendant Slifer, I would have gladly sacrificed a few more disciples to appease her."

The surrounding cultivators began quaking in fear. They looked at each other with wide eyes, realization dawning on them. *This is Master Slifer, the rumored new Ascendant cultivator?* They thought collectively, cursing their rotten luck as they quickly followed their sect master's lead, dropping to the ground. As a smaller righteous sect, lacking an Ascendant cultivator of their own, they had no choice but to swallow this bitter pill of humiliation.

And who said I had dogshit luck? Slifer cleared his throat, giving them a displeased look that sent shivers down their spines. "My disciple informed me you were bullying her," he said slowly.

Their eyes widened at the mention of "disciple." It was truly unheard of for a beast to be considered a disciple, but given the unpredictable behavior of Ascendant cultivators, they dared not question his choice. In their desperation to appease, they began kowtowing fervently, their heads thudding against the hard ground with each bow, leaving red marks on their foreheads.

Feeling emboldened by the turn in events, Val puffed out her tiny chest proudly as she stood on Slifer's shoulder.

"You bully Val!" she accused, trying to sound as righteous as possible.

The cultivators exchanged anxious glances. *Bully?* they thought incredulously. *She was the one who attacked us unprovoked!* They remembered how she'd ambushed a disciple in the forest, and when reinforcements arrived, she'd gobbled them up without hesitation. She had even made a snack out of an elder at the Nascent Soul Realm! But they held their tongues, not daring to argue with the stubborn creature. With lowered heads, they mumbled, "Yes, we . . . bullied you."

Slifer, suppressing a smile, turned to Val. "How do you think they should be punished?" he asked.

Val's face scrunched up in thought. After a moment, she responded with an innocent pout. "Val weally hungwy."

CHAPTER THIRTY-SIX

The men's faces went ashen at Val's innocent declaration. Slifer quickly weighed the pros and cons in his mind. *If I let her try to eat them, they'll fight back . . . and they will realize I'm not the Ascendant cultivator they believe me to be.* He cautiously mulled over their options. "Besides that," he suggested to the baby dragon, trying to steer the conversation away from something that could end badly for him.

Val scrunched up her face in thought. "Val wike tweasures," she finally declared with a nod.

That might actually work, he pondered. *If I let them go without any action on my part, it would seem out of character for the original Slifer they know. But demanding treasures . . . it's a middle ground. Not too aggressive to provoke retaliation, yet assertive enough to fit my perceived image.*

Slifer's expectant gaze settled on the men, who hesitated only for a moment before they started to empty out their storage rings. A plethora of items soon littered the ground: jade pendants glowing with soft light, orbs infused with condensed elemental energy, and pills sealed in exquisite vials.

"P-please, find it in your mercy to accept these humble offerings," stammered one of the Nascent Soul cultivators, sweat beading on his forehead.

The Nascent Soul elder, whose grandson had been devoured, stepped forward with a forced smile, his body quivering like a leaf in the wind. "May the heavens bless me with more grandchildren," he said through gritted teeth, "so that Master Slifer's esteemed disciple can partake in more . . . gourmet feasts." The words tasted like poison on his tongue, but he knew that his survival depended on it.

The leader, with a resigned sigh, unhinged a splendid sword with an emerald handle from his waist, laying it beside the rest. He had once lost an invaluable heirloom to Slifer, and now, history was mocking him with its repetition. He then performed one last kowtow, his forehead lightly thudding against the ground. "Master Slifer, I will never forget this graciousness."

That sounded more like a veiled threat than a sign of gratitude. Lucky for him, I'm not an Ascendant cultivator; otherwise, a slap would've been the least of his worries, Slifer thought wryly as he dismissed them with a casual wave of his hand, the trembling men scampered away without a backwards glance.

"Tweasures!" Val squeaked as she transformed, her form expanding enormously. The change in form seemed to have sped up the digestion of the cultivators she devoured because a Mid-Nascent Soul aura came off her in waves, making Slifer flinch at the intensity.

Ding!
Your Disciple Val Has Broken Through
Reward: 100 Karmic Credits

Great, 100 Karmic Credits. Not enough to make up for the loss, but it's a start.

"Val's! Val's! All Val's!" She began to gobble up the treasures, each item disappearing with a satisfied gulp.

"Spit it out!" Slifer commanded, his expression stern. He realized that despite Val's current loyalty, she was still a wild beast at her core. Even though he saw her more of a child than a pet, she was still a higher-level being, albeit a baby version. A dragon's pride was tremendous, and he needed to show her that he was in charge; an out-of-control adult Val would not be something he would be able to handle.

I can't only blame her, she doesn't know any better, I need to do a better job as a parental figure.

Val's ears cowered back, and she reluctantly spat out the treasures she had eagerly consumed.

"Master told you to stay out of trouble."

"Val sowwy."

Slifer shook his head. "Sorry isn't enough," he said, pausing for emphasis. "You'll need to make up for the trouble you caused. You are to complete ten missions for me. And no humans as a meal unless I allow it, understood?"

Ding!
Your Disciple Val's Loyalty Has Increased By 5%
Ding!
You have received 20 Karmic Credits for disciplining your disciple.

Hmm, seems like I made the right choice.

"Val will be good this time."

A full sentence from the dragon surprised Slifer.

Has the breakthrough to the Mid-Nascent Soul stage affected her mental age? If before, Val was equivalent to a five-year-old, she now seemed more similar to an eight-year-old—but this was all guesswork from Slifer, he didn't really know enough about kids to be certain. *When she breaks through to the Origin Realm, would she be in her teens?*

The relationship between Val's cultivation and her mental age was comforting, Slifer didn't know the first thing when it came to taking care of a kid.

As for a teenager? Slifer mused, a smirk playing on his lips. *First, there's the angst phase, where everything is the worst thing ever. Then, the obsession with the opposite sex—or the same. Ah, and can't forget the rebellion stage.* "You're not my real master!" *That'll be a fun one.*

Shaking his head, Slifer turned his attention to the spoils.

I'm rich!

For a supreme elder; he was, in fact, living in poverty but his true cultivation was at the Foundation Establishment Realm so in reality he was drowning in riches.

As the treasures flowed into his storage ring, he felt a strange connection to one of the items. It was the sword the Origin Realm expert wielded. On closer inspection, Slifer's eyes widened.

Activating his Insight skill on the sword, the information presented stunned him.

Name: Skyfade Emerald Blade

> Rank: Heaven Rank Treasure
> Realm: Adaptable to User's Cultivation Base
> Condition: Perfect

Now, this is a pleasant surprise, he thought, his fingers tracing the intricate carvings on the sword.

Unlike the sword Elder Olakin had given him, which demanded an Origin Realm cultivation to even handle, this Skyfade Emerald Blade was perfect for him. It was adaptable, a treasure that grew with its master. Slifer couldn't help but murmur, "I should probably pay that old man another visit sometime. Who knows, he might have another treasure tucked away."

Just as the thought crossed his mind, Val shrank down to her petite form. Hovering over to Slifer, her face displayed a mix of confusion and embarrassment. "Master . . . why was Val scawed? Dwagons are never scawed," she mumbled, her voice tinged with a hint of shame.

Slifer put two and two together, realizing she'd been overwhelmed by the emotions transmitted through their Soul Bond. *Ah, she felt my fear and assumed it was her own.*

Gently patting her head, he reassured her, "Val is just a baby dragon. It's okay to be scared sometimes. But remember, Master will be here to protect you and then when you're big enough, you will protect Master."

"Master is Val's favowite." She looked up at him with teary eyes.

Slifer chuckled, ruffling her scales affectionately. "Then you should stop causing so much trouble for your favorite master."

Val puffed her cheeks out, nodding vigorously. "When Val is big, Val will protect Mastew!"

Hughie was waiting in Slifer's courtyard, he had finally gotten the hang of the Dimensional Slide technique, landing him in the sect rather than in another near-death experience. He didn't know if his luck could save him a third time. Beside him, Li Fenghao, trapped within a spiritual ring, was mid-rant, boasting about how he'd make Hughie's master bow before him.

"And then," Li Fenghao's voice crackled from the ring, "your master will be so impressed he'll happily hand you over to me."

"I'm not some ornamental pot to be handed around," Hughie retorted, though a part of him felt oddly flattered. He'd always imagined being fought over by jade beauties, not crotchety old men.

Suddenly, the silhouette of a dragon appeared on the horizon, winging its way towards them. It was Val!

Li Fenghao began to laugh. "Watch and learn, brat." But his voice faltered as his eyes narrowed on the figure riding the dragon. The old man's voice turned to a strangled wheeze. "H-how is this possible?"

Hughie, surprised by the old man's reaction, asked, "What's got your beard in a twist?"

"Keep my existence a secret," Li Fenghao managed to croak out, his earlier bravado evaporating like morning mist.

Hughie raised an eyebrow. "I thought you were going to 'show my master who's boss'? Why is the *great immortal* so scared all of a sudden?"

"This is no time for jokes, you brat!" Li Fenghao snapped, his aura retreating into the ring, shrinking smaller and smaller until it was imperceptible. "Humph, I'll explain later."

Hughie sighed in exasperation. "Great," he mumbled to himself. *Even this old geezer doesn't want to be anywhere near my master.*

Slifer and Val descended into Slifer's courtyard, where Hughie was already waiting with an uneasy expression. *How did he get here before us?* Slifer wondered.

Dismissing Val, Slifer walked up to his disciple.

Hughie, seemingly lost in his own thoughts, snapped back to reality and hastily greeted Slifer with a bow and clasped hands.

"Rise," Slifer said, noticing Hughie's discomfort. "Your senior sister was quite worried about you."

Hughie, feeling a twinge of guilt, awkwardly scratched his head. "I . . . um . . ."

Slifer waved off his concerns. "You have done well," he said, referring to Hughie's efforts in protecting Amelia.

Hughie shifted uncomfortably. He knew that when his master acted nice, he generally wanted something.

Slifer, curious about the Heaven Rank treasure Hughie found, probed further. "Did anything interesting happen while you were away? Perhaps you . . . found a treasure?"

Hughie stifled a nervous gulp. "If I had found one, I'd offer it to you, Master." But internally, he grumbled, *I'm tired of "lending" my stuff to Master.*

Knowing that Hughie was lying to him, Slifer glanced at the loyalty stats of his disciples. Hughie's number flickered, settling at a disheartening thirty-five percent.

I guess the loyalty stat isn't just a useless number after all, Slifer mused with a frown. This sparked a troubling thought. *Is someone trying to poach my disciple?* He felt a twinge of unease. *Could it be the handiwork of that greater immortal?*

To clear his suspicions, Slifer started scrutinizing Hughie for any trace of the greater immortal. With his cultivation, he would be a fool to believe he would be able to spot anything. That was where the Insight skill came in handy, he doubted even a greater immortal could hide itself from the System.

Meanwhile, Hughie's face flushed. *Why is Master looking at me like that?* His master's gaze felt uncomfortably intense, and when a strange look appeared on Slifer's eyes, Hughie felt a shiver down his spine. *I need to say something. I can't let Master think he can just . . . ogle me like this.*

Just as Hughie mustered the courage to voice his thoughts, Slifer's eyes narrowed, causing him to swallow his words. *Can Master read my mind?* he thought, feeling more self-conscious. Clearing his throat loudly, he asked, "Master, is there . . . something on my face?"

But Slifer's attention was firmly on the System message that had just popped up:

Name: Soul-Bearing Ring (occupied)
Rank: Heaven
Condition: Poor

Occupied? A grim realization dawned on him—someone was trying to poach *his* disciple, and it was an old man trapped in a ring!

Focusing on the ring, Slifer once again activated Insight.

Name: N/A

Realm: Greater Immortal
Known Techniques: N/A
Disposition: N/A

Of all the clichés, Slifer thought with a silent groan. *Is this one of the benevolent types, or the evil kind who'll devour Hughie's soul?* Either way, Slifer was determined not to let anyone, especially a grandpa-in-a-ring, snatch away a protagonist under his watch.

Maybe the greater immortal provided Hughie with a technique, Slifer wondered. That would be a cunning way to poach his disciple.

Mirror Mastery!
Name: Dimensional Slide
Rank: Obsidian
Description: Allows the user to transverse through the Void Realm.

Obsidian Rank? Slifer pondered with a furrowed brow. *What on earth is an Obsidian Rank technique?* The highest rank he was familiar with was Heaven. His mind raced as he tried to fathom how a Core Formation Realm cultivator like Hughie could use such an overpowered technique. *That explains his sudden appearances. Protagonists really don't play by the rules.*

With a mischievous glint in his eye, Slifer thought, *Well, if it's up for grabs . . .* Without hesitation, he activated the Mirror Mastery Skill, and the technique's knowledge began to imprint itself onto his mind.

−500 Karmic Credits
Mirror Mastery Skill: Technique Copied—Dimensional Slide

As expected, no credit conversion needed for righteous techniques. Nice. Slifer's lips curled into a satisfied smile.

Almost immediately, another System notification chimed in:

Mirror Mastery Level Up
Mirror Mastery Level 2: Copying a Disciple's Technique Will Be 20% Cheaper
You have gained 100 Karmic Credits!

Slifer mentally gave himself a pat on the back. *This is exactly why having protagonist disciples pays off. They do all the heavy lifting, and I get the spoils.*

Slifer's restrained his excitement, the old man likely still had access to his cultivation even if it was limited, Slifer knew he had to mask his discovery. *The last thing I need is for him to recognize me. If he recognizes me from the little life essence incident, I'm toast . . .*

"Hughie, you were saying?" Slifer coughed, feigning ignorance, his tone as casual as he could manage.

"Master, I asked if there was . . . something on my face?" Hughie shifted uncomfortably, his master had been silently staring at him for the past minute, that coupled with the strange expressions on his face only worried Hughie further.

Slifer blinked, abruptly realizing how his actions must look. "Ah, no. Just . . . checking for . . . injuries," he replied, waving his hand vaguely.

Hughie, rattled by his master's lecherous behavior, vowed inwardly, *I need to get stronger so I can fend off . . . whatever this is.*

Ding!
Your Disciple Hughie's Loyalty Has Fallen to 30%
Warning: If a disciple's loyalty falls below 30%, there is a high risk of betrayal.

CHAPTER THIRTY-SEVEN

*S*hit, Slifer thought.

He desperately needed to find a way to increase Hughie's loyalty. The most straight-forward approach would be to get rid of that pesky ring and ensure Hughie remained close. However, he knew that couldn't be done. One, he was certain the greater immortal would smite him, and two, the ring would undoubtedly find its way back to Hughie—possibly due to some "Heaven's Will" or other such nonsense.

Suppressing a sigh, Slifer lamented to himself. He didn't possess any technique or hidden treasure to win over Hughie. If only he had an abundance of Karmic Credits, then he could buy his disciple's loyalty. *Dammit, I really don't have anything to give . . .* Suddenly, an idea sparked. *Val!* Perhaps, letting Val spend some time with Hughie might stabilize his loyalty. While it might not significantly elevate it, at least it could hover above that risky thirty percent.

Hughie, who had been waiting for his master to dismiss him, couldn't help but think, *What's with Master these days? Ever since his breakthrough, it's either he's been getting distracted mid-conversation, leering at me oddly, or staring into space . . .* He couldn't help but think of the grandpa in the ring and his strange behaviors, and sighed. *Cultivation sure does a number on one's brain. Hmm, I wonder if anyone thinks the same about me . . . Nah, I'm sure that only happens once you reach the Nascent Soul Realm.*

Slifer coughed, breaking the silence. "As the Disciple Selection Ceremony is approaching, I want you to remain within the sect," he instructed.

Hughie opened his mouth to protest, but Slifer continued, "Since I will be choosing a disciple, I expect all current disciples to be present."

Hughie's protest died in his throat, and he lowered his head.

"Also, Val has been . . . getting into trouble recently. And as her juni—"

Hughie shot him a skeptical look, and Slifer quickly corrected himself.

"As her *senior* brother, it's your duty to discipline her."

Hughie couldn't help but roll his eyes. *Yeah, right, that's "my" job.* But all he said was, "Of course, Master. I'll look after Val."

Slifer opened his mouth to offer further guidance, but Hughie was already racing off, calling over his shoulder, "Actually, I'll do that right now!"

Watching Hughie's retreating figure, Slifer couldn't help but scoff. "Low loyalty indeed," he muttered under his breath.

Now alone in the courtyard, Slifer decided it was the perfect time to experiment with his new technique. He closed his eyes and focused, recalling the information about the Dimensional Slide technique. It required him to channel qi to the ends of his fingers or feet. He would need to manifest the qi, then transmute it into space qi, and finally use it to tear open a rift in space.

Slifer opted for the finger method, because, well—*Fingers seem less embarrassing if this goes south*. Following the instructions, he successfully focused his Anima Qi—the life force within every cultivator—to his fingertips. But the next step was trickier.

Anima Qi could be converted into elemental qi, like fire, water, or wind. However, transitioning it into something as complex as Space or Time Qi was on a whole other level. It was akin to turning water into wine; you needed a certain divine touch.

It probably sounds harder than it is. He consoled himself, recalling Hughie's dismal comprehension stat of 2. As he tried to convert it into Space Qi, he was met with resistance. He grunted with the effort, sweat beading on his brow. "You're a stubborn fella," he muttered. The only reason he had managed to handle Light Qi was because he had glimpsed its essence during an Enlightenment experience. But Space Qi was proving to be an entirely different beast.

"Come on, Space Qi . . . Be a good little qi and transform," Slifer coaxed, waving his finger as if trying to lure a stubborn cat.

But, like a cat, the qi seemed to have a mind of its own, completely ignoring Slifer's attempts at persuasion.

He concentrated harder but no matter how much he tried, it remained stubbornly Anima Qi. "Maybe if I just . . ." he murmured, flicking his finger in what he hoped was a space-tearing motion. Instead of a rift, all he managed was to flick a pebble across the courtyard.

Slifer gazed at the space in front of him, utterly flabbergasted. "Hughie, with a comprehension of two, mastered this in a day?" he muttered, raking his fingers through his hair. "If that's the case, then is my comprehension stat one?"

He pondered momentarily. A zero would likely mean one's brain was akin to a potato. That unsettling realization made Slifer groan. "Great, I'm nearly a sentient vegetable. Just what the realm needed."

He tried to shake off the disheartening thought. *Until the System reveals my stats, there's no point getting worked up. Maybe Space Qi just . . . isn't my thing*, Slifer reasoned, though not entirely convinced.

With a resigned sigh, he decided it was time to check the cost of leveling up the technique through the System. He had avoided this path before, as the System had a penchant for exorbitant charges. *Last time I checked the prices, I nearly had an aneurysm . . .*

He shook his head, trying to clear it of negative thoughts. "The Dimensional Slide is crucial. It's my get-out-of-jail-free card, and with my luck, I'll need it sooner rather than later. And let's be honest, who else in the human realm can boast about wielding an Obsidian Rank technique? It could be my best shot at escaping a dire situation before I reach the Immortal Realm."

Teleporting . . . he thought wistfully, recalling the movies and comics that had fueled his childhood fantasies. *Just like in* Jumper, *or Nightcrawler from the X-Men . . .*

A soft chuckle escaped him. "I mean, who wouldn't want the convenience? Get to the fridge without moving an inch. Perfect for a former couch potato . . . or a nearly sentient vegetable." Taking a deep breath, he steeled himself. "Okay, let's rip off this Band-Aid," he whispered, ready to see the cost of upgrading the technique.

Focusing intently on the Dimensional Slide technique, he was presented with three distinct options in bold:

Impart
Sell
Upgrade

"Let's see the damage." He sighed heavily, hesitating just a moment before selecting "Upgrade." The anticipation was killing him; he half expected to see a price that would make his heart stop. "Please don't make me regret this, System," he mumbled, fingers crossed for good measure.

Cost: 500 Karmic Credits

He gritted his teeth; it was as he expected. No matter the technique, upgrading from level 0 to level 1 always cost 500 Karmic Credits. This might not seem like much, but each subsequent upgrade only got more ridiculous, doubling each time. Normally, Slifer would rather spend a few days practicing a technique to reach level 1; after all, it wasn't like he did much else. His disciples were usually the ones farming the credits.

Months could go by, and I still might not get it, Slifer thought with a heavy sigh.

Resigned, he clicked "Buy."

He felt a strange sensation, akin to the Enlightenment phase but more like a mini-enlightenment period, as his understanding of space and the technique improved. *Ah, that makes more sense!* He laughed as he finally understood why he wasn't able to convert his qi into Space Qi before.

Ding!
Dimensional Slide Technique Level Up

Closing his eyes, he focused on the instructions of the Dimensional Slide technique. His qi flowed to his fingertips and transformed into Space Qi. With a swift tearing motion, a small portal materialized before him.

"Now, that is awesome," he exclaimed with a chuckle.

Ding!
New Affinity Unlocked
Light (20%)
Fire (5%)
Space (2%)

So, the System wanted me to begin learning three elements before deciding to add it to my stats? Slifer shook his head at the System's strange and seemingly arbitrary requirements.

Just as he was about to step into the portal, he hesitated. *Better safe than sorry. Who knows what's waiting for me in the Void Realm?* Activating the Nascent Soul Armor, smoky black armor enveloped his body. He took a deep breath and stepped through the portal, which snapped shut behind him.

Moments later, Caelum appeared in the courtyard with a flash of qi, his expression fraught with distress. "Master, this useless disciple needs your h—" He cut off abruptly, realizing that Slifer was nowhere to be seen. Frowning, he muttered to himself, "I swear I sensed Master here a moment ago . . ."

"It's over, it's over, I'm finished," Li Fenghao rambled, pacing in the ring like a caged beast. High above him, Hughie, perched on his flying sword while scanning the skies for Val, sighed heavily.

"What are you grumbling about now?" Hughie called down.

Li Fenghao pointed a shaky finger to the sky, mumbling, "Life essence, you can't just absorb it! There are heavenly rules!" His eyes widened as he added, "But your master's technique . . . It doesn't care about such rules!"

Hughie chuckled. "So what? That just means my master is more awesome than we thought . . . which is honestly a sentence I never imagined saying."

Li Fenghao shook his head wildly. "No, no, no! Any cultivator who can ignore the laws set by the heavens is not simple. They go on to do great things . . . scary things. Ascendant cultivator? Your master is no Ascendant cultivator!"

Hughie's eyebrows shot up in surprise. "Wait, are you saying Master's been hiding his cultivation? He hasn't truly reached the Ascendant Realm?"

"No, you fool," Li Fenghao said, his voice dropping to a whisper. "Your master is not a mortal. He's at least an immortal, but most likely a greater immortal." He fell silent, his eyes darting around as if expecting Slifer to pop out of thin air.

"Master . . . an immortal?" Hughie blinked in disbelief. "That can't be possible. Are you sure you haven't had too much spirit wine, old man?"

Li Fenghao glared at him, suddenly looking deadly serious. "He sensed me. I felt him stare right into my soul. Do you think a mere mortal has that kind of power?"

Hughie, taken aback by the outburst, raised his hands in a placating gesture. "Easy there, old man. Take a deep breath."

Li Fenghao heaved a sigh, his shoulders slumping. "It doesn't make sense," he mumbled. "Why would your master let me live? If he used that technique at the Immortal level, he could have drained me dry of life essence."

Chuckling, Hughie teased, "Sounds like the 'mighty' greater immortal is a bit rattled."

With a scowl, the erratic elder retorted, "In my prime, I could've slapped your master into the next realm! But . . ." He paused, glancing around nervously. "For now, let's be a tad wary of him, alright?"

"Be wary of Master?" Hughie questioned, raising an eyebrow. The idea was absurd to him. Sure, there were those recent instances where his master showed a bit too much interest in his disciples, particularly in Hughie. That had led Hughie to speculate, with a shudder, that maybe Master had . . . different tastes. But despite tales of his master's ruthlessness, he had never harmed his own disciples, at least not intentionally. Neglect, maybe, but not harm.

"Why should I trust a grandpa trapped in a ring over my own master?" Hughie shot back

"Your master is definitely hiding some secrets, brat!" Li Fenghao retorted.

Hughie snorted. "Which cultivator doesn't have a closet full of secrets?"

Li Fenghao shook his head vigorously. "No immortal being would willingly hide in the Mortal Realm unless they're planning something major. Either that or they've lost their marbles. But your master seems to have all his faculties intact."

Seeing that Hughie wasn't convinced, Li Fenghao whispered, "I sensed great desire from your master when he stared at you."

Hughie's face paled, and he gulped audibly. So, he wasn't just imagining things. "I guess . . . being careful can't hurt," he muttered, his voice barely above a whisper.

Li Fenghao nodded, he was reluctant to deplete the qi he had painstakingly restored over countless millennia of confinement. However, he recognized the gravity of facing a greater immortal, particularly one that followed the demonic path.

I would rather blow us all up than fall into the hands of one of "them."

Slifer appeared in the Void Realm with a disoriented blink. "This looks like a black-and-white movie," he commented, surveying the eerie landscape that made him slightly uncomfortable. It was a deadland—no trees, no living beings, nothing. Just a barren, desolate expanse. "It's depressing," he muttered to himself, feeling a shiver run down his spine.

Shrugging, he decided it was time to leave, the technique was a great way to move around unhindered but this place was too . . . creepy.

With a casual flick of his wrist, Slifer expected the familiar swirl of the Dimensional Slide technique to materialize instantly. But instead of the usual portal opening, there was nothing—just the empty air where a gateway should have appeared. His confident expression faltered, turning into a mix of surprise and disbelief as he stared at the empty space.

"That was . . . unexpected."

Shaking his head, he repeated the gesture once more, then again, and yet again.

"Why isn't it working?" Slifer frowned, a twinge of panic creeping into his voice. He paused, his eyes widening in horror. "Don't tell me I'm stuck here . . ."

The very thought of being trapped in this lifeless realm sent shivers of dread through him. Being alone here would drive him mad, and if he wasn't alone—well, that was an even worse prospect. *The only beings that would reside here are beings that could squash me like an ant, killing me without even realizing they stepped on something*, he thought, his face paling.

Slifer let out an awkward laugh, which quickly turned into an ugly grimace. "Don't tell me this is karmic retribution for copying a protagonist's technique . . ."

His musings were abruptly interrupted by a roar. But this wasn't any ordinary roar—it was a ghastly sound that made his skin prickle with fear. Instinctively, he turned towards the sound, his eyes widening at the sight of two behemoth-sized, dementor-like figures in the air having a standoff.

"Holy spirit stones . . ." Slifer whispered. His breath caught in his throat; he felt very small and out of place. *How can they be so far away yet look so . . . big?*

Slowly, Slifer began to edge backwards, every muscle in his body tensed. *I need to get out of here and hide*, he thought, tiptoeing as quietly as possible in the opposite direction.

Suddenly, the ghastly roar escalated into ear-piercing screeches as the two dementor-like beings clashed. The shockwave from their collision sent Slifer flying forward, tumbling through the air. As he sailed uncontrollably away from the battle, a begrudging sense of gratitude washed over him.

At least it's pushing me away from those two, Slifer thought grumpily. *No wonder no one wants to live here . . .*

CHAPTER THIRTY-EIGHT

F enlock felt like it was time to return—killing ten demonic cultivators should be enough to meet his master's expectations. A sigh slipped from his lips as he stepped onto the sect grounds. Unlike many others in the sect, he never found joy in tormenting the weak. Engaging with cultivators at the same cultivation had always been a walk in the park for him, particularly since his specialization in sound cultivation often gave him an unexpected edge.

His master had sent him on this mission, perhaps hoping it would steel his resolve against his senior brothers' so-called "bullying"—a term Fenlock found exaggerated. In his view, restraint was a virtue; sharp words were something he could bear with without lashing back.

Senior brothers aren't bullying; they're just . . . giving advice, he rationalized.

Shaking his head, he admitted to himself that his nature had always been to sidestep conflict—a trait that had put him at the receiving end of many beatings from his former master, Elder Fron.

Lost in thought, Fenlock was suddenly jolted from his reverie by a sudden appearance. A silver-haired girl appeared before him, her abrupt presence making him tense instinctively.

Oh, what does she want now? he thought, barely suppressing a sigh.

"*Junior* Brother, you're back!" she exclaimed, a mischievous gleam in her eyes.

Fenlock nodded slowly, opting for silence. He had learned the hard way that his *junior* sister, Amelia, had a knack of looking for a petty excuse to instigate a fight. *Less talk, less trouble with her.*

"Master is out. He went to fetch Hughie," she said, her excitement palpable at the mention of their junior brother.

Fenlock found her enthusiasm strange. *Why is she so excited about Hughie?* he wondered, but then shrugged it off, it was not his problem to worry about. *Perhaps Hughie's her next target.*

He realized that his master had been right; he *was* being bullied. But it wasn't by his senior brothers. No, the real bully was the little silver-haired tornado standing in front of him. Yet, confronting her seemed more trouble than it was worth. Ignoring the girl was, after all, the path of least resistance.

Amelia's chatter blended into the background as Fenlock's mind drifted away. However, a few moments later, a voice snapped him back to the present, breaking through his haze. "Hey, Fenlock, where have you been hiding? It's been a while since we've seen you."

Both Amelia and Fenlock turned, spotting three male cultivators approaching them. The leader, a tall man with black hair streaked with silver, was flanked by two others—one slender with a quick, darting gaze, the other more muscular and carrying a large halberd.

"Senior Brother Zonrak," Fenlock greeted with a bow, clasping his hands together in respect. Zonrak was more than just a fellow cultivator; he was Fenlock's unofficial relationship guru. *Without his advice, I'd have never mustered the courage to ask out Junior Sister Lenvari.*

Zonrak chuckled heartily, patting Fenlock so hard on the shoulder it almost made him stumble. "Ah, Fenlock, still as stiff as ever!" he laughed.

Amelia's brows furrowed slightly at this interaction, but she remained silent.

Zonrak's teasing then took on a sharper edge. "Still meddling with that sound cultivation, huh? That's . . . hardly a man's art."

The slender cultivator chimed in, "Yes, it's rather . . . enchanting, in a way." He giggled.

The larger cultivator added, "A method more suited to serenading ladies than real combat, I'd say."

Fenlock, ever-oblivious, mistook the jibes as genuine advice, nodding in appreciation. "True, I always look for ways to enhance it."

Amelia's face twisted into a scowl, her short temper getting the better of her. With a sudden push, she sent Zonrak stumbling back. "Do you think I'll just stand here and let you bully my junior brother like that?" she spat out.

Fenlock waved his hands in a placating gesture. "Senior Brothers are only offering their guidance," he tried to explain.

Amelia scoffed. "If you think that's advice, then you're more naive than I thought."

Zonrak, red-faced from the unexpected shove, retorted, "Mind your place, little girl!"

Amelia's laughter chilled the air. "You won't find me 'little' when I stand over your corpse," she sneered. With each word, her appearance shifted horrifically. Her skin paled as her eyes hollowed out leaving a blue glow. Black veins snaked across her face and neck. Her mouth opened grotesquely, revealing a maw filled with jagged, menacing teeth. "I bet," she whispered, her voice echoing as if from a deep cavern, "your soul tastes delicious."

Zonrak's stance shifted subtly, betraying a hint of unease. Not because of Amelia's grotesque transformation, but due to her notorious reputation. The girl was infamous for her random assaults on disciples. Lately though, she had been suspiciously quiet, but Zonrak couldn't shake off the unsettling feeling that he might be her next target.

In the meantime, Fenlock stepped in, the peacemaker between two rising storms. "Senior Brother, Junior Sister, please, this is unnecessary," he urged, hoping to defuse the tension.

Amelia released a resigned sigh as she let her ghastly features revert to her usual delicate appearance, the last thing she wanted was for her master to catch her attacking another *innocent* disciple. Her master's prohibition against bullying had been a thorn in her side so she had hoped to goad Zonrak into a fight, giving her the perfect pretext to claim his soul. But unfortunately, her plan had failed.

Seeing Amelia back down, Fenlock's shoulders sagged in relief. He wasn't entirely confident in restraining his junior sister, she did have a tendency to . . . lose control.

However, Zonrak's pride had taken a blow, and seeing Amelia stand down only boosted his confidence. "Look at the mighty predator." He sneered, eyeing her small stature. "Barely taller than a child."

Fenlock's heart raced, well aware that height was Amelia's sensitive spot. He quickly spun around, confronting Zonrak. "Senior Brother, she stepped back. Let's leave it at that."

Zonrak scoffed dismissively. "Perhaps you're accustomed to being spoken to like that by a woman, but I am a *real* man."

Fenlock's brow furrowed in confusion. *What does being a man have to do with this petty squabble?* He suspected Zonrak's pride was clouding his judgment.

Unsatisfied with Fenlock's lack of response, Zonrak pushed further, a wicked grin on his face. "Perhaps a real man should keep Junior Sister Lenvari company tonight, instead of a mere sound cultivator like you, hmm?"

The color drained from Fenlock's face, replaced by a deep blush. His threshold for personal insults was high, but dragging Lenvari into this . . . that was a different matter entirely. The fire in his eyes revealed a rare anger.

A slight smirk curled the corners of Amelia's lips, which went by unnoticed as Fenlock's mouth opened and an ear-piercing sound erupted forth. The waves of sonic energy caused Zonrak and his cohorts to clamp their hands over their ears, their faces contorting in agony.

Fenlock honed the sound on Zonrak, amplifying its intensity. The senior brother crumpled to his knees, blood trickling from his ears as his screams punctured the air. The pained cry snapped Fenlock out of his blind rage, and he quickly closed his lips, his expression morphing into one of shock.

Zonrak lay slumped on the ground, whimpering in pain, as Amelia delivered a hearty slap on Fenlock's back. "Master would be proud," she exclaimed with a wide grin.

Fenlock shook his head, a look of regret washing over him. "This . . . this isn't me," he whispered.

They were interrupted by a soft thud. A bald man, Boss Morvran, glided down gracefully from his sword.

Amelia's face lit up at his sight. "Boss Morvran!" she greeted.

Morvran's sharp eyes darted between Amelia, the fallen trio, and Fenlock, his expression serious. "Your master won't be pleased when he hears about this," he warned as his gaze returned to Amelia.

Amelia, always one to relish in mischief, declared, "Oh, this wasn't my doing." She pointed at Fenlock. "It was all him."

Attacking fellow sect members . . . Fenlock's thoughts churned, he had always felt a sense of loyalty to his sect, but for what reason, he could not explain. *Cultivators outside the sect are one thing, but this . . .*

Morvran's eyes widened ever so slightly. "Didn't peg you for the type, kid. Always thought you were too . . . gentle," he remarked.

Fenlock's gaze fell to the ground, the afterimage of his actions etching themselves into his conscience. *This isn't the path I wanted to walk . . .*

Morvran remembered Slifer's instructions to Fenlock on how the boy needed to learn to stand up for himself. Approaching the conflicted disciple, he offered what he felt was encouragement, "You've showed a spine for once, but it isn't over yet."

Fenlock looked apprehensively at Morvran. *I've already done too much!* he thought.

Unperturbed by Fenlock's silence, Morvran pressed on. "I wasn't too pleased with your performance in our last lesson. I expect more from you this time." He paused, eyeing Zonrak's bloodied ears. "Sound attacks seem even better than breaking bones," he muttered to himself. Turning to Fenlock, he commanded, "Well? Don't stop now!"

Fenlock's head shook vehemently. *No. I won't be pressured into torturing my own sect members. Not again.*

Morvran's frown deepened at Fenlock's reluctance. It was then that Amelia stepped in, her smile beaming with mischief. "I'll heal Zonrak, so Junior Brother doesn't have to worry about accidentally killing him," she volunteered cheerily.

Without waiting for a reply, she positioned herself beside Zonrak, her hands radiating a green hue as she channeled the Essence Mend technique. Typically, the technique would soothe and heal, but as Amelia applied it, Zonrak's screams of pain pierced the air as he regained consciousness.

Amelia's smile only widened at the sight, it was no fun when they weren't awake to feel the pain.

Morvran, observing the scene, couldn't help but nod in approval. "Healing to inflict pain . . . The juniors these days are indeed creative in their methods of torture," he remarked.

Amelia beamed at the compliment, her mind wandering. *Perhaps Master made me learn healing arts for this very reason?* she pondered. She always found it strange that her master wanted her, a demonic soul cultivator, to learn healing.

During this exchange, the other two disciples, sensing an opportunity, began to slink away discreetly. Although Morvran noticed their exit, he made no move to stop them, his attention focused on Amelia's unique application of her skills.

Nodding his head a few times, Morvran then turned to Fenlock and studied him intently before speaking. "To survive in a demonic sect, or even in the vast immortal world, one can't avoid the darker aspects." He sighed, attempting to be encouraging. "At least today marked progress for you."

Fenlock remained silent, he had accepted that it was useless to argue with *crazy* people.

"Oh yes, the real reason for my visit," Morvran suddenly recalled. "Your master has yet to return to the sect. As his disciples, you're required to attend the Disciple Selection Ceremony in his stead. Follow me."

Amelia's eyes lit up, thinking about the possibilities of a new junior brother to toy with. She leaned down to Zonrak's semiconscious form and whispered menacingly in his ear, "I'll be back for you, big boy."

Pulling back slightly, her lips brushed against his in a mockingly tender kiss. She hummed appreciatively. "Mmm . . . delicious," tasting the lingering fear and pain that clung to him.

A feeble groan escaped Zonrak as he trembled under her soft touch, his vision dimmed as he once again lost consciousness.

Fenlock, trailing behind, couldn't help but shudder at the sight. His head hung low, a thought crept into his mind. *Would life have been easier if an immortal cultivator had discovered me instead?*

In the desolate expanse of the Void Realm, Slifer's expression darkened as an unexpected System notification appeared before him.

Ding!
Your Disciple Fenlock's Loyalty Has Decreased By 10%

Ten percent? What the devil did I do? Slifer nearly let a curse slip. He was baffled at the drop in loyalty when he hadn't even interacted with Fenlock.

CHAPTER THIRTY-NINE

The Verdant Serenity Valley was a sight to behold, lush and vibrant, cradled within towering mountains. It was here that the Black Rose Sect's Disciple Selection Ceremony took place.

After the ceremony, the sect master would traditionally claim the privilege of first pick among the new disciples, followed by the five grand elders and then the Nascent Soul elders. Those not chosen but talented enough might be taken in as Outer Sect disciples, where they would serve as servants with dreams of one day ascending into the Inner Sect—the only true disciples of the Black Rose Sect.

At the heart of the valley stood a large pagoda in which the grand elders were seated. The main seat, however remained empty as it was reserved for the sect master, who had yet to exit closed-door cultivation.

Grand Elder Darius, who sat at the right-hand side of the seat of authority, scoffed. "Where is that brat? Just because he has broken through to the Ascendant Realm doesn't give him the right to show us such disrespect."

Grand Elder Tenzin, attempting to soothe the situation, replied, "Perhaps there's something holding the supreme elder up. I believe he'll be here shortly." His eyes shifted, betraying a slight hint of anxiety.

Grand Elder Lydia remained silent amidst the bickering. *Arguing as always, like hatchlings in a nest*, she mused. Her gaze was fixed on the sea of participants below, searching for a successor to the Medicine Hall. *Amelia had promise, yet her violent streak was more suited for the battleground than the healing gardens.* The Medicine Hall demanded cultivators who could temper their inner demons, a trait Amelia sadly lacked.

Grand Elder Wyatt, a bald man with a long white goatee who had the frail appearance of a scholar but the shrewd gaze of a seasoned manipulator, let out a weary sigh. "If the supreme elder doesn't arrive within the next fifteen minutes, we shall commence the ceremony without him. Unfortunately, we simply cannot delay any longer."

Grand Elder Tenzin frowned. He had emphasized the importance of the ceremony to Slifer, but the supreme elder remained absent. Even Slifer's servant, the bald fellow, seemed to have vanished without a trace after being dispatched to fetch him. *Just where did he disappear to?* he wondered.

Breaking the mounting tension, Grand Elder Lydia finally spoke. "Grand Elder Wyatt, may I have a look at the jade slips?"

"Of course," Wyatt replied, handing over the jade slips to her. Jade slips were crucial at such events. There were over a thousand participants, and each had a jade slip detailing their background and character. It was vital that their character was suited to becoming a demonic cultivator, or they showed signs that they could be molded into one. The Black Rose Sect couldn't afford to nurture a disciple who might later spew righteousness at every turn.

* * *

The participants looked around nervously, exchanging whispers and speculative glances as they awaited the commencement of the selection ceremony. Over a thousand hopefuls from cities under the Black Rose Sect's dominion were present.

"I heard the Jexlarin Clan sent their top three talents this year," murmured a tall youth with striking silver hair.

"Pfft, they're nothing compared to the Vexorin Clan from Wick City," sneered a girl with piercing green eyes.

While major cities like Wick, Kaizer, and Rizarian were well-represented, there were also participants from smaller villages and towns within the Black Rose Sect's territory.

Just my luck to stand out like a sore thumb, thought a young man in white robes. His attire was a far cry from the extravagant silks donned by those from the major cities. But while his clothes spoke of simplicity, his eyes held a sharpness that belied his humble origins.

Every so often, a collective gasp or murmur would rise from the crowd.

"Look, that's Ivor from the Zyrklon Clan. They say that he is descended from a Thunder Eagle."

Amidst the murmurs, the shared dream was palpable. To be chosen by the sect master was a rare opportunity. Yet, the name on everyone's lips was not the sect master but Elder Slifer. Rumors had spread like wildfire about his cultivation level.

"Do you really believe that Elder Slifer has reached the Ascendant Realm?" a young woman from Kaizer City whispered.

"It's more than just a rumor," said another, looking around cautiously before leaning in. "My cousin in the Wizeron Clan said it's true. Can you imagine training under him?"

A third chimed in, "Sure, he's known to be ruthless, but the chance to study under an Ascendant cultivator? Who wouldn't risk it?"

William Wick stood tall amidst the crowd, his robes of deep blue embroidered with threads of gold that showed off his status as a spoiled young master. His youthful face, framed by raven-black hair, was alive with laughter as he chatted with the scions of the Vexorin and Zyrklon Clans.

Suddenly, his laughter was cut short as a boy bumped into him. William stumbled, catching himself just in time. His face flushed with a mix of embarrassment and anger. The eyes of his peers were upon him, waiting to see how he would react.

Straightening his robes, William turned sharply to face the clumsy offender. Before him stood a plump boy, his eyes wide with alarm.

"I-I'm so sorry, I didn't mean to—" the boy stammered, bowing apologetically.

The cheap fabric of the boy's attire was enough for William to grasp the full picture. With a disdainful sneer, he reached out and slapped the boy, causing him to lose balance and fall onto the muddy ground. "How dare a mere village bumpkin touch me," he said, sneering as he brushed off his robes with exaggerated disgust.

Laughter erupted around them. "Look at the fatty!" one of the Zyrklon Clan members jested.

Tears welled up in the village boy's eyes as he touched his reddening cheek. *I didn't do anything wrong*, Dusty thought bitterly. The weight of his oversized robe had been his downfall. His mother, in her eagerness to send him off looking presentable, hadn't considered the practicalities of such attire.

"I-I was just looking for my friend," Dusty muttered, his voice barely audible over the mockery.

The onlookers whispered and chuckled, enjoying the spectacle. William stood tall, a smug smile playing on his lips. "Let this be a lesson," he said loudly. "In the world of cultivators, your place is beneath our feet."

Dusty was aware of his ignorance. The city boys around him spoke of realms and cultivation as if they were common knowledge, while he knew next to nothing. And now he found himself face down in the dirt, humiliated. *I-I thought this was a ceremony for an immortal sect.* His mind raced. The realization that he was in a demonic sect filled him with dread. *But . . . it's too late to back out now.*

The young man in plain robes hesitated, his foot hovering mid-step. He was about to intervene when a voice cut through the tension.

"Hey, leave him alone," a new figure declared, stepping protectively in front of Dusty.

William's gaze slid from Dusty to the newcomer. He was tall, with broad shoulders that spoke of hard physical labor. Despite having an imposing presence, William sensed no spiritual energy from him. "Oh, and who might you be?"

"I'm Nomed," the tall boy stated simply, extending a hand to Dusty, who gratefully accepted it and scrambled to his feet. "And I'm this one's friend," Nomed added.

William, feeling the eyes of his companions on him, forced a sneer. "I thought the Black Rose Sect had standards. But it seems they let any village *riffraff* sully these grounds," he spat out the last word with contempt.

Nomed's eyes narrowed at the insult, but he held his tongue. "Let's go," he said to Dusty, and the two of them began walking away to find a different spot.

William's group burst into fits of laughter, taking jabs at the retreating duo. "Look at those rags!" one jeered. "Probably never seen a silver coin in their lives!" another chuckled.

Yet, deep within, William felt a pang of unease. *That gaze . . .* he reflected, remembering Nomed's cold stare. *Did I make a mistake?* But he quickly pushed the thought away, reassuring himself, *I'm the young master of the Wick Clan. Why should I worry about a village bumpkin?*

As they walked, Dusty whispered, "I didn't think you'd make it in time. The village elder was so worried when he couldn't find you."

Nomed gave Dusty a warm, reassuring smile. "I wouldn't miss this for the world," he declared, pausing briefly before clapping a hand on Dusty's shoulder. "This ceremony . . . it's our ticket to a better life."

Dusty nodded with enthusiasm. *If anyone from our village could impress the sect, it'd be Nomed. He's always been exceptional at everything he tried.*

After the fifteen minutes had passed, Grand Elder Wyatt cleared his throat, drawing attention as he stood up. "We can't wait any longer," he declared.

Grand Elder Tenzin released a resigned sigh. "I agree."

Turning towards the crowd of participants, Grand Elder Wyatt greeted them. His voice wasn't loud, yet it carried effortlessly, reaching every ear with crystal clarity. The participants fell silent instantly, their eyes drawn to the imposing figure atop the pagoda.

"Examinees," Grand Elder Wyatt began, "you have already passed an initial evaluation to stand here today, which deems you qualified to attempt the Black Rose Sect tryouts."

The participants listened intently, hanging on his every word.

"The first of your trials will be the trial of will." He paused, letting the weight of his words sink in. "A formation will transport your souls to an illusory plane. There, you must ascend a mountain. Only those who reach the summit shall pass. Should you fail to do so within six hours, you will be eliminated. Oh, and eight out of ten participants fail this test."

A wave of murmurs, a blend of shock and awe, rippled through the crowd. *Eighty percent fail?* some thought, their confidence wavering.

Sensing the rising anxiety, Grand Elder Wyatt raised his hand for silence. "However," he continued, his voice stern, "those who surmount this trial will be guaranteed entry into the Black Rose Sect." He paused, then added almost as an afterthought, "Even if it is as a mere outer disciple."

This time, the murmurs were different—tinged with excitement and determination. *I will be one of those who succeed,* many thought, their spirits reignited.

"Silence," Grand Elder Wyatt commanded, quelling the rising chatter. "As for the subsequent trials, I will not waste words explaining them now. Only those who pass the first will need to know." His tone left no room for questions.

Nomed, staring up at the grand elder, thought resolutely, *As long as I pass this, nothing else matters.* He didn't care about being taken in as an elder's disciple; he just needed to enter the sect.

Beside him, Dusty shivered. "If I knew it'd be this scary, I'd have stayed in the village herding goats," he whispered to Nomed, trying to lighten the mood. "At least goats don't judge you if you can't climb a mountain in your mind."

Meanwhile, the young man wearing white robes narrowed his eyes, his gaze fixated on the grand elder. *Will is not something I lack,* he thought confidently, looking down at the sword at his waist. *Only the strongest of wills are qualified to wield a sword.*

William snorted dismissively at the first trial. *Just as I was told. A test of will.* He mused further, *If my source is correct, then talent will be next, followed by comprehension.* He wasn't content with mere entry into the sect; his ambitions soared higher.

His gaze flickered across the grand elders, searching for a specific figure. "For this to work, *you* need to be here," William muttered under his breath, feeling a twinge of annoyance. "Just where are you, Supreme Elder?"

CHAPTER FORTY

Exhausted, Slifer found a cave that seemed safe enough to catch his breath. It was a simple cave, adorned with a few vines clinging to its walls, but nothing else of note. Unlike the other caves that looked like they spelled trouble, this one felt warm, almost . . . inviting.

But Slifer knew you could never trust a cave, even an innocent-looking one.

After a thorough check to ensure no monsters were lurking inside, he allowed himself to slump down against the cold wall.

Slifer realized that no matter how far he ran, the dementor-like beings remained in view, never seeming to diminish in size. His earlier comparison of being an ant was disturbingly accurate.

Trying to steady his racing heart, he couldn't shake off the overwhelming sense of dread. It was an intrinsic fear, the kind one feels when facing a superior predator. He had watched in horror as one of the dementor-like beings devoured the other. To his astonishment, the victor seemed to grow larger.

Just how much bigger can these things get?!

Slifer gulped, consoling himself with the thought that he was too insignificant to even be considered a snack for such monstrous entities. *I'd be lucky to even get stuck between their teeth,* he thought grimly.

"What to do now . . ."

After some contemplation, Slifer realized he had three potential ways to escape the Void Realm. The first was to keep trying the Dimensional Slide technique, hoping a portal would form. The second option was to use credits to upgrade the technique and *then* attempt to open a portal. The last was to gamble and pray the System granted him a teleportation card or something similar.

Using the Dimensional Slide technique repeatedly could draw unwanted attention, Slifer thought. *Upgrading it seems sensible, but what if it's only marginally more effective? That would be a waste of a thousand Karmic Credits that could have been used to potentially get a useful card.*

A part of him was tempted to stay, lured by the possibility of acquiring something powerful in this bizarre realm. *This is where protagonists in the stories find their cheats.* Even though he already had the System, he would prefer something more . . . reliable.

In the end, Slifer decided the best course of action would be to find a cave to hide in and gamble with the System.

That's enough excitement for this trip. I'd rather play it safe and maybe win something useful than risk wandering around this unpredictable realm—that's practically suicide! "Let's see how many credits I have, status."

Name: Slifer
Race: Human

Alignment: Demonic
Cultivation: Late Foundation Establishment
Lifespan Remaining: 10 Years
Credits: 3060
Skills: Insight (Basic), Nascent Soul Armor: Level 1
Items: Reversal Card, Peak Slifer Card, Whimsical Wind Card
Affinities: Light (20%), Fire (5%), Space (2%)
Abilities: Mirror Mastery: Level 2
Techniques: Sunrise Slash: Level 2, Stellar Nova Strike: Level 1, Dimensional Slide: Level 1
Weapon Mastery: Sword: 5%

"I have enough Karmic Credits to gamble first. If that doesn't work, I'll just upgrade the technique."

Ding!
Random Card Acquired
Activate now?
(Yes/No)

"Yes!"

Ding!
Unsuccessful
Better Luck Next Time

After over a dozen unsuccessful attempts, Slifer finally acquired a useful card—the staple Critical Block Card. It then only took him several more tries before the familiar ding of success echoed again.

Ding!
Successful
You Have Acquired: Soul Fire
Description: Conjure ethereal flames that burn not the flesh, but the very essence of the soul.
Warning: Can only affect those below the Immortal Realm.

Burning the soul? Sounds like something straight out of a demonic cultivator's handbook, Slifer mused, surprised by the nature of the technique. Didn't the System have some sort of agenda against the demonic path?

After checking its price in the Shop, Slifer found it was worth a staggering 15,000 Karmic Credits. This single card alone made his gambling efforts worthwhile.

Yet, Slifer wasn't comfortable with the idea of using such a technique. *Torturing the soul seems too cruel. If I have to kill, I prefer it to be swift and clean, not drawn out like . . . a certain someone's methods.* Shaking his head, Slifer decided to continue his gambling spree, it was only after another few dozen attempts when he finally won a decent card.

> *Ding!*
> Successful
> You Have Acquired: Reflection Card
> Description: Creates an energy barrier that reflects attacks back at the attacker for 20 seconds.

While Slifer could see its usefulness in battles with other cultivators, he doubted its efficacy against the gargantuan void beasts. *Reflecting their attack is pointless if they just swallow me whole*, he thought. Nevertheless, he welcomed the addition of the Reflection Card to his arsenal.

Just as Slifer was about to purchase another Random Card, he felt a chilling sensation creeping over him. *Something* was wrapping around his body.

This . . . this can't be. I checked this cave thoroughly, there were no creatures here!

Slowly looking down, Slifer's eyes widened in shock as he saw the seemingly innocent vines that had been clinging to the cave walls now crawling over his body.

Vines . . . attacking me? His mind raced, trying to make sense of the situation.

The vines, which had appeared so harmless at first glance, were now tightening around his body, slowly squeezing the life out of him.

I was just thinking I would prefer not to use this on anyone, but you left me with no choice! Soul Fire Card . . . activate!

Instantly, the vines fell to the ground and began to thrash violently. Although there was no visible fire, their reaction seemed as if they were being scorched by intense flames as they let out a strange sizzing sound before falling still.

It must be one enormous vine, Slifer realized when he saw that not a single vine in the cave was left alive. *A regular fire technique would have harmed only a part of it, but a soul attack like this affects the entire being.*

> *Ding!*
> You Have Gained 1000 Karmic Credits

I gained a thousand credits? Just what was its cultivation level? Insight!

> *Ding!*
> Congratulations!
> You Have Discovered an Otherworldly Being
> You Have Gained 100 Karmic Credits
> Name: N/A
> Species: Void Plant
> Realm: Early Ascendant Realm
> Known Techniques: N/A
> Known Affiliations: N/A
> Disposition: N/A

Early Ascendant Realm? Slifer was astounded. *Even a simple-looking vine here is ridiculously powerful. If it wasn't for its . . . overly affectionate nature*, Slifer joked to himself, *I would have been dead without even realizing what killed me. Sure, the Critical Block Card would have kicked in, and then I'd have used the Soul Fire Card, but any normal cultivator would've ended up as vine food!*

Remembering that this cave seemed the safest, Slifer shuddered as he wondered what beings were lurking in the others. Shaking off the unsettling thoughts, he made sure to use insight on every nook and cranny in the cave, even the pebbles weren't let off the hook.

After completing his thorough examination, he let out a long sigh of relief. "Finally," he muttered, a hint of fatigue in his voice. As he stretched his arms high above his head, his exhaustion seemed to vanish, replaced by a gleam of anticipation in his eyes.

"Now, onto the truly crucial and, coincidentally, vastly more entertaining task at hand, gambling!"

Ding!
Random Card Acquired
Activate Now?
(Yes/No)

"Yes!"

Again, the cards Slifer was getting were all duds, but after a while, a smirk appeared on his face.

Ding!
Successful
You Have Acquired: Avatar
Description: Creates a complete clone of the user that can independently cultivate.
Warning: The avatar cannot access the System or its cards.

"My own Kage Bunshin!"

CHAPTER FORTY-ONE

T he trial will now begin!"

With that, the formations on the ground came to life, releasing a blue hue. The participants felt a wave of exhaustion sweep over them, causing their limbs to feel like jelly and their eyelids to droop as they slowly succumbed to unconsciousness.

Within the illusionary realm, a lone mountain rose from the ground. Its peak, covered in mist, reached the heavens. As the mist cleared, figures began appearing at the foot of the mountain, each disoriented and surveying their surroundings.

William blinked rapidly, adjusting to the sudden change. He looked down at himself, flexing his fingers and moving his limbs. "It feels so . . . real. Almost like my very body has been transported here," he murmured. Lifting his gaze, he assessed the mountain ahead and the participants materializing next to him. Not wanting to lag behind, and seeing a few already starting, he took a step forward.

With every step, an increasing weight pressed down on him. Observing those around him, William noticed some participants collapsing, unable to withstand the pressure. He sneered. "Weaklings."

As Dusty appeared in the illusionary realm, he took one glance at the towering mountain and felt his knees buckle. "They can't expect us to scale that monstrosity," he said, his hand self-consciously patting the rolls of fat on his belly. "Look at me! I'll drop dead before I even get halfway."

Nomed, who appeared beside him, laughed, clapping Dusty on the back. "My friend, you could weigh as much as ten oxen, but that won't affect your climb," he said, grinning. "Remember, it's not the flesh that's tested here—it's the spirit, the willpower."

Dusty grumbled, "Well, if they wanted to test my willpower, they should have just checked how many pies I could eat in one sitting. Sounds a lot safer to me. I mean, a pie never hurt anyone."

Meanwhile, in the Void Realm, Slifer, ever vigilant for lurking void beasts, sneezed unexpectedly. He instantly froze, his senses alert for any movement. When none came, he relaxed slightly but couldn't help but think, *Why would I sneeze? It's not like cultivators catch colds.*

Back in the illusionary realm, Nomed shook his head. "Get moving, or you'll have to explain yourself to Grandma Sully if you're sent back." Dusty visibly paled; Grandma Sully's idea of punishment was a strict regimen of fasting, which to him was crueler than any physical torment.

Nomed took a step forward, immediately feeling a whisper of pressure, like the touch of a feather. He would have missed it if he hadn't been braced for some form of resistance.

Dusty, however, instantly turned red as his breaths came in short bursts. "It . . . feels like . . . I'm lugging Grandma . . . Sully on my . . . back again!" He cast a sideways glance at Nomed and the other slender participants who moved with ease. Catching his breath, he continued, "I tell ya, this is unfair. Clearly, this blasted mountain has something against us . . . us heavyweights!"

Back in the pagoda, Grand Elder Wyatt causally waved his hand, causing water to coalesce out of thin air, swirling until it formed into a thousand distinct screens that hovered in the air before them. Each one captured the image of a different participant as they faced the mountain's challenge.

As a cultivator's power grew, so too did their ability to multitask. For those in the Core Formation Realm, watching over thousands of such screens with their spiritual sense was a trivial matter. But for these grand elders, who had entered the Origin Realm, such a feat was not even worth mentioning.

"The clans have indeed sent their finest," Wyatt commented. His eyes paused on one particular screen, where a young man progressed steadily. "Raze of the Rizarian Clan—not only defeated the heirs of both Quorvex and Zion in a single battle but crippled them."

Elder Tenzin, standing beside him, watched the screen with interest. "He has certainly earned his place as the prime seed."

When recruiting disciples, the sect relied on a seed system that ranked potential disciples based on talent and background. Though the brief screening was not infallible, years of refinement had honed the system to a point where its estimations were not too far off the mark.

Grand Elder Darius watched the images before him, a glint of approval in his eyes. "This Rizarian boy would serve well within my Disciplinary Hall," he remarked with a confident nod, eyeing his fellow elders for any sign of contest. But seeing none, a smug smile appeared on his face.

"The next three seeds hail from the Jexlarin Clan," Grand Elder Wyatt's voice cut through the silence, drawing attention once again to the screens. "Bryce, Caelin, and Dara."

Grand Elder Lydia's expression tightened slightly. "And what of the other clans within Kaizer City?" she asked.

"It's the Jexlarin Clan," Grand Elder Tenzin interjected smoothly. "They've been expanding, pouring resources into their youth. They have ambition, the other clans have not been able to keep up."

Wyatt gave a nod of acknowledgment. "In a few generations, we may well speak of Jexlarin City, not Kaizer."

Lydia's frown deepened at this. *The Wizeron Clan's talents in healing are unmatched. It is unsettling that we see no new talents from them of late.*

As they discussed, Grand Elder Wyatt's gaze drifted to another screen. The image of a topless muscular young man appeared on it, his eyes sparked with occasional flashes of bright yellow. "Ivor of the Zyrklon Clan," he muttered.

Grand Elder Darius leaned forward, interest piqued. "Is he the one descended from the Thunder Eagle?"

"Indeed," Wyatt confirmed. *The Zyrklon Clan's bloodline usually runs thin, but this . . .* "Every few centuries, a Zyrklon with a decent bloodline emerges. Ivor's soul shows signs of the Thunder Eagle—signs that are far stronger than any we've seen in a millennium."

Grand Elder Darius eyed the image of Ivor keenly. "Hmm, this scion of Zyrklon also seems a worthy candidate for my Disciplinary Hall," he declared. The other grand elders said nothing, their silence an accustomed response to Darius's assertive nature.

With a deliberate cough, Grand Elder Wyatt shifted the attention to another screen. A young man appeared, radiating arrogance as he walked up the mountain, the youth frequently glanced back with a smirk plastered across his face, as if to mock those behind him. "This is the young master of the Wick Clan, William," Wyatt announced in a neutral tone.

The gathered elders remained unimpressed, having seen too many like him—proud due to their lineage, yet insignificant without it. *Young masters like him often crumble without the support of their clans*, they thought collectively, their eyes scanning past William's image indifferently.

"It appears the trial has truly begun," Grand Elder Tenzin observed, gesturing towards the screens. The images now showed several participants brought to their knees, others sprawled on the ground, their wills broken by the mountain's base. As their souls flickered back to the physical realm, a scornful scoff escaped Darius.

"What weaklings." He sneered with a dismissive wave of his hand. "What has our demonic sect become? Afraid of a few casualties?" He shook his head in disdain at the use of an illusionary realm. *In my days, hundreds such as these would be crushed by the trial—boulders would smash them, falls would claim them. They wouldn't return, at least not whole.*

Grand Elder Wyatt shook his head slightly, his beliefs aligning more with the sect master's progressive vision. "A sect without rules, even a demonic one, is doomed to implode," he muttered quietly to himself.

William was already halfway up the mountain, he was breathing heavily, more from the exertion than he would care to admit. *This is more challenging than I expected*, he acknowledged internally, wiping sweat from his brow. It was crucial that he not only avoid falling behind but also that he do so with the grace expected of a Wick.

He sneered as he glanced back and saw the bulky figure who had stumbled into him at the start of the trial. The overweight man was panting, his hands on his knees in a pitiful attempt to catch his breath. *Struggling so soon? Pathetic*, he thought with contempt. His gaze then shifted to the other villager, the companion of the stout man. To his surprise, the villager was making decent progress, closer to the middle than the base of the mountain. *Impressive for a commoner, I suppose, but still laughable compared to a noble like myself.*

William then scanned the path ahead—as expected, the young master of the Rizarian Clan, Raze, was at the forefront with the three prodigies of the Jexlarin Clan at his heels. Yet, William's expression turned to one of disbelief as he witnessed a white-robed youth overtake them like he was taking a stroll in the park. *T-this can't be, is he somehow cheating?* William pondered with a scowl. *How could an unknown possibly surpass the young masters?*

The white-robed male, known as Kalin, had no interest in the Black Rose Sect under normal circumstances; he was not a demonic cultivator, and the sect offered nothing he could not obtain from his own clan. His sole motivation for infiltrating this event was the chance to observe a sword cultivator rumored to have reached the Sword Will stage—an achievement exceedingly rare in the mortal world. *Even immortals struggle to grasp such a state*, he thought, his curiosity piqued. *Perhaps there is something I can learn from a Mortal Realm cultivator.*

As Kalin continued walking, he overheard the grumblings of a participant behind him but paid them no mind.

"That white-robed guy . . . he just overtook Raze. Who is he?" the puzzled voice questioned.

"He's not even sweating," another murmured to a fellow participant nearby. "You don't think he's . . ."

The other shook his head. "Who can say? But if he's cheating, the elders will surely catch him."

Every now and then, Kalin's hand occasionally brushed against the hilt of his sword and his eyes narrowed. *Let's see if this Sword Will stage cultivator is worth my time.*

"Who is that boy?" Grand Elder Lydia's voice cut through the silence, her finger pointing to a screen showcasing a white-robed youth overtaking the supposed first seed.

Wyatt's brow creased as he extended his spiritual sense to sift through countless jade slips, murmuring, "I do not know him." His eyes narrowed—somehow, the young man had bypassed their meticulous screening.

"How dare this boy infiltrate our sect!" Grand Elder Darius boomed, his face flushing with anger as he rose from his seat, his hands clenched.

"No, let him be," Wyatt interjected firmly, gesturing for Darius to sit. "Let's watch how this unfolds."

An impostor would be revealed by the formations, he reasoned. *Unless this boy is an immortal, he cannot hide his true soul from us.*

Though displeased, Darius resumed his seat, acknowledging Wyatt's crafty mind with a begrudging nod. *Discipline and punishment are my realms, Wyatt knows the subtler arts of control.*

Tenzin's gaze, meanwhile, narrowed on the young man's weapon. "A sword cultivator," he whispered. In the illusionary realm, personal weapons did not manifest, but a sword cultivator's blade in the higher realms was an extension of their very soul, inseparable even in illusion.

Grand Elder Darius's frown deepened at the sight of the sword. *Sword cultivators . . . too stern, too inflexible,* he thought distastefully. And demonic sword cultivators were even worse in his eyes—often they would lose their minds to the very blades they wielded. Both types did little more than sour his mood.

While the attention of the grand elders was split between the young masters and the white-robed male, a humble-looking figure and his pudgy companion were largely ignored. Among the sea of participants that were struggling up the mountain, they were just two more faces.

Nomed slowly trudged up the mountain, a sigh escaping him. The trial before him was laughably simple; he could hardly believe it was designed to test one's willpower. *Is there a flaw in the formation?* he wondered, his gaze sweeping over his fellow participants. They were drenched in sweat, their breaths coming in ragged gasps, while he felt as if he were out for a leisurely stroll.

Stand out too much, and you invite trouble. Fade too much into the background, and you become prey, he reminded himself, feigning a pained expression as he pretended to labor over the next step. *Being average is an art in itself.*

Nomed found this performance—the act of pretending to be an ordinary cultivator amidst the sea of struggling bodies—far more taxing than the trial itself.

His gaze swept the mountain path, taking note of those who were ahead and those who trailed behind, calculating his pace to fall squarely in the middle. The idea of catching an elder's attention was the last thing he wanted. *Keep it average, keep it safe*, he thought.

Glancing back, he caught sight of Dusty, his friend's legs wobbling, his resolve clearly faltering as he paused for another break. *Come on, Dusty. You can't stop now.* He couldn't help but want Dusty to succeed.

"Oi, Dusty!" Nomed called out. "If you linger any longer, the mountain might mistake you for a new peak!"

A ripple of laughter spread through the nearby climbers, and Dusty's face broke into a weary grin. With a renewed spark, he pushed off his knees and resumed his climb, Nomed giving him the nudge he needed.

"Huh, don't underestimate me, I'll race you to the top, and the last one there owes the other a meal!" Dusty hollered back.

Of course, it'd be a meal, Nomed let out a genuine smile, even as he continued his charade. *Just make sure you're not last, my friend.*

Grand Elder Wyatt's fingers ran through his long goatee, his gaze fixed on the white-robed youth on the screen. *Impressive . . . to enter undetected is no small feat,* he thought, his curiosity piqued more by the boy's cunning than his leading position.

Next to him, Grand Elder Darius had his eyes shut, a picture of disinterest. He only occasionally sent out his spiritual sense, sweeping the mountain for a certain presence. *Where is Slifer hiding?* he pondered, itching for the moment he could overshadow the so-called supreme elder.

On another side, Grand Elder Tenzin's eyes moved meticulously, tracking the three talents from the Jexlarin Clan. He nodded slightly, acknowledging their prowess. *The clan patriarch's "donation" might have been unnecessary after all,* he mused.

Grand Elder Lydia, on the other hand, barely concealed her lack of interest. *Healers . . . only they are the true jewels in this mundane lot.* Her mind was already leaping ahead to the trial of comprehension, eager to find those that were worthy of her guidance.

Their silent assessments were abruptly disturbed by the unexpected arrival of Morvran and his entourage. The cultivators on their swords landed with an inelegant thud on the pagoda.

Morvran lowered his head. "Esteemed Grand Elders," he greeted respectfully, followed by nods from Amelia, Fenlock, and Hughie. Even little Val tried mimicking the gesture.

Seeing Slifer's disciples arrive without their master, Darius's features contorted into a scowl, his aura flaring like a storm cloud on the horizon. The pressure it exerted was palpable, heavy as the weight of the very earth.

"Where. Is. Your. Master?" he growled.

CHAPTER FORTY-TWO

Feeling the oppressive force of Grand Elder Darius's aura bear down on them, Amelia's face twisted into an angry scowl. "You won't be acting like this when my master arrives," she snapped back. "Then you'll be on your knees begging for mercy."

Perched on Morvran's bald head, Val puffed out her tiny chest and hissed, "Master slap bad man, Val den eat bad man!" Her baby teeth, more adorable than intimidating, flashed in a display of dragonet bravado.

Watching the scene unfold, Fenlock held back a sigh. Val's behavior was excusable—she was just a baby, and a dragon at that; her pride was as vast as the heavens. *But Amelia . . . why must she always provoke those stronger than us?* He pondered the idea of giving her the title of senior, just to avoid these headaches. *Maybe as a senior, she will learn to hold her tongue . . . actually, come to think of it, she would just drag us down with her.*

Hughie shifted uncomfortably at the prospect of the old man attacking them, with everything that had happened recently, it wouldn't surprise him. He felt Li Fenghao stir within the ring.

The ancient spirit's voice grumbled, "If that insect doesn't stop yapping, I will come out and slap him to death."

Hughie couldn't help but mentally question, "Do you still have the power to do that?"

Li Fenghao muttered begrudgingly, "I've got enough left for a few life-threatening situations." Then, as an afterthought, he added, "But for that buffoon, I might just make an exception."

You'd think someone who's lived for hundreds of thousands of years would be more patient, Hughie thought with a shake of his head.

Grand Elder Wyatt observed Darius's increasingly erratic behavior with a hint of disapproval. *This isn't what we agreed on. We can't allow him to simply bully the supreme elder's disciples; the other grand elders will not ignore such conduct . . . And neither can I, reputation is still a thing to maintain after all.*

With a discreet cough to regain control of the situation, Wyatt's face blossomed into a practiced smile, full of apologies. "Please excuse Grand Elder Darius's impatience."

Turning to Darius, Wyatt's smile remained plastered as he counseled, "I'm sure the supreme elder will have a good explanation when he arrives."

Darius let out a derisive snort and flopped back into his seat. "If the supreme elder even bothers to turn up," he muttered.

Morvran's lips curled into a smile that didn't quite reach his eyes. *As if I would confront an Origin Realm elder without a plan,* he mused, already considering which of his underhanded schemes would best inconvenience Grand Elder Darius. *Perhaps it's time to unleash that wily Dentos on him.*

Dong!

The sound of the bell indicated the end of the first trial, all eyes—both the elders' and the disciples'—shifted to the water screens. The images revealed that two hundred and fifty participants had managed to reach the mountain's summit. At the forefront was the mysterious, white-robed figure, followed by the Rizarian young master. The Jexlarin trio secured the next three spots, with Ivor from the Zyrklon Clan taking the sixth.

"Two hundred and fifty . . . That's a bit higher than the last time," Grand Elder Tenzin remarked, his eyes skimming over the screens.

Grand Elder Wyatt gave a contemplative nod. "Indeed, but the real question remains—how many among them possess true talent?"

In the illusionary world, Nomed offered a hand to Dusty, whose large frame was splayed awkwardly on the ground. "I . . . told . . . you . . . I'd . . . make . . . it," Dusty panted out, his hand clenching Nomed's as he was hauled to his feet. His face glowed red, more from anger than the exertion. *All that work and not a pound lighter*, he lamented silently.

Nomed couldn't help but laugh. "Taking last place is a feat in itself; you've got everyone's attention," he joked, helping Dusty to his feet.

Dusty responded with a scowl, "Who'd have thought you, of all people, would barely make the cut. One hundred twenty-fifth place? I expected more."

Nomed's smile was one of someone who had everything going according to plan. *Exactly in the middle*, he mused silently. Aloud, he simply said, "What matters is we *both* passed."

Dusty nodded, catching his breath. "And I won't have to face Grandma Sully again," he added with a shudder that was only half-feigned.

Nomed couldn't help but laugh at his friend's simple joys. *If only life were as simple as escaping a scolding*, he thought wistfully.

William expression darkened when he overheard the banter between the last-placed Dusty and the middle-ranker Nomed. *To be content with such mediocrity . . .* he thought disdainfully. *I suppose village life dulls one's ambitions.*

His mind wandered to his own performance. Tenth place wasn't shameful among the lot, but it wasn't first either. He felt a pang of anxiety at the thought of facing his clan after such a result. *Being bested by other young masters is one thing, but that unknown swordsman . . .*

As he was lost in thought, the sensation of his body dissolving jolted him back to reality. Panic briefly flickered across his face before settling into understanding: the trial was over, and they were returning to the real world. He materialized back in the valley, noting other participants materializing around him.

Grand Elder Wyatt's voice cut through the chatter and confusion. "Congratulations on passing the first trial," he announced. "You have all earned the right to join the Outer Sect of our Black Rose Sect."

A murmur of relief and triumph washed over the crowd, cut short by the Grand Elder's next statement.

"The next trial," he continued, his gaze sweeping over the young faces, "will decide whether you remain in the Outer Sect or advance to the Inner Sect."

The disciples straightened up at the mention of the Inner Sect. It was well known that the true privileges and resources of the Black Rose Sect were reserved for the inner disciples. Each of the four halls—the Disciplinary Hall led by Grand Elder Darius, the meticulous Medicine Hall under Grand Elder Lydia, the Martial Arts and Spiritual Hall that was

Grand Elder Tenzin's domain, and the Treasure Pavilion, filled with artifacts and managed by Grand Elder Wyatt—represented a different path in cultivation.

"And as for those that perform exceptionally well, the grand elders may take you in as their personal disciple."

As the Grand Elder's words sank in, murmurs of excitement spread through the crowd, the notion of being a grand elder's disciple was too great to ignore.

"I'd rather be Grand Elder Darius's disciple," one participant whispered ambitiously, only to be countered by another with, "Are you mad? Grand Elder Lydia is far more composed. Grand Elder Darius is . . . well, too intense."

Laughter broke out among a small group. "Intense? We're in a demonic sect, friend. 'Intense' is a mild way of putting it."

A more wistful voice joined the conversation. "You all can squabble over the grand elders. My sights are set on the supreme elder."

"Yeah." Someone scoffed. "Like he'd notice any of us. He didn't even show up today."

Grand Elder Wyatt raised his hand, hushing the crowd as the earth itself rose, obeying his command. Five pillars surrounded a large stone that pulsed with a green light appeared in the center of the valley.

"This stone," Grand Elder Wyatt began, "is a Luminaresce Quartz. Its glow will vary with the potential qi each of you can channel."

The grand elder continued to explain that the stone was tied to a formation that linked it to the five pillars. Those that lacked talent would not be able to light up a single pillar, whilst those that were destined to remain in the Outer Sect would only be able to light up one pillar. Being able to light up two pillars would ensure that the participant would be able to enter the Inner Sect.

Yet, it was only by lighting up three pillars that one would be able to catch the eye of a grand elder and attain the title of Core Disciple. If a disciple was talented enough to light up four pillars, then that would be sufficient to draw the attention of an Ascendant cultivator.

Seeing the grand elder grow silent, one of the disciples from the village mustered the courage to ask, "W-what about five pillars?"

"Huh, if any one of you were able to light up five pillars, then an immortal from the higher realms will descend and whisk you away." Grand Elder Wyatt let out a dismissive laugh, in the history of the Black Rose Sect, not a single disciple was able to light up five pillars simultaneously, Wyatt didn't even believe such a thing was possible.

The aspiring disciples exchanged glances. Some wore expressions of confidence, while doubt shadowed others' faces.

I forgot just how poor the talent in this backwards realm is. A small frown appeared on Kalin's face.

Not too far away from him, Nomed's eyes narrowed. *Three pillars? It seems a bit too much, I should aim for two.*

Sensing the shift in the crowd, Wyatt continued. "Each of you has passed our pre-selection process, and it is more likely one of you will light up four pillars than fail to light up one."

A collective breath of relief swept through those that were worried they would embarrass themselves by not being able to light up a single pillar.

However, his words did little to console William, who had never considered the possibility that he, the young master of the Wick Clan, would do worse than a village bumpkin. No, he had his sights on something greater, something that even he was unsure of.

That man said it should trick the stone but . . . would it be enough to light up four pillars? William felt his mouth dry up as the pill under his tongue grew heavy. The future of the Wick Clan depended on him. *If I can't catch the supreme elder's eyes, then . . . the Wick Clan . . . will be . . .*

"The trial of talent will now commence."

CHAPTER FORTY-THREE

One by one, the participants nervously stepped forward when called. However, after placing their hands upon the Luminaresce Quartz, one after another, they walked away with their spirits dampened, having lit only a single pillar.

"Circa," came the next call. A young girl, no older than fourteen summers, her legs shaking, approached the stone. The crowd held their breath as she reached out. The first pillar lit up, and a tentative smile touched her lips, she expected no more than this—an outer disciple at best.

But then, a gasp rippled through the crowd as a second pillar burst into light. Circa's heart leapt into her throat. *Maybe . . . just maybe . . .*

As the light crept up the third pillar, the grand elders leaned forward in their seats with budding interest. Yet, when it became clear the third pillar would not fully ignite, halting midway, they relaxed, disappointment etched into their features.

Circa, however, couldn't contain her joy. "I did it!" she whispered to herself, a grin spreading across her face. She was going to be an Inner Sect disciple!

"After the completion of the final trial, you will choose your path within the sect," Grand Elder Wyatt stated, a hint of warmth in his otherwise stern voice. Circa nodded, her enthusiasm uncurbed, as she skipped back to her place among the crowd.

For most of the participants, passing the second trial was sufficient, a guarantee of entry into the Inner Sect. The trial of comprehension that followed was more a matter for the elders—a chance to spot a disciple tailored for their unique cultivation methods.

As participant after participant stepped up to the Luminaresce Quartz, it became a familiar scene—a single pillar lighting up, sometimes bright, sometimes dim, but rarely more than that. The few who managed to illuminate a second were met with nods of approval from the onlookers, mostly young masters and mistresses from the local clans who held their heads a little higher with the acknowledgment.

"Dusty," Grand Elder Wyatt called out for the next participant to come forward.

Dusty, hearing his name, felt his clothes cling to his ample frame like a second skin as he began to trudge forward.

Nomed, seeing his friend uncharacteristically anxious, gave Dusty an encouraging slap on the back, grimacing at the slick of sweat his hand came away with. *Like patting a wet whale*, he thought wryly, trying to hide his disgust.

Reaching the stone, Dusty hesitated, his hand trembling as he placed it on the cool surface. A hush fell over the crowd, the kind of silence that seemed to amplify the slightest noise. The stone remained dark for a torturously long moment, and whispers began to spread among the other participants.

Seeing no change in the pillars, Dusty's face burned with embarrassment. *He said everyone had talent*, he seethed internally, *what kind of sick joke is this?*

Finally, a weak light emerged, barely illuminating the first pillar. It flickered as though it was the last ember of a dying fire.

"Outer Sect," Grand Elder Wyatt announced, his voice tinged with clear disappointment. Head bowed, Dusty made his way back to Nomed, who enveloped him in a sweaty hug.

"Think of all the amazing food you'll find in the Outer Sect," Nomed consoled, trying to keep the hug brief. "Better than anything we had back in the village."

"I guess, but make sure you sneak out some of those fancy Inner Sect snacks for me, okay?" Dusty managed a small wistful grin.

Their moment was cut short by a sneer from William. "Looks like I'll have new servants soon enough. Don't worry, I can take both of you on."

Nomed's face darkened at the comment, yet he held his tongue. *There's a time and place for everything*, he reminded himself, *and this isn't it.*

As the trial progressed, the few notable participants worthy of mention were the three youths from the Jexlarin Clan. Two of which managed to light up two pillars, securing their place in the Inner Sect. As for the third of the Jexlarin Clan, Bryce, he was able to illuminate two and a half pillars; with Grand Elder Tenzin's intervention it was possible he could gain the title of Core Disciple.

"Nomed!"

Nomed straightened as his name was called, it was finally his turn. However, before he could make his way forward, he noticed, from the corner of his eye, Dusty's sweaty palm approaching him. With a nimble dodge to the side, he avoided the blow leaving his pudgy friend grappling with the air. Unbalanced, Dusty stumbled and tumbled to the ground. Nomed couldn't hold back his laughter; it was more the sweat than his sidestep that was to blame.

"Very funny," Dusty grumbled from the ground, shaking his fist at Nomed's retreating back. Nomed just shook his head with a chuckle, walking towards the stone that would judge his talent.

He took a deep breath, feeling the hidden mark on his chest—a claw-like scar concealed under his simple village attire—pulse with a faint red light. It was so fleeting that not even the keen eyes of the grand elders caught the glimmer. *Lucky for me they have no interest in a nobody like me*, Nomed thought.

Placing his hand on the stone, he watched as the first pillar light up, followed swiftly by the second. As the third began to glow, the grand elders leaned forward, their expressions taut with interest. But then, abruptly, the light from the third pillar snuffed out, leaving only two pillars aglow.

The grand elders exchanged puzzled glances. *Has the stone malfunctioned?* they wondered.

For Nomed, that brief moment when the third pillar fully lit up was heart-stopping. Only when it faded did he allow himself a measured breath of relief. *Two pillars is a safe middle ground*, he consoled himself.

"Inner Sect," Grand Elder Wyatt announced, his voice tinged with a hint of confusion that Nomed was quick to ignore.

A modest smile played on Nomed's lips as he returned to Dusty, who erupted in cheers. "I knew you had it in you!"

"A shame about that third pillar, though." Dusty patted his stomach thoughtfully. "Core Disciples probably feast like kings."

Nomed nodded, playing along. "Inner Sect will do just fine," he agreed, while inwardly he repeated, *That was far too close for comfort.*

Finding no issues with the stone, the grand elder called out the next name, "William Wick."

With a haughty smirk plastered on his face, William approached the stone. *Let this pill work*, he silently prayed, not feeling a tenth as confident as he portrayed. He felt the capsule dissolve beneath his tongue. The pill was a rare treasure known as the Celestial Qi Amplifier, a concoction that could temporarily heighten one's affinity with qi.

Just don't scan me too closely, William thought, hoping the grand elders would refrain from scrutinizing him with their spiritual sense.

As the pill took effect, William felt a profound connection to the energy around him. His pores seemed to open as if thirsty for the qi that permeated the air. He quickly placed his hand on the stone, absorbing its energy.

Instantly, the first pillar lit up, followed swiftly by the second. A halfhearted glow began to creep up the third pillar, hesitating momentarily before ascending to the full height.

Up in the pagoda, the grand elders watched with rapt attention. "We may have underestimated the young Wick," Grand Elder Tenzin remarked, his eyebrows lifting in mild surprise.

"This one might just be cut out for the Disciplinary Hall." Grand Elder Darius grunted in agreement.

Grand Elder Wyatt beamed at William. "You will be considered for a Core Disciple position," he declared. "Should you have a preference for a particular hall, inform us. The grand elders will take your wishes into account during the selection process."

"I would like to study under the supreme elder," William declared proudly, his voice filled with the hunger of ambition and a tinge of desperation.

Grand Elder Darius's expression soured as a disciple dared to choose the supreme elder over him. He unconsciously crushed the armrest of his throne, the wood splintering beneath his grip.

Grand Elder Wyatt, however, maintained his composure, offering a smile that didn't quite reach his eyes. "The supreme elder is presently . . . indisposed," he remarked diplomatically. "However, we shall convey your preference and see what arrangements can be made."

With a nod, William headed back to his original position, letting out a sigh of relief once out of the grand elders' immediate scrutiny. *If only they knew how close I was to not even lighting up three pillars.* A bead of sweat rolled down his temple at the memory—death would be his last concern if a demonic sect such as the Black Rose Sect discovered any cheating.

His thoughts then turned towards the pill causing a frown to appear on his face. *Father will have to go through great lengths to repay that debt but . . . if it catches the supreme elder's interest, it will be worth it.*

Passing by the lesser beings, Dusty and Nomed, William felt his mood lift and he couldn't resist falling back into his arrogant young master persona. "Perhaps a servant from the Inner Sect would be more fitting than one from the Outer Sect, wouldn't you agree?" he asked Nomed.

Nomed's jaw tightened. *What exactly are the sect's rules on inner conflicts?* he pondered, but quickly dismissed the thought as an unsettling presence descended from the pagoda.

All heads turned, eyes widening as Grand Elder Wyatt landed gracefully to the valley floor. Whispers rippled through the crowd. *What could bring a Grand Elder down among us?*

The grand elder stopped before the young man draped in white. "Impressive indeed, for one to slip into our sect unnoticed. But what is to stop me right now from extinguishing your life?"

Unfazed, Kalin met the Grand Elder's gaze head-on, the corners of his mouth lifting into a faint, assured smile. "Grand Elder, there isn't a soul in this sect capable of that feat."

From within the pagoda, Grand Elder Darius's fury erupted like a volcano. "I shall sever your head myself, you insolent pup!" he bellowed, ready to leap into action.

Yet Kalin remained undisturbed as he leaned close to Wyatt and whispered, "Even the Venerable Black Tree Sect would think twice before raising a hand against me."

The color drained from Wyatt's face as the gravity of Kalin's words settled in. The Venerable Black Tree Sect, a demonic sect situated in the Immortal Realm, was the backbone of their own Black Rose Sect.

T-this youth is no ordinary cultivator, Wyatt realized, a flicker of unease passing through his eyes.

Darius found himself sinking back into his seat. If someone's ties made the parent sect of the Black Rose Sect hesitate, even he knew provoking them was to court death.

With a forced chuckle, Wyatt smoothed over the tension. "Well, I suppose our sect can always make room for one more, especially one as . . . unique as yourself." He gestured grandly towards the stone.

Kalin approached the stone, debating internally whether he should conceal his true capabilities. *No, subtlety won't serve my purpose here*, he concluded, dismissing the thought with a mental wave. To garner the supreme elder's attention, he needed to be bold.

The moment his skin grazed the stone, three pillars erupted in a radiant glow, drawing gasps from the other disciples. Without pause, the fourth and then the fifth pillars ignited, bathing the valley with a sight it had never witnessed before.

"F-five pillars! H-how is this possible?!"

CHAPTER FORTY-FOUR

The grand elders in the pagoda exchanged worried glances, each one unsettled by the white-robed youth. "We can't possibly admit him into our sect," Elder Tenzin whispered.

Grand Elder Darius, known for his impulsive decisions, nodded in rare agreement. A disciple of such extraordinary talent was more a harbinger of doom than a boon. Assassination attempts from rival mortal sects were manageable, but the pressure from the Venerable sects of the Immortal Realm was an entirely different matter.

Grand Elder Lydia rose to her feet. "We must inform the sect master immediately," she declared, but Tenzin quickly interjected.

"No, we cannot afford to disturb him during his ascension to the Immortal Realm," he countered urgently. Lydia's expression soured, but she reluctantly sat down, recalling the sect master's strict orders not to be disturbed unless the sect faced imminent destruction.

Down in the valley, William's gaze lingered on Kalin, his envy palpable. Any previous thoughts of the white-robed youth being an unremarkable figure had evaporated. *Could he be from the same realm as* him? The thought sent a chill down his spine.

Dusty, standing nearby, grumbled light-heartedly, "Bet that guy's gonna get the tastiest grub now. Probably never even heard of a potato."

"Maybe he'll share some with you," Nomed chuckled at his friend's comment. "But you'll probably eat it all before it even reaches us."

Kalin, observing the reactions of those around him, second-guessed his decision momentarily. *Did I push it too far?* He quickly dismissed the doubt. *No, this should definitely draw out the supreme elder.*

Grand Elder Wyatt held back a sigh, already having anticipated the outcome the moment the Venerable sect was mentioned. In any other circumstance, the sect would have eagerly concealed the fact that a disciple lit up all five pillars and groomed him in secret, potentially shaping him into the next sect master. But, with the youth's ties with the Immortal Realm, that plan was off the table. Rejecting him outright wasn't an option either; they had to let things unfold as they would.

Clearing his throat, Grand Elder Wyatt addressed the still-stunned crowd, his voice firm yet diplomatic. "Congratulations, young man," he said, pausing for a moment as he waited for the youth to reveal his name.

"Kalin," the white-robed youth responded.

"Very well, Kalin," Wyatt continued, "when the supreme elder returns, you will be under his tutelage."

A faint smile appeared on Kalin's face as he nodded and made his way back to his place among the other participants, he had received the exact outcome he had hoped for.

With a flick of his sleeve, Grand Elder Wyatt flew back up to the pagoda, and with another gesture, thousands of scrolls cascaded down into the valley.

"Next is the trial of comprehension," Wyatt explained. "You'll find scrolls of different types: blue for healing techniques, red for spiritual techniques, black for formations, and brown for martial arts. Choose the one you feel most drawn to. But be warned," he added with a stern look, "each scroll is marked with a unique formation. Attempting to steal them would be . . . unwise."

The warning caused a few shifty eyes to dart away, their plans of making some quick coin thwarted.

"The trial of comprehension will now begin, you have six hours."

The clan youths confidently stepped forward, selecting scrolls that complemented their cultivation paths. But the villagers hesitated, their expressions a mix of confusion and awe. They had never cultivated before and were clueless about which scrolls might suit them. Before they were brought to the sect, they were given a scroll to learn how to temper their body but the Body Tempering realm wasn't included in the realms of cultivation.

Dusty, standing awkwardly at the back with Nomed, whispered, "Which one should we take? I don't even know what I'm good at."

"Maybe something that feels right?" Nomed scanned the scrolls with a thoughtful expression. "I heard that's how some cultivators choose their paths."

"Feels right?" Dusty looked skeptical. "Like how a pie calls to me from across a room?"

"Yeah, something like that." Nomed couldn't help but chuckle at his friend's analogy. "But maybe with less . . . pie."

With a resigned sigh, Dusty joined the other disciples. After aimlessly scanning various scrolls, his attention was unexpectedly drawn to a neglected one lying apart from the others. *It's calling to me . . . just like pie*, he mused with a hint of amusement.

Picking up the scroll titled "The Path of the Gluttonous Titan," Dusty's eyes widened. The technique described would cause him to grow larger the more he cultivated it. *Well, I hadn't made much progress on losing weight anyway*. He shrugged as he sat down to absorb its contents, already picturing himself as a formidable, if large, cultivator.

Nomed watched his friend with a fond smile before turning his attention to a black scroll. Intrigued, he unrolled it to reveal a formation cultivation method named Intricate Matrix of the Guarding Spirits. He skimmed through the details which explained how to enter the Qi Refining Realm. *The first realm of cultivation*, he thought. *I could get a better one from "him," but for now, this will do.*

Meanwhile, William chose a wind spiritual technique—Zephyr's Whisper. It was a natural choice, given the Wick Clan's renowned talent with the wind element. *This should be quick and easy to learn,* he thought.

Kalin, on the other hand, picked up a spiritual technique called Blade of the Dawn. His expression soured slightly upon realizing its quality. *A mortal rank technique?* he thought disdainfully. In the Immortal Realm, even the most basic techniques handed to potential disciples were of a much higher rank. Suppressing his disappointment, he began studying the scroll. *At least this won't take long to master,* he reasoned.

Huddled in a small cave within the Void Realm, Slifer estimated that he had been trapped for approximately a week. The frequent, ghastly roars outside caused him to press himself against the cold cave wall, attempting to become as inconspicuous as possible.

These ghostly creatures seemed to perpetually roam the realm, engaging in fierce battles whenever they encountered one another. *I guess they have nothing better to do.*

Slifer had managed to observe a pattern in their behavior; for approximately one hour each day, they would disappear, giving him a brief window to explore and attempt to use the Dimensional Slide technique to escape. But, frustratingly, every attempt to open a portal back to his world ended in failure.

His thoughts drifted to the whooping 1000 Karmic Credits he had squandered on gambling, cursing the stingy System for not providing anything useful to escape this predicament. *Would a simple teleportation card have been too much to ask for?* he lamented.

Sighing, he looked up at the new cards in his arsenal:

Name: Critical Block Card
Description: Protects user from a critical strike.
Name: Reflection Card
Description: Creates an energy barrier that reflects attacks back at the attacker for 20 seconds.
Name: Peak Slifer Aura
Description: Releases an aura mimicking the original Slifer at his peak.
Name: Another Face
Description: Allows the user to change appearance for up to 6 months.
Name: Avatar
Description: Creates a complete clone of the user that can independently cultivate.
Warning: The avatar cannot access the System or its cards.

Slifer couldn't help but scoff at the Peak Slifer Aura card. *Now that I'm supposedly an Ascendant cultivator, this card is about as useful as a screen door on a submarine*, he thought with a hint of irony. *What am I supposed to do? Scare off Voidwalkers with a Nascent Soul aura?*

The Another Face and Avatar cards, while intriguing, did little to alleviate his current dilemma. The idea of creating an avatar that could cultivate on its own was fascinating and he would make sure to play around with it later, but it wouldn't help him escape this desolate realm.

"Great," Slifer muttered to himself, "a clone in the Void Realm would just be a bonus snack for those Voidwalkers. Two for the price of one, how generous of me."

Slifer released a heavy sigh as he called up the System panel and focused on the Dimensional Slide technique.

Name: Dimensional Slide—Level 1
Rank: Obsidian
Description: Allows the user to traverse through the Void Realm.
Upgrade Cost: 1000 Karmic Credits

This was his last shot; he had hesitated to upgrade the technique before, doubtful that level 2 would make much of a difference.

But now, he had no other choice.

With a mix of reluctance and hope, Slifer selected the upgrade.

-1000 Karmic Credits

A serene wave washed over him as knowledge about the Dimensional Slide technique poured into his mind.

Ding!
Space Mastery: 5%

At least this feels somewhat enlightening, he mused.

Once the influx of information ended, Slifer realized that the description for the level 1 technique had updated. His face turned an unhealthy shade of red as he read about the ninety-seven percent failure rate in the Void Realm due to spatial instability.

Why wasn't this mentioned before? he thought, his fist clenching in frustration. *I wouldn't have dared to jump into this forsaken place with those odds!*

Turning his attention to the level 2 description, Slifer's expression softened slightly.

Name: Dimensional Slide—Level 2
Rank: Obsidian
Description: Allows the user to transverse through the Void Realm.
Success Rate in Void Realm: 60%
Upgrade Cost: 2000 Karmic Credits

Sixty percent . . . Not great, not terrible, Slifer contemplated with a half-smile. *Even with my luck, I should be able to make it work if I keep trying.*

He settled down to wait, planning to escape during that one quiet hour when the void beasts took their daily smoke break.

After an agonizing few hours that felt like days, Slifer couldn't hear any more noises from outside the cave. Slowly, he stood up and tiptoed to the entrance. He kept his spiritual sense reined in, knowing it would be akin to holding up a sign saying, "Free buffet, all you can eat!" in the presence of the phantom beings. His eyes swept the desolate landscape, alert for any hint of danger. Seeing nothing amiss, he let out a relieved breath.

"Time to get to work."

Focusing qi to his fingertips, he made a carving motion as he attempted to rip open a portal through space. A small tear began to form, and a smile started to spread across his face. But just as quickly, the space quivered, and the portal snapped shut.

"I knew it was too good to be true to work on the first try," he grumbled under his breath.

For the next hour, Slifer persisted. Time and again, he tried to create a stable portal, but each attempt ended in failure. At one point, a portal did form, but it vanished before he could leap through.

Slifer knew all too well that probability could be a fickle thing. *It's like flipping a coin. Even with a fifty percent chance, there's no guarantee of an even split between heads and tails . . . or getting the side you want even once,* he thought, trying to rationalize his string of bad luck. *It's all about chance, and right now, mine seems pretty rotten.*

"Come on, come on," Slifer urged himself, his attempts growing more frantic. He was running out of time; the phantom beasts would soon return. Failure was not an option, as opening a portal with those creatures nearby would be tantamount to suicide.

Then, after numerous attempts, a portal began to form again. This time it looked stable. As it fully materialized, Slifer couldn't help but let out a triumphant cheer.

"This place is definitely getting a bad review!" With that, he leaped towards the portal, but mid-jump, something caught his eye—a phantom beast materialized out of thin air, its gaping maw opened wide ready to swallow him whole.

Slifer's heart skipped a beat, and in that moment of sheer panic, he took back his previous statement.

"I'll give it five stars, just let me out of here!"

CHAPTER FORTY-FIVE

Slifer barely made it through the portal, feeling the phantom beast's ghastly roar vibrating behind him as part of it got severed by the closing portal. Landing clumsily in his courtyard, he looked disheveled and far from the composed master he usually was.

"Master!" Caelum exclaimed, getting to his feet in a hurry. "The Disciple Selection Ceremony has already begun."

Slifer quickly adjusted his robe and cleared his throat, trying to regain his usual air of mystery. "Ah, yes, I had almost forgotten about the Disciple Selection Ceremony," he replied nonchalantly, waving his sleeve to summon his sword from the storage ring.

"Let's get going then."

But before Slifer could jump on his sword, Caelum hesitantly interjected, "Master, I . . . I need your help."

Slifer gave him a questioning look, this was the first time any of his disciples had directly asked for his assistance, normally they would do anything they could to keep him out of their business.

Looking visibly uncomfortable, Caelum continued, "Someone has . . . poisoned my mother, and I've had no luck finding the antidote."

Slifer's eyes narrowed at this. *Was someone targeting Caelum's mother to get to him . . . and ultimately to me?* He pondered the possibility, compared to original Slifer, Caelum had no enemies.

Now he faced a crucial decision: ignore his disciple and go to the Disciple Selection Ceremony to fulfill the System's mission or aid his disciple, potentially failing the mission. Slifer wrestled with his thoughts. *What would the System do if I fail the mission?* he wondered. *No, I won't be like their original master. If Caelum's mother dies because I didn't help, I'll never forgive myself.* He nodded to himself, making up his mind. "What is the poison, and what is the antidote?" he finally asked.

Caelum's face lit up with a flicker of hope, he hadn't been sure if his master would care to help him. "The poison is called Cultivator's Bane, and the antidote . . . it's the Essence of Dawn," he replied.

Essence of Dawn? Let's hope the System has it . . . at a cheap price. Slifer quickly opened the System panel.

Shop
Cards
Cultivation Methods
Treasures
Pills and Elixirs
Mystic Techniques

Martial Techniques
Bloodlines and Ancestries
Constitutions
Spirit Roots
Beasts and Familiars
Create

Slifer picked the "Pills and Elixirs" option and began scrolling through the list of items, each sounding more extravagant than the last. *If only this System had a search feature.*

After a few moments, he finally stumbled upon the Essence of Dawn elixir.

Name: Essence Of Dawn
Type: Elixir
Rank: Heaven
Description: Able to counteract Heaven Rank poisons, restoring vitality and purging toxins. Widely known as the antidote for the Cultivator's Bane.
Cost: 2000 Karmic Credits

Two thousand Karmic Credits? That's daylight robbery! Slifer's heart sank at the sight of the price, but he couldn't let Caelum down. He wasn't dumb enough to buy the elixir, at least, not until he confirmed the poison himself. *Not wasting two thousand credits only to find out she needs a good nap!*

Meanwhile, Caelum watched his master, slightly puzzled by Slifer's strange behavior. He often caught his master spacing out, followed by random nods or shakes of the head, sometimes accompanied by strange expressions.

Slifer coughed, and suddenly announced, "We'll get going as soon as Val arrives."

Caelum snapped out of his thoughts and nodded, feeling a wave of relief. *Maybe there's hope for Mother after all,* he thought, watching his master expectantly.

But then, something unexpected caught Caelum's eye. "Master, what is that?" he asked, pointing behind Slifer.

Slifer turned to look over his shoulder and his face drained of color. Clinging to him was a miniature version of the phantom beast he had encountered in the Void Realm. Its form was smoky, almost ethereal.

Every instinct in Slifer screamed for him to run, but he held his ground. The Critical Block Card had yet to activate. *If I startle it . . .* He remained as still as possible, wishing that he had already entered the Nascent Soul Realm so he wouldn't need to breathe.

"Just . . . stay calm, Caelum," Slifer whispered, his voice barely concealing his own unease. *How did this thing even attach itself to me? And more importantly, how do I get rid of it without getting us both killed?*

The little phantom beast cooed innocently, its eyes wide with curiosity as it gazed at Slifer. The unexpected childlike behavior of the creature caused Slifer to ponder. *Could this be a youngling of the phantom beasts?* A memory flashed through his mind—the moment he had escaped through the portal, a part of the large phantom beast was cut off. *Could that be how they reproduce?* he wondered, intrigued by the possibility.

Insight!

> *Ding!*
> Congratulations!
> You Have Discovered a Higher Being
> You Have Gained 10 Karmic Credits
> Increase Your Relationship with the Being to Take It As a Disciple
> Minimum Requirement: 80%
> Current Progress: 10%

Interesting. It has a relationship requirement for discipleship. Slifer recalled that Val had no such requirement, but that could perhaps be due to Val already meeting the requirement. He then turned his attention to its cultivation realm.

> Name: N/A
> Species: Void Being
> Realm: Late Core Formation Realm
> Known Techniques: N/A
> Known Affiliations: N/A
> Disposition: N/A

The little being's cultivation level stunned him—Late Core Formation Realm from birth? *That's higher than Val's initial level,* he mused, impressed. *Good thing I didn't startle it. A Core Formation attack would have definitely triggered the Critical Block Card.*

Noticing Caelum's bewildered gaze, Slifer composed himself and casually remarked, "Oh, this little fellow? Just a . . . friend I thought Val might like."

Caelum nodded, though clearly unsure about his master's unexpected companion.

Their conversation was interrupted by the sound of Val's familiar roar.

"Master! Master is back!" the dragon called out as she descended from the sky, landing with a heavy thud, her gaze immediately focusing on the little phantom being.

The creature, sensing the dragon's Nascent Soul aura, hid behind Slifer, its body trembling in fear.

Slifer, with a gentle smile, carefully picked up the phantom beast, its form phasing in and out of tangibility. "Look, Val, what your master has brought you," he said, extending his hand towards her.

> *Ding!*
> Void Beings have a high mental defense making them almost impossible to tame.
> Warning: You are at risk of being enslaved.
> Hint: Eliminate the threat.

" . . ." *Enslaved?* Slifer made sure to stay still, worried any sudden movement would trigger the ticking time bomb.

"Val love gifts." She sniffed the beast with her enormous snout.

"Gift smell nice."

The creature let out a whimper of fear, shaking uncontrollably, its instincts screaming at it to escape.

Don't explode, don't explode, Slifer prayed.

Just when he thought the phantom being was going to retaliate with a mind attack, Val opened her mouth wide and, in one swift motion, swallowed the little beast whole.

Slifer stood there, mouth agape, a mix of shock and disbelief on his face. *Well, that was unexpected . . .* he thought, slightly taken aback by Val's straightforwardness. He remembered the phantom beasts had a phasing ability; he didn't think Val would deal with it so . . . easily.

Caelum, too, looked startled, his eyes wide as he processed what just happened. *I guess that's one type of gift to get . . .* His thoughts trailed off. He'd thought his master had brought Val a friend, not a snack, however, this did fit more with his master's character.

Slifer continued to watch as Val finished consuming the phantom beast. She then turned to him and thanked him for the "gift."

"I'm glad you liked it, Val."

So much for having a Void Realm disciple, Slifer thought, feeling slightly deflated even though he knew that his little dragon just saved his life. *I should probably give her an actual reward . . .*

Ding!
Congratulations!
Your Soul Bond Creature Has Devoured a Unique Being
Gaining Trait from Being
Randomizing . . .
Trait Acquired: Phase Ability—Allows the user to phase for 30 seconds with a cooldown of 60 seconds.
Current Progress: 10%

Slifer's eyebrows shot up in surprise. *Phase ability, huh?* he mused, feeling better already. *Just like the Flash.*

His attention shifted to his status as more notifications popped up.

Ding!
New Passive Skill Acquired: Void Being Aura
  • Decreases likelihood of detection in the Void Realm.
  • Imposes a 5% debuff on lower realm beings.
  • Provides 50% protection against Mind Control below the level of the Immortal Realm.

Slifer's eyes brightened as he read the description of his new passive skill. *Void Being Aura, huh? That's actually quite handy.* The thought of returning to the Void Realm was still unappealing, but with this new ability, it seemed a bit less daunting.

And that mind control protection could come in handy too. A chill ran down his spine as he kicked himself for not buying some protection earlier. *Credits be damned, skimping on protection never ends well . . . Wow, I sound just like my dad.* Shaking his head, he focused on the few options he had. *The plan was to get Val to fly us to the village but . . .* He decided that using the improved Dimensional Slide technique to teleport directly to Caelum's village was the best course of action. *I can save Caelum's mother and still make it to the Disciple Selection Ceremony in time.* "Val, head back to the ceremony and tell them I'll be there soon," he instructed.

"But why Master call Val then tell Val leave?" She looked down at him with big, sad eyes.

"I wanted to give you that . . . snack."

A friend, a snack. To a beast, what's the difference? He shook his head.

Her gaze didn't waver. "Can Val come too?" she asked, her attempt at persuasion sounding more like a threat due to her enormous, intimidating presence.

"Your mission is just as important, if not more," Slifer replied, tying to appease the little dragon's big pride. However, seeing her still pouting, he added, "I promise, Val. I'll be back soon, and then we can go on trips together, alright?"

Reluctantly, Val nodded, her massive wings beginning to flap. "Okay, but Val miss Master," she said before soaring into the sky.

Caelum couldn't help but feel a bit awkward watching the exchange. His master's soft spot for Val was no secret among the disciples, but he had never seen Slifer so openly affectionate with the baby dragon. It was a side of his master that rarely anyone saw.

Slifer turned to Caelum, no sign of the gentleness present on his face. "Alright, let's save your mother and then find you a new junior brother . . . or sister."

"But Master, how will we get there in time?" Caelum asked, he wasn't sure how fast Ascendant cultivators could travel but crossing such a large distance in such a short time and back seemed quite optimistic.

"Leave that to me."

I didn't think I'd be doing this again . . . especially so soon. With a frown, Slifer executed a tearing motion with his hand, opening a portal.

Caelum's eyes widened in surprise. *I had no idea Master had such an ability.* He realized how little he actually knew about his own master.

"Get in," Slifer instructed, gesturing towards the portal.

Slifer exhaled a sigh of relief as they arrived outside Caelum's village home. The journey had been smooth, thankfully. *If we got stuck in that Void Realm again, I'd probably lose my mind . . . or worse, end up playing a never-ending game of hide-and-seek with those phantom beasts,* he thought wryly.

Using his spiritual sense, Caelum had provided a mental image of his home, similar to sending a photo via a phone. The image was clear enough for Slifer to successfully open a portal directly to their destination.

As they approached the familiar door of his childhood home, Caelum felt his heart rate increase. With a trembling hand, he knocked on the weathered wood. The door creaked open, revealing a middle-aged man whose face showed signed of fatigue and sadness.

For a moment, the man stared blankly, but recognition soon dawned in his eyes. "Caelum!" he exclaimed, his voice broke. As he stepped forward, tears began to spill down his cheeks, and he pulled Caelum into a hug, clutching onto him as if he were a lifeline.

Caelum's eyes misted over and he held back a sob as he wrapped his arms around his father.

"Your mother . . . she's . . . ." Caelum's father pulled back slightly, his body shook as he looked into his son's eyes.

"I know, father. I am here now. Everything will be alright." Caelum gently placed his hands on his father's shoulders, offering a reassuring squeeze.

Turning slightly, he gestured towards Slifer. "Father, remember my master? He's come to help us with mother's situation."

Upon recognizing Slifer, the middle-aged man immediately dropped to his knees, pleading. "Oh, Lord Immortal, please save my wife."

Slifer, caught off guard by the man's actions, quickly helped him to his feet. "It is not appropriate for the father of my disciple to bow to me like this," Slifer said, feeling a bit awkward in the situation.

But Caelum's father shook his head, his eyes filled with desperation. "I would do anything to save her, Lord Immortal."

Feeling uneasy under the weight of the man's expectations, Slifer's gaze wandered around the room, that was when he noticed a portrait hanging on the wall—an older man who bore a striking resemblance to Caelum and his father.

A sharp pang of memory hit Slifer, and he clutched his head, momentarily disoriented.

"M-Master, is everything okay?" Caelum stepped forward.

Slifer forced a chuckle, waving his hand nonchalantly. "Oh, it's just a small headache, nothing to worry about," he said, brushing off his disciple's concern.

I've seen this portrait before . . . must be from when the original Slifer took Caelum as his disciple, Slifer reasoned, trying to shake off the sinking feeling in his gut.

CHAPTER FORTY-SIX

Inside the house, Slifer looked at the frail woman lying on the bed. Despite being only slightly younger than her husband, she appeared old enough to be his mother.

The pills the original gave them should have kept them looking much younger and extended their lifespan, Slifer mused, wondering if the original had given them defective pills. *I wouldn't put it pass the old miser.*

He ignored the father's continuous pleas for help as he approached the woman's bedside. Gently taking her hand, he channeled a sliver of his qi into her body. With his spiritual sense, he watched as the poison aggressively consumed the qi, exacerbating her condition.

Definitely Cultivator's Bane, he concluded, letting go of her hand. The original's memories of the poison were clear . . . perhaps a little too clear.

There goes 2000 Karmic Credits, he thought as he purchased the elixir.

In truth, Slifer didn't feel like he lost anything, Caelum had earned him more than 2000 Karmic Credits already and he would continue to earn more.

The System conveniently deposited it into his spirit ring, sparing him the awkwardness of explaining a sudden, miraculous appearance—though, it would be easy to explain to a mortal, they would just attribute it to fancy immortal shenanigans. However, his more astute disciple might feel suspicious, if not now then definitely the day he became an Ascendant cultivator himself.

Retrieving the elixir, Slifer handed it to Caelum, whose eyes widened in disbelief. "Administer this to your mother."

Caelum, his hands trembling slightly as he gently tipped the elixir into his mother's mouth. The liquid seemed to invigorate her almost immediately. Her frail form began to regain some semblance of vitality. Though her muscles remained weak, there was a noticeable change; she no longer appeared as a woman on the brink of death but more like someone in her forties, albeit severely undernourished.

Caelum's father watched in awe, his eyes moist with unshed tears. "Thank you, Immortal," he murmured, his voice thick with emotion.

Slifer nodded, offering a reassuring smile. "She needs rest and nourishment now. Her body will recover in time," he advised.

Overcome with relief, Caelum turned to Slifer. "Master, how can I ever repay you for this?"

Slifer shook his head, dismissing the notion. "Seeing you fulfill your potential as a cultivator is repayment enough." *The higher your cultivation, the more credits you can get for this old man.*

Unable to hold back his emotions any longer, tears streamed down Caelum's face as he turned towards his mother. "M-Mother . . ." He enveloped her in a tight hug, and soon, his father joined them, wrapping his arms around the family.

Slifer stood by, watching the emotional reunion with an awkward air.

Caelum's father, noticing Slifer's discomfort, gestured for him to join the hug.

I've never been a touchy person . . . Slifer hesitantly stepped forward and joined in, feeling out of place amidst the family's heartfelt moment.

Suddenly, a series of System messages popped up:

Ding!

Congratulations!

Your Disciple Caelum's Loyalty Has Reached 100%

New Option Available: Convert Caelum to a Righteous Cultivator

Reward: A Righteous Disciple Will Earn x3 Credit

Slifer's mind whirred upon reading the messages. *Finally, a clue on how to convert my own disciples,* he thought. But the randomness of the loyalty fluctuations lately made him skeptical about the feasibility of reaching one hundred percent loyalty with his other disciples.

Why couldn't all my disciples' family members be poisoned so I could play the hero? He sighed but then immediately shook off the thought. *No, that would make me paranoid about being the real target or . . . being the cause.*

Ding!

New Mission: One Righteous Disciple Is Worth More Than a Thousand Demonic Trash

Description: Your disciple is ready to join the righteous path. Give him a sermon and ask him to join.

Guess I know what I'm doing after work tonight.

The hug became awkward as Slifer, lost in his thoughts, forgot to let go. Caelum, realizing that his master's thoughts had wandered again, coughed gently, "Master?"

Startled, Slifer quickly composed himself and stepped back. "Ah, yes, of course."

Caelum's mother, now sitting up and looking healthier, turned to Slifer with a grateful look in her eyes. "The heavens truly blessed our family the day you took my son into your sect, Immortal Master."

Slifer offered a strained smile, thinking, *To mortals, what difference does it make if it's an immortal or demonic sect? They're all the same.*

Turning to his mother, Caelum's eyes still red from tears, he made a solemn vow. "I promise you, Mother, I will find out who did this to you and make them pay."

Slifer's face darkened as he nodded in agreement. "An attack on a disciple's family is an attack on myself," he affirmed. *If this was indeed directed at me, I must find out who did this.*

"Please, for my sake, do not seek vengeance," the kindhearted woman pleaded softly, not understanding the harsh reality of the cultivation world.

"I'm sorry, Mother, but I cannot obey you in this matter," Caelum stated. He knew that whoever did this would not stop until they succeeded or . . . were killed.

His father, standing beside him, placed a supportive hand on his shoulder. "Get justice for your mother, son."

Caelum nodded before glancing up, his gaze landed on the portrait of his grandfather. "Why is Grandfather's portrait up?" he asked, a hint of surprise in his voice.

"He . . . he passed away three months ago. I had a painter from the nearby city, Master Leo, come two months ago to draw this portrait. We wanted something to remember him by." His father let out a weary sigh.

The lives of mortals seem so . . . fleeting. Caelum sighed.

Overhearing this, Slifer felt a jolt of realization. *If the portrait was drawn only two months ago, how come it's in the original's memories?* The sinking feeling in his gut continued to grow as he connected the dots—the poisoning, the visit from the original Slifer, and the timing of the portrait's creation.

Attempting to mask his thoughts, Slifer cleared his throat and casually mentioned, "It has been over a decade since my last visit. Apart from the . . . recent mishap, it seems your family is faring well."

The parents exchanged a puzzled glance, clearly wondering what signs of wellbeing Slifer was referring to. Their lives had been anything but prosperous recently: their crops had failed last season, bandits had raided their village, and now the poisoning.

Caelum's mother, however, managed a strained smile, playing along with Slifer's comment. "Lord Immortal is right, the family is doing . . . well," she agreed, though her eyes betrayed her words. "We would be even more grateful if Lord Immortal visited more often."

They are not aware of the original's recent visit . . . That old bastard, he really tried to poison his own disciple's mother!

Looking at the woman, who gazed up at him with expectant eyes, he almost shook his head. *They should consider themselves fortunate that the original Slifer isn't in control anymore,* he thought grimly. *Another visit from him, and the husband would have joined his wife in an early death!*

Outwardly though, Slifer maintained his composure and nodded to the family, giving them a promise that he knew he wouldn't remember to keep. "I assure you, I will make an effort to visit more often."

"Thank you, Lord Immortal."

As the family conversed among themselves, Slifer stood to the side, deep in thought. *Why would the original Slifer target his own disciple's family? What could possibly be gained from harming Caelum's mother?*

He glanced at Caelum, observing his disciple's upright character and demeanor, and quickly dismissed the thought of any hidden animosity between them. *More likely, the original Slifer was scheming against all his disciples,* Slifer pondered. *I need to uncover any other messes he's left before they come back to kill me.*

With a strategic cough, Slifer caught Caelum's attention. "I will look into this matter," he assured him, adopting a stern tone. "As a sword cultivator, you must remain focused on your path. Distractions will only impede your progress. Leave this to your master."

"Are you sure, Master? I don't want to add to your burdens. You always seem so . . . occupied," Caelum replied.

"Do not worry about me, Caelum. Trust that your master will handle this matter appropriately." Slifer tried his best to offer a reassuring smile.

Caelum nodded, though he still seemed uneasy about the situation.

This is how they do it, right?

Dusty sat cross-legged, emulating the posture of the city boys around him. He took deep breaths, his attention on the first step of the Path of the Gluttonous Titan technique—opening up his pores to sense the qi around him.

After a few hours, he was able to sense what he assumed was the ambient qi.

Ha ha, and they said it takes weeks. He grinned. But then, abruptly, a sharp pang of hunger struck him. His eyes bulged, and his face reddened as he panted, "Food . . . I need food!"

Out of nowhere, a piece of beast meat, known as the Celestial Boar steak, fell from the large pagoda above. Without a moment's hesitation, Dusty lunged for it, catching it midair. His eyes glinted with a hint of madness as he tore into the meat in a most uncivilized manner, devouring it with a ferocity that left onlookers in shock.

"As expected from a peasant," William, watching from a distance, couldn't help but sneer.

Dusty's technique involved more than just eating; as he chewed the meat, he actively channeled the technique from the scroll, focusing on digesting and absorbing the qi within the meat. His method was unorthodox—rather than absorbing qi from the environment, he was directly assimilating it from the beast meat. After finishing his feast with a loud burp, a faint wave of qi radiated from him.

"Qi Refining!" someone in the crowd exclaimed, surprised at this unexpected breakthrough.

Dusty laughed heartily, patting his now slightly larger belly. "Outer Sect?" he scoffed mockingly. "You lot can't even begin to understand your father's immense talent!" he boasted.

I-impossible! His talent is awful, how could an Outer Disciple's comprehension exceed mine?! William grit his teeth in envy. Even though he was already a Seventh Stage Qi Refining cultivator, he had never entered the Qi Refining Realm so . . . effortlessly.

Yeah, stare at my awesomeness. Dusty strutted around like a proud peacock.

Nomed shook his head at his friend's antics, he had already broken through to the first stage of Qi Refining but he decided to keep it a secret for now, not wanting to put Dusty down.

Up in the pagoda, Grand Elder Tenzin turned to Grand Elder Darius, who was leaning forward with evident interest. "It's rare for you to share one of your prized food items," Tenzin commented, referring to the spiritual beast steak that Dusty had just devoured, the steak contained the qi equivalent of a Third Stage Qi Refining expert.

"This lad's like a well-fed caterpillar that's about to become an over-fed butterfly!" Darius chuckled.

"Seems you have your eye on quite a few disciples this cycle," Tenzin said with a bitter smile on his face.

"Can I help it if they're all naturally suited for the Disciplinary Hall?" Darius snorted dismissively.

With the disparity in their cultivation, Tenzin knew that he would only be making a fool of himself if he were to challenge Darius over a disciple. *If only the sect master was here . . .*

"That boy has a talent that's otherworldly, quite literally," Grand Elder Wyatt's comment cut through Tenzin's thoughts.

They turned their attention to Kalin who, having already mastered the sword skill in mere minutes, was now casually observing the other disciples.

Grand Elder Darius couldn't help but scoff at the situation. "Let the 'supreme elder' handle that headache," he said dismissively, not particularly concerned about the implications of Kalin's presence.

Wyatt, however, shook his head in subtle disapproval. He understood that any issue involving the higher realms could potentially affect the entire sect, not just the one who took the boy in.

"The trial of comprehension is now concluded," Grand Elder Wyatt announced as the six-hour mark was met.

A wave of mixed reactions rippled through the crowd of disciples. Those who had struggled in vain with their scrolls let out sighs of frustration, their shoulders slumping in defeat. "I just couldn't understand a thing," one muttered dejectedly.

"I was so close . . ." another disciple lamented, his voice tinged with frustration.

In contrast, others wore smiles of relief. "Finally, it's over," a disciple exclaimed, stretching his arms above his head, "I thought it would never end!"

Suddenly, a rip in space appeared before the grand elders' pavilion, drawing everyone's attention.

Hughie, recognizing the technique, mentally reached out to Li Fenghao in the ring. "Hey, old man, didn't you say this technique was special? Why does someone else know it?"

Li Fenghao remained silent for a moment, his mind racing. *How is this possible?* he wondered. When the figure emerged from the portal, Li Fenghao's eyes widened in shock. *This guy again! Who is he really? He . . . he must be from the Immortal Realm!* He nodded to himself, trying to make sense of the situation.

The figure was none other than Slifer.

As he stepped out of the portal, the grand elders all rose to their feet, offering a respectful nod, all except Grand Elder Darius.

He stood up abruptly. "Slifer!" His voice boomed across the valley.

"Darius, not yet!" Grand Elder Wyatt hissed under his breath.

But Darius, disregarding the warning, released an aura that made even the other grand elders pale: the aura of the Ascendant Realm.

CHAPTER FORTY-SEVEN

Slifer's head popped out of the portal. He held back a sigh of relief. He had managed to arrive at the correct location. Leveling the Dimensional Slide technique seemed like a good investment after all.

But before the rest of his body could exit the portal, a booming voice caught him off guard, the force of the shout nearly knocking him off balance.

"Slifer!"

Turning his gaze, Slifer saw a middle-aged man, his robes struggling in vain to hide a muscular physique reminiscent of a character from a video game.

Eh, why is this Tekken-like character shouting at me? Slifer couldn't help but wonder.

Slifer recognized him from the original's memories. The man was Grand Elder Darius, an Origin Realm expert, well, now apparently an Ascendant Realm cultivator, he was supposedly the most formidable cultivator in the Black Rose Sect after the sect master.

A heavy pressure descended upon him, and Slifer fought to keep his body from tensing up under the gaze of his disciples and the grand elders. It would be more than a little strange for the supposed "supreme elder" to soil himself in front of an equal, or to even soil himself in general.

I'm certain Nascent Soul cultivators and above don't have these kinds of . . . bodily functions. Well, I guess wetting myself would be an interesting way to expose myself.

"Ha ha, now that Master is here, he'll teach you a lesson."

Slifer didn't need to turn around to know who that voice belonged to. *This girl*, he thought, frustrated.

He had repeatedly warned Amelia about provoking stronger cultivators but clearly it was useless, he would need to hurry up and increase his cultivation, so he wouldn't need to worry about what problem she was going to create for him next. *With these disciples, in this world, a pie is the least of my concerns.*

Forcing a cough to mask his discomfort, Slifer addressed the enraged elder, who was kind enough to wait for him to finish his internal monologue. "Junior Darius, what did my disciple do this time," Slifer asked as his mind wandered to the potential punishments that would make the troublesome girl finally listen to him.

It has to be something embarrassing, so she knows I'm serious but . . . at the same time not too embarrassing where she adds me to her hitlist. Slifer knew that cultivators had the tendency to jump to slaughtering a whole generation for the tiniest slight, as for Amelia . . . he knew she would go the whole nine generations.

The grand elder's face flushed with anger at Slifer's audacity to address him as "Junior." Despite his middle-aged appearance, he was a millennium older than the so-called supreme elder standing before him.

Darius's mind reeled with thoughts of his contributions and sacrifices for the sect. He had been a key figure in fighting back the demons during the demonic invasion, unlike many others who felt that as demonic cultivators their loyalty should be towards the Nether Realm.

The sect master had hinted many times in the past at Grand Elder Darius being the next in line to lead the sect, but Slifer's sudden rise in cultivation rank posed a threat to his aspirations. While he would never openly admit it, Darius did in fact feel threatened by the recent rapid advancement of the sect master's lapdog.

Taking a deliberate step forward, Darius intensified the pressure bearing down on Slifer. "Now that we're *both* Ascendant cultivators, I'm not your junior," he declared as he began to channel qi into his right arm.

Both he and Grand Elder Wyatt had harbored doubts about Slifer's claim to the Ascendant Realm. How could someone they had watched fail the Origin Realm tribulation suddenly emerge as an Ascendant? It had to be a trick, a treasure, something other than genuine cultivation.

Sensing Darius's intention to attack, Slifer's eyes widened in alarm.

Darius's right arm transformed into a stony appendage with jagged edges and in a blur, he closed the distance between them, his fist aimed squarely at Slifer's head.

In the background, Slifer could hear Amelia's enthusiastic cheers, but his focus was entirely on the incoming attack, an attack that was too fast for him to even see, let alone defend against. Before he could blink, Darius's fist collided with his head.

Ding!
Critical Block Card Activated

An invisible barrier sprang up around Slifer, effortlessly blocking the attack and sending a shockwave that repelled Darius several feet backwards. The force of their clash sent cracks spider-webbing across the pavilion's floor.

What technique was that? Darius looked down at his fist in disbelief. *It wasn't a wind technique;* he hadn't felt any wind aura. *A barrier technique, perhaps?* But his knowledge of formations was limited, that was more in Grand Elder Wyatt's domain.

Grand Elder Wyatt was astonished. *A space-time and barrier technique combined?* Such a feat was beyond even his considerable expertise in formations, it required an intricate understanding of essences. Essences were rumored to be the domain of the immortals, and even then, space and time were known to be of the most difficult to comprehend.

Could the supreme elder have entered the Immortal Realm?

Wyatt's original plan had been to carefully prod Slifer into revealing his cultivation level, to confirm whether he truly belonged to the Ascendant Realm or was relying on an artifact. But Darius, unable to be patient even for a few moments, had ruined that plan.

Darius has dug his own grave, he can get himself out of it. He shook his head, deciding to distance himself from the impulsive fool.

At that moment, Grand Elder Tenzin, sensing that things were getting out of hand, quickly flew into the air, ushering Caelum and the other disciples to follow him. "Come, Darius isn't known for . . . restraint."

Once they were out of the way, the pavilion was left with only Grand Elder Darius and Slifer who were locked in a silent standoff.

If not for those nightmarish days in the Void Realm, I might have been at this madman's mercy, Slifer thought, a wry smile tugging at his lips. It was clear to him now that Darius had been itching for an opportunity to challenge him.

Slifer's eyes narrowed as he noticed a red glow emanating from the Grand Elder's chest, it was in the shape of a crystal. *An Ascendant Crystal . . .* he thought, recognizing the symbol of a cultivator's breakthrough to the Ascendant Realm.

The glow from the crystal caused the air to shift as a realm of stone expanded from the core, it engulfed the pagoda. Slifer, being close to the center, felt the weight of the pressure paralyze him, his body feeling heavier with each passing second.

From his vantage point in the sky, Grand Elder Wyatt released a resigned sigh. His spiritual sense was unable to penetrate the solid domain that now enveloped the pagoda. *Without breaking through to the Ascendant Realm, I'm as blind as an Ozarion Beast here.* All he could do was hope that Darius didn't make a fool of himself.

Meanwhile, the man in question let out a triumphant laugh as he taunted Slifer. "If you don't reveal your domain, you might as well be dead," Darius jeered, watching as Slifer's form began to crystallize. "Do you even possess a domain?"

Slifer remained silent, focusing inwardly. His body was slowly turning to stone under the effect of the domain, but he knew he had only one shot at turning the tables. *Come on . . . just a little longer*, he urged himself, waiting for the right moment.

Misinterpreting Slifer's silence as an admission of defeat, Darius sneered. "So, you're just a fraud after all."

He raised his hand, and a hundred rock spikes began to rise, their sharp points gleamed menacingly as they made eye contact with Slifer. With a flick of his wrist, Darius sent them hurtling towards Slifer, intending to end the charade once and for all.

The rock spikes cut through the air as Slifer braced for impact, his mind racing. *This has to work . . . it's now or never. Activate Reflection Card.*

Ding!
Reflection Card Activated

The rock spikes, which were mere inches from impaling him, halted abruptly in their tracks before reversing direction, now hurtling towards Grand Elder Darius.

As Slifer's body reverted from its stony state, Darius gazed in horror at his own foot, which was rapidly turning to stone. Panicked, he channeled his qi throughout his body, struggling against the petrification. His attention, however, was violently drawn upwards as he saw the hundred rock spikes he had summoned now barreling towards him.

"H-how . . . ?" he gasped, moments before the spikes impaled him. Blood splattered as he fell to his knees, the spikes protruding grotesquely from his body. His domain dissipated, retracting back into him as he coughed up blood.

From everyone's perspective, it only took a few moments for Slifer to force an Ascendant cultivator to his knees.

Wyatt had anticipated an evenly matched duel, not this one-sided display of dominance. *The supreme elder must be on the cusp of the Immortal Realm . . . if not already within it*, he thought, recalibrating his understanding of Slifer's true power.

Amelia's taunting laughter rang out, her voice filled with smug satisfaction. "You should have listened to me, old man," she called out gleefully.

The crowd of disciples and onlookers began murmuring among themselves, their voices a mix of awe and speculation about the supreme elder's strength.

"How is he that powerful?"

"What was that technique?"

"Supreme elder . . . could probably beat the sect master . . ."

Slifer, meanwhile, ignored the comments as he approached the figure kneeling before him, only pausing when a System notification appeared before him.

Ding!

Kill for 1000 Karmic Credits or Spare for 2000 Karmic Credits

---

Slifer weighed out the options and despite being attacked out of the blue, he was not inclined to kill the man. Who knew what life-saving treasures the grand elder possessed, Slifer only had a single Critical Block Card left in his arsenal, the risk was not worth it.

It's probably Amelia's fault anyways . . . or something to do with the original Slifer, he reasoned.

Choosing to spare Darius, he thought, *Maybe one day, I'll turn him into a righteous cultivator. It might seem far-fetched, but I just can't write him off.* From the corner of his eye, he noticed a weak purple hue emanating from Darius's hand. *Wait, what is that?*

His thoughts were interrupted by a searing pain that tore through his head; his vision blurred as he clutched his temple in agony.

I . . . can't . . . think . . .

CHAPTER FORTY-EIGHT

Sleep . . .

Slifer's vision darkened as a voice, soft and gentle like a whisper, echoed seductively in his mind. *You've endured so much these past weeks, my love. It's . . . it's okay to close your eyes . . . just for a little while.*

I can't . . . not now, Slifer resisted, his thoughts cloudy. *I'm . . . trapped . . . insi— No . . . I'm in . . . battle . . .*

But aren't you tired? the voice cooed. *Just a moment of peace, my dear. Let go of your burdens, even heroes need to rest.*

Just a brief rest, then . . . Slifer finally gave in. His eyelids grew heavy, and the world around him seemed to fade into the background, the voice becoming his entire focus.

Yesss . . . sleeeep . . .

Zack didn't know what was going on, his mind was a mess.

One moment, he was vaguely aware of standing within a pagoda, doing something important, what it was, he had no clue, but what he did know, was that his life depended on it.

But now, he found himself back on his couch, a half-eaten pie in his hands, preparing for the upcoming pie-eating competition.

What is going on? he wondered, trying to make sense of the strange sensation of being somewhere else. After a few moments of confusion, he shrugged it off as just another one of his vivid daydreams, he was certain if his life depended on something then he would definitely remember. *And when did I even last go outside?* He laughed at the absurdity of it, after all, it wasn't easy for a man of his . . . large stature to strut around just for the fun of it.

His focus shifted back to the present, to the more pressing matter at hand—the pie-eating competition.

The competition was no small feat, even for someone like him who had a natural affinity for pies. Last year's top five competitors had all managed around thirty pies in ten minutes, with the champion devouring an astounding thirty-nine. Who knew that there were others who not only shared the same hobby as him, but excelled in it!

Only in America, Zack thought with a bitter smile.

He glanced down at the pie in his hand. *This is number twenty-nine, not bad, but not enough.* If he was going to win and prove to his parents that he wasn't the failure that everyone accused him of being, he needed at least forty.

The competition was only a week away, he didn't have time to waste and sit around like this. With narrowed eyes, Zack raised the half-eaten pie and shoved it into his mouth, chewing furiously. *I'll show them all. I'll win, even if it kills me . . . well, maybe not literally. I do want to enjoy that fifty thousand dollars of prize money.*

Caught up in his daydream of showing his parents that they were all wrong about him,

Zack carelessly swallowed a chunk of pie that definitely required more chewing. His face turned a frightening shade of red as his eyes bulged, he desperately clawed at his throat, struggling for air. His vision blurred as oxygen deprivation took its toll.

In a frantic attempt to get help, he tried to stand, aiming for the door, but his pudgy feet betrayed him, and he slipped backwards, his flabby back hitting the wall with a thud.

Ptui—

A loud spit echoed in the room as the offending piece of pie flew out of his mouth. The color of his face slowly returned to normal, and he exhaled a heavy sigh of relief.

Who knew pie could kill a man!

> *Ding!*
> Mental Attack Detected
> Attack at the Immortal Level
> Passive Skill Void Being Aura Activated
> Attack Potency Decreased By 33%

Slifer's mind snapped back to reality, his vision sharpening as he found himself a few feet away from Grand Elder Darius. It didn't take him a second to realize what had transpired.

This guy just tried to fuck with my mind! Slifer's face darkened with anger. He had been willing to spare Darius before, but a mind attack was a different story. He was lucky that his willpower stat was sufficient to defend against the remainder of the attack, otherwise, he would have ended up as a puppet, or whatever it was the amulet was aiming to do. *Unforgivable.*

Darius's face contorted in shock seeing Slifer effortlessly shrug off the mental attack. *The amulet should have worked! How could he . . . ?* His thought was cut short as Slifer opened his mouth, forming a ball of fire.

Firebreath! Even if it is only at the Nascent Soul stage, this will end him, Slifer thought, eyeing the severely wounded grand elder. The body of an Ascendant Realm expert was just like any other below the Immortal Realm, only at the peak of the Body Tempering stage.

"No, don—" Darius began, but his plea was drowned out by the growing intensity of the fire in Slifer's mouth. Desperation painted Darius's face. Unlike his disciples who could rely on him to give them life-saving treasures, he didn't have anyone; all he had was his halberd, a weapon as much a part of him as his own soul. "Come forth, Ignispike!" Darius bellowed with great difficulty.

The halberd, which he had won in his youth in a trial left behind by an immortal senior, materialized beside him. It was a majestic weapon, its shaft decorated with intricate patterns and its blade shimmering with a deadly gleam.

Like those sword cultivators he so detested, Darius had bonded with his weapon. The path of the halberd was less glorified, but no less powerful, and he would kill anyone who dared say otherwise.

Darius would never admit it but every encounter with a sword cultivator left him feeling inadequate, there was something about them, the air they carried around them, as though they were superior due to their use of the sword. The sword strike from Slifer a few weeks ago had only reignited those insecurities.

I will never lose to a sword cultivator! Darius channeled the last remnants of his qi into the halberd, causing fire to dance along its edge.

A last stand, huh? Slifer's expression remained cold and unmoved. *Well, it won't change your fate.*

Tightening his grip on the halberd, Darius swung his right arm. It wasn't his strongest blow—far from it, given his current state, impaled by spikes. *This is all I can manage,* he thought grimly. As the halberd moved, his arm tore painfully at the wounds caused by the spikes, sending jolts of agony through his body.

The fiery halberd clashed against Slifer, who didn't seem the least concerned, his focus fully on the fireball in his mouth which only continued to grow larger.

Darius let out a slight smirk when he felt the strike land, however, the smirk turned into a grimace when he noticed that annoying barrier technique spring to life.

Damn it! Darius hadn't expected Slifer to be capable of simultaneously using that blasted formation technique along with the fireball.

"Aaah." The force of the impact, coupled with Darius's weakened state, was too much for him to handle. His grip faltered, and the halberd slipped from his hands, clattering to the ground.

In that same moment, Slifer spat out the fireball, engulfing the grand elder in flames.

A fleeting look of regret crossed Darius's face as he burned. *I didn't plan to kill him . . . just to humble him.* If Slifer had died in the process, well, then Darius couldn't be blamed. *It is not my fault if he is too weak . . .* But now, it was clear he had miscalculated. Or perhaps, been manipulated.

"Wyatt!" he screamed, realizing too late the true orchestrator of his death.

In a final, desperate act, he shattered his Ascendant Crystal. The crystal, the very core of his cultivation, cracked with a resounding echo. The impending explosion was a last-ditch effort, a vengeful attempt to drag the others down with him.

Seeing the suicidal attack by the madman in front of him, a single thought raced through Slifer's mind: *Shit.*

He didn't have any Critical Block Cards left, a situation like this was the very reason he had initially planned to spare the grand elder, but then the fool had to try and fuck with his mind.

The explosion erupted with a deafening roar, an immense force that tore through the pagoda, reducing it to rubble. The ground shook violently, and a wave of heat and light engulfed everything in its vicinity.

Up above, Grand Elder Wyatt, seeing the explosion heading towards him, swiftly activated a formation.

A shimmering barrier sprang up around him and the disciples, protecting them from the remnants of the explosion. The shield glowed with a faint blue hue, vibrating as the shockwaves battered against it, however, each shockwave made the barrier falter. It seemed it would give out any second.

"*Hold on!*" Wyatt yelled, his voice barely audible over the din.

The disciples below, wide-eyed and terrified, huddled together, feeling the heat and shockwaves around them.

"Thank heavens for the barrier . . ." one of them muttered, awestruck at the devastation before them. Even the remnants of the explosion were sufficient to snuff out their fragile lives.

When the shockwaves stopped, they let out a collective sigh of relief.

"W-what happened to the supreme elder?"

CHAPTER FORTY-NINE

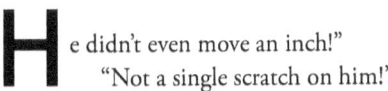e didn't even move an inch!"

"Not a single scratch on him!"

Ding!
Your Disciple Amelia's Loyalty Has Increased By 5%
Your Disciple Young Fenlock's Loyalty Has Increased By 10%
Your Disciple Hughie's Loyalty Has Increased By 15%

Their loyalties better go up, if there was no change in loyalty after that, I might as well give up now, Slifer thought. He then exhaled a deep breath of relief, thankful that his quick thinking to use the Phase ability had paid off without any System hiccups.

Reminds me of that Obito and Konan scene . . .

Ding!
You Have Killed an Ascendant Realm Cultivator
You Have Gained 1000 Karmic Credits

Glancing at the spot where Grand Elder Darius once stood, he noticed that only an amulet remained.

Hmm, let's see how this little thing could mess with my head like that. Insight!

Treasure: Siren's Call
Grade: Immortal Realm
Type: Amulet
Condition: Perfect
Description: Contains the whisper of a siren, can put the target in a passive state.

Sirens, huh? They sound like nothing but trouble. Slifer made a beckon motion with his hand, the amulet flew towards him and disappeared into his storage ring. He did not want to touch anything that could get into his head, at least, not yet. *I need to find ways to increase my mental defense.*

Meanwhile, Grand Elder Wyatt watched with a barely concealed frown as Slifer pocketed the amulet. *That fool Darius,* he thought. *Not only did he fail, but he also lost my amulet.*

As the grand elders, Tenzin and Lydia, descended next to Slifer, Wyatt hastily followed, ready to do some damage control. However, when he opened his mouth, he was immediately cut off by a silver-haired girl.

"Wow, and I thought you were getting soft," she commented, standing uncomfortably close to Slifer.

She'd probably be the perfect candidate for the Siren's Call. Her natural inclination towards soul techniques . . . Slifer shook his head subtly, dismissing the thought almost as quickly as it came. *No, giving Amelia such a treasure would only spell more trouble for me in the long run.*

"Hmm, and that's why you dared to go against my words," Slifer replied to Amelia, his voice hardening.

"But . . . but the old man started it." Amelia shrank back. "He was bullying us!"

Slifer shook his head, knowing that the girl could come up with a thousand excuses, but then Fenlock spoke up.

"Master, she's telling the truth. It seemed the grand . . . the former grand elder had a problem with you . . ."

Unlike his junior sister, Fenlock had a softer character, and Slifer felt that he was a trustworthy guy. Not to mention, Slifer had already narrowed it down to two options: Amelia or the original.

It was only those two who could aggravate an Ascendant Realm cultivator . . . maybe Val too, Slifer added as an afterthought.

"Hmm, you're lucky your senior brother vouched for you," Slifer said, turning his gaze back to the mischievous girl, who immediately began to mutter, "He's not my seni—" but cut herself off when Slifer's eyes narrowed.

Teenagers, Slifer thought with a mental sigh.

"Master left no body for Val," Val pouted as she fluttered around Slifer's head.

I was nearly the one without a body. Slifer shivered as he recalled the explosive ordeal. "When we go on our little trip, you can have as many bodies as you want," he said, trying to appease her.

"Master promise?" Val's big eyes gazed up at him earnestly.

"Yes . . ." Slifer replied, though a nagging feeling told him he might regret this promise. The glint in the baby dragon's eyes seemed to suggest her appetite was far from modest.

Slifer's attention then shifted to Grand Elder Tenzin, who was beaming at him. Slifer nodded in appreciation. "Thank you for keeping my disciples safe."

"Of course, Supreme Elder, it was the least I could do," Tenzin replied, whilst he mentally gave himself a pat on the back. *Aligning with the supreme elder was the right move.*

Even Grand Elder Lydia, who was usually so stoic and maybe even had a slight dislike for the original, gave Slifer a slight bow of her head. Killing an Ascendant cultivator unscathed was no small feat, after all.

"Supreme Elder, I am glad you're okay," Grand Elder Wyatt's voice cut through the air.

Slifer's eyes narrowed as he assessed the suspicious-looking elder in front of him.

Weasel, he thought instantly, reminded of untrustworthy mechanics who'd fix one problem and create ten more. *Definitely wouldn't trust him with my car, let alone the sect.*

"Grand Elder Wyatt," Slifer greeted, his voice carried a frosty edge but internally he was on edge, remembering how the madman had screamed Wyatt's name as he self-destructed. *Is this one going to attack me too?* he wondered apprehensively.

That fool Darius had to drag me into his mess. Grand Elder Wyatt was seething but he maintained his polite demeanor. "Since you are here, Supreme Elder, it would be most fitting for you to lead the Selection Ceremony."

Then through his spiritual sense, Wyatt sent a quick summary of the trials and their notable participants to Slifer. It took Slifer a moment to process the influx of information.

I need to upgrade Insight, Slifer realized, looking up the System status.

Upgrade Insight to Intermediate Skill for 1000 Karmic Credits

With a resigned sigh, he confirmed the purchase.

Skill: Insight
Basic Description: Grants information about an object or person upon focus.
Intermediate Description: Grants the ability to view the stats of the target.

Useful, yet the System's timing is suspiciously perfect, he thought with a tinge of bitterness. He wondered if he upgraded the skill earlier, would it have given the same result or would it have given him something useless.

The surrounding grand elders and disciples exchanged puzzled looks as Slifer stood motionless, seemingly lost in thought.

Amelia's cough broke the silence. "Master, you're spacing out . . . again," she remarked.

Slifer scowled, slightly embarrassed. "Rude girl," he muttered under his breath. Then, turning to face the crowd of disciples, he declared, "I will now choose a disciple."

The disciples straightened up, their eyes filled with anticipation and nervous excitement. The prospect of being selected by the supreme elder, who had just demonstrated his overwhelming power, was both a daunting and thrilling possibility.

As Slifer walked up to each disciple, he activated the upgraded Insight skill, scrutinizing them closely. One after another, he examined dozens of disciples, each time shaking his head due to their stats being insufficient to gain the System's attention.

The disciples felt increasingly uneasy under his intense gaze, especially when he walked away muttering to himself.

Finally, Slifer stood before a white-robed youth, Kalin. *This one's different*, Slifer noted, recalling the information provided by Grand Elder Wyatt. *Mysterious background, possibly from the Immortal Realm, and here for training . . . he seems more like a villain destined for humiliation by the protagonist. Insight!*

Name: Kalin
Realm: 9th Stage Qi Refining
Known Techniques: N/A
Known Affiliations: Black Rose Sect
Disposition: N/A
Comprehension: 9
Luck: 6
Talent: 9
Will: 6

Two stats at nine? This isn't just any character; he's likely a protagonist from his own story in the Immortal Realm.

Clearing his throat and adopting an air of authority, Slifer addressed the youth, "Boy, would you like to be my disciple?"

"Yes . . . Master," Kalin replied with a hint of condescension, it seemed almost as if he was doing Slifer a favor.

From the sidelines, Grand Elder Wyatt suppressed a sigh. *He was supposed to be cautious with this one.*

> *Ding!*
> Disciple slot only available for the target of the mission.
> Taking another disciple without a slot will lead to consequences.

Damn, I forgot about Leah, Slifer realized, mentally kicking himself. *I need to convert her fast to free up a slot.*

Noticing the pause, Kalin raised an eyebrow questioningly.

Slifer didn't want to let go of a disciple with such high stats even if he was on the arrogant side, however, not willing to deal with the consequences that the System could come up with, he coughed awkwardly, scrambling for a plausible excuse to retract his offer.

"Due to your . . . background, I cannot take you as a disciple, but I can offer you . . . some pointers."

The sudden retraction felt like a slap to Kalin's dignity, he felt his ears begin to burn. *If father were he— No!* Kalin forcibly calmed himself, looking down at his sword. *Serenity is key,* he reminded himself, suppressing his pride. Bending slightly, he respectfully said, "I would be . . . honored to receive your guidance."

> Name: Kalin
> Realm: 9th Stage Qi Refining
> Known Techniques: N/A
> Known Affiliations: Black Rose Sect
> Disposition: N/A
> Comprehension: 9
> Luck: 6
> Talent: 9
> Will: 6 -> 7

I was right, the will stat can be changed. Slifer nodded to himself as he watched Kalin, who was on the brink of becoming an arrogant young master, use the path of the sword to reshape himself. *A protagonist, but not my protagonist.* He sighed internally as he turned away.

Nearby, William Wick straightened his posture, sensing Slifer's gaze shifting towards him. His heart pounded with anticipation and anxiety. *This is my moment. I need to impress the supreme elder, not just for me, but for my clan's future,* he thought, bracing himself.

Grand Elder Tenzin, noticing the supreme elder's gaze on the heir of the Wick Clan, piped up, "At just fifteen years of age, young William has already reached the Seventh Stage of the Qi Refining Realm. A rare genius, indeed."

Pride swelled in William's chest as he heard this praise. He couldn't help but smile, believing he had caught the supreme elder's attention, but soon his smile faltered when he heard the silver-haired girl mumble.

"You call this a rare genius? When I was twelve years old, I broke into the Qi Refining

Realm, then at fourteen, I broke into the Foundation Establishment Realm, and I'm eighteen this year, but I have already stepped into the Mid-Core Formation Realm . . ."

Grand Elder Tenzin stood in silence.

Is she trying to belittle me? William thought, his heart pounding with a mix of anger and embarrassment. He felt a hot surge of blood rise to his throat, almost coughing it out, but he held it in, forcing a fake smile, he knew he couldn't offend a disciple of the supreme elder. *But I can't afford to lose face here.*

"Every cultivator's path is unique," William managed to cough out, his voice strained. "I am still learning and growing."

"Yeah, but you should grow faster," Amelia responded as she looked down at her sharp nails, already losing interest in the young master.

How can she be so dismissive? William clenched his fists, trying to control his boiling emotions. *I am the heir of the Wick Clan!*

Slifer spoke up, an air of wisdom surrounding him. "Cultivation is not a race but a journey, some will begin with a gentle pace, steadily ascending to impressive heights, while others resemble shooting stars, blazing brilliantly but fading away in an instant."

Amelia rolled her eyes but stayed silent, knowing better than to argue with her master.

William's heart calmed a bit, grateful for the supreme elder's words. He bowed slightly. "Thank you for your wisdom, Supreme Elder."

It's good to inspire confidence in the younger generation. Slifer nodded to himself as he activated Insight.

Name: William Wick
Realm: 7th Stage Qi Refining
Known Techniques: N/A
Known Affiliations: Black Rose Sect
Disposition: N/A
Comprehension: 4
Luck: 4
Talent: 4
Will: 3

Not even a single five? Slifer shook his head in disappointment, he couldn't believe the kid was able to light up three pillars. His talent clearly wasn't high enough, he could get away with using his clan's resources to breakthrough the stages of the Qi Refining Realm but to trick the Luminaresce Quartz? That was no small feat, it would likely take an Immortal Rank treasure to accomplish.

This one probably has a few secrets, Slifer mused. Since the System didn't require him to take the youngster as a disciple then Slifer would rather pass on him. Secrets in the xianxia world could mean opportunity but they for sure entailed death, and usually a lot of it.

"Nothing special," Slifer muttered to himself as he moved on.

The words stung, crushing the fragile pride that William had managed to rebuild.

Am I really just ordinary? The thought was like a cold blade slicing through his heart. He had worked so hard, pushed his clan's resources to the limits, and yet, in the eyes of someone truly powerful, he was just . . . average.

Unaware of the effect his offhand remark had caused, Slifer's focus shifted to two young village boys, who, when standing side by side, reminded him of the number ten.

Ding!
Target Located
Take the Youth As a Disciple

CHAPTER FIFTY

Seeing the supreme elder's gaze turn their way, Dusty puffed out his chest, his eyes sparkling with anticipation. He nudged Nomed, his voice barely a whisper. "The grand elders thought I had no talent, but it was them who had no eyes," he bragged. Dusty was sure that word had gone around concerning his rapid comprehension of the Gluttonous Titan technique, and now the supreme elder himself was impressed.

Shaking his head at his friend's antics, Nomed remained silent, he felt a strange feeling in his belly as though something bad was about to occur.

As the supreme elder approached, Dusty's grin stretched wider. Looking down at his round belly, he murmured to it, "Stay patient, my friend. Being the disciple of the supreme elder means you can feast to your heart's content." His mind wandered to memories of Grandma Sully catching him stealing chickens from the hen house.

"Dusty, you gluttonous child, those chickens aren't for you to gobble up whenever you please!"

Shaking his head to dispel the memory, Dusty rubbed his healthy-sized belly and whispered, "No cock will be safe after today."

Dusty didn't know what it was, but ever since he could remember, he always had a fascination with cocks—nothing felt better than when he had a cock inside him. And now that he would soon become the supreme elder's disciple, no one would dare stop him. After all, who could complain if the disciple of the supreme elder wanted a cock or two?

But as Slifer walked past him, Dusty's smile faltered, and he watched baffled as the supreme elder stopped in front of his best friend.

A smile appeared on Slifer's face as he looked at the status window.

Name: Nomed
Realm: 1st Stage Qi Refining
Known Techniques: N/A
Known Affiliations: Black Rose Sect
Disposition: N/A
Comprehension: 6
Luck: 7
Talent: 8
Will: 8

These stats . . . the boy's average performance doesn't match his stats at all. A hidden gem . . . or is this perhaps the storyline where the protagonist hides his true talent to infiltrate a sect for some secret mission, he mused silently, a knowing glint in his eyes.

If stats were all it took to gain the System's interest, then the System would have identified Kalin as a potential disciple. Slifer suspected that there were more requirements, he just couldn't figure out what they were, and the System was more than happy to *not* help him.

Nomed, feeling the supreme elder's unsettling smile linger on him, tried not to fidget. *I did everything I could to remain unnoticeable, but this old man still noticed me!*

Looking at the young man's innocent, simple face, Slifer couldn't help but assume, *This kid probably entered the demonic sect hoping to turn it into a righteous one from the inside, much like how some girls think they can transform their leather-jacket-wearing, motorcycle-riding boyfriends into card-carrying members of the "Pajama Party Posse."*

Eh, it doesn't matter if he hid his talent intentionally or there were some other reasons why he performed terribly, what I need to do now is make a good first impression and complete this mission.

Standing tall with his hands clasped behind his back, Slifer raised his chin slightly. With his eyes half-closed as if peering into the depths of the universe, he subtly activated the Whimsical Wind Card, a card he had previously thought was useless.

A gentle breeze began to swirl around him, causing his robes to flutter dramatically. For teens who had almost no experience with cultivation, the effect was striking. The naïve disciples began to gasp in awe.

"Look at the supreme elder's aura."

"He . . . he looks like an immortal!"

"I . . . I want him!"

Pretending as though he didn't hear the last comment, Slifer coughed as he focused his attention back on the protagonist before him. "Young man, would you . . . would you like to be this old man's disciple?" he asked.

The surrounding disciples' awe turned into shock.

"This nobody has caught the supreme elder's eye?"

"How lucky!"

"This . . . I refuse to believe this!" One of the city boys even began to repeatedly rub his eyes in disbelief.

As for the grand elders, they exchanged confused glances. They couldn't fathom the thoughts of the supreme elder; Nomed was so . . . average. However, recalling how Slifer had effortlessly killed Grand Elder Darius, they wondered if there was something in the boy that they couldn't see.

Nomed, feeling slightly overwhelmed by the sudden attention, was frantically trying to think of a way to reject the supreme elder's offer. He realized, with a sinking heart, that there was no logical reason he could give that would be accepted without drawing more attention to himself.

Why is it so hard to stay low-key? he lamented inwardly.

Forcing a smile, he tried his best to appear excited and bowed repeatedly. "Thank you, Master."

Slifer, observing his new disciple's enthusiasm, stroked his beard in satisfaction. *It's always good to have loyal disciples*, he thought. From the simple look of the kid, Slifer could tell he would be a loyal one.

Ding!
New Task
Complete Master-Disciple Ceremony

Success!

All Slifer had to do was complete this annoying ceremony and then he would gain the mystery reward for completing the mission. The task had been far easier than Slifer expected. He had initially worried the System would pick someone with typical xianxia protagonist problems: tragic pasts, vengeful enemies, or cursed bloodlines that attracted calamity. Thankfully, so far Nomed seemed refreshingly normal, just a village boy whose family had yet to be wiped out.

"Grandma Sully was right, I don't deserve any cock."

The whisper from the fatty beside his new disciple brought Slifer out of his thoughts. *W-why are the words "grandma" and "cock" being used in the same sentence . . . ?*

"Master, would it be possible for you to also take Dusty as your disciple?" Nomed asked, not able to bear the look on his friend's face.

Slifer frowned slightly. He knew that the System wouldn't allow him to take in more disciples; if it did, he would have chosen Kalin. But he didn't want to upset his new disciple so soon. That would happen later when Nomed realized he was being worked like the sla— disciple that he was.

Turning to look at Dusty, Slifer activated Insight.

Name: Dusty
Realm: 1st Stage Qi Refining
Known Techniques: N/A
Known Affiliations: Black Rose Sect
Disposition: N/A
Comprehension: 3 (8)
Luck: 8
Talent: 2
Will: 2

Eight in parentheses? Hmm, his normal comprehension must be pretty low, but if he has affinity with the technique then his comprehension shoots up to eight? Sounds about right. Slifer stroked his beard as he looked at the meatball-shaped human pouting at him. *But he is a lucky one, it couldn't hurt to have him on my side . . .* "I have someone else in mind for him," Slifer mumbled as he sent out a spiritual transmission.

As if on cue, the disciples heard a grunt from above, they looked up to see a fat, bald man jumping down from a sword. Landing with a heavy thud next to the supreme elder, the man bowed deeply and said, "Master."

"Morvran," Slifer acknowledged with a nod. He then pointed to Dusty and instructed, "I want you to take this one as your disciple."

Morvran's eyes narrowed as he surveyed Dusty. "This one looks like he needs a lot of work, Master, but I will try my best."

Dusty, feeling slighted, shook his chubby hand at Morvran. "Don't imply I'm fat, I'm only big-boned," he protested.

Morvran shook his head, his expression serious as ever. "You're not worthy of being called fat, boy," he replied as he puffed out his belly to demonstrate his own impressive girth. "You have much more growing to do."

Dusty's eyes widened in awe. "Wow, you must have had a lot of big cocks," he exclaimed.

A rare sense of pride appeared on Morvran's face. "No one in the Mortal Realm has had more cocks than me," he boasted.

Morvran's statement seemed to ignite a new fire in Dusty. He looked at Nomed, his eyes once again shining. "Nomed, I'm gonna be just like this fat guy!"

I never thought I'd witness a competition of . . . cock consumption, Slifer thought, a smirk threatening to break his "wise master" façade. However, he knew that the two were deadly serious.

Cocks, in the cultivation world, were reputed to be greatly beneficial, especially for those who cultivated their bodies. He recalled a tale from the Immortal Realm about a colossal cock, a creature so formidable that even immortals would flee at its sight. Legend had it that this immense cock had sired numerous offspring, and consuming the meat of these various descendants could potentially unlock the rare bloodline of the Great Cock.

From the vague memories he inherited, Slifer remembered that the original had given Morvran a cock-related cultivation method. *The old man must have wanted Morvran to unlock the Great Cock bloodline*, Slifer deduced. Why that was, Slifer didn't know, but knowing his predecessor, it wouldn't have been out of goodwill.

Shaking his head, Slifer decided not to question Morvran's teaching methods. *If Morvran wants to teach his disciple the Way of the Cock, who am I to disapprove?*

The Disciple Selection Ceremony continued, with the other grand elders making their selections. Grand Elder Lydia found two suitable disciples for the Medicine Hall. Although they lacked the innate talent of the Wizeron Clan's usual recruits, they held enough potential for her to invest her time in.

Grand Elder Wyatt chose William as his disciple. Slifer, only half-paying attention, noted that Grand Elder Tenzin selected a boy from the Jexlarin Clan, but he couldn't recall the boy's name. *They all look the same*, Slifer thought, grateful for the Insight skill. *Without it, I might have walked away with some random kid thinking it was Nomed.*

William clenched his fists as he watched the supreme elder depart with his new disciples. *How could he overlook me for a mere village boy? A boy who is only fit to be my servant!* Despite his rage, William forced himself to focus on the bigger picture. He had successfully entered the sect, fulfilling the "man's" orders. *As long as I follow his instructions, my clan will remain safe.*

"I hope you don't regret your choice, Supreme Elder."

In a dark cave, void of any natural light, five spiritual figures stood in a circle. Each figure was cloaked in a hooded robe, their identities obscured by the shadows that clung to them like a second skin.

"The plan was successful," one member announced, their voice echoing off the walls, "the agent has entered the Black Rose Sect."

Another member, their voice tinged with a hint of arrogance, retorted, "Like I said before, the Luminaresce Quartz is not difficult to trick. If those old fools in the sect had listened to me, there wouldn't be such glaring holes in their defense."

The first figure hesitated before speaking again. "Even though the Luminaresce Quartz was tricked, the outcome was not what we were hoping for."

A third figure shook its head. "No matter, as long as the disciple entered the sect, that is what's important."

The fourth one, agreeing with a nod, added, "You need to make sure they secure one of the spots for the Sealed Realm."

Then, the fifth figure, who had been sitting quietly, stood up. "Once the Awakening is successful, war will follow." The figure's voice caused the spiritual forms of the others to tremble instinctively as though they were in the presence of a higher being.

The figure paused and took its time to look at each of the other figures, its gaze piercing through their blurred forms. "Prepare for war," it commanded.

One by one, the spiritual figures nodded. Then, as if they were mere mirages, their figures slowly dissipated into the air.

As the last of the figures vanished, a strange mark appeared on the cave floor. It was a tree, its branches twisted and gnarled. In the center of the trunk was an eye, unblinking and unsettling, as if it were watching everything.

The eye bled a crimson tear before it too disappeared.

CHAPTER FIFTY-ONE

One day later.

"Remember, Caelum, the path of righteousness is not just a choice, but a commitment to uphold justice and virtue in all your actions."

Caelum listened intently, his eyes fixed on Slifer, absorbing every word like a sponge. He had never expected to hear those words from his master. Recently, his master's actions didn't make sense, the change in character, the Ascendant level cultivation, just who was the real Slifer?

"The righteous path values harmony and order. It's about making sacrifices for the greater good, even when it's hard."

At this rate, I'll have my own church in a few years, Slifer thought, barely holding back a sigh. The idea of guiding more followers along a path he didn't believe sounded exhausting, but what was a poor man supposed to do? He needed the credits.

"But, Master," Caelum interjected, "what truly separates the righteous from the demonic?"

This time Slifer was unable to hold back the sigh. *How do I explain that the lines are not always so clear? Everyone has a different idea of what differentiates a righteous cultivator from a demonic cultivator.*

"In truth, Caelum, the cultivation world is complex. There are demonic cultivators who act more righteously than those so-called righteous cultivators. Many of them will do anything in their quest for immortality, whilst other demonic cultivators have limits that they will not cross. The same applies to righteous cultivators, but they like to justify their actions with their self-righteousness."

The System's view is too simplistic, Slifer thought. *It sees the world in black and white, but reality is a spectrum of grays. Even Caelum and Fenlock, labeled as demonic, have shown more righteousness than many of those hypocrites. This System needs an update.*

"The world isn't just black and white," Slifer continued. "Remember, righteous cultivators aren't always righteous, and demonic cultivators aren't always demonic."

"So, how do I know who to trust?" Caelum's eyebrows scrunched up, his master's sermon continued to get more complicated the longer it went on; he felt like they were going in circles.

Slifer shook his head. "Don't worry too much about the labels. Use your own judgment and don't trust anyone blindly." He paused, then added with a slight smirk, "Except for me, of course. So . . . are you ready to embrace the righteous path?"

The decision wasn't too difficult for Caelum. His master had changed his life but more importantly, saved his mother's life. As long as his master didn't instruct him to do something that would violate his Sword Heart then he would follow him, even if it led to his death.

Caelum glanced down at Bloodthorn, they were partners, he couldn't make the decision for the both of them.

Grrrrr, Bloodthorn surprisingly agreed.

Looking back up at Slifer, Caelum nodded firmly. "Yes, Master. I will follow the righteous path."

Name: Caelum Card
Description: Once a day, you can activate any of your loyal disciple's techniques.
Warning: If your disciple's loyalty goes below 100%, you will lose access to this card.

Sweet, it's a better version of the ability from the Soul Bond.

Ding!
Would you like to promote Caelum to Core Disciple?

Erm . . . sure.

Ding!
Your disciple Caelum is now a Core Disciple!
Core Disciples can allocate tasks to inner and outer disciples.

Is the System glitching? Why is it being so nice of all a sudden?

He didn't expect the change in a disciple's status to have much of an effect, the System was making it too easy for him recently to accumulate credits.

"It's been a long time since I have promoted any of my disciples, but I believe you are ready to be promoted to Core Disciple."

"T-thank you, Master." Caelum didn't expect this from his master. *Ever since issues began between Master and Senior Brother, Master stopped promoting us. We didn't think he would anymore, especially so soon . . .*

Seeing the look Caelum was giving him, Slifer assumed the boy was expecting something. *Oh, right. Core Disciples usually get a technique from their master.*

He coughed awkwardly, trying to buy time. "When you activate your Sword Domain, only then will I gift you a personal technique," Slifer stated, hoping to make it sound like that was his plan all along.

No big deal. I can just purchase a technique from the System for him later, Slifer thought. Once Caelum worked the other disciples, he would feel more comfortable spending some credits for a gift. *But not now. Caelum will value it more as a reward for a significant breakthrough.*

"I understand, Master. Comprehending the Sword Domain will be my priority."

"As a Core Disciple, you now have new responsibilities," Slifer continued, seizing the chance to recruit Caelum to his pyramid scheme. "You will assign tasks to your juniors, but remember," he paused for emphasis, "they must be righteous tasks. If you must trick them into righteousness, then do so."

Caelum's expression hardened slightly at the mention of his juniors. *Amelia, in particular, doesn't like taking orders, let alone righteous ones. But I will do what is necessary, I'll make Master proud.*

"I will keep that in mind, Master," Caelum responded dutifully. "Righteousness will guide my actions and decisions."

"Good, good." Slifer waved him away.

Caelum bowed deeply and then turned to leave. *A Sword Domain . . . a significant step indeed. But with Master's guidance, I will achieve it and earn my technique. A technique from an Ascendant Realm cultivator . . .*

As Caelum's figure disappeared, Slifer let out a breath he hadn't realized he'd been holding. *That went well enough.*

Slifer's thoughts turned to his new disciple. He had hoped to complete the Master-Disciple Ceremony quickly, but Nomed had ran off as soon as they left the valley. *He wants his grandmother's blessing first. A superstitious lot, these people.*

As for Kalin, the white-robed youth who lingered like a shadow, Slifer had managed to keep him at bay. "I will offer you some pointers," Slifer had told him, "but only after I've sorted out the sect's affairs."

Slifer didn't have any sword techniques that could impress the youth or even the credits to buy one, but luckily for him, the death of a grand elder left issues that would take a while to deal with.

Wyatt should be here any moment with the other grand elders.

When a disciple was called to the Disciplinary Hall, it was a foregone conclusion that they would spend a few sleepless nights within the sect's prison. If they were lucky, they would only have to undergo three rounds of torture before being let go, and that was only if someone remembered to release them.

The chamber itself was grand and imposing, at the far end stood a large throne. This was where Darius, the now deceased grand elder, used to laze around.

He really enjoyed feeling important, Slifer thought as he reluctantly took his place on the throne.

The leader of the Disciplinary Hall had to deal with those who broke the sect's rules, they were the judge, jury, and executioner; it was a lot of responsibility to place on one man's shoulders.

Now that responsibility had fallen to Slifer. He wasn't exactly thrilled about it.

This is just taking time away from cultivating and learning new techniques, he thought, a hint of annoyance in his mind.

The role of a supreme elder, which Slifer held, was typically that of the sect's protector, free from the day-to-day responsibilities of sect management. *I was hoping to avoid any real work, especially since there hasn't been a battle since the demon invasion centuries ago.*

Yet, here he was, forced into this position because of Wyatt's cunning suggestion in front of the other grand elders. *Sneaky weasel. I couldn't really say no in front of them all without raising suspicion. And I do feel a bit guilty . . . Darius had it coming, but still.* Shaking his head, Slifer focused on his plan. *I'll be the leader in name only. I'll let the old guy handle the actual work.*

The "old guy" was a Peak Nascent Soul elder named Fred, currently briefing Slifer, who was half-listening at best. *Fred, of all the powerful names . . . Fred. It's almost laughable. A man capable of leveling countries on Earth, and he's named Fred.*

"Due to the actions of the late grand elder, the disciples of the Disciplinary Hall have a reputation of bullying the weak, and if this were to continue, I am not sure if there will be any disciples left to discipline. I made numerous suggestions, but the grand elder refused to listen, I was wondering what you think of the following . . ." Fred continued listing off one recommendation after another, clearly he had been waiting a long time for such a moment.

Ding!

The sound of the System notification brought a smile to Slifer's face.

The old man's face darkened, mistaking Slifer's reaction as a dismissal of his recommendations. *It seems the Disciplinary Hall will remain unchanged, continuing to cause the very problem it was meant to solve*, he thought bitterly.

Meanwhile, Slifer, oblivious to the elder's thoughts, beamed even brighter.

Ding! Congratulations on becoming the leader of the Disciplinary Hall! Disciplinary Hall Panel Unlocked You Have Gained 250 Karmic Credits

A management feature for the Disciplinary Hall . . . interesting.

Disciplinary Hall Panel	
Number of Members	
Nascent Soul	3
Core Formation	11
Foundation Establishment	65
Qi Refining	55
Current Tasks	0
Credits Gained	0
Credits Lost	0

As Slifer read the System's message, the smile turned into full-blown laughter. The new feature allowed him to use disciples of the hall to farm Karmic Credits on a larger scale. Each task they completed earned him between 3 and 9 Karmic Credits, but with over a hundred disciples in the hall, credits would quickly accumulate.

If I become the sect master, will I be able to farm the entirety of the Black Rose Sect?

Noticing that the panel recorded the credits lost, Slifer frowned. *Credits are lost when members abuse their authority?* Slifer shook his head. *Demonic disciples are all bullies, preying on the weak is how these sects are run.* Trying to stop his own disciples from bullying others was difficult enough, just how hard would it be to enforce that on such a large scale? *Guess I'll have to take a more direct role after all.*

"Fred, from this day forth, if any member of the Disciplinary Hall abuses their power, they will be punished severely. Send them to the Shattered Chasm," Slifer declared firmly.

The Shattered Chasm was a notorious place within the sect, a deep, dark pit where those sent there were subjected to the constant pressure of spiritual energy, crushing their will and breaking their spirit. The deeper one went into the pit, the greater the pressure.

A few decades ago, a Nascent Soul elder was condemned to the depths of the Shattered

Chasm. When he emerged, his mind was no longer his own. It was said that the elder could often be seen wandering around the sect's grounds, talking to rocks and plants as if they were his old comrades. He would meticulously organize pebbles, believing he was rearranging the stars in the sky. On one occasion, he burst into fits of laughter after seeing his own shadow, the old man then challenged it a duel . . . only to end up losing.

"With these changes, there will be peace in the sect, and we will be able to use each other to grow stronger, not devour each other," Slifer continued.

Fred nearly choked, his heart clenching in frustration. *This is what I've been suggesting all along, and now he claims it as his own idea!* He sighed inwardly, realizing the higher one's cultivation, the more shameless one became.

Whilst Fred was stewing over the unfairness of the situation, Slifer was deep in thought, devising a new System to acquire as many credits as possible. *I'll create a System where they can complete righteous tasks. For each task, I'll set aside a third of the Karmic Credits I get. Hmm, I can call them points.*

Even though they would only earn a single credit or point from the tasks that gave Slifer 3 Karmic Credits, these tasks were quick and easy to complete so they would accumulate. Anything more than a third was too much for the stingy Slifer but if he didn't offer them anything then they wouldn't be motivated to complete the tasks.

Using the stick by itself is not sufficient, you must dangle that carrot.

Slifer decided to put up a list of treasures, techniques, and more from the System, he would claim it was from his own collection. The disciples could use their earned credits to purchase these items.

"Fred, I need you to create a leaderboard tablet," Slifer instructed, detailing his idea. "It will record the points each disciple has earned."

Fred nodded, understanding the strategy. "I'll have it set up, Supreme Elder. What shall we call this tablet?"

"The Karmic Ledger," Slifer replied immediately, he felt the name was appropriate. "I'll send over a list of items that can be bought with the points."

As Fred left to execute the orders, Slifer pondered over possible suspicions from the grand elders. *They won't question the number of items I have. It's normal for an Ascendant cultivator to possess riches equal to a mid-level sect. But the tasks . . . their righteous nature could raise eyebrows.*

After a moment, he came up with a solution. "The tasks are related to my new cultivation method."

That's close enough to the truth, it's not like they know what it takes to reach the Immortal Realm.

There was a lingering concern about the sect master, currently in closed-door cultivation. *Once he's out, he might get suspicious. But by then, I'll have enough credits to deal with that demon.* Slifer's thoughts briefly flashed back to the humiliation he suffered at the hands of the sect master. *I haven't forgotten that day. We will see who bows to whom the next time we meet.*

CHAPTER FIFTY-TWO

Sitting cross-legged in his courtyard next to a serene pond, Slifer was deep in thought, his brow furrowed in concentration. He had set the plans for the Disciplinary Hall into motion. As for the daily matters, they could be handled by Fred, Slifer had a more pressing concern on his mind.

Either the System can see the future, or it's great at manipulating events. More likely, it's both.

Ever since he entered this world, Slifer had felt like a puppet, its strings pulled by the System. He had learned a few techniques to decrease his reliance on the System and focused on increasing his cultivation, but he felt that wasn't enough. He felt confident facing a Foundation Establishment cultivator without any assistance from the System, but that confidence didn't extend to Core Formation cultivators.

"The Dimensional Slide technique is useful if I need to escape, but I can't rely on it too much," he muttered, his gaze drifting across the tranquil water of the pond.

Escaping could only be a last resort; such an action would break the supreme elder façade he had . . . accidentally created. More importantly, techniques that had a chance of failing couldn't be depended on, it honestly wouldn't have surprised him if they failed him when he most needed it.

Skills . . . techniques.

Slifer had long since noticed that the System categorized some abilities as skills and others as techniques. Initially, he didn't pay much attention to it but after some experimentation, he was able to figure out the difference between the two.

Skills, like cards, did not rely on Slifer at all, whether that be his qi capacity or comprehension of the skill, it had total reliance on the System. On the other hand, techniques relied wholly on Slifer; if his understanding or qi capacity were lacking, he would be unable to perform the technique.

Even if I use the System to level up a technique, I gain the knowledge to use it without its help.

Each time Slifer activated a skill, he felt his body following the will of the System allowing him to perform the skill. *I could use this experience as a guide to comprehend the skill until the System recognized it as a technique*, he thought. *It's like learning to ride a bike with training wheels and then without them. Let's see which skill to test this out on. Status!*

Name: Slifer
Race: Human
Alignment: Demonic
Cultivation: Late Foundation Establishment
Lifespan Remaining: 100 Years
Karmic Credits: 4300
Skills: Firebreath, Insight (Intermediate), Mirror Mastery (Level 2), Nascent Soul Armor

> (Level 1), Phase Ability (Level 1)
> Items: Reversal Cards, Peak Slifer Card, Peak Slifer Aura Card, Another Face Card, Avatar Card, Caelum Card
> Affinities: Light: 20% Fire: 5% Space: 5%
> Techniques: Sunrise Slash (Level 2), Stellar Nova Strike (Level 1), Dimensional Slide (Level 2)
> Weapon Mastery: Sword: 5%

The Phase ability was an extremely useful defensive skill that he would need to convert into a technique one day, however, with his current comprehension of space at only at five percent, that day was far away.

One skill stood out to him—the Nascent Soul Armor card. *Though it only lasts ten seconds, it would be enough to kill any Core Formation cultivator, maybe even an Early Nascent Soul cultivator if I caught them off guard.* For higher-level cultivators, he had to be more cautious. *For now, I'll rely on the System's cards and make . . . smarter choices to avoid trouble.* He shook his head, smiling ruefully. *It seems I'm often cleaning up after my disciples' messes or dealing with issues left by the original Slifer.*

Just as he was about to dismiss the blue box, he remembered the new card he had acquired, the Caelum Card.

Wait a minute, my "theory" should apply to cards too, especially one that imitates a Core Formation cultivator's technique.

Slifer decided to activate the Caelum Card. The ability to use any of his disciple's techniques intrigued him, and it could come in handy, especially when his disciples grew more powerful.

> Name: Caelum
> Realm: Late Core Formation
> Known Techniques: Serenity's Embrace, Nine Celestial Phantoms, Sunrise Slash, Thorned Lash, Valor's Crimson Surge
> Known Affiliations: Black Rose Sect
> Disposition: N/A
> Pick A Technique

Well, I'm glad the System automatically converted Caelum's demonic techniques into their righteous version. Slifer had been worried that using his disciple's techniques would result in the System penalizing him, in that case, he would only use it as a last resort and not for training.

But many of Caelum's techniques rely on his sword's abilities, would the technique work without a weapon? Even though he rarely needed a weapon, he did have one, the Skyfade Emerald Blade. However, since his blade was usually in his storage ring, activating the technique without it would reduce a step, and a single second could be the difference between life and death.

"Let's try a technique he received after breaking through to the Sword Soul Realm." He was hoping using such a technique would give him an insight into the sword realm three ranks higher than his own. Who knows, he might even experience a breakthrough.

"Valor's Crimson Surge."

He closed his eyes, feeling the card activate. Sword Qi coursed through his meridians, and with a slashing motion, a small stream of white qi burst forward. The qi grew rapidly as it traveled, swelling to the size of a house by the time it reached the training dummy. In an instant, the massive wave of qi obliterated the dummy.

Training dummies were enchanted with runes, depending on the option selected, they would simulate cultivators. Better yet, unlike cultivators, these dummies were able to regenerate. This particular dummy was set to the level of a Peak Core Formation cultivator; however, the overwhelming power of the attack left no room for regeneration.

" . . . "

Slifer's eyes widened in awe at the sheer destructive power of the technique. The fact that one of Caelum's techniques could surpass an Early Nascent Soul attack shocked him. In the novels he had read, fighting across a major realm seemed as easy as a seasoned warrior swatting away a bothersome fly, but reality was far different. Only with exceptional advantages, such as the Sword Soul Realm, could such a feat be feasible.

"Focus on how it felt."

Once again, Slifer closed his eyes, he recalled the surge of Sword Qi appearing within him. He focused on how the qi was compressed within his meridians, building pressure like water in a tightly sealed pipe. The intensity continued to increase until it was near bursting point. Then, once released, it rushed out with immense force, expanding rapidly as it left the confines of his body. The qi then ballooned in size as it moved, like water gushing from a burst pipe, gaining momentum and power, until it reached the Nascent Soul Realm.

This mental exercise helped Slifer understand the technique's nature—controlling the buildup of energy and then skillfully releasing it for maximum impact by the time it reached its target.

> *Ding!*
> Sword Mastery Increased By 10%

Ten percent? He knew that progress would only be slower as he continued to use the same method, but it would be many times faster than learning it the normal way.

> *Ding!*
> Caelum Card Locked for 24 Hours

"If there was no limit, I could probably breakthrough to Sword Soul Realm in a day or two." He sighed.

> *Ding!*
> Congratulations on your breakthrough to Sword Qi Realm!
> Reward: 100 Karmic Credits

"Sword Qi Realm?"

The Sword Qi Realm was the second stage of sword cultivation.

Once a practitioner refined their Sword Intent up to a certain level, they were able to condense it into tangible Sword Qi. This energy could then be channeled through a sword to enhance techniques. Previously, Slifer had used Light Qi, as a substitute for Sword Qi, for his Nova Strike technique but now he had the real deal.

With a wave of his hand, a blade materialized from the storage ring, he extended his hand and caught it effortlessly midair. Gripping the hilt firmly, he channeled his qi into the blade, the Skyfade Emerald Blade hummed happily in response.

Slifer turned his attention to a training dummy positioned around twenty feet away and made a casual slashing motion. The Sword Qi burst forth, a visible streak of energy slicing through the air. It moved with such speed and precision that it seemed to blur the space between him and the dummy. In a blink, the dummy's head was cleanly severed, falling to the ground with a dull thud, while the body remained upright for a moment before toppling over.

With Sword Qi enhancing my strike, I can take down an Early Core Formation cultivator. He nodded in approval. *And that's all without relying on the System!*

His gaze shifted to the decapitated training dummy as it regenerated before his eyes.

A perfect training partner, he mused.

Shaking his head, Slifer focused on a skill that could enhance his offense, defense, and agility!

"Nascent Soul Armor."

A smoky armor wrapped around him like a protective cloak.

Closing his eyes, Slifer tuned into his spiritual sense. He could feel the qi coursing through his body, weaving an intricate pattern that formed the armor around him. But as the armor began to fracture and weaken, his eyes snapped open.

In a blur, he moved, appearing in front of a training dummy. With a swift, powerful punch aimed at its head, the dummy's head shattered, wooden shards flying in all directions.

Watching the remnants of the armor dissipate, he nodded in approval. "Impressive."

Ding!
Nascent Soul Armor Skill Locked for 24 Hours

Closing his eyes again, he tried to recall the sensation of the qi moving through his body. He attempted to mimic it, envisioning the Nascent Soul Armor forming around him. Hints of the armor started to appear, bringing a smile to his face. But his smile quickly faltered as the armor disintegrated almost immediately.

A wave of fatigue washed over him. *I was right. My body isn't strong enough to sustain the technique without the System's aid. When activated through the System, it offers protection, but only for a limited time.*

"I need to strengthen my body further."

Ding!
Nascent Soul Armor Technique Level 0 (10%)

Hmm, ten percent after one attempt, not too bad. Slifer nodded. He was right, the System now recognized it as a technique. Once the technique reached level 1, he would be able to use it for ten seconds before it strained his body.

Forget about level 1, I want to go straight to level 2, he thought. The difference between the two levels was not the power of the technique but the duration. All he had to do was make a few breakthroughs in body cultivation and practice, shouldn't be too difficult, right?

"Time to put the title of supreme elder to use!" Slifer grinned as his thoughts turned to the sect's resources.

CHAPTER FIFTY-THREE

Ah, Supreme Elder, what brings you here."

Slifer eyed the weasel-looking man in front of him with mild distaste.

Just my luck to see this guy three times in the span of a few days! Slifer would rather have avoided this particular elder, but unfortunately, he needed access to the sect's resources, and this man, Wyatt, held the keys.

"Grand Elder, I was just nearby and thought I might relieve you of some . . . items," Slifer said, trying to sound casual. The less he spoke to the man the better, if any of the grand elders were to see through his façade, it would be the shrewd man before him.

"And what did you have in mind?" Wyatt asked, his tone carefully neutral.

It wasn't like the supreme elder to visit the Treasury, Wyatt couldn't help but feel curious. Well that and he didn't like Slifer lingering around his turf. As the treasurer, Wyatt had the privilege of using the treasures in times of crisis, and who else but him decided what counted as a crisis. But now, if the supreme elder were to take a Heaven Rank treasure, that was one less Heaven Rank treasure that Wyatt could *borrow*.

"Anything related to body cultivation."

Wyatt looked at him strangely, he didn't know that the supreme elder delved in body cultivation. It was rare for a cultivator to choose that path, especially so late in their cultivation.

Unless he plans to cultivate to the Ascendant Realm, it would be pointless to waste time on cultivating the body, Wyatt thought, skepticism evident in his mind. *What is it that he is hiding?*

"I'll see what we have that might suit your needs," Wyatt said, leading Slifer into the depths of the Treasury.

Despite his thoughts, Wyatt knew he couldn't deny Slifer's request. As a supreme elder, Slifer had rights to the Treasury that even Wyatt couldn't oppose.

The vast hall of the Treasury was lined with shelves of numerous artifacts and scrolls, too many for Slifer to count. After a few minutes of silence, they finally stopped at a small room set aside from the main Treasury. Inside, the room was packed with items dedicated to body cultivation—vials of pills, aged scrolls, and various other tools and elixirs.

"Is this all there is?" Slifer frowned as he surveyed the room.

Wyatt nodded. "The Black Rose Sect isn't known for body cultivation. That's more the Black Heart Sect's specialty," he explained.

Activating his Insight skill, Slifer scanned the items:

Ding!
Name: Vitality Surge Pill
Rank: Low Earth
Description: Enhances physical strength temporarily.

Ding!
Name: Essence Rejuvenation Elixir
Rank: Low Earth
Description: Accelerates body recovery.
Ding!
Name: Iron Body Technique Scroll
Rank: High Earth
Description: Strengthen physical resilience.
Ding!
Name: Gravity Seal
Rank: High Earth
Description: Apply to the body to increase weight for training. Contains nine levels.
Ding!
Name: Qi Lock Seal
Rank: High Earth
Description: Restricts qi flow in Nascent Soul cultivators and below.

They were all Earth Rank items, useful but not exceptional. With a wave of his hand, Slifer sent everything flying into his storage ring.

Wyatt's eyes widened in shock. "Supreme Elder, you can't just—" he stammered.

Slifer waved him off. "From the dust here, it's clear these aren't being used. They'll be of better use with me." He could feel Wyatt's hesitation but knew the man wouldn't dare to object.

Wyatt closed his mouth, unable to argue.

Slifer left the Treasury, his mind already considering how best to use these new resources. *I thought the sect would have better resources; I guess I'll just have to buy a Heaven Rank Body Cultivation Method from the Shop.*

Slifer sat on his cultivation pillow in his quarters, scrolling through the System's list of cultivation methods. He focused exclusively on body cultivation methods, dismissing the sect's collection as too low-level.

Why bother with anything less than a Heaven Rank method? he thought, clearly having been spoiled by the System. *And demonic methods aren't of any use to me.*

As for the mysterious Obsidian Rank methods, he likely needed to upgrade the System to Version 2, but for now, he settled on finding the best Heaven Rank option available.

He noticed that Heaven Rank Body Cultivation Methods were more expensive than their spiritual counterparts, but he attributed that to the rarity of body cultivation methods.

After some time, he found three that caught his eye.

Name: Agony's Embrace
Rank: Mid-Heaven Rank
Description: Inflict pain upon yourself, the greater the pain, the greater the foundation you can create.
Cost: 1400 Karmic Credits

Slifer quickly dismissed it. *I'm no masochist. Why endure unnecessary pain?*

Name: Beast Feast Cultivation
Rank: Low Heaven Rank
Description: Consume beast meat, the higher the quality of the meat, the more qi can be absorbed to strengthen the body.
Cost: 1000 Karmic Credits

This one sounds ideal, especially for someone like me who appreciates a good meal. Unfortunately, its lower rank made him hesitant. *If only it were a High Heaven Rank.*

Name: Predator's Vigor
Rank: High Heaven Rank
Description: Consume beast meat, the higher the quality of the meat, the more qi can be stored. Then through rigorous exercise, absorb the qi to transform the body.
Cost: 1500 Karmic Credits

Predator's Vigor . . . It's a mix . . . Consume and then exercise. Not as easy as the second, but still doable. "Looks like I have to decide between ease and efficiency," he muttered to himself. He weighed his options, considering the pros and cons of each method.

The first is too painful, the second too weak, and the third . . . well, it's a balance of both. He knew he had to choose wisely, as the right method could significantly accelerate his progress.

"I'll go with Predator's Vigor. It's the best choice for advancing my cultivation without unnecessary suffering." Slifer nodded to himself, satisfied with his decision.

Ding!
You Have Bought "Predator's Vigor"
-1500 Karmic Credits

"My first High Heaven Rank method." His spiritual cultivation method was only a Low Heaven Rank method, back then it hurt to even look at Heaven Rank methods.

"Hmm, a list of exercises," he mumbled as a barrage of information relating to the technique entered his mind. *I feel exhausted just reading them.* He shuddered.

One particular exercise involved carrying large boulders under a waterfall, all without using qi. *A middle-sized boulder is manageable, but a large one under a waterfall? That's pushing it,* he thought, shaking his head. *No, if I give in to the laziness, I'm only signing my death warrant,* he scolded himself. He knew that to keep up in this ruthless, dog-eat-dog world, he couldn't just be Zack, the couch potato who binge-watched anime all day.

"Well, at least I can enjoy the fun part!" Slifer laughed as he sent a spiritual transmission to Morvran for the highest rank beast meat the sect had.

Ding!
Due to the Actions of the Disciplinary Hall Member Alphie
You Have Gained 3 Karmic Credits

Seems like my plan with the Disciplinary Hall members is paying off, Slifer thought, pleased. He had been receiving similar notifications the whole day.

"Master, I have brought the delicacies," Morvran called from outside Slifer's quarters.

That was quick, Slifer thought, surprised. "Come in, Morvran," he said aloud.

Morvran entered and waved his hand, and suddenly, ten different cooked meat dishes appeared before Slifer.

Slifer's eyes widened in delight. "How were these prepared so quickly?" he asked, genuinely curious.

"After you . . . disposed of the Grand Elder Darius, I took the liberty to retrieve his possessions," Morvran explained.

Slifer had not thought much about Darius's belongings after the grand elder's storage ring was destroyed in the blast. *I was too caught up in the aftermath to consider what he might have hidden away.*

"You did a good job." Slifer nodded at Morvran, it was good to have lackeys who could think for themselves.

"Thank you, Master."

"Hmm, did you acquire anything else?"

Slifer was hoping the grand elder had some treasures or pills that could be useful or maybe something similar to that strange amulet, a man that could enter the Ascendant Realm couldn't be simple.

"I did find something. It's a . . . letter." Morvran handed over a worn piece of paper.

Darius? Letter?

Slifer unfolded the paper and began to read:

"Dear Sweetest Flame, your eyes are like stars in the darkest night, guiding my soul. My heart beats only for you, as fierce as a dragon, yet as tender as a morning dew. Your voice is a melody that intoxicates me more than the finest wine. I long for the day we can unite under the eternal sky. Yours forever, Darius."

This . . . this is just embarrassing to read. Slifer's face twisted in discomfort.

From what the little Slifer knew of the Tekken-like cultivator, he seemed more like a battle-crazy maniac than a romantic.

"Is this an attempt at humor, Morvran?" Slifer asked, looking up at the bald man with disbelief.

"I assure you, Master, it is not," Morvran replied, stoic as usual.

I knew it was impossible for someone with a physique like Darius to be single! Slifer's mind raced as he considered the implications. *Could this woman be the voice I heard, the siren?* He paled at the thought. *If Darius had a lover in the Immortal Realm and she finds out what happened to him . . . I'm a dead man. But for now, there's nothing I can do. If she's going to come after me, she'll come. I just need to be prepared. I need more credits!*

Slifer hated relying on the System but against immortal-level threats, that's all he could do, at least for the time being.

"Master, should we investigate this . . . Sweetest Flame?"

"No," Slifer replied quickly, then added, "not yet. Let's keep this between us for now."

He lacked the means to investigate a potential immortal, and given his precarious status within the sect, he couldn't use the sect's intelligence. If someone like Wyatt were to discover the existence of the "Sweetest Flame," they would only lure the danger towards him.

I still haven't forgotten the last words Darius said, "Wyatt."

"You can leave, Morvran." Slifer was certain Morvran would be relieved to avoid what was about to unfold. Indulging in a good meal was the ultimate way to lift one's spirits and Slifer needed his lifted.

Just as the door closed behind Morvran, Slifer attacked the first dish—a succulent roast of fiery phoenix thigh, glazed in a sweet and spicy sauce that tantalized his taste buds. He devoured it with the ferocity of a homeless man who hadn't eaten in weeks, tearing into the tender, juicy meat as if it were his last meal. The flavors exploded in his mouth, a perfect blend of heat and sweetness that made him reach for the next piece without a second thought.

This is incredible. If this was all there was to cultivation, I would have surpassed the Greater Immortal Realm by now.

With a hearty burp, Slifer patted his now swollen belly, feeling like he was on the verge of bursting. He had completed the first part of the cultivation method—eating an enormous amount of food. Now came the part he dreaded the most: exercise.

Retrieving his sword from his storage ring, he groaned as he jumped onto it, the recent meal making the movement uncomfortable. He flew off in search of a waterfall.

After a few minutes, he found a suitable waterfall and landed nearby. He scanned the area for a large boulder, the kind the method described as weighing around 5,000 kilograms—a weight impossible for even a Body Tempering cultivator to lift.

He finally found one that met the requirements, it was as big as a shed . . .

Approaching it, Slifer placed his hands on the massive rock, straining to lift it. His wiry muscles tensed and trembled under the effort, but the boulder didn't budge.

This is crazy. How is anyone supposed to lift this? he thought, frustrated. Letting go of the rock, Slifer shook his head. *Maybe a little "cheating" won't hurt.* He wrapped his qi around the boulder, levitating it effortlessly. *It's like having a spotter in the gym, not that I would know. Gyms and I were never on good terms.*

He positioned himself under the waterfall, feeling the water pelt him with relentless force. He sighed, levitating the boulder above him. Following the cultivation method's instructions, he manipulated his qi in a spiraling pattern around his body, preparing to absorb the pressure.

"Here goes nothing," Slifer muttered, his voice laced with resignation. Activating the qi lock seal, he suddenly lost access to his qi. The method didn't require him locking away his qi but it did mention it would increase the efficiency.

The boulder came crashing down. With a grunt, Slifer caught it, holding it above his head and back. The weight was immense, pressing down on him like a mountain, making his knees buckle. Water from the waterfall hammered down on him, only making things worse.

I really hate exercise. But if it makes me stronger . . . Slifer thought, gritting his teeth as his face turned an unhealthy shade of red.

Caelum was flying on his sword, lost in thought. *Master wants me to be a righteous cultivator, but he hasn't taught me any righteous techniques. How can I call myself a righteous cultivator if I only know demonic ones?* He was also puzzled by Slifer's instructions to keep his conversion to the *enemy's* side a secret. *Perhaps Master's grand plan is to turn the demonic disciples into righteous ones, but why?*

He remembered his master's words from years ago, insisting that all righteous cultivators were hypocrites and not to trust a single one. *Why the sudden change?* Caelum wondered, shaking his head to clear his thoughts.

Flying through the trees, Caelum suddenly spotted a topless old man under a waterfall, holding a massive boulder above his head. The man's arms were thin, his body frail-looking, but with an oddly huge belly.

Landing near him, Caelum hesitantly greeted, "Master?"

The man's eyes met his, and before Slifer could reply, his belly shrank dramatically. The fat transformed into muscle, redistributing across his body. In moments, Slifer no longer looked frail but lean and fit.

> *Ding!*
> Congratulations!
> You Have Broken Through to Foundation Establishment Realm
> Reward: 200 Karmic Credits

Slifer smirked, now at the Foundation Establishment Realm for both spiritual and body cultivation. He released the qi seal and casually hurled the boulder away, sending it flying through the air with ease.

"What brought you here?" Slifer asked, turning to Caelum with a smile.

Caelum coughed, composing himself before bowing. "Master, all my techniques are demonic. I require righteous techniques."

> *Ding!*
> Your Disciple Caelum Has Come Looking for Guidance
> Teach Him the Righteous Versions of His Techniques
> Reward: 100 Karmic Credits Per Technique

My bad . . . I probably should have taught him some righteous techniques last time. Slifer's eyes narrowed in contemplation. *But then, would the System have rewarded me for it?* "Ah yes," he responded to Caelum's request. "I'll teach you a righteous version of each of your techniques." He paused, then added, "But I will only show you the technique once a day."

Caelum looked at him, a hint of confusion in his eyes. Slifer quickly explained, "With your level of comprehension, I believe once should be sufficient."

"Very well, Master, I am ready to learn." Caelum bowed. *I like it when Master is strict. It shows he cares about my progress.*

Slifer, noticing Caelum's positive response, barely held back a sigh of relief. *Thank goodness. The System only lets me use the Caelum Card once a day. Even if his comprehension was dog shit, that's all he would get.*

"Good. We'll start n—"

> *Ding!*
> Your Disciple Fenlock Is Breaking Through to the Nascent Soul Realm
> New Task: Act as a Dharma Protector

Nascent Soul Realm! Well, I guess Caelum will have to wait a little longer . . .

CHAPTER FIFTY-FOUR

Why didn't that boy inform me he was attempting a breakthrough to the Nascent Soul Realm? Slifer thought as he soared through the air.

Fenlock's hasty actions irked him. Tribulations at the level of the Nascent Soul Realm were serious matters, and Fenlock had only recently reached the Peak Core Formation realm.

"Remember to let your master know whenever *you* are planning to face a tribulation." Slifer turned, reminding his now favorite disciple, Caelum. "As your master, it is my job to act as your Dharma Protector."

"Yes, Master." Caelum nodded respectfully. Caelum knew that Slifer, despite not being the best teacher in traditional terms, always pushed them hard in their cultivation. *He does take our breakthroughs seriously, even if he overdoes it sometimes*, he reflected.

As Slifer continued his flight, he couldn't help but be skeptical. *Acting as a Dharma Protector, huh? Does the System really think I'd fall for that? Fenlock's rash decision is likely to backfire, and I'll have to step in.* He remembered his last tribulation vividly, how the System had locked the Shop at a crucial moment. *I guess it's time to stock up on some life-saving cards,* Slifer decided. He preferred to waste his credits on cards he might not use than risk his life—or his disciple's—in an unprepared tribulation.

Slifer had 3130 Karmic Credits and he knew exactly what to spend them on!

Critical Block Card
Cost: 900 Karmic Credits
Description: Protects user from a critical strike.

Considering he already possessed the Phase ability, offering thirty seconds of attack immunity, other options like the Impeccable Card seemed redundant.

Why waste twelve hundred credits for mere ten seconds of protection when I can get thirty for nothing? he reasoned.

So, the only useful card left was the Critical Block Card.

Purchasing three Critical Block Cards would provide ample security for most situations. *Unless Fenlock somehow triggers a Celestial Prism Tribulation, these should suffice.*

Ding!
You Have Bought 3 Critical Block Cards
-2700 Karmic Credits

Now, to play the hero, Slifer thought, ready for action.

But then, another notification startled him:

> *Ding!*
> Warning: Your Disciple Young Fenlock Is in Mortal Danger
> Task: Save Young Fenlock
> Reward:
> - Disciple Loyalty Increases
> - 5,000 Karmic Credits

Mortal danger? It better not be the Celestial Prism Tribulation . . .

Fenlock let out a deep sigh as the blue sky slowly transformed into a golden hue.

"Golden Crown Tribulation."

During his breakthroughs to the Foundation Establishment and Core Formation realms, Fenlock had faced the Crimson Wave Tribulation. Those had been challenging, and the thought of facing the more formidable Golden Crown Tribulation, with lightning strikes at the Nascent Soul Realm stage, filled him with apprehension.

However, he knew with the added risk came a greater reward, the opportunity to enter the state of Enlightenment and create his own sound technique. Due to the lack of popularity, sound techniques were few and far between, especially those that were at the Earth Rank or higher.

As a devoted sound cultivator, the chance to become a pioneer for the obscure path filled him with excitement. Yet, for Fenlock, there was an even deeper motivation driving him to overcome the tribulation.

"For Junior Sister Lenvari, I must succeed," he muttered, his fist clenched so tightly that his knuckles whitened.

Lenvari's hesitation about advancing their relationship to a more serious level had left Fenlock in a dilemma. She believed that twenty was far too young for immortals to contemplate marriage.

But how can I face my parents and tell them I'm with a girl, and we're not even betrothed? he thought. The mere idea of admitting that to his traditional parents was horrifying.

And the idea of waiting, of not being bound to her immediately, was unbearable.

Breaking through to the Nascent Soul Realm, that will surely sway her, Fenlock convinced himself. *Once I achieve that, she'll see. She'll understand. And then I can finally bring her to meet Mother.*

Driven by this belief, Fenlock had hastened his breakthrough, accelerating the onset of a tribulation that he was ill-equipped to deal with.

Fenlock closed his eyes, focusing on the intense feelings he had for his junior sister, he brought the flute to his lips.

As he played, a melody rich with emotion flowed forth, each note tinged with a hint of sadness and longing. The sound resonated in the air, weaving an intricate tapestry of qi which quickly coalesced into a protective bubble that enveloped him.

The heavens roared as three azure lightning strikes formed, their electric arcs crackling with intense energy. The lightning bolts zigzagged through the air, heading straight towards Fenlock. They struck his qi barrier with a resounding clash. The bubble shook violently under the impact, but surprisingly, it held firm.

Sweat poured down Fenlock's forehead but he played on, reinforcing the barrier with more qi.

Then, the clouds churned again, this time releasing three crimson lightning strikes. They came down one after another. As they collided with the bubble, each strike felt like a hammer blow against the barrier. Fenlock could feel the force of each impact, his qi shield quivering under the relentless assault but the force of the crimson strikes was too much for the barrier to handle.

The barrier shattered and Fenlock was sent hurtling backwards, flying through the air like a leaf caught in a storm.

I . . . I can't fail already, he thought desperately.

With great effort, Fenlock managed to twist his body midair, reorienting himself to land on his feet. He stumbled slightly upon landing but quickly regained his balance.

Looking up at the heavens, a hint of fear appeared in young Fenlock's eyes.

The final three strikes of the tribulation were approaching, and they were at the Late Nascent Soul level.

Can I really withstand such power?

The sound barrier, his most potent defense, had just barely held against a Mid-Nascent Soul attack. The probability of succeeding the tribulation was slim.

Failing a tribulation didn't always mean death for the cultivator, but it almost always involved severe injuries. Such a setback could lead to the creation of a Dao demon, especially in those with weaker willpower, potentially stagnating their cultivation forever.

But I have to try. For my future, for Lenvari. Fenlock grit his teeth, bringing the flute back to his lips.

The heavens let out another roar, forming another three crimson lightning bolts which quickly merged into a single, formidable bolt. The crimson lightning bolt turned golden and like a spear hurled by the gods, it pierced the sky, heading straight for Fenlock.

I . . . I can't survive this . . .

Just as Fenlock lost hope, an old man in orange robes appeared out of nowhere. With a swift, powerful slap, the old man deflected the bolt. The bolt shot back towards the heavens.

With his back facing Fenlock, the old man stood tall and imposing, his gaze fixed firmly on the heavens as he exuded an aura of unshakable confidence.

"M-Master . . ."

Slifer released a sigh as he looked down at his scorched hand, which was already rapidly healing. The Peak Slifer Card had elevated his cultivation to the Half-Step Origin Realm, but that was in terms of spiritual cultivation, not bodily.

If not for my superior quality of qi, that slap would have cost me my hand, he thought.

He hadn't wanted to use his last remaining Peak Slifer Card, but upon arriving with Caelum and witnessing the final lightning bolt descending on Fenlock, he had no choice. With only a Foundation Establishment cultivation, reaching Fenlock in time was impossible. Crushing the card was the only option.

Turning to Fenlock, Slifer asked sternly, "Why would you face the tribulation without informing me?"

Fenlock's head drooped, his voice soft with regret. "I'm sorry, Master. Forgive me."

His previous master, Elder Fron had never shown any interest in acting as a Dharma Protector for his disciples, Fenlock had assumed the same for his new master, and his desire to break through further clouded his judgment.

Slifer shook his head. "You'll make it up to me later," he said, then softened, placing a reassuring hand on Fenlock's shoulder. "But let Master handle this now."

Ding!
You Have Interfered in a Heavenly Tribulation
Warning: You Are Facing Heaven's Wrath
Task: Survive
Reward: 2000 Karmic Credits
Note: Shop Locked

Survive? Oh, I plan to.

Slifer turned back to face the heavens just as the golden clouds swirled into the shape of an old face, its expression one of wrathful fury. The face roared down at them, and a golden lightning bolt began to form in its mouth, clearly at the Peak Nascent Soul stage.

I don't want to waste a Critical Block Card on this, Slifer thought. His own techniques, even if powered by his Half-Step Origin Realm qi, couldn't match a technique comprehended to the Nascent Soul Realm.

Multiple demonic techniques would only cost me 25 Karmic Credits. That's far cheaper than wasting a card. He prepared himself, channeling his qi and readying the original Slifer's techniques to counter the attack.

As the golden lightning bolt surged towards Slifer, black flames erupted around him, forming a protective barrier.

"Darkflame Ward, it's been a while," Slifer sighed, feeling the force of the lightning bolt clashing against the barrier.

The flames held out against the attack until the lightning deteriorated into harmless sparks. Seeing the attack fail, Slifer let the barrier fade away, it would be of no use against the following attacks.

Slifer's eyes hardened as he sensed an Origin Realm attack forming in the heavens. None of the original's techniques could save him from such a strike.

Laughing, he stretched out his hands, challenging the heavens. "Do your worst," he taunted.

Another roar echoed from the heavens, and a golden lightning bolt with specks of black shot down towards him. The strike hit, enveloping the area in a cloud of dust. When the dust settled, Slifer was standing unharmed, his form flickering in and out of existence.

Twenty-five seconds left of the Phase ability, Slifer noted, glancing at the timer.

Multiple Origin Realm attacks rained down on him, but he stood calmly, the Phase ability shielding him. Luckily for him, before the time limit was up, the attacks from the heavens paused, gearing up for another round.

Slifer eyed the cooldown timer for the Phase ability.

Sixty seconds . . . I hope three Critical Block Cards are enough. He swallowed the lump in his throat, observing the size and intensity of the lightning bolts forming in the Heavenly Face's mouth.

T-these next attacks are at the Ascendant level!

"Leave, now!" he shouted to Caelum and Fenlock. "The barriers will protect you outside the quarters. I don't want you caught in this."

Caelum and a guilt-ridden Fenlock nodded, vanishing in a flash.

Slifer turned around in time to come face to face with a black lightning bolt.

Before the lightning bolt could pierce through his head, a shimmering barrier materialized around him. The impact was colossal, devastating the entire courtyard and quarters.
Trees were uprooted, walls crumbled, and debris flew in all directions, the scene resembling
the aftermath of an explosion.

Only two cards left, Slifer thought, steeling himself for the next wave of attacks.

As the heavens unleashed two more attacks, Slifer was shielded by the remaining Critical
Block Cards. But with his last card used up, a bead of sweat trickled down his forehead as
he gazed upwards.

The celestial face transformed dramatically, morphing into a colossal golden dragon
made of lightning. Its details were intricate and majestic, with scales shimmering like molten gold and eyes blazing with ethereal fire.

This dragon makes big Val look like a hatchling, Slifer thought, awestruck.

The dragon roared, a sound so powerful it pushed Slifer back several feet, then it dove
down towards him.

Slifer glanced at the timer; only one second remained before he could activate the Phase
ability.

As the dragon drew closer, its massive form filled his entire field of view, its maw opened
wide, ready to swallow him whole.

T-this is too close . . .

CHAPTER FIFTY-FIVE

The golden dragon, a manifestation of Heaven's Wrath, swallowed Slifer whole as it crashed into the ground, exploding into a shower of lightning sparks. The explosion was catastrophic, decimating the surrounding areas.

Caelum and Fenlock, who had been watching from a distance in the air, were caught off guard by the sheer magnitude of the blast, the shockwave almost knocked them out of the sky!

"M-Master!" Fenlock cried, not knowing how their master fared against the attack due to the thick heavenly qi-laden dust obscuring their vision. He had witnessed Slifer's nonchalance in the face of danger before, but this was unlike any other threat they had faced. *This is Heaven's Wrath, not just some Early Ascendant attack like that grand elder*, Fenlock thought, fear gripping his heart.

Caelum, seeing the regret and worry on his senior brother's face, placed a hand on Fenlock's shoulder. "Trust in Master."

Fenlock nodded, trying to calm his racing heart. Moments later, he let out a sigh of relief. There, amidst the rubble and within a newly formed crater, stood their master. His robes were slightly singed, but he was otherwise unharmed.

Either Master has an indestructible body or he's a master of space techniques. Either way, it's incredible, Fenlock thought in awe.

Seeing his master risk his immortal life to intervene in a Heavenly Tribulation changed his perspective; the regret he had felt earlier, about being a disciple in a demonic sect, began to fade.

"Not many masters would do what he just did," Fenlock mumbled in disbelief, his previous complaints seeming trivial now. He realized while the righteous sects often preached about self-sacrifice and duty, very few actually lived up to those ideals.

Ding!
You Saved Your Disciple's Life
Reward: 5000 Karmic Credit, Fenlock Card (x3)
Ding!
Your Disciple Fenlock's Loyalty Has Reached 90%
Ding!
What Hinders Complete Trust in Young Fenlock?
Task: Discover the key to gaining Fenlock's utmost trust.
Reward: Unlock "Convert" Option
Ding!
You Have Survived Heaven's Wrath
Reward: 2000 Karmic Credits

Slifer ignored the System's notification as he stood frozen, the fabric of his robes clinging to his skin. The dragon's mouth had closed around him just as he activated his Phase ability, he could still feel its hot breath breathing down on him.

That was too close. If it renewed even a fraction of a second later, I would've been toast, he thought, the realization of his narrow escape sending a shiver down his spine.

Suddenly, the residual golden lightning coursed towards him, it entered his body and merged seamlessly with his cultivation, expanding his qi capacity and increasing its potency.

Ding!
Congratulations on your breakthrough!
Reward: 250 Karmic Credits

Peak Foundation Establishment Realm. Slifer sighed, he hadn't expected a breakthrough so soon. Turning to his disciples, he watched as the lightning poured into Fenlock like a torrential stream, elevating him into the air, his body surrounded by a luminous golden glow.

A tiny Nascent Soul, resembling a miniature version of Fenlock himself, appeared above his head. It had its eyes closed and seemed to be in a deep, peaceful slumber.

Slowly, the tiny soul began to merge into Fenlock's body causing Fenlock's eyes to snap open as the aura of the Nascent Soul Realm pulsed around him in waves.

"I . . . I did it," Fenlock whispered as he landed on the ground.

Ding!
Congratulations!
Your Disciple Fenlock Has Broken Through to the Nascent Soul Realm
Reward: 500 Karmic Credits

"Thank you, Ma—" Fenlock's words were cut short as his eyes took on a glazed, distant look.

Fenlock? Just as Slifer was about to inquire about the sudden change in his disciple, an overwhelming wave of dizziness hit him.

Clutching his head, Slifer struggled to maintain his balance. A few seconds later, his vision cleared and he found himself in an endless expanse of white. He recognized the place—he was in the state of Enlightenment!

Noticing his master and senior brother's blank stares, Caelum immediately realized what was going on. He quickly sent a spiritual transmission to Morvran, requesting the death warriors to surround the remnants of Fenlock's quarters.

It was rare for a cultivator to enter Enlightenment even once in their immortal life, Caelum had never met someone like his master, for whom Enlightenment seemed like a daily routine. Gripping the hilt of Bloodthorn, Caelum whispered, "Stay vigilant, my friend." The sword growled in response.

Back in the endless expanse, a flood of information poured into Slifer's mind, but it was less overwhelming than his previous experience. He quickly assumed a meditative position, focusing intently.

I know exactly what to do with this enlightenment, he thought determinedly. *A space technique!*

The essence of space was notoriously difficult to comprehend but that didn't put Slifer off, as in the state of Enlightenment, it was very much possible. *If I can increase my understanding of space and integrate it into my techniques, it will give me a significant edge.*

He knew this was his chance to be like those protagonists that could defeat enemies across multiple realms.

I need an offensive sword technique that incorporates the concept of space, Slifer thought, closing his eyes to better concentrate.

He sifted through the influx of information, searching for anything related to space. As he delved deeper, he began to grasp the essence of space—its vastness, its fluidity, and its potential to alter the very fabric of reality.

Even in the state of Enlightenment, the essence of space was too profound for him to comprehend fully but he was able to derive one concept.

Space is not just an empty void; it's a canvas where distances can be manipulated, and reality can be bent.

Ding!
Space Mastery: 20%

Now I get why those xianxia protagonists have those "Aha!" moments over simple things like fire. Here I am, geeking out over space and it's actually working!

With this newfound understanding, Slifer started to craft a unique sword technique. He envisioned a sword strike that could transcend the limitations of physical space.

If the sword attack could vanish from one point and reappear within an opponent's body, no one would expect that, it would be unstoppable!

He imagined the attack's trajectory, not as a straight line, but as a path that could fold space itself. The sword attack would slip into a spatial rift at one end and emerge from another, directly inside the target.

It's like threading a needle with the sword, except the needle's eye is a momentary gap in the fabric of space.

This technique would require precise control and a deep understanding of spatial dynamics. Slifer visualized the flow of qi in his body, redirecting it to align with his sword. He saw the qi wrapping around the blade, forming a cocoon that could pierce through the spatial layers.

The strike wouldn't just be fast; it would be instantaneous. From the perspective of the opponent, it would appear as if the sword materialized within them out of thin air.

Excitement coursed through Slifer as the technique took shape in his mind. He named it the Void Piercer—a sword technique that utilized the essence of space to deliver a strike that defied conventional defenses.

Ding!
Sword Mastery: 20%
Ding!
Congratulations on creating a new technique!
Reward: 1000 Karmic Credits
Technique Name: Void Piercer

Rank: High Heaven
Description: Manipulates space to allow sword strikes to phase and hit targets from inside.

Feeling a tugging sensation at the back of his mind, Slifer realized that the Enlightenment period was ending and sighed as he returned to reality.

He found himself surrounded by his disciples and numerous masked figures. The sight of the masked figures made him tense before he realized who they were.

Death warriors. "Congrat—" Slifer started to speak, but he was abruptly interrupted as Fenlock dropped to his knees and clung onto Slifer's leg.

"Thank you, Master, for saving me!" Fenlock cried out, tears streaming down his face. "I'm so sorry, please forgive me."

Slifer looked down at Fenlock, who was gripping his leg tightly. He tried to gently shake his leg free, but the newly minted Nascent Soul cultivator's hold only tightened as he continued to weep.

Slifer let out a resigned sigh. "Fine, I forgive you. But don't think you're off the hook," he said, shaking his head. *I haven't thought of a suitable punishment yet . . . I'll decide on that later.* He knew he had to discourage this kind of simp-like behavior.

Fenlock, still clinging to Slifer's leg, nodded as he wiped his eyes. "I understand, Master. I deserve punishment."

"Exactly how long have I been in Enlightenment?" Slifer asked, trying to change the subject and regain some normalcy.

"It's been six hours, Master," Fenlock replied, finally releasing Slifer's leg and stepping back, his eyes still red from crying.

"Six hours?" Slifer echoed, genuinely surprised.

It had felt like mere minutes to him. Suddenly, a wave of fatigue washed over him. *I need a snack . . . No, a feast . . . Maybe those spicy noodles, or that grilled fish I love so much. Oh, and dumplings. Definitely dumplings.*

Whilst Slifer was almost salivating at the thought of the delicacies waiting for him, Caelum looked at his master in amazement.

Six hours in Enlightenment? Caelum thought in awe. Fenlock's Enlightenment only lasted two hours, which was similar in length to his own experience, the longer the state lasted, the more taxing it was on the mind and body. *But then, it's Master. I shouldn't be surprised anymore.*

Slifer's belly grumbled hungrily, bringing Caelum out of his musing. Coughing awkwardly, Slifer waved his hand, signaling everyone to disperse, they didn't need to be traumatized by the ravenous side of their master.

This is, well, it used to be my quarters, and Master is dismissing me from it. Fenlock hesitated, wondering if he should actually step away.

Slifer chuckled, realizing his mistake. "Right, I should be the one leaving," he said and then jumped onto his sword.

Fenlock watched as his master soared off, a smile tugging at his lips. *Even though Master doesn't need a sword to fly, he still uses one. Such humility is rare.* He reminisced about his initial impressions of Slifer. *I never expected the notorious demonic elder to be like this when I first became his disciple.*

* * *

Slifer sat comfortably in his quarters, leisurely munching on a dumpling. He had already indulged in a lavish feast, but he felt a few extra dumplings wouldn't hurt. He took a bite, savoring the juicy filling and the soft, chewy texture of the dough, nodding in satisfaction.

Nothing beats the simple pleasure of eating dumplings, he thought, relishing the moment of peace. *This is the easy life I enjoy.*

Slifer took a pause to address his disciple. "Now that your senior brother is still breathing, we can continue where we left off. So, where were we?"

"Master, you were going to teach me a righteous sword technique," Caelum replied eagerly.

"Ah, yes. Let's start with your signature move, Shadow Slash," Slifer said, wiping his hands. "After having a glance at your technique a few weeks back, I've developed an alternative. I call it Sunrise Slash. I'll bring it down to the Foundation Establishment level to make it easier for you to grasp."

Slifer had only managed to comprehend the Sunrise Slash technique to level 2, which was equivalent to the Foundation Establishment Realm. Teaching Caelum a Core Formation version would require using a Caelum Card, something he couldn't afford at the moment, given the card's renewal time was still a few hours away.

Caelum nodded, remembering the time he saw Slifer use the technique. *Master saw my technique once and created an improved version. His swordsmanship is truly on another level.*

"This technique harnesses the essence of light to enhance the speed and precision of the strike," Slifer explained. "The key is to channel your qi in a way that it resonates with the natural light around you, creating a burst of speed and power."

Slifer didn't know how helpful his explanation was, he didn't really understand the intricacies behind it, activating the technique was almost instinctive and didn't require any mental effort.

Caelum listened intently, his eyes widening with each detail. *Master's ability to simplify and explain such a complex technique . . . It's incredible. He truly is an exceptional teacher,* Caelum thought, impressed by Slifer's profound understanding.

"Okay, now I'm going to demonstrate. Pay close attention."

Slifer closed his eyes and activated the technique. In a flash of light, he appeared behind a training dummy. With a swift, fluid motion, he sheathed his sword. As if delayed by magic, the dummy's head then fell off.

He managed to hold back a smirk. *I always loved that moment in anime where the swordsman sheathes his blade, and then the enemy falls after a slight pause. Classic.* Composing himself, Slifer turned to Caelum with a serious expression. "Was that rusty demonstration enough for you?"

Caelum nodded vigorously. "It was perfect, Master," he replied, his voice filled with awe. *Master calls that "rusty"? His standards are incredibly high. Even perfection isn't enough for him,* Caelum thought, marveling at Slifer's skill and modesty.

Slifer nodded in response before his eyes briefly lost focus. A few seconds later, he turned back to Caelum. "Good. Now you practice. I have some . . . *matters* to handle."

As Slifer jumped on his sword, his eyes narrowed in annoyance. *Some Bart fellow dares to stir up trouble!*

CHAPTER FIFTY-SIX

Ding!
A Disciplinary Hall Member, Bart, Has Abused His Authority
Credit Deduction: 3 Karmic Credit
Ding!
Task: Discipline the member and make an example of him!
Reward: 100 Karmic Credits

Slifer sat on his throne in the Disciplinary Hall, his head resting on his hand. The hall's member, Bart, had dared to violate the rules Slifer laid down. The disciple probably thought he could escape notice, not realizing the System would notify Slifer of his actions.

"Master, we should flay him alive," Amelia suggested. "Peel his skin inch by inch, ensuring he feels every shred of pain but remains conscious throughout the ordeal. The conscious part is really important!"

Slifer raised an eyebrow at her suggestion. "Maybe I should consider such a punishment for you when you disobey me," he retorted dryly.

Amelia visibly recoiled at Slifer's words, retreating into the shadows and trying to blend into the background.

Minutes ticked by until a young man entered the hall. He had black hair, wore black robes, and his face carried an annoyingly smug expression. "Supreme Elder, you summoned me," Bart bowed, barely concealing a smirk. He had recently entered the Core Formation Realm and assumed the news had caught the supreme elder's ear. *He must want to recruit me, no doubt impressed by my talent.*

Slifer scoffed at the disciple's demeanor. "Since taking over, I implemented a new System for you, the members of the Disciplinary Hall, to win cultivation resources from my personal collection at a more than reasonable price. But there are rules." Slifer paused, fixing his gaze on Bart, whose face drained of color when he realized he had *not* been summoned to be recruited.

"What was the rule I commanded all of you to follow?" Slifer asked.

Swallowing hard, Bart managed to reply, "Not to abuse our authority, Supreme Elder."

"And yet, you felt emboldened to break this rule. Why?" Slifer's tone turned icy.

Sweat beaded on Bart's forehead as he began to falter. "I haven't done anything, I—"

"You dare lie to my master!" Amelia's voice cut through the hall as she emerged from the shadows, her face flushed with anger.

Slifer was baffled at the blatant act of hypocrisy taking place before him. Amelia had no qualms about disobeying and deceiving him, yet she seemed personally affronted when another disciple did the same?

Bart glanced at the silver-haired girl, his legs trembling slightly. He knew her by reputation—the "demon girl," as others called her.

"Senior Sister, I—" Bart stammered, but Amelia sharply cut him off.

"For the blatant disrespect you showed my master, I should rip out your tongue and feed it to you," she snarled as she advanced, her face twisting into a more ghoulish visage with each step.

Bart's eyes widened in terror, taking a step back. He knew it wasn't an empty threat, the innocent-looking girl had once done that to a Core Formation expert when he spoke ill of Amelia's master.

"Or perhaps I should flay your skin slowly, layer by layer, letting you feel every excruciating moment." Standing right in front of him, her face now fully transformed, and her long tongue extended, she whispered, "Let me just taste your soul, just a little lick. It won't hurt much . . . I promise."

Bart, almost crying in fear, blurted out, "I did it, I'm sorry!" He turned desperately to Slifer, "Please, Supreme Elder, protect me!"

Ding!
Your Disciple Amelia Disciplined Bart
Reward: 3 Karmic Credits

Slifer, nonchalantly waving his hand, signaled for Amelia to retreat. She backed off, her appearance reverting to normal.

At that moment, a white-robed youth entered the hall—Kalin. Slifer had summoned him; he had delayed the youth's request for too long, it was time to throw him a bone.

Two birds with one stone, Slifer thought, looking between Kalin and Bart.

Releasing his Peak Foundation Establishment aura, Slifer stood up from his throne. The disciples exchanged confused glances but remained silent. They knew better than to be fooled by the old man's aura; after all, they had recently witnessed him effortlessly defeat an Early Ascendant Realm cultivator.

"Kalin, you wanted to see my sword skills. Today, you'll witness them," Slifer announced, his voice echoing through the hall. "And as for you, Bart, you'll serve as an example of what happens to those who break my rules."

Kalin's eyes lit up with anticipation, a move by a sword cultivator at the Sword Will Realm? He couldn't afford to blink.

"I will not use my higher cultivation realm to bully you as you did to that disciple," Slifer continued. He didn't know exactly what Bart did, but the disciple's demeanor suggested typical cultivation world nonsense, like bullying someone weaker. "In fact, I'll limit myself to the Foundation Establishment Realm and still defeat you . . . in one blow."

"Master, allow me to handle this!" Amelia interjected, a twisted smile playing on her lips. Her silver hair writhed around her like sinister tendrils.

Slifer shook his head, this was a great opportunity to test out his new technique, Void Piercer. But more importantly, he wanted to make a statement.

He thinks he can defeat me in one blow? Bart thought incredulously. He felt the supreme elder was underestimating him, he wasn't just any cultivator with subpar techniques; he was one of the Black Rose Sect's most talented youths.

He only respected the supreme elder due to the vast gap in their cultivation realms. But now, with Slifer lowering his power below Bart's own level, he saw an opportunity to outshine the elder, and if it meant humiliating the supreme elder in the process, then so be it.

"It would be an honor to spar against the supreme elder," Bart said, bowing respectfully while concealing his true thoughts. *Today, I, Bart, will make a name for myself by defeating the supreme elder.*

Slifer merely nodded in acknowledgment. He turned to Kalin. "Watch closely, Kalin. I'll demonstrate this technique only once."

Unlike Bart, Kalin had no illusions regarding an Ascendant cultivator's prowess. He already knew the outcome; he was more interested in witnessing the supreme elder's sword skills.

A sword materialized in the air, and Slifer caught it effortlessly with one hand. Turning towards Bart, he commanded, "Begin."

Bart's face contorted into a menacing smirk, his left arm enveloped in qi, transforming into a demonic, enlarged red limb that rushed towards Slifer with alarming speed.

In a swift, almost imperceptible motion, Slifer slashed with his sword and then sheathed it back.

The very moment Bart's mutated hand was about to collide with Slifer, the disciple's eyes shot open in shock. Blood spurted from his mouth as his hand reverted to normal. He collapsed to his knees, clutching his stomach in pain. He had no visible wound, yet he couldn't stop spewing blood.

As Slifer had predicted, it only took one move.

Ding!
You Punished a Demonic Cultivator
Reward: 1 Karmic Credit
Ding!
Completed Task: Discipline the member and make an example of him!
Reward: 100 Karmic Credits

Not bothering to spare his fallen opponent a glance, Slifer turned to Kalin. "Did you catch that?" he asked.

Kalin's face paled. He had expected a display of Sword Will, but never had he thought to witness a technique infused with the space element, at least not in the Mortal Realm.

The fact that Slifer, a mere Ascendant cultivator, had demonstrated such mastery over both Sword Will and space manipulation was beyond extraordinary. Such cultivators tended to break past even the Greater Immortal Realm!

A genius like this . . . even the Venerables would fight over such a talent! Kalin thought in awe.

Slifer's gaze rested thoughtfully on the white-robed youth.

Once Val manages to soften Leah up a bit, I should be ready to attempt converting her to the righteous path. Then, I'll have a spare disciple slot to take this one in.

Slifer turned his gaze towards Amelia. He thought back to the 3 Karmic Credits gained when she intimidated Bart and realized that he had been dealing with her wrong the entire time. Instead of constantly trying to rein in her sadistic tendencies, why not channel them for a more . . . constructive purpose?

"Amelia, from now on, you'll be in charge of dealing with rule-breakers in the hall," Slifer announced, watching her reaction closely.

A wickedly bright smile lit up Amelia's face, and she produced a dagger from seemingly nowhere, already sharpening it with eager anticipation.

"But remember," Slifer added with emphasis, "you can only punish those whom *I* have judged guilty."

Amelia let out a small sigh, obviously disappointed by the limitation, but she nodded. Her master had a knack for knowing when people lied to him, she decided it was better to obey him. At least with this new role, she could have a little fun with some poor disciple once in a while.

As Slifer settled back into his throne, he dismissed the group with a wave of his hand. Kalin and Amelia gave respectful nods before vanishing from the hall. But Bart, who was still severely injured, struggled to stand and eventually had to resort to crawling away, leaving a trail of blood in his wake.

Slifer made no move to assist him; in the world of demonic cultivators, mercy was seen as weakness. Power was what commanded respect and today's actions would serve as a warning to anyone foolish enough to think they could slip under his or, more precisely, the System's radar.

Resting his head back, Slifer closed his eyes, pondering the future of the Disciplinary Hall. *When will the first member accumulate enough credits to redeem a treasure?* he mused. *The carrot and the stick . . . that's how you manage people.*

"Master, I have returned."

Slifer's eyes snapped open, focusing on the figure before him.

CHAPTER FIFTY-SEVEN

The figure was Nomed, who had returned from the village after gaining the blessing of his parents.

Great, I can put this one to work sooner than expected, Slifer thought, a mischievous smile playing on his lips.

"I'm here too!" Dusty wheezed, panting heavily as he entered the hall. His eyes widened at the sight of the leftover delicacies. He rushed forward, almost knocking over his best friend in the process.

"S-Supreme Elder, can I have some, just a little?" Dusty's mouth watered at the delicious aroma.

Slifer observed the hungry boy with a raised eyebrow. Though he was reluctant to share his meal, he didn't want to ruin Nomed's impression of him, at least not yet. Slifer waved his hand dismissively and the fat boy wasted no time, diving headfirst towards the dishes.

Slifer couldn't help but show a disgusted expression at the messy display. Turning his attention back to Nomed, Slifer asked, "Have you prepared the Master-Disciple Ceremony?"

Nomed, recovering from the embarrassment caused by Dusty's behavior, nodded and swiftly retrieved teacups from his storage ring. Pouring tea into a cup, he offered it to Slifer with both hands.

Slifer accepted the tea and took a small sip. After a moment, he nodded and declared, "From today onwards, you are my disciple."

"Thank you, Master." Nomed bowed.

Ding!
Congratulations!
Nomed Is Officially Your Disciple
Reward: 250 Karmic Credits
Ding!
Reward: Time Reversal Card
Description: Sends the user through the river of time, the user will retain their cultivation.
Warning: The user will exit the river of time at a random point.
Warning: Use of the card will render the System locked, this effect is temporary.

Time travel!

Slifer was elated. Even though it would send him to a random point in the past, the card was invaluable. It basically gave him a second chance at life!

But for the System to gift me this card . . . His eyes narrowed in suspicion. He knew how the System was, for it to hand him such an OP card for such an easy task, it meant he would definitely need it, and likely soon. *I need to keep an eye out and note down any significant events*. He nodded to himself, preparation was key for a regressor.

Dusty, not even halfway done with his impromptu feast, belched loudly, startling Slifer out of his musing.

Is this what I look like to others? Slifer thought with a disapproving expression.

He was glad he dismissed his disciples before spending some *alone* time, the last thing he wanted was for them to think of him as a savage. Shaking off a shiver of disgust, Slifer got ready to send Nomed off to complete some righteous tasks and take his fat friend with him, when he suddenly remembered Grand Elder Tenzin's words. The Inter-Sect Tournament was approaching, and with it, the chance to enter the Sealed Realm.

The Black Rose Sect had two slots for the Sealed Realm, one of which Slifer could allocate as he wished. The other slot would be decided by the grand elders, however, Slifer knew that the grand elders would most likely give the slot to the sect master's disciple, Zhen.

Zhen was a genius, there was no doubt about that. The boy had reached the peak of the Core Formation Realm at the age of sixteen and was only one step away from the Nascent Soul Realm. He had deliberately suppressed his cultivation, waiting for the opportunity to enter the Sealed Realm.

Slifer looked at Nomed, who was still bowing. Nomed was only at the Qi Refining Realm, and he had only a few months to enter the Foundation Establishment Realm if he wanted to have a chance at entering the Sealed Realm. Even if Nomed was a prodigy, Slifer wasn't sure if the kid could do that without his help.

It's time to act like the master I'm pretending to be.

Ding!
Your Disciple Nomed's Loyalty Is at 20%
Warning: If a disciple's loyalty falls below 30%, there is a high risk of betrayal.

Oh yeah, since he's a new disciple, I have to work on increasing his loyalty. Hmm, what better way to solve both of my problems than gifting him a Heaven Rank Cultivation Method!

"Nomed, as your master, I have a responsibility to guide you on the path of cultivation." Slifer cleared his throat. "You have a good aptitude and a pure heart, but you lack a suitable cultivation method. The one you are using now is too low-grade and slow. It will only hinder your progress and limit your potential. So, do you have any preference on the type of cultivation method?"

It would be counterproductive for Slifer to just hand Nomed a random Heaven Rank Cultivation Method and expect results as cultivators had varying talents for the elements, those with a particular high talent would feel some comfort or familiarity when they were around their element.

"Master, might there be a light element cultivation method suitable for me?"

Light element? Slifer's eyes narrowed. *A demonic disciple requesting a righteous cultivation method—how strange!*

But Slifer then remembered these boys were mere villagers. Categorizing them as righteous or demonic was meaningless when they were blank slates ready to be molded. This was, after all, why the System wanted Slifer to take in a disciple in the first place.

But why does the System still label him as a demonic cultivator? Slifer shook his head, it was useless trying to understand the logic behind the System's criteria in differentiating between righteous and demonic cultivators.

"Hmm, I'll see what Light cultivation methods I have," Slifer replied as he opened the System panel.

After a minute of awkward silence, Slifer found three methods that could suit his new disciple.

Solemn Sunfire Sutra: By assimilating the essence of solar qi, this method generates a sequence of nine miniature suns within the cultivator's dantian. The initial three signify the early stage, followed by the middle stage represented by the subsequent trio, and the ultimate three suns mark the late stage of cultivation.

Candlelight Meditation Scripture: Absorb Light Qi from celestial bodies to create a flame within the dantian, cultivate the flame to increase breakthrough.

Cathedral of Celestial Radiance Scripture: Build a cathedral within the dantian where divine light converges.

Slifer gave a basic explanation of each method and then asked, "So, which one would you prefer?"

"Ah, they all seem incredible, Master! Maybe I could cultivate all three?" Nomed asked, scratching the back of his head.

All three Heaven Rank methods? Slifer almost rolled his eyes. *This boy should be grateful for even one!*

Outwardly, he adopted a sagely demeanor.

"It is not a good idea for a new cultivator like yourself to experiment like this," Slifer quickly made up an excuse, hoping it sounded believable. "Mixing cultivation methods can disturb the foundations."

"Oh, I see . . . then the third method suits me best."

A holy method? That's . . . surprising. Slifer was wary with any method related to gods, which were most likely just higher-ranked cultivators loaning out their qi to those in the lower realms, and like most loans, it probably came with interest!

Slifer did not fancy handling an incensed deity chasing interest payments.

Eh, maybe I'm wrong. Nomed is a protagonist-like figure, he'll be okay . . . I'm sure of it.

Name: Cathedral of Celestial Radiance Scripture
Rank: Mid-Heaven
Description: Build a cathedral within the dantian where divine light converges.
Cost: 1500 Karmic Credits

Fifteen hundred? Slifer's eyes almost bulged out of their sockets. It was more expensive than his own cultivation method!

No matter, no matter, it's an investment, Slifer consoled himself as he reluctantly purchased it.

Details relating to the method flooded his mind causing Slifer to close his eyes as he began to process it. After a few moments, Slifer opened his eyes and retrieved a scroll from his storage ring.

To Nomed's surprise, the supreme elder began writing down the entirety of the holy cultivation method!

Cultivators were known to have amazing memories, and the higher one's cultivation, the stronger the memory. However, cultivation methods were notoriously difficult to memorize fully and only someone who had mastered a method could transcribe it.

Remembering that his master had not only given him three options to choose from but also the choice of the element itself, made Nomed look at his master in a different light. *Just how many methods has the supreme elder mastered?*

> *Ding!*
> Your Disciple Nomed's Loyalty Has Increased By 2%

Slifer ignored the message as he handed the scroll over to Nomed, who bowed in thanks.

"If you require any guidance on comprehending this method, you need only ask me," Slifer stated, as he realized it might be daunting for Nomed to ask him for help. The title of supreme elder could be intimidating to new disciples.

> *Ding!*
> Your Disciple Nomed's Loyalty Has Increased By 8%

Only eight percent? I feel like it should have increased a bit more, maybe like thirty percent. Slifer held back a frown. *Kids these days really are ungrateful.*

"Of course, Master." Nomed then turned to leave before pausing. He coughed lightly to get Dusty's attention. The plump boy was still busily stuffing his face.

"We're leaving," Nomed said pointedly.

Dusty pouted, giving the food a longing look. But under Nomed's expectant gaze, he reluctantly got to his feet and trudged after Nomed out the door.

Good riddance, no more of that annoying whale to disturb me, Slifer thought, gazing at the remaining delicacies.

He frowned when he saw that there was barely anything left!

Muttering curses under his breath, Slifer picked up a half-eaten roasted chicken leg and bit into it with gusto, savoring the juicy meat and crispy skin. The Predator's Vigor activated, absorbing the spiritual essence of the chicken into his body and using it to nourish his meridians.

> *Ding!*
> Congratulations!
> Your Disciple Hughie Has Broken Through to Peak Core Formation
> Reward: 100 Karmic Credits

Faster than I expected. Slifer raised his eyebrows at the notification. *Is it related to the grandpa?*

> *Ding!*
> Warning: Your Disciple Hughie's Loyalty Has Decreased to 20%

Well, that answers my question . . .

> *Ding!*
> You Can Purchase a Hint on How to Increase Hughie's Loyalty
> Cost: 500 Karmic Credits

Five hundred credits just for a hint? Slifer shook his head at the System's shamelessness, but knowing he had no choice, he purchased the hint.

> *Ding!*
> Hint: Your Disciple Hughie Has a Mortal Lover That Lacks Aptitude

"A mortal lover? Hughie?" Slifer scratched his head, puzzled. That was not the hint he was expecting; he had always assumed that Hughie was the type of protagonist to end up with a harem of jade beauties.

"She lacks aptitude, so I guess all I have to do is buy a treasure from the Shop that can make her a cultivator?"

Slifer imagined Hughie's immortal grandpa imparting him techniques, seeking to undermine Slifer's authority. But the joke would be on him—Slifer would gain a devoted disciple and more Obsidian techniques for his troubles.

Chuckling, he began browsing through the Shop's inventory for a suitable treasure.

CHAPTER FIFTY-EIGHT

After a few minutes of browsing, Slifer found a few treasures that caught his eye. The first was the Celestial Awakening Pill, it gave a mortal a talent of 1, which was the bare-bone requirement to cultivate.

Next was the Divine Blood Essence, a vial of thick crimson liquid that could ignite the mortal physique and bestow spirit roots that gave a talent of 2.

One thousand and twelve hundred Karmic Credits? Not too bad. Slifer nodded, pleased that the System was finally displaying some reasonable prices.

However, one item gave him pause—the Wheel of Fate, a talisman that was worth 2,000 credits. When activated, it would give an entirely random cultivation talent to the mortal.

Since the girl has strong karmic ties with Hughie, her luck should be quite good, Slifer reasoned. Decision made—he purchased the talisman. It materialized inside his storage ring.

Slifer then sent a spiritual transmission to Morvran. "Come see me at once."

After a few seconds, the bald man appeared and bowed. "Greetings, Master."

"I have a task for you. It seems Hughie has found himself a mortal lover."

Morvran's eyes widened in surprise. "A lover? I would not have imagined Young Master Hughie distracted by such things." He shook his head in disappointment. "I hope he does not end up obsessed like that other one."

"I was surprised too. I did not think one girl could steal the young lad's heart. Anyways, I would like you to find her."

"Of course, Master. I will dispose of her quickly." Morvran cracked his knuckles menacingly.

Slifer was taken aback. He quickly clarified, "No, no, don't kill her!"

Morvran looked puzzled. "My apologies, Master, I think I may have misheard. You wish for me to . . . *not* kill her?"

Slifer rubbed his temples, wondering how many hapless souls had met their end due to Morvran's hearing issues. "That's right, no killing. Just find her and do not make contact."

"I see, I will . . . locate the girl." The words felt strange coming out of Morvran's mouth.

Morvran bowed, though his expression remained conflicted. *No matter, I shall carry out Master's will. If he wishes to have that wench join, then I will find her for him.*

Slifer had given Morvran quite a few talks about how violence wasn't the only option, but it seemed it still hadn't gotten through to him.

The original had truly done a tremendous job of brainwashing his followers.

"Good. You are dismissed." Slifer leaned back in his seat, steepling his fingers together as his thoughts turned to Hughie's mysterious lover. Who was this mortal girl who managed to capture his disciple's affection? Did she possess some alluring charm that the jade beauties in the sect lacked? No matter—he would find out soon enough once Morvran located her. Then her path of cultivation would begin and Hughie would once again be in his clutches.

That'll teach that grandpa for trying to steal my disciple!

* * *

"Are you sure this is safe?" Slifer asked, glancing down at the strange concoction before him.

The bath water had an odd, murky green color, looking more like a cursed swamp than any therapeutic soak. Tendrils of steam curled up in wispy trails, carrying a pungent, herbal scent.

Slifer never liked the smell of medicine, his previous health problems ensured that he had an . . . intimate relationship with hospitals.

"Yes, yes, Supreme Elder!" The alchemist, an elderly man named Lorgren, waved a hand in dismissal. "I have been perfecting the art of bath cultivation for over three centuries. This mixture of herbs and ores will increase your qi absorption tremendously."

Lorgren's back was hunched from decades of leaning over mixing potions and reading scrolls. His bald head and liver-spotted scalp gave him a rather vulture-like look. But his eyes still shone with youthful enthusiasm, especially when babbling on about alchemy.

Despite the assurances, Slifer still felt skeptical. Blindly mixing various mysterious concoctions didn't seem the most scientific approach. But then again, the workings of this world differed greatly from Earth. If the alchemist swore that it was safe, who was he to argue? After all, such "cultivation baths" were common tropes in fantasy stories.

"Now, I must warn you—the temperature is quite hot initially," Lorgren cautioned. "But the body adjusts quickly. Simply relax and allow the elixir infusion to work its magic!"

Lorgren was surprised that the supreme elder had never bathed in a cultivation tub before, but then he remembered hearing how some geniuses didn't require cultivation resources and could reach great heights through meditation.

The supreme elder must be one of those, come to think of it, he never really went out much. Lorgren nodded to himself.

"Very well. You may take your leave." Slifer dismissed the alchemist with a wave of his hand.

Alone in the steam-filled room, Slifer activated Insight.

Name: Jade Cleansing Bath
Rank: Mortal (Upper)
Effect: Cleanses impurities, boosts physique, increases qi absorption rate by 23%.

Useful but nothing impressive, Slifer mused. He planned to use credits to purchase better spiritual herbs and medicines to concoct an even more potent bath in the future. But for now, the resources he had taken from Grand Elder Wyatt would do. "Let's test this out," he murmured, taking off his lower garment and stepping gingerly into the tub.

Immediately, the scalding water stung his skin, practically boiling him alive.

This is insane! He wanted to leap out instantly, but Lorgren's warning rang in his mind. Gritting his teeth, Slifer forced himself to remain stay put. Gradually, his body numbed to the extreme temperature. As the minutes passed, a soothing warmth penetrated his muscles making him feel drowsy. *I'll just rest a little bit,* he thought as he leaned back and closed his eyes.

"Supreme Elder, a disciple has accrued enough points to redeem a treasure." The spiritual transmission from Elder Fred caused Slifer's eyes to shoot open, bringing him out of his slumber.

Finally!

Slifer had been waiting for this moment ever since implementing the credit reward system. Unfortunately, the original wasn't known for his honesty, so some members were hesitant to carry out tasks that didn't involve killing or maiming innocents. Slifer hoped that after the first member successfully retrieved a treasure, word would spread that he wasn't handing out false promises, which would encourage the other members to complete more tasks, resulting in more credits for himself.

Ding!
Congratulations on breaking through to the Mid-Foundation Establishment Realm!
Reward: 100 Karmic Credits

Nice, I'm catching up to my spiritual cultivation. Slifer wondered if having both spiritual and body cultivation at the same level would give him some sort of reward.

Glancing down through the now lukewarm water, he noticed that his swollen belly had receded and been replaced by another layer of muscle.

As much as he liked his original physique on Earth, it did tend to be a bit of a hindrance from time to time, an example being the repeated trips to the hospital . . .

I could get used to this. Slifer smirked, flexing his biceps as he stepped out of the tub.

A fresh set of robes and slippers greeted him outside the room. Inhaling deeply, he caught traces of a delicious aroma. Following it led him to a tray stacked with an expertly cooked meal waiting just outside his chamber. Heavily seasoned chicken and lamb, cream sauces, and even dumplings!

About time those lazy servants figured out my preferences! Slifer's mouth watered at the sight. He wasted no time digging in, his hands reaching for the chicken leg, spending any time looking for utensils for a meal like this would be criminal. *Ohhh, so delicious!* Between mouthfuls, Slifer made a mental note to reward the chef. Just as he licked his lips and went in for a final bite, his eyes caught an unexpected movement from the corner of the room. There, hidden beneath his bed frame, was a familiar face peeking out at him. Slifer's hand paused midair, mouth still agape. Before he could react further, the intruder spoke.

"Master!" the young man greeted cheerily, as though appearing under the supreme elder's bed was perfectly normal.

It was none other than Dentos, the overly eager disciple who had previously begged to be taken as a student.

Slifer quickly masked his surprise, dabbing his mouth casually with a cloth. "Ah, Dentos. I was wondering how long you would hide under there." He kept his tone nonchalant, as though he knew the brat was hiding under his bed all along.

Dentos blushed, surprised that the supreme elder remembered his name.

Though Slifer maintained an impassive façade, inwardly he was reevaluating his impression of this gangly teen. Successfully sneaking into the supreme elder's forbidden quarters, which was heavily guarded by death warriors, was no small feat.

I can't detect him with my spiritual sense! Slifer wondered if his eyes were fooling him and had conjured the image of the young man. He quickly dismissed the thought. If he were to conjure anyone to his chamber, it would be one of those jade beauties who couldn't resist giving him the googly eyes!

There must be more to this Dentos than meets the eye . . . Insight!

Name: Dentos
Realm: Peak Core Formation
Known Techniques: N/A
Known Affiliations: Black Rose Sect
Disposition: N/A
Comprehension: 3
Luck: 9
Talent: 4
Will: 9

Two nines and he still got rejected by the System! Slifer shook his head, he had assumed Hughie was the main character, but it was this dumb-looking kid. *Shame I can't take him as a disciple . . . yet.*

"You clearly have some abilities," Slifer remarked. "But tell me, to what end? Why risk such a stunt?"

Dentos's face lit up. "For the chance to be your disciple of course!" Noticing Slifer's frown, he quickly added, "But also, I wanted to see if you enjoyed the meal I prepared!"

"You cooked this?" Slifer's eyebrows shot up in surprise.

Dentos rubbed his neck bashfully. "Yes, Master. Boss Morvran finished the last meal I cooked so I had to make sure it actually reached you this time!"

A betrayal of this magnitude by Morvran . . . that was not expected. Slifer couldn't wrap his head around the fact that his loyal lackey had attempted to stop him from experiencing this culinary masterpiece firsthand!

"I hope it was to your liking . . ."

Slifer waved a hand, feigning nonchalance. "Barely acceptable," he muttered, but internally he was shocked—this kid could rival the six-hundred-year-old head chef!

Seeing Dentos's crestfallen look, Slifer sighed. Perhaps a minor compliment would avoid crushing the boy's spirit. "The flavors were . . . adequate," he conceded. "You may have some natural talent."

At even this faint praise, the youth instantly perked up, beaming from ear to ear. "Thank you, Master! Your words are worth more than ten thousand compliments!"

Slifer shook his head at the dramatic reaction. Clearly, this kid was obsessed with gaining his favor. Still, better to have a loyal fanatic than an enemy lurking in the shadows, especially with luck and will stats both being at nine, a dangerous combination.

"Enough idle chatter," Slifer said. "I trust you did not sneak in solely to cook me dinner?"

"Ha ha, nothing escapes Master, I've come to redeem the reward."

Reward? Dentos is a Disciplinary Hall member? Slifer glanced at the Disciplinary Hall Panel.

It was true, the boy really was a Disciplinary Hall member, he had joined recently.

A thousand points in ten days? Slifer was shocked at the number of tasks the kid had completed, it was worth 3000 Karmic Credits. The System thankfully had a mute function so he didn't have to see a notification every time one of the members completed a task.

"So . . . which reward would you like?"

"To become your disciple!" Dentos exclaimed. Seeing Slifer's eyebrow raise, the boy quickly amended, "But the Wings of the Roc will do for now."

Slifer's eyes narrowed thoughtfully. Cultivators below the Nascent Soul Realm were unable to fly without the assistance of treasures. The Wings of the Roc would remain useful until the Origin Realm.

Paired with Dentos's strange ability to escape spiritual sense, the boy could become exceedingly troublesome to deal with for anyone below the Origin Realm should his motivations ever shift.

But on the other hand, if Slifer were to hang the title of disciple, he could turn this boy into a credit generating machine . . .

If I can't have him as a disciple, then a walking ATM sounds good to me. Slifer spent the 1000 Karmic Credits to purchase the Wings of the Roc.

Retrieving the item from his storage ring, Slifer handed over the talisman paper to Dentos, explaining how to activate it. The talisman paper would melt into his back, inscribing a rune in the shape of wings, which would expand into genuine wings on activation.

"Thank you, Master! I'll see you . . . soon."

As Dentos turned to leave, Slifer raised a hand to stop him. "If you ever sneak into my quarters again, you will never get the opportunity to be my disciple."

Dentos paled, stammering out hasty apologies and assurances it would not happen again. As much as the warning terrified him, it also kindled a fragile hope. For the supreme elder to even suggest he might accept him one day filled his heart with joy.

How do I attract such . . . characters? Slifer shook his head. Keeping these unpredictable followers in line would be no easy task.

Ding!
Your Disciple Is Ready to Breakthrough
Bring Your Disciple 3 Peak Core Formation Souls
Reminder: Righteous Souls Will Result in Credit Deduction
Reward: 200 Karmic Credits

I guess it's time to pay Amelia a visit . . . Slifer sighed.

The dungeons of the Black Rose Sect were not designed for comfort. Rough stone walls enclosed windowless chambers lit only by flickering candlelight. The air was heavy with the metallic tang of blood.

In the center of the largest chamber knelt a boy no older than sixteen. His face was swollen and bruised almost beyond recognition as he whimpered for mercy.

Standing before him was young silver-haired girl. A cruel smile twisted her lips as she leaned in and whispered, "Don't worry, sweetie, we're almost finished here."

The boy shrieked as she pressed a glowing brand to his skin.

"Amelia."

Hearing the familiar voice, the innocent-looking girl's bloody hands paused their work.

"Master!" Amelia greeted Slifer as she turned around. "What brings you here?"

Slifer suppressed a shiver at her nonchalance towards the tortured, sobbing boy. "Amelia, you are close to another breakthrough. I will allow one week's leave from the sect so you can fulfill the . . . requirements."

What he chose to keep to himself was the contingent of Nascent Soul elders who would secretly shadow her every move, ten should be enough to guarantee her safety. He would have sent more, but Nascent Soul cultivators were the backbone of the sect, some needed to remain behind in case the sect was attacked.

After the mess caused during his closed-door cultivation, he had prohibited any of his disciples from leaving the sect without his permission. But, for his disciples to grow as cultivators, they would need to leave the sect and get more life experience. He couldn't just keep them locked up within the sect their whole lives, that would not only make them incompetent but also breed resentment.

And the last thing he needed was a protagonist after his head.

"A whole week? Thank you, Master!" Amelia's eyes shone as she rushed forward to give him a hug.

Slifer quickly raised his hand, stopping her in her tracks, he'd literally just come out of a bath, he didn't need Amelia to bathe him in blood.

"Just remember to follow the rules."

"I will!"

After Amelia skipped off, Slifer took a deep breath of the slightly less oppressive air of the hallway. Dealing with that unpredictable girl always left him feeling drained.

Well, it looks like her new "job" is keeping her satisfied and obedient.

Shaking off the lingering unease her presence evoked, Slifer began to walk up the winding staircase, but he only made it halfway when a spiritual transmission caused his face to darken.

"Supreme Elder, the Ascendant Meet is in three days. Since the sect master remains in secluded cultivation, the duty to represent Black Rose falls unto you."

Wyatt waits till now to inform me . . . Slifer's eyes narrowed at the dangerous game the grand elder was playing.

From the memories of the original, Slifer learned that the Ascendant Meet was a gathering of the Ascendant cultivators of each sect before a grand event such as the Inter-Sect Tournament. Attendance was nonnegotiable. Failure to attend would be seen as forfeiting their sect's slots to the Sealed Realm.

For a mere Foundation Establishment cultivator like himself to attend was like a newborn lamb strolling into a den of starving wolves. He would be shredded to pieces if the Ascendant beings even sensed a whiff of weakness.

Heart pounding, Slifer racked his brain for a solution. But the more he pondered, the clearer it became—he was trapped and defenseless against such beings—he would need to rely on the System!

Ding!
Task: Awe the Ascendant cultivators!
Reward: 1000 Karmic Credit for Each Ascendant Cultivator Awed
Failure to Hide Your True Identity: Death

Most likely a long, gruesome death . . .

This mission would require luck, wits, and an insane amount of bluffing.

Slifer had barely survived a few encounters with Origin Realm cultivators by pretending to be the old eccentric but would that enough to fool demi-immortals?

I guess I'll find out soon . . .

Gripping the stone railing for support, Slifer took a deep breath and steeled himself. Ready or not, he had a role to play. The show must go on.

Okay System, let's see what you got!

CHAPTER FIFTY-NINE

Slifer shook his head in frustration as he scrolled through the System Shop. The treasures and cards that could actually rival an Ascendant cultivator's power cost upwards of fifty thousand credits! If the meeting was in a few weeks, perhaps the work of the Disciplinary Hall members would have been enough to buy something worthwhile.

"Couldn't you throw a starving cultivator a bone?" Slifer grumbled under his breath.

The Shop interface flickered mockingly before disappearing.

Slifer sighed, forcing himself to look on the bright side. At the very least, he was able to purchase the means to physically get to the Ascendant Meet itself. An Obsidian Rank item!

After not finding any mention of Obsidian Rank cultivation manuals, he had assumed that the System wouldn't give him access to the Obsidian Rank until it leveled up, but surprisingly it was there for treasures. As for why that was, Slifer had no idea and he doubted he would find out anytime soon.

Version 2 better come with a search function! At least I've finally got myself a boat.

Name: Divine Azerion Ark
Rank: Obsidian
Condition: Critical
Cost: 5000 Karmic Credits
Description: Crafted by an immortal, the Ark now limps through the heavens. Its body, marked by old fights, is barely able to hang on.
Warning: Some functions may be unavailable due to critical condition.

For an Obsidian Rank treasure, it wasn't even that expensive! Sure, it is in critical shape but that is a critical shape for an Obsidian Rank item.

The ship would do the job . . . he hoped.

The Ascendant Meet was always held in the clouds of the Seventh Heaven, far beyond the reach of those below the Ascendant Realm. From what Slifer gathered, the Mortal Realm had nine heavens, it was said that breaking through the Ninth Heaven would lead to the Immortal Realm.

As for the Seventh Heaven, the air pressure and elemental forces present at such altitudes would crush anyone under the Ascendant Realm, unless they had access to a vessel or artifact that could protect them. And apart from the ship, there was nothing else Slifer could afford that could take him there.

But having the physical means to reach the Meet was the easy part. Actually surviving the gathering of powerful Ascendant Realm cultivators was another matter entirely.

Slifer didn't really know what to expect. The original, as a Nascent Soul cultivator, had never qualified to attend such a gathering before. But Slifer knew how these things went—as the new guy, he fully expected the other Ascendant cultivators to try him.

He had no illusions about his chances without the System, just a sneeze from an Ascendant Realm cultivator could turn him to dust. After all, he was like an ant arriving at a convention of giant boot-wearing humans.

And he couldn't even bring along bodyguards, even if the grand elders were loyal—which they were far from—they wouldn't even qualify as meat-shields!

With my cards, I'm not totally helpless. Slifer smiled, looking at the few Critical Block Cards and the single Reflection Barrier card he had bought. *Are they enough though? I should probably try my luck at gambling, who knows, I might just get lucky . . .* Slifer nodded to himself, he would rather use his credits now than get one-shotted later. Those thousands of credits would be useless then.

Ding!
Random Card Acquired
Activate Now?

"Yes!"

Three days later.

The streets of Riarn bustled with life, flooded by crowds going about their daily business. Vendors called out from stalls lining the roads, advertising various goods from exotic places. The smells of roasted nuts, fresh bread, and fragrant spices melded together, saturating the air. Children laughed and played, ducking around grumbling laborers.

Two boys chased each other when one suddenly tripped, tumbling forward. His knee scraped painfully against the ground, and he yelped, clutching his leg as tears welled up in his eyes.

Before the boy could cry out, a hand gripped his shoulder.

"Are you alright, lad?"

The boy looked up into warm brown eyes set in a gentle face. The man had short chestnut hair and appeared to be in his late twenties, he wore simple but well-made clothes.

The boy sniffed loudly and shook his head as he struggled to hold back tears.

"Let me see, little one."

The boy tentatively showed his injured leg, a tiny amount of blood trickled down the scrape.

The man placed a hand above the wound and soft red glow emanated from his palm, easing away the stinging pain.

"See there, good as new!"

The boy stared wide-eyed. "Y-you're an immortal?" he whispered in awe.

The man smiled. "Ha ha, not yet but . . . I'm getting there."

He ruffled the boy's hair affectionately. As he did so, a faint, intricate pattern momentarily appeared on the boy's head. It quickly faded away without leaving a trace.

"What do we say?" the man prompted gently.

"T-thank you, sir."

"You're quite welcome, lad. Now, do be more careful in the future."

As the man turned to continue on his way, the boy stared after him, dumbfounded.

Nearby pedestrians who had seen the exchange smiled and whispered to one another. "That was Lord Ulric, wasn't it?"

"Yes, he is so compassionate and humble. If only more nobles were like him."

One figure lurked in the shadows of a nearby alley, face hidden by a hooded cloak. They watched the encounter closely, lingering even as Lord Ulric disappeared into the crowds. After several long moments, the mysterious observer faded away into the darkness.

A few hours later as the sun dipped low over the city's rooftops, the boy from the market wandered alone down an empty alley. His eyes lacked the usual spark of life and curiosity that one would expect in a child. His footsteps dragged as he shuffled forward until he reached the end of a dark alley.

Rotting wooden boards blocked the windows of the last building, the boy paused before its door, swaying slightly as though he was in a trance. As he stared blankly ahead, the door creaked open.

The kind stranger from the market stood in the doorway, though there was nothing kind about the smile that stretched across his face.

"There you are. Come in, come in, the others have been waiting for a while already."

As the boy stepped forward, the door slammed shut behind him.

In center of the room sat eight other children arranged in a circle. Though they faced one another, their blank eyes stared right through each other. Their new addition joined the circle. He did not speak or even glance around. None of the children so much as blinked.

Ulric clasped his hands together. "Perfect, perfect! Nine souls, ripe for the taking!"

He scurried to the center of the circle, nudging the children's limbs as he positioned them to his liking.

"The book said nine boys, and here you are!" Ulric continued muttering to himself as he drew intricate patterns on the children's foreheads using a vial of ink. "Following its guidance, I should have no trouble forming a Nascent Soul. Yes, no trouble at all!" He retrieved a scroll from his robes. "Now let's see, first I must corrupt their souls."

Closing his eyes in concentration, a red glow emanated from his palms, coalescing into pulsating tendrils of energy. They snaked towards each child before boring into their chests in a misty haze.

The children convulsed, faces contorting in silent agony as the purity was leeched from their souls. After a few sickening seconds, their bodies slumped to the floor.

"Excellent, that should sufficiently corrupt and weaken them." Ulric opened his eyes. "Now to extract their souls. If I can harness the souls of nine innocent boys, I'll finally break through to the Nascent Soul Realm. Oh, I can almost taste it!"

Looking down at the young boy from earlier, Ulric laughed. "And I'll be one step closer to being an immortal!"

He then retrieved a wicked curved dagger and poised it above the first child's heart.

Just as Ulric was about to plunge the dagger down, the sound of splintering bones and tearing flesh filled the air.

Ulric froze, dagger slipping from his fingers. Looking down in horror, he saw a claw-like hand emerge from the center of his chest, staining the floorboard with blood.

"You didn't think you'd be the only one having fun, did you?" a ghastly voice hissed into his ear. A foul breath tickled the back of his neck, sending an icy chill down his spine.

Ulric whipped his head around, mouth opening to scream, but only a strangled gurgle escaped his lips.

Before him stood a girl, perhaps sixteen, with skin so pale it appeared translucent. Dark veins spiderwebbed across her face. Her eye sockets were hollow, and they let off an otherworldly blue glow.

As her mouth opened impossibly wide, the woman inhaled deeply. An unseen force, like an invisible hand, seized the demonic cultivator's soul, pulling it from his body and guiding it towards her gaping maw.

Ulric convulsed weakly, his eyes rolling back in their sockets.

With a wet squelch, the girl withdrew her hand from Ulric's back, examining the blood staining her pale fingers.

The lifeless corpse slumped to the floor.

Dragging her thumb across her lower lip, the young woman purred, "Delicious," smacking her lips together in satisfaction. As she turned her attention to the unconscious children, the dark veins receded, and color returned to her cheeks.

"As much as I'd love to claim your little souls as well, Master would be really mad if I did that," Amelia murmured. With a resigned sigh, she took a step towards them, intending to return them to their homes.

No sooner had her foot touched the ground than the wall behind her exploded in a shower of dust and splintered wood. She leapt back as a crescent blade of solidified air whistled through the space her head had just occupied.

Whirling around, Amelia's eyes narrowed at the figure now stepping through the new hole in the wall. He was a young man who looked to be in his early twenties, with a strong, muscular build and shoulder-length raven hair. His handsome features were twisted into a vicious scowl, and his emerald eyes glinted with a predatory light.

"Just who do you think you are, barging in here?" Amelia growled.

The corner of the man's lip curved up mockingly.

"Ziven."

Ding!

Alert: Your Disciple Amelia Is in Battle Against a Son of Heaven

Win Reward:

If your disciple defeats the Son of Heaven, your luck will be restored to its normal state. If she manages to kill the Son of Heaven, your luck will be significantly enhanced and you will gain a random bonus reward.

Loss Consequences:

If your disciple is defeated but survives the encounter, your luck will decrease.

If she dies, you will suffer the consequences of a disciple death.

CHAPTER SIXTY

The moon hung low in the night sky, casting an ethereal glow on the sleeping city below. Ziven stared down the young girl before him. He had spent months on the run, worried her master would send cultivators after him. He finally got some news that one of the old man's disciples were in the city, he couldn't pass up on such an opportunity.

I'll send "him" her head. Ziven sneered, releasing his Peak Core Formation cultivation base.

Amelia met his gaze unflinchingly, completely unintimidated. She let out an unladylike burp as a similar aura of Peak Core Formation erupted from her slender body, pushing back Ziven's oppressive aura. She wasn't sure why this handsome stranger had decided to attack her, but if he wished to offer up his soul, who was she to refuse such a gift?

After all, Master had made it clear that self-defense was fair game. And anyone stupid enough to pick a fight with me deserves what they get.

Amelia's lips curved into a wicked smirk as her beautiful features morphed into an inhuman, ghoul-like countenance—skin growing paler, dark veins surfacing across her face, eyes hollowing into glowing blue sockets.

Ziven's scowl deepened at the sight of the girl's transformation, she was a monster, just like her master. "You have your master to thank for your death today, demon," he spat, his emerald eyes flashing bloodred. "Did you think I would ever forget how he cut down my brother Xander?"

The image of his best friend Xander's vacant eyes staring lifelessly up at the sky flashed through his mind. His hands curled into fists, nails biting into his palms.

"We were like brothers. He was the only family I had left in this world after bandits slaughtered my parents. Even if he joined the bandits, I could have made him understand! I could have saved him—!"

The young man's speech was cut off abruptly as a blade of soul energy came slicing through the air towards his head, forcing him to jerk to the side. The attack left a burning gash across his cheek.

"A Soul cultivator!" Ziven's spat as he felt his soul recoil in pain. The one thing Ziven hated more than demonic cultivators were demonic cultivators who messed with souls. That was unforgivable.

Amelia let out an exaggerated yawn, clearly unimpressed by the young man's tragic backstory.

"I don't really care why you're so eager to let me have your soul," she drawled, idly examining her nails. "Now are you going to keep whining, or are we going to have some fun?" To emphasize her point, Amelia launched two more blades of condensed soul energy towards Ziven.

Ziven dove and rolled, avoiding the attacks by a hair's breadth. He came up in a crouch, lips peeled back in a disgusted sneer. How dare this monster interrupt his righteous quest for vengeance against her master? She would pay for such insolence.

Directing the Wind Qi to his hands, Ziven sent a volley of wind blades slicing through the air towards Amelia.

But the pale girl merely threw back her head and laughed, purple wings unfurling from her back. With a powerful flap, she took to the air, evading the wind strikes with ease.

Hovering in midair, Amelia peered down at Ziven's dumbfounded expression with a smug grin. After her close call with the Nascent Soul cultivator, she had worked tirelessly to develop this Soul Wing technique. Now nothing could touch her!

Craning his neck to glare up at the hovering girl, Ziven grit his teeth in frustration. Fighting an aerial battle was not his forte—his mastery over the wind element was not yet advanced enough to engage her at range. He would need to get creative to bring her back down to his level.

That is a weakness I need to fix after dealing with this wretch, Ziven thought as he gathered his qi towards his palms and then thrust them upwards.

A spiraling column of wind erupted towards Amelia, catching her off guard and slamming her violently back down to earth. She crashed into an old oak, the trunk splintering under the impact.

Not wasting a second, Ziven appeared before Amelia, a claw of wind wrapped around his hand as he stabbed down towards her chest.

At the last instant, Amelia managed to twist aside. The wind claw only grazed her left shoulder instead of piercing through her heart.

Hissing in pain, Amelia stumbled back, clutching the injury.

To Ziven's disgust, rather than show any distress, a look of pleasure crossed her face as she lifted her bloodied hand to her lips and took a long, slow lick.

"Mmm, now this is starting to get fun," she purred, flashing her bloodstained teeth in a wicked grin.

Ziven tensed, a chill running down his spine at the sight of the unhinged glee in her eyes. He had to end this, fast. But before he could make another move, Amelia's blue eyes flashed brightly. An overwhelming pressure seized his mind, leaving him momentarily stunned.

Capitalizing on her opponent's confusion, Amelia shot forward with incredible speed.

Move! Ziven mentally screamed but his body refused to obey him.

In the blink of an eye, she closed the distance and grasped him by the throat and, with terrifying strength, slammed Ziven's head viciously against the pavement. The cobblestones cracked under the impact, pain exploding through Ziven's skull.

Standing over Ziven, Amelia grinned down at him, revealing a long, snakelike tongue that flicked excitedly. "I bet you have a delicious soul, handsome," she purred, taking a deep breath. "The self-righteous ones always do."

An irresistible pull tugged at Ziven's spiritual core, slowly extracting his soul from his body. Mind still reeling from the pain and disorientation of Amelia's attack, Ziven struggled to resist the soul-draining force. As his soul slipped further away, panic threatened to overwhelm him.

N-no! It can't end here, not before I get my revenge!

Just before his soul detached fully from his body, a black marble shot out from within Ziven's chest. It slammed into Amelia with an explosive burst of energy, sending her flying into the air. Her body reverted to its normal delicate appearance as she crashed to the ground dozens of feet away.

Dazed, she pushed herself up from the rubble and debris. She blinked in confusion, scanning the street only to find no trace of the righteous fool. *That coward talked so boldly of vengeance but fled like a dog with his tail between his legs at the first sign of real danger.* She punched the ground in frustration.

Why did they always run away?

Unbeknownst to the seething girl, ten figures hid in the shadows, watching the entire exchange unfold. These were the Nascent Soul elders, assigned by the Slifer to keep an eye on Amelia during her mission. They had been ordered not to interfere unless her life was in imminent danger.

When it became clear the black pearl would be whisking Ziven away to safety, the elders had briefly considered moving to prevent his escape. But before they could act, Ziven had vanished.

One elder shook his head in amazement. "Those two are really only at the Core Formation Realm? Their battle seemed more appropriate for those at the Nascent Soul Realm like ourselves."

His companion nodded in agreement. "The youngest generation always seems to eclipse us. It won't be long before this pair leave us completely in the dust."

The Seventh Heaven stretched as far as the eye could see, an endless expanse of wispy white clouds.

Astrid tapped her foot impatiently, arms crossed as she sat on a thick, golden-hued cloud. The black and white stripes of a tigress adorned her robes, she was the supreme elder of the White Tiger Sect. With her stern face framed by two tight buns, she looked ready to discipline any fool who dared to test her patience.

"That oaf Malachar is late yet again," Astrid grumbled. "Have they no concept of punctuality in the Black Rose Sect?"

Beside her, Leontius, the supreme elder of the Pure Soul Sect gave a sympathetic smile, the corners of his eyes crinkling.

"It appears the Black Rose Sect Master has secluded himself in closed-door cultivation," he said gently. "The newly ascended supreme elder will be attending in his stead."

Astrid harrumphed. "More likely lazing about. In my sect, such disregard for others' time would be met with ten nights in the pits of Azaras."

"You're too harsh." Leontius clasped his hands together. "We all journey at our own pace."

On a nearby red cloud, Zofia, the supreme elder of the Heaven's Light Sect, let out a derisive laugh. With her ornate blue and gold robes, she appeared almost delicate, but the enormous broadsword across her knees dispelled that notion immediately.

"You're too soft as always, Leontius," Zofia said, not pausing as she sharpened her sword. "When that demonic scum finally shows up, I'll be sure to give him an appropriate . . . *reward*." A vicious gleam entered her eyes at the thought.

Leontius frowned. "There is no need for conflict. We are all cultivators seeking the same destination, though our paths may differ."

"Hah!" Astrid barked. "Don't waste your breath on sentimentality, old man. The strong flourish, and the weak perish. That is the way of cultivation." She gave an approving nod at Zofia.

The Black Heart Sect Master, half-hidden in the shadows of a dark cloud, watched the exchange between the righteous sects in silence. A cruel smile played at his lips as he imagined the humiliation awaiting the Black Rose Sect's supreme elder. That fool Slifer had killed an Origin Realm elder and multiple Nascent Soul cultivators from his sect!

Let him suffer at the hands of the righteous hypocrites.

As a demonic cultivator himself, Kaelius knew Zofia's self-righteousness hid the same lust for power that drove him, she just hid it better.

Leontius means well, but his naïvety will be his undoing. As for Astrid . . . Kaelius mentally acknowledged her uncompromising strength and felt a touch of kinship with the other supreme elder. In another life, perhaps they could have been allies.

A pulsating aura interrupted his thoughts as all four Ascendant beings sensed a foreign presence approaching. Their heads turned, following the qi signature.

In the distance, an arc-shaped vessel limped through the clouds, pieces breaking off and falling into the open sky below. It looked as if it had been pieced together from the scraps of a dozen other ships, metallic patches of varying sizes haphazardly welded over gaping holes in the hull. One of its three sails hung in tatters, barely clinging to the mast.

As it drew closer, the elders could make out the name engraved along its side: Divine Azerion Ark.

Zofia threw her head back and laughed. "This is humiliating enough! Is this wreck even capable of flight?"

"It seems not even the heavens favor the Black Rose today," Kaelius sniggered.

Astrid wore a look of disgust. "Only a fool would rely on such garbage. I'd turn right back if I came in that heap."

Leontius furrowed his brow at the comments. "Come now, friends, let us reserve judgement until we meet them. Power lies also in perseverance."

The Ark suddenly veered left as a mangled engine on its right side sputtered, leaking smoke. The movement caused its broken left wing to finally tear free completely. The now useless slab of metal spun towards the clouds below.

As the elders watched the crippled ship desperately try to stay aloft, an ear-splitting roar resonated across the Seventh Heaven.

Their heads swiveled towards the sound.

Approaching rapidly from the north was a massive, winged beast covered in crackling electricity. Spanning over fifty meters, from its three savage heads to the tip of its scorpion-like tail, the Ascendant-level lightning chimera emitted a crazed bloodlust. Each of its three heads sported a thick mane that flickered from white to blue to purple.

Leontius's eyes widened. "A Heavenly Beast? Here?"

Heavenly Beasts were creatures forged out of natural elemental qi that accumulated in certain areas of the upper heavens.

Based on the chimera's aura, Leontius estimated it to be at the Late Ascendant Realm. A difficult opponent for any of the present cultivators to handle alone.

Yet the chimera ignored the elders, its gaze fixed on the damaged Ark sputtering through the clouds. Opening all three of its fanged maws, the beast released an earth-shaking roar and shot towards the ship like a bolt of lightning.

"It appears this will be over quickly." Astrid raised an eyebrow.

"That wreck is done for." Zofia grinned wildly.

Kaelius and Leontius remained silent as they watched the chimera rapidly close in on the crippled Ark.

Nothing good ever came from angering a Heavenly Beast. This chimera would never stop hunting the Ark until it or the cultivator was dead.

On the Ark's crumbling deck, Slifer's eyes widened at the sight of the monstrous chimera barreling towards him, electricity cackling around its three sets of gnashing teeth.

"You have got to be kidding me," he groaned, staggering as the ship listed to one side.

He had spent almost all his credits on preparing to face the Ascendant beings, and now a crazed beast wanted him dead before he could even make it to the Meet?

Ding!
Your Disciple Amelia Has Defeated the Son of Heaven
Your Luck Has Returned to Its Normal State
Reward: 500 Karmic Credits

With my luck no longer being dog shit, I can see if this card works!

It was time to show the overgrown kitten what true lightning was.

"A ninety-nine percent chance of failure, what could possibly go wrong?" Slifer laughed as he crushed the card.

CHAPTER SIXTY-ONE

Have a taste of Heavenly Tribulation!" Slifer roared.

A blinding pillar of white lightning tore through the clouds, hitting the beast in the chest. The impact sent the chimera tumbling away with a pained screech, but the beast righted itself quickly, shaking off the daze with a vengeful glare.

The Heavenly Tribulation Strike Card had failed to do any real damage.

Of course it wasn't the Ascendant level bolt I needed—just my crap luck at work as usual. He grimaced. That had been a measly Origin Realm strike at best. Still, it had stalled the beast for the moment. *Time to put the real plan into motion.*

Slifer scrambled into the hold of the Ark, nearly tripping over his robes. He slid into the control seat of the main cannon, glancing at the mess of levers and buttons that controlled the ancient weapon.

Now where was that blasted firing manuals? Ah, never mind, no time to figure this thing out properly.

Slifer closed his eyes, channeling his qi into the cannon. With a lurch, a building hum filled the chamber as energy gathered within the enormous barrel. *Come on, it just needs enough power to roast the overgrown pigeon . . . there!*

BOOM!

The deafening blast nearly burst Slifer's eardrums, but he grinned as the cannon fired an orb of condensed qi out into the open sky. His smile quickly disappeared though as the blast sailed clean over the chimera, continuing towards the gathering of Ascendants.

"Whoops . . ." he muttered, wincing as the blast closed in on the female elder.

To her credit, Zofia reacted quickly to the surprise attack. With an elegant spin, she swung her broadsword in a wide arc, deflecting the cannon blast skyward where it burst harmlessly amongst the clouds.

"My apologies for the friendly fire!" Slifer called out as he returned to the Ark's deck, but Zofia's only response was an icy glare. Clearly he owed her one now—*wonderful.*

Well, no time to worry about that now.

The chimera had recovered and now dove towards the Ark with renewed fury, jaws crackling with electricity. Two of its heads snapped at the ship's hull, tearing off large chunks of metal plating as if it were paper. The other head targeted him.

Slifer again channeled his qi, steadying his aim before launching another cannon blast towards the chimera. The chimera tried to twist out of the path of the beam, but it was too late! The orb exploded against it, blasting off one of the heads into a cloud of gore. Direct hit!

"Ha! Not so confident now, eh?"

But despite the missing head, the chimera refused to give up. With an enraged howl it lunged towards Slifer once more.

"Just die already!" Slifer yelled, infusing the cannon with all the power he could muster.

Too slow—the chimera was nearly on him!

At the last possible second the cannon discharged, catching the chimera mid-roar with a massive orb of qi directly down its throat.

This time the damage was beyond recovery. The chimera seized up as electricity discharged randomly from its spasming body. Then, all at once, the light left its eyes and the massive beast began to plummet from the sky.

Ding!
You Have Gained 1500 Karmic Credits

"You're mine!"

Slifer flew the limping Ark beneath the falling chimera; he wasn't about to let anyone take his hard-earned spoils. With a heavy thud, the metal deck dented under the weight of the beast.

"There we go, all in a day's work." Slifer grinned, quickly storing the corpse into his spatial ring.

The materials harvested from a Heavenly Beast would fetch a hefty profit, not to mention the beast core. This lucky break almost made up for his unlucky encounter with the chimera in the first place. Almost.

Now to deal with the peanut gallery watching his display. Slifer turned to face the supreme elders, noticing the looks of approval. Power spoke loudly in the cultivation world after all.

Leontius smiled, clearly impressed that Slifer had eliminated such a dangerous threat on his own.

Astrid gave a thoughtful nod, she acknowledged that she had underestimated Slifer and his damaged ship.

Kaelius's expression remained neutral, but a hint of greed crept into his dark eyes. That ship, as broken as it was, seemed interesting. *Though it would probably be more useful in my hands.*

But Zofia . . . Slifer noted nervously that her beautiful face had twisted into a scowl. He swallowed hard. That did not bode well.

"Hmph! So you got in a lucky shot while hiding away on your junk pile," Zofia snapped, crossing her arms. "If I had an Ascendant weapon like that, I could have roasted that beast just as easily!"

The other Ascendant cultivators looked at each other awkwardly, then Leontius spoke up, trying to steer past the hot-headed girl's comment.

"Come, let us get the meeting started." Leontius gestured to an open cloud where Slifer could join the others.

But Slifer shook his head, remaining aboard the battered Ark. "I appreciate the offer, but I need to stay on the ship to maintain its functions."

A half-truth at best, since he lacked the protective qi to withstand the Seventh Heaven's pressure, if he even took one step off the ship, he would be flattened to a pulp.

But the elders didn't need to know that little detail.

" . . . "

"I wasn't finished talking!" Zofia rose swiftly into the air, landing gracefully upon the deck across from him. Up close, the intensity of her presence was even more apparent. This woman was not one to let grievances go unaddressed.

"What do you want?" Slifer's eyes narrowed, not pleased that she had entered his personal space.

"Humph, let us get to the point then. Your handling of the beast was adequate, I'll grant you that much." Zofia's razor tone left no room for argument. "Yet something puzzles me. For a supposed *Ascendant* cultivator, your aura seems awfully . . . limited."

She tilted her head as if puzzling over a complex problem. "An esteemed supreme elder such as yourself should have no trouble proving your cultivation. So . . . let us see it."

The challenge was clear—prove that you're an Ascendant cultivator or get the hell out of here.

Leontius interjected gently. "Now, let's not fight among ourselves. I'm sure Supreme Elder Slifer has his reasons." But Zofia ignored him, continuing her tirade as she leveled her sword at the Ark.

"You hide behind your ships and treasures like a coward. I say you have no right to be here unless you can prove your cultivation level, fight me!"

Slifer shrugged, keeping his carefree mask in place while silently cursing. Zofia clearly suspected him of hiding his low cultivation. He would have to handle this carefully to avoid exposing himself.

"Bold words," he replied lightly. "But I'm not one for pointless fights. Our sects are here to cooperate, after all."

Astrid found herself agreeing with Zofia. If Slifer was in fact not an Ascendant cultivator, then that would free up another spot for the Sealed Realm, a spot that the White Tiger Sect disciples would happily take.

"Enough talk," Astrid interrupted the duo. "If you both believe so strongly, then let us settle this simply. An exchange of three strikes to test your skills should suffice."

"I won't even need three strikes to expose this fool!" Zofia scoffed.

"I'll try not to embarrass you too badly." Slifer yawned. If this arrogant woman wished to be humiliated, who was he to deny her the privilege?

Zofia bristled at the dismissal, cheeks flaming. "Humph, since you're so confident, let's make this interesting," she retorted, eyeing the Ark's cannon. "When I win, I'll be taking this scrap heap off your hands!"

Slifer raised an eyebrow at the bold wager. "And what do I receive when you lose?"

Zofia let out a derisive laugh. "As if that would happen! But sure, if by some miracle you win, you can have this." She retrieved a glowing red cube from her robe—an Essence of Fire!

The other elders stared in disbelief. Essence cubes were exceptionally rare, containing the very mysteries of a specific element. They proved invaluable when comprehending an element, which was crucial for Immortal Ascension. And this arrogant woman gambled one so casually?

Though Slifer kept his face an impassive mask, inwardly he trembled with excitement. His comprehension of fire was only at five percent, using an essence cube so early in his cultivation would give him a chance to comprehend a fire domain before even reaching the Origin Realm!

"Ladies first," Slifer said with a mock bow.

Zofia's eyes narrowed, storing away the cube. She channeled her qi into the sword, causing crimson flames to cover the blade. In a blur, she appeared before Slifer, slashing directly at his head with unbelievable speed.

Yet Slifer didn't even twitch, standing calmly as death whirled towards him.

When the strike was a mere inch from his face, a translucent barrier materialized and blocked the blow.

> *Ding!*
> Critical Block Card Activated

The backlash knocked Zofia backwards several steps.

"You . . . you're a space cultivator!" she spat accusingly. If she had known his affinity, Zofia would never have challenged him; space cultivators were known to be tricky to deal with. *Damn those slippery rogues!*

Kaelius and Astrid gave each other looks of astonishment. Leontius merely nodded, having already suspected there was more to the new Ascendant. Controlling space itself was no meager feat.

"One strike down, two to go," Slifer reminded her cheekily.

Face still burning with embarrassment and rage, Zofia took a deep breath to calm herself. She would need absolute focus now—this opponent was far trickier than she anticipated.

Activating Sword Heart increased her perception. Now his tricks would prove useless before her foresight. Her qi came off her in waves, trapping Slifer in her Sword Domain. A thousand gleaming swords materialized around her, ready to attack.

With a decisive slash of her blade, the endless sword rain descended upon Slifer from all directions. But before they found their mark, his spherical barrier flashed into existence once more. The wild tempest of blades glanced off harmlessly.

> *Ding!*
> Critical Block Card Activated

"One strike left. Make it count," Slifer said, examining his nails in feigned boredom.

Gripping her sword with white knuckles, Zofia uttered an invocation. The blade ignited into a massive conflagration, scorching the very air. "Burn all things . . . Zelihima!"

She slashed with all her might, unleashing the enormous firestorm point-blank towards Slifer, vaporizing metal and cooking the clouds beneath their feet. If he wished to play with fire, she would grant his wish!

But instead of incinerating Slifer, the raging inferno simply vanished, absorbed into his barrier. Zofia's eyes widened in disbelief. How had he nullified her ultimate technique?

> *Ding!*
> Reflection Barrier Card Activated

Slifer dusted off his robe casually. "Now then, I believe that concludes your three strikes. Allow me to demonstrate how it's done . . . in one strike."

Zofia shook her head in denial. "Impossible! No one except the sect master could . . ."

Her objection died on her lips as Slifer waved his hand, splitting open reality itself. From the yawning rift emerged Zofia's own firestorm, redirected right back at her!

"N-no . . . how is this possible?"

Raising her sword defensively, Zofia poured every ounce of power she had into resisting the hellish flames. But her defense paled before her most powerful technique, the raging firestorm easily overpowered it, slamming into the woman with the force of a collapsing mountain.

By the time the blaze cleared, Zofia remained standing through sheer force of will alone, swaying and half-naked amidst the ruins of cloth and armor. Her flawless skin now appeared cracked and blackened. Through the haze of pain, one thought dominated her mind: *How? How could she have lost to this nobody?*

"Hmm, I expected . . . more."

Silence descended on the Seventh Heaven as Slifer's words sunk in. This unknown newcomer had just casually trounced one of the most powerful women alive. With her own attack, no less.

Ding!
Task Complete: Awe the Ascendant Cultivators
Reward: 1000 Karmic Credit for Each Ascendant Cultivator Awed
Credits Gained: 4000 Karmic Credits

"I'll be taking the cube now," Slifer declared, extending his hand towards Zofia.

Despite the agony, Zofia lifted her head and glared at Slifer with eyes burning nearly as hot as the flames. With a pained grunt, she retrieved the promised essence cube from her storage ring and tossed it towards Slifer's outstretched hand.

Catching the pulsing cube, the Black Rose supreme elder graced Zofia with a small nod. "You have my thanks for the generous *gift.*"

In response, Zofia spat a glob of red phlegm to the deck before limping back to her cloud. Only once settled upon its surface did she retrieve a medicinal pill and consume it. Slowly, muscle and skin began to regrow across her ruined body as the medicine worked its magic.

Ignoring her seething glare, Slifer addressed the remaining Ascendants. "Now then, are we done here?" His tone carried an unspoken warning—no more games. Any other challengers would face similar consequences.

But inwardly, Slifer was praying that they fell for his bluff, he had no more cards that could save him, the two Critical Block Cards and the one Reflection Barrier Card were all he had! Seeing the Ascendant cultivators refuse to meet his eyes, Slifer held back a sigh of relief, the bluff had paid off.

"In that case, let the meeting begin."

CHAPTER SIXTY-TWO

A s we all know, the Inter-Sect Tournament takes place once every century, to decide which disciples enter the Sealed Realm," Leontius continued. "Each sect is allowed a number of guaranteed places, based on how many Ascendant cultivators they possess."

"The Heavenly Light Sect has three Ascendants, so we get three guaranteed slots," Zofia interrupted, sitting taller.

As one of those three Ascendants, she would definitely claim a slot for her personal protégé. The girl showed promise, and the resources of the Sealed Realm would aid her growth immensely.

"The Pure Soul Sect has two Ascendant cultivators, so we shall claim two slots," Leontius said.

Slifer had yet to meet the Pure Soul Sect Master. He wondered what sort of righteous paragon they must be, to match someone like Leontius.

"One slot for the White Tiger Sect," Astrid declared. She had already chosen which elite disciple would inherit that coveted spot. The boy showed exceptional talent with the White Tiger and deserved the chance.

"And the Black Rose Sect will have two slots," Slifer commented.

All eyes turned to Kaelius, waiting for him to claim the Black Heart Sect's allotment. "One slot for my sect as well," he said after a pause.

In truth, Kaelius wished he could claim more slots. Unfortunately, the Black Heart Sect only had himself at the Ascendant level currently. A deficiency he was working to remedy, the only issue being he didn't trust his grand elders enough to help them break through.

"Excellent. That leaves ten remaining tournament slots, to be contested by the most talented disciples of each sect," Leontius said. "Now we must decide which sect shall host the Inter-Sect Tournament this time."

At his words, Zofia shot to her feet. "The Heavenly Light Sect will be hosting the tournament, of course!" She stated it as if it were already decided. "We hosted the last two tournaments, so by tradition the honor falls to us again.

"Also," Zofia continued, "our Cloudrise Arena is the largest and most renowned dueling ground in the Mortal Realm. Its facilities and protections are unmatched, perfect for such a competition."

Her tone left no room for argument. After all, who could possibly object to the most powerful sect in the Mortal Realm?

Slifer listened to her ramblings with a detached interest, leaning casually on the railing of his ship. He weighed the pros and cons of the Black Rose Sect hosting the prestigious tournament.

The main advantage would be avoiding an unfamiliar environment filled with potential threats. Slifer disliked leaving the relative safety of his own territory; venturing into another sect's domain meant surrendering control. And it would be twice as difficult to hide his identity there.

Not to mention needing to interact with more self-righteous cultivators . . . I would rather not.

Remaining within the Black Rose Sect's headquarters also granted the home advantage for their disciples. Familiarity with the terrain could prove the difference between victory and defeat during critical rounds.

It's like in sports, teams always do better when they play at home.

However, being a host had disadvantages as well, if any conflicts arose, as the supreme elder, it was expected that he would intervene.

I can't just slip away . . .

Also, entertaining a horde of cultivators just sounded exhausting.

But at least I'll be in my element.

"Actually, I believe it's the Black Rose Sect's turn to host the tournament this time."

His casual interjection cut off Zofia's building momentum. She turned on him, eyes blazing.

"Absolutely not! There's no way I'd let a bunch of demonic cultivators organize something so important! It is the Heavenly Light Sect's duty to steer the righteous path forward."

She emphasized "righteous" while looking disdainfully in Slifer's direction. In her eyes, he and his whole demonic sect were a blight needing to be cleansed.

But Slifer only shrugged, not bothered by her scathing tone, she was just another hypocrite in his eyes. "Don't be petty."

He tapped his fingers against one of the cannons before continuing. "As the newest supreme elder, I wish to prove my sect's capabilities by hosting this tournament. Don't you agree, honored elders?"

Slifer directed the last part to the other Ascendants. Outnumbered, Zofia fumed but stayed silent, waiting to hear their reactions. *Surely they wouldn't actually consider allowing those vile demonic cultivators to host something so important?*

Surprisingly, Astrid was the first to respond. "The White Tiger Sect has no objections." She ignored Zofia's shocked look. "If Supreme Elder Slifer believes his sect is ready for the responsibility, we shall not stand in his way."

After her initial dismissive attitude towards Slifer, even Astrid found herself gaining respect for the mysterious man. The way he handled the earlier crises earned her vote.

Leontius smiled reassuringly at the spluttering Zofia. "Come now, let us give him a chance. The Inter-Sect Tournament is meant to be an opportunity for all the sects to come together in fellowship."

His gently chiding tone made Zofia duck her head grudgingly. When the kindly supreme elder phrased it like that, even she couldn't continue arguing so stubbornly. At least not without losing face.

Kaelius merely nodded. "I have no objections either. The Black Heart Sect will respect whatever is decided here."

His bland words gave no hint of his true thoughts. In truth, Kaelius looked forward to visiting the Black Rose Sect territory. It would grant him a rare opportunity to investigate the Black Rose Sect Master who was rumored to be close to Immortal Ascension.

Realizing she stood alone, Zofia slowly retook her seat. "Fine! The Heavenly Light Sect will . . . tolerate this break from tradition just this once," she bit out as though she had a say in the matter.

Slifer got the sense that it physically pained her to make that concession. Well, letting go of petty grudges was an important lesson for one to learn, one he assumed someone so old should have learned by now.

"Then it's decided. We shall reconvene in one month's time at the Black Rose Sect for the official start of the tournament." Leontius smiled.

The Pure Soul elder's faith in harmony between the sects shone through.

He seems oddly naïve for someone whose lived a few millennia. Slifer hoped Leontius's idealism wouldn't backfire one day. *Or maybe this is all an act . . . wouldn't surprise me.*

With the matter of the tournament settled, the Ascendants exchanged a few more pleasantries before gradually dispersing.

Back in the Disciplinary Hall, Slifer leaned back and stretched out on his throne, finally relaxing his stiff shoulders. Dealing with those insufferable elders had been utterly exhausting.

At least the meeting had accomplished its purpose—the Black Rose Sect would host the Inter-Sect Tournament. As Slifer reached for a steaming bun from the feast laid out on the table beside him, the doors to the hall creaked open. Glancing up in annoyance at the interruption, he saw Grand Elder Wyatt shuffle inside.

Ah yes, time to deal with another nuisance. Slifer's eyes narrowed as he recalled Wyatt's attempt to sabotage him by lying about the time of the meeting.

Slifer only realized when Zofia commented that he had turned up late . . . three days late.

"To what do I owe the pleasure, Grand Elder Wyatt?" Slifer asked mildly, setting down the bun. "Have you come to beg forgiveness for your lapse in judgment earlier?"

Wyatt froze mid-step as Slifer's words registered, his wrinkled face paling. *So the brat realized I intentionally tried to make him look foolish before the other elders!*

"S-Supreme Elder, of course not!" Wyatt sputtered, sweat beading on his forehead. The events of the Ascendant Meet had reached his ears; he never expected that the supreme elder would be able to defeat Zofia, supreme elder of the Heavenly Light Sect in one move!

"It was merely . . . an oversight on my part, no harm was intended!"

"Hmm, likely story," Slifer snorted. "But intentions matter little, only results. And your bungling nearly cost this sect greatly." *But more importantly, nearly cost me! If Amelia could whip some sense into this old fool that would be perfect. Unfortunately, our cultivation is just too low to beat up this old man.* "However, the matter resolved itself nicely," Slifer continued. "I'm feeling rather magnanimous at the moment, so I believe no further punishment is required."

Wyatt sagged in relief. *Thank the heavens for small mercies!* Perhaps he could still salvage something out of this mess. "You are too kind, Supreme Elder," he fawned. "Truly, your generosity knows no bounds!"

Slifer rolled his eyes at the blatant flattery before fixing Wyatt with a piercing stare that instantly silenced his groveling. "However, steps must be taken to avoid any further . . . oversights," he continued. "Effective immediately, I will be taking control of the Treasury, *temporarily.*"

Slifer knew the old man wouldn't allow him to take it permanently; if Slifer pushed him into a corner then the grand elder would retaliate with another scheme. And Slifer did not need Wyatt monitoring his actions.

"What? You can't!" Wyatt burst out before catching himself. He attempted to smooth over his outburst.

"Er, that is to say . . . the Treasury has always been under my discretion during the sect master's reclusion. To disturb the natural order over one small mistake would be premature, don't you agree?"

Wyatt forced a placating smile, though inside he seethed at this outrageous demand. Relinquishing control of the sect's wealth was untenable! He would lose all standing.

But Slifer was unmoved by his arguments, the grand elder needed to understand that he wasn't a pushover.

"While I understand this may disrupt our 'natural order,' extreme circumstances call for extreme measures. Let us call this an . . . insurance policy, to avoid potential catastrophes during my handling of the Inter-Sect Tournament."

Recognizing there was no convincing Slifer, Wyatt bowed. "Of course, Supreme Elder. I . . . I shall begin the process immediately. The Treasury will be fully under your command within the hour."

"See that it is." Slifer leaned back casually, popping another dumpling into his mouth.

Wyatt took the cue and quickly bowed out of the hall, but not before his wrinkled face briefly twisted into a ferocious scowl once his back was turned.

That impudent brat! Wyatt cursed silently before schooling his features back into a mask of subservience. *Patience is required here, a lot of patience.*

With the sect's power structure now firmly under his thumb, Slifer retired to his private chambers. An important matter required his attention—preparing for the Sealed Realm.

He had already given Elder Fred responsibility on arranging the intricate details of the tournament, the old man didn't seem too pleased with the added work, but Slifer had to admit Fred was quite efficient.

Slifer looked at the card floating in front of him.

> Avatar Card: Create a complete clone of the user that can cultivate independently.
> Warning: The avatar cannot access the System or its cards.

Slifer nodded thoughtfully. If he created an avatar, it could enter the Sealed Realm competition legitimately.

The avatar would enter the competition and earn their sect another slot in the Sealed Realm. Then Slifer could reap the benefits and keep his identity hidden. It was a foolproof plan.

But there was one obvious problem—without access to the System, the avatar would not have access to any cards. It would need to cultivate through traditional methods.

No pain, no gain. Slifer shrugged. *Also, it would be a useful lesson in discipline . . . for the clone.*

First though, he needed to disguise his avatar's appearance. Having a second elderly Slifer running around wouldn't help his cause.

He had the perfect solution—Another Face Card!

> Another Face Card
> Description: Allows the user to change appearance for up to 6 months.

Activate!

A character customization panel materialized before him, and Slifer clapped his hands together.

It's just like a video game!

After adjusting the various sliders and toggles, an appearance emerged that he felt would be worthy of his avatar: a handsome young man, around eighteen years old, with tousled black hair and piercing green eyes. The lean athletic physique with six stone-hard abs certainly didn't hurt either.

This guy could easily pass for a model! Handsome little bastard.

With another wave of his hand, Slifer confirmed the new look. Before his eyes, his wrinkled hands smoothed, and white hair darkened. Glancing at his reflection in a nearby water basin, Slifer nodded in approval at the roguish teen smirking back at him.

"Not bad, not bad at all," he mused, turning his face this way and that as if admiring a work of art. After a few moments enjoying his temporary makeover, it was at last time to create the clone.

This time, when Slifer activated the Avatar Card, the process went smoothly. On the floor before him materialized a perfect copy of his new look, bare skin layered over lean muscle, limbs sprawled haphazardly, it looked like the clone was just waking up.

With a soft groan, the clone opened his eyes—the same vivid green as Slifer's temporary ones—and slowly stood, gazing curiously around the chamber.

"Well now, let's see what we have here," Slifer murmured, beginning to circle the clone closely as if inspecting a prize stallion.

The resemblance truly was uncanny, from the unruly dark hair down to the elegant hands and feet. In fact . . . Slifer's gaze dipped lower, and his eyes widened in surprise.

"Wow, is that what I look like under all those robes?" He let out an impressed whistle. "I chose well during character creation!"

The clone followed his gaze downwards and chuckled. "I know, I'm gorgeous. What can I say? We have excellent taste." His voice emerged as a deeper echo of Slifer's own.

Slifer laughed out loud at that. Perhaps creating a clone wasn't such a bad idea after all. It seemed they shared the same witty sense of humor.

I have my own Kage Bunshin!

After testing the clone's capabilities, Slifer was glad to find it an exact copy in every way except for System access. The two of them could even share thoughts and experiences if Slifer activated that function.

This meant Slifer could share any insights or techniques he uncovered with his clone, and vice versa. It was like having a customizable player two by his side!

Now there was just one problem—what to name his new disciple? Somehow "Little Slifer" didn't seem quite right.

The clone pursed his lips. "What about . . . Zack?" he eventually suggested.

Slifer froze in surprise. *Zack* . . . that had been his name before all this cultivation business began.

"Zack, eh? I like it. Has a nice ring to it," Slifer laughed, clasping the avatar's shoulder. "Don't think I'll go easy on you just because you're my copy."

Zack gave a wry grin at that. "Wouldn't dream of it."

The two shared a look.

"Welcome to the Black Rose Sect . . . my disciple."

"I'm at your command . . . Master."

Yes, Slifer had a good feeling about this partnership.

CHAPTER SIXTY-THREE

Slifer stood shirtless beneath a waterfall, the crashing water pounding down on his shoulders. In each hand he held a massive boulder, their rough surfaces digging into his palms and fingers as he focused on maintaining his grip.

As much as he hated working out, he couldn't let his body cultivation fall behind.

After a few more minutes, Slifer heard a distinct crack as the tendons in his arms stretched and expanded. He could feel the Beast Meat Qi coursing through him, assimilating into his body. His lean muscles grew tighter, more defined.

> *Ding!*
> Congratulations!
> You Have Broken Through to the Late Foundation Establishment Realm
> Reward: 250 Karmic Credits

Just one more sub-realm then my spiritual and body cultivation will be the same!

Slifer planned to enter the Core Formation Realm as a double cultivator.

Laughing, he turned off the qi restricting cuff.

With the limiter removed, the boulders now felt like mere pebbles in his hands. He casually flung them out towards the lake with a flick of his wrists.

The massive rocks went flying out in a blur, kicking up huge spouts of water as they skipped across the surface.

One of the boulders zoomed to the shore where Nomed was walking. At the last second, he noticed and leapt out of the way. The boulder hit the shore with explosive force, sending debris flying in all directions.

Is . . . is he trying to kill me?

Nomed clutched at his chest, breathing heavily. He glanced back towards the waterfall just in time to see his master waving, apparently oblivious to how close he'd come to crushing his own disciple.

"Ah, Nomed, you're finally here." Slifer gestured for Nomed to come closer, as he reached for a robe hanging from a nearby tree.

Earlier, Slifer had dismissed his avatar to go cultivate in seclusion. He planned to eventually introduce Zack as a new disciple, but first he needed to deal with Hughie's wavering loyalty. So, he decided, whilst he waited for Morvran to return, he would do some training and check up on his new disciple.

The young man quickly gathered himself and rushed over, going down on one knee before Slifer.

"Master, you called me?"

"Yes, how goes your cultivation with the Cathedral of Celestial Radiance Scripture?"

As part of the Qi Refining stage, Nomed had to construct a cathedral within his dantian to store qi.

Nomed shifted awkwardly, rubbing the back of his neck. "Truth be told, Master . . . my progress has been slower than I would like. I've only managed to finish about half of the cathedral so far. I suppose that puts me at the peak of the fifth level of Qi Condensation. My talents are meager compared to my Senior Brothers."

No, talent isn't the issue. Slifer's eyes narrowed.

With a talent of 8, Nomed should have been at the Seventh Stage of Qi Refining by now.

The Cathedral of Celestial Radiance Scripture just isn't compatible with Nomed, I should try to convince him to pick a different method. He's only just begun his cultivation journey; it would be better to change methods now than later.

"Have you considered switching to a different cultivation method? The Scripture of Broken Shadows may complement your constitution better . . ."

But Nomed rapidly shook his head. "No, Master! It . . . it has to be this one!"

Slifer held back a sigh. The boy's stubbornness was admirable, yet counterproductive. But then again, the boy was a protagonist-like figure, it was best to let him decide his own path.

I just need to give some advice when I can.

"The path of cultivation is yours to walk, and you must follow your heart," Slifer said sagely. "Keep working hard, and you may earn a chance to enter the Inter-Sect Tournament and . . . maybe even the Sealed Realm."

At the mention of the Sealed Realm, Nomed's eyes lit up, though he quickly hid it.

"I will try my best, Master."

Slifer nodded, stroking his beard when a thought suddenly occurred. "Come to think of it, I haven't yet imparted any techniques to you, have I?"

While a cultivation method provided the core foundation, supplementary techniques were needed for offense, defense, and movement. Without any techniques, a cultivator was a sitting duck!

Slifer waved a hand, summoning one of his death warriors.

"Escort Nomed to the Treasury. He can pick one attack skill, one defense skill, and one movement technique." The death warrior bowed in acknowledgement.

Now that Slifer controlled the sect Treasury, he could freely hand out techniques to his disciples without needing to waste credits. But he was careful not to overwhelm Nomed by giving too many options right away. One of each type would be enough for now.

But it wouldn't hurt to dangle a few more for encouragement.

Turning back to Nomed, Slifer said, "If you can break through to the Foundation Establishment Realm before the Inter-Sect Tournament, I'll let you pick another set of techniques."

"Thank you, Master!" Nomed bowed before following the death warrior.

Nodding to himself, Slifer reflected on how smoothly everything was proceeding. Perhaps he had a knack for this whole "master" business after all.

Ding!
Your Disciple Nomed's Loyalty Increased By 3%

Only three percent? Oh . . . maybe I'm not so good at this after all.

As he was lost wondering what went wrong, Morvran appeared before him.

Slifer's face cracked into a smile at the sight of his bald lackey. "How was the mission?"

Locating the hidden village of his wayward disciple's secret lover had proved unusually difficult. But if anyone could accomplish it, it was Morvran. There was a reason he was the original's right-hand man.

"It was a success, Master." Morvran relayed the village's exact coordinates.

"Ha ha, excellent work!"

Morvran flushed at the praise. "Think nothing of it, Master. Serving you is this one's sole purpose."

As good as that is for me, it is a . . . sad life.

"Nonetheless, I am grateful," Slifer replied. "Come, let us pay this young lady a visit."

With a rippling motion of his fingers, Slifer opened a portal. He strode through, with Morvran close behind. The gateway sealed shut after them.

They emerged along a dusty road on the outskirts of the village. The common folk milling about the street froze at the sudden appearance of two immortals. A young child pointed and squealed, "Look mama, immortals!"

The mother quickly gathered up her child, eyeing the strangers warily. "Hush now, don't stare . . ." she murmured.

Slifer raised his hands in a peaceful gesture, offering what he hoped was a disarming smile. "We're only here to visit Oliviare. Could anyone point me in the right direction?"

The villagers looked at one another. The old man in front of them had one of those faces that you just couldn't trust.

After a brief pause, one of the villagers spoke up. "That'd be the place there, Lord Immortal," he said, pointing to a modest but well-kept cottage down the lane.

"Here." Slifer flicked a golden coin to the villager, who fumbled to catch it.

"Bless you, Immortal!" the man cried in delight, quickly pocketing the coin. The other villagers murmured in relief, seeing that the immortals were not like the other ones that visited their village a few months back.

Villagers really are simple. Slifer allowed himself a small smile at winning them over so easily.

Approaching the front door, Slifer rapped his knuckles against the wood. He thought it was better not to simply barge into the home unannounced like most immortals would have done.

A few seconds later the door creaked open, revealing a petite girl with chestnut hair and sapphire eyes set in a heart-shaped face of flawless cream.

"..."

N-no wonder Hughie fell for her! Slifer sucked in a sharp breath. She was the very image of a classical jade beauty.

After a few moments of awkward silence, the young woman bit her lip anxiously. The strange old man was just . . . staring. Had she opened the door to some senile vagrant?

"C-can I help you, sir?"

Slifer coughed, realizing his gawking had nearly frightened the poor woman away.

"Oliviare, is it? I'm Hughie's master."

At the mention of Hughie, the girl seemed to relax. A faint blush colored her cheeks. "Oh yes, that's me. Is Hughie here?" She craned her neck trying to see behind Slifer. Finding only a plump baldy there, her face fell.

Slifer shook his head. "No, I'm afraid not. But I was hoping to speak with you. Can we come inside?"

"Oh, please come in!"

Walking inside, Slifer immediately noticed an older man sitting by the window, whittling away at a small block of wood. He had thinning white hair and resembled Oliviare somewhat. The man looked up, taking in Slifer's cultivator robes. His expression darkened.

"Oi, girl! What're you thinking, inviting a strange immortal into our home?" Brom stood protectively in front of his daughter.

Slifer couldn't help but agree with the old man—as soon as Hughie's name was mentioned, the girl was a little too quick to let her guard down.

Not that she could have done anything to protect herself from an immortal. Slifer held back a sigh. The disparity between mortals and cultivators was too great of a chasm, resistance against an immortal was useless.

"This is Hughie's master, father."

At the familiar name, the old man relaxed slightly, though his eyes remained suspicious. "Hmph. And what business does he have here?" A thought seemed to occur to him, and his scowl deepened. "If you've come to snatch my girl, you can turn right back around!"

Slifer's brows shot up in surprise. He had expected curiosity, perhaps suspicion given their immortal status, but not outright hostility.

And such assumptions! Though it was common knowledge that old immortals loved to kidnap young girls. *I'm not actually an old man! And I'm definitely not dumb enough to steal a protagonist's lover . . .*

"It is nothing like that, I would like to take Oliviare into my sect as a disciple."

Since Slifer wasn't planning on taking Oliviare as his own personal disciple, the System would have no issue with it. In truth, Slifer didn't care which of the elders took her in, as long as Hughie was happy, that was all that mattered.

And then we can work together to deal with that grandpa . . .

Oliviare's eyes grew round with surprise at the offer. She never imagined she might have the talent to become an immortal herself.

"The hell she will!" Brom snapped, jabbing his carving knife towards Slifer. "I'll not have some immortal coot taking my daughter away, no matter how grand he thinks he is! Your kind brings nothing but trouble."

At his side, Morvran bristled angrily. "Mind your tongue, mortal! You are talking to the supreme elder of the Black Rose Sect. Show respect!"

Slifer gently motioned for Morvran to be calm. Personally, Slifer was more shocked than offended. This sort of defiance was . . . intriguing. The old Slifer would have just killed the insolent fool on the spot.

Most mortal parents would be overjoyed at the prospect of their child joining a sect. Just how was he to persuade this stubborn old bastard? Brute force clearly wasn't the answer.

As he pondered this dilemma, a loud gurgling sound erupted from Slifer's stomach.

Oliviare's eyes widened at the sound, she made a move towards the hearth, saying, "You must be hungry, Master! Please allow me to prepare something quickly."

"No . . . there's no need for that." An idea was forming in Slifer's mind. "In fact . . . I believe a celebration is in order tonight. A feast for the entire village!"

"A fine meal won't be enough to sway me." Brom narrowed his eyes. "You immortals always want something in return for your 'generosity.'" He spat the last word.

Morvran once again took a step forward, but Slifer held him back. As much as he liked Morvran standing up for him, antagonizing the man further wouldn't help matters. No, he would need a soft touch here.

"This is merely a small gesture of goodwill, nothing more." Slifer gave his most innocent smile.

The old man continued glaring but said nothing more. Slifer mentally counted this as a minor victory. He had planted the first seeds. Now he just needed to help them grow.

Night fell, and the village square was lit up with lanterns and a great bonfire. The air was filled with music, laughter, and the mouthwatering smell of roasting beast meat.

Slifer sat in the seat of honor with Morvran standing dutifully behind him. Slifer had tried to encourage Morvran to sit down and join them, but Morvran refused, saying something about how he needed to stay sober whilst at work.

Food does drive him crazy . . . hmm, probably something to do with the Great Cock bloodline . . .

To Slifer's left were Oliviare and her father Brom, eating with somewhat less enthusiasm than their neighbors.

The villagers were thoroughly enjoying the rare treat of beast meat and fine wine. The children ran about playing games, while adults chatted and sang merrily. Many bowed or waved in thanks towards Slifer for his generosity. He nodded and smiled in return. He had to give off the impression that he was approachable and not a recluse with zero social skills. They were the ones known to resort to kidnapping.

Overall, his plan seemed to be working smoothly. The villagers were warming to him, and Brom was even engaging in small talk with him.

Just a little more time and effort, Slifer mused, *and the girl will be mine . . . Err, I mean, Hughie's.*

As Slifer took a sip of the Immortal Wine, his spiritual sense detected something in the darkness beyond the village outskirts.

Multiple somethings, in fact. And headed this way.

"Well, well," Slifer murmured under his breath. "Right on schedule . . ."

CHAPTER SIXTY-FOUR

T*hirty minutes later.*

And my daughter Calista, oh you must meet her!" Vilhelm bellowed, swaying tipsily as he gestured towards a plain-faced girl across the village square. "A true beauty, ripe for the picking! Strong hips, perfect for bearing many sons. You won't find a better bride in the region, I tell you!"

The old man laughed uproariously, as if he'd just told the most hilarious joke in history. Slifer nodded along politely, only half-listening as he tore into a juicy beast leg coated in savory sauce. Slifer loved food, but dry meat was the bane of his existence.

As for the drunken villager's ramblings or his daughter, Slifer had zero interest. Mortals were often quiet in the presence of cultivators but a drink or two was enough to change that.

Best to simply let the man prattle on.

Most of Slifer's attention was focused out beyond the edges of the village, where his spiritual sense tracked the multiple figures closing in through the darkness. Nine to be precise, they surrounded the village from all directions. And their cultivation . . . Core Formation at least.

Slifer's eyes flicked to Morvran, and with a subtle tilt of his head, signaled for his companion to take no action yet. Morvran gave an almost imperceptible nod in response. They would wait for the other party to make the first move.

"A fine strong lass, my Calista!" Vilhelm rambled on, oblivious to the silent exchange happening right in front of him. "Sturdy, obedient, and skilled in all the womanly arts—"

A bloodcurdling scream tore through the air. The music and chatter died abruptly as all heads turned towards the cry. Vilhelm blinked sluggishly, wine sloshing from his cup.

"Eh? What's all this then?"

He peered at the seat beside him, only just realizing it was now empty. That strange immortal who'd been there moments before had vanished. And his grim bald sidekick too. Odd, very odd.

Brom and Oliviare exchanged tense glances from where they sat nearby.

"I warned you these immortals would bring trouble," Brom grumbled.

"We don't know that, Father. Don't be so quick to judge." Oliviare shook her head but her voice lacked conviction. Her father did have a point, whenever immortals visited the village, trouble seemed to follow. Always.

"Humph, stay close to me, girl," Brom ordered, standing protectively by her side as they began carefully making their way back to their house.

Meanwhile, the screams had come from the far side of the village, where a young woman who had decided to leave the feast early was now cowering behind the corner of a building.

Before her stood a hulking black beast, with the sleek fur and feline features of a panther. Violet, predatory eyes gleamed with bloodlust as it stalked towards the frozen girl, razor fangs bared.

With a guttural snarl, the beast sprung forward, lethal claws extended to tear through flesh and bone. But faster than a blink, a blinding arc of silver flashed through the air. Blood sprayed, and the panther's headless body crashed to the ground with a heavy thud, its severed head rolling away into the shadows.

Behind the corpse stood an elderly man in orange robes, face grim as he flicked the residual gore off the blade.

The young woman looked up at the old man and tried to say something—her mouth was working, but no sound emerged.

Slifer wrinkled his nose at the stench of voided bowels.

Always unsightly business, that.

"Go inside where it's safe," he instructed before shifting his focus back to the matter at hand.

Ding!
You Killed a Core Formation Beast
25 Karmic Credits Gained
Ding!
You Killed a Core Formation Beast
25 Karmic Credits Gained
Ding!
Save the Villagers
Reward: 100 Karmic Credits
Current Progress 4/9 Beasts Defeated

Slifer's spiritual sense rapidly swept the area, taking stock of the situation. There were five panther-like beasts left, and Morvran was making quick work of them.

Slifer recognized the beasts from the original's memories, they were known as Pantherions. They typically hunted in groups, known as prides. The pride that was attacking the village were at the Core Formation Realm.

Slifer's eyes narrowed in consideration. These beasts were clearly more cunning than the average wild animal. They had been patiently stalking this village, waiting for the right moment to strike. The scent of roasting beast meat from tonight's feast must have lured them in prematurely.

In truth, this surprise attack aligned perfectly with Slifer's own intentions for the night. He had known the panther beasts were lurking nearby and planned to draw them out in order to display his strength and protection to the villagers. Now they could witness for themselves what would have befallen them without the cultivators' intervention. A necessary step to softening old Brom's stance against the sect taking in his precious daughter.

"But Core Formation beasts attacking a simple village . . ."

Typically only Qi Condensation or Foundation Establishment creatures would actively hunt mortals. Those at Core Formation and above required the rich spiritual energy found in cultivator cores to advance.

The Pantherions were stealthy, opportunistic hunters, but mortals were essentially useless to them, so why were they here?

The chilling sound of a low, rumbling growl snapped Slifer from his musings. Whirling around, he saw another Pantherion creeping from the shadows. It moved cautiously, muscles tensed as it sniffed the air. Its eyes landed on the headless corpse of its fellow panther and widened in shock.

"Oh good, you're finally here. I was starting to think you got lost on the way to the feast." Slifer waved his bloodstained sword in a beckoning gesture.

The Pantherion tensed, fangs bared threateningly. But it hesitated to attack.

Slifer's cultivation level was only at Peak Foundation Establishment, after all. By all rights, these Core Formation creatures could make short work of him. Yet this human exuded an air of absolute confidence, even eagerness for battle.

It was . . . strange.

The Pantherion paced, its eyes locked onto the human. The prudent thing would be to retreat for now. But its pride stung at abandoning its fallen comrade so easily.

Sensing its indecision, Slifer laughed. "As much as I'd love to play with you all night, I've more important matters to attend to."

With that, Slifer lunged forward and swung his sword towards the Pantherion's head. The beast yowled in surprise and narrowly dodged the attack, leaping aside at the last instant. Its eyes lit up as it realized that its prey was slower than it expected. Perhaps it had overestimated this human.

It pounced, claws extended, and fangs bared as it aimed for the vulnerable flesh of Slifer's neck.

But Slifer's face showed no hint of fear at the incoming assault. Instead his lips pulled back in a fierce, mocking grin just before the killing blow could land. "Gotcha."

In the next instant, the panther's claws and fangs passed harmlessly through Slifer's body as though it was an illusion. Its eyes went wide with shock as it stumbled and slammed into the ground where the human had stood only a heartbeat ago.

Before the disoriented beast could react, Slifer's form solidified behind it and neatly slashed through the vulnerable back of its neck with a precise swing of his sword. With a final snarl, the light faded from the beast's eyes and its lifeless body collapsed to the dusty ground.

Ding!
You Killed a Core Formation Beast
25 Karmic Credits Gained

"Heh, love that trick," Slifer chuckled to himself as he flicked the blood from his blade. The phase technique was incredibly useful. And if he was being honest, it made him feel pretty badass too.

If only I could spam it like Obito did . . .

Just as Slifer got caught up admiring his handiwork, his spiritual sense picked up a powerful aura and it seemed to be heading towards Oliviare's house.

"Shit!"

As Oliviare stepped inside the house, Brom quickly shut the door behind them and slid the iron bolt securely into place. He doubted such measures would stop a rampaging beast, but the action provided some meager comfort nonetheless.

"There now, we should be safe enough here," Brom said, attempting to inject confidence into his voice. Inside, his heart pounded against his ribs.

"Do . . . do you think everyone else is okay, Father?" Oliviare asked softly, voicing the worry gnawing at both their minds.

Brom chose not to voice the bleak thoughts swirling through his mind. The others likely weren't okay. When beasts attacked settlements this small and remote, rarely did anyone escape with their lives. Instead he merely grunted, settling on a stool by the hearth and attempting to project a calm demeanor. He had to be strong for his daughter.

"All we can do is wait here for now and pray," he rumbled wearily, removing a chunk of wood and a small paring knife from his vest. Fighting against these beasts would be suicide and he would not risk his daughter's life. Focusing on the familiar task of whittling would help settle his nerves.

The rhythmic rasping of blade on wood filled the heavy silence as he carefully shaved curling strips from the block clutched between calloused fingers.

"That man—Hughie's master—he seemed kind," Oliviare said after a while. "Surely he would help protect the villagers."

Brom's steady strokes paused briefly at the mention of the white-bearded stranger. "Humph . . . or he and his portly companion ran at the first sign of danger," he muttered darkly.

Before Oliviare could offer any rebuttal, Brom's head jerked up, the hairs on his neck and arms standing on end. The air had changed—grown heavier somehow.

It was here.

Oliviare gasped softly as she too sensed it, eyes darting fearfully between the door and her father.

Together they rose slowly from their seats, Brom placing himself between his daughter and whatever lay in wait beyond that feeble wooden barrier. His palms grew slick around the grip of his carving knife. Memories of the last time monsters had visited their village flickered through his mind, bringing bile to the back of his throat. His wife . . . she . . . no, he would not let that happen again.

A floorboard just outside the door creaked under some tremendous weight. Brom's breath stalled in his lungs. Silence hung for a torturous moment. Then with an ear-splitting crack, the barred door exploded inwards, shredded by claws longer than a man's arm.

A huge Pantherion stalked inside, lips peeled back to reveal jagged teeth capable of crushing bone. Hot saliva dripped from its maw as violet eyes focused on the cowering mortals. Powerful limbs tensed, ready to pounce and tear these humans apart in an instant.

But quick as a flash, Brom lunged forward with a wordless cry. Years of handling sharp tools had honed his reflexes and precision.

But the resistance of a mortal was futile.

Massive paws batted Brom aside as easily as one might a bothersome fly. The old carpenter flew across the room and hit the far wall with bone-jarring force before crumpling to the floor.

"Father!" Oliviare cried, dodging around the thrashing monster. She fell to her knees at Brom's side, desperately pressing her apron against the deep gashes torn across his abdomen by those razor talons. Blood seeped hot over her fingers no matter how hard she tried to stanch the flow.

Seeing the brute turn towards them, Oliviare curled over her father's body protectively. She squeezed her eyes shut, bracing for the inevitable as the Pantherion towered over her.

Hughie's master, where are you?

CHAPTER SIXTY-FIVE

Slifer reappeared inside Oliviare's cottage just in time to see an enormous, clawed paw pressed down on Oliviare's back.

The Pantherion was easily twice the size of the others, with fur the deep purple of twilight. It turned its head towards Slifer. A low snarl emanated from its throat.

The message was clear. One wrong move from him, and the girl would pay the price.

Slifer clenched his jaw, weighing his options.

Of all the ways this could have gone, getting caught in a hostage situation ranked pretty low on the list. I didn't even know beasts were smart enough to take hostages!

From the weight of leader's aura, the Pantherion King had clearly reached the Nascent Soul stage. Slifer then remembered that Pantherions were able to reach human-like intelligence earlier than most beasts. Negotiating safely out of this predicament wouldn't be easy.

"Seems we've found ourselves at an impasse here," Slifer called out mildly. "So, what do you want?"

The Pantherion rumbled again in response.

Right, no baby dragon around to conveniently translate. I'll just have to wing it.

Slifer tried to decipher meaning from the Pantherion's noises and body language.

The beast appeared reluctant to actually make good on its threat unless provoked. It seemed like it knew that its ambush had failed and that Slifer wasn't the Foundation Establishment cultivator that his aura indicated he was. Now the beast just wanted to secure safe passage for the remaining members of its pride.

As for why it targeted Oliviare, either the beast was intelligent enough to sense that the girl was the only villager Slifer cared about, or Slifer just had dog shit luck.

No matter what happens, I can't let her die . . . Hmm, I think I can work with this.

"How about we make a deal?"

The Pantherion scoffed at the notion of cooperating with the man who'd slaughtered half its kin. As if reading its thoughts, Slifer laughed.

"Look, you attacked us first. If I was set on killing you all, would any of your pride still be breathing? I'm offering you a chance here."

Grudgingly, the Pantherion had to acknowledge the logic in his words.

Among beasts, it was kill or be killed. Temporary alliances were common when mutually beneficial. And right now, with most of the male members of his pride dead, the females and cubs were vulnerable. Perhaps this arrangement could work. But how could this human help him, and what exactly was being asked in return?

Sensing he needed to show his worth, Slifer subtly adjusted his aura until it surpassed even the Nascent Soul beast—stopping just short of Half-Step Origin Realm.

Who knew the Peak Slifer Aura Card would be useful.

Immediately the Pantherion tensed, claws flexing as that oppressive pressure settled over it.

"Let me sweeten the deal. Swear your allegiance, and I'll help you rule the nearby lands." Slifer smiled.

The Pride was in a precarious situation. Before the ambush, the Pantherion Pride was one of the weaker beast groups in the area, had it not been for their speed and intelligence, they would have been wiped out long ago. If what the human was promising was true . . .

After a stretched silence, a fire of ambition lit up the Pantherion's gaze. It dipped its head and stepped away from Oliviare.

Well, I'm glad that worked out, and here I thought I'd have to waste another card.

Crisis averted. For now, anyway.

Slifer's aura dissipated as he approached the girl and her father. He pulled a small brown pill from his sleeve.

"Here—he needs to take this quickly."

Brom's eyelids fluttered weakly at the sound of Slifer's voice. With Oliviare's help, he managed to tilt his head back enough to swallow the medicinal pellet.

The effect was immediate—color returned to Brom's cheeks as the bleeding stopped and torn flesh began knitting back together. Within moments, only faint scars remained across his abdomen.

As Brom struggled to rise on still-shaky legs, he eyed Slifer warily. "I suppose you think yourself quite clever then?" he huffed, nodding pointedly to the hulking Pantherion King. "Lure the beasts here with a feast, only to play the hero?"

Slifer raised his brows, looking vaguely offended by the accusation. "The Pantherion Pride has been stalking your village for some time. I sensed them closing in even before we arrived. It was mere coincidence that provided an opportunity to . . . ah, kill two birds with one stone."

Brom's expression remained skeptical. Slifer tilted his head towards the Pantherion King. "Ask it yourself if you don't believe me."

After a moment of what seemed like silent communication between man and beast, Brom grunted ambiguously. "It seems you weren't lying. But the arrival of you immortals always brings trouble. You can't blame an old man for being cautious."

Cautious? That's a . . . nice way of putting it. The old man was downright rude, but Slifer didn't care enough to argue, he did see the old guy's point.

"I understand. I know you only want to keep your daughter safe, but left unprotected, even a peaceful village such as yours can become prey." Slifer placed a hand gently on Brom's shoulder. "The path of cultivation could give her the power to defend herself, when you no longer can. Is that not worth thinking about?"

Brom stared silently at the ground. When he finally spoke, his voice was heavy with resignation. "You may be right. I'm just an old fool, I can't decide for her. The girl must choose her own path now."

Oliviare clutched her father's arm, smiling up at him brightly. "Don't say such things, father. But becoming an immortal could help keep our family and village safe. With your blessing, I will try my best."

Brom patted her hand. "You have it, though it pains me to see you leave. Do an old man proud."

Slifer had considered changing Brom's mortal fate, but he knew that it would be extremely difficult for the old man to cultivate at his age. The Body Tempering stage was too difficult—most mortals couldn't bear it, some even described it as torture.

If it was like my situation, where he would be recultivating, that would be a different situation.

Seeing the father and daughter pair embrace, Slifer motioned to the Pantherion King to follow him.

On the way to Morvran, the Pantherion King recovered corpses of its kin. When they finally found Morvran, they arrived in time to see the bald steward grinning savagely as he smashed the heads of two Pantherions together repeatedly.

The Pantherion King growled at the sight.

"Had enough fun?" Clearing his throat, Slifer got Morvran's attention.

Morvran, realizing that the Pantherion King had submitted to his master, let the beasts go.

The beasts immediately scurried over to cower behind their leader, letting out whines of complaint.

"Ah, Master. We're done?" Morvran wiped the blood off his hands.

With a slight shake of his head and chuckle, Slifer nodded. "We are. The sect can dispatch someone to deal with the rest."

A Nascent Soul elder would be sent to guard the village until the Pantherion deal was secured.

Together, they returned to Brom's cottage, where Oliviare waited for them.

Slifer tore open a portal back to the Black Rose Sect. There was one final piece of business before this night's work was concluded.

"It's time to see Hughie!"

Slifer sat casually in his courtyard, orange robes draped loosely across his shoulders as he nibbled on a freshly-steamed pork dumpling. Beside him stood Morvran, hands clasped behind his back. As usual, the plump baldy looked ready to beat someone up at the slightest provocation.

Across the courtyard, standing alone near an ornamental rock garden, was a young woman in pale blue cultivator robes. She fidgeted nervously with the fabric, eyes downcast and cheeks flushed.

Oliviare's heart pounded as she waited for Hughie. She was eager to see him after so long apart, but what if he reacted poorly to her presence here? What if there was another girl? *Maybe coming to the sect had been a foolish wish . . .*

Noticing the girl's nervous fidgeting, Slifer smiled to himself. *Ah, young love . . . how nauseatingly sweet.*

No matter the realm, some things never changed.

A faint whistle sounded from above. Slifer tipped his head back lazily, catching sight of a dark figure rapidly descending from the sky.

Right on time. Slifer popped the last dumpling into his mouth just as Hughie landed on the ground and bowed.

"You summoned me, Master?"

Hughie's dark eyes flicked briefly to the shy, brown-haired girl standing off to one side. He did a double take. *Was that . . . ? No, it couldn't be.*

"Allow me to introduce our newest recruit." Slifer rose and gestured to the blushing young woman. "This is—"

"Oliviare?" Hughie blurted out in disbelief.

Oliviare's eyes widened at being addressed so directly. A pretty blush colored her cheeks as she gave a nervous nod.

"Y-yes. Greetings, Senior Brother Hughie," she stammered, gaze fixed firmly on the ground.

Now that she was a member of the sect, Hughie would be her senior brother and she had to address him as such, he wasn't just her Hughie anymore.

Hughie stared, mouth agape. He seemed torn between rushing forward to embrace her and remaining rooted in place out of shock.

Meanwhile, Slifer watched on in amusement.

Ah, to be young and in love again. Takes me back to my first girlfriend, Kylie. Or was it Kaylie? Hmm, can't seem to recall her name, probably wasn't important. There are probably more realistic AI models now anyway.

"I don't understand." Hughie finally found his voice. "Oliviare doesn't have the aptitude to cultivate. Why is she here?"

At his words, Oliviare's smile faltered. *After all this time, that's the first thing he says?* Oliviare bit her lip and turned away before Hughie could see her eyes water.

A lover's spat? I guess it's up to me to fix it! Slifer cleared his throat. "Yes, well, it's true she doesn't have a spiritual root. But after hearing how my *favorite* disciple had lost his heart to a mortal girl, what sort of master would I be if I didn't help my disciple out?"

Slifer paused, eyebrow cocked as if waiting for some praise at his benevolence. When there was no reaction, he huffed and continued.

"As I was saying, a lack of spiritual roots poses no real obstacle for someone like myself. She'll have some spiritual roots soon enough, then you'll be free to pursue your, ahem, romantic interests openly."

"You really found a way?" Hughie breathed, scarcely daring to hope.

"Of course! Why else would I have brought her all the way here?"

"Humph! Your master lies. No treasure in the mortal realms could awaken a non-existent spiritual root," Li Fenghao scoffed from within the ring.

Hughie ignored the skeptical immortal spirit, too focused on Slifer's words to care. All that mattered was the possibility of a life with Oliviare. He dropped to his knees before Slifer. "Master, I beg you, please help make Oliviare a cultivator!" His voice cracked with emotion.

Slifer looked profoundly uncomfortable with this sudden display of gratitude. He waved his hands frantically. "Alright, alright, that's enough bowing. Just doing my duty as your master, no need for all this." His face slightly flushed, he quickly rummaged through his storage ring. "Now let's get this over with."

He retrieved an unremarkable circular medallion on a long cord and gestured for Oliviare to approach. "Here, place this on your forehead and close your eyes," he instructed gently.

Oliviare glanced nervously at Hughie, who smiled and nodded encouragingly. With a small gulp, she raised the talisman to her brow.

The talisman pulsed with a soft blue glow the moment it touched her skin. Gasps echoed around the courtyard as glowing runes began flowing outwards, slowly enveloping Oliviare's body in an intricate web of light.

The runes spun faster, weaving together to form the image of a massive wheel rotating around and around her slender frame.

Hughie stared transfixed as the hypnotic patterns swirled, holding his breath.

After several moments, the runes flickered and faded. The now-dark talisman slipped from Oliviare's brow as her knees buckled.

Hughie darted forward just in time to catch her limp body before it hit the ground. Cradling her close, he frantically swept his spiritual sense over Oliviare.

"She's alright," he announced with clear relief. A smile broke across Hughie's face. "No, more than that—she has a spiritual root now. I can't believe it!"

Overjoyed, Hughie spun Oliviare's slumbering form in an impromptu dance across the courtyard.

"Yes, the Wheel of Fate talisman is remarkably effective, if a bit rough on the user," Slifer remarked. "She will probably sleep for a few hours. When she wakes up, she will be at the Qi Refining Realm."

He was rather curious what sort of root the girl had awakened. But using spiritual sense without permission to scan another's body was rude, especially when their lover was right there.

Eh, I can just ask later when she wakes up.

Hughie paused his celebratory jig. "You mean she'll skip the Body Tempering stage completely?"

Slifer simply chuckled. "This sleep is her tempering. When she wakes, she can begin refining spiritual energy. Consider it a bonus for having such a benevolent master," he finished with a roguish wink.

"Master, thank you. This means more than I can say."

Ding!
Congratulations!
Your Disciple Hughie's Loyalty Has Reached 100%
New Option Available: Convert Hughie to a Righteous Cultivator
Reward: A Righteous Disciple Will Earn x3 Credit

Finally, it's done. Slifer let out a tired sigh. His plan had worked.

Ding!
New Mission: One Righteous Disciple Is Worth More Than a Thousand Demonic Trash
Description: Your disciple is ready to join the righteous path. Give him a sermon and ask him to join.

Hughie carefully set Oliviare's sleeping form on a bench. He turned to face his master once more, his expression turning serious. "Master, there is something important I need to tell you."

"Don't you dare, boy!" Li Fenghao shrieked. "Have you mushrooms for brains?"

But Hughie didn't care what the grandpa thought.

No more lies. No more hiding. It's time for Master to learn everything.

CHAPTER SIXTY-SIX

. . ." Hughie faltered, dropping his gaze. "I haven't been fully honest with you, Master. There are things I've kept hidden."

Is this what I think it is? Slifer raised an eyebrow.

"Back when you were in closed-door cultivation, Oliviare gave me this . . . ring as a parting gift," Hughie confessed. "I didn't think much of it at first, but then I realized there was an immortal spirit trapped inside."

Li Fenghao let loose a string of expletives, cursing the boy's foolish honesty. Hughie winced but pressed on.

"His name is Li Fenghao. Apparently, he is some kind of greater immortal . . ."

Hughie kept his gaze fixed firmly on the ground, unable to meet his master's eyes. Would Slifer be angry? Would he punish Hughie?

For a long moment, Slifer simply looked at Hughie with an unfathomable expression. Then, he threw back his head and laughed.

"Yes, yes, I've known about your ghostly roommate for a while now."

"You . . . you did?"

Seeing Hughie's dumbfounded expression, Slifer chuckled. "Did you really think anything could escape my notice?"

Relief washed over Hughie in a great wave. Of course his master had already known. Slifer's abilities were beyond comprehension. Hughie silently berated himself for doubting him.

"I'm sorry for not telling you sooner, Master. After everything with the treasures . . . I was worried you might take the ring for yourself." Hughie's cheeks reddened. "But you've . . . changed a lot recently. I should have trusted you."

Slifer waved off Hughie's concern. The original *had* taken advantage of Hughie on more than one occasion. He couldn't blame the boy for being reluctant.

"It's fine. I am just glad you felt comfortable enough to open up to me now."

Now I just need to check this Li Fenghao out myself and find out if he is a threat. Can't have parasitic grandpas leeching off my disciples.

With no cards that could protect him, Slifer had been reluctant to interact directly with the immortal spirit. However, now that Hughie had opened up to him, Slifer had to basically do a "security check" if he didn't want to come off as suspicious.

Even if he is evil, if I only send my spirit sense into the ring, the worst that could happen is it gets destroyed. And then, I'll stock up credits until I can get a card powerful enough to kill the old man . . .

"I'd like to have a chat with this . . . grandpa of yours," Slifer said lightly. "Just to make sure he isn't up to any funny business."

Hughie shifted his feet awkwardly. "Actually, Master, I can't sense his presence right now. I think he's hiding . . ."

Hiding? Wait a minute . . . is the immortal grandpa scared of me?
This was unexpected.

An indignant squawk sounded from the ring. "*Hiding?* This old man hides from no one!"

"Oh wait, never mind!" Hughie laughed. "He's back."

"Great. Let him know I only want to chat." *The last thing I need is for this grandpa to go all kamikaze on me . . .*

Hughie nodded. "Just . . . go easy on him, okay? He's very . . . proud, but I don't think he means any real harm."

Slifer held back an eye roll at Hughie's naïvety. Clearly the boy had gotten attached to the ring spirit. *Doesn't matter—I'll just assess the situation myself.*

Closing his eyes, Slifer sent a wisp of spiritual sense into the ring. When he opened them again, Slifer found himself standing in an endless white void.

Strange, he thought. He had expected at least some attempt at a pocket dimension illusion. *This "greater immortal" was either incredibly weak or astronomically lazy.*

Perhaps a bit of both, Slifer amended, catching sight of a robed figure floating towards him.

Despite not having a physical form, the weight of Li Fenghao's aura was immense, causing Slifer's spiritual projection to tremble.

This guy . . . he isn't simple, Slifer thought, keeping a tight grip on his spiritual form.

"You are not what I expected," Li Fenghao said, brow furrowing. "The boy thinks you're only an Ascendant cultivator, yet your abilities far exceed any mortal cultivator. In fact, some of your skills should be impossible even in the Immortal Realm . . ."

The old man drifted closer, scrutinizing Slifer intently. "Even standing before me now, you seem like a genuine Foundation Establishment cultivator!"

Slifer remained silent, allowing Li Fenghao's monologue to continue. No need to interrupt an immortal fond of hearing his own voice.

From his experience in this world, the greatest lesson Slifer learned was that the more he talked, the greater the chance that he would slip up.

"Just . . . what are you? Have you surpassed the Great Immortal Realm?" Li Fenghao's eyes widened.

Interesting. The old man thinks I'm hiding my strength. Guess it's time to pretend to be something that can scare even a greater immortal. Slifer adopted a mysterious air. "The Mortal Realm, the Immortal Realm—such things are beneath my notice. The world is far more vast than you know."

He let that hang in the air for a moment.

Nothing Slifer had said was a lie, this whole xianxia world was just one of many worlds, another being Earth. Even if the immortal had an ability that could call out lies, it didn't matter.

Li Fenghao looked vaguely offended but also intrigued.

It's working! Time to reel him in. "In fact, with your *limited* perspective, I doubt you could understand even if I explained it to you."

It was just vague and mystical enough to reinforce Li Fenghao's assumptions without making any definitive claims. *Hah! Eat your heart out, Gandalf.*

The immortal spirit bristled, pride stung. But he could not refute Slifer's words. He'd witnessed the mysterious cultivator's inexplicable power many times.

After a lengthy pause, Li Fenghao rubbed his beard. "I see . . . I apologize . . . Senior."

Phew, it worked. Now I can get some answers of my own.

"What do you want from Hughie?"

"I . . . I just wanted his help getting a new body."

"Hmm, is that so? Then you haven't been secretly plotting to make Hughie your disciple the moment you escape this prison?" Slifer replied, one brow raised.

"I—well—that is—" Li Fenghao spluttered, indignant denials dying on his tongue. With a scowl, he switched tactics. "The boy shows promise. I didn't want you demonic sc—"

Insight!

> Name: Li Fenghao
> Realm: Peak Greater Immortal (Sealed)
> Known Techniques: N/A
> Known Affiliations: N/A
> Disposition: N/A
> Comprehension: 8
> Luck: 7
> Talent: 9
> Will: 6 (8)

As expected from a greater immortal, he's got protagonist-level stats.

But Slifer wasn't too bothered with the grandpa's stats, the only reason he used the Insight skill was to give the grandpa a little scare. The higher the cultivation, the more aware a person was of their soul. Slifer assumed a greater immortal would feel an uncomfortable sensation as he used Insight, especially since Slifer activated it so blatantly.

It's . . . it's that look again. A bead of spectral sweat trickled down the old man's brow as he snapped his mouth shut.

Slifer's gaze made Li Fenghao feel as if the demonic cultivator was peering through his soul; compared to the previous time, this was twice as intense, he felt like he was laid out utterly bare. He felt insignificant. As a greater immortal, he couldn't remember the last time he felt like this.

"I'm s-sorry," he coughed. "I won't try to steal your disciple." Li Fenghao also couldn't remember the last time those words left his mouth. It galled him to humble himself this way. But the life essence technique weighed heavily on his mind. He could not risk provoking this man's wrath.

Satisfied that his scare tactic had succeeded, Slifer inclined his head. "Take good care of my Hughie. And don't try to turn him against me. It would be . . . unwise."

With that, Slifer's projection faded away.

The immortal spirit sagged in relief. Dealing with beings of higher cultivation was always stressful, even for someone at his realm. And this Slifer unnerved him more than most.

"Still, perhaps I can use this to my advantage," Li Fenghao mused aloud. "The boy has gotten closer to me. If I help him out more, I might be able to curry more favor from his master . . ."

The opportunity to gain a few words of advice from a being who had surpassed the Greater Immortal Realm was too great to pass up. Even if Li Fenghao escaped the ring, he didn't have the confidence to succeed in breaking through. His only hope was this mysterious immortal.

Yes, that should work nicely.

* * *

Back in the courtyard, Slifer, unaware of the old man's plan to kiss up to him, withdrew his spiritual sense and turned to Hughie with a reassuring smile.

"The grandpa won't be any trouble. In fact, you could learn a thing or two from him. Just be careful if he tries turning you against your master." Slifer's expression turned sly. "Not that he could hide such a thing from me, of course."

Allowing Hughie to keep the ring was a calculated risk. The boy's loyalty was high, but prolonged exposure to Li Fenghao's influence could become a problem.

I'll need to monitor the situation closely. At the first sign of wavering loyalty, the ring goes.

"Thank you, Master." Hughie shoulders relaxed. He felt a bit guilty for revealing Li Fenghao's presence without permission. But it seemed things had worked out for the best. Neither Slifer nor the immortal spirit had come to blows at least.

"Oh, there is one more thing before you go," Slifer added casually.

Hughie looked at him quizzically. "Yes, Master?"

"It's time for you to walk the righteous path."

Hughie's eyes bulged. Had he heard that right? His demonic master, suggesting he become a righteous cultivator? It was the last thing he would have ever expected.

"But why?" he asked uncertainly. "You've always followed the demonic Dao . . ."

Slifer smiled. "My own path doesn't matter—what is important is helping my disciples reach their full potential. Your heart has turned to the light, even if you remain afraid to show it."

He cast a meaningful glance at where Oliviare still slept peacefully on the courtyard bench. A small smile tugged Hughie's lips as understanding washed over him.

Slifer nodded sagely. "Love is the light that guides us through the dark." *Wow, that one gave me goosebumps. I really need to write these down!*

"Master, I . . ." Hughie faltered, overcome with emotion. "You're right. After meeting Oliviare, I have felt conflicted about being a demonic cultivator. I don't want her to see me as a . . . monster."

"Ha ha. There's no need to suppress your righteous urges anymore. Follow your heart from now on!" Slifer clasped his shoulder.

"Thank you, Master! I will be a better man!"

Ding!
Hughie Is Now a Righteous Cultivator
Ding!
Name: Hughie Card
Description: Once a day, you can activate any of your loyal disciple's techniques.
Warning: If your disciple's loyalty goes below 100%, you will lose access to this card.

Phew, just three left . . .

Over the next few weeks, Slifer spent many hours trying to convert Leah.

While their relationship had grown less hostile, the brooding girl remained skeptical of Slifer's intentions.

Looks like converting her will take more than just a few heart-to-heart chats with her father's killer, Slifer mused wryly. Still, the occasional playful smirk or snippy comment gave him hope she would come around eventually.

The girl just needed more time. But with the Inter-Sect Tournament looming, time was in short supply right now.

Slifer sighed. He could only do so much. The rest was up to Leah and the mysterious workings of karma.

As the Inter-Sect Tournament approached, Slifer spent more time training.

I hope it's enough to win the tournament, he thought, sitting in his courtyard and biting into an apple.

His disciples, who sat in a circle around him, glanced at each other in confusion before resting their gazes on their master. This was the first time they had seen him even touch a fruit.

I've not checked my status in a while, it wouldn't hurt to have a look.

Name: Slifer
Race: Human
Alignment: Demonic
Lifespan Remaining: 100 years
Karmic Credits: 11,570
Skills: Firebreath, Insight (Intermediate), Mirror Mastery (Level 2), Nascent Soul Armor (Level 2), Phase Ability (Level 1), Void Being Aura (Level 1)
Items: Reversal Cards, Peak Slifer Card, Critical Block Cards x5
Affinities: Light: 25% Fire: 15% Space: 20%
Abilities: Mirror Mastery: Level 2
Techniques: Sunrise Slash: Level 3, Stellar Nova Strike: Level 2, Dimensional Slide: Level 2, Nascent Soul Armor: Level 1, Void Piercer: Level 1
Weapon Mastery: Sword: 20%

Over 10,000 Karmic Credits . . . finally. Slifer smiled.

The credits were all thanks to the tasks completed by the Disciplinary Hall members, his new farming system had played out perfectly.

It's mainly due to that Dentos fella, he's always number one on the leaderboard . . .

Slifer then took a look at his skills.

Leveling up the Sunrise Slash and Stellar Nova Strike was the right call, both techniques will let Zack finish fights quickly.

Slifer's gameplan was for his avatar to show as little of his arsenal as possible. The similarity between their techniques could be explained through their master-disciple relationship, but some of the other Ascendants may grow suspicious and suspect that Zack was a clone.

The armor will be my trump card. Slifer nodded to himself as he looked at the level 2 Nascent Soul Armor technique.

Through grueling practice, Slifer was able to increase the duration to thirty seconds if he activated it through the System. Without the System's aid, he was only able to use it for ten seconds. It still wasn't much, but a few seconds could make all the difference in the tournament.

Ptui! Slifer spat out the apple. *Never again.* He had noticed quite a few disciples in the sect eating apples, he had to admit they did look juicy, he couldn't resist trying one for himself. He had thought that maybe they tasted different in this world but no, he was wrong. It tasted just like a regular apple. *Nothing can compare to the satisfaction of real food, like, uh, dumplings!*

"You have all trained hard these past weeks," Slifer began, wiping his mouth with the edge of his sleeve. "Well, for the next two days you can relax!"

The disciples all nodded enthusiastically; the Inter-Sect Tournament was starting in three days. Their master had warned them that they needed to give their bodies a few days' rest. Participating in the tournament when injured or tired could ruin what was likely their one and only chance to enter the Sealed Realm.

"I'm sure we'll dominate the tournament and secure the most spots for the Sealed Realm," Slifer went on, "but it's not just you four I'm relying on . . ."

Here he paused for dramatic effect. His disciples leaned forward, wondering what or who their master was referring to.

"Allow me to explain," Slifer chuckled.

With a flourish, Slifer gestured towards the entrance to his quarters. All eyes turned. For a long moment, nothing happened. Then a figure emerged into the courtyard.

It was a young man who looked to be in his late teens, with artfully tousled brown hair and chiseled features that would make the statues of celestial immortals weep with envy. He had the sort of ridiculous physique that could only be achieved through years of cultivator training—wide shoulders tapering to a narrow waist, with muscular arms that looked as though they would burst through the thin robes at any moment.

The disciples gaped. Just who was this absurdly handsome newcomer?

"Hey, I'm Zack."

CHAPTER SIXTY-SEVEN

Please, no need to fawn. There's plenty of me to go around." Zack flashed a roguish wink, the motion parting his robes further to reveal impressively sculpted abs that caused Amelia to make a strangled noise low in her throat.

Hughie shook his head; he was just relieved *not* to be the sole focus of Slifer's attentions anymore.

Watching this exchange, Caelum barely restrained an eye roll. So, they had a cocky junior brother now. Wonderful. As if keeping Hughie and Amelia in check wasn't work enough.

Ignoring their odd reactions, Slifer clapped Zack on the back.

"I must admit, I too was blown away at first by this young man's talents." Slifer nodded.

He had decided to go down the "Zack is a prodigy among prodigies" route, it would explain why Zack used similar technique to himself. Not to mention, giving yourself a few compliments here and there couldn't hurt, right?

"Master, I heard you have a slot for the Sealed Realm . . . I . . . *we* were wondering . . . which one of us will be getting it?" Nomed piped up.

Slifer remained silent as he looked at his disciples, who looked at him expectantly.

"The slot will go to . . . . none of you!"

" . . ."

The disciples glanced at each other in confusion, if they were not getting the slot, then who was?

Hughie noticed that the new disciple, Zack, nodded smugly. Just what did Master's new favorite know?

Nomed held back a frown, he *had* to enter the Sealed Realm, but as an Early Foundation Establishment cultivator, he was at a clear disadvantage.

Despite there being five slots and a separate tournament for Foundation Establishment cultivators, most participants would be at the Late or peak stage, and that was just their apparent cultivation, their battle prowess likely reached the Core Formation Realm.

And now, he also had to compete against a new prodigy.

At his master's words, Fenlock shrugged. As a Nascent Soul expert, the tournament didn't concern him, only those below the Nascent Soul Realm were able to enter the Sealed Realm.

Whilst his juniors were busy training, Fenlock took Junior Sister Lenvari on date after date—he really felt like he was making progress. Who knows, if the heavens smiled down on him, he might even be a married man by the end of the year!

"Don't worry about the free slot, I want each of you to focus on earning a slot for yourself," Slifer continued.

He knew better than to give any of his disciples a free slot. Some of them, like Hughie or Amelia, would be tempted to grow lax and not prepare, and this was something Slifer knew pretty well. After all, he was guilty of it during his school exams.

The disciples slowly nodded. Their master may have changed but it seemed like he was still the stingy old Slifer they knew and loved.

"Cheer up!" Slifer laughed at their dismay. "Your master isn't going to leave you empty-handed."

As the Black Rose Sect oversaw the tournament, Slifer was privy to what trials would be involved. More accurately, Elder Fred consulted Slifer before preparing each trial.

Slifer would be a fool *not* to take advantage of that knowledge, and perhaps the trials happened to favor his disciples, it was not like anyone would dare question an Ascendant cultivator over such matters.

It was expected.

It wasn't without reason why the Heavenly Light Sect were adamant with wanting to host the tournament. During their time as the host, they had used every trick in the book to increase their disciples' chances of entering the Sealed Realm, they weren't the most powerful sect in the land for nothing.

Cracking his knuckles, Slifer grinned savagely. "So, here's what we're going to do . . ."

Two days later.

The Black Rose Sect was bustling with activity. Disciples scurried to and fro, busy making last-minute preparations. Pennants and banners in the demonic sect's signature dark rose color decorated the normally stark walls and archways.

For the first time in its long history, the Black Rose Sect would be hosting the prestigious tournament. It was a great honor, but also a grave responsibility. Slifer had given Elder Fred free access to the sect's resources to ensure they displayed their best to their guests.

The Inter-Sect Tournament was designed to allocate slots for the Sealed Realm; however, it was also an opportunity for sects to feel each other out. Presenting a strong front was necessary if they wanted to avoid war.

Despite Slifer never having experienced war back on Earth, he had read about it. The pains and tribulations of war were not something he wanted to partake in, especially in a world where beings could destroy stars with a flick of the wrist.

Not to mention the hundreds of thousands of credits that he would need to spend to survive one, wars in this world could easily last centuries. It was the last thing Slifer wanted.

Three young female disciples struggled under the weight of a huge ornamental urn, bickering and snapping at one another as they lugged the cumbersome pottery towards the sect's front gate. It was said to be a Heaven Rank treasure, containing the remnant spirit of a demonic general.

In the main square, two disciples were busy hanging up banners when one turned to the other. "Can you believe they're actually letting us host the tournament this year?" he said with a grin.

His friend laughed. "I know, right? The righteous sects must have lost their minds!"

They chuckled together as they worked. Nearby, a group of female disciples swept the ground diligently. One girl paused and leaned on her broom.

"Hosting the tournament is a big responsibility," she said seriously. "We have to make sure we represent the Black Rose Sect properly."

The other girls nodded in agreement. As a demonic sect, they rarely got opportunities like this. They couldn't mess it up.

As the disciples worked, a commotion at the sect entrance drew their attention. A group of cultivators had arrived, all dressed in white robes embroidered with the image of a tiger.

"Ugh, look who it is," one of the Black Rose disciples muttered. "The goody-goody Tigers."

At the head of the White Tiger group was a beautiful young woman with long blonde hair and piercing blue eyes. She wore an arrogant expression as her gaze swept disdainfully over the Black Rose disciples.

"This place is even uglier than I remember," she said loudly. "I can't believe the sect master approved these demons hosting the tournament."

Her White Tiger disciples tittered obnoxiously. One of the Black Rose disciples scowled, dropping the lantern he was hanging.

"You're not wrong, Elder, I can practically smell the stench of demonic energy here," one of the white-robed men complained, wrinkling his nose.

Angry mutters broke out amongst the Black Rose disciples. How dare these self-righteous fools insult them in their own sect!

One stocky Black Rose disciple stepped forward, an angry flush on his cheeks. "You come to our home and dare insult us? If you think you'll only get a beating for those words, you're wrong. I'll take your life!"

He unleashed his Late Core Formation cultivation base, prepared to attack. The White Tiger disciple paled initially but quickly matched the aura with his own, refusing to back down in front of the elder.

The blonde woman watched with an amused smile, always eager to see demonic cultivators put in their place. Things were just getting interesting.

But before it could escalate further, a sudden gust of wind blew through the square. A figure appeared between the two groups.

"Still starting trouble wherever you go I see . . . Liora," the man sighed, shaking his head.

Liora's eyes widened briefly in recognition before narrowing. "It's you! Don't think I've forgotten what happened!"

The young man wore the black robes of the Black Rose Sect, he regarded Liora calmly.

"If I remember correctly, you were the one who challenged me last time. And you couldn't defeat me."

A faint blush colored Liora's cheeks at the memory. It had been utterly humiliating that she hadn't been able to defeat the youth in one move. She had only recently reached the Nascent Soul Realm, while Caelum was still in the Peak Core Formation stage. Yet he was still able to fight evenly against her somehow.

"That was just luck," she snapped. "If the grand elder hadn't stopped the fight—"

"Excuses," Caelum interrupted. He cast a meaningful look at the other White Tiger disciples, who were still glaring daggers at the Black Rose Sect members. "How can I expect you to keep your disciples in check when you can't even control yourself."

Liora trembled with rage; she wasn't used to being spoken to in such a manner. How dare this demonic scum lecture her on etiquette!

With great difficulty, she reined in her anger. As much as she itched to put Caelum in his place, she could not afford to lose control. As an elder, she needed to set a good example.

"Hmph. You're lucky that I don't qualify to enter the tournament," was all she said. The look in her eyes promised that this wasn't over between them. Not by a long shot.

Caelum simply inclined his head politely in response. Though inwardly, he was surprised by Liora's restraint. Seemed like the proud girl had matured, even if just a little.

Before either could say more, a sudden spike of energy drew their attention. In the distance, the unmistakable sounds of battle could be heard. Caelum and Liora exchanged a glance, and with a burst of speed, they raced towards the source of the commotion. To their surprise, it led them right to the doors of the Disciplinary Hall.

A crowd had gathered, kept back by several black-robed disciples.

"Alright people, nothing to see here!" one disciplinary member called out. "Just a minor disciplinary issue, the boss is taking care of it."

At the mention of this "boss," the other disciples nodded sagely.

"That's our boss, always so diligent!" a short, pudgy disciple gushed. "Never have I seen someone so devoted to upholding sect rules!"

Caelum and Liora exchanged puzzled glances. Just who was this "boss" they spoke so highly of?

Noticing Caelum, the disciplinary disciples quickly moved aside to let him through. As one of Supreme Elder's personal disciples, he warranted some respect around here.

Stepping past the doors, Caelum was greeted by the sight of a skinny young disciple mercilessly whaling on another student. The victim was a boy in golden robes—likely a disciple of the Heavenly Light Sect based on his attire.

"Please, stop!" the Heavenly Light disciple cried, covering his head. Blood dripped from his broken nose and split lip.

Nearby, more disciples in golden robes were pinned face down by the Disciplinary Hall members, unable to come to their comrade's aid. They struggled and shouted curses but could not break free.

"That's it boss! Teach that punk a lesson!" one of the Disciplinary Hall members yelled. The others shouted their own encouragement.

Liora watched in disgust. Despicable. This is exactly why demonic cultivators cannot be trusted. However, since it wasn't any of her men, she decided not to get involved. She could even sense auras that made her tremble hidden within the hall.

Caelum remained silent, eyes narrowed as he took in the situation.

The Heavenly Light disciple being beaten sniffled loudly, snot mixing with the blood on his face. "It's not fair," he whined. "That Black Rose disciple was causing problems too. Why am I the only one being punished?"

The lanky youth paused his assault, smiling creepily down at the crumpled form beneath his foot. "Patience, friend. I will get to him."

With two final punishing strikes, the boss stepped back, examining his handiwork. The Heavenly Light disciple lay groaning at his feet, face swollen and purpling.

"You know the rules—no fighting during the tournament," the lanky youth said calmly, as if he hadn't just tenderized the boy's face mere moments ago. "But it seems you needed an extra lesson."

He looked to the side where a Black Rose disciple was restrained, his eyes widened in fear. The lanky youth beckoned him closer with a crooked finger.

"As do you." The boss grabbed the Black Rose disciple and slammed him viciously into the wall.

"No, please, I don't want any trouble!" The Black Rose disciple tried getting back up, but the Disciplinary Hall members grasped his arms tightly.

Other disciples watched on with pale faces as the lanky man continued pummeling the poor disciple.

"Does he have to be so harsh to his own sect member?" one muttered fearfully.

"That's just how Boss Dentos is. Ruthless, even to us," another replied.

So, this was the notorious Dentos who had rapidly risen to number one on the Karmic Ledger. Caelum had heard the rumors of his methods but seeing the sheer sadistic glee on his face as he unleashed such violence reminded him of a certain junior sister.

When Dentos finally stepped back, both disciples lay moaning on the ground. He rubbed his hands together, as if dusting them off after a job well done.

"Hopefully that will prevent any further incidents," he said lightly. "If not, I'm always happy to provide another lesson. But next time, I might not be so nice."

"You're lucky it was me who found you." He leaned in close. "And believe me, you don't want Senior Sister Amelia to be the one to find you instead."

At the mention of Amelia, the other Disciplinary Hall members visibly shivered. One leaned to whisper to his companion, "Not sure who is worse—Boss Dentos or Senior Sister Amelia. They're both completely deranged."

"Too true," the other agreed.

Dentos tossed the two disciples aside carelessly to land in a groaning heap.

One of the Heavenly Light disciples helped his friend up, throwing a venomous glare back at Dentos. "Just you wait. Once our senior brother hears of this, you'll regret it!"

The other conscious Heavenly Light disciples were quick to chime in.

"Yeah, Senior Brother will crush you for this!"

"He just joined our sect, but he is a never-before-seen genius!"

"Broke through to the Core Formation stage faster than anyone on record!"

"Defeated numerous senior brothers one after another in sparring matches!"

"Even Nascent Soul experts can't hold a candle to him!"

Their words blurred together as all the disciples began yelling about the incredible talents of their senior brother. Surely someone so cool and gifted could put this demonic beast in his place.

But Dentos didn't seem phased by their threats. He crossed his arms, staring down at the disciples.

"I don't care if he's the Son of Heaven himself," Dentos said flatly. "No one will cause any problems here while I'm in charge."

For a brief moment, his eyes took on a distant, almost haunted look. "I won't allow it . . . I can't," he muttered to himself as he thought of an old man in orange robes.

He shook his head sharply, regaining focus. He was given a job to do, and failure was not an option. He would enforce discipline with an iron fist.

"He . . . he's here!"

The nearby disciples quietened down as approaching footsteps echoed down the hall.

They parted to allow a tall, muscular young man with shoulder-length black hair to pass. His golden robes had the insignia for the Heavenly Light Sect. He emanated an overwhelming aura of confidence.

It was the genius senior brother!

The youth glanced around coolly, taking in the scene. When his eyes found Dentos, he raised one eyebrow. "So, you're the demonic scum causing trouble?"

Dentos met his gaze calmly. "And who might you be?"

The corner of the man's lip curved up mockingly.

"I'm Ziven."

CHAPTER SIXTY-EIGHT

Ziven smirked, sure that he would easily put this demonic scum in his place. But before he could make a move, Dentos suddenly vanished. Ziven's eyes widened in surprise—where did that weirdo go?

A split second later, Ziven felt a strong hand clamp down over his face as Dentos reappeared directly in front of him. With lightning speed, Dentos tried to smash him down towards the ground. Caught completely off guard, Ziven only just managed to twist his body and blast out a surge of qi to counter the attack. The force was enough to throw Dentos back.

Ziven touched his face and scowled as he regained his footing. "I should have expected such a cowardly sneak attack from demonic filth like you," he spat.

Dentos merely smiled, a true demonic cultivator didn't care about honor. Honor only led to a swifter death.

"I'm going to wipe that smirk off your face," Ziven said, concentrating qi into his legs. In the blink of an eye, he appeared right in front of Dentos, hand formed into a sharp wind claw aimed right for his face.

He would return the favor.

But Dentos easily avoided the blow, his movements smooth like flowing water.

"H-how can you be this fast?" Ziven's eyes narrowed in frustration.

He was renowned for his speed, yet this lanky guy with a dumb-looking smile not only matched his speed but exceeded it!

Ziven knew this was a bad matchup, but with so many eyes on him, he couldn't just walk away now. It wasn't easy for him to enter the Heavenly Light Sect and rise to the level of Legacy Disciple, he couldn't fail, not yet.

Before Ziven could attack again, his senses screamed at him to move. He immediately did a backflip, just barely dodging a blast of purplish energy that tore through the space he had occupied only a moment before.

Ziven growled as he recognized the energy; there was only one person he knew that used soul-based attacks. He turned to face the silver-haired woman.

"You!" he snarled.

Amelia smirked, her long silver hair flowing behind her like a snake. "I'm surprised you have the audacity to show your face here after you scurried away with your tail between your legs last time," she laughed.

"Y-you bitch!" Ziven's face flushed red with embarrassment and anger at the memory. After some fortunate encounters, his own battle prowess had increased tremendously since their last meeting. He was certain he could wipe that annoying smirk off that girl's face now.

But looking between the troublesome Dentos and the infuriating Amelia, Ziven noticed a black-robed youth reaching for the sword in his scabbard.

He's not like the other two, he's dangerous . . .

Cursing internally, Ziven took a step back. "Just you wait—in the tournament, you won't have anyone to bail you out," he declared. With that, he strode away, the other Heavenly Light disciples hurrying after him.

As they retreated, the other disciples shot their own heated glares and curses.

"You just wait, demon scum! Our Senior Brother Ziven is invincible!"

"He'll crush you all when he gets serious!"

"Yeah, he was only playing with you!"

Their arrogant words faded into the distance.

Amelia turned to Caelum as the Heavenly Light group disappeared from view. "Master was right. That brat really did find his way into the tournament," she said.

Caelum nodded, releasing his hold on Bloodthorn.

Their master had warned them to be on the lookout for Ziven, instructing them to kill him if they encountered the arrogant youth in the competition. Killing him before the tournament began would cause more than a ruckus. The strongest sect in the Mortal Realm, the Heavenly Light Sect would not let that slide.

If he doesn't die in the tournament, then I'll just end him in the Sealed Realm . . .

Even though Caelum was now a righteous cultivator, he didn't shy from killing when it was necessary.

He shouldn't have attacked Amelia . . . and he definitely shouldn't have threatened Master.

"I will go inform Master of this development," Caelum muttered as he walked away.

As he left, he heard Dentos calling out behind him, "Don't forget to let Master know what I did here, them two troublemakers won't be walking for a few weeks at least . . . and the same with the arrogant kid when I next see him."

Caelum just shook his head, wondering, not for the first time, about the eccentricities of those that surrounded his master.

Zack soared through the sky atop his flying sword, wind whipping through his hair. The Inter-Sect Tournament began tomorrow, but he still had one final task from the Main Body—reach the Peak Foundation Establishment stage as a dual cultivator.

Zack smirked to himself. As an avatar rather than the main consciousness, he could act however he wanted without damaging Slifer's image.

While the Main Body had to play the part of an all-powerful old man, Zack could be cocky and carefree, kinda like a high school student. And he planned to enjoy every moment of it!

If only I knew my stats, then I could see how I compare to the disciples . . .

The Main Body had tried using his Insight skill on Zack, hoping to learn his stats and cultivation level. But unfortunately, the only information that came up identified Zack as Slifer's clone.

At least he bought me some cool stuff.

Now that they had a steady influx of Karmic Credits, the Main Body no longer had to be stingy. He had purchased a High Heaven Rank spiritual cultivation method for himself, and another for Zack as well.

Having two separate methods was better than sharing the exact same skills. After all, what was the point of an avatar if it was just a carbon copy? Different cultivation methods provided unique abilities to develop. And since Zack didn't have access to the System, he needed to rely on cunning rather than brute force.

So, the Main Body had chosen methods well-suited to Zack's needs.

The High Heaven Rank Thunder Wings focused on speed enhancement—perfect for Zack's preference to dodge rather than block attacks.

Not to mention it sounded incredibly cool. Who wouldn't want wings, even Amelia loved wings! Grinning, Zack leaned back and rested his hands behind his head. The wind whipped through his hair dramatically. *Oh yeah, I bet I look so cool right now!* After a few moments, Zack coughed. He couldn't get distracted, no matter how handsome he looked. *I need to keep my spiritual cultivation at the Foundation Establishment Realm.*

Zack could feel it itching to break through to the Core Formation stage. But he firmly reined it in. For the tournament, he intended to compete at the Foundation Establishment level where he would have the greatest advantage. There was no need to rush into the Early Core Formation stage against all those Peak experts.

Thanks but no thanks, Zack thought, nodding to himself.

He planned to simply make the breakthrough inside the Sealed Realm instead. That's why reaching Peak Foundation Establishment now was so crucial. As a dual cultivator, Zack knew he wouldn't be quite so outmatched when the Core Formation cultivators entered the Nascent Soul Realm.

With the treasures the Main Body gave me, I should be able to achieve my goal in the Sealed Realm.

Arriving at his destination, Zack looked down at the scroll in his hand, checking the instructions one last time. His body cultivation level already hovered at Late Foundation Establishment from the Main Body passing the early stages.

Now it was time for the final push to Peak.

Zack hovered over the base of the Lightning Peak Mountain, a place coveted by all lightning-aligned cultivators. The very core of the mountain was said to harbor a rare Heaven Rank treasure that attracted heavenly lightning, the strikes growing even more frequent and intense the higher one ascended.

Though impressive, such lightning tempering grounds could be found in all the top sects across the Mortal Realm. The reason why it was so common was because the benefits were limited to those below the Origin Realm.

But that's good enough for me.

The Lightning Peak Mountain was separated into nine sections. The first two sections were for Qi Refining cultivators, the third and fourth sections were for Foundation Establishment cultivators, the fifth and sixth sections were for Core Formation, whilst the seventh and eighth sections were for Nascent Soul cultivators.

As for the ninth section . . . it was for the breakthrough to Origin Realm.

All Zack had to do was bear with the fourth section.

Doesn't sound too bad, hopefully it isn't too painful . . . well it doesn't really matter, I better start climbing!

Lightning flashed overhead in agreement.

Zack landed lightly on top of the rocks. Immediately a bolt of lightning cracked down from above, splicing through the space he had just occupied. Zack didn't move, allowing the violet fork to splash over his body.

Rather than turning him to ash, the lightning was rapidly absorbed. Zack closed his eyes briefly, sensing the lightning qi flowing in a spiral as it circulated through his meridians, subtly enhancing his muscles, organs, and bones.

Opening his eyes, Zack continued onward. The strikes came faster and stronger in the second region, though still manageable. Only at the third section did he need to slow his pace, each Foundation Establishment level bolt requiring more time to temper his body without harm.

Finally entering the fourth section, Zack had to stop completely after each step, the force of the blows nearly buckling his knees.

Gritting his teeth, Zack stood his ground.

Immediately a thick cord of lightning crashed down, the impact driving him to one knee. His teeth ground together as he desperately channeled the Thunder God cultivation method, trying to subdue the volatile energy before it destroyed him.

For those several heart-pounding seconds, Zack grappled with the lightning. It was like a raging dragon, trying to break his will. His meridians felt like they would rupture, his organs were on the verge of liquification.

But Zack only threw his head back and laughed maniacally. "You think that's enough to make me quit? I'm Zack! A little lightning won't stop me!"

How could he return to the Main Body as a failure? He was the avatar; he was created for this exact purpose!

His robes, despite being buffed by runes, had turned to ash, but he wouldn't give up.

Better it than me . . . but this . . . this is enough.

With a roar, Zack summoned his sword from his storage ring and launched himself into the sky, sweat dripping off his face.

It was done. His task was complete.

He had become a Peak Foundation Establishment dual cultivator.

Being an avatar was such exhausting work!

Slifer was back under that frigid waterfall with four massive boulders over his head. The waterfall not only helped strengthen his body but also muffled any embarrassing noises he made as he pushed his limits.

Ding!
Your Avatar Zack Broke Through to the Peak Foundation Establishment Realm
Karmic Credits Gained: 250

Slifer burst out laughing, the boulders shaking over him. "I've lost against myself!"

He and Zack had made a challenge to see whose body could reach the Peak Foundation Establishment stage first.

Since I'm the Main Body, whenever the avatar wins, so do I. Slifer nodded to himself.

With a final loud grunt, he felt his body break through the bottleneck, the telltale sign of popping tendons announcing his advancement.

> *Ding!*
> Congratulations on the breakthrough to the Peak Foundation Establishment Realm!
> Karmic Credits Gained: 250

Only a few seconds late . . .

With a wry grin, Slifer tossed the huge rocks aside and stretched. It always felt strange when he experienced a breakthrough; his body would naturally adapt to the sudden increase in power. Well, as long as he wasn't breaking through multiple stages at once.

> *Ding!*
> Your Spiritual and Body Cultivation Are Now Equal
> You Have Unlocked a Perk
> Dual Cultivator Perk: Combining Both Cultivations in Attacks Increases Battle Prowess By 35%

Slifer's brows shot up in surprise. He had hoped that something would happen when both his spiritual and body cultivation reached the same stage, he just hadn't expected a perk. He didn't even know the System even had such things as perks, it certainly wasn't in the Shop.

Hmm, maybe it's saved for Version 2. Reading the description, he nodded to himself. *So this explained the legendary fighting ability of dual cultivators at the same stage. An innate buff was granted to anyone meeting the criteria. Just one more hidden advantage among many it seemed.*

As the supreme elder of the Black Rose Sect, it would be foolish for him not to read the stories of the exceptional cultivators that graced this world. The stories were not only interesting, but gave him a few ideas on how to increase his battle prowess without having to rely on the System.

At least Zack now has another trump card.

His avatar was already set to dominate the Foundation Establishment tournament. But inside the Sealed Realm, Zack would need to face the top Core Formation—and even Nascent Soul—experts.

A thirty-five percent power boost could prove invaluable, especially when he used some of the toys that Slifer provided him with.

Now I just need a few cards that could keep me alive, his eyes narrowed. The thought of being in the company of the other Ascendants for any duration of time unnerved him.

Now that I have a modest number of credits, I don't have to rely on my luck gambling, he thought as he brought up the System. *But the smart thing to do would be to save some credits, who knows, luck may save me once again.*

Thirty minutes later.

Slifer laid back as he closed the System's interface. Since he entered this new world, he had relied on cards, cards that disappeared after one use.

Now that he wasn't dirt poor, he had the chance to go a . . . different route.

"Master, the Ascendants . . . they've arrived . . ."

"Ah yes, Morvran. I'm ready."

More than ready . . .

CHAPTER SIXTY-NINE

S upreme Elder Slifer, nice of you to finally grace us with your presence," Zofia said sarcastically, eyeing the orange-robed man as he strode into the grand hall.

Slifer waved a dismissive hand. "Ah, my apologies, as the sole supreme elder of the Black Rose Sect, I actually have responsibilities to attend to," he retorted.

Inwardly, Slifer laughed. Most of those so-called responsibilities he pawned off on his underlings. Wasn't that what they were for after all?

Let them handle the tedious day-to-day affairs while he focused on the important stuff, like pretending to be an Ascendant cultivator when he had just reached the Foundation Establishment stage.

Zofia's face darkened at Slifer's flippant response, and for a moment it looked as if she might lunge across the table and throttle him. She was too used to letting her fists do the talking whenever she couldn't best someone verbally.

But one humiliating defeat at this man's hands was enough, no matter how much his nonchalant attitude grated on her nerves.

Sensing the tension, Leontius stepped forward, raising his hands in a calming gesture. "Now, now, let's not argue. It is an honor to be here at the esteemed Black Rose Sect."

Slifer raised an eyebrow. *Is this guy being serious?* he thought.

Kaelius leaned forward. "So won't the Black Rose Sect Master be hosting the tournament himself?"

Slifer shook his head. "I'm afraid he is still deep in closed-door cultivation."

Kaelius nodded slowly, a calculating look in his eyes. "I see. How . . . unfortunate."

"Yes, quite unfortunate indeed," Slifer agreed mildly. "But we will manage somehow in his stead."

"Enough wasting time on pleasantries," Astrid cut in impatiently. True to her no-nonsense personality, she wanted to get right down to business. "Just show us to our quarters already so we can rest and prepare for the tournament."

Slifer nodded. For formality's sake, he only came to greet them. He turned to lead them out of the hall. But before he could take a step, Zofia spoke up.

"By the way, it seems the Black Death Sect really isn't participating this time around."

The supreme elders exchanged glances. This was unprecedented—never before had one of the major sects declined to join the tournament and lose their chance to enter the Sealed Realm.

Astrid scowled, crossing her arms. "If the Black Death Sect doesn't attend, how will we open the gateway to the Sealed Realm? We each hold a piece of the key. Without their piece . . ."

Each of the major sects held a fragment of the key needed to open the path to the Sealed

Realm. Without all the pieces united, it would be nearly impossible to breach its defenses, even for Ascendant cultivators.

"I contacted their sect master after he failed to appear for the Ascendant Meet," Leontius explained. "He assured me that if the Black Death disciples do not come, he will send an envoy with their key fragment."

"If?" Zofia echoed, one elegant eyebrow raised.

"It seems there is still a chance they may participate after all," Kaelius mused.

Astrid shook her head firmly. "Missing the Ascendant Meet is the same as forfeiting their right to join the tournament. If they want to enter the Sealed Realm, they'll have to do it through the one guaranteed slot allowed for their sect."

"I agree," said Zofia. "The rules clearly state—"

"Now, let's not be too hasty," Leontius gently interrupted. "I'm sure if we give them a chance to explain themselves, this can all be resolved amicably."

Zofia whirled on him. "If I didn't know how naïve you Pure Sect cultivators are, I'd think you were secretly a demon yourself with how much you defend them!"

Leontius simply sighed and shook his head. There was no reasoning with that woman once she got an idea in her mind.

Slifer observed all this whilst trying to hold back a laugh. The politics of the so-called righteous path were endlessly entertaining.

Zofia seemed satisfied that the matter was settled, at least for now. She turned her gaze back to Slifer. "Well, what are you waiting for? Lead the way."

Suppressing a sigh at the pushy woman, Slifer proceeded out of the hall, the four Ascendant cultivators trailing behind him.

This was going to be a long month.

William laid awake in bed, staring up at the ceiling. Tomorrow morning was the start of the Inter-Sect Tournament—his chance to secure a slot to enter the Sealed Realm.

Just thinking about it made his heart race with anticipation. And nerves. Mostly nerves, if he was being honest.

Could he actually win one of the open slots? As an Early Foundation Establishment cultivator, the odds were stacked against him. The field would be packed with Peak Foundation Establishment opponents.

William gritted his teeth, hands clenching the blankets.

He wasn't confident. And William hated feeling uncertain.

Ever since that night when that "man" visited his family home, William's cocky confidence had wavered. It was the first time he truly comprehended how powerless he was, how fragile his family's lives hung by a thread at the whims of those stronger than himself.

If he wanted to protect them, he had no choice but to become a puppet on the "man's" strings. Securing a spot in the Sealed Realm was the first step, though William still did not fully understand the "man's" ultimate goals.

The Black Rose Sect's resources were the only reason he managed to break through to the Foundation Establishment stage at all. But would that be enough?

You don't have a choice, he reminded himself. His family's safety depended on him securing a spot in the tournament. The "man" had been very clear—succeed, and his family would be spared. Fail, and . . .

William shoved that thought away. He refused to fail.

At least the "man" had provided some resources to help him accomplish that goal: treasures and talismans that William could activate once inside the Sealed Realm itself.

The rules of the Inter-Sect Tournament forbid the use of external tools, restricting cultivators to only their personal skills and weapons.

A buzzing sensation in his mind interrupted William's brooding. *The communication talisman!* Heart racing, he jumped out of bed and hurriedly threw on a dark robe.

The sensation grew more intense as William slipped out of his room, keeping to the shadows as he navigated the dim halls. Despite the late hour, the sect was still bustling with activity as disciples finished their preparations for tomorrow.

He spotted several Disciplinary Hall disciples patrolling the grounds, on the lookout for any troublemakers. William held his breath as he snuck past, praying they wouldn't sense his presence.

After what felt like an eternity, William made it through the sect entrance and escaped into the forest. Only once he was certain he hadn't been followed did he dare pull out the glowing talisman.

"Yes, I'm here," he whispered into the stone.

A deep voice came from the talisman. "Is everything prepared?"

William's jaw clenched. "Yes. As you instructed."

The voice chuckled. "Excellent. Remember, activate it as soon as you get near the target. This is almost over—succeed, and your family will be safe."

" . . . I understand," William bit out, even as doubts flooded his mind. Could he really trust the word of this mysterious man?

But what choice did he have?

Clenching the talisman tightly, William steeled himself for what was to come. Soon, everything would change—for better or worse.

"Man, you're so lucky you got your own place," Dusty said through a mouthful of bone as he lounged back on Nomed's bed. "You've got your own chef, no chores, servants to boss around whenever you want."

Nomed smiled at his plump friend. To Dusty, this luxurious lifestyle must seem like paradise compared to the rugged training under his strict master.

"It's not all fun and games," Nomed replied lightly. "Being alone can weigh on you after a while. I'm grateful for Master Slifer's generosity, but I do miss having you around to liven things up."

That seemed to delight Dusty. Beaming, he chomped down on another bone from the pile on the bed. Nomed wasn't sure where his friend kept getting these bones from, and he wasn't certain he wanted to know. Dusty's cultivation method seemed to have some . . . unique aspects.

"Well, you don't gotta worry about me and Master Morvran!" Dusty declared, bits of bone flying. "He's got me on this special training regimen to help my cultivation. Although . . ." Here, Dusty scowled. "He's making me grow my own food! Can you believe it?"

Nomed raised an eyebrow curiously. "What do you mean 'grow' it?"

"It's part of my new cultivation method—the Way of the Cock," Dusty explained through his perpetual mouthful of food. "I gotta raise chickens from eggs, care for 'em and stuff, let 'em grow big and healthy. Then, when the time's right, I absorb their energy to aid my cultivation!"

Nomed frowned, not quite following Dusty's rambling explanation. "But can't you just buy full-grown chickens from the market and use those? Seems much easier than raising them yourself."

Dusty adamantly shook his head, strands of his black hair swinging. "Nah, doesn't work like that. The method said I gotta raise 'em myself, from eggs to chickens. Something about the process strengthening my spirit or whatever." He shrugged. "Mainly it's just a lotta boring work. But Master Morvran said it's necessary, so I gotta do it."

"Huh," Nomed replied. "That's quite an unusual method. Are you making much progress with it?"

At this, Dusty laughed sheepishly. "I dunno. See, the first chicken I raised, Ol' Clucky . . . me and him got kinda close, y'know? Spent every day together, fed him the best seeds and bugs. I'd chat with him while we walked the grounds."

Dusty's expression turned reflective. "Ol' Clucky was a good listener. Squawked back now and then, but mostly let me ramble."

Nomed nodded as he listened patiently.

"So yeah, me and Clucky got to be buddies," Dusty continued, snacking on a rib bone now. "But then, when it came time for the ritual harvestin' . . . I dunno what happened exactly. It's all a blur. But next thing I knew, I was surrounded by bloody bones, hands covered in feathers, and one very satisfied belly."

He blinked at Nomed. "Weird, huh?"

Nomed stared. That was certainly not the heartwarming conclusion he anticipated. Trust Dusty to turn a charming tale into something much more macabre.

"Well, Master Morvran said that was a good sign!" Dusty went on cheerfully. "Means my cultivation instincts are developing well. Anyway, now I'm raising Clucky the Second. Hopefully the harvest goes smoother this time."

"I see," Nomed said slowly. "Well, I'm glad your training is progressing, if a bit unconventionally."

Nomed felt relieved his friend would not be participating in the tournament. As an Early Foundation Establishment cultivator, Dusty didn't meet the qualification standards to enter the tournament. The Sealed Realm would be dangerous enough without Dusty losing himself in some feeding frenzy at an inopportune moment.

As if reading his mind, Dusty flopped back on the bed with a sigh of content. "Yep, no big tournament for me! Don't gotta worry 'bout fighting other disciples or crazy life-or-death battles. Too much effort. I'm happy sticking to my chickens."

Nomed chuckled. "It does sound exhausting. Best leave the glory-seeking to the others."

Inwardly though, his thoughts took a more somber turn. Dusty was right to be grateful he could avoid the tournament. With everything looming on the horizon, it was better if his friend remained far away from the coming storm.

Nomed repressed a wince as a familiar burning sensation erupted across his chest. Speaking of his role, it seemed events were being set in motion once again tonight.

He hid his discomfort behind an easy smile. "It's getting late," Nomed said apologetically. "I should rest before tomorrow."

"Oh yeah, good idea!" Dusty said, sitting up and brushing bone fragments off the sheets. "Big day comin' up. You're gonna kick butt in that tournament! I know you got this."

"Thank you, my friend," Nomed replied. "I'll do my best."

After Dusty left, Nomed waited several minutes before slipping a black robe over his sleep clothes and disappearing into the night.

Kaelius sat stiffly on the cushion the Black Rose Sect had so generously provided, gazing around his lavish quarters with thinly veiled disgust.

This place dares call itself a demonic sect?

The environment was fit for royalty, not proper demonic cultivators.

In Kaelius's own Black Heart Sect, disciples lived in harsh conditions like inside a volatile volcano.

And rather than wasting resources on such useless luxuries, the Black Heart Sect's funds went towards more practical things—like weapons, assassination equipment, and information gathering.

Not that they needed money when anything they desired could simply be taken by force.

It was survival of the fittest—the weak culled out quickly in the merciless environment. Only the strongest, most ruthless cultivators thrived.

Kaelius curled his lip contemptuously. *The Black Rose Sect was soft, an insult to everything demonic cultivation stood for. They even allowed laughter and cheer in their streets—outrageous!*

He wondered if their disciples even killed each other over treasure. They behaved more like a righteous sect.

Well, he wouldn't have to tolerate it for much longer. Closing his eyes, Kaelius extended his spiritual sense past the confines of his room, stealthily probing through the sect. He took care to avoid the residences housing the other Ascendant cultivators; no need to arouse undue suspicion.

Satisfied he wasn't being observed, Kaelius's mouth curved into a razor-thin smile. In a blur of shadow, he slipped out into the night.

Kaelius flitted through the Black Rose Sect under the cover of darkness, disdainfully eyeing the ostentatious buildings and perfectly manicured gardens. *How disgustingly decadent.*

One figure caught his eye—a young man dressed in dark robes making his way towards the sect gates.

How curious . . . what business did he have sneaking away on this eve of all nights?

Examining closely, Kaelius saw the youth had only reached the Early Foundation Establishment Realm. In other words, a nobody. Whatever mischief he was up to, it would have no impact on someone of Kaelius's stature.

Dismissing the matter, Kaelius shifted his attention elsewhere. There was little of interest occurring within the disciples' residences. No, what Kaelius sought was information on the Black Rose Sect's greatest secret—their sect master.

Rumored to be secluded in attempt to reach the immortal stage, the sect master's hidden location was not known to anyone. But Kaelius was not so easily deterred.

If the Black Rose Sect Master was in the middle of a breakthrough, then that would be the best time for him to strike!

Devouring his cultivation will be enough to attempt my own breakthrough . . . Kaelius grinned.

Extending his spiritual sense towards the sect headquarters, Kaelius searched for anything out of the ordinary. He knew all sects had secret chambers and facilities hidden away, even from their own members.

There—along the edge of his sense, Kaelius detected several powerful energy signatures that were trying to appear inconspicuous gathered in one area. Upon closer inspection, they were shockingly all at the Origin Realm!

For so many Origin Realm masters to be clustered together could only mean one thing: they were standing as guards over something . . . or rather, someone.

Found you at last.

Locking onto the Origin Realm experts' positions, he traced their presence deeper into the sect. Their trail led to a hidden cave entrance secreted away in a remote mountain valley.

How delightfully sinister, Kaelius thought, lips curling. Finally, something befitting the alleged demonic nature of this sect.

He dissolved into shadow and slipped past the entrance, descending into the cavernous tunnels below.

Immediately, a powerful demonic aura blasted his face, so concentrated it was nearly tangible. Kaelius's cultivation method activated as it greedily drank it in.

Delicious . . .

The farther in he went, the more the demonic energy grew.

An unsettling roar echoed up ahead, reverberating off the stone walls.

This is no ordinary demonic cultivation. Kaelius hesitated. *Just what is the Black Rose Sect Master doing down here?*

Before he could proceed further, an enormous cavern opened up before him. Kaelius's pupils contracted to pinpricks, and he inhaled sharply.

Lurking in the shadows was a hulking form, crimson eyes glowing as they fixed on him.

"Demon!" he choked out before the world went dark.

CHAPTER SEVENTY

Zack walked into the grand arena, casually taking in the sights around him. The massive stadium had been hastily constructed by the Black Rose Sect in preparation for the upcoming Inter-Sect Tournament.

The entire structure looked freshly cut from black marble, with towering stands that would soon be filled by thousands of spectators.

It was clear that the Black Rose Sect had spared no expense when it came to hosting the tournament.

Despite the early hour, the stands were already beginning to fill as disciples and spectators alike fought for the best views of the tournament stage below. Excited chatter hummed through the crowds as friends called out greetings and rivals traded taunts.

Zack's gaze swept over the disciples gathered in the arena's center, all clustered in their sect groupings. He spotted a few familiar faces from the Black Rose Sect and walked over to join them.

"Junior Brother Zack!" a cheerful voice called out.

Zack turned to see Hughie elbowing his way through the crowd towards him, a wide grin splitting his face.

Once he reached Zack, Hughie clapped him on the back. "Man, can you believe this place? The tournament's gonna be epic!" Lowering his voice, he added, "And when you make it into the Sealed Realm, your senior brother's got your back. My luck's gotta rub off on you at some point!"

Zack laughed. Having Hughie's notorious bouts of fortune on his side certainly wouldn't hurt. He still remembered how it saved the Main Body's hide a few times. "I'll hold you to that, Senior Brother."

To Zack's surprise, he and Hughie got on quite well. Unlike with the Main Body, Hughie seemed quite laid-back and relaxed around him, he even made a few jokes here and there.

Noticing two more familiar figures, Hughie waved them over. "Caelum! Amelia! Come join us!"

As the two walked over, Amelia gave Zack a slow, heated once-over that made him resist the urge to take a step back.

Really, being cursed with such devilish good looks can be a hassle at times. Zack sighed as though it wasn't the Main Body who meticulously crafted his body. *Well, I guess with great power comes great responsibility.*

"Let's join the other disciples in the waiting area," Caelum suggested. He gestured towards the tunnel leading under the arena floor. "We'll be summoned when it's time."

The group nodded, moving to follow the steady stream of disciples. Zack glanced around, realizing that one disciple was missing.

"Has anyone seen Nomed?"

The disciples glanced at each other and shook their heads.

"You know how he is, always wandering off on his own for who knows what," Hughie said. "I'm sure he'll turn up sooner or later."

What was that kid up to when he vanished like that? Zack wondered. *Eh, it's not my problem, keeping disciples in check is the Main Body's job!*

Shaking his head, Zack turned his attention to the other disciples filling the tunnel. With over a few hundred Foundation Establishment contenders, seeking out potential troublemakers would prove tricky.

Someone's watching me . . . A prickle on the back of his neck made him glance over to find none other than Ziven staring back at him. *No, he's not looking at me.*

The Heavenly Light disciple was actually glaring at Amelia—the animosity was nearly palpable even from a distance.

Glare all you want; you don't have long to live anyway.

Scanning the crowds again, Zack spotted another knot of disciples gathered around one Heavenly Light disciple in particular. The slender youth ignored those vying for his attention, though his posture suggested that he enjoyed the fawning.

It was none other than Arkan, a well-known prodigy even in the Heavenly Light Sect. According to Morvran's intelligence reports, the youth resented Ziven for stealing some of his limelight as a newcomer to the sect.

Now there's a possibility worth entertaining, Zack mused. *Stoking the flames of rivalry to spur Arkan into confronting Ziven during the tournament could produce some entertaining chaos and who knows, it may even weaken the Son of Heaven. If you want to kill a Son of Heaven, you gotta play dirty.*

Before Zack could further ponder this, shouts erupted from his left. Whipping his head around, he spotted a hulking White Tiger Sect disciple stomping through the passageway. Zack guessed that he had to be at least seven and a half feet tall.

As the White Tiger disciple strode by, even some of the Core Formation competitors shuffled out of his path. The man's cultivation base fluctuations identified him as a solid Peak Foundation Establishment Realm cultivator.

A dual cultivator! Zack felt a spike of excitement.

He hadn't expected to see another cultivator like himself.

The White Tiger Sect was notorious for producing beast-like combat fanatics.

And a dual cultivator had "difficult opponent" written all over him.

An image of the huge disciple and Zack exchanging earth-shattering blows flashed through his mind.

Smirking to himself, Zack decided finding the opportunity to face off against this brute in the arena could make the tournament somewhat less monotonous.

The Main Body wants me to breeze through the competition, but where was the fun in that?

Zack's musings were cut short by another commotion, this time it was to his right. He glanced over to see a cultivator from the Black Heart Sect go flying through the air before crashing into the wall.

"Keep your filthy hands to yourself, worm!" a familiar voice snapped.

Zack blinked in surprise to see Amelia standing there, wiping her hands as she glowered at the fallen cultivator.

Interesting.

He had naturally assumed the girl must have started the altercation given her . . . volatile temperament. Apparently, there was more to the situation.

Slowly sitting up, the Black Heart disciple wiped blood from his mouth with the back of one hand. The air around him rippled with qi as he fixed Amelia with a venomous glare.

"You should be grateful that I would even spare you the slightest notice," the man spat.

Zack scrutinized the disciple, sensing the cultivation base of a Peak Core Formation Realm cultivator.

Not bad, but I don't think he has what it takes to beat Amelia.

Before the man could stand, a sudden pressure slammed down on him, forcing him back to his knees.

Caelum's eyes had sharpened, bearing down on the Black Heart disciple with over-whelming intensity. Even though he knew Amelia could handle herself, he couldn't help but get involved, he hated those who preyed on women.

"A sword cultivator!" someone exclaimed.

Only someone who had attained the rare Sword Soul Realm could exert such formidable pressure without leaking the slightest bit of energy.

Sneering, the Black Heart disciple moved to stand but before things could escalate further, an ear-splitting chime rang out through the arena.

"Take your places, disciples! The first competition will soon begin!" Elder Fred's voice boomed overhead.

"Guess playtime's over," Hughie said, cracking his knuckles. "Let's go prove why our sect's the best!"

Zack took one last sweeping look across the arena, imprinting the faces of the more *interesting* opponents to memory.

When next they met, it would be as enemies.

"Right," he murmured. "Let the games begin."

Five minutes ago.

Seated comfortably in the highest booth overlooking the arena, Slifer stroked the scaly head of the baby dragon perched on his shoulder.

Little Val peered down at the bustling crowds below, her slitted eyes bright with curios-ity. "Why can't I join the tournament too?" she said, turning her big eyes up at Slifer. "It looks like fun!"

Slifer chuckled, reaching up to pet her. "I'm afraid not, little one. The tournament is only open to human disciples below the Nascent Soul stage."

And Val was neither human nor below Nascent Soul.

Her eyes rounded in surprise. "Oh! Val is too strong for humans?"

Slifer laughed. "Yes, far too strong for them, I'm afraid. You'd gobble them all up without even trying!"

He tickled her belly, and she released a small burp of flame in protest, though she looked rather pleased by the assessment of her skills.

"So Val can't play with them?"

"If you played with them, it could be considered bullying," Slifer explained patiently. "We need to let the others have a fair chance to compete as well."

The lie rolled smoothly off his tongue. The tournament was rigged to favor his disciples, Slifer didn't care about playing fair. Playing fair in a xianxia world only got you killed.

But Slifer didn't enjoy lying, especially to little Val. However, it was his job to turn her into a righteous dragon.

If there even is such a thing.

Val mulled over Slifer's words for a few seconds before nodding. "I don't want to be a bully," she declared. "Master said being a bully is bad."

"Exactly right," Slifer praised, smiling at this small sign of moral development. He popped a cinnamon candy from his robe pocket into her mouth as a reward.

It wasn't the human meat she craved, but it would do the job.

For now.

One by one, the Ascendant cultivators from the other sects began filing into the adjoining booths reserved for them. Slifer greeted them lazily through half-lidded eyes.

When the last booth remained empty, Astrid broke the silence. "Where is Kaelius? Did anyone see the Black Heart Sect Master arrive?"

The other Ascendants shook their heads. None of them had seen the Black Heart Sect Master since yesterday.

"Funny you should mention that," Slifer remarked lightly as he reached into his spatial ring.

He brought out an item—a gold key etched with black runes.

"One of my patrols found this dropped near our sect's southern border."

Zofia's eyes narrowed. "Why do you have Kaelius's key fragment? What have you done with him?"

"Now hold on," Leontius interjected gently. "Let's not jump to conclusions. I'm certain there's a reasonable explanation."

"Was there any other sign of Kaelius?" Astrid butted in.

Slifer shook his head, keeping his expression neutral. "My men scoured the region thoroughly but found no traces. As you know, when an Ascendant truly does not wish to be found . . ."

He trailed off with a shrug. The implication was clear—if Kaelius had gone into hiding, no one short of an Immortal Realm expert would be capable of locating him against his will.

"Preposterous!" Zofia snapped, crossing her arms. "You expect us to believe an Ascendant cultivator just happened to disappear without a trace while visiting your sect? Do you take us for fools?"

Ah Zofia, always quick to think the worst of people. Slifer resisted the urge to rub his temples at the headache he could already feel developing.

However, he couldn't blame her, it did sound suspicious.

He had known revealing Kaelius's key would arouse the others' suspicion. But if he had withheld it only to produce the artifact later during the opening of the Sealed Realm, it would have made him appear even more untrustworthy.

If he was the Ascendant cultivator that he pretended to be, then avoiding conflict wouldn't matter to him.

And unfortunately there was simply no graceful way to handle the Black Heart Sect Leader's unexpected disappearance.

"While I don't claim to know what happened to Sect Master Kaelius, I can assure you I played no part in it," Slifer said evenly, meeting Zofia's hostile gaze. "Are you really suggesting I have the ability to overpower and dispose of a cultivator of Kaelius's level without anyone else detecting anything?"

Zofia's eyes flashed, but she held her tongue.

Cultivators at their level *could* be defeated by others in the same realm, but they were incredibly difficult to kill, they just had too many life-saving treasures.

And for one to go missing without being able to alert anyone? Even she knew that sounded ridiculous.

"Enough speculation. If the Black Rose Sect intended to attack us, why wait until now? They could have ambushed us from the beginning." She eyed Kaelius's key fragment. "All that matters is we have his piece. I'm sure Kaelius will turn up eventually."

With a huff, Zofia settled back in her seat. Unless the Black Rose Sect Master completed his breakthrough, the Black Rose Sect simply didn't have the qualifications to threaten any of the other major sects.

And if such a breakthrough were to occur, then the mysterious phenomenon that accompanied it couldn't be hidden.

Crisis averted. Slifer held back a sigh.

"Please inform us if you learn anything more of Kaelius's whereabouts," Leontius requested.

"You have my word." Slifer inclined his head, though he was skeptical whether the word of a demonic cultivator meant anything.

He certainly wouldn't be naïve enough to believe it.

Slifer had his suspicions about the Black Heart Sect Master's sudden disappearance. But voicing them now would only rouse further suspicion.

Better to keep it to himself for the time being.

Satisfied that the Ascendants were appeased, Slifer signaled for Elder Fred to commence with the opening proceedings.

It's showtime.

Right on cue, the tunnel entrances around the arena's perimeter shuddered open. What appeared to be a solid stone wall slid apart, revealing the competitors standing ready in the passageways.

"Welcome to the Inter-Sect Tournament!" Elder Fred's voice boomed through the arena. "You have met the criteria to enter the tournament. Now is your chance to earn a slot to enter the Sealed Realm!"

The disciples below stood straighter, pride and excitement on their faces. Entering the Sealed Realm could change their fates, those that were destined to die as mediocre could become the rising stars of the younger generation.

"Two parallel tournaments will take place simultaneously over this coming month," Fred continued. "One for the Core Formation disciples, and one for Foundation Establishment."

The disciples listened intently. The tournament structure was familiar to them already.

"Five total spots to enter the Sealed Realm will be awarded to each group," the elder said, holding up five fingers. "Now, onto the first stage." He waved a sleeve, conjuring glowing images of two contrasting environments. "It will take place in two pocket realms we have prepared."

Pocket realms were similar to mini-sealed realms. Like the name suggested, they were much smaller in size. It was normal for sects to have a few in their possession.

"The Foundation Establishment group will be entering the Forest of Whispering Shadows." The image depicted a misty, gloomy woodland. "As for the Core Formation group, they will enter the Valley of Scattered Flames." This realm showed a fiery landscape of lava flows and smoky fissures.

"Participants will be divided randomly into teams of three. Each team will be sent into separate pocket realms containing one Yin scroll and one Yang scroll." Fred allowed a dramatic pause before continuing. "And of course, all team members must remain alive to pass. The rules are simple—work together and survive."

This announcement was met by muted mumbles as the disciples sized up potential allies and enemies. Teams would cut across sect divisions, forcing cooperation with rivals.

The demonic cultivators in particular seemed disgruntled. Trust did not come naturally to them under the best circumstances. Relying on unknown teammates could prove disastrous.

For once, the righteous cultivators shared their reluctance. How could they place their fates in the hands of those who walked the demonic path? Even with rules compelling cooperation, they still hesitated to trust those deviants.

Could they truly cooperate?

Raising his hands for silence, Elder Fred went on. "The team assignments will now be determined."

With another gesture, a wooden barrel etched with glowing symbols appeared on the ground. "Each of you, come forth and draw a marked stone. The number will assign you to your team."

Before the first eager disciple could rush forward, a powerful pressure abruptly weighed down on the arena, stopping everyone cold. Gasps and shouts erupted as all heads craned skyward.

There, a flying ship broke through the clouds before descending towards the tournament grounds. The disciples could make out a dark, hooded figure standing atop the deck.

A cloaked man leapt over the side, landing catlike on the booth holding the Ascendant beings. Pulling back its hood, the figure revealed itself, it was the Black Death Sect Master!

"What is the meaning of this, Vowron?" Zofia demanded, on her feet. "The Black Death Sect forfeited their tournament rights by not attending the Ascendant Meet."

The Black Death Sect Master chuckled, unbothered by her attitude. "Come now, let's not fuss over technicalities between friends." He walked towards the empty booth. "Surely one more competitor would make things . . . interesting."

"Absolutely not," Astrid declared, rising to join Zofia. "The rules clearly state any sect absent from the Meet relinquishes their entry eligibility."

"It sounds like you're making excuses, do you fear facing true competition?" Vowron raised an eyebrow.

"Why you—!" Zofia looked ready to leap down and throttle the man herself. Only Leontius's hand on her shoulder kept her rooted in place.

But the Black Death Sect Master merely smirked at the Ascendants. "If you brought the Heavenly Light's esteemed sect master, I may have backed down," he purred. "But against the likes of you? I think not."

To emphasize his point, he unleashed the full pressure of his cultivation base. The sheer power forced Zofia and Leontius back into their seats. Only Astrid managed to remain standing, though uneasily.

Peak Ascendant Realm!

The Ascendants all turned to Slifer. Not only was he supposedly the most powerful amongst them but he *was* the host, this was his mess to deal with.

Dammit, why does this keep happening? What should I do? I can't afford to reveal my trump cards, at least, not so soon.

CHAPTER SEVENTY-ONE

*I*nsight!

> Name: Vowron
> Realm: Half-Step Immortal Realm
> Known Techniques: N/A
> Known Affiliations: N/A
> Disposition: N/A
> Comprehension: 5
> Luck: 5
> Talent: 6
> Will: 5

So, the man already has a foot in the Immortal Realm. It seems this tournament just became a little less boring. Slifer held back a frown.

He wasn't happy.

Boring was good, boring was safe!

Based on Vowron's attitude, Slifer guessed that the Black Death Sect Master likely aimed to goad him into a confrontation, then use him as a punching bag to show off his new cultivation to the other sects.

However, Slifer had no desire to be anyone's puppet, least of all a punching bag!

Like hell I'm humiliating myself for your amusement, Vowron.

As much as Slifer wished to put the arrogant devil in his place, he knew revealing his trump cards this soon would be unwise.

Diplomacy it is . . .

Rising to his feet, Slifer felt the anxious gazes of the other Ascendants fix on him, anticipating and perhaps even desiring a clash between the two.

"Vowron is absolutely right," Slifer declared, flashing a carefree grin. "The more competitors we have, the more exciting the tournament will be!"

Vowron's eyebrows shot up in surprise. This was clearly not the reaction he had expected.

Slifer smiled and waved a hand invitingly. "By all means, join us! I look forward to seeing what your disciples can do against the best of our sects."

Recovering quickly, Vowron returned Slifer's smile. "You are too gracious, Supreme Elder," he said smoothly. "I appreciate you seeing reason."

The other Ascendants exchanged wary glances, suspicion etched on their faces. Clearly they wondered whether the two demonic cultivators were in collusion against them.

Little Val tugged worriedly on Slifer's sleeve. "Master, that strange man feels scary," she whispered.

I agree! he cried internally. However, outwardly, he smiled and gave the dragon a reassuring pat. "Not to worry, I won't let anyone hurt you, little one." He slipped her another cinnamon candy to distract her.

It worked.

Val's small face immediately brightened. "Master is the best!"

With Vowron now seated, the Black Death Sect disciples disembarked from the flying ship and joined the other competitors on the arena floor. Slifer watched as the team allocation process resumed.

When it came time for Hughie to draw his number, Slifer had to resist a knowing smile. Through a bit of trickery beforehand, Elder Fred had secretly marked the stones corresponding to the qi of Slifer's disciples.

Just as Slifer anticipated, Hughie picked up a stone carved with the number nine.

Excellent. Now to get the other two on the same team.

Shortly after, Amelia approached and also selected the stone marked with the number nine. She shot Hughie a smile as she came to stand beside him. Finally, Caelum drew the same stone.

"Well, well, what a fortuitous *coincidence*," Zofia remarked drily, casting Slifer a pointed look. "One might even say this assignment process seems downright rigged."

Slifer simply laughed. "Come now, Zofia. You can only blame the heavens for my luck."

He glanced down at Val who bobbed her head in fervent agreement. "Master said lying is bad. He would never ever cheat!"

Slifer nodded, ignoring the twinge of guilt he felt at the baby dragon's trust in him. *Sometimes cheating is necessary*, he reassured himself.

"Of course not," Zofia said flatly, clearly unconvinced. With a resigned sigh, she settled back into her seat.

A sect securing small advantages for its own members was simply expected when hosting tournaments such as these. Zofia's own Heavenly Light Sect had certainly rigged things in their favor during previous tournaments.

At least the teams appear evenly matched otherwise, Zofia noted.

The random assignment process resulted in most groups comprised of disciples from different sects. In comparison, Slifer's handpicked team consisted solely of top Black Rose disciples. She hated to admit it, but Slifer's sect did have a distinct edge this round.

Thirty minutes later.

With the Core Formation teams allocated, it was time for the Foundation Establishment disciples. Slifer watched idly as they approached one by one to draw their numbers. Most knew better than to outwardly react to their new teammates, though Slifer noticed more than a few poorly concealed grimaces.

When William stepped up, Slifer observed closely. He remembered William. During the Disciple Selection Ceremony, the other grand elders expected Slifer to take him on.

However, Slifer knew that whilst the boy's stats were decent, they were not enough to catch the eye of a grand elder, let alone a supreme elder. He didn't know how he did it, but Slifer knew that William had cheated.

He was a motivated young man, willing to do whatever it took to succeed. And that was what Slifer was looking for.

He could be a good teammate for Zack.

William drew a stone engraved with the number three. Though he kept his face impassive, his breathing quickened. Slifer could sense the boy's anxiety. William knew that passing the first stage greatly depended on having good teammates.

Ha ha, don't worry lad, I've got that sorted for you. Slifer held back a laugh, he could get used to playing the strings behind the scene.

A few more disciples were given their numbers before Nomed, who had arrived just before Elder Fred's announcement, stepped forth.

Slifer wasn't surprised when Nomed also selected the stone marked three.

Zack, Nomed, and William . . . Together, they should be one of the stronger groups in the Foundation Establishment Realm.

William's eyes narrowed slightly. He did not like or trust Nomed. Though he would never admit it aloud, he felt inferior to the talented village boy who had risen so quickly through the sect. However, remembering his family's fate depended on him entering the Sealed Realm, William swallowed his pride. Nomed's skills could help him pass this stage.

I guess I could partner up with a village boy, William thought, giving Nomed a slight nod as the other disciple joined him.

After several more team allocations, it was finally Zack's turn!

Zack sauntered up to the stone barrel, fully expecting the number three to be etched into the one that called to him. The Main Body already rigged this entire process in his favor, after all. This would be child's play.

He plunged his hand inside, grabbing onto the fragment that he felt calling to him. Without even glancing at it, he turned to head towards William and Nomed's side. But halfway there he froze, smile disappearing as he read the number on the fragment—five.

Five! How was that possible? Did the Main Body somehow make a mistake? Zack snuck a look at Slifer, who, with his wrinkly face, couldn't look anymore disinterested. But Zack could tell by the slight twitch on his forehead that the Main Body was just as stunned as him.

The Main Body didn't know . . . which means . . . sabotage! Someone or something interfered. Has my identity been exposed? But why target something so trivial as team assignments? It . . . it doesn't make sense! Unless . . . A chill ran down Zack's spine. *Could this be the work of Heaven's Will itself? Striking back against the Main Body?*

A pointed cough from Elder Fred jolted Zack from his spiraling speculation. "If you're quite done gawking, boy, move along now. Others are still waiting for their turn."

"Er, right. Sorry." Zack shook himself out of his stupor and headed over to join the other disciple who drew stone number five.

As he took his place, Zack looked at his new teammate—a pale, silent girl from the Black Death Sect.

She spared him a single impassive glance before turning away.

Zack resisted the urge to scowl. *Well, isn't this just fantastic . . . nothing says "fun times ahead" like getting partnered with the living embodiment of a K-drama gothic vampire.*

Hopefully the third member would be more talkative. As much as Zack enjoyed listening to his own voice, talking to himself grew tedious and would probably draw unwanted attention that he did not need.

After several more students, a tall, wiry Black Death disciple shuffled over to join them. Sharp cheekbones, sunken eyes, sallow complexion—*yep, definitely some undead blood in this one. Maybe a zombie?*

Plastering on a friendly grin, Zack stuck out his hand. "Name's Zack! Let's all get along now."

The boy ignored his outstretched hand, face expressionless. Zack let his arm drop, smile growing strained.

Okay, then. Looks like sparkling conversation is off the table.

Noticing the unexpected grouping, Vowron called over to Slifer, "It seems our disciples will be teammates. How fortunate!"

Slifer forced a smile. "Yes, my disciple is lucky to have yours." Inwardly, he thought the opposite. He did not trust these Black Death disciples one bit.

Vowron shook his head. "Come now, let us not pretend luck had anything to do with this." His knowing look made Slifer's eyes narrow.

The Black Death Sect only arrived as the Inter-Sect Tournament was beginning, they didn't have time to interfere with the stone markings.

Unless . . . there's a traitor!

It wasn't unusual for spies to be hidden within the ranks of sects. Only a foolish sect master would refrain from sending spies to other sects. What troubled Slifer was that the traitor was targeting Zack or maybe . . . him?

The Black Heart Sect Master's disappearance . . . the traitor targeting me . . . Slifer's eyes flashed. Ever since he had entered this world, it was one problem after another. He wasn't surprised that the tournament was no longer a simple tournament. Something was going on, and he needed to find out what.

"Morvran, I need you and Kalin to . . ."

With all the teams decided, Elder Fred raised his hands. "The first stage will now begin!"

He lifted two cubes in his palms—one fiery red, one emerald green. With a flick of his wrists, he sent them flying towards the disciples below. The red cube landed amongst the Core Formation competitors, while the green one reached the Foundation Establishment group.

"Take hold of the cube with your team to activate the teleportation portal," Elder Fred explained. "Do not let go until you have crossed over, or you may become separated."

Cries of shock and excitement rang out as the disciples hurried to follow his instructions.

Hughie, Amelia, and Caelum grabbed hands around their cube.

"I've got a bad feeling about this," Hughie muttered. "Going through weird portals never ends well for me."

"Oh, stop whining." Amelia snatched his hand along with Caelum's. Before Hughie could protest further, she channeled her qi into the cube.

"Hey, wait a sec!" Hughie's panicked voice echoed back right before a fiery portal enveloped the trio.

Zack watched as the Foundation Establishment teams disappeared into green portals. Elder Fred's words rang in his head, if he didn't keep a hold of his teammates, he would be separated.

The criteria to pass the first stage stipulated that all team members must be alive. But . . . it never mentioned anything about being crippled.

He shared the Main Body's suspicion. He knew that demonic cultivators should never be trusted but something about these two was dangerous, very dangerous.

And Zack *definitely* did not want to be trapped alone with them.

As much as he craved excitement, Zack did not want to die.

No! I'm too young to die, I'm only a few weeks old!

The Black Death disciples closed in on either side of Zack, each grabbing one of his arms just before the jade stone arrived.

So, they ignore me when I want a handshake, yet this is okay? Zack sighed, feeling their grips tighten around his wrists like iron shackles.

These guys are too shady and I don't have any cards to keep me safe, I need to get out of here! Zack decided as the stone's teleportation field enveloped them.

He quickly jerked his arms free and leapt backwards.

The Black Death Sect members' expressions darkened, reaching forward to grab him.

"See you never," Zack laughed, waving as he disappeared into the vortex.

CHAPTER SEVENTY-TWO

Valley of Scattered Flames

Hughie let out a startled yelp as he tumbled out of the portal, landing face-first into a pile of thick, mushy muck.

"Ugghh, gross!" he exclaimed, scrambling to his feet. His face was covered in sticky, pungent gunk. He grimaced as he tentatively sniffed the foul substance.

"Oh no . . . is this what I think it is?"

Of course he would land smack into a pile of Silverspine Ape dung—known throughout the realm for producing the largest, smelliest piles of feces.

They weren't even native to warm terrains, what was the bloody ape doing here?

"This is why I hate portals!" he groused miserably.

The old man's laughter rang in his head. "Serves you right for not jumping in yourself, boy! A little crap will do you good."

Scowling, Hughie looked around for something to clean himself with. Finding a clear puddle, he hurriedly bent down to splash the water on his face.

"That's much better—" He broke off with a strangled yelp as Amelia emerged behind him, biting back a smile.

"Pretty sure that puddle is ape piss, Hughie."

Hughie reeled back, every inch of his face burning with humiliation. Just his luck—shit and piss in one fell swoop.

This day just keeps getting better and better.

Seeing his expression, Amelia laughed.

Oh yeah, laugh it up! Hughie shot her a venomous look as he desperately wiped again at his face.

This was all her fault for shoving him into that blasted portal.

As the two bickered, Caelum emerged from the portal. His gaze swept over the fiery landscape—rivers of lava, plumes of toxic gas, jagged cliffs—taking in the Valley of Scattered Flames.

It was a harsh, unforgiving environment.

Caelum closed his eyes, extending his spiritual sense out in all directions. As a sword cultivator, he had honed his spiritual perception to extend exceptionally far.

Amelia watched Caelum closely, arms crossed. "Any other teams close enough for me to play with?" she asked. Though her tone was nonchalant, her eyes glinted with that familiar sadistic gleam.

After a long moment, Caelum opened his eyes and shook his head. "No one else seems to be nearby," he reported. Given the vast size of the pocket realm, he hadn't really expected to detect anyone right away. "We appear to be alone for the time being."

Amelia sighed. "That's a shame. I was hoping to get my hands on some arrogant righteous disciples." Cracking her knuckles, she added, "I would have enjoyed teaching them some manners."

Having finally cleaned himself off using a non-urine puddle, Hughie walked over to them. "Alright, we made it here in one piece. What's the plan?"

Caelum paused, considering their options. Master had informed them that the scrolls they needed were protected from traditional spiritual sense somehow. However, he did give them a map.

A map that marked the location of several scrolls!

Normally, Caelum frowned on cheating. As a sword cultivator that now followed the righteous path, he valued honor and fairness.

Master said we must do whatever it takes to succeed, he reminded himself. *For the greater good.*

Pulling out the map, Caelum pointed to a spot circled in red ink. "A scroll is hidden somewhere near here. It's close by, so we'll start our search there." He traced a finger along the route. "Stay within signaling range in case of trouble," he advised. "There could be dangerous beasts about . . . or worse, humans."

Hughie nodded seriously. After his face-first introduction to the local wildlife, he was taking no chances.

Caelum stored the map back inside his storage ring. "Let's begin. And remember, do not take any unnecessary risks."

The three disciples split up, moving deeper into the scorched valley.

Hughie picked his way carefully over the rugged terrain, not daring to fly. Caelum had warned him that it would only expose him to any beasts hidden on land.

The earth rumbled beneath his feet, and he eyed the bubbling lava pits warily. One misstep would cook him quicker than a chicken drumstick at a barbecue. The thought made his stomach grumble—when was the last time he'd eaten?

"Scared, boy?" Li Fenghao sneered in his mind. "And to think you joined a demonic sect!"

Hughie scowled. Just because he didn't want to plunge to a fiery death didn't mean he was afraid! He was just being careful. Caution was perfectly rational.

"If you say so," Li Fenghao said, clearly unconvinced. "Just focus on finding that scroll."

Hughie nodded, extending his spiritual sense, looking for signs of the hidden scroll. His search proved fruitless.

Master was right. He sighed.

The scroll had a concealment inscription which prevented detection through spiritual sense.

I guess I'll have to locate it the old-fashioned way.

A hiss was his only warning before a snake lashed out from the shadows. Hughie yelped, narrowly evading the surprise attack. The serpent's fangs grazed his sleeve as he leapt aside.

A tiny, brightly colored snake lay coiled a few feet away, flicking its tongue. Hughie snorted—this little thing was six inches at best? How cute.

"I'm a little big for you fella, don't you think?" He laughed as he raised his foot.

He prepared to stomp the Late Core Formation stage reptile to death, but the little thing was a slimy one, easily dodging his attacks.

The two got into a stalemate where neither was able to touch the other.

Noticing the acidic venom spat by the snake, Li Fenghao facepalmed.

The boy was confident, too confident. He clearly needed more humility beaten into him. But the old man stayed silent. Better to let the boy learn from experience.

"Nice try little guy." Hughie laughed as he slipped past another venomous strike. "Now, ta—"

Suddenly, the ground beneath Hughie's feet trembled and began caving in! "Whoa!" He quickly leapt onto his flying sword, staring around in bewilderment as a sinkhole began to form.

What was going on here?

"The snake's venom targeted the ground, you fool!" Li Fenghao snapped.

"So? I can fly just fi— GAH!" Hughie's retort ended in a strangled yelp as an ear-piercing shriek rang out. He jerked his head up just as a dark shape plummeted from the smoky sky towards him. Talons slashing, the hawk-like beast barely missed disemboweling him as he desperately rolled his sword aside.

"Okay, flying—very bad idea." Hughie clutched at the long gash torn in his shoulder. "Where the hell did that come from?"

Li Fenghao sighed loudly. "Do I need to explain everything, boy? Use that lump on your shoulders called a brain."

"Uh, yes, please explain," Hughie said sheepishly. He knew he could be dense sometimes. "I'd appreciate it, Master Li."

The greater immortal pinched the bridge of his nose before responding.

"Clearly that pathetic snake has been hiding from that hawk-like creature," Li Fenghao lectured. "It lured you into the air to make you bait it out."

Hughie's eyes widened in understanding as he glanced around for the now-vanished serpent. "Ooohh, so it made me a distraction to escape! Clever girl."

"No, it didn't escape. It's hiding, it wants *you* to deal with the bird."

"Sneaky little bastard," Hughie grumbled. "Oh well, I'll leave Feathers up there to Caelum. Fighting airborne sucks."

Hughie shot a quick pulse of qi into the sky to summon his senior brother.

Moments later, Caelum burst into view, sword at the ready as he took in the situation. His gaze flicked from Hughie's bleeding shoulder to the circling hawk beast and back again.

"I'll handle this," Caelum said calmly, deflecting an aggressive swoop from the hawk. "You focus on the scroll."

As the two squared off in a blur of feathers and steel, Caelum added, "This is the serpent's territory, so the invader was likely brought in here by the sect." He swerved around the predator's claws. "Check its nest, the scroll is probably there."

Brows furrowing, Hughie asked, "Wait, how can you tell this is the snake's turf? Couldn't the bird be the native one?"

Caelum concealed his exasperation, focusing on the battle. "The acidic venom spatters on the ground are characteristic of the Diamondback Trickster snake, they are quite common in this realm. As for the bird, it is a Heartclaw Battlehawk, native to the Desolate Mountains, *not* here."

The hawk screeched in fury as Caelum's sword strike interrupted its attack. It pulled up sharply, circling around for another dive.

Caelum turned back to Hughie. "Does that satisfy your questions? Now, go find that nest while I handle this."

Seeing Hughie's blank look, Caelum's eye twitched. "Did you not even read the briefing scroll Master gave?"

Hughie chuckled awkwardly, rubbing the back of his head. "Ha ha, maybe skimmed it. But hey, that's what I've got you for, Mr. Encyclopedia!"

Caelum sighed deeply but Hughie was already scampering off.

Turning his focus back on the bird, he gripped Bloodthorn tightly. This was no ordinary hawk—it had clearly reached the Half-Step Nascent Soul Realm.

He would need his full concentration for this battle.

Amelia was annoyed.

She had specifically chosen to venture out further than their agreed area in hopes of encountering stragglers.

Sadly, her search only yielded stupid beasts so far.

A rumbling growl reverberated from down a rocky passage just as she had the thought. Amelia's eyes lit up. Perhaps this time it would be something interesting! She slipped silently towards the sound, pressed against the canyon wall. Peering around a boulder, she spotted the source—a hulking Goronox foraging through a pile of bones and debris.

What a beauty . . .

Standing over six feet at the shoulder, the giant armored boar was known for its wicked tusks and ill-tempered manner. Few would dare approach this Late Core Formation beast for the fun of it.

Come to mama. Amelia smiled, accepting the challenge. She enjoyed playing with beasts almost as much as cowardly disciples.

With a laugh, she launched herself from cover right onto the oblivious Goronox's back. The beast snorted in surprise, immediately bucking and thrashing to dislodge the unwelcome rider. But Amelia's legs locked tightly around its bulk as she clung on.

"Let's have some fun, piggy!" She blasted its unprotected ears with a soul attack, laughing as it squealed in pain.

Whipping its huge head around, the Goronox managed to clamp its sharp tusks onto her calf.

Amelia's smile deepened at the pain. She ripped a horn from its armored skull, raising the makeshift weapon high. But rather than stabbing down, she threw the horn into the sky.

The Goronox followed the flying object with its beady gaze. As the Goronox was distracted, Amelia unleashed her Soul Render technique, a blade of soul qi slashed the creature's legs. With a surprised squeal, the huge boar toppled over.

Catching the horn, Amelia leaned on the beast's head, letting her blood fall onto its face. The Goronox thrashed its head in frustration.

"Aw, tired already?" she mocked. "But I'm just getting started!"

Ignoring its muffled squeals, Amelia examined the ugly horn she held. Its jagged edge could do some beautiful damage on soft flesh. She traced it almost lovingly across the beast's face, leaving faint red lines in its rough hide.

Maybe if she was lucky, some disciples would come investigate the pained cries. Amelia smiled dreamily at the thought. She couldn't wait to see their faces when they stumbled into her playtime.

Humming cheerfully, she carved elegant spirals into the Goronox's tough armor. Their little game was just getting fun.

Forest of Whispering Shadows

Zack tumbled out of the portal, transitioning smoothly into a roll before springing back onto his feet.

"Ha! Nailed the landing!" He grinned, dusting himself off.

His smile faded as he took in his gloomy surroundings. Murky fog shrouded the damp, marshy woods around him. A bog stretched out nearby, surface shimmering with oily black water.

"Lovely place." Zack grimaced, glancing back at the empty space that once occupied a portal. "Yeah . . . this looks like a fantastic place for a vacation. Maybe I should build a summer home here."

Shaking his head, Zack fished out his map, scanning for telltale markings. None. "Damn. No scroll here," he muttered, returning the map to his ring.

Sloshing noises drew his gaze back to the swamp. An enormous, beady-eyed creature surfaced, jaws gaping wide to swallow him whole!

Zack immediately channeled lightning qi into his legs, the energy crackling over his skin as he nimbly jumped clear of the attack. "Whoa, now! No need for that."

The beast sunk below the murky waters once more, glaring at Zack before slowly submerging.

Zack wagged a scolding finger. "Ah ah ah, too late to back out now. You wanted a snack, well, now I'm not leaving until I get a new pair of boots."

That sneak attack sealed this dumb creature's fate.

Clenching his fist, Zack channeled his qi into a glowing orb of lightning. With a casual flick, he lobbed it into the swamp waters, where it exploded in a brilliant flash.

The entire bog lit up with branching arcs of electricity as the energy surged through every living thing in the murk. A chorus of strangled croaks and hisses rang out as the swamp dwellers spasmed and thrashed before falling still, roasted by the lightning blast.

Zack made a tugging motion with his hand, and the creatures' corpses rose to the surface, floating over to pile at his feet.

"Perfect. Plenty of materials to work with here." He casually stashed the dead beasts away into his storage ring. He never knew when creature parts might come in handy for pills and the like.

Just then, Zack sensed three figures entering the range of his spiritual sense. Masking his presence, he slipped into the cover of the trees and silently observed the group pass by a few minutes later.

"I'm telling you, we need to split up! It's our best shot at grabbing two scrolls before the others," argued the burly, dark-robed boy Zack recognized from the Black Heart Sect.

The slender blonde girl in blue Heavenly Light Sect robes shook her head firmly. "No, we barely know anything about what we'll be facing. It's too risky alone."

The final member of their team, a tall White Tiger disciple, nodded in agreement. "She's right, we stand a better chance sticking together."

The Black Heart boy scowled but didn't argue further. "Whatever, we do it your way. But when your plan inevitably costs us this stage, don't say I didn't warn you."

The White Tiger disciple spoke up hesitantly. "Well, splitting up might not be the best idea . . . but we're not totally unprepared." He patted the bronze medallion hanging around his neck. "I have a treasure-seeking artifact from my sect. It can locate precious items under Nascent Soul level."

The Black Heart disciple's glare transformed into a greedy gleam at this news, though he quickly masked it. "An intriguing trinket," he remarked casually. Too casually.

"That's great! We can track down the scrolls with no problem then," said the Heavenly Light girl happily.

But the White Tiger boy shook his head. "Not exactly. The medallion doesn't register the scrolls as treasures—those don't give off an aura. It's only helpful for locating a second artifact once we have the first scroll."

The Black Heart disciple sneered. "Then what good does it serve now? Seems you've wasted everyone's time boasting about useless junk."

"It's not useless!" the other boy protested. "It can still help with the second scroll later. I just wanted to let you both know it's an option."

"Enough bickering," interjected the Heavenly Light disciple. "We focus on securing one scroll first. Your medallion can assist us after that. Agreed?"

Both boys nodded in agreement.

"Maybe we should just ambush whoever finds the first scroll and steal it?" suggested the Black Heart boy casually. "Save us the trouble of searching."

His teammates quickly vetoed this idea, refusing to stoop to such *dishonorable* tactics. Their argument faded into the distance as the mismatched trio moved off.

From his hidden perch, Zack chuckled and rubbed his hands together. "Oh, this is just perfect! Duty calls, idiots."

He would follow these three buffoons until they acquired the first scroll, then take it along with that delightful treasure-seeking trinket.

How generous of them to hand over such useful tools! Whistling cheerfully, Zack stealthily trailed after the group.

CHAPTER SEVENTY-THREE

The mismatched trio trudged through the murky woods, boots squelching in the damp earth.

The Heavenly Light disciple wrinkled her nose at the dank atmosphere. "What is that awful stench?"

"It's the natural musk of the swamp, princess," Leif said with a smirk. "Not all of us grew up in cozy temples and libraries."

The blonde girl shot the Black Heart disciple a withering look. "My name is Isolde, not princess. And I'll have you know the Heavenly Light Sect temples require grueling physical training."

"Oh yes, grueling training in how to properly fold robes and recite poems about rainbows, no doubt."

"I wasn't asking for your opinion, Leif." Isolde gave an exaggerated sniff. "Honestly, what kind of name is that for a big, scary demonic cultivator anyway? It sounds like you should be the one frolicking in flower fields."

Leif bristled, his face flushing an angry red. "Hey! It's as intimidating as any other name!" He jabbed a finger at Isolde. "Why don't you make yourself useful for once and scout ahead instead of complaining, Little Miss Sunshine?"

"Little Miss Sunshine? Why you—" Isolde began hotly before Orion stepped between them.

"Enough bickering. We need to focus on the task at hand," the tall White Tiger disciple said sternly.

Leif rolled his eyes but didn't argue. Isolde bit her lip. Orion was right, but that arrogant demonic cultivator just rubbed her the wrong way.

"So where to next?" she asked Orion, pointedly ignoring Leif. "Any signs of beasts ahead?"

The older boy crouched, examining a disturbed patch of mud. Running his fingers over the imprints, his eyes narrowed thoughtfully.

"These are feline tracks, most likely a large predatory cat of some sort," Orion reported. "But something isn't right."

"What do you mean?" asked Isolde. Beside her, Leif scowled impatiently.

"Well, if I'm right then the tracks belong to a Stonestalker tiger, but . . . they typically prowl mountain ranges, not swamplands," Orion explained, rising back to his feet. "I believe someone deliberately released it here to guard something."

Understanding dawned on Isolde's face. "The scroll! This must be on the right track then."

She turned eagerly to Orion. "Think we can sneak past the tiger and grab the scroll without a fight?"

"What's the matter, afraid to break a nail?" Leif snorted. "We're cultivators, not helpless maidens."

Isolde bristled at his mocking tone. "I'm not scared," she retorted. "I'd . . . I'd rather avoid a deadly battle this early if we can."

Before Leif could respond, Orion stepped in. "I'm afraid confrontation is inevitable. Stonestalkers are clever beasts, it will detect us once we're within its territory."

Leif cracked his knuckles, an eager glint in his eyes. Isolde took a deep breath and smoothed her robes. She really hoped Orion knew what he was doing.

Guided by the tracks, it wasn't long before the trio found themselves peering into a rocky overhang sheltering the tiger's den. Snarls echoed from within the darkness.

Isolde tensed. "Definitely our tiger friend in there," she murmured.

Peering inside, her breath caught at the sheer size of the beast dozing just inside. It was as big as a carthorse! But that wasn't the worst of it, that aura . . .

She met Orion's stare with her own wide-eyed one and mouthed, "Pseudo Core Formation!"

Isolde trembled slightly—she had never faced anything above Foundation Establishment before. They were insane to consider this.

Orion clasped her shoulder, whispering, "Don't worry, we can handle this challenge together."

Leif just snorted at their words. Weaklings, both of them. If they experienced the ruthless lives of demonic cultivators, they would not be hesitant so quickly at danger.

"Let's just get this over with," he muttered. Without waiting for a response, the Black Heart disciple slipped into the cave entrance, sticking to the shadows as he stealthily circled around behind the tiger.

Isolde and Orion had no choice but to follow suit. They split up to surround the predator before it noticed their presence.

Unfortunately, their efforts proved futile as the tiger suddenly lifted its shaggy head, pupils dilating. Letting loose an earth-shaking roar, it bounded towards the cave opening to confront the trespassers.

Isolde cringed as the gale nearly bowled her over. So much for stealth!

The Stonestalker swiped a massive paw at Orion. He narrowly dodged the blow meant to decapitate him.

"Aim for its legs!" he shouted, unleashing a series of claw quick strikes to the beast's shoulders. "Slow it down!"

Leif nodded, sweeping his leg out in a blazing arc. "Cinder Whip!"

A fiery lash coiled around the tiger's hindquarters. It snarled in pain but kept charging towards Isolde. She froze for a tenth of a second before her training kicked in.

Twisting aside, she pointed her palms at the oncoming beast. "Solar Flare!" Dazzling light exploded forth, blinding the Stonestalker. It veered off course, smashing into the cave wall inches from Isolde.

Her joy at her success quickly morphed to alarm as the tiger shook off the collision and rounded on her once more. Before she could react, a swat from its massive paw sent her flying across the cave.

"Isolde!" Orion cried. His distraction cost him as the beast pivoted, clamping its jaws around his left arm. Cursing himself for lowering his guard, Orion jammed his fingers into the tiger's eye. It reared back with a pained yowl, releasing his bleeding arm.

Leif darted behind the Stonestalker, hands flying in a complicated pattern. "Death by a Thousand Cuts!"

Razor-thin discs of qi sliced across the tiger's hindquarters. It spun, catching Leif's shoulder with an extended claw. He rolled away, clutching the deep gash.

Isolde struggled to her feet, shaking off the dizziness. Her heart leapt when she spotted a scroll tucked into a rocky crevice. That had to be it!

Before she could move, the wounded tiger rounded on her once more. Thinking fast, Isolde pointed her fingers like a gun. "Solar Shot!" A pulsing orb of light burst forth, catching the beast right in its snarling mouth.

It reeled back, pawing at its muzzle. Seizing the opportunity, Isolde lunged for the scroll. Her fingers had just grasped it when an enormous paw slammed down on her leg.

Isolde's agonized screams echoed through the cave as the bones splintered under the tiger's crushing weight. Orion and Leif rushed to help, but the Stonestalker easily swatted them aside.

Pinned and helpless, Isolde feared the end had come.

Then Orion stepped forward, his entire body beginning to ripple and transform. Fur sprouted across his skin as his face distended into a fierce muzzle. Claws tore through his fingertips as he dropped to all fours.

Within moments, a hulking white tiger with the aura of a Pseudo Core Formation beast stood before them.

"I can hold this form for three minutes," Orion growled. "Get the scroll now!"

With the Stonestalker's attention fixed on this new challenger, Isolde gritted her teeth and dragged herself free. Cradling her mangled leg, she clutched the scroll to her chest.

They'd done it!

Orion and the Stonestalker collided in a whirlwind of fangs and claws. Evenly matched, the two tigers battled fiercely, neither willing to up give an inch. Isolde watched anxiously as Orion narrowly avoided the repeated swipes at his neck.

Leif circled the two beasts, waiting for an opening. When the Stonestalker reared up to slash at Orion, he struck.

"Phoenix Arrow!" A spear of condensed flame shot forth, piercing deep into the Stonestalker's chest. It sank to the ground with a final anguished roar, blood splattering the rocky floor.

Panting heavily, Orion's body rippled and reverted to human form. He looked down at the dead beast. "You fought well, brother tiger. May your spirit run free in the heavens."

He then turned to his teammates. "Nice work, you two," he said, pulling out an Earth Rank healing pellet from his ring. "Here, it's not enough to completely heal that leg but it should be enough to travel."

"Thank you," Isolde swallowed the pellet.

As for Leif, his gaze lingered on the corpse. "Do either of you mind if I harvest materials from our fallen friend? Waste not want not, as they say."

Isolde shrugged indifferently as she watched her injuries heal. "Go ahead, better you than leaving it to rot."

Orion turned away, he didn't like killing tigers, let alone harvesting them. However, he knew it wasn't his place to force his beliefs on the others.

After Leif had salvaged what he could from the corpse. The trio were ready to depart.

One scroll down, just one more to go!

* * *

Hidden in the upper branches of a tree, Zack watched the trio emerge from the cave. His eyebrows rose when he spotted the happy expression on their faces.

"Well, well, it looks like they brought me a scroll," he murmured. "How kind of them."

Circulating his qi, Zack prepared to drop down and ambush the unsuspecting disciples. Caught up in their victory, they would never see him coming. This was just too easy!

He tensed, ready to strike . . . then paused. Faint qi signatures approached from the right, steadily moving closer.

Another group? Interesting. Zack's eyes narrowed.

Stilling his breath, he calmed his aura and observed the scene unfolding below.

Moments later, an ice spear burst from the woods straight at Isolde. Crying out, she tried to dodge but it still grazed her shoulder, drawing blood.

"Ambush!" Leif yelled, hands blazing as he whirled to face their attackers. Beside him, qi covered Orion's hands, forming claws.

Three teenage boys walked out from the trees.

Zack recognized the Black Heart robes on one burly boy and the flowing white garments of a Pure Soul disciple. The third, a tall, handsome lad in rich black and red robes, was apparently from the Black Rose Sect if his arrogant expression was anything to go by.

Not wasting time on pleasantries, the Black Rose disciple pointed a finger at Orion's group. "Hand over the scroll if you wish to keep your lives." Icy vines burst from his sleeve, slithering towards them.

With her injured leg not ready for battle, Isolde could only defend as the vines entangled her. But Leif quickly conjured a wall of flames to keep the ice at bay.

"Back off, Torin," he snapped at the Black Heart disciple. "This is our scroll."

Torin laughed coldly. "Oh Leif, you know it doesn't work that way." He hurled a fireball towards Leif's face. "We're all enemies here."

But the Pure Soul disciple stepped forward, trying to convince the other group. "Please, don't make us kill you! Just surrender the scroll and you can walk away unharmed."

Torin scoffed. "Where's the fun in that? I intend to leave a trail of bodies behind me before this trial ends." He laughed at his companion's baffled reaction.

"Fight now, regret later! Take them out, Mael!" Torin ordered.

The Black Rose disciple—Mael—nodded and sent another icy spear flying at Isolde. But this time Orion intervened, deflecting it with a swipe of his paw.

"We won't make this easy," he shouted.

Despite not having the ability to activate the partial transformation again in such a short timespan, he would not back down without a fight.

With a roar, he charged at Mael, his claw-like hands glowing brightly. Caught off guard, Mael hastily raised an ice spear to block the slash at his throat.

Meanwhile, Leif squared off against Torin, both hands wreathed in flames. "Let's see who the better pyro really is!"

Torin just smirked, casually blocking Leif's fireballs with his sleeve. "Still just a helpless whelp. You bring shame to the Black Heart Sect."

With a howl of rage, Leif launched himself recklessly at Torin, only to be ensnared by thorny vines bursting from the dirt.

"I don't want to kill you," the white-robed youth said. "Don't make me."

He flicked his wrist and the vines tightened, making Leif cry out in pain.

Isolde hung back near the cave. She was in no shape for another fight after that tiger battle. All she could do was hope her teammates could defend her.

The clash was brutally one-sided. Orion only had one good arm left but still tried to shield Isolde. A well-placed spear thrust sent him crashing down with a hole in his thigh.

Seeing an opening, the black-robed boy sent a coil of icy vines shooting towards Isolde. She screamed as they wrapped tight around her wrist.

"Give us the scroll or I start removing pieces," he giggled. "We can do this the fun way, or the really fun way."

Sobbing, Isolde removed the scroll from her storage ring. This was all her fault! She should have listened to Leif.

The black-robed boy reached eagerly for his prize, grinning with glee. Victory was at hand! These fools had practically gift wrapped this scroll for him.

Until a bolt of lightning sliced through the air, severing Isolde's hand at the wrist in one clean strike.

Everyone froze in disbelief as her severed hand and the scroll it held were snatched out of the air by a newcomer.

In the blink of an eye, the twisting bolt of lightning solidified into an unfamiliar young man.

"Yoink! Thanks for doing all the heavy lifting, suckers."

Stashing the scroll in his ring, the boy darted over to Orion. Before anyone could react, he ripped the medallion free from Orion's prone form.

"I'll take this too. Pleasure doing business with you all!" With a jaunty wave, the lightning boy took off into the woods, leaving behind a severed hand.

For one heartbeat, both groups just stared after him in absolute shock. Then Torin roared in outrage.

"After him, fools! We can't lose that scroll!" The three boys immediately abandoned their attack on Orion's team to give chase.

Alone now, Isolde could only pick up her severed hand and sob. They had lost everything in one ambush. She had never felt so hopeless and defeated.

This trial was surely over for them now.

Zack ran through the shadowed forest, grin still stretched wide. Things had played out even better than he had hoped!

One scroll, one tracking medallion, zero effort. Those idiots made it too easy. No one thought to look up and be wary of a surprise aerial strike.

Trees blurred past as he rapidly increased the distance from his three pursuers. Their angry threats echoed behind him. As if those losers had any hope of catching a lightning cultivator in the woods!

Still, no reason to take chances. Zack changed direction abruptly, heading towards one of the Yin scroll locations.

Let those idiots run themselves ragged chasing a cold trail. With his two precious new tools, Zack could easily find the next scroll!

CHAPTER SEVENTY-FOUR

Three young cultivators were making their way through the valley. One wore the robes of the Black Rose Sect, while the others bore the insignia of the Pure Soul and White Tiger Sects respectively.

As they searched for the scrolls, a faint squealing reached their ears. The three exchanged glances, debating whether to investigate.

The White Tiger disciple closed his eyes, extending his senses. "There's only one aura over there," he reported, brow furrowing. "They're at Peak Core Formation level."

He opened his eyes, glancing between his companions. "For someone to be alone, either they're overconfident . . ." He paused meaningfully. "Or extremely dangerous."

The two Late Core Formation cultivators shared a cocky look.

"Please, the three of us can easily handle a lone Peak Core Disciple." The Black Rose disciple scoffed. "Don't tell me you're scared?"

The White Tiger disciple shook his head sharply. "Fear just breeds defeat. If we work together, we can overcome anyone in this mini-realm."

The three exchanged confident nods before heading towards the strange sounds. As they drew closer, the muffled squeals grew louder and more pained. The Pure Soul cultivator couldn't help but cringe at the cries.

"What kind of freak enjoys inflicting pain like that?" he muttered uneasily. But he didn't dare suggest turning back now, he didn't want to propagate the already wide-spread belief that Pure Soul cultivators were cowards who would do anything to avoid confrontation.

Turning a corner, the three disciples froze at the sight before them. A silver-haired girl sat casually on top of a massive, armored boar. In one hand she held a jagged horn, using it to slowly carve patterns into the squealing beast's hide.

The pattern looked like a name . . .

The Black Rose disciple's face drained of color. "Amelia!" he choked out. Before the others could react, he spun on his heel and fled back the way they'd come.

The White Tiger and Pure Soul disciples stared after him in confusion. Over his shoulder the fleeing cultivator cried, "Run, it's her!"

Exchanging bewildered looks, the two disciples ran after their companion. Once they'd put some distance between themselves and the crazy cultivator, they grabbed the Black Rose cultivator's arm.

"What are you doing?" the White Tiger disciple demanded. "Don't tell me you're afraid of a little girl?"

The Black Rose disciple shook his head frantically, still trembling. "You don't understand! That's one of Supreme Elder Slifer's personal disciples."

The other two looked even more puzzled.

"So what?" asked the Pure Soul disciple. "She's still just one cultivator."

The Black Rose disciple's eyes were wide with fear. "You don't get it. Amelia's not just strong, she's completely insane! She loves torture and pain." He shuddered. "We can't beat someone like that in a fight and if she gets a hold of us . . ."

The White Tiger disciple shook his head firmly, he did not take kindly to cowardice. "You should never run from someone just because they're stronger. Don't you have any courage?" He turned to the Pure Soul disciple. "With the three of us, we can handle her."

But seeing the Black Rose disciple's stricken face, he felt the first twinges of doubt. Someone who could inspire such primal fear in a demonic cultivator was clearly dangerous.

The Black Rose disciple seemed near tears. "You don't understand, I've heard Amelia's defeated even Nascent Soul cultivators before. We wouldn't stand a chance!"

The White Tiger disciple paled slightly at this revelation. As a Peak Core Formation cultivator himself, he was quite confident in his strength, he knew he was only able to match Half-Step Nascent Soul enemies currently. Having help could allow him to stalemate a weak full Nascent Soul . . . but defeat one? Impossible.

The Pure Soul disciple nodded slowly. "Ah, I see. Well in that case, good call on retreating," he said, clapping the Black Rose disciple's shoulder. "I'd rather not tangle with someone unhinged enough to torture beasts for fun."

The Black Rose disciple nearly sobbed in relief at their understanding. But a chill suddenly ran down all three of their spines.

"Oh? Who are you calling unhinged?" a soft voice questioned from right behind them.

They whirled to find Amelia standing there, idly playing with the bloody boar horn. An unsettling smile graced her lips as she tilted her head at them.

"Demon!" The Black Rose disciple yelped, nearly tripping over his own feet to get away. The Pure Soul disciple also backpedaled furiously. Only the White Tiger disciple stood his ground. He raised his sword warily at the girl.

"Though I'll agree, I do take pleasure in certain . . . acts," Amelia continued lightly. But her gaze turned hungry as it passed over them. "I'd be happy to show you just how much, if you're interested."

Caelum's eyes narrowed as he was pushed back by the hawk-like beast. It let out an ear-piercing screech, claws swiping dangerously close. He sighed, raising his sword defensively. Through his master's teachings, Caelum had converted some of his demonic techniques into righteous ones—but unfortunately not all of them.

Hopefully I won't need to resort to any demonic techniques to defeat this creature, he thought.

As the hawk swept in for another strike, Caelum activated his Sunrise Slash technique, vanishing and reappearing behind the bird. He slashed at its head with his sword, but the hawk somehow sensed the blow coming and dodged aside at the last second. It immediately countered, its talons grazing Caelum's arm and nearly tearing through the sleeve of his robe. He leapt back just in time, grimacing slightly at the near miss.

"Tch, this thing's instincts are too sharp. Nine Lights Mirage," Caelum muttered. Suddenly, eight identical images of him appeared, each wielding its own sword. They surrounded the hawk in a circle, then attacked simultaneously from all sides.

The hawk let out an enraged screech, pushing back several of the images with a powerful wind blast. Though it destroyed three of the images, the technique allowed two of the real Caelum's sword strikes to land. The hawk squawked in pain as gashes opened along its flank.

Finally!

Caelum's lip curled in satisfaction, but it quickly turned to alarm as the injured hawk's eyes suddenly burned red. With an echoing shriek, its aura began climbing exponentially, quickly reaching the power of an Early Nascent Soul cultivator.

It's still climbing! Caelum's eyes widened. He couldn't allow the beast to fully enter its berserk state! At this rate, it would become too powerful for him to handle without suffering from severe injuries. He had to end this now.

Hissing through his teeth, Caelum thrust his sword forward. "Thorned Lash!"

The blade seemed to shoot forward, extending and elongating until it struck the frenzied hawk directly in its thick neck. The razor-sharp point pierced deep, cutting off the creature's building scream.

Caelum quickly retracted the whip-like weapon back to its normal sword form as the mortally wounded hawk collapsed, its aura fading away.

"Just more death . . ."

As a former demonic cultivator, Caelum was no stranger to violence. Yet he would avoid ending lives when he could.

He let out a soft sigh, watching almost sadly as a long, tongue-like appendage emerged from his sword, devouring the beast's qi.

Though Caelum now followed the righteous path, Bloodthorn would always remain a demonic weapon. Swords couldn't change their nature even if their master wanted them to. He made a mental note to seek out a righteous blacksmith to see if the sword could be reforged.

Or maybe Master could help, he gifted Bloodthorn to me in the first place. His master had a knack for surprising others, pulling out miracles left and right. If he could turn a mortal girl into a cultivator then perhaps he could show a sword the righteous path.

But before then, Caelum was handicapped. Fighting with a demonic sword whilst using a righteous technique didn't give him the opportunity to bring out the full extent of his battle prowess. However, the bond between the two was too strong for him to consider using a replacement.

"We live and die together," Caelum whispered as he flicked the blood from his blade.

Bloodthorn growled in agreement as it continued to feed.

Reflecting on the battle, Caelum sighed. *I still have far to go before I can call myself a true righteous cultivator. This battle only proved how reliant I still am on my demonic abilities.*

As Bloodthorn burped in satisfaction, Caelum suddenly sensed a spike of energy from the direction Hughie had gone.

"Hughie," he muttered, quickly flying towards the disturbance. Whatever trouble his junior brother had found, Caelum only hoped he wasn't too late.

Hughie picked his way carefully across the fiery valley, focused on finding that hidden scroll.

Caelum was off battling some giant bird, which sounded way too troublesome. As for Amelia, he honestly had no idea what his senior sister was up to, but it likely involved a lot of screaming . . . and not the good kind.

"You're supposed to be cultivating a heart of iron, boy," Li Fenghao's voice rang out in Hughie's mind. "Yet a mere walking pace has you wheezing like an old man!"

Hughie scowled, but couldn't deny the complaint. The rocky terrain combined with the oppressive heat was sapping his energy fast. Which made him feel uneasy—a Core Formation cultivator feeling tired just from walking? Something was off.

"Hey, give me a break! This place is like a bloody furnace," he grumbled. "I'd like to see you do better in this heat, geezer."

The immortal's disdainful huff nearly blew Hughie's eardrums out. "Excuses, excuses. Focus on your mission or I'll double your training."

Since his master had that conversation with the greater immortal, the old man had been motivated in Hughie's training. Far too motivated.

What a greater immortal considered adequate training, Hughie considered torture.

That threat spurred Hughie to quicken his steps. The temperature seemed to climb even higher in response, and he grimaced at the sweat dripping down his back. *Ugh, disgusting.* At this rate, he'd pass out from heat stroke before ever finding the scroll.

Just then, his foot snagged on a half-buried boulder, sending him sprawling face-first onto the ground. "Owww, son of a . . ."

Hughie's voice trailed off as his gaze landed on the object his fall had inadvertently revealed—a small chest tucked into a cleft in the rocks. Heart pounding, he scrambled over and wrenched it open.

There, nestled inside, was a scroll sealed with crimson wax!

The Yang scroll!

"Ha, yes!" Hughie cheered, pumping a fist in the air. "Who's the man? I'm the man!"

Li Fenghao snorted. "Yes, truly your intellect is unparalleled. Falling on your face and blind luck, a masterful strategy."

"Hey, a win's a win," Hughie shot back, ignoring the sarcasm. He had done it! Wait until he showed Caelum the scroll. His senior brother would be thrilled. But more importantly, he could tell Oliviare how *he* was the reason why they all passed the first stage.

She'll be so impressed! I can already imagine the look on her face!

Tucking his prize safely away into his storage ring, Hughie's facial expression turned serious as he glanced around cautiously. Other teams could be lurking, looking for an easy ambush. He needed to regroup with the others immediately.

Suddenly, Hughie sensed a flash of movement overhead. He looked up just as a dark figure plummeted from the smoky sky towards him.

Twisting desperately, Hughie narrowly avoided the diving kick aimed at his head. He caught a glimpse of black robes and a porcelain mask etched with a black skull.

"A Black Death disciple!" he gasped, ducking under a flurry of punches. What rotten luck to run into one of them here, and a crazy aggressive one at that!

But Hughie quickly realized something was off about his attacker. Rather than using any techniques, the person stuck solely to physical strikes, as if . . . holding back?

Cryptic words continued spilling from behind the mask between attacks. "Fight . . . me . . . useless . . . die!"

Hughie's danger sense blared as he sidestepped an elbow strike at his throat.

Who is this weirdo?

CHAPTER SEVENTY-FIVE

The three young cultivators scrambled to get away from Amelia, but she continued trailing after them. She wouldn't let her prey off so easily.

"Leaving so soon?" she called out in a sing-song voice. "But we were just starting to get to know each other!"

The Black Rose disciple risked a panicked glance over his shoulder, only to find the silver-haired girl less than ten feet behind, still casually twirling the bloody boar horn in her hands.

He pumped his legs harder, internally cursing his luck. Of course they'd run into one of Elder Slifer's deranged disciples!

The Pure Soul disciple ran alongside him, wheezing slightly from exertion.

She vanished, reappearing directly in their path. The Black Rose disciple yelped, nearly crashing into her.

"Come on, at least introduce yourselves before running off," Amelia chided, tilting her head. "It's only polite."

The Black Rose disciple paled, stumbling back a step. The Pure Soul disciple grabbed his companion's arm, urging him to keep moving.

"Let's go, don't engage with her," the Pure Soul cultivator muttered under his breath.

Amelia's smile turned predatory as she watched them try to skirt around her. Every time they changed direction, she flickered in front of them again. It was like a twisted game of cat and mouse.

The White Tiger disciple's expression darkened with each repetition. His companions pleading glances did little to curb his rising irritation.

He'd had enough.

The White Tiger disciple stood his ground and glared at Amelia. "It seems you have no intention of letting us leave. If you want a fight, then stop these childish games and face me properly!"

"Oh? Don't tell me you're actually planning to fight me?" Amelia looked him up and down. "How brave . . ."

"If you won't let us pass freely, then we'll force our way through," the White Tiger disciple stated evenly.

The Black Rose disciple clutched at his sleeve. "Don't be stupid! We need to run!"

Shaking him off, the White Tiger disciple flourished his sword. "A tiger never retreats from a battle. If I must stain my hands with more blood to reach the Nascent Soul stage, then so be it!"

Without warning, he suddenly plunged the tip of the blade into his own stomach. The Black Rose and Pure Soul disciples recoiled in shock as blood leaked from the gaping hole that was staring right at them.

"Have you gone insane?!" the Black Rose disciple shouted.

But then the hilt began melting into the White Tiger disciple's skin, merging with his flesh. Strange black and white striped markings started spreading across his body from the entry point of the sword.

His muscles bulged and a bestial aura erupted from him, it quickly climbed to the level of a Nascent Soul cultivator. The White Tiger disciple's handsome features grew longer and more feral as he shouted, "I am the claw that shreds the heavens!"

White fur sprouted all over his body and sharp claws protruded from his fingers. With a roar that shook the entire valley, the transformation was complete.

In the White Tiger disciple's place now crouched a massive white tiger, easily over ten meters long. It fixed its predatory gaze on Amelia, baring its gigantic fangs.

"Oh my, I wasn't expecting that," Amelia remarked, looking genuinely delighted.

The White Tiger disciple was able to combine his sword cultivation with his transformation; it was a rare feat.

This was going to be fun.

"I've got some tricks of my own."

She closed her eyes, and when she opened them again, only glowing blue sockets stared back at them. Her creamy skin paled to an unnatural white as dark veins ran across her face. When she grinned this time, it was with a mouth full of jagged teeth.

"A demon's Ghoul Transformation!" The Pure Soul disciple recoiled with a gasp.

Amelia's aura rose in waves as her cultivation base also ascended to the Nascent Soul stage, matching the White Tiger beast. She cackled, flexing her elongated claws.

"Now then, who wants to play first?" she purred.

With a roar, the tiger lunged towards Amelia, but she easily danced out of reach, her speed doubled by the transformation.

"Ah ah, too slow!" Amelia chided, wagging a clawed finger. Then she casually flicked her wrist, sending a ribbon of purple energy slicing towards the beast.

"Soul Render!"

The tiger tried to dodge, but the technique still grazed its side, making the beast yowl in pain.

The Pure Soul disciple's expression turned grim at the sight. "A demonic soul technique! Be careful, if it lands clean, it could destroy your soul completely!" Turning, he began tracing glowing symbols in the air around his companions. A soft blue light enveloped them both as one of his protective soul techniques took effect.

"Oh, how precious! Look at you two helping each other." Amelia laughed, leaping backwards. "But don't think your little soul shields can stop me. I'm not a one-trick pony."

To demonstrate, she curled the fingers of one hand. A ball of flames sparked to life in her palm. The Pure Soul disciple paled at the sight.

"Burn!" Amelia cackled, sweeping her arm out. The fireball went flying, exploding against the canyon walls. More flickering flames joined it as she sent them spraying recklessly in all directions.

The White Tiger beast snarled, trying to slash through to reach her, but Amelia revealed a pair of purple wings from her back. Beating them once, she launched into the air, easily evading each swipe.

"You said she was unhinged, but this is just absurd!" the Pure Soul disciple cried. He should have expected that the sadist was also an arsonist!

The Black Rose disciple grit his teeth in frustration, he wanted to flee, it was a hopeless situation. But if either of his companions died here, it would eliminate all of them from the tournament.

He couldn't give up, not yet.

Clenching his jaw, he stopped hesitating and joined the fray. "Fireball Barrage!" he shouted, sending a dozen flaming orbs at the ghoul.

Amelia laughed wildly, retaliating with her own fireballs. "Yes, let's burn it all!"

The two fireballs collided, exploding violently. The Pure Soul disciple struggled to maintain the soul barriers against the shockwaves as flames rained down around them.

Over the roaring of the explosion, Amelia's shrieks of glee could be heard as she evaded the white tiger's increasingly sluggish strikes as it tried to reach her in the air.

The beast was too large to fly on a sword!

After mocking them from the air, she noticed that the Pure Soul disciple was left unguarded. "You're mine!"

She dove down and clasped her claws around the Pure Soul disciple's face before he could react.

"Gotcha!"

She then slammed him face-first into the rocky ground. The soul shields around his companions shattered as he lost consciousness.

Amelia crouched over him, claws digging into his cheeks almost gently.

The white tiger froze mid-swipe, its eyes locked on the fallen Pure Soul disciple.

"Ah ah ah, don't move now," she cautioned, tilting her head with a smile. "You don't want me to crush his pretty head, do you?"

Panting heavily, the great tiger lowered its head, it had failed.

The time limit on the transformation had run out. Dark markings began receding from its body. Its muscles shrank and the fur shed until only the ordinary human form of the White Tiger disciple was left.

The Black Rose disciple, seeing this, sighed. There was no point in further resistance. Clearly this fight was over.

"There now, that wasn't so hard. Just be good boys and you might live to see tomorrow."

She extended a hand towards them. "Now then, I believe you owe me a little something. Hand over your scroll."

The Black Rose and White Tiger disciples exchanged uneasy glances.

"We uh . . . don't actually have any scrolls on us," the Black Rose disciple admitted.

Amelia blinked. For a moment her smile faltered. Then it returned, brighter than before as she thought of an idea.

"Well then! It seems you'll have to work for me until you can obtain one." She clapped her hands together. "Oh, this will be fun—my own little worker bees!"

The White Tiger disciple bristled, pride stung. "A tiger cannot be tamed so easily!"

But the warning look from his companion made him swallow his protests. They clearly had no choice in this matter.

Gritting their teeth, both disciples bowed their heads.

Amelia's smile turned satisfied as she studied them. So this was how her master felt, having others bend to his will.

Yes, she could definitely get used to it.

* * *

Hughie grunted in pain as another series of quick jabs connected with his chest, driving him back several feet. The Black Death disciple pursued him relentlessly, not giving him a chance to catch his breath.

"Gah, what's with this guy?" Hughie wheezed, narrowly dodging a knee aimed at his stomach. The attacks themselves weren't too powerful, but the constant barrage of punches and kicks was keeping him completely off balance.

He'd barely lasted thirty seconds against this weirdo and hadn't even had a chance to activate a proper technique!

It was the classic advantage body cultivators held over those focused on spiritual power—the ability to unleash attacks instantly compared to the split second needed to activate arts and techniques. And this Black Death cultivator was exploiting that gap masterfully.

Another fist hammered into Hughie's chest, blasting him backwards and knocking the breath from his lungs.

"Oof!" Inwardly, he cursed as he gasped for air.

"Pathetic, truly pathetic!" Li Fenghao's voice boomed in his mind. "Is this the limit of your skills, boy? To be tossed around like a ragdoll?"

Hughie scowled, leaping back to avoid an elbow jab at his throat.

"Oh shut it, you senile geezer! This freak's not normal," he shot back mentally.

But couldn't help but agree with the old man; being constantly rocked around by someone using only basic punches and kicks was just embarrassing!

The Black Death disciple hadn't said a word since appearing and ambushing him. The voice that taunted out earlier phrases was clearly being distorted by some artifact in the mask.

Hughie just couldn't wrap his head around this guy's deal. One moment mocking him for being weak, the next holding back on actually hurting him or using any techniques. It made no sense!

"Excuses as always!" Li Fenghao harrumphed. "A true warrior would have defeated this stick figure in the first exchange."

Hughie ignored the old man, he didn't have time to deal with him.

But thinking about it, the immortal did have a point. This Black Death cultivator didn't seem to be emitting the sort of overpowering physical aura one would expect from someone who had only trained their body.

So what's going on here? Hughie's eyes narrowed as he continued evading the barrage of strikes. There was definitely something off about this guy. And he was going to find out what it was!

To do that, he needed to fight back, but the Black Death cultivator refused to back off even an inch or give him any room to activate a technique!

Well, if that is how the creeps wants to play it . . .

When the next punch came rocketing towards his face, rather than dodging, Hughie stepped forward to meet it head-on. The devastating impact exploded against his face, fracturing his cheek bone and launching him like a ragdoll through the air.

Finally!

He ignored the white-hot pain and wetness of blood, focusing on activating his go-to technique.

"Bloodforge Ascension!"

The malignant red qi of the demonic art swirled around Hughie's body as he flew through the air. His muscles bulged and the injuries knitted back together.

He landed with a heavy thud, the impact causing spider-webbing-like cracks on the rocks beneath him.

Hughie's eyes flashed a demonic red as his hulking figure emitted the aura of an Early Nascent Soul cultivator.

"Let's fight for real now!"

For the first time, the Black Death cultivator seemed startled.

"A demon's art!"

But Hughie didn't give the disciple the chance to react. He instantly appeared before the disciple with a roar, delivering a punch directly into his midsection.

The disciple doubled over with a grunt as the force of the blow lifted him off his feet and tossed him into the air. But he managed to flip and land in a crouch, one hand braced on the ground.

"Tch, not bad," the figure admitted, straightening slowly. He seemed unaffected by the attack that would have pulverized a normal Peak Core cultivator.

Hughie's eyes narrowed. Just what was going on here?

Trading more blows, it quickly became apparent Hughie's enhanced state gave him a sizable advantage in strength and speed. Yet oddly, the Black Death cultivator continued to rely only on punches and kicks to fight back.

I can't maintain this for long . . .

It was getting harder for Hughie to stay in control as the demonic technique stoked his bloodlust.

Sensing this, Li Fenghao's voice echoed in Hughie's mind. "Control yourself, boy! Don't lose your soul to mindless violence."

At the reminder, Hughie grit his teeth, reigning in the dark impulses trying to cloud his mind. Oliviare's smiling face flashed in his mind's eye. For her, he would get through this!

Across from him, the Black Death disciple seemed to come to some sort of decision.

"I can't waste any more time, I need to end this now," the Black Death cultivator whispered.

Bloodred qi flared around him.

The porcelain mask cracked and fell away, revealing red skin and bulging black veins beneath.

That aura . . . that qi . . . this guy is a real demon! Hughie's eyes widened.

Demonic cultivators had red qi that contained hints of black and other colors; only a true demon had pure red qi.

Hughie tensed as the Black Death cultivator's demonic eyes glared at him from a face that could give babies nightmares for life.

No wonder the creep was hiding his techniques. Hughie realized his opponent must have been trying to conceal the fact that he wasn't human.

"You will die here today, abomination!" the demon growled. Crouching low, it suddenly launched itself at Hughie in a blur of claws and fangs.

Grunting in surprise at the sudden boost in power and being called an abomination, Hughie raised his arms barely in time to block the strikes. He skidded back from the force of the blows.

This is bad! The demon is easily at the Mid-Nascent Soul stage now. Hughie could already feel his defense weakening.

"Fool, use your transformations before he rips you apart!" Li Fenghao snapped urgently.

Li Fenghao didn't understand the boy at all, why beg him to teach techniques if he wasn't going to even use them?

The boy does have a knack for transformation techniques, maybe he could turn this around . . .

Cursing under his breath, Hughie quickly activated the first transformation. Fur erupted all over his body as he shifted into a black wolf easily the size of a small house.

Before the demon could react, the ginormous wolf's powerful jaws closed around its torso.

Howling in rage, the demon smashed into the ground hard enough to form a crater. But despite the heavy blow, it didn't seem majorly injured.

Hughie realized his mistake too late as he was blasted away by a shockwave of force from the demon.

Right, this thing was finally using its own techniques.

Hughie really was outclassed here.

The gigantic wolf crashed into a boulder a few hundred meters away. As it struggled back to its feet, the form blurred and morphed into an equally massive three-eyed toad.

Not waiting for the demon to attack again, Hughie shot out the toad's long tongue. It wrapped around the demon's torso in an iron grip.

Got you now! Hughie thought, swinging the tongue down to smash the demon repeatedly into the ground.

"Ahhh!" Hughie yelped, tongue instinctively retracting.

The demon lit itself on fire!

Panting, Hughie resumed his human form. This wasn't good at all. His transformations let him fight toe-to-toe against the demon, but none of his attacks were powerful enough to severely injure a Mid-Nascent Soul Realm demon!

"Boy, you need to run! Use your movement techniques to escape."

Hughie shook his head stubbornly. "Ain't no way I'm running from this freakshow! I'll fight him till my last breath if I have to."

He was only putting on a show of bravery; he was in fact more than ready to run if he had to, but the old man didn't need to know that.

A surge of pride appeared in the old man's voice, believing the brat had finally developed some courage. "Spoken like a true warrior. But this is one battle you can't win, it's better to—" The immortal grew quiet before continuing, "Never mind, boy. Help is coming."

Help? Hughie blinked in confusion. But then a minute later he sensed it too—a wave of power approaching rapidly, like the blade of a guillotine plummeting down.

In the next instant, a figure dropped from the sky, sword raised high and wreathed in killing intent.

Hughie's eyes widened in recognition and relief. "Senior Brother, you made it!"

The demon froze mid-charge, its red eyes darting between the two figures before it. It was certain it could defeat the funny-looking one, but it felt a dangerous aura from the newcomer . . .

"Ha ha, it's over for you now! Even a Mid-Nascent Soul cultivator can't touch my senior brother!"

CHAPTER SEVENTY-SIX

Caelum's eyes narrowed as he looked at the strange creature before him. It was human-oid in shape, but with bloodred skin, bulging black veins, and a monstrous, inhuman face that had two horns protruding from its skull.

This was no beast or cultivator, but a true demon.

He couldn't rely on righteous techniques as he did with the hawk earlier. This creature would require his full power.

"Demon," Caelum muttered, gripping his sword tighter. The dark aura radiating from the blade intensified as he channeled his qi into it.

"Crimson Vortex!"

Bloodthorn erupted with demonic energy, enlarging until it was easily ten meters long. The massive sword sliced through the air, aimed to cleave the demon in two.

The demon leapt backwards, avoiding the worst of the strike but still losing an arm in the process. It let out an enraged howl, clutching the bleeding stump as it looked around for an escape route.

Seeing it preparing to flee, Hughie rushed forward with a fierce grin, shifting mid-leap into a wolf. He landed with a loud thud directly in the demon's escape path, cutting off any chance of retreat.

They couldn't let this thing get away without figuring out why it was here, and what it wanted with the Black Rose Sect.

"Going somewhere?" Hughie growled, baring his fangs. Behind the demon, Caelum strode forward, sword resting across his shoulders. His handsome features were set in a cold, calculating expression.

"I wouldn't try running just yet. We have some questions, and you have answers."

The demon's eyes darted between them warily before settling on Caelum.

"Your aura . . . you're close to awakening a domain," it rasped.

It could feel the oppressive aura of a pseudo-domain pressing down on it, restricting its power. If it wasn't for the suppression ability of the domain, it wouldn't feel so helpless right now. It couldn't believe its eyes, a Core Formation cultivator at the verge of awakening a domain was almost unheard of!

"Perceptive." Caelum's let out a smile that didn't quite reach his eyes. "But I'm not the one being interrogated right now."

With blinding speed, he appeared behind the demon and lashed out with Bloodthorn. The elongated sword left a deep gash across its back. Howling, the demon stumbled forward, right into the waiting jaws of the wolf.

Razor-sharp teeth dug into the demon's torso as Hughie violently thrashed his head, trying to rip it apart. But with a snarl, the demon enveloped itself in flames once again, forcing Hughie to release it or be burned.

Skidding backwards, the demon rasped out a guttural incantation in a language unfamiliar to the two humans.

Dozens of fireballs materialized around it, shooting towards Caelum.

It needed to distract the sword cultivator if it wanted a chance to escape.

Caelum's blade danced as he deflected the fireballs.

"Is fire all you've got?" Caelum taunted. "Then you've already lost!"

"Nine Shadows Mirage!"

With a surge of qi, illusory copies of himself split from his body. In the blink of an eye, nine identical Caelums now surrounded the demon.

The demon's red eyes widened in alarm. It tried to block and evade the sudden onslaught from all sides, but stood no chance against the perfectly coordinated assault.

In seconds, Caelum and his shadows had left countless more wounds across the demon's body.

Snarling in pain and outrage, it slammed both palms down towards the ground. "Inferno Purgatory!"

Roaring flames erupted in a dome around the demon, rapidly expanding outwards as they burned away Caelum's mirages. When the flames died down, the panting demon was surrounded by scorched earth and molten rock. It stared at Caelum in disbelief, not understanding how he had weathered its strongest attack unharmed.

This youth really was no ordinary cultivator!

"Thorned Lash!" Caelum appeared before it in a blur of movement.

Bloodthorn extended impossibly long, stabbing clear through the demon's chest and out its back in one smooth motion. Howling in agony, the demon could only claw helplessly at the air as the blade lifted it up, then ruthlessly smashed it back down again.

And again.

After the third heavy impact left the demon dazed and motionless, Caelum retracted his blade.

Breathing heavily now, the demon could only watch as Hughie once again blocked its escape route.

"Last chance to answer my questions. What are you doing here, demon?" Caelum asked.

When it just spat a glob of black blood at him in response, Caelum's eyes narrowed.

"Bloodthorn Feast."

A long, bright red tongue suddenly shot from his sword, wrapping around the demon.

The demon thrashed violently but couldn't break free as the tongue tightened around it. Helpless, it could only scream in agony as Bloodthorn greedily sucked away its precious demonic energy.

Caelum's jaw tightened, holding in the urge to scream himself. The potency of pure demonic qi was far beyond anything he had absorbed before. It took all of his willpower not to lose control.

Eventually, the demon went limp, drained to the brink of death. Caelum severed the connection then, swaying slightly from the strain. Bloodthorn, now sated, rumbled happily.

Stepping forward, Hughie clamped his jaws around the semiconscious demon's body, holding it in place.

"I'll ask one final time. Why are you here?" Caelum asked.

The demon's glassy eyes struggled to focus on him. Then the bloodied mouth twisted into a grin.

"You cannot stop . . . what is coming," it rasped.

Before Caelum could demand an explanation, Li Fenghao's voice echoed urgently in Hughie's mind. "Fall back, now!"

Trusting the immortal's warning, Hughie immediately released the demon and shifted back to human form. "Senior Brother, move!" he shouted to Caelum.

They leapt away just as the demon self-detonated in a blinding explosion. The shockwave blasted out in all directions, scouring the earth and leaving a smoking crater behind.

Caelum and Hughie landed lightly. Caelum stared at the devastation with wide eyes. He had sensed no buildup of demonic energy before the blast.

Just what was going on here? What did it mean by "what is coming"?

Clearly there were unknown forces at work plotting against the sect.

Caelum and Hughie glanced at each other.

Master needs to be informed!

Amelia strolled through the forest, humming to herself with a faint smile on her face. Trailing reluctantly behind her were the three cultivators who had become her companions.

There was Jumpy, the nervous wreck from the Black Rose Sect who flinched if you so much as looked at him. Then there was Stripes, the White Tiger disciple who fancied himself a great warrior but had gone down with barely a fight. And finally Timid, the frail little Pure Soul disciple who spent most of his time staring at the ground.

Yes, Amelia had chosen fitting names for the trio of misfits that fate had dropped into her lap. And as much as they claimed to hate their new nicknames, they were stuck with her until they could obtain a scroll.

"Come along, my little worker bees," Amelia called out. "We mustn't dawdle if we want to claim our prize!"

"Are you certain a scroll is even here?" Timid asked nervously, cringing a bit as Amelia turned her bright smile on him.

"Of course! Have I let you boys down yet?" She giggled at their unimpressed looks. "Oh don't be like that. This is so much more fun than wandering around aimlessly, isn't it?"

"Let's just get this over with," Stripes grumbled.

"Shhh now." Amelia pressed a finger to her lips as they approached a rocky clearing. "I hear something up ahead!"

They crept up and peered down at the skirmish below.

Two Pure Soul disciples and one Heavenly Light disciple were battling a monstrous, ape-like creature easily fifteen meters tall. And in one of its massive hands was a scroll!

Amelia had to stop herself from laughing out loud at their luck. This was even easier than she'd hoped!

"Alright boys, time to earn your keep," she whispered. Before any of them could react, she gave Jumpy a shove, sending the Black Rose disciple tumbling down into the middle of the fight with a shriek.

The other two disciples quickly followed, either pushed by Amelia or leaping down of their own will.

Giggling, Amelia sat down on a nearby boulder to watch the show unfold.

The three disciples were not happy at the sudden interruption and turned their attacks on the new arrivals. For a few moments, it was a complete free-for-all brawl between all six cultivators and the hulking beast.

Jumpy got punched in the face almost immediately but managed to stay on his feet. Face pale, he retaliated with a series of fireballs that scorched the beast's fur but barely slowed its rampage.

Stripes activated some White Tiger transformation technique, sprouting claws, fangs, and fur all over his body. Roaring, he launched himself at one of the other disciples, and the two became locked in a vicious melee.

Meanwhile, Timid struggled to dodge the various techniques and bodies crashing chaotically all around him. But he managed to get close to the beast holding the scroll and landed a desperate palm strike to its leg that made it stumble.

Unfortunately, the giant creature immediately backhanded poor Timid in retaliation, sending the slim cultivator flying into a tree trunk with a sickening crunch. He collapsed in a limp heap at the base of the tree, clearly out of the fight.

Amelia watched all this with great amusement, casually throwing the occasional fireball or a soul blade into the fray whenever she felt like it, not caring who she hit.

After a few minutes, with a blow to the head, Stripes managed to knock the Heavenly Light disciple out. He then turned to face the beast, leaping onto its back.

The ape roared as it tried to shrug him off, but Stripes sunk his canines into its neck until it finally toppled over dead, the scroll falling to the ground.

Leaping down, Amelia landed in front of Jumpy and Stripes. "Thanks for the help, boys. I'll take that now," she said sweetly, picking up the scroll from the ape's corpse.

Jumpy and Stripes stared at her, both looking like they wanted to attack her and take back the scroll. But ultimately, they stayed back, not willing to risk it.

Good choice.

Amelia hummed thoughtfully, tapping one long nail against her chin. She could keep her new pets longer, force them to get her another scroll too . . .

But no, Caelum and Hughie would worry if she took too long. It was better to return now. She had what she wanted anyway.

"It's been fun, boys. But I should get back to my team now. See you around!" Amelia blew them a kiss.

Caelum paced within the cave hideout, a deep frown on his normally calm features. Hughie leaned casually against the wall, watching his senior brother with a hint of amusement.

"Come on, Senior Brother, I'm sure she's fine," Hughie said lightly. "You know our little hellcat can handle herself."

"That's not the point, Hughie. We're supposed to be a team, but she ran off on her own without any consideration for us."

"But that's just Amelia."

Caelum shook his head. "What if I hadn't gotten to you so quickly against that demon? Amelia should have been there watching your back, that's what teammates do!"

Hughie opened his mouth, then closed it again, realizing he had no real counterargument. Caelum was right, it had been irresponsible of Amelia to abandon them like that.

Their master had thought that Hughie's near-death encounter made Amelia more of a team player but that didn't seem to be the case.

At that moment, a silver-haired girl strolled into the cave.

"Hello boys, did you miss me?" Amelia called out. Her smile faltered a bit after seeing Caelum's stony expression.

"Where have you been?"

"Oh. Senior Brother, don't be such a worrywart! I was just having a bit of fun." She tried to drape herself casually over his shoulder.

But Caelum shrugged her off. "Our master entrusted me with keeping everyone safe during this trial. Your carelessness could have led to Hughie's death."

Amelia frowned, unused to being scolded so harshly by him. She tried to think of some glib response to brush it off, but Caelum wasn't done.

"We're supposed to be a team, but you abandoned us for your own amusement," he continued. "As your senior brother, I expect better from you."

Amelia's mouth twisted unhappily. She clearly wanted to argue back but could tell Caelum wouldn't bend.

"You're right, of course," she admitted quietly. "I didn't think through how my actions might impact you both. It was selfish of me, and . . . I'm sorry."

Caelum's stern demeanor softened slightly, and he gave a nod.

Eager to break the tension, Hughie spoke up. "Check out what I nabbed us."

He held up a scroll triumphantly. Amelia's eyes lit up as she saw it was a Yang scroll.

"Excellent work Hughie! Now we can fina—" She broke off, smile freezing in place as she seemed to remember something.

Slowly, she reached into her ring and pulled out . . . another Yang scroll.

"Ugh, I can't believe my useless servants didn't grab a Yin scroll," Amelia grumbled under her breath.

Hughie chose not to ask for details.

"Guess we'll need to trade one of these for a Yin scroll," he said.

Instantly, Amelia was shaking her head. "Oh we don't need to bother with that! We can just take a Yin scroll from someone; it'll be easy. I saw some nice targets earlier—"

"No," Caelum shook his head. Despite the battle against the demon looking easy, utilizing a pseudo-domain as a Core Formation cultivator was draining. "We're not wasting time and energy fighting others for no reason. The next stage starts immediately after this one."

"I'm with Senior Brother." Hughie nodded. "I've had my fill of battle for one day."

Seeing she was outvoted, Amelia let out a sigh. "Fiiine. I suppose we can do this the boring way."

Suddenly she perked up.

"Oh, I know just the stick-in-the-mud to wheedle a trade out of! Come on boys, let's go find him!"

"Find who?" Hughie asked.

"Dentos!"

CHAPTER SEVENTY-SEVEN

Atrius struggled to prevent his legs from trembling as he followed the two Black Rose disciples through the fiery, volcanic terrain. The chubby one with the buzzcut wasn't so bad—for a demonic cultivator, Xavier seemed nice enough. But the tall, lanky one with the wild hair and crazed eyes . . . Atrius shuddered just thinking about him.

Dentos.

Atrius had witnessed the madness of the Black Rose disciple firsthand. He'd seen Dentos go toe-to-toe with Ziven, the Heavenly Light Sect's Legacy Disciple and Son of Heaven. And if Atrius was being honest . . . Dentos had been getting the better of the duel before it was interrupted.

Even more terrifying than his skill was Dentos's complete lack of morals. Atrius had watched in horror as the demented cultivator ruthlessly tortured not only disciples from rival sects, but also members of his own Black Rose Sect! It was clear Dentos didn't differentiate between friend and foe when it came to inflicting pain.

Up ahead, Dentos suddenly stopped walking.

Oh no, what now? Atrius froze, his heart pounding.

But the Black Rose disciple wasn't looking at him. Dentos's gaze was fixed on a small group of Heavenly Light disciples who had just emerged from behind a boulder.

Atrius thought he recognized one of them—*Isn't that Leo, one of Ziven's friends?* His stomach dropped. *If Dentos decided to "play" with them too . . .*

Sure enough, an unsettling grin spread across Dentos's face. He pointed at the group. "Xavier, fetch."

"You got it, boss!" the chubby disciple responded with a grin, cracking his knuckles. He ran towards the unaware Heavenly Light disciples.

Atrius averted his gaze, not wanting to watch the impending carnage. Though he couldn't block out the screams that soon pierced the air.

After a few minutes, Xavier returned, dragging two semiconscious disciples by their collars. He dumped them on the ground in front of Dentos, who crouched down with interest. Atrius noticed Xavier was sporting quite a few new burns and cuts.

"Good job, Xavier," Dentos praised, patting his subordinate's shoulder. "Now let's see what secrets our new friends can share, shall we?"

Atrius's insides twisted with anxiety and guilt as Dentos proceeded to "persuade" the two disciples to reveal any information they had about Ziven's current location and plans. The methods the demented cultivator used made Atrius want to vomit.

He thanked the heavens that Dentos had not used such tactics on him. As soon as Atrius realized who he was dealing with, he had spilled everything he knew about Ziven without hesitation.

Loyalty to the Heavenly Light Sect be damned—I want to make it through this trial alive!

"Here, catch!"

Atrius instinctively caught the object Dentos tossed to him. He looked down to see it was a scroll—a Yin scroll.

So far, thanks to Dentos's terrifying efficiency, their group had already collected three Yang scrolls and three Yin scrolls. Atrius didn't understand why the Black Rose disciple continued hunting for more scrolls when they only needed one of each to advance.

Was he trying to decrease the competition that'll make it to the next stage?

Atrius didn't dare ask.

Dentos strolled back from where the two disciples lay crumpled on the ground, having gotten everything he could out of them. He jerked his head towards the north.

"Let's go. Ziven was spotted heading that direction."

Atrius gulped and nodded. So they were going after Ziven for payback.

Fantastic.

As they set off, Atrius noticed Xavier following Dentos's every command without hesitation.

Right, Xavier had mentioned Dentos was ranked number one on something called the Karmic Ledger within the Black Rose Sect's Disciplinary Hall. Crazy bastard seems like a star among Black Rose enforcers.

Whenever they encountered another Black Rose team with a Disciplinary Hall member, that person would salute Dentos and call him "boss."

Lost in thought, Atrius almost slammed into Xavier's wide back when Dentos came to a sudden stop. He silently cursed himself for being distracted.

Dentos stood still, head cocked. Then without warning he activated the Wings of Roc on his back and shot upwards, narrowly avoiding the purple energy blade that struck the earth where he'd just stood.

That was close. Too close, Atrius thought as he took a step back.

A girl's laughter rang out. Dentos reappeared directly in front of a silver-haired girl and bowed his head.

"Senior Sister Amelia."

Atrius's mouth fell open. This was the first time he'd ever witnessed Dentos bow his head to anyone.

The girl—Amelia—smirked. "Still as quick as ever, I see, Dentos."

"Thanks to Master."

Two more Black Rose disciples emerged to stand beside Amelia—a handsome, raven-haired youth, and a mischievous looking teen.

"Was it necessary to attack him?" The handsome sword-wielding cultivator frowned slightly.

Amelia shrugged. "We like to keep each other on our toes in the Disciplinary Hall."

Dentos nodded in agreement.

Atrius sensed there was some history between him and this dangerous beauty. From what he knew, Amelia had recently started working at the Disciplinary Hall as well, often partnering up with Dentos in his . . . interrogations.

In return, she had apparently promised to put in a good word about Dentos to their master, Supreme Elder Slifer. It seemed both these demonic cultivators shared similarly twisted tendencies.

"Yes, I suppose I should have expected as much from you two," Caelum sighed.

Clapping her hands together, Amelia turned her gaze back to Dentos. "Right, let's get down to business." She held up two Yang scrolls. "Care to trade?"

Dentos motioned for Atrius to step forward. Nervously, Atrius presented three Yang scrolls and three Yin scrolls to the Black Rose disciples.

The younger teen let out an impressed whistle. "Wow, you guys have been busy!"

"All thanks to Boss Dentos!" Xavier declared proudly.

Caelum shot Amelia a pointed look. "If only you were half as efficient as Dentos, we wouldn't have had any issues."

Amelia barely refrained from rolling her eyes. She had yet to meet anyone whose ability to quickly accomplish objectives could match Dentos. The lanky cultivator was like a machine—singularly focused and ruthlessly efficient.

Though his reasons for wanting a master still eluded her . . .

Oblivious to her thoughts, Dentos spoke up. "You're welcome to take all six scrolls. We can easily get more." He motioned for Atrius to hand them over.

Atrius nearly choked in disbelief. Hadn't obtaining these scrolls been difficult and dangerous? Why was Dentos so quick to just give them away?!

But he wasn't foolish enough to question his leader's decision out loud.

"One Yin scroll will be enough."

Dentos nodded and passed him a scroll. The mischievous teen—Hughie, Atrius had gathered—pumped a fist in the air.

"Alright! Now we've got what we need to advance!"

"Speaking of which, have you had any luck finding our slippery friend yet, Dentos?" Amelia let out a predatory smile.

Friend? Atrius frowned in confusion. *Who is she talking about?*

"I've been tracking him, but the Son of Heaven remains . . . elusive," Dentos replied. "It seems he is evading us."

Amelia let out an annoyed huff. "Talks a big game, but runs like a coward when it comes down to it." Her lips curved into a cruel smirk. "But his luck is about to run out."

Atrius blood ran cold. *Son of Heaven . . . she had to mean Ziven! Are they going to gang up on him?*

Caelum nodded. "Let's work together to deal with this nuisance before the first stage ends." He leveled a stern look at Amelia. "Remember, Master ordered us *not* to engage Ziven alone. We need to work together and overwhelm him immediately. No playing around this time."

Amelia rolled her eyes. "Yes, yes, I know. Don't worry your pretty little head, I can behave." A chilling glint entered her eyes. "That rat won't slip away so easily this time."

The two groups nodded, turning north. Atrius could only follow, praying he survived to the end of the trial.

Just what have I gotten myself caught up in?

Slifer sat in the private booth, not paying much attention as the disciples from the sects competed in exhibition matches and tests of skill.

He wished he could head back to his fine quarters but as the host, he couldn't excuse himself.

It's the xianxia equivalent of a talent show. Slifer stifled a yawn. He had never enjoyed talent shows back on Earth—*Like dad used to say, I have no talent. Well . . . that's not true anymore.*

The situation was different in this new world, this time around, he had been given a more *fortunate* hand.

Sitting in place for seven days . . . I can't feel my legs, he thought, tapping his hand against his knee. *At least there's only twenty-four hours left before the real fun begins!*

The elders of the other sects also sat meditating. All except for one.

Zofia sat scowling with her arms crossed.

"I cannot believe the *esteemed* Black Rose Sect does not present the first stage," she remarked. "Are your disciples' talents so pathetic you wish to hide them even now?"

"Now Zofia, it is their right to maintain secrecy." Leontius opened his eyes. "Your own sect has done the same in the past."

Zofia's scowl deepened, but she held her tongue.

Slifer resisted the urge to smirk. He was familiar with the hypocrisy of so-called righteous cultivators, so he would let those two argue it out.

Slifer had two reasons for blocking outside observation of the first trial round. First, it allowed his avatar, Zack, to use any techniques without worrying about being exposed.

But there was another, more pragmatic reason.

Slifer's gaze darkened, thoughts turning to the thorn in his side—Ziven, beloved Son of Heaven and Legacy Disciple of the Heaven's Light Sect. The arrogant whelp was crazy, clearly he would do anything to get revenge on Slifer.

Yes, Ziven needed to be removed, and soon. The first stage provided the perfect opportunity, away from any watchful eyes.

The Heavenly Light Sect would likely take offense at their darling prodigy being ganged up on and eliminated. And Slifer didn't want to deal with the headache they would cause when they retaliated. But with the first stage hidden, they could never prove Slifer's involvement even if they suspected it.

Hopefully they finish their hunt quickly. Slifer sighed. *Ziven's luck can't hold out forever, especially when he will be facing multiple protagonists.*

CHAPTER SEVENTY-EIGHT

Ziven rode through the Valley of Scattered Flames on a horse-like creature, which he had nicknamed "Blaze."

Blaze was an Ash Courser. Standing at fifteen feet tall, it had a muscular build covered in ash-colored fur that allowed it to blend into the surroundings. Its hooves were strange, almost resembling talons, they gave the beast traction on the loose volcanic terrain.

"You're a good boy," Ziven leaned forward, patting Blaze's neck affectionately.

It was only appropriate that he, a Son of Heaven, had such a magnificent companion.

He had discovered Blaze skulking around in the third day of the trial, no doubt driven down from its mountain home by the influx of disciples invading its territory.

He'd always had an affinity with beasts and creatures since childhood; it hadn't taken much for him to earn Blaze's trust, only a few dried strips of meat.

The Ash Courser now followed his every command, which was convenient now that he was on the run.

As soon as Ziven realized that he was being tracked, he had abandoned his two teammates and fled with his new mount.

One of those teammates had been a Black Rose disciple—there was no way Ziven could trust anyone from that demonic sect. Not when he intended to kill their supreme elder.

Ziven brushed his fingers over the ring on his right hand, there were two scrolls stored inside—one Yang and one Yin. He didn't dare hand the scrolls to either of his useless teammates. At their pathetic cultivation levels, the scrolls would've been stolen from them in minutes.

No, the scrolls were safest with him.

His face darkened as unwanted thoughts of the Black Rose disciples filled his mind. Hunted like a wretched dog, all because those demons wanted to stop him from carrying out Heaven's justice.

One day, I'll personally exterminate every last one of those foul cultivators, ridding the realm of their evil for good! Ziven clenched his teeth.

Sensing its master's fury, Blaze let out an uneasy whine. Ziven quickly softened his expression, gently stroking the Ash Courser's neck.

"Easy boy, it's not you that I'm mad at."

Blaze nodded before its ears suddenly pricked upwards, nostrils flaring. The Ash Courser's head swiveled, fixated on a rocky outcrop they were approaching.

The beast possessed sharper senses than any human. If it smelled trouble ahead . . .

"So it's time then, is it?" Ziven's eyes narrowed, looking around warily.

Six figures walked out. Black Rose disciples formed a circle around him, cutting off any chance of escape. But one figure hung back—*Is that Atrius?*

"Atrius," Ziven growled at his fellow Heavenly Light disciple. "What is the meaning of this?"

Atrius lifted his hands, taking a step back. "Z-Ziven, I don't want any trouble. I just need to pass this trial."

Before Ziven could respond, a silver-haired girl stepped forward. "There's nowhere left to run, little rat," she purred.

Ziven regarded the beauty before him with contempt.

Amelia.

She was the worst of the lot.

"Swarming me like a pack of rabid beasts." Ziven sneered. "Have you no sha—"

In that instant, Caelum struck without warning. His sword extended, ready to impale the Son of Heaven through the chest.

Relying on his instincts, Ziven twisted sideways at the last second. Instead of his heart, the blade pierced through his left shoulder. Face contorting in pain, he barely swallowed back a scream.

"All together now! Leave nothing to chance!" Caelum shouted.

Ziven paled. He was hoping to stall as he knew the first stage would be ending any moment. But the Black Rose disciples were clearly done wasting time.

Grimacing, he yanked Bloodthorn free, then leaned down to stare into Blaze's eyes.

"Rampage," he commanded.

As the enraged Ash Courser's cultivation rose to the Half-Nascent Soul Realm, it charged forward. Ziven leapt and rolled from its back, sprinting for cover behind a boulder while clutching his wounded shoulder.

Blaze's roars and the sounds of battle erupted behind him. Ziven glanced back to see the Ash Courser engaging Xavier and Hughie in battle.

But Caelum, Amelia, and Dentos had their sights locked on their real target—him.

Cursing under his breath, Ziven continued running.

No matter how arrogant he was, half a dozen Peak Core Formation cultivators, including Slifer's direct disciples, were not enemies he could fight head-on.

His figure blurred as he activated a movement technique, Wind Descent. Yet as he continued to flee, every time he glanced that, he saw the Black Rose psychos clinging to his trail like leeches.

Ziven twisted around, throwing a wind blade back at Amelia to slow her down. She deflected it with a wave of her hand.

From his other side, Caelum's blade came slashing in again. Ziven darted right to avoid it, the sword slicing through the hem of his robes.

Too close . . .

Up ahead, Ziven spotted an opening between two large boulders. He immediately threw himself into the gap, hoping it would force his pursuers into single file. Ziven kept low to the ground as he scrambled on all fours through the tight space, careful not to get wedged.

Just as he pulled himself free on the other side, a giant crimson vortex filled the crevice. Ziven crouched behind one of the boulders, narrowly avoiding Caelum's attack. Moments later, Dentos emerged from the gap, followed closely by Amelia.

Ziven took off again. He wove between rocky outcroppings, leapt over smoldering chasms, ducked flying blades and beams of purple energy. But no matter the evasive maneuvers he used, his three pursuers matched him move for move.

Up ahead, Ziven spotted a large active geyser shooting steam high into the air. Seizing the opportunity, he sprinted straight into the scalding vapors, hoping to obscure himself from view.

Seconds later, three dark silhouettes emerged from a cloud of steam. Ziven barely rolled to the side in time to avoid Amelia's Soul Render as it came cleaving through the vapors.

I need a new strategy, and I need it now!

"I see you, little mouse!" Amelia called in a sing-song voice.

Ziven immediately switched direction as her next soul blade obliterated the path ahead. But in his haste to avoid it, he skidded out into open ground.

Suddenly, the air around Ziven warped and distorted.

What sorcery is this?

An enormous transparent cube formed, trapping him inside. A lanky cultivator stood just outside the cube, controlling its creation through his paintbrush.

Dentos!

"Now! Attack together!" Caelum yelled.

Amelia, Caelum, and Dentos unleashed their techniques simultaneously. Amelia's Soul Render, Caelum's Crimson Vortex, and Dentos's Painted Spear combined into one massive roaring column of destructive energy, aimed directly at Ziven's heart.

No! It can't end like this! Ziven thought desperately. *Not until I get my revenge! I will get my revenge!*

Just as the attacks were about to connect, the world around Ziven blurred and dissolved. He felt a strong pulling sensation, and then everything went black.

Zack was lazing high up in a tree, relaxing after having found both the Yin and Yang scrolls needed to pass the first stage of the exams.

"Unless one of those two weirdos die," Zack muttered to himself as he juggled the scrolls. He felt quite confident that his strange teammates would survive. If they could make him feel uneasy, they could definitely handle the other Foundation Establishment cultivators in the trial.

If anything, Zack felt bad for anyone unlucky enough to encounter them.

Though, he had been worried that the Black Death disciples would hunt him down, so he had stayed on the move. He didn't know what they wanted with him, and he did not want to find out.

But with only an hour left until the first trial ended, he could finally take a breather.

Well, a short one anyway. Never hurts to stay vigilant.

As he began to doze off, Zack's eyes suddenly shot open. A prickle of unease crept down his neck. He sat up, instantly on alert.

Now hold on just a darn minute . . . this is usually the point where everything goes spectacularly wrong! Just when the protagonist thinks they're safe, bam! Ambush out of nowhere!

Zack wasn't about to fall for that cliché. Time to be proactive.

He closed his eyes and activated a new technique the Main Body had learned called Mind's Eye. It was a surveillance technique that Slifer thought would come in handy for situations like this.

A barely perceptible pulse of qi radiated out from him, sweeping the forest. It traveled more than twice as far as his spiritual sense could reach.

There!

Two hundred feet to the east, partially obscured from his spiritual sense. Two figures stealthily approaching his position.

Zack's eyes snapped open, immediately focusing east. Were they his creepy teammates? It would explain how they evaded his initial spiritual probe.

His question was answered a second later when two beams of inky black qi came hurtling directly at him.

Cursing, Zack instantly manifested his lightning wings technique, launching himself into the sky right as the attacks struck the tree he'd been lounging in just moments before.

The tree let out an awful groan before crashing down, leaves withering and bark decaying from the residual death qi.

Zack's eyes narrowed, wings beating to keep him in the air. The attacks were similar to the Reversal Card's life-draining properties, but instead of absorbing life essence, they corrupted with pure death qi.

Below him, two black-robed figures emerged from the tree line. Zack frowned. Yep, definitely his shady teammates from the Death Rose Sect. Though he'd nicknamed them Vampire and Zombie in his mind.

Well, no time like the present for a cheerful reunion!

Zack pasted a sunny grin on his face and called out, "Yo, guys! Fancy meeting you here. What took you so long?"

The Vampire girl frowned up at him. "Why did you run from us before?" she demanded.

Zack laughed. "Oh, I just wanted a head start, no biggie!"

As he chatted, his eyes scanned his surroundings, looking for any escape routes. Staying too high up made him an easy target.

There—fifty feet to the west lay a thick bundle of trees. And if he could just make it over that rocky overhang to the south, he'd find plenty of caves to duck into.

And with caves come opportunity!

Now he just needed an opportunity to escape to one of those spots without getting hit by another blast of deadly miasma.

Meanwhile, Zombie spoke up. "We have some questions for you," he said slowly, "about your master, Slifer. There are . . . inconsistencies."

"Sorry to disappoint, fellas, but you're barking way up the wrong tree." Zack waved a hand. "An Ascendant like him? That's crazy above your pay grade."

The male disciple continued staring at him like a creep. "We also have questions for you. You seem to have appeared from nowhere. Who exactly are you?"

"Me?" Zack plastered on an oblivious look. "I'm nobody important, just some disciple. Nothing worth digging into there."

The Vampire girl took a step towards him, and Zack realized she was about to attack again.

Crap! Time for me to scram!

Zack immediately dove towards the escape route he had picked out earlier.

He had no desire to actually fight these two. He had no idea which techniques they had in their arsenal, even if he was able to defeat them, he doubted he would come out unscathed.

Unlike the Main Body, who had his cards to save him, I need to look out for myself!

A streak of inky darkness shot through the air, narrowly missing his wing as Zack barrelrolled out of the way.

He plunged into the trees as the Black Death disciples followed in pursuit. They fired off more attacks, decay spreading wherever their qi touched. Zack just managed to dodge them, the blasts grazing past close enough to tear his robe and leave bloody furrows across his shoulder.

Gritting his teeth against the pain, Zack clamped one hand over the wound. That stuff was nasty—he could feel the death energy trying to corrupt his own qi.

As he sprinted through the underbrush, Zack focused on containing the spread before it could contaminate his dantian and meridians.

This crap is strong!

Sweat beaded his forehead from the effort. Zack knew he couldn't suppress it forever.

He soon found a thick tree to lean against and catch his breath.

Closing his eyes, he prepared to cycle his qi in cleansing patterns, only to suddenly freeze as a pulse of Mind's Eye qi returned two life forces rapidly closing in.

"Damn, how do they keep finding me so fast?" Zack muttered. He opened his eyes to see the pair standing before him.

"I tried being nice, but it seems you two are just ungrateful," Zack said, narrowing his eyes. His cheerful demeanor vanished. *I need to hit them hard and fast!*

But before Zack could act, the marking on his palm—the one he had used to touch the teleportation cube earlier—suddenly flared with light.

A portal appeared out of thin air, sucking all three of them inside.

"Well, crap—" was all Zack had time to say before disappearing.

CHAPTER SEVENTY-NINE

The arena was buzzing with excitement as the spectators leaned forward in their seats, eyes glued to the empty stage below. Any moment now, the first stage of the tournament would come to a close.

Only the teams who secured both the precious Yang and Yin scrolls, while keeping all three members alive, would progress to the next round.

In the highest booth, on the most impressive seat, sat Slifer, lazing around like he had no care in the world.

He had no doubt that his disciples would pass the first trial with ease. They were the elite of the Black Rose Sect, handpicked and trained by the original personally.

But more importantly, they were either protagonists or pseudo-protagonists, it would take more than some average Core Formation cultivators to deal with them.

No, Slifer was far more interested in whether his followers had succeeded in disposing of that pesky cockroach, Ziven.

"My, my, someone's awfully sure of themselves."

Slifer didn't bother turning his head at the voice coming from two seats over.

Zofia leaned towards him, an impish grin on her face. "Getting a bit complacent, are we?"

When Slifer continued ignoring her, Zofia let out a frustrated sigh.

"It's rude not to look at someone when they're talking to you. Didn't your master teach you any manners?"

"You're the rude one!" Val bared her fangs. "Stop annoying Master, he wants nothing to do with an old hag like you!"

Old hag? Now where did she learn language like that? Was it Amelia? Slifer wondered.

As nice as it was for Val to come to his defense, he didn't want to spoil her with crude language like that, she was just a baby after all.

Zofia's eye twitched, but her smile remained fixed in place. "Still hiding behind your little bird, I see."

"Bird? Val a dragon!"

On Slifer's other side, Black Death Sect Master Vowron turned to him with a smile.

"The results of the first stage may surprise you, Supreme Elder," he said. Though his words sounded innocuous enough, Slifer's senses prickled.

Surprise me? What was the man getting at? Slifer nearly frowned. None of his disciples had fallen in the trial, he was certain of that much. The System would have notified him instantly if that was the case. *Just what are you plotting?* His gaze sharpened, and he stared intently at the Black Death Sect Master's face.

He had yet to receive any updates from Morvran or Kalin regarding the Black Death Sect's movements, so he had decided to add Fenlock to hunt.

It's not like he has anything better to do . . . all he does is spend time with his junior sister.

Slifer shook his head. Fenlock's strange relationship was not something he wanted to delve into at this moment. *But I do think gaining his complete loyalty is related to that junior sister of his . . .*

Any further thought was interrupted as dozens of spatial portals sprang into existence around the arena.

Slifer sat up straighter, an eager glint entering his eyes.

Here we go! Let's see how they did!

Hundreds of cultivators came tumbling out of the portals onto the platform. Many had injuries or torn clothes.

Slifer immediately focused on scanning the mass of disciples for his own. He held back a sigh of relief as he spotted Amelia's silver hair, then Dentos's lanky frame, followed by the rest of his team. They seemed a little battered but overall intact.

Good.

Satisfied his disciples had passed, Slifer turned to shoot Vowron a pointed look. The Black Death Sect Master had the grace to appear surprised.

Interesting . . . it seems he really didn't expect my disciples to return.

This gave Slifer pause. There was a big difference between sabotaging group allocations and attempted murder. Unfortunately, he had no idea what the demonic sect master was up to.

If only I could buy the answer from the System . . .

Ding!
Congratulations!
Your Disciples All Passed the First Stage
You Have Gained 400 Karmic Credits

It's always nice to get credits without having to move a muscle.

Slifer's eyes then narrowed as his gaze landed on a familiar muscular figure with dark shoulder-length hair.

Ziven.

Somehow that tenacious cockroach had survived. Slifer shouldn't be surprised. The heavens seemed to favor their precious son no matter what obstacles were thrown his way.

Much like actual cockroaches, Ziven just kept crawling back time and time again.

Slifer hid his displeasure and schooled his features into indifference. He couldn't let anyone guess the extent of his hatred, or was it fear, towards the Heavenly Light Sect disciple. A supposed Ascendant cultivator targeting a mere Core Formation cultivator would bring about too many questions.

A spiritual transmission from Caelum stole his attention.

"Master, I'm sorry we failed the mission. But there is something important we found out. The Black Death disciples are . . ."

When the blinding light of the portal finally receded, Zack found himself dumped onto the floor of an arena. Groaning, he rolled over and sat up, blinking rapidly as his vision adjusted.

One sweep of the surroundings and Zack instantly recognized where they were—the Inter-Sect Tournament grounds.

Hundreds of other cultivators were also pulling themselves up from the ground around him, some letting out sighs of relief whilst others complained.

"Ugh, finally. I never want to see another lava pit again!"

"Just thank the heavens we made it out of that nightmare!"

"Feels like we barely escaped with our lives. Are trials normally this deadly?"

Zack stretched his back, wincing as his joints popped. He was battered, hungry, and desperately in need of a bath, but otherwise no worse for wear.

A burning sensation in his shoulder proved him wrong immediately.

Oh yeah, I've got to get that sorted before it becomes a real problem.

Zack's eyes turned to his two teammates, who were rising to their feet as well. The male and female Black Death disciples stared at him with their usual blank, creepy expressions. Zack suppressed a shudder.

"Well ain't this just an awkward reunion." He laughed nervously.

Their last encounter in the trial space had been . . . tense, to say the least. The pair had gone from seemingly ignoring his existence to abruptly trying to murder him.

And they had pursued Zack relentlessly, despite his attempts to lose them. It was as if passing the trial meant nothing compared to their desire to kill him, which made zero sense!

Just what beef do they have with me? I'm obviously an amazing dude, but still!

Before Zack could ponder the mystery further, he sensed a familiar tugging at the edges of his spiritual awareness. It felt as though strands of his recent experiences were being gently extracted from his consciousness.

Ah, this again!

He had grown accustomed to the out-of-body sensation that accompanied the Main Body syncing their experiences and memories.

"Hope you're happy, bossman. The first round wasn't exactly a picnic," Zack muttered internally. Images of the deadly black miasma the two Black Death disciples wielded flashed through his mind. "Send me the antidote before my arm falls off!"

The booming voice of Elder Fred interrupted Zack's complaints.

"Attention! All participants, stand with your teammates immediately!"

Zack grimaced. Well, time to get up close and personal with his murderous buddies again. He dragged his feet over to join the Black Death cultivators, carefully positioning himself out of arms' reach. Their lifeless gazes followed his every move.

Yeah, this isn't creepy at all . . .

"Right!" Elder Fred bellowed. "The teams with both a Yin and Yang scroll, present them now!"

Grinning, Zack took out the scrolls from his interspatial ring, holding them up proudly. He spotted Caelum and Dentos doing the same, along with a few other talents like William and Nomed.

Nice, the whole squad made it through.

"The ten teams that secured the scrolls from both the Core Formation and Foundation Establishment divisions shall advance." Elder Fred's tone hardened. "The rest of you, scram!"

Angry mutters broke out among the eliminated disciples at the dismissal.

"This isn't fair, we didn't even get to show our strength!"

"They can't just fail us without seeing what we can do!"

But under the oppressive pressure of Elder Fred's Nascent Soul cultivation, nobody dared protest further. Shooting dirty glances at the passing teams, the losers quickly filed out.

"Now then! The second trial will consist of one versus one battles. And just like before, the Core Formation division shall compete separately from the Foundation Establishment division."

"There will be five brackets of six competitors each," Elder Fred continued. "The six cultivators in a bracket will battle each other in turn. A win earns you three points, a draw earns one point, and a loss earns zero points. The cultivator in each bracket with the most points will advance and secure a slot to the Sealed Realm."

Mumbles of annoyance spread amongst the participants.

"Only five slots, out of all of us?"

"Seriously? One loss and you're basically out of the running."

"They expect us to battle tournament style right after the first trial?"

"Yeah, we've not had any time to rest!"

"Enough!" With a wave of his sleeve, Elder Fred silenced them as he produced a glowing orb of water. "The matchups will now be decided!"

He caused the liquid to separate into five smaller orbs, each holding six names. With motions from his fingers, he stirred the names within each orb, randomizing the order.

Watching closely, Zack noted with satisfaction when the Black Rose disciples each ended up in different brackets, just like the Main Body had promised.

With a round-robin style tournament bracket, there's no chance of the gang accidentally knocking each other out of the competition. And with a bit of luck, we'll be able to monopolize all five slots to the Sealed Realm!

Finally, Elder Fred flicked his wrist, solidifying the pools into brackets.

Let's see who I'm up against first . . . Zack scanned the Foundation Establishment list.

"The first match will be Zack versus Varoom!" Elder Fred announced.

Varoom? What kind of name is that? It sounds like one those little toy vehicles kids race around . . . what were they called again? Hot Wheels? Ah well, no use making jokes the poor guy won't even understand. I'll just have to throttle him quickly instead!

Zack cracked his knuckles as he stepped forward, ready to face the nobody from the Black Heart Sect.

CHAPTER EIGHTY

This scrawny pipsqueak doesn't look like much. He probably hasn't even reached the Mid-Stage of Foundation Establishment, Varoom scoffed, looking down at his opponent.

"Boy, I won't even need any techniques to beat you. I'll just slap you to death!"

"Give it a try, big guy," Zack responded with a smirk.

Varoom grunted. This kid was clearly all talk, and that smug attitude just made Varoom want to pound his face in even more.

Without warning, Varoom flickered out of view. In the blink of an eye, he appeared directly behind Zack, already swinging a massive fist towards the back of his head.

But to his shock, Zack reacted instantly, whipping around and casually catching his punch with one hand.

"Too slow," Zack said, clicking his tongue. With his free hand, he delivered a lightning-fast jab straight towards Varoom's nose.

Varoom stumbled back, blinking rapidly. How could this pipsqueak stop his full-powered punch with just one hand? Just how strong was this guy?

After gathering himself, Varoom spat out, "So you're just a freakish body cultivator, is that it?"

"Something like that," Zack said, rolling his injured shoulder with a slight wince. *Can't play around for too long with this bum arm.*

Gritting his teeth, Varoom changed tactics. He slammed his foot down, sending a spike of stone shooting up beneath Zack's feet.

But Zack merely raised an eyebrow at the incoming attack. With a sigh, he thrust out his palm, meeting the stone spike head-on.

"Thunderclap Palm!"

A resounding shockwave boomed out, obliterating the spike into tiny pebbles.

Varoom's eyes narrowed as understanding dawned on him. This was no ordinary Foundation Establishment cultivator. The kid's comprehension and control over elemental forces was clearly at the level of Core Formation at least!

Zack considered bringing out a sword and using Sunrise Slash to end the fight quickly. But no, that would definitely rouse suspicion about his true identity. For now, he'd have to rely only on his own techniques.

"Let's wrap this up, shall we?" Zack inhaled deeply before letting out a roar. "Dragon Roar of the Thunderous Sky!" Visible shockwaves rippled through the air, crackling with lightning.

Just before the attack could land, a bolt of pain shot through Zack's injured shoulder, disrupting his control. The thunderous roar fizzled out pathetically mid-flight.

"Crap!" Zack cursed under his breath.

"Pathetic!" Varoom seized the opportunity.

Stomping again, he raised up earthen walls in a spherical formation around Zack, creating a stone prison. Rune inscriptions along the prison walls rapidly siphoned away Zack's qi.

Looking through the prison's single barred window, Varoom smirked. "Not so cocky now, are you? That's what you get for underestimating me."

Inside the cell, Zack grumbled in annoyance. He had let himself get too carried away showboating. Now he was stuck in this stupid rock box like a misbehaving child sent to the naughty corner.

Meanwhile, in the spectator stands, Slifer watched the situation unfold with a shake of his head. Zack was acting just as rash and short-sighted as Slifer himself tended to be. But unlike Slifer, who had to restrain himself constantly for the sake of his supreme elder image, Zack had no such obligations.

It's strange seeing myself from a different perspective . . .

Ding!
New Task: For every battle your disciples win in the first round, you will gain 150 Karmic Credits!

One hundred and fifty Karmic Credits just to bully others, why not? Slifer smirked.

"My, it seems your disciple has gotten himself into quite the predicament," Zofia laughed.

Slifer waved a hand dismissively. "I thought someone of your cultivation would be more . . . perceptive."

Zofia's smile froze. She opened her mouth to snap back with a retort, but then a distant rumbling suddenly drew her gaze to the sky.

A massive thunderbolt tore through the clouds, descending rapidly towards the arena grounds. With a resounding crack, it struck the stone prison, blasting it to pieces in an instant.

As the dust settled, Zack stood smirking amidst the rubble, wisps of electricity still dancing across his skin.

"A useful little trick, that one."

The Celestial Lightning Tribulation technique let him call on one lightning bolt from the heavens. He normally used it to temper his body, but it worked in situations like this, after all, lightning was the weakness of earth techniques.

"How?" Varoom stumbled back in shock.

No matter what he tried, this kid seemed to have the perfect counter. Just what would it take to defeat him?

Sensing his injured shoulder continuing to worsen, Zack sighed. "Sorry, big guy, but I'm gonna have to wrap this up quick before my arm falls off."

In a flash, Zack appeared behind Varoom, electricity cackling from his wings. Varoom hurriedly raised a stone barrier, but Zack's Thunderclap Palm blasted straight through it and slammed into his chest.

Varoom soared backwards through the air.

"The winner is Zack!" Elder Fred declared.

Satisfied, Zack made his way off the arena stage, slowly rolling his bad shoulder. That fight had been way too close for comfort. He sent a reminder to the Main Body. "*Yo, bossman, gonna need that poison antidote pronto before my whole arm rots off!*"

* * *

William watched as Zack strolled casually from the arena.

Zack had come out of nowhere and somehow managed to become the supreme elder's disciple. William didn't understand how a nobody like Zack deserved that honor when he, a young master, did not.

But what grated on William even more was how talented and powerful this newcomer seemed to be, much more so than William himself.

It was unacceptable!

No!

William shook his head; he couldn't keep thinking like this. It was this attitude that had gotten his family involved with that "mess" in the first place.

"Next match—William versus Alfie!" Elder Fred announced.

William grit his teeth. Just his luck to face a Heavenly Light disciple at the Late Foundation Establishment stage right off the bat. As an Early Foundation Establishment cultivator, he was definitely at a disadvantage.

Walking onto the platform, William kept his nerves hidden. He would not let this opponent sense any weakness.

"Begin!"

Alfie smirked, not even bothering to take a battle stance. "This should be quick. I hope you've made your peace, kid."

William's face burned, he wasn't used to being talked down to like that, but he kept his anger in check. Losing his cool now would only lead to a quick defeat.

"If you are done talking, let's fight."

"Don't say I didn't warn you," Alfie taunted. He casually summoned flames to his hands and tossed a fireball at the boy. "Here, catch!"

As the fireball flew at him, William executed the Gale Force Palm, shooting out a gust of wind from his hand. The wind collided with the fireball, causing a small explosion between them.

"Not bad," Alfie remarked, clearly just toying with him. "But wind techniques won't get you far against my Phoenix Immolation!"

Alfie thrust his palms forward, unleashing a massive firebird. The phoenix screeched as it shot towards William with terrifying speed.

Reacting quickly, William activated his Wind Step technique, using the wind to propel himself out of the phoenix's path. He appeared twenty meters to the left, barely avoiding the collision.

But Alfie simply turned and sent the phoenix chasing after William once more. "You can't run forever!"

William was forced to keep evading the phoenix, using all his speed and agility to avoid its swooping attacks.

Alfie just stood back with an amused expression, controlling the phoenix's movements with casual flicks of his fingers.

After a few minutes of this cat and mouse game, William was panting heavily. Alfie seized the chance to attack again.

"Try my Phoenix Talons!" he cried, morphing the firebird into two gigantic claws of flame. The talons shot forward to grab a hold of William.

Reacting on instinct, William sent a Spiraling Wind Blade towards the left claw, disrupting its form and causing it to dissipate. But the right talon remained intact, slamming into William's side.

"Argh!" William cried out as the intense heat seared his robe and flesh. Dropping to one knee, he quickly patted out the flames before they could spread. Gritting his teeth against the pain, he stood back up to face Alfie once more.

By now, Alfie looked slightly annoyed that the match was still continuing. "Just give up! You'll never win with that pathetic cultivation of yours."

William frowned, mind racing for a solution. Alfie was clearly the superior cultivator in terms of pure power. William's only advantage lay in the natural counter that wind held against fire. If he could just exploit that somehow . . .

When Alfie sent another fireball whizzing towards him, a plan formed in William's mind. He deflected the first fireball with a wind palm, then watched closely as Alfie followed up with a second, larger fireball.

Just before impact, William executed his Wind Accelerator technique. This greatly enhanced the speed and power of the oncoming fireball, sending it crashing straight into its unsuspecting caster.

"Arghhh!" Alfie screamed in shock and pain as his own fireball exploded against him with twice the force. The Heavenly Light disciple fell to the ground, frantically trying to pat out the flames that now devoured his own robes.

After a few minutes, the fire finally died out, leaving Alfie groaning on the floor with smoke rising from his clothes.

"The winner is William!" Elder Fred announced.

One down, four to go . . . William sighed as he walked off the stage.

If it wasn't for his quick thinking, he would have been the one rolling around on the floor.

Still, he had expected no less from someone of his standing. This Alfie had learned the hard way not to underestimate a young master.

Watching from the stands, Slifer nodded in approval. It seemed this William fellow wasn't as stupid as Slifer first thought. The boy had managed to snatch victory from the jaws of defeat by using his opponent's strength against him.

Maybe I was too quick to dismiss him . . .

"Next match: Hughie of the Black Rose Sect versus Paddy of the Pure Soul Sect!" Elder Fred called out.

"Alright! It's finally my turn!" Hughie whooped, leaping down into the arena. Across from him, a young man in white robes stepped forward.

"I take no pleasure in violence, but do not believe I will hold back," Paddy said gently, bowing.

"Bring it on, pretty boy!" Hughie shouted, bouncing on the soles of his feet. "I'm gonna mop the floor with ya!"

CHAPTER EIGHTY-ONE

Hughie glanced up at the spectator stands, spotting Oliviare among the sea of faces. She gave him a small wave.

"Gotta give the people a good show!" Hughie said with a grin. "Especially with my number one fan watching."

Paddy followed Hughie's gaze up to Oliviare. "Ah, there is a jade beauty cheering you on. So, you do not wish to disappoint her?"

"You bet!" Hughie thumped his chest. "Nothing's gonna stop me from winning now that my lady is watching!"

Oliviare blushed at the declaration, clasping her hands together as she prayed for Hughie's safety. She knew he could be reckless in battle.

"Then come," Paddy said, settling into a graceful battle stance, palms outstretched. "Show me what you can do."

"Yeah, I'll show you all right!" Hughie shot forward, cocking back a fist. He aimed a punch straight at Paddy's face, putting his full weight behind the blow. But his fist passed harmlessly through empty air as Paddy's form flickered and vanished.

"An illusion?" Hughie realized too late. A sweeping kick to the ribs sent him sprawling.

"You must see through deception to land a blow on me," Paddy whispered, his body wavering like a mirage.

Hughie growled, bouncing to his feet. He didn't need a lecture from his opponent, he got enough from the old man as it was!

He charged again, throwing a flurry of blows, but each one met only air as Paddy's illusionary form flickered around him.

A sharp elbow to the back of Hughie's head made him stumble. Hughie whirled, lashing out behind him, but again struck nothing.

In the spectator stands, Oliviare watched anxiously, hands clasped together. *Be careful, Hughie!*

Sensing her worry, Hughie gave a small wave. "No need to worry, Liv! I got this!"

Oliviare shook her head, but couldn't help a small smile. *That fool . . .*

"Do not divide your attention in battle," Paddy chided. "It will cost you dearly."

As he spoke, ten exact copies of Paddy suddenly appeared, surrounding Hughie in a wide circle. Hughie's eyes darted around warily.

"Let's see you find the real me now," the Paddys spoke in unison, their voices overlapping from all directions.

Reminds me of Senior Brother's technique . . . but only a knockoff version!

Hughie cracked his knuckles, a grin spreading across his face. "I'll just smash through all of you at once!"

Spinning rapidly, he unleashed a barrage of wild punches and kicks, plowing through the ring of illusory Paddys. They flickered and vanished under his attack, but the real Paddy remained untouched.

Before Hughie could stop spinning, a heavy blow slammed between his shoulders, driving him down into the arena floor with a crash. Hughie groaned, momentarily stunned.

Up in the stands, Oliviare winced at the impact.

"Are you alright, Hughie?" she called down worriedly.

"Ha ha, I'm just getting warmed up!" Hughie laughed, flashing a thumbs-up despite his stinging back.

He leapt back to his feet and dropped into a fighting stance. But internally, he was annoyed at himself. *Gotta take this more seriously or I'll end up embarrassing myself in front of Liv!*

As the battle intensified, the ring on Hughie's finger suddenly pulsed, and a grumpy voice echoed in his mind.

"Pathetic! Is this the best you can do, boy?" the Immortal Li Fenghao scolded. "You fight like a brainless ox! Use your techniques!"

Hughie scowled. "I don't need advice from some old fart!"

Li Fenghao huffed indignantly. "Insolent brat! I was slaughtering enemies while you were still in diapers! You must exploit your opponent's weakness."

"Their only weakness is their ugly mug!" Hughie shot back, launching himself at the nearest Paddy.

He grappled with the illusion briefly before it dissolved into smoke. Li Fenghao sighed.

"His weakness is specialization," the immortal lectured. "This boy relies too much on illusions. Find a way to break his illusions and he will fold."

Hughie paused, glancing down at the ring. "Huh, I guess you've got a point for once, gramps."

"Do not call me gramps!"

Hughie decided to change the flow of the fight, he would need to go big. Crouching down, he channeled his qi before exploding upwards.

"Black Wolf Transformation!"

Fur sprouted across Hughie's body as he morphed into a giant black wolf. Letting out an earth-shaking roar, Hughie swiped his clawed hands in wide arcs, shredding two of the illusion Paddys. But once again, the real Paddy evaded by a hair's breadth.

Hughie bared his fangs in annoyance. "Stand still, will ya?!"

"If you insist," Paddy replied. He stopped moving as Hughie charged towards him.

At the last second, Paddy thrust out his palms. "Spirit Shackling Chains!"

Glowing blue chains materialized around Hughie, their spectral links clanking as they wrapped around his limbs and torso. The sudden stop sent Hughie crashing face-first to the ground with a yelp.

He thrashed violently, but the spirit chains held fast. Paddy glanced down at him impassively.

"Do you submit? This battle is over."

"Like hell it is!" Hughie snarled. With a roar, he poured all his strength into shattering the chains. They cracked and splintered until they gave way.

Hughie jumped to his feet. His earlier playfulness had vanished, replaced by a ferocious glare.

"No more playing around. I'm taking you down!"

He charged, claws outstretched towards Paddy's throat. But faster than he could blink, Paddy disappeared, reappearing twenty meters away.

"My apologies, but it seems like you will not give up, so I must end this for both our sakes," Paddy sighed.

He formed a diamond with his thumbs and forefingers. "Soul Crushing Prison."

A blue pyramid materialized around Hughie. The translucent walls rapidly closed in, trapping him within the tiny space.

Hughie panicked, his wolf form scrabbled desperately as he tried to escape but his claws simply slid off the walls of solidified spiritual energy.

Sweat beaded Hughie's brow as his breaths came in shorter, harsher gasps. It felt like the very life was being squeezed from his lungs. He could hear the cheers and shouts from the spectators, but they sounded strangely muted and distant, as if he was hearing them from underwater.

Suddenly, a clear voice cut through the haze in his mind.

"Come on, Hughie, you can do this! I believe in you!"

Oliviare!

Hughie's gaze snapped up, meeting Oliviare's from across the arena. Her hands were clasped worriedly against her chest, eyes brimming with concern. But she kept her focus fixed on Hughie, mouthing silent words of encouragement.

Hughie clenched his jaw. No way was he going to fail and embarrass himself in front of his girl!

Mustering every ounce of power, Hughie slammed his palms against the pyramid's walls. "Get . . . OFF!"

With a final explosive push, the prison shattered into fading wisps of spiritual energy. Hughie collapsed to his hands and knees, sucking in deep gulps of sweet air. His black fur was matted with sweat, but his amber eyes still burned fiercely.

Across from him, Paddy's eyes widened in surprise. "How? You should not have been able to break that technique . . ."

Hughie barked out a strained laugh as he struggled back to his feet. "Never underestimate a Black Rose disciple!"

His legs wobbled dangerously and he had to dig his claws into the stage floor to remain standing. Dark splotches blossomed across the front of his robes where blood seeped from numerous gashes and lacerations on his chest and limbs, caused by the prison's crushing force.

"You are gravely injured. Let us stop this pointless battle so you can receive medical aid."

Hughie scowled. "Ain't . . . pointless," he panted out. "We got spectators . . . relying on us for a good show. And I aim . . . to deliver!"

"Bloodforge Ascension!"

Hughie's veins bulged and skin flushed an angry red as the berserker transformation overtook him. His muscles swelled until he was a hulking beast of a man, the wolf features of his previous transformation mutating into something more closely resembling an ogre— but somehow even more terrifying.

"I'm gonna take your head!" Hughie roared. Faster than before, he dashed at Paddy in a red blur.

Paddy's calm expression finally broke into one of surprise as he frantically blocked and evaded the onslaught of crushing blows. Even he was forced onto the defensive against such overwhelming power.

But Hughie's strikes came even faster, Paddy's guard began to slip. A particularly devastating punch broke through and caught him full in the stomach.

"Gah!" Paddy cried out, slamming backwards into the arena barrier so hard it cracked. He slid to the ground, clutching his midsection in agony.

Hughie paused, chest heaving as he regained control over his bloodlust. He really hoped he hadn't overdone it and seriously injured the guy.

Slowly, painfully, Paddy climbed back to his feet. Swaying slightly, he gave Hughie a weary smile.

"It seems . . . I underestimated you," he panted.

As Paddy prepared himself to continue, Hughie suddenly had an idea.

"Check out my next trick!" he announced. There was a burst of black smoke, and when it cleared, a gigantic three-eyed toad croaked on the arena floor, a large tongue lolling from its mouth.

"Pretty cool, huh?"

Before Paddy could respond, the toad's tongue shot out quicker than the eye could follow, looping around him. With a sharp yank, it hoisted Paddy high into the air, leaving him dangling upside down by one leg.

"Do you submit?" the toad croaked at the struggling cultivator trapped in its tongue.

Paddy wheezed helplessly. Seeing no escape, he reluctantly nodded.

Hughie released him and transformed back into human form, pumping his fists. "Yeah! That's what I'm talking about!"

Up in the stands, Oliviare breathed a sigh of relief. Thank *goodness.*

Elder Fred stepped forward. "Victory goes to Hughie of the Black Rose Sect!"

The crowd erupted into applause as Hughie took a bow. Paddy picked himself up off the ground, brushing dirt from his robes with as much dignity as he could muster.

"You beat me fairly," Paddy conceded, offering Hughie a bow. "Well played, friend."

Hughie slapped him on the back with a grin. "You put up a good fight too, buddy! No hard feelings, eh?"

Paddy managed a small smile in response before limping from the arena, massaging his sore ribs. Hughie waved cheekily until his opponent was out of sight.

As Hughie walked back to the waiting area, Li Fenghao spoke up once more.

"What kind of harebrained fighting was that? You made a complete fool of yourself out there!"

"I still won, didn't I?" Hughie grumbled under his breath.

"Winning through sheer dumb luck and transforming does not make you a skilled fighter," Li Fenghao lectured. "You were appallingly slow to enter your Bloodforge state despite struggling earlier. And your blows had no finesse or strategy, you were just flailing around blindly!"

"Hey, I kept him on his toes, didn't I?" Hughie argued. "Unpredictability is my style!"

Li Fenghao scoffed. "That was not unpredictability, that was just sloppy improvisation and wasted energy. You must have a clear plan of attack tailored to your opponent's weaknesses. Never show your full hand right away either, make them underestimate you first before striking the finishing blow."

"Ugh, whatever, backseat battling is real easy." Hughie rolled his eyes. "I'd like to see you do better from inside that dinky ring, oh mighty one."

"Why you arrogant little—!"

"—Next match, Caelum versus Antonio!" Elder Fred announced.

Ding!
Your Disciple Hughie Has Won
150 Karmic Credits x3
450 Karmic Credits Gained

That one hundred percent loyalty multiplier coming in handy.

Slifer watched as Hughie pumped his fists, celebrating his victory over Paddy. While the battle had been entertaining for the spectators, Slifer couldn't help but feel that Hughie's reckless fighting style had mostly been down to luck.

If it had been Slifer's avatar in the ring instead, such carelessness could have easily led to defeat or knowing his luck, death. Zack couldn't rely on blind luck to win his fights.

Now if only my other self took the fights more seriously . . .

"Next match, Caelum versus Antonio!" Elder Fred announced.

The two disciples stepped into the arena. Caelum stood with his hand resting on the hilt of Bloodthorn.

"Try not to embarrass yourself too badly," the Heavenly Light disciple taunted. "Wouldn't want that pretty face of yours all bruised for the victory ceremony."

Caelum didn't respond, ignoring the jab. He knew words were meaningless here—only strength mattered.

"Begin!" Elder Fred declared.

Antonio immediately blasted towards Caelum in a blur, cocking back a meaty fist. Just before it could land, Caelum sidestepped, the blow sailing past his cheek.

Antonio's momentum carried him stumbling several feet beyond. He whirled around with a growl. "Don't run away, dammit!"

Caelum remained silent, hand still resting casually on his sword hilt.

With another roar, Antonio launched a frenzied series of punches and kicks. But Caelum flowed between the attacks like water, barely exerting himself as he ducked and wove with minimal movement. Antonio struck nothing but air, his frustration visibly growing.

Finally, Caelum went on the offensive. His sword sang as he drew it faster than the eye could follow, slashing across Antonio's chest.

"Gah!" Antonio cried out at the sudden blaze of pain. He leapt backwards, clutching the deep gash now marring his chest. "You bastard!" he spat. "I'll kill you!" Face twisted in rage, he lifted one hand towards Caelum, palm outstretched. Yellow qi coalesced rapidly before him. "Vajra Fist!"

A massive projection of a golden fist rocketed towards Caelum. But Caelum didn't flinch. With a single upwards sweep of his sword, the fist split cleanly in half, dissipating harmlessly.

Antonio gaped at the casual display of strength. He desperately channeled more qi, materializing four huge fists that hovered around him defensively.

"Try getting through this!" he challenged.

Caelum's features remained impassive. Without a word, he stabbed his sword into the ground before him. "Thorned Lash."

Before Antonio's eyes, Bloodthorn seemed to come alive. Its blade lengthened impossibly as it shot out in Antonio's direction. It wrapped around two of the golden fists, constricting tightly. The fists warped and cracked under the pressure before shattering.

"Shit!" Antonio dispelled the remaining fists and tried to dodge, but the sword was too quick. It coiled around his limbs and torso, razor edge digging into his skin as it lifted him up. Antonio thrashed helplessly several feet above the ground. "Let me go!" he roared.

Caelum made a slight pulling motion with one hand and Bloodthorn instantly retracted, slamming Antonio down hard enough to leave cracks in the stage floor.

Elder Fred hurried over and checked Antonio's condition before raising his hand. "Winner, Caelum!"

Ding!
Your Disciple Caelum Has Won
150 Karmic Credits x3
450 Karmic Credits Gained

As expected of Caelum. Efficient, controlled, and not toying with his opponent like Hughie. Slifer nodded approvingly from the stands as he noted the similarity between his disciples' battles. *I just hope Hughie realizes that Caelum was teaching him a lesson there.*

"Next match—Olive versus Kuwi."

While half-listening to the other matches, Slifer opened up the System Shop. He needed an antidote for Zack's injured shoulder. That Black Death cultivator's corrosive death technique was still causing issues for Zack. Slifer had initially wanted Zack to deal with it himself, but his avatar had made it clear that he was making no progress.

The attacks of the Black Death disciple were not simple.

Hmm, what do we have here . . .

The first antidote that popped up was called Rejuvenating Phoenix Balm, a medicinal paste that could cleanse all wounds and regenerate destroyed meridians.

Useful, but Zack's meridians are fine . . . Slifer swiped to the next option as he purposely ignored the 10,000 Karmic Credit price tag.

Next was Life-Sealing Pill, at only 100 Karmic Credits, it was able to forcefully suppress any malicious qi or toxins within the body.

Tempting, but I'm not trying to suppress anything, I need to get rid of the problem!

Finally, he found what he was looking for—Essence Cleansing Serum. This liquid could purge both external and internal injuries by liquefying them and flushing the corruption from the body's essence channels.

Five hundred Karmic Credits, not bad. He quickly purchased the serum and had it sent to his storage ring. *Perfect. Now to inform Zack.* He closed his eyes and delivered a message directly to his other self.

"*Hey, I got you something to fix that messed up shoulder. It's in the ring.*"

In preparation for the Sealed Realm, Slifer had spent a handsome amount of Karmic Credits to link two rings so that they shared the same pocket dimension.

One thousand Karmic Credits is definitely worth it! Whilst Zack is in the Sealed Realm, I can just buy items and send them over. We'll see how the other protagonists deal with that, ha!

With his job done, Slifer returned his full attention to the tournament stage as the next match was announced.

"Ziven versus Katherine!"

CHAPTER EIGHTY-TWO

Slifer watched with interest as the next two contestants stepped into the arena—Ziven of the Heavenly Light Sect, and Katherine of the Black Rose Sect.

The cocky Son of Heaven wore a smirk as he faced Katherine across the arena. "Try not to bore me too quickly, will you?"

Katherine bristled, flames already dancing along her fingertips. "We'll see who's bored after I burn off that stupid grin!"

"Begin!" Elder Fred announced.

Katherine immediately leapt at Ziven, propelling herself forward on jets of fire from her feet. With a fierce cry, she hurled a massive fireball straight at her opponent's head.

But faster than she could react, Ziven thrust out a palm, conjuring a swirling vortex of wind that swallowed up the fireball. With his other hand, he made a squeezing motion.

"Wind Lock!"

Before she could retreat, the air around Katherine condensed with an audible crack, forming into glowing green chains that clamped onto her limbs and held her suspended in the air.

"Already?" Ziven yawned. "What a disappointment."

He flicked his wrist, and the chains flung Katherine against the ground, then up into the barrier wall. Over and over her battered body smashed back and forth between the two surfaces as she screamed.

Finally, Ziven recalled the chains, dropping Katherine to lie crumpled on the floor, barely conscious. He prodded her with the tip of his boot.

"Pathetic. Is this the best your wretched sect can muster?"

Elder Fred hurried over and checked Katherine's condition. Her face was badly bruised, and blood dripped from her nose and mouth. With a shake of his head, the elder raised his hand.

"The winner is Ziven!"

The Heavenly Light disciples erupted into deafening cheers for their victorious sect brother. Chants of "Son of Heaven! Son of Heaven!" rang out from the stands. Even spectators from the other sects looked impressed by Ziven's swift and utter demolition of his opponent.

As for the Black Rose section, it was silent except for a few muttered curses.

Hughie slammed his fist angrily against the railing. "He's cocky now but wait till I face him!"

"That is the fate of all demonic cultivators!" Ziven declared loudly enough for all to hear. "To be crushed underfoot by the righteous!"

More cheers erupted from the Heavenly Light disciples. Slifer resisted the urge to roll his eyes. *Protagonists were always one for dramatic speeches.*

"I quite like his style," Vowron chuckled.

"As expected of our finest. None of the disciples here can match Ziven," Zofia said with a proud smile on her face.

So he defeated some no-name scrub, big deal. My own disciples are far more entertaining to watch. And he's already lost against Amelia before anyway.

As if sensing Slifer's thoughts, Elder Fred stepped forward for the next announcement.

"Amelia of Black Rose Sect versus Adrian of White Tiger Sect!"

A petite silver-haired girl stepped into the arena with an innocent smile on her face. Adrian towered over her, rippling with muscle.

"I'll try not to hurt you too badly, little girl," Adrian laughed.

Amelia's smile grew even more innocent as she clutched her hands to her chest. "Oh my, you're so big and strong! Please be gentle with me!"

Slifer had to resist the urge to snort out loud. The little minx was laying it on thick with her act. He could already predict what was about to happen.

As expected, the moment Elder Fred announced the start of the match, Amelia's entire demeanor changed. Her innocent smile twisted into a vicious grin and her hand snapped out, backhanding Adrian across the face before he could react.

The White Tiger disciple reeled back with a startled shout, clutching his cheek. "Why you little—!"

Amelia immediately schooled her features back into a mask of terror.

"I'm so sorry!" Amelia exclaimed. "But I got scared, forgive me!"

"I . . . I didn't even atta—"

But Amelia was already on him, hands covered in purple qi.

"Spirit Severing Claw!"

Her nails elongated into wicked talons that she raked across Adrian's chest in a blurred series of swipes. Blood sprayed as Adrian's robes were shredded, five deep gashes slicing across his torso.

He stumbled back with a cry of pain as his soul burned. "Damn you!"

Amelia dropped her innocent act as a cruel smile appeared on her face. "Mmm, not bad," she murmured as she licked the blood from her claws. "But big strong men always taste the sweetest when their arrogance turns to despair."

"Y-you bitch!" Adrian shouted as he activated his sect's signature White Tiger transformation. Muscles bulged and white fur sprouted across his body as he dropped on all fours, morphing into a massive tiger. Razor-sharp claws dug into the arena floor as he pounced with a deafening roar.

But Amelia darted around the wild strikes, looking almost bored. As Adrian passed by, she delivered a slap to his bottom.

"Bad kitty! You need to be punished for that little temper tantrum."

She grabbed the tiger by the tail and slammed him down hard. Adrian yowled as the arena floor cracked under the impact.

But Amelia was just getting started. Still holding him by the tail, she swung the helpless Adrian around like he weighed nothing, building momentum before releasing him. He sailed through the air, crashing headfirst through the arena barrier.

Watching Amelia's antics, Slifer sighed internally. *She's never going to learn respect or mercy at this rate. It will take someone finally giving her a taste of her own medicine before she changes. And even that might not be enough . . .*

Astrid, seeing one of her sect members being tortured like this, frowned. "This level of humiliation is unnecessary. She has already clearly won, there's no need to drag it out."

"Oh, I don't know, I'm quite enjoying the show." Vowron laughed.

Adrian had finally reverted back to human form and was now being spun overhead by his ankles before being pile-drived back down.

"While technically allowed, this does seem rather . . . excessive," Leontius winced.

"What else can be expected from demonic scum. They have no honor!" Zofia sneered down her nose.

Slifer frowned. He may not approve of Amelia's methods either, but he wouldn't stand for outsiders criticizing his disciples. That was his job!

"Amelia is still young," he said. "She has much to learn in controlling her . . . enthusiasm during battle." *That's probably the understatement of the century.*

The words had barely left his mouth when Amelia leapt onto the semiconscious Adrian's back. "Giddy-up horsey!" she cackled, slapping his sides as she pretended to ride him around the arena like a bucking bronco.

I give up. Slifer pinched the bridge of his nose. *She's hopeless.*

Amelia then hopped off and proceeded to repeatedly smash Adrian's face into the ground like she was grinding pepper.

After grinding Adrian's face into the dirt several more times, Amelia seemed to grow bored. With a dismissive sniff, she dusted off her hands and walked away, leaving her opponent in a whimpering heap.

Elder Fred awkwardly raised his arm. "Um . . . victor, Amelia of Black Rose Sect."

Ding!
Your Disciple Amelia Won
150 Karmic Credits Gained

Well, at least she won. Guess I'll have to give her a lecture about "respecting your opponent," for all the good it will do.

Amelia curtsied to the cheering Black Rose disciples. Then she turned and gave a wink straight at Ziven, blowing him a kiss. The Son of Heaven looked like he wanted to murder her on the spot.

The remaining matches of the first round passed by fairly quickly. Dentos, as efficient as usual, defeated his Black Heart Sect opponent with several well-placed strokes of his paintbrush. The poor cultivator found himself sealed inside a painting of a serene meadow for the remainder of the duel.

Nomed got lucky with his matchup, facing off against a Pure Soul Sect cultivator at only the Mid-Foundation Establishment Realm. The mismatch was obvious to everyone as Nomed battered his opponent into submission in less than a minute.

It will take more than a gap of one substage in cultivation to defeat a protagonist.

"Next match—Zack of the Black Rose Sect versus Urion of the Heavenly Light Sect!"

Let's see how my other self does. Slifer straightened up in his seat with interest.

Ding!
New Task: For every battle your disciples win in the second round, you will gain 200

Karmic Credits!

Wow, if I get credits for every battle they win in the rest of the tournament, just how many credits would that be?

Zack strolled into the arena wearing a confident grin as always. Despite Slifer healing his shoulder, he still wore bandages wrapped around one arm for show.

Urion smirked when he saw the bandages. "Just give up now. With you already half-crippled, I'd hate for you to embarrass yourself out there."

"Funny, I was hoping to get matched against one of you Heavenly Light peacocks." Zack's eyes glinted dangerously. "Can't wait to pluck those arrogant feathers of yours."

"You da—!"

"Begin!"

CHAPTER EIGHTY-THREE

Zack and Urion circled each other slowly. Zack continued pretending that his shoulder was still injured by favoring his unbandaged side.

"I'll show you!" With a roar, Urion charged forward surrounded by halos of light. Just before reaching Zack, he thrust out both palms.

"Heavenly Radiance Burst!"

Rays of golden light erupted towards Zack. But Zack was ready as he jumped into the sky. "Dragon Wings!"

With a crackle of electricity, lightning wings sprouted from Zack's back. With a single flap, he easily evaded the Heavenly Radiance Burst as it scorched the ground where he had been a moment before.

From above, Zack smirked down at Urion. "Too slow!"

He then dive-bombed straight towards his opponent, fist cocked back.

"Thunderclap Palm!"

Urion crossed his arms, manifesting a shield of light to block the blow. Zack's palm collided with a resounding boom that shook the entire arena. Urion slid back several meters from the force, but his shield managed to absorb the worst of the attack.

Up in the stands, Slifer shook his head as he watched the battle play out. It was obvious to him that his avatar was merely toying with the Heavenly Light disciple. After all, what could someone at the Peak Foundation Establishment Realm truly do against the full power of his avatar?

The difference between their battle prowess was like an adult wrestling with a child. No matter how crafty the child was, victory would require a miracle. Or utter carelessness on the adult's part.

In other words, Zack could end this battle anytime he wished. The only question was how long he wanted to draw things out for the spectators' entertainment.

Judging by the theatrical performance so far, Slifer guessed his avatar planned to milk this for all it was worth.

Eh, let him have his fun.

Down below, Zack landed back on his feet. "Not bad," he said to Urion. "Now it's my turn!"

Once more he took to the air on wings of lightning, zigzagging randomly around Urion. Confused, the Heavenly Light disciple tried to track Zack's erratic movements, but it was hopeless.

Zack suddenly dove, appearing right in Urion's face. "Boo!"

"Gah!" Urion shouted in surprise, stumbling backwards.

Zack laughed and resumed zigzagging overhead. "What's wrong? Eyes too slow to keep up?"

Urion growled in frustration. Losing a battle was understandable but it was humiliating being toyed with like this.

"Try my Heavenly Gaze then!" Closing his eyes, Urion channeled his qi. When his eyes opened, they glowed with an azure light. Everything seemed to slow down as his vision locked onto Zack's lightning-fast form, allowing him to perfectly track the movements.

"Woah, cool dōjusts—!"

Just before Zack could finish, Urion thrust out a palm.

"Heavenly Snare!"

A glowing lattice of light manifested in midair right in Zack's flight path. Too fast to change direction, Zack smashed right into it. The snare instantly coiled around him, completely immobilizing his limbs no matter how much he struggled.

Urion smirked, closing his fist. The snare contracted, crushing Zack in its grip.

"How's that?" Urion leered up at his captive. "Still having fun?"

Zack groaned dramatically. "Oh no . . . I can't get out and my shoulder . . . it hurts." He made a show of clutching his bandaged arm.

For a moment, a flicker of hope appeared in Urion's eyes. Was it actually over?

But in the spectator stands, none of the elders seemed particularly concerned by the sight of Zack trapped. If anything, most looked mildly amused.

"Supreme Elder, your disciple has some skill," Leontius remarked. "His mastery over lightning at such a young age is really quite impressive."

"This Zack . . . he seems interesting," Vowron murmured.

The only one not looking impressed was Zofia. "Do not be taken in so easily," she warned. "He may have some meager talent for his age, but in the end, no demonic cultivator can match the Heavenly Light Sect."

Slifer bristled slightly at that, but held his tongue, he didn't let it stop him from feeling smug under the praise. Even though it was aimed at his avatar rather than himself, he still enjoyed the attention.

Down in the arena, Zack's eyes narrowed. Playtime was over. With a pulse of lightning, the Heavenly Snare imprisoning him shattered into sparks.

Urion stared, dumbfounded. "But how—"

Before he could react, Zack shot forward and landed a solid kick to Urion's chest, knocking him flat on his back.

"You peacocks are all flash and no substance," Zack said, standing over him. "Time to pluck those feathers for real."

Urion shakily rose to his feet. He took a few steps back from Zack, no longer so bold.

"D-don't get cocky!" he shouted, though it sounded like he was trying to convince himself. "I'll show you the ultimate power of our Heavenly Light techniques!"

Taking a deep breath, Urion adopted a wide stance. He brought his palms together in front of him as brilliant halos of light sprang up around his body. The arena shook from the sudden spike in spiritual pressure.

"Behold the Heavenly Radiance Cannon!"

Between Urion's hands, a small orb of light appeared, deceptively innocent at first. But it quickly expanded, intensifying into a miniature sun that grew larger and larger, until Urion finally thrust it forward with a roar.

The orb transformed into a massive beam of blazing light, seeming to set the very air aflame as it annihilated everything in its path.

In the stands, Zofia smiled proudly. This was one of the Heavenly Light Sect's strongest techniques. No mere Foundation Establishment cultivator could possibly withstand a direct hit. This match was over.

But Zack did not look worried. As the Heavenly Radiance Cannon bore down on him, his posture shifted. His injured arm dropped back to his side. With his functional hand, he calmly unsheathed his sword.

"Stellar Nova Strike!"

Zack's sword blurred as he executed a blinding series of slashes. Each cut left behind a trail of light that hung in the air.

Within seconds, Zack was enclosed inside a dome of condensed starfire. At the same time, the Heavenly Radiance Cannon struck.

But the Stellar Nova barrier easily swallowed up the attack, diffusing it harmlessly.

"How . . . that's impossible!" Urion gaped as he fell to his knees.

His strongest technique had been completely overpowered. At this point, he knew he had no chance of victory.

Up in the stands, Zofia's smile had slipped into a look of astonishment. She too was having difficulty comprehending what she had just witnessed.

Zack blew out a breath, scattering lingering motes of starlight as he shook his head.

"Not gonna lie, I thought you'd put up more of a fight. But if that's really all you've got . . ."

In an instant, he flickered out of sight, reappearing directly behind the stunned Urion, sword lightly resting across the Heavenly Light disciple's neck.

" . . . then this match is over."

" . . . I submit," Urion choked out.

Zack released him and spun his sword around before sheathing it. He patted Urion on the shoulder.

"You've got decent skills. Work on that temper though, and don't underestimate your opponent next time."

With that, he strolled away, leaving behind a dumbfounded Urion. The Heavenly Light disciple stared after him for several seconds before his knees gave out and he plopped down hard on his behind.

Just how? That lightning, the spatial teleportation, the sword and light techniques . . . he wielded them all perfectly. Urion shook his head in disbelief. He couldn't understand how someone at the same realm had outclassed him.

Stumbling to his feet, he quickly retreated from the arena without another glance back. There were murmurs and whispers from the Heavenly Light section.

Ziven in particular looked outraged. "How could he use light techniques?" he spat, knowing just how hard it was to gain access to the light element, it was one of the reasons he himself joined the sect. "He must have stolen our sect's secrets somehow!"

But Zofia shook her head as her voice carried down to him. "No. His skills did not come from our sect. I'm not sure where he learned these techniques, but they do not originate with us."

Inwardly, she was more troubled than she let on. Even though the light techniques demonstrated were only at the Foundation Establishment level, she could see their potential, they were at least Mid-Earth Rank techniques. Now how did a demonic sect acquire such high-level light techniques?

Up in the participant waiting area, Caelum shot to his feet, staring down at the arena with shock written across his normally stoic features. Sunrise Slash!

Zack's at the Sword Qi Realm at the very least . . . and that other sword technique? He really is Master's protégé.

"Ahem." Elder Fred cleared his throat, drawing everyone's attention. "Victory goes to Zack of the Black Rose Sect!"

Cheers erupted from the Black Rose section as Zack lapped up the attention. He spotted Amelia blowing kisses at him from the waiting area and responded with a roguish wink.

As he made his way off the arena stage, Slifer leaned back. His avatar's performance had certainly made an impression on the other elders.

While part of him enjoyed the prestige, he also hoped no one looked too deeply into things. He trusted Zack not to break character unless absolutely necessary. Still, the more eyes on them, the greater the risk someone might uncover their secret.

Even though I don't trust the System, it is good at what it does. And if that old man Li Fenghao hasn't noticed, then I have nothing to worry about here.

For now, Slifer decided to just enjoy his sect's momentum. One victory at a time. After all, this was only the second round of a five-round tournament.

Ding!
Your Avatar Zack Won
200 Karmic Credits Gained

Let the games continue.

CHAPTER EIGHTY-FOUR

Slifer watched with amusement as the Heavenly Light disciple scheduled to face Ziven walked onto the arena stage, took one look at the Son of Heaven, and promptly turned right back around to exit on the other side.

"I forfeit this match!" the disciple called out, not even sparing a glance backwards.

Slifer chuckled under his breath. Clearly that disciple knew Ziven by reputation and decided the only wise choice was to avoid fighting the monster entirely. Not a bad strategy when the difference in power was so vast. Better to lose a match than end up crippled or dead.

Elder Fred raised an eyebrow but made the announcement. "Er . . . by forfeit, victory goes to Ziven of the Heavenly Light Sect."

The Heavenly Light section erupted into loud cheers and chants of "Son of Heaven! Son of Heaven!"

Slifer thought it was rather silly to celebrate what was essentially a non-battle. But he supposed that was the privilege of being the protagonist. Even your opponent surrendering without a fight was seen as an achievement.

As for the Son of Heaven himself, he looked mildly annoyed at being denied his fun, but he didn't argue. No doubt he had been expecting his opponent to tremble in fear. His ego would recover soon enough.

"Next match, Caelum of Black Rose versus Pollus of Pure Soul Sect!" called out Elder Fred.

Both disciples entered the arena and faced each other. Caelum wore his usual impassive expression while the Pure Soul disciple Pollus gave a friendly smile.

"Good luck to you," Pollus said politely with a slight bow. "May this be a good match."

Caelum simply nodded in return. He had no interest in exchanging pleasantries. His focus was only on the fight ahead.

But instead of assuming a fighting stance, Pollus turned and bowed towards the Pure Soul section.

"My apologies, but I too must forfeit this match!"

Murmurs of surprise rippled through the crowd.

Slifer frowned. *Another walkover victory? How strange.*

But glancing over at Leontius, the supreme elder of Pure Soul Sect didn't look angry or upset. If anything, the old man seemed vaguely approving of his disciple's choice.

Hmm, so it was a deliberate strategy on their part. Slifer realized that by forfeiting the second round matches, the Pure Soul disciples preserved their strength for the later battles when the stakes were higher. *Not a bad plan.*

"Caelum wins by forfeit," Fred announced, slightly exasperated. He was no doubt hoping to officiate some actual fighting.

Slifer had to admit, two consecutive concessions did make for somewhat dull viewing. Oh well, he was certain things would get more exciting soon. After all, they were still only in the second round. No doubt the other elders shared his thoughts, based on the politely hidden looks of boredom on their faces. Even the audience seemed to be growing restless.

Time to deliver something a bit more thrilling.

As if on cue, Fred stepped forward for the next announcement. "Amelia of the Black Rose Sect versus Krikoff of the Black Heart Sect!"

Now this should be interesting, Slifer thought as both disciples leapt into the arena.

Usually Amelia liked to toy with weaker opponents, but he sensed something different about her demeanor this time. There was no playful smirk on her face as she stared down the Black Heart disciple. If anything, her pretty features were set in an uncharacteristic scowl.

Krikoff on the other hand looked thrilled at this matchup. He leered across the arena at Amelia, his eyes roaming hungrily over her petite form.

"Well hello there, beautiful, fancy seeing you again," he called out loudly. "This time, I hope you'll be more receptive . . ."

Slifer's eyes narrowed. He knew exactly why Amelia looked ready to murder the fool. In their last encounter, the lecher had tried to grope her, and she'd responded by blasting him through a wall.

That perv was lucky not to have lost that hand.

Apparently the creep had yet to learn his lesson. But it seemed he would receive a refresher course today. Slifer almost felt pity for what was about to happen to the arrogant idiot.

Almost.

Amelia's scowl deepened at the taunt. With a flick of her wrist, a black dagger appeared in her hand. Slowly, she dragged her tongue along the flat of the blade while maintaining eye contact with Krikoff.

"Let's see you touch anyone with those filthy hands after today," she spat.

Krikoff simply laughed, making a show of looking her up and down again. "Ooh, feisty. Don't worry, I like it rough. You'll be screaming my name before long!"

With that he cracked his knuckles, his Peak Core Formation power rolling off him in waves. But Amelia did not so much as blink.

"Begin!" Fred shouted, before quickly retreating from the stage. He did not want to be caught between those two right now.

Krikoff wasted no time as vines burst out of his sleeves, aiming to restrain her.

But Amelia was ready. With a swipe of her dagger, she severed the vines before they could touch her. In the same motion, she slipped right through Krikoff's fingers like smoke, appearing behind him within the blink of an eye.

The Black Heart disciple spun with a snarl. More vines erupted from his body, lashing towards Amelia in thorny tendrils. She flipped backwards out of reach, but the vines pursued her, reluctant to let her go.

Realizing he couldn't restrain her fast enough this way, Krikoff changed tactics. With a roar, massive vines burst out of the ground beneath Amelia's feet. But she had already read the intent, pushing off the instant before they erupted. She landed lightly on top of one of the swaying vines.

Before Krikoff could react, she dashed down the length of it, her smaller frame letting her twist out of the way as thorns snapped at her. Within a second, she had reached the end and pushed off, throwing herself straight at Krikoff.

"Soul Render!"

At this distance, Krikoff had no chance to evade the blow, he was barely able to cross his arms to block the attack. But even then, he slid back from the force, face scrunching in pain. The purple qi blade had shredded right through his robes, directly attacking his soul.

"Dammit!" He clutched his chest and tried to scramble away. But Amelia pressed on.

Forced completely on the defensive, Krikoff's arrogance rapidly unraveled. Just defending against Amelia's attacks took all his focus. Even using his vines only delayed the inevitable by seconds.

By the end of it, Krikoff was panting heavily, whilst his soul felt like it was on fire, Amelia had yet to suffer so much as a scratch. His cocky attitude had evaporated completely, replaced by pain and rage . . . and fear.

Slamming his palms down, he sent a pulse of qi into the ground.

"Entangling Undergrowth!"

Thick vines exploded outwards, warping into spiked whips that filled the entire arena with a writhing mass of greenery.

Amelia leapt over one vine, severed another, then flipped to the side to avoid a third. But the density of attacks was rapidly increasing. Her expression shifted slightly for the first time, her eyes narrowed as she looked for an opening.

"Merge!"

Krikoff condensed all the scattered vines into one last thorny tentacle and sent it spearing straight towards Amelia with all his strength behind it.

Too focused on her footing, Amelia did not react quickly enough this time. The massive vine whipped around her torso, thorns biting deeply into her flesh as they coiled tight. She bit back a scream, the black dagger still clutched tightly in her hand.

"Got you now, bitch!" Krikoff exulted. With a savage jerk, he hauled Amelia off her feet, smashing her down hard against the arena floor.

Again and again he whipped her into the earth. Amelia's head snapped back with each blow, chest constricted by the vines.

Up in the stands, Slifer leaned forward, eyes narrowing. *Now things are getting serious.*

In the arena, Amelia regained enough sense to start hacking at the vine crushing her. But the thorns dug in deeper in response, she bit back a hiss of pain. She could feel her strength rapidly draining.

Krikoff grinned maliciously, savoring this moment. "What's wrong? Thought you were going to chop off my hands?" he taunted between slams. "I think it's your arms that will be separating from your worthless body!"

With a final heave, he brought Amelia down on her head with a stomach-turning crack. Her struggles weakened and the dagger fell from her hand.

Gloating at his seeming victory, Krikoff began slowly reeling Amelia's semiconscious form towards him like a fish on a line. "Maybe I won't kill you just yet, though." He licked his lips. "First, I think I'll take my time paying you back for humiliating me before I finish crushing the life out of you. Oh, I'm really going to enjoy this!"

He reached for her as soon as she was close enough, hands twisting towards her chest.

"Don't touch me!"

In that instant, Amelia's head jerked up, eyes flashing purple. An inhuman snarl tore from her throat. Before Krikoff could react, her fingers locked around his wrist like a steel trap.

With a sickening crack, she crushed the bones in her grip. Krikoff's shriek of pain turned into a gurgle as her free hand whipped forward, shoving down his throat and ripping out his tongue in a spray of blood.

Not even waiting for him to fall, Amelia grasped the vine still entangling her and channeled her qi. The vine blackened and dissolved into ash under her corrosive touch.

With a thud, she landed on her feet. When she looked up, her beautiful features had morphed into something inhuman—skin growing paler, dark veins appearing across her face, eyes hollowing into glowing blue sockets, and a pair of smoky wings unfurling from her back.

She had activated her Ghoul Transformation!

Krikoff tried to crawl away, clutching the bloody hole that had been his mouth. But Amelia descended on him in the blink of an eye, no longer playing around. She grabbed his right wrist, placing her foot on his forearm.

Krikoff's eyes pleaded for mercy, but only agonized gurgles escaped as Amelia twisted his hand off, spraying more blood.

She tossed the hand aside and moved to the other arm, repeating the process. All the while, her face remained emotionless.

Armless and unable to scream, Krikoff writhed on the ground in sheer mindless agony. Amelia watched his pathetic struggles for a few moments before taking a step towards him.

I'm sorry, Master, but he needs to die!

Purple qi flickered around her fingers as she leaned down, pressing them lightly against Krikoff's forehead.

"Soul Collapse."

The Black Heart disciple's back arched in a silent scream as he gasped his last breaths, eyes rolling back before his body went limp.

Amelia straightened slowly, flicking the blood from her hands. The light gradually returned to her eyes as her wings receded and her face reverted to its normal delicate appearance.

"Pathetic filth," she muttered before making her way off the stage.

A hush had fallen over the entire arena. Many spectators looked on with horror, while others seemed quietly satisfied that arrogance had received its just rewards.

From the participant viewing area, Hughie winced and gave a low whistle. "Remind me not to get on her bad side!"

Next to him, Caelum simply nodded without taking his eyes off his junior sister. Amelia was usually without mercy once someone crossed her, but for once, Caelum could understand. If she hadn't dealt with the pervert, Caelum knew that he would. He had to. No one touched his family!

Ziven, on the other hand, was staring at Amelia with pure disgust.

"This is what demonic scum do!" he spat. "Torture, cripple, and kill! I just don't understand how no one else sees it!"

Up on the stand, Slifer kept his face impassive, but internally he was wincing. This was exactly the kind of unrestrained brutality he had hoped to curb in Amelia. Killing the fool was one thing, but she had clearly taken things too far out of a desire to inflict pain and humiliation.

. . . *Still, the imbecile brought it upon* himself. Slifer decided to give her a pass just this once. *Luckily, the Black Heart Sect Master has gone missing. If he was present, then maybe I would have had to step in to protect her. But then again, with demonic cultivators, you never know. Hell, it wouldn't surprise me if he told her she went too easy on the perv and then gave her a live castration demonstration . . .*

Ding!
Due to Your Disciple Amelia's Actions You Have Gained 1 Karmic Credit
Ding!
Your Disciple Amelia Has Eliminated a Demonic Cultivator
25 Karmic Credits Gained

Slifer dismissed the notifications as he turned to see the reaction of the elders beside him.

The elders seemed divided in their reactions. Leontius in particular seemed appalled.

"That level of torture was completely unnecessary." He frowned. "Supreme Elder, I fear the heart of your disciple is blacker than the name of your se—"

But before he could finish, Slifer held up a hand. "That young man has harassed and even laid a hand on my disciple. She showed remarkable restraint until now, all things considered."

He left the exact details ambiguous, but the meaning was clear. The female elders in particular immediately looked outraged on Amelia's behalf.

"Is that so?" Zofia said, eyes narrowed dangerously. "Then he deserved worse than what he got. Do not waste pity on those who prey on women."

Leontius looked taken aback while Vowron simply chuckled. Astrid nodded in agreement with Zofia.

"She taught him a lesson he earned," the White Tiger elder declared. "I have no sympathy for such trash."

Leontius fell silent, unwilling to criticize Amelia further given the circumstances. In truth, he was conflicted. Justice had perhaps been served, but the methods still unnerved him.

Down in the arena, Elder Fred finally stepped forward as Krikoff's mangled corpse was carried out.

"Victory to Amelia of the Black Rose Sect!"

CHAPTER EIGHTY-FIVE

A shton of the White Tiger Sect versus Rai of the Black Heart Sect!"

Ashton stepped into the arena. At over seven feet tall, he was a giant, with bulging muscles that seemed ready to tear through the white robes straining to contain them.

Up in the waiting area, Zack's eyes lit up. The winner of this battle would face him in the next round!

Now that's more like it! No more wasting time with these weak sauce appetizers. I want the main course!

He could already feel his blood pumping faster at the thought of battling someone with Ashton's sheer physical prowess. Most cultivators relied too heavily on their techniques in Zack's opinion. He wanted to see what this dual cultivator could do with that monstrous body of his. Because Zack knew that when it came to hand-to-hand combat, no one could match him.

Let's see those tiger claws go up against my fists! Just try not to go down too quickly, big guy. I plan on putting on a good show for the crowd.

Across from Ashton, a lanky cultivator with flame-red hair entered the arena—Rai. He wore a cocky grin as he sized up his opponent, clearly unintimidated by Ashton's massive form. With a scoff, Rai produced a black rose from within his robes and tossed it at Ashton's feet.

"I'll lay you to rest on a bed of ashes, White Tiger," Rai declared, flames already dancing along his fingertips.

Ashton said nothing in response, settling into a solid ready stance, palms open and facing Rai. He had no need for flashy threats or posturing.

The time for talk was over.

"Begin!" Elder Fred shouted.

Rai instantly went on the offensive, hands flying as he threw waves of black fire at Ashton. But with startling agility for his size, Ashton twisted and turned, avoiding the attacks. He then countered by slamming both palms forward.

"Quaking Palm Blast!"

A powerful shockwave erupted from Ashton's hands, shattering the black flames and slamming into Rai. The Black Heart cultivator managed to cross his arms right before impact, shielding himself from the worst of the hit. But the force still sent him skidding back several meters, heels digging into the arena floor.

Undeterred, Rai pressed his attack once more. "Hellfire Dragon!"

The black flames swirled and expanded before him, taking the shape of a gigantic serpentine dragon. It reared back its head and shot towards Ashton, mouth opened wide, ready to swallow him whole.

But Ashton held his ground. Clenching his right hand into a fist, he punched out as the flaming dragon bore down on him.

"Ironbreak Fist!"

Empowered by a surge of qi, Ashton's fist plowed straight through the Hellfire Dragon's head, dispersing it completely. Residual flames licked harmlessly across his White Tiger robes but failed to do any damage.

"Is that all you've got?" Ashton rumbled.

"Let's see you block this!" Rai snarled.

Drawing back both hands to his side, he concentrated his qi into a swirling vortex of black fire between his palms. The flames spun faster and faster, condensing down into an orb. With a shout, Rai thrust his palms forward, firing off the concentrated blast.

"Black Fire Cannon!"

The orb shot towards Ashton, but Ashton remained calm, clasping his hands together. A visible wave of qi radiated out from his body as all his muscles flexed at once.

"White Tiger's Fortitude!"

The black fire cannon struck Ashton head-on, swallowing him in an inferno. The arena shook under the force of the detonation.

Slifer turned to see the White Tiger supreme elder's reaction but found that there was not a flicker of concern on her face.

Yeah . . . I think that Rai fella is screwed.

As the smoke cleared, Ashton stood in the same spot, completely unharmed. He hadn't bothered moving or defending; he simply relied on the durability granted by his qi enforcement technique and his physique.

Rai stared in dismay. Just what kind of monster was this guy? His strongest attack didn't even make him flinch!

Among the crowd, looks of astonishment crossed more than a few faces. For Ashton to so casually overpower a Peak Foundation Establishment cultivator's techniques with just the force of his body . . . very impressive.

"My turn," Ashton said. Crouching down, he slammed both palms flat on the ground.

"Tectonic Upheaval!"

A shockwave rippled out from Ashton's hands, cracking and buckling the arena floor. Caught off guard, Rai was knocked off his feet and landed hard on his back with a grunt.

But Ashton wasn't done yet—the White Tiger disciple suddenly crossed the distance between them in two huge strides. Before Rai could react, Ashton's massive hands clamped down on his shoulders.

Rai struggled helplessly as he was lifted clean off his feet. Ashton held him up with one hand as though he weighed nothing. Then with a roar, Ashton flung Rai straight up into the air.

"White Tiger Meteor Smash!"

Bouncing off the very tops of the arena barriers, Rai shot back down like a fiery comet, unable to stop or change direction. At the last possible second before impact, Ashton spun and delivered a devastating punch to Rai's stomach as he descended.

The Black Heart cultivator spat out a mouthful of blood as his body absorbed the massive blow. He was sent rocketing across the arena in a high arc until he smashed upside down into the barrier wall, leaving a man-sized crater on impact. Then he slid down and collapsed on the ground.

Elder Fred hurried over to examine Rai. After confirming he was still alive, albeit likely nursing several crushed organs, the elder raised his hand.

"Victory goes to Ashton of the White Tiger Sect!"

A deafening cheer rose up from the White Tiger section. Even disciples from the other sects looked impressed by the total domination displayed.

A team of Pure Soul Sect healers gently carried the whimpering Rai out on a stretcher. Ashton clasped his hands together and bowed deeply to his opponent.

"You fought well. I apologize for any excessive force. Please recover swiftly."

Up in the stands, Astrid smiled proudly as her disciple displayed the might of their sect for all to see. None could match the White Tiger Sect's bodily cultivation techniques when it came to pure physical toughness, and who better than a dual cultivator to showcase that.

In the waiting area, Zack was on his feet, clapping and laughing. "Now that's what I'm talking about! Skills and brawn, the total package!"

Finally, a real challenge! None of those squishy, robed weaklings. Soon it'll be time to see who the real dual cultivator is around here! He eyed Ashton hungrily as the White Tiger disciple left the arena.

Slifer observed his avatar's eager reaction and suppressed a sigh. He knew nothing he said would make a difference once Zack got all fired up. That bull-headed enthusiasm of his was a strength in its own way, but Slifer didn't want his avatar throwing caution and strategy to the wind.

From his memories of stage one, he was quite cautious, but maybe I'm underestimating him . . .

"Arkan of the Heavenly Light Sect versus Surian of the White Tiger Sect!"

The two disciples stepped into the arena.

While Surian may not have been as large of a giant as his junior brother, he was still a towering slab of muscle compared to normal sized humans. He flexed his muscular arms and cracked his neck from side to side.

"You saw what happened in my Junior Brother Ashton's match, didn't you?" he chuckled. "That Black Heart fool was crushed within minutes. You'd be smart to surrender now if you don't want to be carried out on a stretcher."

Arkan gave a flick of his long blonde hair and smiled. "You're not at my level, you should take your own advice."

Up in the stands, the female Heavenly Light disciples were going crazy, screaming Arkan's name.

"He's so dreamy!" one squealed.

"And that gorgeous hair! I just want to run my hands through it all day!" Another fanned herself.

Arkan paid them no mind, his gaze moving to the participant's area where it locked with Ziven's. The Son of Heaven stared back at him, eyes narrowed.

In the Heavenly Light Sect, Ziven was a newcomer who had swiftly defeated many Core Disciples to become a Legacy Disciple. Arkan wished to face him in the tournament, to show everyone the difference between a newly raised Legacy Disciple, and one born into the role like himself.

Surian grunted in annoyance as he realized his opponent wasn't even looking at him anymore.

"You underestimating me, pretty boy?" he growled. "I'll claw that smug look right off your face!"

Arkan just sighed in response, he saw no benefit in arguing with a beast.

"Begin!" Elder Fred shouted.

Immediately, Surian attacked. "Wind Blade Palm!" He thrust out both hands, generating twin gusts of cutting wind. The razor-sharp air blades shrieked towards Arkan.

But Arkan didn't move. As the wind blades neared, rays of dazzling light materialized around him to form a barrier. The Wind Blade Palms glanced off harmlessly.

Surian's eyes narrowed. So, it wouldn't be that easy. With a shout, he leapt into the air, qi surging as his body expanded and morphed. White fur sprouted across swelling muscles as claws and fangs elongated. Within seconds, the White Tiger cultivator's transformation was complete, leaving an enormous white tiger in his place.

The tiger slammed back down, arena floor cracking under its weight. Lips peeling back from saber-like teeth, it let loose an earth-shaking roar and pounced at Arkan, seeking to tear through his defenses through sheer brute force.

The heavenly shield rippled under the blow, but held firm. Arkan didn't even blink.

Snarling in frustration, the white tiger began circling the barrier, searching for any weak points to exploit. Finding none, it came to a stop directly in front of Arkan and opened its mouth. Then, drawing in a deep breath, the tiger let out another roar, this one concentrated with sonic qi vibrations projected straight towards Arkan's head.

The sound-based attack pierced flawlessly through the light shields, wreaking havoc on Arkan's equilibrium as it hammered his eardrums.

For the first time, cracks appeared in the Heavenly Light disciple's tranquil façade. Face contorting in irritation, Arkan raised one hand, fingers poised to snap.

"Be quiet, beast!"

Snap.

A circle of glowing daggers formed around him.

"Heavenly Barrage."

At his command, the daggers shot forward, impaling themselves into the white tiger's limbs. The tiger roared in pain, the sound attack breaking off as blood poured from its wounds.

Arkan summoned another object into existence—a whip of sunlight. He wrapped it around the injured tiger's neck, making the creature yowl and thrash, but no matter what it did, it could not break free.

Seconds later, it went limp, reverting back to Surian's human form as he slumped to the ground, unconscious.

"Should have taken your own advice." Arkan yawned, dismissing the light whip.

The Heavenly Light female disciples broke out in excited squeals again.

"So strong!"

"He's amazing!"

"Senior Brother, I'll be your pet next!"

"No, use that whip on me next time!" another cried out boldly. This drew gasps from the others.

Arkan paid them no mind, elegantly sweeping his hair back as he turned to leave the arena. But not before his eyes passed briefly over Ziven once more. The message was clear—your time will come.

"A flawless display of power, as expected of a Heavenly Light disciple," Zofia praised from the spectator stands once Arkan had left. "Perhaps only Ziven could hope to match him in this tournament."

Beside her, Vowron made a thoughtful noise. "The boy shows promise, I grant you that."

"As usual, the Heavenly Light disciples cannot be underestimated." Leontius nodded.

In contrast, Astrid sat stiffly, lips pressed thin. After Ashton's dominating performance earlier, she had been riding high. But now, after her own sect member had been toyed with and defeated without Arkan even needing to move, her pride had taken a hit. However, she swallowed down her bitterness and held her tongue. Getting emotional would not change matters.

As for Slifer, he kept his face impassive. But internally, he was contemplating. Soon, his avatar would face off against both Arkan and Ziven inside the Sealed Realm. *And he knows just how to make those arrogant peacocks turn on each other.* He suppressed a sly smile.

"Next match! Ironius of the Black Death Sect versus Powl of the Pure Soul Sect!" Elder Fred announced the last match of the second round.

Slifer sat up straighter, watching with interest as a pale, red-eyed youth stepped into the arena. According to Ironius's status window, he was also a hidden demon like the one who attacked Hughie.

Let's see what tricks this demon has up its sleeves . . .

CHAPTER EIGHTY-SIX

Powl was a thin, gentle-looking man, he gave a small bow as he entered the arena.

"Let us have a fair and honorable match."

Ironius said nothing in response, staring back impassively. Like most of the Black Death disciples in the tournament so far, he seemed a man of few words.

"Begin!" Elder Fred shouted.

Immediately, Ironius exploded into motion. With startling speed, he closed the distance to Powl in two quick steps and launched a blistering combo of palm strikes and kicks.

Powl's eyes widened in surprise at the ferocity of the opening assault. He quickly raised his arms to defend, but Ironius's attacks came from tricky angles that made them difficult to anticipate and block.

A palm strike to the shoulder sent Powl stumbling back.

A sweeping kick took his legs out from under him.

A follow-up knee to his stomach knocked the wind from his lungs.

Powl wheezed and clutched his midsection, but he had no time to recover before Ironius pressed in again, raining down punches and elbows.

Up in the stands, Leontius stroked his beard as he watched the battle. "Most impressive. Supreme Elder Vowron, it seems your Black Death disciples have quite a high level of skill in martial arts."

"There has recently been an increased emphasis on martial arts training in our sect," Vowron smiled. "I felt it was an area we needed to improve upon."

"An unusual decision," Zofia muttered, frowning. "Martial arts have limited usefulness for spiritual cultivators. Our true strength lies in spiritual techniques. No number of kicks and punches will overcome that gap in power."

"Sometimes going back to basics provides unexpected benefits," Vowron replied vaguely.

Slifer nearly laughed out loud. *Focusing on martial arts training, my arse! He's just making sure his demon disciples keep their qi suppressed. Can't have them losing control and revealing their true natures after all.*

Down in the arena, Powl finally managed to disengage and put some distance between himself and Ironius.

Placing his palms together, he began chanting under his breath. A soft glow emanated from his hands.

"Soul Snare!"

A pair of glowing purple bands shot out towards Ironius. But the Black Death disciple twisted his body to narrowly avoid one band while slapping aside the other.

"Soul Shockwave!"

Ripples of violet energy pulsed from Powl's palms, distorting the air as they sped towards Ironius. The vibrations slammed into the Black Death disciple's body, causing him to stumble briefly. But after a second, Ironius shook off the disorienting effects of the spiritual attack. His red eyes narrowed, and he resumed his advance.

"Im . . . impossible . . ." Powl stared, dumbstruck.

A brutal side kick crashed into Powl's torso, cracking ribs and sending the Pure Soul disciple flying backwards.

Up in the stands, Slifer shook his head as he observed the one-sided thrashing taking place below.

As a soul cultivator, Powl was at an inherent disadvantage in this matchup. Demons possessed greater soul strength compared to humans at the same cultivation level. Powl's soul techniques were simply not potent enough to threaten a demon like Ironius.

This battle's outcome had been decided the moment the two stepped into the arena.

Down below, Ironius moved in a blur of motion, raining down an endless barrage of punches and elbow strikes on the overwhelmed Powl. The force of the impacts could be felt even in the spectator stands.

Within seconds, Powl had been battered into a daze, barely able to stand. With Powl totally exhausted, Ironius delivered the finishing blow—a devastating palm strike that exploded against Powl's chest.

A visible shockwave rippled out from the point of impact. Powl let out a choked gasp as he doubled over and crumpled to the ground.

Elder Fred flew over to check on him. Powl was still breathing, but blood leaked from his nose and mouth. The elder waved his hand.

"Victory to Ironius of the Black Death Sect!"

"A pity for young Powl. He fought bravely, but was simply outmatched," Leontius sighed.

"I'd like to see how Ironius would fare against one of my disciples who use martial arts to enhance their spiritual techniques," Astrid remarked.

"As would I," said Zofia, a small frown on her face. "Relying solely on physical techniques seems . . . limiting."

Vowron simply smiled and said nothing more. The less attention drawn to his disciples, the better.

"The second round is now complete! We will begin the third round in fifteen minutes. Disciples, take this time to rest and prepare yourselves," Elder Fred announced.

There was a general murmur through the crowd as spectators and participants took the opportunity to stand, stretch, and gossip about the battles seen so far.

Slifer inclined his head to the other elders. "If you'll excuse me, I should check on my disciples' conditions before the next round." He made his way down to the Black Rose waiting area. Though he maintained an air of calm authority on the outside, his mind was racing.

The tournament so far had gone smoothly, with his disciples scoring victory after victory as expected. Yet Slifer could not shake the feeling that something was off. There was an undercurrent of tension in the air that left him uneasy. He didn't know whether it was due to the presence of so many powerful sects gathered in one place . . . or the fact that his own impostor status left him constantly paranoid of being uncovered.

I feel like something big will go down once the tournament ends . . . that Vowron fella, he doesn't seem too concerned about the results of the matches. Is he going to make a move when the Sealed Realm opens?

Slifer wasn't sure but either way, he still had a few insurances he could rely on to deal with Vowron, even if the Black Death supreme elder was a half-step immortal.

Upon entering the Black Rose waiting area, Slifer was not surprised to find Zack practically bouncing on the balls of his feet as he grinned at Caelum.

"Did you see that, Senior Brother? That big white tiger dude was a beast! I can't wait to throw down with him next."

"Ashton does possess both formidable strength and skill." Caelum offered a rare smile. "You will have quite the challenging battle ahead."

"I know right?" Zack laughed. "These Heavenly Light chumps and random fodder are getting real old. I wanna fight someone who can actually give me a workout, you know? Get the blood pumping! Maybe if I'm lucky, I'll finally get to cut loose for real out there!"

"An admirable desire for challenge," Slifer cut in smoothly as he entered the room. "But do not let eagerness make you careless. Facing a powerful opponent requires an even sharper mind, not just greater strength."

Zack spun around, immediately standing straighter. "Master! Uh, I just meant I'm tired of holding back so much. Testing myself against strong rivals is the only way I can improve."

Slifer studied Zack for a moment, and a part of him couldn't help but envy his avatar. Unlike himself, the avatar was able to act more carefree and have a bit of fun. "Remember, your safety is the priority, I would rather you forfeit than die . . ."

After all, I can always give myself the free slot for the Sealed Realm, this tournament is just so I can gain some battle experience. But if Zack dies so soon, then that's just an Avatar Card wasted, and who knows when I'll get another one?

Zack looked slightly abashed. "Yes, Master. I'll stay safe."

Satisfied, Slifer patted him on the shoulder and then checked on the others. Amelia was practically glowing following her last victory, while Dentos looked unharmed, though mildly disappointed his opponents had not put up much of a fight.

As for Hughie, he seemed to be in the middle of an argument with that immortal grandpa of his.

"What do you mean play it safe?" Hughie suddenly exclaimed to the air. "We're talking about me here! Quadrupling my strength and speed is like my whole thing!" He nodded along absently for a few seconds. "Okay, sure, no need to get personal, just saying—I look way more badass when I'm over eight feet tall and rippling with muscles . . . It really shows off these."

Hughie flexed an arm and kissed his bicep.

"Anyway, you know caution isn't my style, gramps. I'm the 'punch first, ask questions while punching' type."

He mimed a series of jabs and uppercuts.

"Uh-huh, uh-huh, I hear you but—"

Not wanting to get involved, Slifer made his way back up to the spectator stands. The third round was just about to begin.

The third round saw the remaining contestants whittled down even further in both the Foundation Establishment and Core Formation tournaments.

In the Foundation Establishment tournament, William took the stage against a Black Heart Sect disciple. The battle started off fairly evenly matched, but slowly began turning against William's favor as his opponent unleashed several elemental techniques that William struggled to counter.

Gritting his teeth, the young prodigy somehow endured a combination of quick thinking and raw talent, managing to reverse the tide at the last second to barely eke out a win. He left the stage looking quite battered. The difference in cultivation levels was beginning to show against the more talented Peak Foundation Establishment opponents he faced, but at least he won.

Nomed's fight went much smoother. His protagonist-like strength allowed him to dominate the matches. He calmly weathered the desperate attacks of his third-round challenger before picking him apart with surgical precision.

In the Core Formation tournament, the matchups were quite lopsided.

Ziven's opponent took one look at him and immediately forfeited. The man's legs had been shaking so badly, he likely would have collapsed if he tried to fight.

Caelum was also awarded an automatic win as his opponent from Black Heart Sect refused to set foot into the arena.

As for Amelia, when her name was called, the female disciple meant to face her stared wide-eyed for several seconds before fleeing from the waiting area, screaming about not wanting to die.

"Well, that's unfortunate, I was so hoping for some playtime," Amelia pouted.

Elder Fred could only shrug helplessly. "Er . . . victory to Amelia by forfeit."

Slifer kept his poker face on but was chuckling inside. His little sadist was carving out quite the dreadful reputation for herself.

"Hughie of the Black Rose Sect versus Anne of the Heavenly Light Sect!"

In the elder's booth, Zofia leaned forward with interest. Anne was one of their sect's most gifted illusionists. Even Nascent Soul cultivators sometimes found themselves ensnared by her techniques. This Black Rose brute didn't stand a chance.

"Oh yeah!" Hughie cheered as he jumped down into the arena. He rolled his shoulders and neck, loosening up in preparation for the fight.

Across from him, his opponent Anne descended the steps gracefully. She was a cute blonde girl who looked to be around sixteen or seventeen years old.

"Please go easy on me, okay?" Anne smiled, blinking her big blue eyes at Hughie.

Hughie froze momentarily, rubbing the back of his neck. "Oh, uh . . . well, I wouldn't want to hurt a little girl like y— OW!"

He yelped as a phantom smack upside the head made him stumble. *Right, gramps is watching too.* The old man hated when Hughie went soft on female opponents just because they were cute.

Hughie straightened back up. "Er, what I mean is, this is a tournament. We should both do our best and have a fair match."

Anne looked slightly disappointed, but she nodded. "You're right, my apologies."

Up in the stands, Oliviare felt a small frown form on her face as she watched the blonde interact with her Hughie. There was just something about Anne's body language that seemed overly friendly and familiar.

And is Hughie blushing slightly? Oliviare's frown deepened. She didn't like how openly this Heavenly Light girl was flirting with her man.

"Begin!"

CHAPTER EIGHTY-SEVEN

Immediately, Anne's innocent smile shifted into a ruthless smirk. Her hands flashed in an incantation gesture.

"Dancing Lights of Deception!"

A dozen glowing orbs materialized around Hughie, surrounding him in a circle. The orbs began to spin faster and faster, trails of light blurring together until all Hughie could see was a hypnotic kaleidoscope of colors.

He blinked hard, trying to shake off the disorientation. But the moment he opened his eyes, a crushing vertigo slammed into him. The world seemed to flip upside down as the ground vanished from under his feet.

Hughie stumbled, barely catching himself before faceplanting.

"Ugh, not this again!" he groaned. Why did all his opponents insist on using illusions against him? Hughie hated having to play mind games during a fight. All he wanted was a good old-fashioned brawl, fist against fist! Was that too much to ask?

Squinting against the nausea, Hughie looked around, trying to spot his opponent amidst the swirling lights. But he could barely even tell which way was up anymore.

Anne's giggles echoed around him as glowing light blades materialized in the air. The blades shot towards Hughie with blinding speed. He tried to dodge, but the world kept spinning crazily, throwing off his coordination.

Several slashes carved across Hughie's body, making him howl in pain. Blood dripped down his arms and chest.

Inside the ring on his finger, Li Fenghao shook his head sadly. It was a repeat of the last match. The lad was trying to brute force his way through the disorienting illusion when he needed patience and calm focus. But the stubborn oaf probably wouldn't listen even if Li tried advising him now. Perhaps he should let the boy learn his lesson the hard way this time.

Hughie growled, features distorting in rage. That was it! He was done playing nice.

"Let's see your pretty lights stop me now!"

With a roar, he transformed into a giant three-eyed toad. His long tongue lashed out, smashing craters into the arena floor as he thrashed around trying to hit Anne. But between the chaotic lights still spinning around him and his muddled sense of direction, he couldn't land a single strike.

Watching from the spectator stands, Oliviare bit her lip anxiously. That devious hussy might look sweet and innocent on the outside, but here she was, mercilessly tormenting her poor Hughie! Oliviare's hands clenched into white-knuckled fists. She wished she could jump down there and rip Anne's pretty little face off for hurting her man.

Anne arched an eyebrow, looking mildly impressed that Hughie had broken through the first layer of her illusion. But he was still trapped within the larger web she had woven. Time to get serious.

Drawing in a deep breath, Anne began chanting under her breath. A glowing spear of light appeared in her palms.

"Piercing Lance of the Heavens!"

She flung her arm forward, launching the spear straight at the toad's chest. It punched clean through Hughie's thick hide and erupted out his back in a spray of blood.

Hughie let out an agonized croak, body convulsing.

Anne prepared another Piercing Lance, taking aim at Hughie's head this time. She smirked, savoring his pained noises. The big lug was finally learning just how outmatched he was.

But then, Hughie's croaks shifted into roars as his rage peaked. The severe injuries triggered his signature technique, Bloodforge Ascension.

Red lines spiderwebbed across Hughie's gray skin as all his veins bulged, muscle mass doubling, then tripling in size.

Though the disorienting lights still surrounded him, Hughie began flailing his limbs with even more reckless abandon, his enhanced strength smashing craters into the arena floor with each miss. Anne backed away warily, forced on the defensive.

Then, with one lucky strike, Hughie's giant fist clipped Anne's shoulder, sending the girl flying halfway across the arena. She slammed into the ground with a pained shriek, her concentration shattering.

The hypnotic lights finally vanished.

Hughie's vision cleared, sights and sounds snapping back into focus. Letting loose a roar of victory, he lumbered over to where Anne lay sprawled on the ground, one arm hanging limply. She looked up at the giant toad looming over her, eyes wide with fear.

Immediately, Anne's expression shifted back into an innocent, tearful look.

"P-please, you've won! Just don't hurt me anymore!" Her voice quivered. Anne even managed to make tears well up in her big blue eyes for added effect.

Buying time, she slowly slid her uninjured hand behind her back, preparing another illusion technique. Just one opening and she could trap this brainless brute again.

But before Anne could cast her illusion, an unexpected voice rang out.

"Don't fall for it, Hughie! She's trying to trick you again, finish her off now!" Oliviare yelled.

Hughie blinked in surprise, not expecting his girlfriend to encourage violence. But her voice was enough to snap him out of his brief hesitation. Letting out a rumbling growl, he reached down and wrapped one gigantic webbed hand around Anne's throat, cutting off her chanting with a choked gurgle.

Hoisting her up, legs dangling helplessly, Hughie brought Anne close to his massive toad face. His three bloodred eyes bored into her terrified blue ones.

"S-submit!" he growled out.

Face purpling, Anne frantically tapped his arm in surrender.

Satisfied, Hughie released his grip. Anne dropped to the ground like a rag doll, coughing violently.

After making sure she wasn't getting back up, Hughie finally allowed his Bloodforge Ascension and toad form to recede. Muscles deflated and skin smoothed back to normal as he shrank down to his regular size.

Elder Fred descended to the arena floor, prodding the groaning Anne with his foot before nodding.

"Victory goes to Hughie of the Black Rose Sect!"

Li Fenghao let out a long-suffering sigh. As expected, the thick-headed oaf had ignored strategy and only won through luck. If not for that fortunate hit triggering his brute strength technique, the boy would certainly have lost. How many times would it take for him to learn proper focus and control?

Back down in the waiting area, Hughie plopped down on a chair with a tired groan. "Phew, that took a lot outta me! Man, I hate having to bust out the big guns just to beat some sneaky illusionist."

"If you possessed a calmer mind, you could have broken her illusion," Li Fenghao scolded. "But instead, you got slapped around like a helpless whelp, just like in the first match! If not for that lucky hit, you would have lost badly. Do not always rely on brawn over brain, boy."

Hughie waved a hand dismissively. "Yeah, yeah, I get it, gramps. We can't all be genius strategists like you." Then he paused, looking thoughtful. "But you know, maybe you've got a point for once. I really need to work on fighting illusions better."

The admission took Li Fenghao aback. Perhaps the lad was finally maturing a little.

"Hmph. Of course I'm right, I am a greater immortal!" Li quickly covered his surprise with boastful bluster. Though frankly, it pleased him to see a glimmer of wisdom in the young fool.

Up in the elder's box, the others were discussing the match with interest.

"What a pity for young Anne, she had the right approach but couldn't finish it." Zofia clicked her tongue. "That Black Rose brute has no finesse at all. Just a messy brawler."

Leontius sighed. "Yes, Hughie relies far too much on transformations and brute force. He lacks . . . refinement. Still, both disciples fought with admirable passion."

"I'm more surprised he didn't adapt quicker, given that he faced an illusionist in his first match," Astrid said. "Carelessness like this could get him killed."

Vowron said nothing, merely staring down at Hughie with an unreadable expression.

As for Slifer, he kept his face blank. But internally, he was chuckling. Hughie was such a stereotypical protagonist—bull-headed and oblivious, but gifted with incredible luck and tenacity. Brute forcing his way through things was just part of his charm! Not the cleverest approach perhaps, but if the heavens were on your side, then it worked.

Ding!
Your Disciple Hughie Won
600 Karmic Credits Gained

"Ahem." Elder Fred spoke up. "Let us proceed with the next match. Dentos of the Black Rose Sect versus Avery of the Black Death Sect!"

Dentos walked into the arena, his eyes fixed solely on Slifer seated in the spectator stands above. This was his chance to prove himself. If he could secure one of the slots to the Sealed Realm for the Black Rose Sect, and perhaps even return with some treasure or resource that would aid Slifer, then maybe, just maybe, the Ascendant cultivator would finally accept him as a disciple.

It was a slim hope, but one Dentos clung to with almost desperate fervor. Ever since he had joined the sect, he had been consumed by the desire to gain a master, someone who would teach him, someone who would take care of him.

The supreme elder was the only person Dentos felt understood his uniqueness. Where others saw madness or instability, Slifer saw potential.

Across from Dentos, a girl with snow-white hair entered the arena. Her features were delicate and doll-like, with skin as pale as porcelain. But it was the empty, lifeless look in her eyes that seemed unusual.

"My apologies, miss, but in order to impress my future master, I'm afraid you'll have to endure a significant amount of pain. Try not to take it personally."

As expected, Avery said nothing in response, merely staring back at him.

Elder Fred's voice rang out. "Begin!"

Immediately, Avery exploded into motion, rushing straight for Dentos. Her hands moved in a blur of precise strikes aimed at vital spots—it was the same brutal martial arts style Dentos had witnessed from that Ironius fellow earlier.

But Dentos had sparred countless times against his fellow disciples of the Disciplinary Hall. He easily flowed around Avery's attacks, parrying what he could not dodge, before countering with a casual backhanded slap that sent the girl stumbling back.

A flicker of surprise passed through Avery's empty eyes. As a demon, her physical body should have been far stronger than a human's, even whilst suppressed in a human guise. Yet this scrawny boy had so easily turned aside her assault.

Undeterred, Avery dove in again, her strikes even swifter than before. But once more, Dentos spun and weaved between her blows with practiced ease. Despite his opponent being physically faster and stronger than him, to his senses, her movements seemed sluggish, almost easy to read.

With another slap, he knocked Avery across the arena floor.

Up in the Black Rose Sect's stands, the Disciplinary Hall members broke out into cheers for their boss.

"As expected of the boss! No one can match him in martial arts!"

"Did you see that backhand? So classy!"

"He's toying with that Black Death chick. This fight's already over."

"Boss! Boss! Boss!" they chanted. Their leader was putting on quite a show.

Over in the elders' booth, Vowron watched the battle with narrowed eyes and thinned lips. Beside him, Zofia chuckled.

"My, my, it seems your disciple is having some difficulty despite your sect's recent interest in martial arts."

Vowron's jaw tightened, but he gave no other visible reaction.

Beside Vowron, Slifer allowed himself a small smirk. "Young Dentos may be unorthodox in his ways, but he is an exceptional disciple. The boy excels in all areas."

"Oh? He is one of your personal disciples then?" Leontius asked.

Slifer's smile turned awkward. "Er, well . . . not exactly. The truth is, Dentos does not actually have a master."

"No master?" Astrid cut in. "Why not? The child clearly possesses ample potential to be nurtured."

"Yes, that is quite true." Slifer sighed. "Unfortunately, some find Dentos's unique personality and penchant for . . . eccentric acts . . . somewhat difficult to accept. I'm afraid not many have had the patience required to look past the external to see the talent buried within."

Here he gave a helpless shrug, as if to say, "What can you do?"

Down in the arena below, Dentos decided it was time to stop playing around. With a flick of his wrist, his signature paintbrush appeared between his fingers. With a few quick strokes, he brought his art to life.

The painting peeled itself off the page and transformed into a massive spectral hand that swatted Avery aside like an insect.

The white-haired girl tumbled roughly along the ground. She started to push herself back up, eyes flashing red for a brief instant as rage crossed her face at being slapped around by a mortal. But then she caught herself and schooled her expression.

"I . . . surrender," Avery forced out as she picked herself up off the ground one last time. She would remember this humiliation.

"Victory goes to Dentos of the Black Rose Sect!"

As he left the arena, Dentos risked a glance upwards at Slifer, hoping to gauge the Ascendant's reaction. But the supreme elder's face remained impassive, not a single hint of being impressed.

Dentos's shoulders slumped. It seemed he had failed to make an impression on the one person whose opinion truly mattered right now.

"The first match of the fourth round will begin in five minutes," Elder Fred announced, breaking Dentos from his gloomy thoughts. "Disciples, Zack of the Black Rose Sect and Ashton of the White Tiger Sect, be ready!"

Swallowing his disappointment, the boy shuffled back towards the Black Rose pavilion, mind churning with ideas on how to grab Slifer's attention in the next fight. He had to think bigger, flashier, really go all out . . .